CATHY GILLEN THACKER

Lost and Found

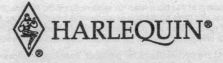

HARLEQUIN®

TORONTO • NEW YORK • LONDON
AMSTERDAM • PARIS • SYDNEY • HAMBURG
STOCKHOLM • ATHENS • TOKYO • MILAN • MADRID
PRAGUE • WARSAW • BUDAPEST • AUCKLAND

HARLEQUIN BOOKS

by Request—LOST AND FOUND

Copyright © 2003 by Harlequin Books S.A.

ISBN 0-373-18517-0

The publisher acknowledges the copyright holder of the individual works as follows:
BABY ON THE DOORSTEP
Copyright © 1994 by Cathy Gillen Thacker
DADDY TO THE RESCUE
Copyright © 1994 by Cathy Gillen Thacker
TOO MANY MOMS
Copyright © 1994 by Cathy Gillen Thacker

This edition published by arrangement with Harlequin Books S.A.

CATHY GILLEN THACKER

is a full-time wife/mother/author who began
typing stories for her own amusement during
"nap time" when her children were toddlers.
Twenty years and more than fifty published novels
later, Cathy is almost as well-known for her witty
romantic comedies and warm, family stories as she
is for her ability to get grass stains and red clay out
of almost anything, her triple-layer brownies and her
knack for knowing what her three grown and nearly
grown children are up to almost before they do!
Her books have made numerous appearances on
bestseller lists and are now published in seventeen
languages and thirty-five countries around the world.

CONTENTS

CONTENTS

BABY ON THE DOORSTEP

Prologue

Damn, but it felt good to be home again, Alec Roman thought as he steered his silver Lotus into the garage. Grabbing his briefcase and carry-on bag with one hand and his McDonald's takeout sack with the other, he vaulted out of the driver's seat, strode purposefully across the cavernous garage, past the custom outfitted four-wheel-drive Jeep, the Mercedes, and the restored '63 Corvette and into the main house. He'd only been in Asia three weeks this time, but as usual, it had seemed like an eternity.

Whistling and grabbing a light beer from the refrigerator as he passed by, Alec took his dinner into the den. Not one to waste time, he went through his mail as he ate. Fortunately, there was almost nothing of a personal nature today. That suited Alec just fine. He didn't have time for a personal life anyway. These days, his life revolved around the computer firm his father had started. Since taking over the fledgling company fifteen years ago Alec had turned it into an international powerhouse that one day soon would compete with the likes of Apple and IBM.

Alec opened up his briefcase and began going over the contracts he had negotiated while in Japan. He had just become absorbed in the fine points when the doorbell rang. Frowning at the interruption, he pushed his chair back and strode to the front door of his Philadelphia mansion.

On the porch was a heart-shaped red wicker basket decorated with stenciled cupids and a huge white satin bow. For a moment, he couldn't think why anyone would have left such a thing on his porch; he wasn't exactly a hearts-and-flowers kind of guy. Then he recalled it was Valentine's Day. He frowned even more as he wondered which of his many female admirers the gift was from.

It seemed women would stop at nothing these days to pick themselves up a rich husband. He'd had women jump naked out of bushes at him, and others had asked him outright to marry them when they knew he didn't love them. Weekly, he received incredibly intimate and imaginative photographs in the mail. While Alec had nothing against sex, these fortune hunters, working with his well-known reputation as a play-boy, all wrongly assumed he was so base and stupid as to be driven by his hormones. Little did they know, Alec couldn't be swayed by desire. Sex was great, but it had nothing to do with the professional goals he had set for himself.

Thankful that there seemed to be no one around to go with the holiday "gift basket," Alec bent to pick it up, then frowned as he got a closer look at the contents. "What the hell?" he murmured, perplexed.

Swathed in white wool blankets was a small baby with a cherubic face and big blue eyes. Seeing him, the baby let out a yowl loud enough to wake the dead. "Hey!" Alec yelled impatiently out into the night, as he straightened and searched for any sign of movement along the sweeping circular drive or immaculately manicured front lawn. "I don't know what you're thinking, leaving this kid here, but this isn't an or-phanage! I don't know anything about babies. I can't possibly take care of this kid."

Unfortunately, there was no reply. Alec tried once more to get whomever had left the baby to reconsider, then gave up and decided to take the baby inside.

After a frustrating couple of moments in which Alec seemed to be all thumbs, he discovered that beneath the cum-bersome white cashmere blanket the baby was wearing a light blue sleeper with embroidered bunnies on the front. There was a typewritten note taped to the sleeper, addressed simply, *"To Andy's Father."* It read, *"Own up to your mistakes!"*

His heart pounding frantically, Alec glanced from the baby to the note and back again. No, it couldn't be, he thought as he stared down at the baby with dark unruly hair so much like his own. Lots of people had dark curly hair. It didn't mean anything. This was just another scam, but it was one that was destined to fail. "I don't care what the note says, kid. You are not my baby!"

Chapter One

The door to Jade Kincaid's downtown Pittsburgh office swung open with a whoosh and a bang. She glanced up, startled, then paused, her heart in her throat. Her unexpected visitor was tall—at least six three or four—athletic, with raven black hair. He had a solid male build from head to toe. But even more interesting than the thirty-something man's sexy uptown appearance, however, was the darling little baby in his arms. Swaddled in a white cashmere bunting outfit and matching hat, the baby couldn't have been more than six or eight weeks old. He was sound asleep against the man's broad shoulder, and the expression of utter bliss on his cherubic face was completely at odds with the disgruntled look of the man carrying him.

"May I help you?"

The sexy stranger nodded at her gruffly by way of introduction, then continued as if he hadn't a second to waste. "Alec Roman. Where's your sister, Ms. Kincaid?"

Uh-oh. Here comes trouble.

"Where's yours?" Jade volleyed back lightly. Nothing beat buying a little time. Judging from the aggrieved look on Alec Roman's face, she was going to need it. *What had Nicole done now?* she wondered uncomfortably.

His sensual lips thinned. "I'm not kidding around here, Ms. Kincaid," he said quietly.

"Okay," Jade replied lightly, ignoring his increasingly uptight attitude, "we'll shelve the jokes for now. What do you want with Nicole, Mr. Roman?" *As if I really want to know.*

His expression became distressingly remote. "I'd prefer to discuss that with her."

"That's fine with me." Jade turned to her computer screen and went back to calculating calories. She didn't want to be involved in another of Nicole's romantic-liaisons-gone-wrong anyway.

Unfortunately, Alec Roman didn't show himself out, as she had half hoped he would when she resumed her work. Instead, he walked wordlessly to the conference table at the far side of the room and set the combination baby carrier/car seat he had brought in with him on the center of it. For a moment he just stared at the carrier. Finally, he took a deep breath and put one hand behind the baby's neck and head, the other underneath his bottom. Looking almost as if he didn't dare breathe while attempting such a tricky maneuver, he lowered the baby toward the carrier and finally slipped the sleeping infant into the padded seat.

The baby was situated nicely. Unfortunately, Alec Roman's hands were trapped between the baby and the carrier. For a moment, Jade thought he wouldn't be able to extricate his hands without waking the baby, but after several equally awkward, tenuous moves, and some more breath-holding, Alec Roman finally managed to get his hands out from beneath the baby and strap the baby in. All without waking him.

Finished, Alec heaved a sigh of relief. Once again looking completely at ease with himself and his surroundings, he circled authoritatively around Jade's L-shaped work area. His attention focused solely on Jade, he leaned over her computer, his hands on either side of her, and shot her another appreciative male glance. "There's a slight problem. I have to find Nicole before I can talk to her," he explained, as if speaking to the village idiot.

Jade ignored the unsettling way her senses stirred at his close proximity. "That's your problem, not mine," she coun-

tered, refusing to allow herself to be sidetracked by the dark
woodsy scent of his after-shave. Uncomfortable with his
closeness, she pushed her chair back a very necessary six
inches.

Attractive men were a dime a dozen in her business, but
it wasn't often she found herself responding to one on such
an intimate level. Just looking at his patrician features made
her palms dampen and her heart race. She didn't want to
imagine what it would be like to be held against his tall strong
body or kissed by those soft, sensual lips.

She could handle this, she told herself firmly, pushing the
last of her surprisingly evocative fantasies about him to the
furthest recesses of her mind. "Now if you don't mind, Mr.
Roman, I've got a month of menus to prepare."

To her dismay, Alec Roman showed no signs of leaving,
despite her less than gracious hint. "You're in on this, too,
aren't you?" he asked so suddenly that it took her breath
away.

Every muscle in her slender body went stiff with tension.
Beginning to feel thoroughly exasperated, she swiveled
slightly to face him and felt his hot gaze slide over her from
head to toe, before returning with heart-stopping accuracy to
her face. "In on what?" she questioned coolly, wishing fervently all the while her heart would stop its telltale pounding
and resume its normal beat.

"This scam."

"What scam?"

He quirked a disbelieving brow and folded his arms in
front of him. His entire body was a study in impatience.
"You're telling me you know nothing about this scam Nicole's trying to pull?"

If there was anything Jade hated, it was being held ac-
countable for her grown sister's mistakes. Her jaw took on a
stubborn tilt. "In case you haven't noticed, I'm not telling
you anything at the moment, loverboy."

"Oh, I've noticed all right. What I want to know is *why*
you're not telling me anything."

"Maybe because I want *you* to tell *me* something."

His gaze narrowed in silent challenge. "Ask away."

Jade picked up a pencil and restlessly tapped the eraser end against her chin. "Just what is it about me that makes you think I'm as wild and reckless and generally untrustworthy as my younger sister?" When he remained stubbornly silent, Jade couldn't resist throwing down the gauntlet. She sat back in her chair and crossed her legs primly. "Is it the way I wear my dark shoulder-length curls in wild, loose disarray that puts that crazy imagination of yours right into overdrive?"

He leaned across the computer console, taking full advantage of his view of her legs before returning his gaze to her eyes. "A more apt description of that hairdo of yours couldn't be had," he replied with a lazy smile that sent shivers of awareness racing down her spine.

Afraid if she gave him any more of an opening, he'd take over the meeting completely, Jade continued in the same vein. "Or perhaps it's the Ravishing Red tint of my lipstick that has impugned my character in your eyes," she guessed lightly, trying to make him see, through a bit of glib humor, how ridiculous he was being!

"Nope. I like that, too," Alec drawled with easy familiarity as his gaze lowered and fastened on her mouth. His eyes traced her bow-shaped lips. Jade didn't know quite how it happened, but one look, one long lazy survey from him, and she felt as if she'd just been kissed...by an expert! Her lips tingled. She was dizzy and trembling inside. Her limbs had that fluid sexy languor, coupled with an almost immediate wish for more.

Fortunately for both of them, she reassured herself swiftly, that wasn't going to happen. Not in this lifetime.

His unchecked amusement combined with his lazy appreciation of her looks worked together to get her back on track. "Or maybe it was just the outfit I wore to work today," Jade continued as she resisted the urge to pull the hem of her skirt down, closer to her knees.

Alec tilted his head. His frankly male appraisal sent prick-les of awareness through Jade. "I don't know about any im-pression that outfit of yours is supposed to send, other than that you're one sexy woman," Alec countered in a lilting voice filled with wickedness before beaming her another megawatt smile.

Jade watched him straighten lazily, wondering all the while how he had turned the banter she'd begun to *his* advantage. Not that it mattered…she wasn't giving up her attempts to better him. "Then again, maybe it's just the taupe shadow on my eyes that brands me and my sister liars and con artists in your mind?" she finished softly.

She expected outrage, sputtered denials to the contrary, but Alec only grinned. "You don't have any trouble speaking your mind, do you, sweetheart?" he asked softly at last, then surprised her by touching the side of her face with the palm of his hand. It was warm, slightly calloused; his touch at once very gentle, and very sure. All in all, a devastating combi-nation. Or would have been, Jade thought, had she not had all her defenses securely in place.

"No, and neither do you apparently," Jade answered tartly, pulling away from his touch as serenely as if she had hardly noticed it.

Again, Alec smiled. Desire, pure and simple, was in his eyes. "No, I don't, do I?" he said softly.

Her pulse still racing, Jade stared at him. There was a part of her, a very small part of her, that would've liked nothing better at that moment than for him to come all the way over that console and take her in his arms.

But he merely straightened and folded his arms in front of him decisively, letting her know in a second that the time for matching wits and trading insults was now over. "Then you'll understand when I tell you Nicole left that baby on my doorstep last night," he said quietly, his expression implac-able.

Jade knew her sister was irresponsible to a fault, but she

was also sure Nicole hadn't left Alec Roman with that adorable baby.

She regarded him evenly. "It's a little early for April Fools' jokes, isn't it, Mr. Roman?"

Unperturbed by her disbelief in his ridiculous claim, Alec calmly pulled a piece of paper from his inside coat pocket. "The baby's name is Andy," he told her in a flat unperturbed tone, "and he came with this note."

Jade hesitated, then took the paper that was still warm from his touch, and studied it reluctantly. The typewritten page was rimmed with tape. Miniscule tufts of soft blue cotton that might have come from a baby's sleeper stuck to the clear tape. "I don't see my sister's name anywhere on this note," she said as she handed it back, and watched him pocket it once again. "Anyone could have typed this note."

"It has to be Nicole," Alec retorted firmly, as if there was no question at all in his mind.

Jade glanced back up at him, wondering what he knew about her flighty, irresponsible sister that she didn't. "And how, pray tell, do you figure that?"

Alec regarded her smugly. "Because she's the only woman I was with last spring who could've been pregnant in the interim without my knowing about it. Not that I believe this baby is actually mine for one instant," he added, seemingly as much for himself as for her.

"Why not?" Because Nicole slept around and they both knew it?

"Look, despite the innocent way she looks in her photos and commercials, we both know your sister is no angel," Alec Roman said gruffly.

Did they ever! Jade thought. From the moment Nicole had left the womb she'd been nothing but trouble. The only difference now was that for the past five years, since their parents' death, Jade had been the only person cleaning up after her sister's messes.

Not wanting Alec Roman to know how much the pressure of trying to control the wild Nicole had gotten to her, however, Jade smiled and reminded him in a less than cordial tone, "Few of us are angels, Mr. Roman."

Alec was silent. Thinking perhaps of his own foibles and flaws? Of the penchant for carefree lovemaking and commitment-free liaisons she saw reflected in his face?

"Nicole told me you were the only family she had," he said finally. "You *must* know where she is."

"Sorry," Jade answered in a clipped tone of voice, not wanting to get into the details of her ongoing quarrel with her twenty-six-year-old sister. "I don't."

"But you could find her if you wanted to," Alec insisted.

"Not necessarily."

"You could still try."

Jade faced him in silence, a little in awe of his tenacity. It was easy to see why Nicole had fallen for this guy. Physically, he was, quite honestly, one of the sexiest men she had ever seen. His broad shoulders and firmly muscled chest were shown to stunning advantage beneath the crisply starched olive dress shirt, matching Italian suit and tie. On some men, the stark singularity of color would have been too much. On Alec Roman, it was just right. His finely chiseled profile, arresting dark brown eyes and windblown black hair combined to make him look more all-American than gangster. Although, from what little she had seen of him so far, she had the feeling he was just as dangerous as a gangster, and just as darkly alluring.

He was also one of the most persistent, determined men she had ever met, and Jade knew a lot of men, in fact worked almost exclusively with male clients. Most of whom were outrageous bounders and rakes! Briefly, she wondered if Alec Roman fell into the same class, then she pushed the thought aside. Whether Alec Roman slept around or not, was not her problem. The concern at hand was the baby he had brought in with him. She couldn't quite make herself believe it was Nicole's.

Jade pushed away from her desk and circled around to the file cabinets across the large spacious room. "Look, Mr. Roman, I'm sorry but I don't know anything about that baby over there or why he was left on your doorstep."

He quirked a brow and watched her restlessly roam her office. "Sure about that?"

The way his sensual, experienced glance roved roguishly over her trim suede skirt and white poet's shirt made Jade wish she'd worn a skirt that fit a little less snugly, a blouse with starch instead of a silky drape.

Drawing a bolstering breath, Jade mustered a cool, officious smile. "Yes, I'm sorry. So, Mr. Roman, since neither of us knows where that baby came from, never mind who he really belongs to, why don't you just go to the police and give the baby over to them? I'm sure someone in the Pittsburgh—"

"Philadelphia," he corrected.

"—police department would know what to do," Jade finished.

Alec shook his head contentiously, nixing her suggestion on the spot. "And have this on the front page of every newspaper in America? I can see the headlines now. Computer Magnate Finds Lost Heir On His Doorstep. No thanks. I'll pass on the publicity."

So he was *that* Alec Roman, Jade thought. The up-and-comer who'd made Roman Computer into a household name. Which meant he had to be fabulously wealthy. "Is bad publicity all you're worried about?"

He checked out her late-model IBM computer with a frown. "Naturally, I want to see this baby reunited with his mother." He looked her straight in the eye. "Will you help me?"

It seemed more a command than a request. "Nicole's troubles are not my problem, any more than that baby is, Mr. Roman."

He quirked a disgruntled brow. "Meaning?"

Jade backed up without looking where she was going and collided with the file cabinet. To cover her growing unease, she folded her arms in front of her. "I stopped being Nicole's keeper two years ago, and I have no intention of starting up again.''

He studied her implacably. ''You really *don't* like your sister, do you?''

Jade knew how cold and unfeeling she sounded, but she was unable to help it. Being cold and unfeeling, when it came to Nicole and all her problems, was the only way to survive. If Jade spent all her time trying to fix the myriad problems her sister created for others, she'd have no time for her own life. And at age twenty-eight Jade wanted her own man to love, and her own baby. She didn't want to be worried about Alec Roman or the baby her sister had allegedly dumped on his doorstep.

''I know why I'm furious with Nicole. What'd she do to you to make you so hot?''

Color heated Jade's cheeks, but she kept her head high. ''That is none of your business!''

''Sure?''

''If you want to find her, I suggest you contact the Renown Modeling Agency in New York City.''

''I already have. They won't tell me anything. Apparently, Nicole gets calls from men there all the time.''

''Did you tell them why you wanted to know?''

Alec shrugged. ''I asked if she'd had a baby recently.''

''And?''

''They hung up on me.''

''Imagine that.''

He ignored her sarcasm pointedly as he stepped close enough for her to smell the dark, woodsy scent of his after-shave. Because the file cabinet was at her back, Jade couldn't get away from him without it looking as if she were running away.

''Call them for me,'' he urged in a soft, persuasive voice that sent ripples of sensual awareness up and down her spine. His warm fragrant breath stirred her hair. ''You're her next of kin. They'll probably tell you what they know.''

Jade knew she wasn't going to get rid of Alec until she

did what he wanted, and she was desperate to get rid of him. Senses reeling, she nodded her acquiescence reluctantly, waited until he gave her room to maneuver once again, then went to do as bid.

"Well?" Alec asked, long moments later when she'd returned from her phone call.

Jade sat on the corner of her desk and tried not to notice the interested glances Roman kept throwing at her legs. "I talked to Myra Lansky herself, the head of the agency. She told me Nicole hasn't worked at Renown for the past six months."

Alec frowned and turned his appreciative glance away from her knees. His eyes met hers. "Why not?"

"She wouldn't say." Jade played with the large gold hoop in her ear, pretending to adjust the tightness of the clasp as she stared into his magnetic sable brown eyes. "I had the feeling there was some kind of trouble between Nicole and the agency, but Myra wouldn't say exactly what it was."

Alec cursed, his frustration with the situation evident.

Despite her own strong desire to stay well out of this mess, Jade felt her heart go out to him. She supposed the least she could do was to help him work out some of this problem. Then she would get rid of him. "Let's presume you're right. Let's presume Nicole left this baby on your doorstep. Why would she have waited until now to contact you, especially if she was pregnant and couldn't work? Why wouldn't she have contacted you months ago?"

Alec rubbed his right shoulder with powerful strokes of his hand. "How the blazes should I know? Maybe she wanted to live off her savings. Maybe she knew the baby wasn't mine—it's common knowledge your sister has a short attention span when it comes to men. Or maybe it was because of the way our liaison happened."

"I don't think I want to hear this."

Alec rounded the desk and stepped inside the L swiftly. The next thing she knew, his thighs were brushing her knees, creating warm tingles of sexual awareness, and his hands were on hers. Tightening his grip, he kept her from covering her ears with her hands or moving away.

"Well, you're going to hear it," he said as he held Jade squarely in front of him, apparently oblivious to the havoc he was causing deep inside her. "I met Nicole at a party in Japan last year. She was there promoting Ingenue soap. I was there on business. We were both homesick, and she went back to my hotel with me after the party. I admit we had a wild time but neither of us had any illusions about what was happening that week." He frowned, released her, and stepped back. "We were only together during that trip. I never saw her again."

Jade's hands were suddenly chilled, as were her knees. She told herself the loss of his touch did not leave her feeling bereft. "Was that her choice or yours?" she asked.

"A little of both, I suppose. She was still on that promotional tour. I had a business to run, deals to make." He shrugged again and an ambivalent silence fell between them.

Finally, Jade sighed. "Well, I guess under the circumstances, I don't blame her for dropping out of sight." As she slipped off the desk, her heels hit the carpet soundlessly. "I'd be embarrassed to be pregnant by a man I barely knew, too."

Alec gave her a sharp look, then glanced away a long moment. When he turned back to her, he said in a voice that was flat with remorse, "Okay, Jade, you've made your point, and so has Nicole. *I should have been more responsible.* Now how much is it going to take?"

Jade blinked, sure she hadn't heard right. *"What?"*

"How much cash will it take to end this scam here and now?" Alec Roman spoke with deceptive patience, pushing the words through a row of white, even teeth.

Jade stared up at him incredulously. "Let me get this straight. You're offering to pay me to take this baby off your hands?"

The sensual edges of his mouth pulled down into a censuring frown. He stepped closer, which in turn forced her to back up until her hips connected with the edge of the desk once again. "Give me a break, sweetheart." The edges of Alec's mouth hovered just above hers. "You know what I'm doing."

Trying to kiss me? Jade thought dizzily as she propped one hand on the desk beside her for balance, and planted the other squarely on his chest. Which was, she soon discovered, as solid and warm and hard as it looked.

"I'm trying to stop this extortion and blackmail scheme of yours before it goes any further," Alec continued, pressing even closer despite the continued resistance of her palm. "So I repeat. What'll it take?"

Jade didn't know whether to laugh or give him a shove that would send him all the way to China. She flashed him a brittle smile. "I hate to be the one to break it to you, Alec Roman, but I am not attempting to extort anything from you."

"And Nicole?" he probed silkily, his dark gaze thoughtfully caressing her face.

"I can't speak for her."

His brown eyes darkened, as if he had been expecting as much. He leaned closer and planted a hand palm-down on the desk on either side of her. "Then hear this. Your scheme is not going to work, even if the baby is mine, and at this point I'm far from convinced of that."

Jade flushed. It was all she could do to catch her breath. "You're calling me a con artist?"

He shrugged. "If the shoe fits."

A harsh silence fell between them. Slowly, he drew back. Jade realized she was shaking. "Anyone ever tell you you're a great judge of character?" she asked, relieved to find she sounded far more in control of the situation than she felt.

Alec ignored her sarcasm. "Listen, sweetheart, you've got a lot to learn here—"

"Do I?"

"I don't know what you think you know about me, but this isn't the first time a woman's come forward with such a claim and attempted to run a scam on me—"

"How many illegitimate children do you *have?*" Jade broke in, aghast.

"None. I married a woman who claimed to be pregnant with my child," he muttered in reluctant explanation, shoving a hand through his thick black hair. "Only she wasn't. The divorce cost me plenty and I've got no desire to be taken for a ride again."

"I can't imagine you would," Jade murmured, surprised to find herself suddenly sympathetic to his plight. "Unfortunately—" She stopped and bit her lip uncertainly.

Alec frowned. "What?"

She moved carefully away from the edge of the desk, determined not to put herself in such a physically vulnerable situation with him again. "You're right in your assessment of my sister's character." Jade paused and gave Alec a frank look. "Nicole's been looking for a wealthy husband for a long time."

Alec's frown deepened.

"But as for anyone letting Nicole borrow their baby to use as bait indefinitely... It's far more likely she had this baby herself and then turned him over to you, hoping you'd get attached to him, and then offer cash. Maybe even marriage. I don't know."

Alec studied her carefully, his emotions hidden from view. "You really think it could be my baby?"

Jade pressed her lips together pensively. As much as she hated to admit this, she knew she had to be honest with him. "I think it bears further investigation, yes."

Chapter Two

Jade put the phone down with a sigh. "There's no answer at Nicole's apartment."

Alec had expected as much. All he ever got was an answering machine, too. "That settles it then. You have to go to New York with me."

She smiled at him in bemusement. "I've got news for you, Alec Roman," she informed him in a sweet, soft voice laced with temper. "I don't have to do anything I don't want to, and I certainly don't want to go to New York."

Too bad, Alec thought. He didn't want to be saddled with an orphaned child he couldn't even be sure at this point was really his, but he was. Like it or not, until Nicole was found, he and Jade were in this together.

Not that he minded being with Jade all that much, he amended silently to himself. She was a pretty woman, with a quick wit and a lot of style.

"So find someone else to help you locate Nicole," she continued.

"Fine," Alec said. Deciding a different tack was called for to enlist Jade's cooperation, he gave her an easy smile. "I'll hire a private investigator. Run full-page newspaper ads in Pittsburgh, Philadelphia, and New York. I can envision them now. A big picture of Nicole. The caption under it would read, Have You Seen This Woman? I could set up an 800 number, maybe offer a reward."

She looked at him, temper simmering in her pretty jade eyes. "I thought you didn't want publicity."

He still didn't, given the choice. "I have the feeling neither do you. Besides, I can run ads looking for Nicole without saying why I'm looking for her."

True, Jade thought. Unfortunately, if he ran ads about Nicole, there would be questions. Plenty of them. And her business, which was just now coming into full flower, might be damaged as a résult. The players she counseled wouldn't care, but the team owners and the public relations people might not want their players linked to a family with a major scandal brewing. She put her hands on her hips and asked with open asperity, "Now who's blackmailing whom?"

Alec shrugged unapologetically. "I'm determined to find your sister. To that end, I'll do whatever is necessary."

"As well as publicly embarrass me?" Jade asked coolly.

Alec held her glance, trying all the while not to notice the soft disarray of her wildly curling dark brown hair or the ripe softness of her wide sensual mouth. God knew under the circumstances he didn't want to be attracted to Jade Kincaid, but a man would have to be blind not to see the womanly allure in her tall willowy frame. But it was more than just the sexy way she looked. It was the intelligence in her dark green eyes. The way she matched wits with him. As president and CEO of Roman Computer and one of Philadelphia's most eligible single men, he was used to being accommodated and sought after, not sassed or challenged.

"I'll only embarrass you if you leave me no choice," he promised bluntly. He was hoping she'd decide to help him of her own volition, just as he was hoping they would one day be free of this mess with her sister so he could pursue Jade the way he wanted to pursue her—all out.

Jade muttered an impolite description of Alec, one he was sure she wanted him to hear, then picked up the phone and punched in a number with quick, angry jabs. "Tim Johnson, please. Hi, Tim. Jade. I'm not going to be able to see you today. I know. I've got to go out of town. No, I'm not coun-

seling any of the Jets or the Giants." She grinned and added,
"Yet, anyway." The rich melodious sound of her laughter
filled the office.

Alec wondered idly what it would be like to have the full
power of her flirtatious nature aimed at him, then pushed the
thought away. He had more pressing matters to attend to than
getting involved with Nicole's sister. First, he'd see to the
baby, then business, then Nicole. And then he could chase
after Jade.

Jade flirted some more, either not caring or not noticing
the way he was watching her, then hung up. She gathered up
her purse, coat, and keys. "Ready to go?"

Alec walked over to retrieve Andy, who was still sleeping
peacefully. "Just like that?"

She reached past Alec to tuck the blanket closer around
Andy. "I presume you have a private jet?"

Alec nodded. "And a limo waiting at the curb."

Once they had settled in the car and were making the short
trip to the airport, Alec couldn't resist asking. "Was that *the*
Tim Johnson you were talking to on the phone just now?"

Jade nodded. "'Perfect Pass' himself. He's a really nice
guy, a lot of fun. Always teasing."

"How is it you know the quarterback of the Pittsburgh
Steelers?" he asked curiously. Was she dating Tim Johnson?
And that wasn't jealousy he was feeling, was it? He never
got jealous. Even when it came to women he was currently
dating. His concern was probably due to the possible com-
plications any previous romantic liaison Jade had would cre-
ate for him and Andy now.

"I know all the players on all the pro sports teams in both
Philly and Pittsburgh. I'm a registered dietitian. I counsel
them all on diet and nutrition."

"Nice job, if you can get it."

"Yes—" she smiled smugly "—it is."

As Alec had feared, Andy woke up as they boarded his
jet. He had to be strapped in for takeoff, and that made him
all the more furious. By the time they had reached their cruis-

ing altitude for the trip to New York, he was wailing at the top of his lungs.

Alec rummaged in the diaper bag he'd brought along with him and took out a ready-to-use bottle of formula he'd picked up at the pharmacy. But Andy would have none of it.

"Maybe if you heated it up a little," Jade suggested.

"The pharmacist said I didn't need to. He said room temperature is fine."

"Try heating it up anyway. Just don't get it too hot."

Willing to do anything to stop Andy's crying, Alec went off to the galley. When he returned a minute and a half later, Jade was changing Andy's diaper with brisk but soothing efficiency. He had stopped crying and was listening intently to her soft, maternal whispers. Finished, she snapped Andy back into his flannel sleeper, swaddled him in a receiving blanket, and scooped him up in her arms.

"How'd you do that?" Alec asked, amazed. The only times Andy had stopped his loud verbal protests were when he was sleeping.

"Do what?" Jade said, accepting the bottle. She shook a drop of formula on her wrist, found it just right, then began giving him the bottle. Andy sucked down the formula greedily.

Unable to take his eyes off Jade and the baby, and the sweetly maternal picture they made, Alec sat opposite her and leaned closer. "How do you make him smile and coo like that?"

She shrugged. "I don't know. Maybe he just wants a woman's arms around him. Maybe he misses his mother."

Somehow, Alec couldn't see Andy being any happier in Nicole's arms.

Jade finished giving Andy the bottle, then lifted him to her shoulder, where she had placed another flannel receiving blanket. She patted him gently on the back until he burped, then held him close to her heart, rubbing his back tenderly all the while. Her blouse clung to her breasts, outlining the soft full globes and jutting nipples with disturbing accuracy, which confirmed Alec's earlier guess that she wasn't wearing a bra but a camisole or teddy of some sort. The mental image sent even more blood rushing to his groin. Alec shifted uncomfortably in his seat and adjusted the overhead air vents, turning up the heat.

"Thanks," Jade said, as the warm air blew down on them both. "I was getting a little cold."

I noticed, Alec thought. Steering his thoughts to safer less intimate ground, Alec said the first thing that came into his mind. "You're good with babies. You'd make a good mother."

Jade immediately sent him a censuring glare. "Unlike Nicole?"

"I didn't say that."

Color highlighted her cheeks. "You didn't have to."

Alec shrugged. "Okay, now that you mention it, your sister didn't strike me as very maternal."

"She's not," Jade returned calmly, holding his gaze. "That doesn't mean she couldn't learn."

Aware Andy was sound asleep again, Jade transferred him gently to the car seat and strapped him in securely. She covered him lightly with a blanket, then turned to Alec. "Got any coffee or anything?"

Alec nodded. "Come on back to the galley. You can take your pick of the different blends and I'll brew us a pot."

To his disappointment, she bypassed the many exotic blends and selected decaf. "Afraid to live dangerously?" he teased.

"Too much caffeine gives me the shakes," she told him.

Alec wondered what else would make her tremble, then pushed the unexpectedly amorous thought aside as he set about routinely making coffee. He didn't need to be fantasizing about what it would be like to have Jade Kincaid in bed beneath him, her arms and legs wrapped around him as she eagerly returned his kisses. Any more than he needed to be fantasizing about what she would look like, clothed only in a lacy teddy.

"So why haven't you ever married?" he asked conversationally, once the coffee had started to brew.

Jade's chin lifted contentiously. "How do you know I'm not?" she asked.

He nodded at her soft, slender yet capable hands. "No ring."

She turned her back on him and stared out the jet window at the gray winter clouds below. "I guess I haven't found Mr. Right."

"Haven't found him? Or haven't looked?"

Jade turned back to face him. "Can we get off this subject?"

Appreciating the annoyed sparkle in her dark jade eyes, he persisted despite her plea. "I'm curious."

Jade crossed her arms at her waist. "Yeah, well, remember what curiosity did to the cat," she advised him flatly.

He laughed, not the least bit put off. "Were you and Nicole close growing up?"

Jade sighed and paced the small galley restlessly while they both waited for the coffee to brew. "Not really."

Again, Alec was consumed with a depth of curiosity he couldn't ignore. "Why not?"

Jade lifted her face to his. She studied him openly for a moment, then admitted with a beleaguered sigh, "Nicole could never refuse the challenge of trying to steal my boyfriends from me, which, as you can probably imagine, ruined it for both of us with the men in our lives. Nicole couldn't understand what the problem was, so we grew apart."

Despite her candor, Alec had the feeling she wasn't telling him everything. "And that's it?" he probed.

"Isn't that enough?"

No, Alec thought, it wasn't. "Jade, there's no reason for you to be jealous of your sister." He couldn't even figure out why she was.

"I'm not—"

"Because the two of you aren't even in the same league,"

Alec said, and then he acted purely on instinct, doing what he had wanted to for hours now.

The next thing Jade knew his arms had closed around her waist and brought her close. She tipped her head back and opened her mouth to protest, only to have his own lips clamp down firmly on hers, silencing the fervent protest she was about to make. At once she was aware of so many things, the softness of his lips, the sheer male insistence of his kiss, the invasion of his tongue.

There had been many women in Alec's life. Nameless faceless women who had spent hours, sometimes even days, in his bed. But none of those women, no matter how pretty or clever, had ever affected him the way Jade Kincaid did.

One touch and he was on fire. One caress of her lips against his turned him to molten lava. The scent of her, all wildflowers and sunshine, drove him wild.

He had known her mouth would be soft. He hadn't counted on her being so quick to respond to him. He had expected to have to woo her with sweet gentle kisses, but she had surprised him by opening her mouth to him right away. And once he'd felt her surrender, felt the softness of her body pressed against his, there was no stopping with just one kiss. No pretending that something extraordinary wasn't happening between them....

Jade had known from the second Alec Roman charged into her office, baby in arms, that he was a dangerously determined man. She just hadn't expected his ambitions to include seducing her. And even though she knew she should be resisting his incredibly tantalizing kisses, she couldn't seem to summon up the willpower needed to call a halt to his lusty embrace.

At least not right away, not when he knew just how to kiss her, just how to make her go all soft and hot inside. She had never felt so sensual, never responded so openly, never been kissed and held quite so masterfully. Yearning swept through her in sweet wild waves and for just the slightest moment, a moment that seemed forever suspended in time, Jade allowed herself to mold her body against him and kiss him back. Not just once, but again, and again, and again.

"Damn, but you feel good, Jade," Alec whispered against her mouth. His hands threaded through her hair, tilting her face up to his. He held her mouth under his as he inundated her with kisses, with the warm security of his tall strong body.

I know, Jade thought, as the passion swirled and dipped around her, drawing her into its mesmerizing depths. *You feel good, too, Alec.*

"But not here," Alec continued softly, as he left a hot trail of kisses from her ear, down the nape of her neck, across her jaw, and back to her mouth again. "There's a bed in the rear cabin," he said impatiently, his mouth hovering over hers as he reached for the buttons on her blouse. "We can—"

His attempt to undress her brought her swiftly back to reality. Realizing what was about to happen, what she had encouraged him to do, Jade placed both hands on his chest and pushed him away from her. "I can't believe you just said that!" Her low voice reverberated with hurt, as the sensual mist receded and her sanity returned. *I can't believe what we almost did!*

Alec stood very still. He was aware he was close to losing everything here. And he didn't even know what he'd done. "It's a crime to want to be comfortable?" he asked softly.

"It's a crime," she corrected sternly, "to seduce unsuspecting women on your playboy jet."

"Wait a minute," Alec interrupted. For the first time he could remember, he felt completely at a loss with another human being. "This is a business plane, Jade."

She crossed her arms in front of her and regarded him wryly. "Now I suppose you'll tell me what just happened was business, too?"

"No, of course not," Alec countered, exasperated she was being so deliberately dense. "There's a bed on this jet because I frequently take twenty-four-hour flights to the Far east, and I sleep en route."

"Are you finished?" Jade demanded tightly, her patience both with him, and the situation, obviously exhausted.

Figuring she'd cool down if he could just kiss her again, Alec reached for her. "I don't have to be," he whispered softly, wanting only to feel her in his arms again, all warm and clinging.

But that, too, was the wrong thing to say and do.

Jade batted his hands away and glared at him, her chest heaving as her temper flared out of control. "Damn you, Alec Roman! After all I just told you about the history between Nicole and myself, how dare you try and seduce me into your bed!"

"What do you mean?" Alec volleyed back "How dare I try and seduce you? You know damn well it didn't start out that way. It started out with a kiss, Jade. A simple kiss."

"One that never should have happened." She pivoted on her heel and pushed past him.

"Maybe not," Alec conceded as he followed her back to her seat, "but it's not as if I actually seduced you, either."

"Given half a chance, you would have," she pointed out coolly. "Had I allowed you to kiss me again, you would have taken me back to your bed and made love to me without a second's thought."

"Yeah, well…" There was no getting around that, so Alec didn't even try. "I'm not going to apologize for wanting you, Jade."

"Then perhaps you should apologize for acting on that desire," she advised, the rigid set of her spine and shoulders thrusting her soft breasts up and out.

Alec tore his gaze from the soft globes and focused on her face. Her lips were still pink and damp and swollen from his kisses. He ached with the desire to kiss her again and it irked him no end to be denied that opportunity. It wasn't as if he had set out to rob her of her purity deliberately, he thought.

Working to keep his voice at the same soothing level, he reminded her, "That desire, as you so primly put it, Jade, was mutual."

Jade tossed her head and ignored his steady glance. "*Was* being the operative word here, I believe."

Alec felt his jaw tighten. Normally, he was a patient man, but Jade had a way of pushing his composure to the limits. "You're telling me it won't happen again?"

She held herself stiffly. "I'm telling you you're deluding yourself if you think it will."

Alec shook his head, watching as she refastened her seat belt. This was precisely why he made it a practice to steer clear of complicated entanglements with women. He hated emotional scenes, and an emotional scene with a woman he might be able to care about was even worse. "I should have known you'd react hysterically," Alec muttered beneath his breath, still unable to shake the feel of those kisses, the memory of the way she'd felt and smelled and tasted, the way she kissed him back, with absolutely nothing held in check.

He felt…led on.

He felt…disappointed.

"I should have known you'd be too good to be true."

"What?" Jade snapped, her eyes flashing in a way that told him she'd caught only part of what he'd just said.

For a second, Alec almost told her. But guessing how she'd react if he tried to tell her what they'd just shared had been special made him decide against it. There was no use wasting words that were going to fall on deaf ears. He'd talk to her later—maybe—when she calmed down. *If* she calmed down. Right now he even had his doubts about that.

"Never mind," Alec said brusquely. It was his dumb luck to fall head over heels in lust with one sister while in the midst of chasing down the other. He never should have made a pass at a woman like Jade the same day they'd met…. He should have waited. Maybe if he'd waited, he thought as the jet banked and prepared to land, she wouldn't resent him now.

Jade was silent as the jet landed at La Guardia. Figuring it was best not to try to engage her in conversation, Alec used the lull to do some work on his laptop computer. As always, immersing himself in business soothed him, and he was in a positive frame of mind when the three of them disembarked.

He had arranged for a limousine to meet them at the airport. It took them promptly to the Renown Modeling Agency. Because Jade was there, Myra Lansky agreed to see them.

"I'll be frank," Myra Lansky began, when they were all settled in her office. A tiny slip of a woman, she had a short, sleek cap of hennaed hair and uneven features that had been expertly made up to enviable sophistication. "Things weren't good the last time I saw Nicole." Myra smiled at baby Andy, who Jade was holding, and took his little hand in hers.

"Why weren't they good?" Jade asked.

Myra frowned, still looking a little distracted as she continued to play with the baby. "Nicole had been gaining weight and she looked a little bloated around the face. Like she had been partying too much or hitting the dance clubs every night."

Either that, or she had been secretly pregnant with Alec Roman's child, Jade thought uncomfortably.

"The bottom line is, the lousy care she was taking of herself showed," Myra Lansky continued without an ounce of sympathy for the model whose career she had handled for the past twelve years. She sat back and looked at Jade. "There was no makeup that could hide the circles under her eyes, or the faint wrinkles beginning to appear around her mouth. But then again, she was twenty-six. She had already put in a good twelve years before the cameras. Aside from the Ingenue soap contract, she had no other job offers coming in on a regular basis. It was easy to see that it was time she began to move on. I suggested she lose some weight immediately and start looking at other long-term avenues of employment. Perhaps a career as an actor. She told me she had no ambition or talent in that area, so I suggested she go back to school."

Despite the differences between them, Jade felt her heart go out to Nicole. She didn't envy her sister, being in a profession where looks were the only thing that counted, and where people were as disposable as yesterday's trash. Jade swallowed around the lump of empathetic emotion in her throat, and forced herself to ask calmly, "How did Nicole react to this?"

"Badly. For two weeks, she terrorized everyone in the office. She was already in trouble with the Ingenue soap people. Listen, would you mind if I held that baby? He's just so adorable."

Jade looked at Alec, not sure how he'd feel about that. "Sure," he said. He watched as Jade handed baby Andy over to Myra. She clucked over him and made goofy faces and smiled, finally getting a little sound that just might have been a giggle—or something close to it—out of him.

Taking advantage of Myra's infatuation with Andy, Alec asked genially, "Why was Nicole in trouble with the Ingenue soap people? I thought they loved her. They're always running her commercials. You know, the ones where she sits in a sunlit meadow—"

"Looking like an angel," Myra smiled.

"—and confesses that the secret of her beauty is Ingenue soap."

"Those commercials are very successful." Myra paced back and forth, Andy gurgling in her arms. "But there's a lot more involved in being a spokesmodel than just appearing in print or television ads. There are personal appearances to be made."

"And that's where Nicole screwed up," Jade guessed.

Myra nodded. "Nicole skipped a couple of receptions in her honor when she was in Japan last spring on a whim, and offended her Japanese hosts. The Ingenue people were embarrassed. And angry, as they had every right to be."

Jade slanted a look at Alec and noted he had the grace to look faintly embarrassed, which confirmed her guess he'd had something to do with Nicole's absences from those receptions.

Myra continued grimly, "They're talking about not renewing her contract when it comes up again in April. If she loses that she'll have nothing. Since she only tours for Ingenue from April to August anyway, I gave her the advice I would have given my own daughters. I suggested Nicole take a month or so off to think about her future. So she did. Unfortunately, she never came back to the agency or let us know where she is.''

"So when did you last see or hear from her?" Alec asked. Looking restless now himself, he stood and took the baby back.

"Seven months ago."

"And you haven't heard from her at all since?" Jade asked tensely as she struggled to push the image of Nicole, alone, pregnant, scared, and unemployed, from her mind. "Not even a postcard?"

"No." Myra began to look concerned, too. She paused. "Surely the two of you got together at Christmas? I mean, I know you were the only family she had, Jade."

"No, we didn't," Jade said tightly, as she struggled unsuccessfully to deal with her guilt. How had it come to this? That she was completely cut off from the only family she had left?

Myra sat on the edge of her desk. Briefly, she looked as shocked and concerned as Jade felt. "Well, look, you know what a survivor Nicole is," Myra stated finally. "I'm sure she's okay. Maybe she'll get in touch with us in April, at tax time."

Alec frowned. "That'll be too late. We need to talk to her now."

Myra Lansky quirked a hennaed brow and regarded Alec curiously, before she went back to studying the baby again. "What's the rush?"

"It's a personal matter," Alec answered quietly.

Jade asked, "When does Nicole's Ingenue soap contract expire?"

"April sixth." Myra looked at them both. "I'm sure she'll want to know if her contract has been renewed."

But what if she wasn't selected to be the Ingenue girl

again? Jade wondered. What then? Nicole had no other skills. No other way to get a job.

Alec handed the baby to Jade, then reached into his pocket and withdrew a business card with his name and number on it. "If Nicole should call prior to that, will you tell her I'm looking for her?"

Myra Lansky nodded before she gave baby Andy a last fond look. "Certainly. But don't hold your breath, because the chances of that are slim."

"NOW WHAT?" Jade asked Alec once they were out on the sidewalk again. Andy cuddled in her arms contentedly.

"Nicole had an apartment in town, didn't she?" Alec asked as he ushered them into the warm, waiting limousine. "Let's go there."

It only took fifteen minutes by cab to get to Nicole's apartment on the Upper West Side. To Jade's relief, only one of Nicole's five old roommates, Tawny Blair, was around—the others were all off on assignment in Europe, Africa, and South America. The apartment was beautifully furnished but Alec, damn him, seemed to be aware of nothing except the statuesque model with the wild mane of salon-streaked hair, and the information he hoped to get from her.

"Nicole split, still owing her share of the rent," Tawny reported matter-of-factly to Alec and Jade, as she fixed herself a health-food shake in the blender. "She didn't tell us she was leaving, either, so the rest of us are royally hacked off at her. Her stuff is in the basement storage."

Jade's brow furrowed as she shifted the sleeping baby in her arms. Something was wrong here. Nicole cared as much about her possessions as she did about her looks. "Nicole hasn't been back for any of it?" she asked, concerned.

"No." Tawny stuck a straw in her drink and carried it around the apartment, sipping as she went.

"And no one here has heard from her?" Alec asked.

Tawny paused in front of a window and opened the venetian blinds. "Hey. We're not exactly her mother," she said as late-morning sunlight poured into the room. She strode barefoot over to the pine armoire in the corner. "Here's her mail, though."

As Jade had expected, the stack was all bills, most of them long overdue. She sent a tentative look at Alec, wishing he didn't look quite so much like a man to lean on in times of stress, then swung back to face Tawny, bumping into Alec's chest in the process. He lifted a hand to steady her. The gesture was an innocent one, but it still reminded her of his kisses and her own unexpectedly tempestuous response to them. Jade still couldn't believe she had almost made love to him, a man she had just met.

Working to keep the flush of physical awareness from her cheeks, Jade focused on Tawny as she regained her balance, and then stepped away from Alec once again. "Do you mind if we go down to the basement and take a look at Nicole's things?" she asked. Maybe there would be some clue as to where Nicole had gone down there.

"Be my guest," Tawny said. She gave Alec a dazzling smile, which he returned. "I'll get the key. Listen, if Nicole's not coming back, and you want to move the stuff out, we'd appreciate it."

Jade stuffed Nicole's mail in her bag, then Alec, Jade, and Andy went down to the basement. The storage locker was a mesh six-by-six square, filled with garbage bags full of what appeared to be clothing and boxes of shoes.

Alec unlocked it and pulled out a slant board. Jade sat down on one end of it, primly tugging her skirt down to her knees. Alec sat on the other, and this time pretended gallantly not to look. Trying not to show her relief that he was no longer indulging himself with leisurely visual tours of her legs, Jade suggested, "Before we go any further, let's go through this mail, piece by piece, just to make sure it's all what it seems."

"Good idea," Alec said as Jade handed him a stack of the bills, careful not to disturb the sleeping baby on her lap.

Fifteen minutes and some rapid calculations later, they

were astounded by what they had found. "She's got over thirty-five thousand dollars on her credit cards alone," Jade concluded, shocked.

"Not to mention that she's in the soup with her bank. This last statement says that her account had been grievously overdrawn."

Jade released a slow breath as her anxiety built. Even if she wanted to help Nicole out of this mess, and she still wasn't sure how involved she wanted to get with her wild baby sister again, Jade knew she couldn't. It was all she could do to pay back the bank loan she'd taken out to start her business. What little she could loan Nicole wouldn't begin to make a dent in credit card charges like these. "When was the last deposit or withdrawal made?" Jade asked tensely.

"Last August. About the same time she disappeared."

They sat in silence for a moment, both unhappy, both worried. "If she was pregnant, and knew she couldn't work," Jade speculated aloud finally, "her disappearing kind of makes sense."

"If that were the case, if she really were in trouble, why didn't she try to get support out of me then?" Alec asked. "After all, she knew how wealthy I was."

Jade shrugged and neatened the bills into a tidy stack. "Maybe she thought she could do it alone. Maybe she planned to live on her credit cards for a few months. Are there any recent charges on any of these credit card bills?"

"Nothing. Not that that's a surprise. She was over her limit on all of them."

Jade held the sleeping Andy even closer. "Obviously this situation was much more serious than I realized," Jade said softly. She lifted her eyes to his, and just for a moment, let herself drown in the kindness she saw in the dark sable brown depths. What would it have been like, she wondered, if the two of them had just met another way? Not that there was any use speculating on what could have been, she reminded herself sternly.

"I hadn't realized Nicole was so deeply in debt." Jade

frowned, turning her attention to the huge pile of bills once again.

"And maybe hoping to find someone wealthy enough to bail her out of the mess." Alec scowled. Was it possible, he wondered, that Nicole had gotten pregnant with his baby deliberately, hoping he would bail her out financially, not just now, but for the rest of her life?

Jade sighed and leaned toward Alec, careful to keep her voice low, so as not to disturb the baby. "Well, whether or not Nicole was planning to come back to New York at some point, I don't understand why she left all these clothes behind."

Alec shrugged, not sure he cared about Nicole, baby or no, half as much as he cared about Jade. But like it or not, there was a problem to be solved and he sensed he wouldn't get anywhere with Jade until the problem was completely taken care of and Nicole was a closed chapter in his life.

Turning his attention back to the locker contents, Alec speculated freely, "If she were pregnant, the clothes in this locker would not have done her much good. At least not until after she'd had the baby, and even then, she might not be able to fit into them, particularly if she were gaining weight as quickly as Myra Lansky indicated to us."

"True."

For a moment, their glances meshed. Alec felt strangely at peace. He hadn't talked so freely with a woman in a long time, even if it was largely about someone else.

Her whole body stiff with accumulated tension and worry, Jade lifted Andy in her arms, stood and handed Andy back to Alec.

She was filled with conflicting feelings. There were so many things she should have done and said, she saw now in retrospect. Maybe if she had just tried to work out this problem with Nicole and her boyfriends earlier, Nicole never would have seduced Clark away from her. Maybe they wouldn't have had this breach in their relationship. But she couldn't tell Alec about Clark and the stinging humiliation

Jade had felt when her relationship ended. It was bad enough he knew as much dirt on Nicole as he did.

Jade sighed and shook her head in mute self-remonstration. "I'm sorry, Alec."

Again, Alec slid his free hand under her elbow to steady her. She felt the tantalizing warmth of him through her clothes. As his grip tightened, the sensation intensified. Tremors started deep inside her. Lower still, there was an insistent ache.

"Sorry for what?" he asked softly, as he continued to cradle Andy in one arm and hold onto her with the other.

For allowing myself to be attracted to you, Jade thought. *For allowing myself to kiss you like nothing else, no one else, mattered, when all along I knew better.* Maybe she was more like the reckless Nicole than she thought!

Aware her heart was pounding, Jade withdrew her arm from his light grasp and stepped back. She had to put these crazy thoughts aside.

Swallowing to relieve the dryness in her throat, Jade said, "I think I inadvertently ignored Nicole's plea for help. Last summer, Nicole left several urgent messages on my answering machine. I never returned her calls because we were quarreling."

Alec's black brows drew together. "About what?"

"It doesn't matter." Jade averted her eyes.

"If you sensed she was in trouble, why didn't you return her calls?" Alec asked softly.

Jade flushed. "Because she was always asking me for money, which was ridiculous since she earned double what I made as a nutritionist."

Alec continued to regard her steadily.

"Look, I think under the circumstances, until we find Nicole, I had better take the baby," Jade said finally. Maybe she couldn't change the past, but she could do better in the future. And she could start by doing right by Andy.

Alec held Andy closer to his chest, looking very much at that moment like a protective new father. "No way!"

Jade's spine stiffened. He was acting as if she had no say in this matter—after he had not only dragged her into it, but proved with his clumsy handling of Andy that he knew next to nothing about babies. The familial responsibility she'd felt all her life came back to hit her, full force. "Look, Alec, Andy's my sister's baby. I have a responsibility here, too."

"And that is?"

"To look out for Nicole's interests, just as you want to look after yours."

"I'm not quarreling with that," Alec asserted, his expression intractable. "I understand you care about the baby, Jade. Andy's so cute he'd be hard not to love. But if you want to watch Andy, Jade—"

"And I do!" She owed her parents, Nicole, and her tiny nephew that much.

"—you'll have to do so under my roof."

Chapter Three

"Look, I know what's worrying you," Alec said as he surveyed the distressed look on Jade's face that had appeared that moment he'd stipulated their care of Andy be jointly managed, under his roof. "You're thinking about the way we kissed back on the jet—"

She smiled at him sweetly. "And you're not?"

"—and worrying it'll happen again," Alec continued matter-of-factly, resisting what seemed to be an ever present desire to haul her into his arms and kiss her senseless once again.

Suddenly seeming able to read his mind all too well, Jade gave him a skeptical look. "And you're promising me that it won't," she surmised flatly.

"Something like that," Alec drawled, hoping against hope he could tease Jade into seeing the humor of the situation, instead of the potential for romantic crisis.

"Not good enough, Alec. Not nearly."

"Well, that's too bad. Because it's the best I can do right now." It was the end of a long day that had been filled with tension, worry, and travel. Yet Jade still looked fresh as a daisy. She'd asked him earlier what it was about her that he based his impressions on. Was it her hair, the soft, sensual clothing she wore, the color of the lipstick on her soft, bow-shaped lips, or even the tight dark brown curls that tumbled Nicole Kidman-style to her shoulders? Alec couldn't say precisely what it was about her that he found so very compelling. He only knew he wanted her, and that the yearning he felt got stronger with every second that passed.

But he also knew they'd just met, only kissed one time. Already Jade was making way too much out of those kisses, acting as if their one necking session was a damn marriage proposal instead of a simple exchange of affection between new friends. That alone was a danger sign. Coupled with the accusing glances she was giving him...

"You never should have tried to seduce me," she continued, reproaching him softly.

Alec heard the underlying note of steel in her hushed voice, and smiled. He wasn't so sure he'd been the only one doing the seducing, but because he was a gentleman, he let her remark pass. For the time being, anyway. "Meaning what?" he asked in mild exasperation. "That the necking we were doing was okay? If I'd just stopped there, you wouldn't have gotten mad at me, and we wouldn't be quarreling now?"

"You know very well the incident was not appropriate for our situation," Jade replied tightly as a fresh wave of color flowed into her cheeks.

"Then what would have been okay?" Alec persisted, frankly curious as to how her mind worked. "One kiss? Two? Or only the closed-mouth variety? Was it the French kissing, Jade," he whispered silkily, "or the fact I started to undress you that really got you hot under the collar?"

"You're making a joke out of this," she accused, her green eyes throwing daggers at him, her soft mouth forming a pretty pout.

The rigidity of Alec's lower body told him this was no joke. He stepped nearer and ran a caressing hand up the length of her sleeve. "And you're taking what happened earlier much too seriously," he said, cupping her shoulder warmly. His eyes lasered down into hers as he continued in his softest, most reasonable voice. "You're acting as if we were committing some criminal act, instead of..." He floundered, not sure exactly how to put it.

Jade was as still as a statue as she studied his face. "What?"

"...getting to know each other a little better," Alec finished, knowing she'd likely take offense at whatever he said.

Jade lifted a discriminating brow. "Is that what you call it?"

Helpless to do otherwise Alec watched Jade slip out of his grasp and walk away from him. "Well, I know it wasn't a damn marriage proposal," he called to her retreating back. She pivoted to face him. The look she gave him was one of fury. Knowing they couldn't go on quarreling this way, Alec lowered his voice. "Look, Jade, I enjoyed kissing you," he told her, stepping nearer once again. "And unless I miss my guess, you enjoyed it, too."

To his surprise, Jade voiced no denials. "Has it occurred to you," she asked defiantly, lifting her chin, "that your situation with my sister and Andy is complicated enough without factoring me into the equation, too? Has it occurred to you that even though I'm highly attracted to you I might want my own man to love, someone who doesn't have a previous sexual history with my sister?"

No, he hadn't thought about that. "I hadn't looked at the situation that way," Alec admitted reluctantly.

"Well, I have," Jade retorted emotionally as she planted both hands on her slender hips.

"Okay, look," he conceded with a sigh as Jade turned and walked away from him. "You have my promise I won't put the moves on you again. Unless you want me to, that is."

Jade sent him a skeptical look over her shoulder. "I already told you I don't," she reminded him frankly.

"I'll let you retain the right to change your mind," Alec offered generously, recalling what she'd just said about being "highly attracted" to him. As for the problems, problems were always there. Problems could be worked around.

"I won't change my mind," she warned.

Alec warmed to her passionate nature. "We'll see. In the meantime—" his voice softened seriously "—I promise I

won't rush you again." Her expression was so feisty he
couldn't help grinning. "What's the matter?" he teased.
"Don't you believe me?"

Arms folded at her waist, she continued walking away
from him. "I don't know you well enough to believe you or
not at this point," she said irritably, then swung around to
face him once again. Her legs braced a foot apart, her high
heels digging into the floor, she lifted her chin and studied
him contentiously. "Besides, I don't want you making promises you might not be able to keep."

Alec knew what she meant. Just seconds ago, he had promised not to kiss her again. But already, he was itching to get
his hands on her, to feel that sweet soft mouth of hers crushed
under his, and see what was under that slim suede skirt and
billowy white blouse. Was she as golden all over, and as soft,
and scented with perfume? With effort, he clamped down on
his erotic thoughts. His eyes boring into hers, he asked,
"What makes you think I won't be able to keep that promise?" *If I set my mind to it,* he added silently. He wasn't sure
he really wanted to do that, either.

The corners of her sensual mouth curved upward in exasperation. "Baby Andy, for one thing," she replied sweetly.

He released a short, exasperated breath and tried not to
notice the way her feisty stance emphasized the slim sexiness
of her legs. "I explained that to you," Alec repeated with as
much patience as he could muster. "It was an exceptional
situation."

"Do tell," she replied with a sweetness that set his teeth
on edge.

Alec frowned. "You know what I mean, Jade."

He liked sex as much as the next person, hell maybe more
than the next person, but he wasn't in the habit of going home
with women he barely knew. That had just happened. And
though he didn't regret it, if he had it to do all over again he
didn't know if he'd repeat the indiscretion. Especially now
that he'd met Jade....

"Well, this is also an exceptional situation, Alec Roman,"

she reminded him fiercely, then added, "and I don't want to make it any more exceptional than it already is. Not to mention the fact that I have a business in Pittsburgh."

"Yeah, right." He pressed his lips together in regret. He hated to see her go, but maybe she was right, maybe it was time. Certainly he didn't need to be tempting fate, risking an involvement with another sexy Kincaid sister.

"Well, you've certainly done your part," he allowed cordially. "I'll see you back to Pittsburgh, and then take care of Andy on my own." Alec rubbed a hand across the back of his neck. Damn, but he was tense today. "I'm sure I can hire a baby nurse to watch him for me. I've got a business deal pending anyway."

"Are you trying to cut me out?"

"I handle my own problems." Alec loosened the knot of his tie and unbuttoned the first button on his shirt.

"Meaning?"

He brushed past Jade and went toward the galley. "I don't need anyone meddling in my private life, thanks," he said over his shoulder. "I can take it from here." He reached into the refrigerator and pulled out a can of Coke.

"You're a one-man army?" she guessed when she'd reached his side.

It wasn't a compliment, but Alec pretended it was anyway. "Something like that," he said smugly.

She watched him take a long sip. "I don't think so. And you really should be drinking fruit or vegetable juice or even water instead of soda."

"I'll take that under advisement." Alec leaned against the stainless steel counter. "As for Andy, he's not your problem anymore."

Jade took a step closer to him. "Look, Alec, I did not want to be involved in this, but now that I am, I'm not just going to walk away from my nephew."

Alec grimaced and took another long draught of the icy liquid. "I don't think you have a choice here, Jade." He gave her a level look, trying not to notice how thick and velvety her eyelashes were, or how well they framed her wide expressive jade green eyes. "Andy isn't your baby."

"But he is my nephew," Jade countered firmly. She took another step nearer, inundating him with the wildflowers and sunshine scent of her perfume. "And that makes him a part of my family. If I have to, I'll fight you for temporary custody of him."

Alec ignored the feelings of desire generated by her closeness. He had been afraid this would get ugly all along, afraid there would be a price to pay for allowing himself even the slightest intimacy with Jade Kincaid. But fool that he was, he had allowed it anyway. "I thought you wanted to avoid a public scandal," he said.

"We both do. That's why we're going to continue to work together on this until we find my sister."

Alec took another long drink of cola, wishing that the idea of staying so close to Jade, of perhaps even kissing her again, carrying her to his bed, and making wild passionate exhausting love to her, was a little less appealing to him. "What about your work?" he queried softly.

"I'm sure I can watch Andy and still get things done, although I'm going to have to juggle some of my appointments with clients. I'll just pack up my stuff and bring things to Philadelphia. I assume you have room for me at your place, since it was your idea we both be under one roof?"

It had been his idea, all right, Alec realized with chagrin. He had never really figured she'd take him up on it. "Right," he said gruffly.

Jade knew how he felt. She didn't want to live with Alec Roman for one day, even if it was for Andy's sake. But whether she liked it or not, she had a responsibility here, Jade told herself firmly. She had to see that Andy was all right. She had the feeling that Alec Roman's idea of proper child care was hiring a nanny so he could go back to building his empire and forget all about the tiny son he had sired. Having been raised by a distant, workaholic father herself, she wasn't about to let the same thing happen to the adorable little baby who had already snagged her heart in a very fundamental way. She had to make sure he was very well taken care of and had at least had the chance to be reunited with his mother.

"You're determined to do this?" Alec asked grimly.

Jade nodded. "Very."

His mouth tightened even more. "Then let's get to it."

After that, everything happened with amazing swiftness. Alec flew her to Pittsburgh to retrieve enough clothes for a week—although they were both hoping it wouldn't take nearly that long to locate Nicole—her portable fax machine, cellular phone, and computer. And then back to his home base of Philadelphia. During both flights, he dragged out a briefcase, laptop computer, and phone. He spent the whole time completely immersed in Roman Computer business. Jade spent the whole time cooing over Andy.

By midnight Saturday, they had landed in Philadelphia and were en route to his home on Society Hill. As they entered the open wrought iron gates and drove up the circular drive, Jade couldn't help but catch her breath. Located in a picturesque area with cobblestone streets and plentiful parks, the three-story red brick home boasted a mansard roof with dormer windows. Pine green shutters adorned every window. The front door was painted a glossy white. Smokestacks had been built at each end of the house. Tall hedges and an abundance of mature trees provided privacy while adding to the elegant, pastoral setting.

Inside, the ivy-covered, century-old mansion was everything Jade would've expected. A sweeping staircase dominated the marble-floored front hall. A chandelier sparkled overhead. To the right was a banquet-sized dining room, to the left, a formal living room filled with antiques. To the rear of that was a paneled study with a huge fireplace, and a gourmet kitchen that was a cook's dream.

Well, this explained further why her sister might have set her sights on Alec Roman, Jade thought. His mansion was made for entertaining. And as owner of one of the most successful computer firms in the country, he certainly had the money for it. Nicole was such a party animal, she had to see the endless possibilities in marrying such a man.

"You can have your choice of bedrooms," Alec began as he led the way up the narrow back staircase to the second floor.

"What's the difference?" Jade asked as she shifted Andy to her other arm.

Alec cast a look at her over his shoulder. "Color schemes and decor, mostly. Each bedroom on the second floor has its own private bath."

Thank goodness for that, Jade thought. She wouldn't be running into a scantily clad Alec before or after his shower. She needn't discover if he slept sans clothing or in silk pajamas or Jockey briefs, if he looked as sexy just getting out of bed in the morning as he did in the middle of the day, or late at night.

"Where is your room?" she asked, making a mental note to find out where he was quartered and then avoid going that way as much as possible.

"Right here, on the left." He paused in the doorway, and again, Jade was surprised. She didn't know what she had expected of the sexy CEO. A king-of-Siam decor, maybe. Something appropriate for a bachelor on the prowl. But there were no mirrors on the ceiling, and there was no Jacuzzi built up on a platform beside the bed. The bed was a cozy double, not a king. The oak furniture was plain and masculine. The only hint of his personality was in the color scheme. Everything in the room—drapes, upholstery, carpet, bedspread— was done in the same steely blue shade. It shouldn't have worked, and yet—like his clothes—it did.

There was a beautiful cradle standing in the corner. "I had Andy in here with me last night. I was afraid I wouldn't hear him if he woke, otherwise. Not that he slept all that much." Alec frowned.

"You should get a baby monitor at the store. That way

you'll be able to hear him even if you're not with him,'' Jade suggested.

Alec stepped closer and she caught the green woodsy scent of his cologne. "They make those?" he asked.

Jade smiled. "They're more popular than walkie-talkies.''

Again, Alec looked surprised.

"But I'll take Andy tonight, since you had him last night,'' Jade said, aware her heart had started to pound again as she contemplated the night ahead of them. "So if you want to move that cradle down to whichever room you want me in, Alec, I'll—''

"All the beds in all the rooms are made up,'' Alec interrupted, already sounding a little bored with their arrangement as he lounged in his bedroom doorway. "You choose.''

Alec knew it was too late to be having second thoughts about this arrangement, but dammit, he *was* having second thoughts. Maybe it wasn't such a good idea, having Jade underfoot. He didn't mind sharing a bed with a woman for a couple of hours, but sharing a breakfast table with someone was another matter entirely. He liked his privacy. He didn't want anyone telling him what to eat or when to eat it. And he didn't want to see Jade Kincaid in anything more revealing than the business clothes she had on, for fear what would happen if either of their hormones unexpectedly kicked into high gear again. Alec's body tightened painfully just thinking about the way she had responded to him, the way she kissed. How the devil was he supposed to forget all about that? Jade apparently had, if her cool collected expression was any indication of her inner feelings.

"You're sure it doesn't matter to you which room I take?'' Jade asked, searching his face.

"Not at all.''

Andy still in her arms, Jade backed out of his bedroom and continued her survey of the second floor, until she reached the far end of the hall.

Aware Alec was calmly, methodically, assessing every move she made, she selected a pink, rose, and white bedroom next to the back stairs. Alec made no comment on her selection, merely carried the cradle in and put it in the corner, where Jade directed. Once it was settled, she put Andy down and covered him with a blanket. He stirred slightly, let out a soft whimper that had Jade and Alec both holding their breaths, then settled heavily back into an exhausted, travel-weary sleep.

"I'll go down and get your suitcases," Alec said.

While he did that, she took her cellular phone in the bedroom across the hall and called her answering service in Pittsburgh.

When he'd finished, he joined her. "Any word from your sister?"

"None."

"Isn't there somewhere else you can look? Or anyone else you can call, now that you've had time to think about it?"

"Offhand, I can't think of anyone," Jade admitted reluctantly, "and believe me, I've wracked my brain." Nicole was breathtakingly beautiful, but she didn't have a lot of true friendships with other people. Jade sighed her own frustration and gave Alec an empathetic look. "I feel sure we could clear this up swiftly, if only we could talk to her."

"Maybe, maybe not," Alec predicted cryptically. "Any woman who would abandon her own child—"

He was interrupted by a soft, halfhearted whimper from the cradle in the next room.

"Guess he's not as sleepy as we thought," Jade said. Retracing her steps, she set her cellular phone on the nightstand.

Beside her, Alec was already rushing to the rescue. "Maybe if you hadn't held him the whole time we were in the air," Alec drawled, "he wouldn't have slept the whole way home and be awake again now."

"It's impossible to spoil a baby, Alec," Jade countered as she went to stand beside Alec. "They just like to be held, same as adults."

"Gotta hand it to you, Andy, you've got the right idea,

wanting to spend most of the afternoon and all of the evening snuggled up against a pair of warm female breasts.''

Jade flushed despite her decision not to. ''Very funny.''

Alec wiggled his eyebrows at her. ''I thought so. You know, maybe we should get one of those thingamajigs,'' he suggested as he awkwardly picked up Andy.

Jade tried desperately to follow what he was saying, which wasn't easy, given their close proximity and his maddening lack of specificity. When he was that near to her, all she could think about was what a wonderful body he had, so hard and strong and tall. ''A baby carrier, you mean?'' she asked.

Alec shrugged and continued to try to get a better hold on the squirming baby in his large, capable hands. ''I don't know what it's called,'' he said, exasperated. ''You wear it like a sling in front of you.''

''That's a baby carrier,'' Jade told him as she went to get a clean diaper. ''Not a bad idea for a complete novice.''

''Hey, Andy, hear that? I just got high praise from our in-residence baby pro,'' Alec retorted dryly as he gingerly lowered Andy toward the double bed. At the tentative handling by his father, Andy's tiny brows knit together in concern for his own well-being. He peered up into Alec's face, looked over at Jade, and then let out a wail loud enough to wake the dead.

''Okay, that's it. I gave it my best shot.'' Alec handed Andy over to Jade. ''Take him before he wakes the entire neighborhood.''

Jade cradled Andy close to her chest. ''You're being ridiculous, Alec. Andy's crying has nothing to do with your gender.''

''The heck it doesn't.''

''There, there, now,'' Jade soothed Andy, steadfastly ignoring Alec's smug gaze. ''It's all right, sweetie. No need to cry.'' Andy quieted almost immediately. After several jerky tries, he managed to stuff his tiny fist into his mouth. He sucked noisily, his eyes huge and watchful as they focused on Jade's face.

For not the first time in her life, Jade felt a pang of regret that she hadn't yet had any children of her own. She had always thought by this time in her life she would have three or four babies. But it hadn't worked out that way.

"Yeah. And whether you're willing to admit it or not, he also likes women better than men," Alec said, watching as Jade efficiently changed Andy's diaper.

"Yes, I know, because we have breasts," Jade recited, determined to beat Alec to the punch line this time.

Alec's sable eyes darkened sexily. "And because you're so deliciously soft," he agreed, tweaking the billowy white sleeve of her poet's shirt.

Alec smoothed Andy's downy hair with soothing, gentle strokes of his hand. "We men are too hard, right fella? A baby can't get comfortable against a chest like mine."

I didn't have any trouble getting comfortable against that chest, Jade thought. She also couldn't help but recall how a sleeping Andy had snuggled against Alec's chest that morning. "He seemed to be resting quite comfortably there this morning," she retorted.

"Only because he was exhausted from being up all night. And he had no choice. Now he knows he's got one."

"Nonsense," Jade corrected as she swiftly buttoned him back up into his sleeper. "He knows when he is being picked up by a pro, that's all." Taking note of how unsure of his parenting abilities Alec was, Jade reassured him gently, "But you'll learn."

Alec frowned. "I'm not so sure about that. A baby is a lot of responsibility. I'm equipped to handle business."

"And very little else?"

"It would seem that way, wouldn't it?"

They stared at one another in mute dissatisfaction, Jade wondering what Alec hoped to get out of this arrangement besides a live-in nanny to his son. A little no-strings-attached sex on the side? Maybe not even that? And what would she do if Alec brought home another woman to bed down with while she was in residence? How would she feel about that?

The silence in the room was broken by the shrill ring of the cellular phone. Collecting her thoughts swiftly, Jade handed Andy back to Alec. He let out another wail, but she ignored him as she retrieved her phone and popped it open. She put up the antennae just in time to hear a familiar female voice demand, "Just what the hell do you think you're doing, Jade, asking questions about me all over New York?"

Relief flowed through Jade. Finally, they were getting somewhere. "Nicole, where are you?" Jade demanded.

"Does this mean you're no longer mad at me?" Nicole said.

I didn't say that, Jade thought, then chided herself for continuing to hold a grudge. "Listen, this is going to sound crazy, I know, but I have to ask you something."

"Can't wait for that," Nicole quipped sarcastically.

Jade took a deep breath and, all too aware of Alec's dark brown eyes upon her, critically assessing her, she turned her back to him and plunged on. "Have you had a baby recently?"

"Why would you ask me that?" Nicole shot back in the uneasy voice she always used when she wasn't quite ready to tell the truth.

"Just answer the question, Nicole."

Nicole swore like a sailor on leave. "For heaven's sake, Jade! There's a morals clause in my contract. I can't have a baby out of wedlock—"

"I'm not asking if you can," Jade interrupted, as Alec walked around to face her. "I'm asking if you already have."

Nicole was silent an ominously long moment. In front of Jade, Alec swayed back and forth, soundlessly rocking a newly quieted Andy while patting him gently on the back all the while. "Who wants to know?" Nicole demanded.

Jade swallowed and hated herself for wishing that Nicole and Alec weren't so involved. "Alec Roman," she replied.

There was another silence, this one even longer. "The wealthy computer dude?" Nicole asked after a moment, sounding stunned.

Maybe you have a future as an actress after all, Jade thought sourly, recalling all the times her wild sister had used the "innocent act" on her in the past, just to get her own way. But this time, Jade thought, Nicole was not going to get away with it.

"Yes, Alec Roman."

"*The* Alec Roman?" Nicole gasped.

"The one and only," Jade confirmed dryly, recoiling slightly as Alec strode closer. His expression was so grim it made her heart race. "You met him last spring in Japan," Jade reminded. She watched as Alec went to the diaper bag, and rummaged through it until he found a pacifier.

"I remember Alec," Nicole said in that faintly mysterious, dreamy voice she always used when she was interested in a man.

"Well?" Jade demanded impatiently, aware her eyes were still locked with Alec's as they did a silent dance around the room, with her spinning and turning and reeling back, out of reach, every time he got the slightest bit close. "Did you have his baby or not?" she asked as Alec offered Andy the pacifier and he accepted it greedily.

"Where'd you get an idea like that?" Nicole responded suspiciously.

"From Alec Roman himself."

Another silence, this one anything but pleasant. "Really," Nicole remarked sarcastically at last. "And why, pray tell, would the great loverboy himself think that?"

Jade watched uneasily as Alec once again settled Andy in his cradle. "Because someone left a baby on his doorstep on Valentine's Day, that's why!"

"I bet he was surprised," Nicole replied unsympathetically.

"Did you have anything to do with that baby showing up on Alec's doorstep?" Jade asked her sister. The sooner they got to the bottom of this game playing, the sooner she could leave. Get back to her own life, away from Alec.

Nicole's voice turned sulky. "You always suspect me of the worst," she accused Jade.

Jade fought to hang onto her skyrocketing temper as Alec straightened away from the cradle and turned toward her. "Maybe because you give me reason," Jade told her sister.

"I knew it," Nicole said grimly.

Soundlessly, Alec closed the distance between them, reached out and took the phone.

"You're still angry at me about Clark, aren't you?" Nicole said.

At the mention of Clark, Alec's brows raised in silent inquiry.

Jade grabbed the phone back. "Clark has nothing to do with this!" Jade told her sister, her face heating with an involuntary flush. Ignoring Alec's increasingly interested look, Jade continued firmly, "And I don't want to talk about that!"

"It wasn't my fault!" Nicole protested anyway, in a voice loud enough for both Alec and Jade to hear.

Jade flushed an even deeper pink and averted her gaze from Alec's probing stare. "Listen, Nicole, about Alec Roman—"

"I've got nothing to say to him," Nicole stated flatly.

Jade closed her eyes. She could just imagine the hurt, sulky look on Nicole's face. The look Nicole always got when things weren't going her way. "Well, he wants to talk to you," she said tightly.

"How do you know?" Nicole asked impatiently on the other end of the line. When Jade didn't answer right away, Nicole stormed, "Don't tell me you're moving in on him!"

Jade only wished it were something as simple as revenge motivating her. "As if I want to steal your beau!" she shot back, losing it completely as she massaged her temples.

Alec grabbed the phone again. "Nicole—"

"Alec!" Nicole gasped—loud enough for them both to hear.

"You're damn right about that much, you little minx!" Alec said.

Nicole swore vituperatively. "What is this, Jade? Payback for Clark?" she shouted.

"Who the hell is Clark?" Alec asked, as the two of them tussled for the phone. His grip was so superior, Jade knew she'd never have a chance to regain her phone…at least not as long as she played fair.

"That is none of your business!" Jade told him hotly as she stomped on his foot. Alec released his grip on the phone with a yelp of surprise and pain.

Jade dashed into the closet and shut the door behind her. She threw her weight against the door. Not caring that it was dark, or that Alec was on the other side of the portal, pushing furiously, Jade exclaimed, "Nicole, we have to talk!" She dug in her heels and found herself moving forward anyway.

"I don't think so," Nicole said coolly.

Jade knew her sister thought she was trying to steal Alec from Nicole's legion of admirers. And though Jade had to admit there might be perverse pleasure to be found in doing just that, she would never stoop that low. "Nicole—"

"I have to think, Jade," Nicole interrupted, briefly sounding more panicked and upset than Jade could ever recall. There was a click as the connection was broken, and then the annoying hum of the dial tone.

Jade stepped back and let go of the door just as Alec threw his weight against it. He came crashing in, almost knocking her to the floor with him. Only the closet wall saved them. They both swore simultaneously and struggled to right themselves. "Are you satisfied?" Jade snapped.

Alec pushed her back against the closet wall and held her there with his body. He glared down at her. "Not yet," he promised in a silky voice that arrowed straight to her soul. "But I will be before we're through here!"

Chapter Four

"Let me go!" Jade said, pushing the words through gritted teeth.

Alec held her against the row of empty wooden shelves at the far end of the walk-in closet. His hands cupped her shoulders and he was leaning into her, using the brunt of his weight to hold her still. "Not until you tell me the truth," he said very, very softly.

Everywhere they touched, Jade felt solid male muscle and a disquieting warmth. Remembering what had happened the last time they were this close further unnerved her and sent a shiver of pure sensual awareness down her spine. Alec wasn't hurting her, not in the slightest, and yet she knew she wasn't getting out of there unless he wanted her to leave. And that made her feel trapped. Wary. Impatient. And, she was ashamed to admit, very much aroused.

She uttered a sigh. "I have told you the truth."

He studied her skeptically. "Yeah, right," he agreed matter-of-factly. "What did your sister say just now?"

Jade tilted her head back another notch and glared up at him defiantly, determined to come out the winner in this battle of wills if it killed her. "Thanks to you, almost nothing," she replied sweetly.

"Did she say the baby was hers?"

"Not exactly," Jade said curtly. Feeling her pulse skitter and jump, she turned her head to the side. She wished she hadn't noticed how aroused he was, but she had and there was no denying how hard he was, or how well their bodies seemed to fit. No wonder Nicole had let herself be seduced by him, she thought. A man with as much raw energy and sex appeal as Alec Roman would be hard to resist.

The hands on her shoulders tightened impatiently. "Did Nicole say the baby wasn't hers then?"

With effort, Jade forced herself to meet his dark, probing gaze. It disappointed her to discover he was thinking only of her sister. Her spirits, already low, fell even more. "Not exactly."

"Did she at least say she was the person who left Andy on my doorstep?"

"No," Jade answered and Alec cursed. "But she didn't say she didn't leave him there, either."

"Then why did she call you?" he demanded.

"She heard I was looking for her."

"And?"

"And that's it!"

Alec shook his head at her in silent remonstration. "You know, if the two of you are going to make a career out of this, you'll need to get a lot better at it. And you could start by trying to get your stories straight!"

Jade decided they had played cat and mouse long enough. She put her hand flat on his chest and pushed, hard. "I don't care what you think or what it looks like. I am not trying to jerk you around! But if that's what you want to believe," she finished, albeit a little breathlessly, "then go ahead!" She'd given him no reason to mistrust her. In fact, she had gone out of her way to assist him in discovering the truth. It galled her to have him questioning her motives now, after the hellish, tiring day they'd both put in.

His expression thoughtful, Alec moved back slightly. The maneuver gave her some breathing room, but he didn't let go of her shoulders.

Alec's mouth tightened. "Is Nicole trying to con me, Jade?"

How the hell was she supposed to respond to that? Jade hadn't the slightest idea what her wild sister was up to now. "I can't answer for her," she said calmly. *I don't want to answer for her.*

"Then call her back and let her answer for herself," Alec advised gruffly.

His implacable attitude, the sense that he felt all he had to do was wish for something and it would be done, pronto, grated on her already ravaged nerves. "I can't do that," Jade replied tightly.

"Why the hell not?" Alec demanded.

"Because I don't know where she is!"

He backed off completely and swore vituperatively beneath his breath. "I don't believe this! You didn't ask where she was?" Alec folded his arms and regarded her incredulously.

Jade looked past him, toward the only way out of the closet, and contemplated making a break for it. Deciding swiftly it would be better to wait him out than risk a tussle that could easily turn into something much more intimate and dangerous, she turned back to him with a censuring glare of her own. "I didn't have time."

"You expect me to believe that?"

"I don't give a flying fig what you believe," Jade asserted quietly, as she tucked her hair behind her ear. "It's the truth."

He looked as if he were about to explode at any minute. "I'm warning you, Jade. I am not an easy mark. I am not about to be taken for a ride. Not by you. Not by Nicole. Not by anyone."

Her heart thudded against her ribs. Although the situation was not of her making, Jade felt as if she had just grabbed a tiger by the tail. Too stubborn to grovel for understanding, however, she adopted an insouciant stance, leaning back against the shelves and crossing one high-heeled foot across the opposite ankle. "How nice to hear," she said with exaggerated pleasantness.

His eyes scanned her hotly from head to toe. "If you want

to end this scam you and your sister have dreamed up here
and now—''

"I said it before. I'll say it again. There is no scam."

Their eyes clashed.

Alec had believed her before the phone call. Now he
wasn't so sure. If the sisters weren't working together, was
it possible they'd somehow put him in the middle of their
quarrel, right alongside Clark—whoever the hell *he* was? It
was time to put Jade's motives to the test.

Alec reached into his suit jacket and removed a checkbook
from the inside breast pocket. His gaze still holding hers, he
asked calmly, "Would fifty thousand end this? No? How
about a hundred thousand, then?"

"How about a million and a half?" Jade replied, just to
gauge his reaction.

To her disappointment, he appeared to think her demand
was serious. "You're insane," she muttered. Where did Alec
Roman get off, thinking he could buy her cooperation?

"No," Alec corrected as he closed the distance between
them swiftly. He gripped her hands and hauled her close.
"*You're* insane if you think you're going to get one red cent
out of me over this."

Jade struggled out of his grasp and regarded him stonily,
a pulse throbbing wildly in her throat. "Get this straight,
Roman," she retorted with as much control as she could muster, "I don't want your money."

Alec studied her with an expression that bore only the
slightest hint of relief. "Then what do you want?"

Answers, Jade thought fervently. *A man of my very own.*
Because she could have neither, at least here and now, she
replied calmly, "A good night's sleep. Since it's already well
after midnight, I suggest we both think about turning in."

"I guess you're right." Alec shoved a hand through his
hair, rumpling the thick raven strands even more. "Until Nicole shows up, if she shows up—"

"She will," Jade interrupted. If there was something to be
gained, she knew her sister would show up.

"Meantime," Alec continued with only a hint of grumpiness in his voice, "there's no point in the two of us going round and round."

Jade released a sigh. "You're right about that much." These confrontations with him were making her edgy. And they were also reminding her how long she had been alone. Up until now, that had been her choice. After the Clark fiasco, she hadn't wanted another relationship. Now…now, she did. It was as simple, and complicated, as that.

"About the baby," Alec began. He studied her bluntly, then plunged on. "I know we said you'd keep him tonight, but maybe it'd be better if I had him."

Jade blinked. "The cradle's already in my room. Andy could wake up again if he's moved."

Alec was striding out of the closet, toward the hand-carved cradle. "I'll risk it."

Jade caught his arm before he could reach for Andy, and tugged him back. "You distrust me that much?" she said, trying hard not to show her hurt.

Alec looked down at her hand on his arm, then covered it absently with his own. "I just don't want to risk anything happening at this point."

Jade pulled her fingers free. "Such as?" she prodded quietly.

Alec's eyes held hers. "You or maybe even Nicole walking off with him in the middle of the night."

The hell of it was, Jade knew Alec had every right to be wary. Just as she had every right to completely lose patience. "Fine, Alec. Move the cradle back to your room, and you keep Andy tonight."

ALEC SETTLED ANDY onto his shoulder as the first pink lights of dawn streaked across the sky. His son was warm, dry, fed, and fussy as all get out. He didn't want to rock. Didn't want to be walked. Didn't want his pacifier. At a loss, Alec had decided to rock Andy anyway. Sooner or later one of them would get sleepy.

Andy let out another wail just as Jade walked in. Wrapped in a thick terry-cloth robe, her hair a riot of tumbled bitter-sweet chocolate curls, she looked sleepy and warm and soft in a womanly way that made Alec's heart race and his loins tighten. He knew he couldn't afford to get involved here, not until he was sure he could trust Jade. But that didn't stop him from wanting to discover just what was beneath that thick terry-cloth robe of hers.

"I thought I heard you, Andy," Jade murmured in that gentle singsong voice mothers used. She cast around, spying the baby blanket on the bed. She straightened it into a flat square, then walked over to Alec and held out her arms for the baby. "I'll show you a trick."

Willing to try anything at this point, Alec handed Andy over. Andy continued to fuss as Jade carried him to the bed, talking softly all the while. She laid him down gently in the center of the blanket, then starting at the bottom, folded a triangle of cloth over Andy's feet. A triangle from the left covered his chest, and so did another triangle from the right. By the time she had finished, Andy was wrapped up like a mummy. Jade carried him back to the rocking chair and stood over Alec. "May I?"

Alec nodded. "Be my guest."

Jade cradled Andy in her arms and sank down in it. Telling him about the hard couple of days he'd had, she continued to rock gently back and forth. Short minutes later, she had worked the miracle Alec had been seeking for two hours now. As soon as Andy was asleep, she carried him back to the cradle and put him down in it.

Alec followed her out into the hall. "Where'd you learn how to wrap him up like that?"

Jade paused midway between their rooms. She leaned back against the wall and folded her arms in front of her. "I baby-sat a lot when I was a kid."

Silence fell awkwardly between them. She glanced at him, then glanced away. He saw her look at his night clothes again. Alec almost never wore pajamas, but last night he had

dug out some blue and red paisley silk pajama pants someone—a woman, maybe?—had given him years ago, and covered it with the black monk's robe he pulled on after his
showers. "I know," he said before she could speak. "The
colors clash."

"That wasn't what I was going to say."

His brow lifted. She drew a deep breath and rushed on,
"About last night. I'm sorry I snapped at you, Alec. I know
how it looked when Nicole called me. And I have an idea
what you've been through the past thirty-six hours. You had
a right to be upset by the turn of events, just as I had a
responsibility to maintain my calm."

"You did a pretty good job," Alec put in, unable to help
but think how pretty Jade looked in the morning, or fantasize,
just a little, what it would be like to wake up with her in his
house every day.

"But not good enough." Jade threaded her fingers through
her thick curly hair and lifted the weight of it away from her
face. "It's just…" She floundered a moment as she tucked
her hair behind her ear. "Dealing with Nicole makes me
tense."

Me, too, Alec thought.

"I'll take Andy for a while if you want me to," she offered, then frowned as he hesitated. "Still afraid I'm going
to walk off with him?" Hurt glimmered in her eyes.

"Look, I'm all for you and I splitting the care."

"Just as long as I do it in your presence," Jade said bitterly.

Alec paused. Despite all the evidence to the contrary, he
did want to trust Jade, but he also had to protect his son. "If
your sister calls—" he began autocratically, only to be cut
off once again with an arch look from Jade and a beleaguered
sigh.

"Knowing Nicole, and how she likes to go for optimum
drama in any and every situation, I doubt very seriously that
she will call you anytime soon," Jade interrupted.

"Nevertheless, when she does call again, I want to talk to her," Alec declared firmly.

"Why? So you can scare her off again before I have a chance to get anything concrete out of her?" Jade snapped. She started to walk away.

Alec blocked her path. "You're intimating I'm the problem here?"

Jade shrugged, eyed his stance, then leaned back against the wall. "If the shoe fits…" she drawled, then smiled when Alec's mouth tightened in irritation.

"Cute, Jade."

She grinned back at him smugly, perversely pleased with the way his sable eyes had darkened. She was getting to him, just the way he was getting to her. It was easy to see why her sister feared dealing with Alec. He seemed to let no one get in the way of what he wanted, and right now he wanted his son. The question was, what did Alec really want from her here? Just someone else who was also on the premises, and reliable enough to help take care of Andy, plus lure Nicole back to the fold, or was Alec really looking for someone who would also take care of him in bed? Jade pushed her disturbing thoughts away. One way or another they would find Nicole. Then this would no longer be her problem. She could write herself out of the equation and go back to a normal life.

"Jade?" Alec interrupted her thoughts. He rubbed a hand across the stubbled underside of his jaw. "If Nicole calls again—"

Jade pushed away from the wall. "I'll ask if she wants to talk to you, Alec. But that's all I can or will do." She refused to notice how sexy he looked. "The rest is up to you and Nicole."

"Fair enough," Alec said as she breezed past him.

"In the meantime, I'm going to shower and go shopping. Andy needs clothes, a Portacrib, diapers. Do you have a car I can borrow, or should I call a cab?"

Alec followed Jade as far as the door to her bedroom.

"I've got a Jeep you can drive and a credit card for whatever Andy needs. It's still pretty early, though."

"Don't sweat it, Alec," she assured him as she shut the door and turned the lock. "By the time I'm ready and there, the stores will be open."

"DID YOU BUY OUT Wanamaker's or just Philadelphia in general?" Alec asked dryly as Jade carried in yet another bundle of boxes and bags shortly after one o'clock that afternoon.

He got a whiff of perfume as she moved past, her strides swift and purposeful. He'd thought she'd been sexy in a skirt. He hadn't imagined how she would look in hunter green flannel slacks that hugged her slender bottom or a matching V-neck cashmere sweater that did equally wonderful things for her high, delectably round breasts. But it was her long-lashed eyes, made to look even greener by the hue in her clothes, that really held his attention. Maybe it was crazy, but he couldn't help but wonder how it would feel if Jade looked at him as tenderly as she often looked at Andy. Just as he couldn't help but wonder why she'd been gone so long.

Not that much had happened in her absence. He'd carried the cradle down to his study, and worked on Roman Computer contracts while Andy slept.

"I don't recall you saying anything about a credit limit when you handed me your Wanamaker card," Jade asserted, breezing past him and heading back for the Jeep, which was crammed nearly to the ceiling with packages and boxes. She ducked beneath the open tailgate and leaned into the back of the Jeep, one long shapely leg extended behind her.

Looking at the graceful arch of her body, Alec felt his mouth go dry. "The limit was implied."

"Was it?" Jade's voice was muffled. She dragged out the baby crib mobile box and several bags. Her eyes fastened on his. "Or is this just an excuse to give me a hard time?"

Her accusation hit home. Alec was feeling a lot of frustration. About a lot of things—Jade, the baby, Nicole. But he'd been taking it all out on her, and that wasn't fair.

"Sorry," he offered. Money wasn't the issue here anyway. He'd been worried about her because she'd been gone so long—almost four hours. Now that he saw what all she'd purchased, the long absence made sense.

"I'm sure whatever you bought was fine."

Jade's expression gentled. "Now that's more like it. And you're right. Andy did need a lot of things." She filled his arms with bags and boxes, then picked up another load for herself. "Sleepers, toys, blankets, diapers. I even got a bassinet and a Portacrib, so we won't have to keep lugging that cradle from room to room or make him sleep in the baby carrier. I know it looks comfortable enough but it can't be good for him, sleeping sitting up all the time."

Minutes later, they had carried everything in. Alec knelt beside Jade on the floor to go through her packages. She had done an admirable job outfitting Andy. The kid would be prepared for any situation. Alec fingered a ribbon-wrapped bundle of soft white cotton. He figured there had to be a hundred tri-folded diapers in that stack. "Why did you get cloth diapers instead of disposable?" he asked.

"They're better for the environment. And softer, too."

"Oh." He hadn't thought of that, particularly since Andy had arrived wearing disposables.

Maybe he had been wrong to assume she was exactly like Nicole. After all, he reasoned, from the little he'd overheard last night, Nicole hadn't sounded very friendly to Jade. Deciding there was no time like the present to start over, informally at least, he asked, "Have you eaten lunch?"

"No."

He was already reaching for his keys. "I was just going to go out and pick something up."

"Let me guess," she said dryly, her disapproval with his diet evident. "McDonald's."

He made no apologies for liking fast food. "Want something?"

Her eyes gleamed with liveliness. "After the morning full

of exercise that I've had, I guess I could live dangerously this once.''

Now she was talking, Alec thought.

"I'll have a McLean, a salad, and—heck, why not?—an apple bran muffin for dessert.'' She flashed him a saucy grin. "Your treat, of course.''

Alec smiled. Despite her penchant for healthy food, his initial reservations about her, and the difficulty of the situation, he was beginning to like Jade more and more. Maybe one day, when all this was over, they could at least be friends. Maybe more than friends, if luck was really with him. "One healthful McDonald's lunch, coming right up.''

"ALEC, WHY IS THERE a cloth diaper in the trash can?''

Alec tore his eyes reluctantly from the computer screen in his study. Although he and Jade had ostensibly been "sharing'' care of Andy for the afternoon, except for one diaper change, she had ended up doing most of the rocking and feeding and singing. While Jade was very satisfied with the mobile she had also managed to assemble, she was not at all satisfied at what she had just discovered outside the back stoop.

"What were you doing in the trash?'' Alec asked.

"Taking out the McDonald's bags from lunch.''

Alec's brows knit together in a puzzled frown. "You cleaned up the kitchen?''

"It's a dirty job, but someone had to do it.''

"I know,'' he agreed, his eyes lighting up with bemusement. "But not you. I have a housekeeper, Mrs. Scott. She comes in twice a week and takes care of all that.''

"Well, I'm not about to leave that for her when I have two legs and two arms and a reasonably intelligent mind that allows me to do things like this for myself. And you haven't answered my question.'' Jade moved a stack of papers and sat on the edge of his desk. She wondered how anyone could look so sexy, simply working at a computer. "Why did you put that cloth diaper in the trash?''

Alec shrugged. "It was soiled. I would've had to wash it."

"That is the general idea for using cloth diapers in the first place," Jade said dryly. "You know, we wash them, dry them, use them, wash them, dry them, use them. It's very economical to do it that way."

Alec hit the save button on his computer. He pushed his swivel chair away from the desk, and wheeled it around to face her. "Look," he huffed in a tone of irritation Jade was beginning to recognize all too well. "I've agreed to heat bottles and change diapers and stay up all night if need be, but *I draw the line at washing diapers.*"

Then he was just going to have to undraw it, Jade thought. "Alec, cloth diapers are expensive."

He shrugged. "I can afford them."

"That's not the point."

Alec leaned back in his swivel chair so it was at an angle, and propped his left ankle across his right knee. He was dressed casually, in a lamb's wool charcoal shirt worn buttoned to the neck, charcoal trousers, charcoal socks, and charcoal suede loafers. "Then what is the point?" he asked, looking very citified, and sophisticated and sexy, even in his just-staying-at-home clothes.

Jade crossed her legs at the knee and flushed when his eyes tracked the movement. "Throwing them away is wrong."

Alec put his clasped hands behind his head and continued to look at her. "Why?"

Jade rolled her eyes in exasperation. "Because it's hopelessly extravagant, that's why."

Alec eyed her lazily in a very predatory, very male way. "Not to me, it isn't. I don't want to mess with them. And frankly, sweetheart, my time is worth a whole lot more than what a package of cloth diapers will run me for one day."

Jade had been raised not to waste anything, and seeing someone throw away perfectly good diapers just because they were soiled was more than she could bear. "We could get a diaper service then," she suggested calmly.

Alec made a face. "We'd still have to rinse. No way am I rinsing diapers in the commode, Jade."

She hopped off his desk. Being that close to him had put all her senses in overdrive. "You're impossible!"

"Practical," he corrected, his dark brows lowering like twin thunderclouds over his eyes. "You're the one who's impossible, thinking there is only one way to do things—yours."

Jade flushed even more. "No one on earth would agree with you about this," she shot back. Then she realized uncomfortably that she was wrong. There was someone who would agree with Alec on this—Nicole. Maybe the two of them had more in common than she wanted to admit.

"So?" Alec pushed away from his desk and stood. "I don't care if anyone agrees with me or not." He jabbed a thumb at his chest. "I'm okay with what I am doing, and that's all that matters."

Still locked in the battle of wills, Jade stared at Alec a moment longer. Every inch of her was taut, ready to do combat with him, even looking forward to a fight. Why? So he could kiss her again? She couldn't afford to lose control here, couldn't afford to let this baby-sitting get any more personal than it already had.

Besides, what did it matter to her if he threw away cloth diapers? Even if he was wrong. "Sometimes I wonder what planet you're from," she murmured finally.

"This one," Alec said. He looked beyond her, to the Portacrib in the corner. "Hey!" he enthused, grabbing her elbow. "Did you see that?"

Jade glanced at the crib. "See what?" she asked.

"Andy! He just rolled from his stomach onto his back."

Together, they moved closer. Andy was awake, and grinning from ear to ear. "Hey," Jade said slowly, unable to mask her wonder, "Andy did roll over, didn't he?" Before, he'd been sleeping on his stomach!

"Way to go, champ! Want to do it again?" Alec asked. Andy gurgled in response.

Gently, Alec rolled Andy over onto his tummy. "Okay, champ, let's show Jade what a bruiser you are." His tiny fists pushing hard against the mattress of the Portacrib, Andy raised his head. It wobbled from side to side as he looked from one side of the Portacrib bars to the other. Winded, he flopped back down onto his tummy, bumping is forehead gently in the process.

Jade murmured in tender sympathy. "He's worn out, poor thing." She reached toward their tiny charge, intent on rescue.

Alec caught her hand before she could turn Andy onto his back. "Let him try it again."

Jade's wrist grew warm beneath Alec's hand. She looked up into his eyes and felt herself catch her breath for reasons completely unrelated to the lively infant.

Alec's eyes darkened. Time seemed suspended. Suddenly, there was just the two of them, just this moment. "Tell me you feel this too, Jade," Alec whispered.

Jade told herself to step back, out of reach, but her legs wouldn't move, didn't want to move. "I don't know what you mean," she said breathlessly, her heart pounding so hard she could hear it in her ears.

Alec brushed his thumb across her lower lip. He continued to regard her steadily, his hand on hers growing even warmer. "I think you do, Jade," he said softly. He lifted her other hand to his mouth and pressed a kiss across her knuckles. "Just like I think you know we weren't really arguing about diapers just now. This tension between us is going to continue until we do something about it," he said firmly, his desire for her evident.

"Oh, Alec—"

As she whispered his name, Alec's sable eyes darkened with pleasure. Wrapping both hands around her waist, he caught her against him, so they were touching length to length. "Just one kiss, Jade. One short, simple kiss. That's all I'm asking." He lifted her hand to his mouth, pushed up the sleeve of her sweater, and pressed his lips to the inside of her wrist.

Jade's heart skipped a beat at the soft, sensual feel of his mouth moving over her skin. What would it be like if he kissed her like that all over? "I thought we were going to try and exercise some self-restraint here, Alec," Jade breathed as she felt her insides turn warm and fluid.

He only smiled at her and kissed his way farther up the inside of her arm. "I changed my mind," he said wickedly.

Jade knew she should fight this, fight him, but she let him draw her into his arms. "You're seducing me again," she accused, and felt her breath catch as his tongue darted out to make contact with her bare skin.

"I know." He tunneled his hands through her hair and fitted his mouth over hers.

If the first time he'd kissed her had been impulsive, this time was nothing but deliberate. He rubbed his lips against hers, gently at first, then with growing intensity. She arched against him, hoping for closer contact, but to Jade's growing frustration, he refused her the intimate kiss she yearned for. Tilting her head back, he kissed her temples, her cheeks, her eyelids, over and over and over again, until she felt starved for the passionate contact she craved.

Jade groaned. "You're not playing fair." She'd never wanted to taste and feel a man as much as she wanted to taste and feel Alec at that moment.

Alec lifted his head and smiled. "I'll let you in on a little secret, Jade. There're damn few things in this life that are fair. But there are any number of things to be enjoyed."

"Like sex?" Jade said, sighing softly as another delicious shudder heated her body.

"Like making love," he corrected, his arms encircling her, one hand in the small of her back, bringing her intimately closer. "To me." Giving her no chance to respond to that, he bent his head and gave her a long, thorough kiss designed to shatter her resolve.

She sank into him, knowing it was wrong, but luxuriating

in the tensile feel of him and the tenderness of his kiss. "Damn," she whispered shakily, when Alec finally lifted his head long minutes later. She had never felt such pleasure.

"My feelings exactly," Alec rasped, his compelling gaze riveting her to the spot.

They stared at one another a moment longer, then turned in unison to the crib. Jade was still trembling inwardly, but Andy was back up, pushing his fists against the mattress. With a great deal of effort, he lifted one fist off the mattress, arched his back, and then rolled onto his back. He let out a delighted gurgle and kicked both his tiny feet in the air.

"See?" Alec tightened his arm about Jade's waist, looking as proud as any papa. "I told you he could do it!"

"So you did," Jade said in wonder. She tore her eyes from Andy and looked up at Alec. His attention was no longer on his son, but on her upturned face. Jade's lips parted and she felt her breath catch in her chest. It was happening again. She could feel the desire pouring from them both. Only this time Alec would not be satisfied with a few kisses. And she wasn't ready to take the next step.

Alec dropped his hold on her reluctantly and stepped back. His face was impressive again as he glanced at his watch and remarked casually, "I meant to tell you earlier. We've got company coming."

Company? Jade thought, feeling a little irked he could turn his emotions on and off so much easier than she could. "Who?"

"Jeremy Packard, a private investigator. I've asked him to help us find Nicole."

"Oh. Good." But the mention of her sister left her feeling as if she had just been sucker punched in the gut.

"He should be here any minute." Alec paused. "What's the matter? You look upset."

She was upset. Damned upset. For just a second she had let herself forget about Nicole. And Alec's mistrust of her. She had let herself fall into his arms once again with only a token, teasing resistance. The truth was, she wanted him to pursue her. She wanted him to persuade her to accept his kisses. Just as she secretly wanted him to lure her into his bed. What was wrong with her?

"Don't you want me to hire an investigator?" Alec asked, and then waited, carefully gauging her reaction.

Frankly, she didn't. To her, bringing in a private snoop sounded messy and intrusive. Not that it mattered what she thought in this situation. Alec was bound and determined to lay claim to his son, and the only way he could do that was by finding Nicole, and getting Nicole either to acknowledge and live up to her responsibility to Andy, or relinquish all rights to his son. Either way, Jade would be out of the picture, for as soon as Alec got what he wanted from the Kincaid family, she had no doubts that he would want both Kincaid sisters out of the way, and out of Andy's life.

The doorbell rang. "Do what you have to do," Jade advised finally, in answer to his question.

"I plan to." With a last thoughtful look at her, he went to greet the investigator. When he returned, Jeremy Packard was at his side. Alec made introductions swiftly, then they all sat down.

Jeremy opened up his briefcase. "I got on this yesterday morning, just like you asked," he began.

Yesterday, Jade thought, reeling with the shock. Alec had hired an investigator yesterday and he hadn't even told her?

"I called him right after Andy was left on my doorstep because I knew finding Nicole, either in New York or through you, was a longshot."

"Why didn't you tell me this earlier?" Jade asked, beginning to see how far Alec would go to secure his child. Far enough to use her, too? To somehow get her on his side in case a custody battle eventually came up?

"I didn't see any need to tell you then," Alec explained with a shrug. He turned back to Jeremy. "What have you got?"

Jeremy sighed his frustration as he admitted, "Not a lot so far. Apparently, one of the last things Nicole purchased before she left New York was a one-way plane ticket to Los Angeles. She flew west last September eighth. There's no record of her ever having charged a return ticket to any of her credit cards.''

''Which means she could still be in Los Angeles,'' Alec said.

Jeremy Packard nodded. He looked at Jade. ''Any reason why your sister would've wanted to go to Los Angeles?''

Jade thought, recalling what Myra Lansky had told them. ''She might have been trying to break into the movies. Maybe even television.''

''Had she ever taken acting classes?'' Jeremy asked, making notes.

''No, but she'd never had any experience as a model before she was accepted at the Renown Agency, either.'' Knowing Nicole, and her enormous ego... ''She probably didn't figure she needed any.''

''Nicole might be right about that,'' Jeremy conceded thoughtfully. ''Lots of famous models get hired for their name. Every man in America knows Nicole from her Ingenue soap commercials. Take her out of those sweet-sixteen clothes and put her in a skimpy string bikini and you'd have plenty of people watching.''

Alec raised a brow at the suggestion, and the jealousy Jade had worked so hard to suppress reared its ugly head. Had Alec kissed Nicole every bit as passionately as he had just kissed her?

''On the other hand, it might've been hard for Nicole to get work if she were pregnant,'' Alec theorized bluntly.

''And even more difficult for her to get herself back in shape physically, find work, and simultaneously care for Andy,'' Jade said. Which explained why she had left her son with Alec.

''Yeah, having a baby might've mucked things up for her,'' Jeremy agreed. ''Then again, Christie Brinkley didn't have a problem finding work after she had Billy Joel's kid.

So maybe that sister of yours is hoping the same will happen to her, once she gets set up with a nanny and all that.''

"Which is where I suppose I come in," Alec said. "Money."

Ignoring Alec's derisive remark, Jade asked Jeremy, "Have you checked all the hospitals in Los Angeles, looked at the birth records?''

Jeremy nodded. "I've got people working on it. And I'm going out myself this evening. I should know something more in a couple of days.''

They all stood. As Alec walked Jeremy out, Jade returned to the Portacrib, where Andy had fallen asleep again. With his tiny fist shoved in his mouth, he looked peaceful and very very sweet. It was funny, he'd only been a part of her life for a few hours, but she couldn't imagine her life without him now. Her desire for a baby of her own, always there, grew even stronger. *It must be my biological clock ticking,* Jade thought, *the fact I'm almost thirty.* Her desire for a baby had nothing to do with Alec Roman, or the increasing desire she felt whenever she was around him.

A shadow fell over her. She pivoted to find Alec standing slightly behind her. He looked dark and dangerous, and about as happy as he had been the moment he had first appeared in her office. Wordlessly taking her elbow, he drew her across the room, to the tapestry-covered seats lining the bay window that overlooked the back lawn. "I'm sorry I surprised you about Jeremy, but I can't help but think the sooner we wrap this up, the better.''

"You're telling me." Jade quipped, using sarcasm to mask her hurt. Those few simple kisses hadn't meant anything to him, no matter how passionately they'd been given.

Alec sighed, his own frustration evident. "I know I acted like a jerk last night, grabbing the phone from you, but if Nicole calls again—''

Jade returned his troubled look, her expression suddenly as serious as his. "I'll at least find out where she is if she calls again. I promise.''

He nodded grimly. "Either way, we'll know something soon."

"I know we will," Jade murmured back. That was what worried her. As much as she wanted and needed to know that her younger sister was all right, Jade didn't want Nicole back in her life. She didn't want her causing havoc, coming between her and Andy, or even her and Alec Roman.

"In the meantime, I've got to go to Raleigh on business tomorrow. It's just a two-day trip, down on Monday, back on Tuesday, but I've got to go."

Jade wondered if Alec had a woman down there, too. "You can't put it off?" she asked.

He shook his head. "I'm building a new lab in The Research Triangle and I've got to check on it. I'd take Andy with me but I don't think a construction site in the dead of winter is any place for a baby."

"It isn't."

"I know you were against hiring a baby nurse—"

"I still am," Jade affirmed quietly. "It seems to me that Andy's had enough strangers in his life. Besides, I can watch him easily enough. That is, if you trust me not to abscond with him, and then hold him for ransom or something?" she said dryly.

There was another silence. She knew Alec was weighing his options, thinking ahead. Finally, he sighed heavily, and said in a bemused tone, "I guess there are just some things I'm going to have to take on faith."

Jade met his gaze equably and found herself returning his charming smile. She felt mesmerized by the very male interest she saw in his eyes. "It'd be easier for us both if you would." Plus, with Alec gone, it would give her a chance to look for Nicole on her own. And she had an idea just where to start.

Alec stood. He looked anxious to get back to his work again. "You're sure it won't be too much for you trying to work and handle Andy alone?"

"I'm positive. Trust me, Alec. I can handle everything

here.'' Now, if only she could forget their kisses as easily as he seemed to.

"TIM, I NEED your help," Jade said early the next morning, the moment Alec left for the airport.

"Anything for you, Jade. You know that," Tim "Perfect Pass" Johnson replied cheerfully.

Jade smiled at the low raspy sound of his voice over the long-distance phone lines. The Steelers quarterback was one of the sweetest men she'd ever known, and an incorrigible flirt, but he was also steady as a rock. And right now she needed a rock.

Jade didn't quite understand how she had become so personally involved in this mess. Her five years of working with the pro players on a one-to-one basis had taught her a lot about dealing with rich, sexy men. She knew how to fend off passes! And yet when Alec Roman put the moves on her, she lost all common sense and fairly melted in his arms. When he looked at her, she felt hypnotized by his steady gaze. Whenever he was near her, she tingled inside.

"Jade? You still there?"

Jade started, then flushed as she realized she had been obsessing about Alec again. She sighed. "Yes, I'm here. Sorry. Listen, Tim, I need to find my sister, Nicole." The way things were going, the sooner she got out of there and away from Alec Roman, the better!

"I haven't heard from her," Tim said in a baffled voice, reminding Jade that he was one of the few men around who had never expressed the slightest romantic interest in her wild younger sister.

"But one of your friends might have," Jade persisted calmly. "You know what a thing Nicole has for football players."

Tim laughed. "That's an understatement, kiddo. I think she's dated every eligible player on the east coast at one time or another."

"Well, I have reason to believe she may have started on the west."

Tim was polite enough not to ask for further details if Jade didn't want to give them, and she didn't. "What do you want me to do?" he asked briskly.

"Call around for me. Talk to the players you know in California. Ask if anyone has seen or heard from Nicole recently."

"Will do," Tim promised. "About our appointment the other day—"

"I'm sorry I missed it," Jade apologized readily, "but I can fax you your menu plans and we could go over them by phone."

Tim didn't answer her suggestion right away. Jade knew he sensed there was trouble. He knew she never would have neglected her business, otherwise. "Why not in person?" he asked.

"Well, for starts," she answered dryly, "I'm in Philly."

"The Eagles quarterback getting precedence over me?" he teased.

Jade chuckled softly. "You know me better than that. I love you guys all the same."

Tim laughed with her. "When will you be back?" he asked.

"I don't know." Jade wished she could leave now, before she got in any deeper with Alec. It was only a matter of time before he took her into his arms again. And when he did...well, there was no telling what might happen.

"I may be stuck here for a few days. A lot depends on how quickly I can find Nicole." She hoped it was soon. Damn soon, before she made an even bigger mistake and ended up in Alec Roman's bed.

Chapter Five

"What are you doing up again, sweetie?" Jade asked Andy around a yawn. "Don't you know it's only midnight? Andy merely gurgled at her and waved his arms and his feet in the air.

Jade slipped on her matching ice blue satin robe with the shawl collar, not bothering to belt it, and reached for a clean diaper. When Andy was dry again, she picked him up and headed downstairs for the kitchen. She heated his formula in the microwave, shook the bottle vigorously, then tested it on her wrist. It was lukewarm. "Perfect," Jade said, smiling down at her charge.

"I couldn't agree more," a lazy male voice drawled.

Andy still in her arms, Jade whirled in the direction of the low, sexy and familiar voice. Alec was standing in the kitchen doorway, leaning indolently against the jamb. His navy suit jacket was hooked over the index finger of his left hand and slung over his shoulder. He carried a briefcase and a sack of fast food in his other hand, resting against his thigh. His starched navy shirt and tie were still impeccable, even after what must have been a horrendously long day for him, since he'd left Philadelphia at dawn. Only the faint shadows beneath his eyes and the piratical shadow of nearly a day's growth of dark beard gave him away.

At the dark, sensual, and admiring look in his eyes, Jade's heart pounded. "I thought you were still in Raleigh," she said coolly, trying hard not to notice how good he looked in navy. How sexy, in a crisp, athletic, all-American way. Not many men could carry off such a stark look.

"I was," Alec admitted as he set his briefcase on the floor, tossed his jacket on the counter, and headed toward her. "But I finished my survey of the new lab and my meetings with the new research and development staff we're assembling there, and decided to head on home tonight."

"Can't stay away, hmm?" Jade regretted the words the instant they were out, fearing he'd take her offhand comment the wrong way.

Alec's eyes grew thoughtful. Loosening the knot of his tie with one hand, he sauntered closer. "I admit I've never had a reason to hurry home before." If his words hadn't been so soft and sincere, Jade would have thought they were a come-on. Mesmerized, she watched as Alec held out a hand to Andy, who immediately curled his tiny hand around Alec's little finger. Though he confessed to know little about babies, he had remarkably good instincts and a wealth of tenderness inside.

At her unexpectedly romantic thoughts, Jade drew herself up short. She couldn't let this situation, or Alec, get to her. Sure, it was intimate, being with him like this. Feeling like they were at least a temporary mommy and daddy to Andy. But she had to remember that once Nicole was found, Alec would have no more need of her.

"So, how are things going with Andy?" Alec asked, as Jade began to give Andy his bottle of formula. Still holding onto his son, Alec lifted a hand to his throat and undid the first two buttons of his shirt.

Jade turned to Alec and found herself at eye level with the crisp dark hairs curling out of the opening of his shirt. She tore her gaze from Alec's golden skin. "Everything's fine."

Alec quirked a brow. "He's up kind of late, isn't he?"

"Babies operate on their own schedules, Alec. Midnight, noon, it's all the same to them. If they're hungry, they're hungry."

As Jade spoke, Andy waved his other fist around, hitting first the bottle, then swinging it back out again. His fingers caught a fistful of her satin pajama top, above her right breast. he tugged it close, then pushed it away, inadvertently baring her breast almost to the nipple in the process. Jade was mortified, but there was nothing she could do—one hand was holding Andy, the other the bottle.

Wordlessly, Alec lifted his free hand to her pajama top. His eyes on Andy's face, rather than the exposed creamy slope of Jade's breast, and the hint of pink nipple just beyond the edge of tightly held cloth, Alec wrested the satin from Andy's tiny fingers and smoothed it back into place, giving her maximum coverage once again.

Unfortunately, Jade thought, there was nothing she could do about her braless state, or the way her nipples were now peaking tautly against the satin, or the way she was beginning to heat up inside. And there was nothing she could do about the predatory male hunger she saw in Alec's eyes.

Her face flaming, she turned away from Alec. It was bad enough she was here with Alec in the kitchen in the middle of the night. But she had to be in her pajamas, too, with not an ounce of makeup on her face, or any way to hide the traitorous way her body had responded at his first touch.

"Is that your dinner?" She nodded at the Burger King bag. He ate fast food far too much. When she knew him better, she'd try to do something about that.

Alec nodded. "I didn't have time to eat earlier this evening. I got you a Whopper and some fries, just in case you were hungry."

"Thanks, but I've already eaten."

He nodded, as if he had suspected as much. She watched him pull a light beer from the fridge, sit down, and open the sack containing his dinner.

"Have you heard from Jeremy Packard?" Jade asked, taking a seat opposite him at the oblong oak table.

Alec added ketchup to his fries. "He's supposed to call

first thing tomorrow with a report, if I don't hear from him sooner.''

Silence fell between them, more awkward than before. ''Well, I guess I'll head on back upstairs and finish giving Andy his formula,'' she said, amazed at how calm her voice could sound when all her senses were in overdrive.

Alec nodded tersely. ''Call me if you need me.''

''Will do,'' Jade promised as she got to her feet once again. But the reality was, she had no intention of calling him now or at any other time. They were getting far too close as it was.

Upstairs, in the safety of her own room, Jade sank into the rocking chair and, still holding Andy in her arms, finished giving him his bottle. Though she tried to block it from her mind, all she could think about was the astonished hungry look on Alec's face when Andy had bared the upper slope of her breast to his view.

She was not going to make a fool of herself with Alec. So he wanted to make love to her. So what? He didn't love her. She didn't love him. Wishing she could have a future with Alec wouldn't make it happen, any more than wishing Andy was her child and Alec's, instead of Nicole's and Alec's, would make that so. This interlude in her life would be over soon enough, Jade told herself firmly. All she had to do now was get through it, without getting hurt again in the process.

''JADE?'' ALEC APPEARED in the doorway to her bedroom just as Jade was putting a slumbering Andy down again. ''I've got Jeremy Packard on the phone.''

Jade frowned. ''At this time of night?''

''It's only nine-thirty in Los Angeles. He needs to talk to both of us.''

Jade grabbed the baby monitor she'd bought on her shopping spree, then followed Alec downstairs to his luxuriously appointed study, closing her robe and belting it tightly as she went.

Alec walked over to his desk and pressed a button on the

speaker phone. "Jeremy? Jade is here with me, so go ahead and tell me what you've got."

"Nicole made the rounds of Hollywood agents back in September, just as we guessed, but found no takers among the big agencies," Jeremy reported, his voice crackling over the telephone lines.

Jade moved to the opposite side of the desk, so that the speaker phone was between her and Alec. "Did they say why they wouldn't sign her on?" Had it been because Nicole was pregnant?

"From what I was able to ascertain, the problem was her lack of training and experience. Several of the agents advised her to take up acting lessons, and then come back."

Alec frowned. "Did she take any?" he asked.

"She signed up for some at a prestigious workshop in L.A., but they said she never showed up."

"Anything else?" Alec prodded impatiently.

"The hotel she was staying at—a seedy dive off Sunset Boulevard—kicked her out when her last credit card hit its limit. They said she left no forwarding address, and frankly, I can't find any evidence that she was even in L.A. after September." Jeremy paused. "Any ideas, Jade, on where your sister might have gone if she was as broke and desperate as we think she was last September?"

Jade sighed and shook her head. "No, sorry."

"Well, call me if you think of anything," Jeremy urged. "In the meantime, I'll keep digging out here."

"Thanks, Jeremy." Alec cut the connection.

The conversation over, Jade started to leave the study.

"Wait a minute."

She turned to face Alec. Even with her robe belted securely over her pajamas, she felt ridiculously exposed in the ice blue satin, and wanted only to make a quick exit back to her room.

"Don't you think we should talk about this?" Alec asked bluntly.

"Talk about what?" Jade retorted tensely, still wanting only to flee. "Jeremy Packard said he didn't have anything."

Alec angled closer. "Surely, you must know something—"

"If I did, I would have said so. I don't."

He continued to regard her with that steady, analyzing look. "You're telling me you've made no phone calls on your own?"

Jade thought of her call to Tim Johnson and the others she'd made. It was all she could do not to flush. "Look, Alec, it's been a long day."

He moved, barring her way to the door. "What do you think will be gained here if you find her first?"

I'll find out how she feels about you, Jade thought, a little annoyed by the intensity of her feelings for Alec. "Nothing," she fibbed.

"Now why don't I believe that?" he questioned dryly, moving even closer.

Jade caught a whiff of his cologne and stepped to the side. Her hip bumped the edge of the table. "I don't know. Why don't you believe that?" She tightened her grip on the belt of the robe even more. "Now if that's all—"

"It's not."

They stared at one another. Jade's heart pounded harder at the implacable note she heard in his voice. "What then?" she asked, aware her hands were trembling.

Alec walked to the bar in the far corner of the room and fixed them both a drink. "I think we should talk more about where Nicole might be."

Jade accepted the glass of white wine he handed her and continued to regard her warily. Her shoulders and neck were already drawn tight as a bow. "I've already told you everything I know."

Alec gave her another hard look, then knelt to stir the fire he'd lit while she'd been upstairs with the baby. "Still, maybe if we brainstorm together we'll be able to come up with something."

"Maybe."

"What kind of hobbies does Nicole have?"

"These days?" Jade watched him pick up his glass of wine and prowl the long room that had floor-to-ceiling bookcases. "I haven't the foggiest idea."

"When you were growing up then. What did she like to do in her spare time?"

"Ice skate, ski, read, go to the movies." *Chase boys.* Jade used the tip of her index finger to trace the rim of her wineglass.

"What happened to drive the two of you apart?"

Jade sucked in a breath. "Cut right to the chase, do you?"

"Usually." He flashed her an unapologetic grin.

Jade sank into one of the deep leather chairs before the fire and tucked her feet up beneath her. He was still waiting. But she didn't want to talk about her recent troubles with Nicole. "I guess our problems started when Nicole was fourteen."

"How old were you?" he interrupted.

"Sixteen. Nicole started modeling for the teen department of a local clothing store. It wasn't long after her photos appeared in their newspaper ads that she was discovered by the agency. They wanted her to move to New York and she did."

The mood in the room was quickly becoming too intimate for comfort. Jade left her chair and went to sit at the edge of the window seat that overlooked the landscaped backyard.

"Did you visit Nicole in New York?" Alec asked. Looking a little restless himself, he ambled across the room and took a seat at the far end of the window seat.

"I did at first. But as time went by we had less and less to say to one another." Jade finished the rest of her wine and frowned at the floor. "When she landed the job as the spokesmodel for Ingenue soap when she was twenty-one, she became even more obsessed about her looks." Jade shook her head in silent regret and met Alec's gaze head-on. "I know the pressure was on her to be perfect but all she could think about, talk about, was herself. She wanted to be in the same league as other supermodels like Christie Brinkley and Cindy Crawford. That's when she really began playing on and perfecting this innocent-but-secretly-wild-underneath routine.''

His expression unreadable, Alec drained his own glass and put it aside. ''What does Clark have to do with all of this?''

Jade shot him a sharp glance and lifted her chin. ''Clark is none of your business.'' She jumped to her feet and started to step past him.

He stood and moved with her. ''If you don't tell me the rest of it, I'll just have Jeremy look into that, too.''

Jade stopped where she was and sent him a seething glance. ''You're really a bastard, you know that?''

He gripped her arm above the elbow. ''So what's it going to be? Are you going to tell me about Clark or is Jeremy Packard?''

''If you must know, Clark was my fiancé.''

He let her pull free of his grip without comment. ''What happened?''

Jade felt a new wave of hot color rush into her face. She never talked about this, not with anyone. ''Clark left me at the altar,'' she said stiffly.

''You mean, he broke your engagement?'' Alec ascertained softly.

''Let's put it this way. I was in my wedding dress, coming up the church aisle. Clark was standing at the altar when he suddenly realized he couldn't go through with it. Before the strains of 'The Wedding March' had ended he had dashed back down the aisle, grabbed Nicole's hand, and run out of the church with her. They called me the next day from Vermont to apologize profusely, of course.''

''Bet you told them to go to hell,'' he drawled.

''Among other things,'' Jade confirmed, amazed to find herself grinning back at him. ''Apparently, they expected that, too. But, as Clark explained, there was just no helping what they had done. The two of them were madly in love. And besides, she was so innocent. She needed him.'' Jade recited the facts mechanically. ''Unfortunately, Nicole's 'need' only lasted about two weeks, and then she dumped him.''

"And then Clark came crawling back?" Alec speculated grimly.

"Give the man some credit," Jade went on dryly. "The truth is, I haven't seen Clark since. And I'm very glad of it." *Especially now.*

"And Nicole?"

Jade shrugged her shoulders indifferently. "Except for the telephone conversation late last night, we haven't spoken since the day after my wedding."

Alec's gaze gentled compassionately. "Does Nicole want to work things out?"

Jade lowered her glance away from the kindness she saw in his eyes. "I don't know and I don't care." Jade headed toward the table where she'd left the baby monitor. "My only concern is to see that my nephew is taken care of."

Alec followed Jade over to the table. "So Nicole made a mistake, running off with your fiancé," he said reasonably. "That doesn't have to mean the end of your relationship with your sister."

Jade looked so unhappy that Alec felt compelled to do or say something to make her feel better. He couldn't just let her run back to her room, to brood alone over events that had happened long ago.

She looked at him wearily. "Maybe it wouldn't have been if Clark had been the first beau of mine Nicole had stolen, but he wasn't."

Alec studied her with growing curiosity. "What are you saying?"

"Nicole loves a challenge, and there's nothing more challenging to her than stealing one of my boyfriends. Every time I brought a guy home, Nicole would bat her long eyelashes at him. Having fallen victim to her innocent charms yourself, I'm sure that you know what I'm talking about."

Unfortunately, Alec knew exactly what Jade was talking about. That incredible purity and innocence Nicole exuded not only had attracted men, it had gotten her the million-dollar Ingenue soap contract. The hint that just beneath all that innocence beat the heart of a very wild young woman only made her more desirable.

For Alec, making love to Nicole had been like unwrapping an empty package on Christmas morning. Pleasurable but ultimately unfulfilling. If he hadn't been overseas, lonely, and homesick as hell, he probably wouldn't have gone to bed with her at all. Sensing Jade didn't want to hear that, though, he said nothing. What had happened in the past was over. It was his future that counted now.

"I'm sorry, Jade," he said finally. "I didn't know—"

She fixed him with a cool stare. "Well, now you do."

Alec continued to look at Jade, all the compassion he felt for her reflected in his eyes. "I don't know why anyone would throw you over for Nicole," he said softly, aware once again of the overpowering need to comfort her. It wasn't like him to want to get involved with other people's problems. He had all he could do running Roman Computer. But there was something about Jade he couldn't turn away from. Something about Jade that kept haunting him, day and night.

He gave in to a whim and touched the side of her face with his hand. It felt like hot silk beneath his palm, softer than the satin pajamas she wore. He let his hand slide beneath her hair, to the back of her neck. He tilted her face up to his and felt his heart pound. The way she looked at him, all soft and wanting beneath the veil of thick dark lashes, put his senses in an uproar.

He knew damn well there would be hell to pay later but right now he couldn't help himself. He slanted his mouth over hers and tasted the sweetness that was Jade. She moaned low in her throat as both her hands came up to push ineffectually at his chest.

Apparently, she was totally unprepared for the leisurely quality of his kiss. Good, Alec thought, as her lips opened beneath his and she moved against him pliantly. With a little sigh of contentment, she lifted her arms and wreathed them around his neck, his desire to make love to her deepening as layer by layer, restraint fell away.

Jade arched forward and he tightened his hold on her, crushing the softness of her breasts against his chest. He wanted her, but he didn't want to scare her off. Despite her increasingly passionate response to him, he knew she still felt very skittish.

Alec lifted his mouth from hers and rested his forehead against hers while they both caught their breaths. "Damn, Jade," he whispered against her hair, very much aware they'd done little more than kiss and he was already hard as a rock. "You're incredible." But apparently that, too, was the wrong thing to say.

Jade shrugged away from his touch as suddenly as if he'd burned her. "Don't patronize me, Alec," she said tightly. "I don't need compliments from one of my sister's ex-lovers to make me feel good about myself."

Alec's muscles tensed. "Right, Jade. I'm really into making love as an act of mercy," he drawled. But apparently that was what she believed.

"Forget it, Alec. Your glib words aren't going to cut it with me."

Maybe more decisive actions were called for, Alec thought. Still reveling in the pleasure of their kiss, Alec grinned. "Then how about this to make us both feel good?" He pulled her into his arms once again. Ignoring her soft gasp of surprise, Alec took full advantage of the soft round O of her mouth. Again and again he slipped his tongue inside her, delving deeper each time.

At first, Jade remained stiff and unyielding. But moments later, Alec's persistence was rewarded as Jade again moaned and her head fell back, giving him even fuller access to her mouth. Clamping an arm possessively about her waist, he dragged her even nearer, so close their bodies were almost one. That, too, felt incredibly good, incredibly right, Alec thought. His own body throbbing, he continued kissing her, wooing and seducing, until her whole body seemed to melt and come alive in his arms, until he was sure she wanted him as much as he wanted her.

Needing more, much more, Alec slipped his hand inside the notched collar of her satin pajama top and smoothed his hand from the silk of her shoulder to the silk of her breast. She trembled in response, her flesh swelling to fill his palm.

"Make love with me, Jade," Alec whispered, not sure how much more he could take.

Jade struggled to right herself. He could tell from the stunned, embarrassed look on her face that she felt ashamed of the way she'd just let herself go. "No—"

Alec nearly groaned aloud at the thought of what he had to do. But he knew it was either let her go or continue seducing her and take her right there on the floor of his study in front of the fire, and deal with both their regrets in the morning. Hadn't there been enough regrets in his life? Hadn't hasty lovemaking been what got him into this situation in the first place? With reluctance, he released Jade slowly.

Trembling she stumbled backward and shoved her hands through the riot of her hair, to restore some order. Then she delivered a look that Alec knew was meant to quell him into submission but only made him want her all the more. "I thought I made it clear I don't believe in recreational sex," she said in a decidedly haughty voice that quavered only slightly.

Alec couldn't help it. He grinned, still feeling triumphant about the way she'd responded to him, despite herself. "Then you don't know what you're missing," he teased. She might say she didn't want him to kiss her. She reacted otherwise. Hell, she reacted great. If she reacted that way to just a simple kiss, he wondered how she would react to his lips on her breasts, or his hands on her thighs.... She'd probably turn to wildfire.

"I am not going to be a stand-in for my sister."

At the mention of Nicole, Alec tensed. Exasperation hissed through his teeth as he jammed both hands on his waist. If there was anything he hated, it was being accused of something he didn't do. And he hadn't kissed Jade because he wanted Nicole. "Who the hell asked you to?" he muttered gruffly.

Jade continued to glare at him. "It's very clear to me where this is all going."

The corners of his mouth lifted in a censuring smile. "Then perhaps you'd care to enlighten me," Alec said.

"You want custody of your son. He also needs a mother." She leveled an accusing finger at his chest. "You don't know yet whether or not Nicole is going to give you custody of Andy or want to bring him up with you. You are probably reasonably sure that she isn't exactly maternal."

That was the understatement of the year, Alec thought grimly.

"If it comes to a custody battle over Andy, and it well might," Jade continued with an authoritative lift of her sable brows, "it would probably bode better for you to have Nicole's only family, which is me, on your side. Whether or not it turns out you need me, you strike me as a man who likes to hedge his bets."

Curious as to what she was going to come up with next, Alec folded his arms in front of him. "Go on. This is all getting very interesting."

"You also need someone to help you care for Andy on a permanent basis. Because I'm good with babies and also Nicole's sister, I probably seem like a logical choice. But you're on the wrong track if you think you're going to seduce me into helping you get custody or take care of Andy permanently," Jade finished defiantly, her dark green eyes glittering with a temper Alec found every bit as delicious as her kisses.

Alec took a soothing step nearer. "You're wrong if you think I had any ulterior motive, other than plain desire, for kissing you just now." Knowing he would go mad if he didn't touch her again, Alec took her into his arms and sifted his fingers through the wildly curling ends of her hair. Jade might think she was the responsible one of the two sisters, but right now, she seemed the more deliciously exciting.

"I want you, Jade," Alec stated softly. Needing to see into her face, he hooked his thumbs beneath her chin and tilted her face up to his. If they were going to tell part of it, they might as well both tell it all, he thought, and continued on dangerously, "I want you beneath me. I want you naked, in my bed. I want to be so deep inside you that neither of us knows where you end and I begin. That's how much I want you, Jade," Alec finished on a thready whisper. He lowered his mouth to hers, felt her soft gasp, felt her tense in anticipation. And still, the desire in her was nothing compared to his. "I want you...enough...to do...this."

This time, he let his feelings take over, and allowed the kiss to edge toward desperation. Jade shivered in his arms, but she did not pull away, not until his hand moved toward her breasts again. And then she did pull away—decisively. Once again, he knew he'd gone too far. Jade had evidently decided she could risk necking with him, but no more. Well, the rest would come, Alec reassured himself bluntly.

"You are such a playboy!" Jade scowled at him as she stormed away, snatched up the baby monitor, and held it in both hands. Her mouth was swollen from his kisses and her cheeks were flushed. "Don't you realize that's even worse, to want me strictly out of desire?"

Alec shrugged. He knew he was supposed to feel thoroughly chastised but he didn't. "At least I'm honest," he said. "I would think you'd appreciate that, Jade."

"Being honest and being right are two different things." Without waiting for a reply, Jade turned on her heel and walked out on him.

Alec stared after her. Maybe Jade was right to be so opposed to their getting together. He wasn't a hearts-and-flowers kind of guy. It was lunacy for him to even think of getting involved with such a hopelessly romantic woman. So why did he want it anyway? As practical a person as he was, why did he no longer care about anything except getting Jade in his bed? *Was* he the reckless playboy everyone said? Or

was there something more going on here than either he or
Jade wanted to admit? And if there was, Alec wondered
on a beleaguered sigh, how the hell were they going to deal
with that?

Chapter Six

The sound of Andy's peculiarly weak and feeble crying woke Jade shortly after five. Alec had insisted on taking Andy back to his room after his three a.m. feeding, perhaps as penance for the unrestrained way he'd kissed her. Jade threw on a robe and rushed down the hall to Alec's room. She was sure something was wrong even before she got there, but the look on Alec's face as he bent over the bassinet confirmed it. "What's wrong?" she asked.

"I don't know," Alec replied tensely. "He doesn't want another bottle and he's not wet, but he feels awfully warm to me. I think he's sick, Jade."

Jade joined Alec at the side of the bassinet. She touched a hand to Andy's flushed cheek, her earlier quarrel with Alec over his playboy antics all but forgotten. "You're right," she said softly, concern radiating in her low voice. "Andy is burning up." She picked Andy up and held him against her, soothing the wailing child as best she could with the gentleness of her touch. "Do you have a thermometer?" Jade asked, already working Andy out of the sleeve of his sweat-dampened sleeper.

Still clad only in his pajama pants, Alec headed for the medicine cabinet in his blue tile bathroom. "Not a baby one."

Jade averted her eyes from the splendor of his bare, muscled chest. Now was not the time to be noticing what a beautiful, thoroughly male, body Alec had. "A regular one will do."

Alec returned seconds later. He shook the thermometer down while Jade put Andy on the rumpled sheets of Alec's bed. They were still faintly warm and scented with the intoxicating blend of Alec's cologne, but Andy didn't like Alec's bed any more than he had liked his own bassinet, judging by his immediate wail of indignant protest.

"Come on now, Andy, this is only going to take a minute," Jade soothed as she placed the thermometer in Andy's armpit and held his arm to his side. They had to wait three minutes to get an accurate reading. Andy cried the whole time—short, hiccuping sounds that made tears of commiseration and empathy spring to Jade's eyes.

Finally, the necessary time had elapsed. Jade removed the thermometer from Andy's armpit and read it. "One hundred and three," she said. "Poor darling. No wonder he's crying. He probably feels awful." She picked Andy up again and held him. He cuddled against her, his sobs subsiding only slightly.

His expression deeply worried, Alec declared, "I'm calling Phil Merick."

"Who's that?" Jade followed Alec to the phone.

He was already dialing. "My family physician."

Jade blinked and then moved back slightly from the phone, so Andy's crying wouldn't interfere with Alec's ability to hear. "This early?" she asked, stunned.

"He's an old family friend... Hi, Phil. Sorry to wake you. I've got a sick baby here." Alec paused. "Mine." Another pause. "You weren't the only one. Anyway, Andy's temperature is one hundred and three. Yeah, that's him crying." Alec breathed an enormous sigh of relief. "Thanks, Doc."

He hung up the phone, looking only slightly less worried, and announced, "Dr. Merick is on his way." Grabbing his clothes, he started to shuck his pajama pants. Catching the look on her face, he grinned and took the clothes into the bathroom, but he didn't shut the door behind him.

Jade turned her back. Desperate to think of anything except how Alec would look naked or even nearly naked, Jade asked over her shoulder, "Dr. Merick didn't want us to take Andy to Emergency?" She hadn't realized there were any doctors who still made house calls, even for old family friends.

"No." Alec came out wearing slacks and buttoning his shirt, but he'd done nothing about his sexily rumpled black hair. "He's always come right over if there's a problem," Alec explained, sitting down to put on his socks and shoes. "And conversely, he knows if he has a problem, that I'm every bit as willing to help him as my father was."

"What kind of problem could you help him with?" Jade asked curiously.

Alec shrugged as if it were no big deal. "A couple of years ago the hospital where Merick is chief of staff needed a new wing. I helped raise the money for it." Finished dressing, Alec crossed to her side and looked down at Andy, who was curled against her breast. "Is it my imagination, or is he a little quieter?"

Jade continued soothing Andy with gentle strokes of her hand. "I think he's winding down. Probably from sheer exhaustion. Considering how high his fever is, I doubt he feels any better."

Alec rubbed Andy's back, just as Jade was doing. At the double dose of attention Andy got even quieter. "Poor kid," Alec said softly.

Maybe not so poor, Jade thought, considering how much Alec already seemed to love Andy, and how much she knew she did, too. She had never meant to fall in love with this baby, merely do her duty as his aunt, until her sister could be found. But she had fallen in love with him anyway, and Jade knew it was going to be hard to let go of him emotionally when the time came.

To Jade's relief, Dr. Merick arrived short minutes later. There was a moment's shock when Dr. Merick strode into the study and first took in Jade and Andy. Too late, she realized what the distinguished, bespectacled, gray-haired doctor was seeing: Alec, dressed but looking as if he had just this instant gotten out of bed, Jade in her pajamas and robe, both of them hovering over Andy like worried parents. But Dr. Merick recovered quickly, greeted them both, and then got down to the business of thoroughly examining Andy.

"Andy has a middle ear infection in both ears," Dr. Merick pronounced minutes later. He put his stethoscope away and reached into his medical bag, pulling out a small vial of medicine and disposable syringe. "I can give him a shot of antibiotic to combat the infection and some drops for his ears to ease the pain, but he'll still need to be on oral antibiotics for the next ten days. And then I want to see him in my office to have another look at his ears."

"How long will it take before he feels better?" Jade asked.

"Well, you should see marked improvement in the first twenty-four hours," Dr. Merick instructed them kindly as he carefully filled the syringe, "but it'll probably be a good two days or so before his fever subsides completely, and until that goes away, he isn't going to be what I would call charming company. Just give him plenty of liquids and as much tender loving care as possible."

Jade was pleased to note that Alec listened as intently to Dr. Merick's instructions as she did. It was true Alec still had a lot to learn about babies, probably as much as her sister did, but she couldn't fault him for not trying.

Alec waited until Dr. Merick had finished giving Andy his shot and then walked him to the door. Jade stayed behind in the study to keep Andy out of the draft, but she could hear them just the same in the nighttime silence of the house.

"Call me if Andy doesn't improve," Dr. Merick said. "And Alec? This may be none of my business, but because your father and I were friends for a lot of years, I feel I ought to tell you what *he* would've told you about this… situation…you've got going here. If the two of you are going to shack up together and coparent the boy, you really *ought* to get married."

ALEC RETURNED to the study. Jade's face was still pink with embarrassment. Alec looked a little sheepish, too. "I guess you heard that?" he asked.

"Unfortunately, yes." Jade felt even more embarrassed.

"Phil has a habit of saying exactly what's on his mind," Alec explained.

So I noticed, Jade thought. To her frustration, Alec seemed to take the doctor's meddling in stride. "The commentary on your personal life really doesn't bother you, does it?" Jade put a sleeping Andy back in the Portacrib they were keeping in the study.

Alec shrugged, looking masculine and appealing as he bent to add another log to the fire in the grate. "Dr. Merick may be old-fashioned but he's also right. Andy *does* need a father and a mother, Jade. Every child does."

"Unfortunately, Alec, the situation here is not that simple," Jade warned, her heart pounding. She stepped closer to Alec, careful to keep her voice low.

"Neither is growing up in a one-parent home," Alec replied calmly as he stood and put the poker back in the stand.

It was oddly disconcerting, discovering Alec was dissatisfied with any area of his life. She'd thought he'd always had everything he wanted. Apparently not. "Your parents were divorced?" she asked gently, making no protest when Alec took her hand and led her over to the sofa.

He shook his head and sat down beside her. "My mother died when I was just a baby—cancer. My father did his best, don't get me wrong about that, but Roman Computer took the majority of his time. I was reared by a succession of governesses."

Jade tried to imagine Alec as a small child, being raised in this house. His father off at work, no brothers or sisters to fight with and confide in. No mother to call him on his bad behavior and praise him for his good deeds.

"I don't want Andy to grow up feeling he's missing out on a normal family life, like I did."

"And yet initially you were going to hire a baby nurse to

take care of Andy while you worked,'' Jade pointed out, surprised at how matter-of-fact her voice could sound when her feelings were in such turmoil. The idea of being Andy's mother appealed to her, more than it should. And she wasn't completely averse to the idea of being Alec's wife, at least when she remembered the way he made her feel when he kissed her, all soft and melting and vulnerable.

''I was going to hire a baby nurse only because I had no choice.''

''And no wife.''

Alec stood, looking restless again. ''I still intend to be around for Andy a lot.'' He strode soundlessly over to Andy, checked on him, then satisfied he was still sleeping, came back to Jade's side. He sat on the arm of the sofa, propping one foot up on the seat of the leather sofa. ''Unfortunately, I have a job that requires constant travel. Who'll be here for Andy when I'm not—and don't say Nicole because we both know that she doesn't have a maternal bone in her body.''

''Maybe you should've thought of that before you bedded down with her,'' Jade told Alec coldly as she stood, pulled her robe tighter around her, and moved toward the fireplace.

He gave her an annoyed look. His dark eyes were stony. ''I explained how that happened.''

''And I explained to you how I felt about cleaning up my sister's messes,'' Jade said as heat began to climb from her neck into her cheeks. She clutched the belt to her robe tightly. ''I pitched in here for Andy's sake, because he's my nephew—''

Alec stood and moved toward her persuasively. ''Then become his mother for exactly the same reason,'' he urged softly.

He spoke as if it were all so easy. The romantic part of her wished it were that easy, too, while the sensible side of her knew she'd be a fool to ever let herself consider, even for one love-struck moment, that it could be. ''*Are* you asking me to marry you?''

''What if I were?'' he countered swiftly, his voice cautious and soft. Too soft. She couldn't let herself forget how easily he had kissed her before this very fireplace the night before, or how much the recklessly, wildly romantic part of her wanted him to kiss her again. Just to see if it would be as good the fourth time as it had been the first, and the second and the third....

Pulling all her defenses around her, she sent him a blunt glance and declared, "Then I'd tell you that you were crazy."

He grinned and stepped closer, so there were mere inches separating them. She felt the warmth emanating from his body just as surely as she felt the warmth of the fire in the grate. Trying not to think about how good that strong, hard body of his had felt pressed up against hers, she averted her gaze from his face and stared into the flames again.

"There's nothing crazy about wanting to make a good, stable, loving home for a child," he said in a deep persuasive voice. "We're a good team, you and I." He slid a hand beneath her chin and lifted her face to his. "We just proved it by the way we handled this crisis with Andy."

Had they handled the crisis? Or just gotten themselves in deeper? Her senses in a riot, Jade stepped away from him so he was forced to break his hold on her, and cast another look at the sleeping infant. "The crisis isn't over yet." And it wouldn't be, she reminded herself grimly, until they found Nicole and made her own up to her responsibility. "He's still sick."

"Which is one of the many reasons why I still need you here with me, not just for today, but for a long time to come," he said softly.

His wildly romantic words were like an arrow to her heart because she knew he hadn't meant them to be romantic, even if they were. "Alec." Without warning, Jade felt her throat close up. "Don't."

"Why not?"

"Because I don't want to be used to complete the idyllic Norman Rockwell life you're planning for your son."

"I never said anything about using you." He paused. "You'd get as much out of the arrangement as I would."

"Right. Sex. Credit cards. A handsome successful husband and your family name. What else could a woman want?"

"I don't know." Alec looked baffled. "What else *could* a woman want?"

"How about love and companionship?" Jade countered coolly, as she struggled to contain her disappointment.

He sighed. "Let's be practical here, Jade."

"I know, I know. You're not a hearts-and-flowers kind of guy."

He smiled at her, looking ridiculously pleased she understood him. "Exactly."

Jade sighed. This discussion was over as far as she was concerned. Deciding far too much had been said already, she swallowed hard and turned away from him once again. "Look, Alec. Andy's asleep, at least for the moment. I suggest we take advantage of the peace while it lasts and take turns showering and getting dressed for the day. And since it was my idea, and I've got a ton of work to do today, I'll go first." The sooner she got out of these satin pajamas and into something less intimate, the better.

"Don't feel you have to get dressed on my account," Alec teased in mock seriousness. "I *like* those pajamas you're wearing."

Jade gave him a subduing look. The fact she knew he was teasing did nothing to quell the thrill that went through her at his frankly sexual look. "That's too bad, Casanova," she said sweetly. "Because this is probably the last you're going to see of them." Furthermore, he never would've seen her in her nightclothes at all if he hadn't come back from Raleigh so unexpectedly, and if Andy hadn't gotten sick in the middle of the night.

"Sure about that?" Alec drawled, his teasing grin widening as she headed for the door, her head held high.

No, Jade thought as she disappeared around the corner. She wasn't sure about that. That was exactly the problem.

THE MORE ALEC considered his marriage proposal as he drove to the pharmacy for Andy's medicine, the more he was convinced he'd completely lost his mind. What had he been doing, asking Jade to marry him? So Andy needed two parents. Jade could be a loving presence in Andy's life simply by being his aunt. She didn't need to live with him permanently to do that—although it would help to have her in the same city. So what had gotten into him?

Was it the fact Jade was opposed to casual affairs? The fact he sensed that marriage was the only way he'd ever really have her? Or was it just that he was beginning to see he needed more out of life than work. He needed family.

Alec didn't know. The only thing that was clear to him was that he had to have her. One way or another he had to get her into his life, and into his bed. After that…who knew what would happen? Maybe the two of them would eventually decide to have a child of their own. Andy would probably like having a brother or a sister. He wouldn't mind a daughter, and as enamored as she was of babies, he sensed neither would Jade. She wanted children. They both wanted family. Their getting together made sense. Now all he had to do was get past Jade's romantic notions and figure out how to convince Jade of that, too.

"I'VE GOT THE information you wanted," Tim Johnson announced the moment he walked in for his eight-thirty appointment.

"You really work fast," Jade said admiringly as she led him into Alec's study. Because it was the coziest room in the mansion, not to mention the warmest, and Alec wasn't due back from the morning errands she had sent him on for quite a while, she had decided to work there with Tim.

"Hey." Tim grinned with a glance at the sleeping baby in the crib on the other side of the room. "I've got a reputation to maintain. Is that Roman's kid?"

"As far as we know. We're still trying to piece together the whole story," Jade told Tim as she seated herself next to him on Alec's leather sofa. "That's why we need to talk to Nicole. So what'd you find out?" She leaned forward to pour him a cup of herbal tea.

He accepted the cup she proffered. "Nicole went to a Halloween party out in Los Angeles with one of the Rams, Trey Isaacs." Tim lifted the china cup to his lips and took a big gulp. "Know him?"

"No, but go on."

"Well, and this is the damnedest thing." Tim quickly took another gulp of the steaming, honey-laced tea before he put it back on the table in front of them. "Trey said Nicole went to the party dressed as a pumpkin. And to prove it, he faxed me this photo of her." Tim pulled a slightly grainy fax out of his pocket and unfolded it on the coffee table.

A pumpkin? Her sister would never be caught dead in such an unflattering costume, Jade thought.

But the picture Tim handed her proved otherwise. It was Nicole in the photo, all right. She had on a long-sleeved leotard, tights, high-top sneakers and sweat socks. From neck to knee, she was covered with a blouse material that ballooned out around her like a giant pumpkin. On her head was a hat that looked like a stem. It was a cute outfit, but about as unsirenlike as could be.

"I know, I know," Tim soothed Jade compassionately as he continued to look down at the faxed photo. "I couldn't believe it, either. I mean, who woulda figured Nicole would ever go to a party in something like that? You wouldn't be able to tell if she weighed two hundred pounds beneath it!"

Exactly, Jade thought. What better way to hide an advancing pregnancy? "What did Trey say about her mood? How did Nicole seem to him?" Was she really okay, as Jade hoped despite their ongoing quarrel with one another, or in the midst of some kind of emotional breakdown?

"Well…" Tim sighed. "That was another thing. He said she seemed kind of different, sobered up almost. Not that she'd ever been that much of a drinker, but you know what I mean."

Jade nodded, thinking an unexpected pregnancy would make you grow up and become more responsible whether you wanted to or not. "Yes, I do." Jade paused. "Did she tell Trey anything about what she'd been doing lately?"

"Well, he said she admitted she hadn't been working much. She'd had some trouble with the Ingenue soap people. She'd skipped some reception in her honor in Japan and insulted the hosts real bad. The company was ticked off at her, big-time."

"I know about that."

Tim paused. "I don't want to worry you, Jade, but Trey said Nicole seemed really down. Like something was really bothering her. But at the same time determined, you know. Like she knew what she was going to do, she just wasn't ready to share it with anyone."

That sounded like Nicole, Jade thought sourly. Always looking out for her own best interests. Deliberately, she pushed her resentment of her sister aside. If she was going to help Nicole, help Andy, she had to get over what had happened in the past.

Besides, there was always the possibility that Nicole no longer wanted Alec for herself. If so Jade was free to try to make him see that a real marriage was not something to be feared, but revered. The first step in working all this out would be to talk to Nicole, however, to find out exactly what her intentions were. "Has Trey spoken to her lately?"

Tim shook his head. "Nope. Apparently, she was hanging around a lot of the California teams early on in the fall. You know, back in September. But everyone said she was real subdued. Not the same old Nicole. And, I don't know if this counts for anything, but…everyone said it was obvious Nicole was putting on a little weight, not working out the way she used to."

"I'd heard that, too." Jade got to her feet and moved to the fireplace. Glancing down, she saw Alec had put another log on the fire before he'd left for the store. He seemed determined not to let that fire die.

"What's with the two of you?" Tim asked. He joined her in front of the fireplace and bent down slightly to search her face.

"I'm just worried about her because I haven't heard from her much lately," Jade replied.

"Because of Clark," Tim guessed.

Reminded how long the two of them had been friends, and how good Tim had always been to her, helping her start up her own business as a personal nutritionist, introducing her to fellow athletes, Jade nodded. And then struggled with her guilt.

I let Nicole down. I let the whole family down, dammit, and all because I was too selfish and jealous and unforgiving to see past my own humiliation over Clark. Mother and Dad would turn over in their graves if they knew about this.

Seeing the extent of her distress, Tim put his hands on her shoulders. "Look, I'll keep trying to find her, okay?" he promised as she looked up at him.

"Thanks, Tim," Jade said, and impulsively moved forward in his arms to give the sunny quarterback a hug. "Thanks for everything."

ALEC HEARD VOICES the minute he entered the mansion. Frowning, he followed them to the study and was stunned by what he saw. Jade in the arms of another man, with Andy asleep nearby. Alec had never considered himself jealous, but something about seeing Jade embraced by another man, when she'd been kissing him a few short hours before made a fury unlike anything he had ever felt erupt within him.

Jade was the first to see him. She stepped back, out of the circle of Tim Johnson's arms, took Tim by the hand and led him over to where Alec stood, framed in the doorway of the study. "Tim, this is Alec Roman," Jade said with a cool cordiality that belied the emotion in the room. "Alec, Tim Johnson."

Johnson stuck out his hand. "Nice to meet you," he greeted.

Alec shook the quarterback's hand and nodded back at Johnson. He looked at Jade. "I see you've been busy."

"More than you know," Jade said mysteriously, and surprised him by picking up a paper from the coffee table in front of the leather sofa and thrusting it at him. "Tim brought me this."

His attention temporarily diverted, Alec stared down at the picture of Nicole. Explanations from both Jade and Tim swiftly followed. Alec's heart sank as he realized what all this meant, that Nicole probably had been pregnant in late October. He wanted Andy to be his. He just didn't want Nicole as a mother to his son. Jade was already bothered by his fling with Nicole. He had an uneasy feeling that confirmation of Nicole's maternity would only compound her reluctance to make love with him.

Tim sized up Alec, the way Alec had initially sized up him. "You're looking for Nicole, too, I take it?" Tim ascertained casually.

So Jade hadn't told him everything, Alec thought triumphantly, glad he had the edge on the famous quarterback by at least this much. "Yes," Alec admitted bluntly. "We have some things to work out." He looked at Jade, then back at Tim Johnson. Under normal circumstances he would have relished the chance to talk offensive strategy with the valued NFL player, but after seeing Jade wrapped in the quarterback's arms, the only thing Alec wanted was to get the guy out of his house. "If you two are about finished—" he began.

"Actually, Tim and I have some business to conduct," Jade interrupted. "I canceled an appointment with him the other day to help you find Nicole. So, if you'll excuse us—"

"Sure," he said tightly, unable to completely mask his disappointment. He wasn't sure where this jealousy of his was coming from, but he wished it would disappear as quickly as it had surfaced. He didn't like feeling uncertain of himself. And Jade's reluctance to become involved with him made him feel very vulnerable. Alec forced a smile he knew didn't fool any of them. "If you need me, I'll be in the next room."

"Look, Alec, if the lack of sleep is going to make you this grumpy maybe you should just go upstairs and take a nap," Jade advised him curtly three hours later.

Alec watched as Jade simultaneously cleaned up the mess she'd created in the kitchen making Tim Johnson lunch and prepared a half-dozen bottles of formula for Andy. A half-finished pop in his hand, he leaned against the wall, next to the phone, and watched her indolently. For the first time he could remember, his emotions were in control of him, not the other way around.

"I'm not tired," he stated flatly.

"Well, you act as if you are!" Jade retorted evenly, looking none the worse for wear for the lengthy session she'd spent with Johnson. She'd gone over his menu plans and nutritional needs for the upcoming month, while Alec diapered, fed, and gave the second dose of medicine to his son before putting him back to sleep.

"Furthermore," Jade lectured, her tirade picking up steam, "if you had joined Tim and I for a nutritious lunch of homemade vegetable soup and grilled turkey burgers, as I asked you to, instead of scarfing down yet another burger and fries from the fast-food place around the corner, you'd be feeling a lot better!"

Alec didn't see how sitting at the same table and watching Jade lavish attention on "Perfect Pass" Johnson would have made him feel any better. "You seemed to be handling Perfect's passes just fine without me," he said.

Jade leaned over to put a dish in the dishwasher, the cropped jacket of her sexy fire-engine red business suit hiking up to reveal a hint of creamy skin. "You're out of line here, Roman."

Alec's throat went dry as she straightened and her jacket

slipped back into place. "Am I really now?" he challenged, not sure why he was spoiling for a fight.

"Furthermore," Jade continued calmly, "I resent your implication that my friendship with Tim is anything but platonic."

His own temper soaring, Alec pushed away from the wall and closed the distance between them. "Well, I resent the way you've been driving me crazy since you moved into my house. One minute you're kissing me like you want to go to bed with me and the next you're telling me hands off!"

"I knew it was a mistake for me to move in here!" Jade pivoted away from him, the hem of her pleated skirt swirling about her knees.

"No, Jade. Our mistake has been in denying our feelings," Alec said softly. Feeling pushed to the absolute limit, he moved to block her way out of the kitchen. When she moved to step past him again, he hauled her close, tangled his hands in her hair and brought his mouth down on hers.

The kiss was both harder and sweeter than he'd intended. He wanted Jade to feel as overpowered as he did by what was happening here. He wanted her to feel ravished, on the brink of throwing caution to the wind and making love with him. From the looks of it as she drew away from him breathlessly, he'd been at least partially successful in his goal.

"Don't you have any other way of resolving disputes?" she asked, putting a hand to her throat.

"No." Alec pulled her close once again. He tunneled his hands in her hair and tilted her head back.

"How about hobbies then?" Jade sucked in her breath sharply as his tongue traced down her throat.

"Only this."

Alec's satisfaction deepened as he felt her response. This was all he wanted. *She* was all he wanted. Still cupping her face between his hands, Alec bent his head, gazed deeply into the misty green softness of her eyes and then kissed her again, teasing her tongue with the tip of his until her breath was as short and shallow as his. He wanted to make love to her. He wanted her to feel everything it was possible to feel. He wanted her to experience...everything.... Maybe even teach him something new because God knew it had never been like this for him before, so intensely out of control.

Again, Jade pushed away from him. Her body might have been saying yes, but her eyes were still saying no. "You know," he drawled as he studied her upturned face, and the conflicting emotions he saw there, "if you'd just stop fighting your feelings so much you might get a heck of a lot more pleasure out of this, Jade." *We both might.*

Much more pleasure and she would end up making love with him, Jade thought, and she had promised herself she would not do that. "How do you know what my feelings are?" she challenged lightly.

His sensual lips parted in an enigmatic smile. "Because I feel them in your kiss and I see them in your eyes."

Then he had to know she was vulnerable, too. Much too vulnerable. Jade released a trembling sigh. "Oh, Alec, what am I going to do with you?" Jade asked softly, feeling both flattered by the intent way he was chasing her and wary of him. "You just won't quit." If it were only pleasure his kisses promised her...maybe she would give in...but making love with someone wasn't that simple and she knew it. And she didn't want to be hurt again. Ever.

Alec's smile deepened tenderly as he rubbed his thumbs across her lips and confessed, "You know me, Jade. When I see something I want I don't stop until I get it."

And what he wanted was her, Jade thought. The idea of being his lover was as thrilling as it was disturbing. Allowing herself to be too romantic, to forget the practical side of things would be a big mistake. She still wanted her own man to love. She still wanted marriage, children, a deep and lasting commitment, a partnership that would last the rest of their lives. Alec talked marriage in the abstract. What he really wanted was a business arrangement. Jade didn't want to spend the rest of her life worrying that Alec would tire of her one day and cancel his "contract" with her the moment a "better deal" came along.

Alec felt the change in her. He sighed, making no effort to mask his disappointment. "Back to square one again?"

Jade shook her head. "Did you really think it would be any different?"

"A guy can always hope." He grinned, letting her know he hadn't begun to give up on her. "Unfortunately for the both of us, I've got work to do today, too." Roman Computer was the one mistress that would never let him down.

If Jade wouldn't allow them to make love, he supposed he could accept that. He was a patient man. He knew their time would come. Until then, he'd just have to continue wooing her with kisses and bury himself in work. He'd been neglecting his business anyway.

He started reading. Five pages later, he couldn't recall a word he had read. Alec sighed and wondered what had gotten into him. It was more than just sexual frustration. He should be narrowing the search for the director of the new Roman Computer lab. But all he could think of was Jade. And what he wanted to happen between them.

Alec sighed and sat back in his chair. Being suspicious of a woman was not new to him. He'd been on his guard since the day he'd learned what a farce his first marriage really was. But the feelings of jealousy were. He shook his head, recollecting the intensity of emotion he'd felt when he'd seen Jade hugging the Steelers quarterback.

Where did he get off reacting so proprietorially to Jade? He barely knew her, hadn't even made love to her yet. He wasn't the kind of guy who was known for his possessiveness. Just the opposite. Yet, around Jade he turned into a hormone on legs. All he could think about was getting her into his bed, driving her senseless with passion, taking her to the edge, and then diving over it with her.

It must be the stress, Alec thought, running his hands through his hair. The surprise of having a son in his life...a son who needed a mother, not just a loving aunt. That had to be what was getting to him. That had to be why he had reacted so jealously when he'd seen Jade with Johnson. Because he'd felt, at the moment anyway, that Tim might be interested in Jade, that Tim might just be the kind of guy who'd offer Jade the romantic approach Jade felt she needed.

Well, he'd handle this unexpected development the way he handled every other crisis, business and otherwise. He'd keep a close eye on Jade and the baby. And he'd keep his emotions in check. He could make love with Jade, of course, but he drew the line at further emotional involvement. He would treat this relationship in a practical, businesslike manner from here on out. He would have Jade, but he'd have her on his terms.

Chapter Seven

"I wondered where you two had disappeared to," Alec said early Friday morning.

One hand on Andy's middle, to keep him from rolling off the thick terry-cloth towel she had spread over the bathroom countertop, Jade spared Alec a brief glance. It was only eight in the morning, but he looked ready to conquer the world in his sophisticated khaki dress shirt, slacks, coat, and tie. She, on the other hand, was ready to conquer a much more domestic agenda.

His glance slid over her oversized black and gold Steelers jersey, embolded with Tim Johnson's number, and formfitting gold leggings. "Nice outfit. Looks like official gear," he remarked casually.

Jade didn't know why, but she felt a little embarrassed. "Tim Johnson had it made up for me last Christmas, as a thank-you gift for all I'd done for him and the team."

"A thank-you gift or a this-woman-is-mine gift?" Alec asked.

Jade's head lifted. Her heart was racing, but she forced herself to maintain a serene expression. "I told you there's nothing between Tim Johnson and I except friendship."

"Does he know that?"

Jade released a jagged breath and turned to face Alec so suddenly, her hips grazed the front of his trousers. "Are you always this impossible in the morning, or is it just around me?'' Jade said tartly.

He stepped so close they nudged torsos again. ''You wouldn't be trying to make me jealous, would you?''

It was a serious question, but Jade gave him an amused glance. ''Dream on, sweetheart.''

''Because if you are,'' Alec continued, following her around the bathroom, ''it's not working.''

Jade rolled her eyes. ''Oh, I can see that.''

Teasing lights suddenly appeared in his eyes. ''Just as long as we've got the record straight,'' he declared with a grin.

Their eyes meshed. She felt the warmth of his affection for her, and suddenly all was right with the world. ''As long as you're here, how about giving me a hand with Andy's bath?''

''*Now?*''

''You need to learn the basics.''

''Why?''

''Because as long as I'm staying here, Alec Roman, this is going to be an equal opportunity household.''

''Meaning?''

''Everything I do, you do.''

''Boy, you drive a hard bargain, lady.'' But he was already taking off his jacket and rolling up the sleeves of his dress shirt.

Jade returned his teasing grin, aware she was feeling more lighthearted than she had in hours, and all because she was spending time with Alec again. ''You think I'm tough now,'' she threatened, ''just wait until we get started on your diet. Right, Andy?'' Jade lifted Andy into the lukewarm bath. He kicked and cooed as he hit the water, but didn't cry as Jade soaped his tummy, arms, and legs. She rinsed him with scoops of the warm bathwater, cupped in her hand, then turned to Alec. ''Why don't you give him his shampoo?''

Alec was standing close enough to her that she could feel him stiffen. ''Me?''

''Sure,'' Jade said gently as she turned toward him and inhaled the dark woodsy scent of his cologne. Seeing that

Alec was as nervous as all new fathers everywhere, suddenly endeared him to her. She smiled her encouragement. "I'll hold him, all you have to do is give him the shampoo."

Alec frowned. "What if I get shampoo in his eyes?"

"No problem. It's baby shampoo, formulated not to sting."

"Oh." Alec picked up the bottle of golden shampoo, then turned back to her, for the first time really seeming to trust her. "What do I do first?"

"Wet his hair. That's it," Jade encouraged gently, talking him through it. "Now put on a little shampoo, about a dime-size drop or less, work it up into a lather. And use that cup of warm water to rinse, careful not to get the water into his face. There," Jade said softly when Alec had finished. "Wasn't that easy?"

"Sure, with you holding the little slugger." Alec picked up the thick hooded baby towel and held it out while Jade lifted Andy out of the water. They swaddled him securely, then Jade carried Andy into her bedroom. She placed him gently on the center of her bed, next to the fresh diaper and clothing she had already laid out. "So what's up anyway?" Jade asked, as she sat down, Indian style on the center of the bed. "Why were you looking for me?"

Alec stretched casually across the width of her bed and picked up a baby rattle. "Jeremy Packard has found what he thinks is an important lead on Nicole."

Jade tried to appear happy. After all, this was good news. Once Nicole was back, Jade would be free to leave. The only question was, *did she want to leave?*

"What's the lead?" Jade asked as she unswaddled Andy and began to diaper him.

Alec continued to amuse Andy with the rattle. "There's a doctor out there that Nicole was dating last August. Kurt Xavier. He won't talk to Jeremy about Nicole but Jeremy thinks if you and I go out there that he might talk to us. The only hitch is that Xavier's about to take off for some seminar so there's not much time. Anyway, I was thinking maybe

you, I, and Andy could fly out there together on my jet tonight and spend the weekend.'' He looked up at Jade and
smiled, his sable eyes gently persuasive.

"There's only one tiny flaw with your plan," Jade said.
"Andy can't fly right now because of his ear infection."

Alec's dark gaze narrowed. "Are you sure about that?"

"Positive."

Alec sighed, looking disappointed. "There's no reason this
should put a damper on your plans, Alec. You can still go,"
Jade offered automatically. "I'll stay here with Andy."

Alec studied her thoughtfully. "You wouldn't mind?"

"Not at all," Jade lied, though the thought of Alec chasing
down Nicole personally was enough to set her teeth on edge.
"Anyway, I've got a lot to do myself, work-wise, so I'll be
pretty busy here. I'm supposed to go to the Phillies' spring-
training camp in Florida, week after next, and counsel all
their players. And I'm still preparing menu plans and individual menus for that."

Alec nodded, and fit the rattle into Andy's fingers, curling
them tight around it. He looked back at Jade. "All right, I'll
go by myself, but I'll be back as soon as I can. Maybe even
as soon as tomorrow."

"WE'RE GOING TO HAVE to make this short," Dr. Kurt Xavier
said as he settled into a chair opposite Alec Saturday morning.

Alec had been cooling his heels in a hotel room all night.
Had Xavier agreed to meet him the previous evening, as Alec
had wanted, he could already have been back in Philadelphia.
"Believe me," he said emphatically, "I have no wish to drag
this out unnecessarily."

"Good," Xavier replied, gesturing toward the suitcases
standing packed and ready to go in the entryway of his plush
West L.A. apartment. "Because I'm about to leave for a seminar at Johns Hopkins."

Alec nodded, all too aware how annoyed he would feel if
the situation were reversed. "I understand."

"No, I don't think you do." Kurt Xavier gave Alec a hard look. "I'm not in the habit of discussing my personal life with anyone, and certainly not with the ex-lover of a woman I once dated."

Alec resented Xavier's implication that this fact-finding mission was fun for him. "Normally, I'm not in the habit of asking. But under the circumstances..." Alec began to explain, and when he had finished long minutes later, he had Kurt Xavier's full attention, if not his full cooperation.

"Well, I can certainly see why you're trying to track Nicole down," Kurt Xavier said warily. "I imagine you want to get to the bottom of this...situation."

That was an understatement and a half, Alec thought. "So you'll help me?" he pressed.

Kurt Xavier shrugged. "I don't see how I can. I'm not dating her anymore."

Alec frowned. He'd been afraid of this. Nicole's fickleness when it came to men was legendary. "How long ago did you stop?"

"Months ago. The truth is, I only saw her socially three or four times, over a two-week period in late August."

Alec paused and did some rapid calculations. Nicole would have been five months pregnant by the time Kurt Xavier and Nicole dated, if Alec was the father; he still wasn't one hundred percent convinced of that. Given Nicole's wild behavior, the father could have been anyone. Nevertheless, he wouldn't mind having Andy for a son, as long as he didn't have to have Nicole in the bargain.

"Was she pregnant?"

Xavier's glance narrowed sharply. "This is getting kind of personal, isn't it?"

Alec shrugged. "Paternity is personal."

Xavier said nothing in response.

"You're a doctor," Alec continued impatiently, anxious to get this ordeal over so he could get back to Philadelphia, and Jade. "If she were five months pregnant, surely there would have been signs you could've picked up on, even if she were doing everything she could to hide that fact.''

"That doesn't mean I would share any conclusions I had about Nicole, medical or otherwise, with you," Xavier replied.

"You're telling me you won't help me. Is that it?" Alec asked tersely.

Xavier gave him a stony look. "As I said, Nicole and I stopped dating in late August."

Alec swore silently to himself in frustration, and yet, in a way, he couldn't fault Xavier for protecting Nicole. Had the situation revolved around Jade, Alec would be doing the same. "Is Nicole still in Los Angeles?"

Xavier shrugged. "I haven't run into her socially for months."

Unable to mask his impatience, Alec probed, "Did she talk to you about going anywhere else?"

"No."

This was like trying to get blood out of a stone, Alec thought. "Look, if you see her—"

"I'll tell her you're looking for her." Xavier stood and glanced at his watch. "Now, if you'll excuse me, Roman, I've got a plane to catch."

"WELL? WHAT'D YOU find out?" Jade asked the moment Alec got home late Saturday afternoon.

Alec propped a shoulder against the laundry-room doorway, for a second just savoring the sight of a thoroughly disheveled Jade. Domesticity in any form had never appealed to him—until now. His own disappointment over the lack of results already dealt with and put aside, Alec concentrated on his happiness to be back with Jade and Andy again. Which was another first. Although he always missed the familiarity of home when he was away on business, never before had he been really lonely for anyone in particular, the way he'd been lonely for Jade.

"Practically nothing," he replied finally.

The disappointment in Jade's green eyes deepened. "Where's Nicole?"

Alec shrugged, still marveling that he could miss any one woman as much as he had missed Jade. There hadn't been a moment since he'd left her yesterday that he hadn't wondered what she was doing and if she was missing him, too. "Beats the hell out of me," he replied, then hunkered down beside her, a quizzical expression on his face. "What are you doing?"

She was on her hands and knees on the utility-room floor, mopping up a stream of sudsy water flowing from beneath the washing machine. She was wearing Penn State sweats. Her dark hair was tousled, her face flushed, her lips enticingly soft and bare.

"What does it look like I'm doing?" Jade retorted in obvious irritation. "I'm trying to clean up this horrendous mess."

"I can see that," Alec explained patiently, and refrained from telling her once again that he hired people to do chores like this. "How did it happen?"

"How should I know? It's your washer."

He caught the edge in her voice. Obviously she was ticked off as hell at him for something besides the malfunctioning washer. "Is something wrong?"

"I'll tell you what's wrong," she said, her green eyes flashing. "While you've been gallivanting across the country, chasing down my wild sister, I've been here keeping the home fires burning."

Was that jealousy he heard in her low, sexy voice? Over him? Alec stared at her in bemused wonderment. *I'll be damned,* he thought, feeling oddly pleased and very elated, *it was.* "Did you call a repairman to come out?"

"No. I figured I'd clean up the flood first."

From a practical standpoint, Jade seemed to have the situation under control, and yet she was still very upset. His mood cautious, Alec stepped around several piles of wet towels. "How's Andy?"

"Fine," Jade snapped, giving him another pointed glare. "Now that he's finished spitting up or otherwise soiling everything we both own."

Alec's brow furrowed in concern. "Andy wasn't spitting up when I left yesterday—"

"He got fussy after you left. I couldn't figure out why until last night, when his stomach began acting up. Dr. Merick said Andy was probably having a reaction to the medicine and switched him to something a little easier on his stomach earlier this morning." Jade paused, tugged off a work glove, and ran a hand through the tousled layers of her dark curly hair. "And he's been fine ever since."

"Why didn't you call and tell me this?" Alec demanded, loosening the knot of his tie. "I told you where I'd be staying."

"I didn't want you to worry when you were so far away and there was nothing you could do. Besides, the situation was under control."

Dealing with a sick baby had left her emotionally drained, Alec thought, his heart warming with sudden sympathy. He closed the distance between them, reached a hand down to her, clasped her soft hand in his, and wordlessly helped her to her feet.

"If I'd known you were having trouble with Andy, I would have turned my jet around and come back and said to hell with the meeting with Xavier, Jade."

For a moment, she looked touched, then her chin assumed that stubborn tilt he was beginning to know so well. Jade withdrew her hand from his, but not before he felt her tremble. "It wasn't necessary, Alec."

"Dammit, Jade," Alec retorted, taking her in his arms even as he disagreed with her. Now that he was holding her, it was all he could do not to kiss her. "It was necessary. Don't you understand?" he asked gently as he brushed the hair from her face. "I want to worry right along with you— whether I'm in a position to do anything for Andy immediately or not,'' Alec said, as much to his surprise as hers. "We're in this together.''

"You're wrong, Alec. We are not in this together.'' Jade withdrew her soft warm body from the circle of his arms and stepped back, until she was leaning up against the washer. "You're in this with Nicole. At least until Nicole tells you otherwise. And I'll be frank, I'm not all that sure that's going to happen.''

Alec wanted to disagree with Jade on her assessment of the situation. He wanted to tell her of his plans to buy Nicole off and then send her packing so he could go after Jade and find a way to make a real home, with a real family, for Andy. Deciding these plans were better left unvoiced, for the moment anyway, Alec said nothing.

"I take it you didn't get much sleep while I was gone?'' he asked gently. For someone who had been through baby hell, she sure looked good, he thought. Damn good.

Jade was silent, refusing to acknowledge his attempt to commiserate with her. Impatiently, she rubbed at the back of her neck, then crossed her arms at her waist. Alec knew she was oblivious to the way her contentious stance had tautened the fabric of her sweatshirt over her breasts, clearly delineating the high rounded globes, but he sure wasn't.

"I'm fine,'' she said, dismissing him with a glance.

"Grumpy, you mean,'' he teased, his every protective instinct kicking immediately into overdrive. "But don't worry, sweetheart. I know how to fix that.'' He slid one arm around her waist, the other beneath her knees.

"*What are you doing?*''

A very primitive, very male satisfaction rushed through Alec like a shot of adrenaline as he scooped her up in his arms and positioned her against his chest. "Seeing you get the sleep you need.''

Her arms clung softly to his shoulders. "Alec, put me down,'' she ordered hotly, but there was no real conviction in her voice.

Alec grinned down at her as he swept through the kitchen and up the back stairs. "Gladly, once we reach your bed."

Jade's face assumed a panicked look. "We can't go in my room, Alec. Andy's asleep in there."

"Then you can use mine." He sailed through the doorway to his room and lowered her gently to the bed.

Jade looked up at him, her eyes wide, her lower lip trembling. "You're crazy."

Right now Alec felt a little crazy. He sat down beside her on the edge of the bed and planted an arm on either side of her. "If I'm crazy, Jade, it's because you make me crazy." Her hair was spread out over his pillow. It looked exactly as he had dreamed it would, the corkscrew curls all dark and silky and wild. He closed his eyes and just for a moment, touched his lips to the fragrant silk and inhaled the flowery scent of her hair and skin. "Tell me you missed me, Jade, at least half as much as I missed you," he whispered, feeling intoxicated by her nearness, by the fact she was finally... finally...in his bed.

Jade looked up at him, her green eyes filled with longing and the more urgent need for self-preservation. "I'll tell you no such thing," she said cantankerously, and folded her arms in front of her like a defensive shield.

Alec chuckled. He had figured this wouldn't be easy. "Then you'll just have to show me," he declared.

He leaned over her and lowered his mouth to hers. Her response was immediate and volatile. She grabbed his upper arms, digging her fingers into his biceps, and melted against him. Growling low in his throat, Alec stretched out on top of her. He spread her knees and slipped between them. The V of her thighs cradled his hardness and his sex throbbed against her surrendering softness. He wanted her. Damn, but he wanted her and this time, he could tell by the frantic unrestrained way she was kissing him back, there was going to be no stopping.

His emotions soaring, he slid his hands beneath the hem of her Penn State sweatshirt and pushed it up over her breasts.

She wasn't wearing a bra and she was just as beautiful as he remembered. He cupped the full weight of her breasts with his palms, discovering anew the feel of creamy skin and rosy nipple. The last time she had kept him from going any farther. Not this time. He bent his head and took a nipple into his mouth, sucking lightly on the tender bud. Jade drew in a quick urgent breath and dove her fingers through his hair, holding him close. He loved her with his mouth and hands and tongue until her back arched off the bed. "Alec—"

Her whimpered plea was all the encouragement he needed to take their lovemaking forward another step. Satisfaction pouring through him, he tugged her sweatpants down and off, slipped a hand between her thighs and found the silken core of her. Jade trembled at his touch and uttered a quiet, strangled sigh that nearly drove him wild with desire. But not wanting to proceed any further until she was gloriously wet, gloriously ready, he kept up his tender explorations and urgent kisses until she moaned and buried her face against his shoulder. "Now, Alec, I don't want to wait."

She wasn't the only one who was anxious to have him inside her. Containing his own sense of urgency with effort, Alec shucked his pants and settled over her, the tip of his manhood pressing against the delicate folds. She moved to receive him and he pushed all the way inside. Being a part of her was like being held in the grip of a tight soft glove. He groaned and began to move inside her, slowly at first, then with rapidly escalating pleasure.

"Oh, God, Alec," Jade cried, tightening her arms around his back as she arched her back and spread her thighs, lifting her whole body into the contact. "Don't stop...don't... stop..."

Stop? He could barely control himself as she shuddered and writhed beneath him, her insides clenching around him, urging him on to release. He heard her moan and felt her tremble, and he thrust forward, surging completely and deeply into her, his release coming quickly on the heels of hers.

Feeling completely wiped out by their lovemaking and yet more content than he could ever remember feeling in his life, Alec collapsed on top of Jade and held her close, enjoying the soft warm feel of her. To his surprise, he could already feel her going to sleep. A wave of tenderness rushed through him as he realized how exhausted she was. They'd make love again, later, he promised himself, but only after she had rested. Closing his eyes, he followed her into sleep.

WHEN HE AWOKE an hour or so later, Jade was gone. Alec felt a burst of unaccustomed panic. He had known the shift in their relationship would be difficult for her. He hadn't expected her to just take off without a word. But maybe considering how foreign the idea of a casual affair was to her— if you could call what they'd experienced casual, he amended fiercely to himself—he should have expected this kind of conflicted response from her.

Bracing himself for the inevitable emotional scene to come, he dressed and went to her bedroom. Andy was sleeping peacefully, but Jade was not in sight. He relaxed as he noticed her suitcase, purse, business papers. If that was all still here, she must be, too, he thought with relief.

He went downstairs and checked his study, then the kitchen. Nothing. He finally found her in the laundry room, doing, to his irritation, exactly what she'd been doing when he first arrived home—mopping up the mess the malfunctioning washer had left. "I wondered where you went," he said quietly, a little surprised she hadn't changed out of the Penn State sweats, yet glad she hadn't, too. Just seeing her in them reminded him of all she apparently was now working just as fiercely to forget.

"Well, now you know," Jade said without looking at him.

Alec knelt beside her. He wanted to take her in his arms again and kiss that troubled look away. "What's wrong, Jade?"

"What could be wrong?" she retorted stubbornly. "We both got what we wanted."

Had they? Alec wondered.

"But now that's over, we have some things to discuss," Jade said, putting down her towel, which was saturated, and reaching for a new one. She stood and leaned against the washer. "I assume by the fact you returned alone that you weren't able to work things out with Nicole while you were in California."

Alec had never liked playing games. He preferred to keep his dealings with women open and aboveboard. Clearly, Jade did not operate on a similar level. He pushed aside his hurt that Jade was not as happy about what had just happened between them as he was, however. They did need to talk about what had happened in California. "The trip was a wasted effort," he told her. "Dr. Xavier was more bent on getting to Johns Hopkins for a seminar than helping me. I was never able to come close to locating Nicole, so no, I didn't work things out with her."

Jade looked at him as aloofly as if he were a complete stranger. Alec wished he knew what she was feeling, but her eyes gave him no clue. "Were you at least able to confirm that Nicole was pregnant last fall?" she asked as calmly as if they were talking about the weather.

Alec frowned. "Xavier refused to comment on that but it's possible he didn't know for certain. Nicole couldn't have been more than five months pregnant when they dated last August."

She swore and looked like she wanted to punch something; he knew just how she felt. "I don't believe this," Jade muttered.

Neither had Alec, at the time. Still, there was something in Jade's eyes now that needed to be dealt with. He had the feeling she thought he was doing less than his best where Nicole was concerned. "You think you could have done better?" he asked.

She regarded him with a haughty confidence that surprised him. "I know I could have," she announced.

After traveling six thousand miles in thirty hours just so

he could be with Jade as soon as possible, then making tender love to her, Alec wasn't in the mood for having his competence questioned, in any area. "How would you have done better," he shot back as he lounged negligently in the doorway, "by flirting?"

Color flowed into her cheeks. "I don't have to listen to your insults." Her lips trembling with barely suppressed rage, she jumped to her feet and started to brush past him through the door. "And as for the mess in here, I'm tired of playing housemaid to your lord of the manor. You can clean up your own damn floor!"

He caught her elbow. He knew what was really getting to her—the fact they'd made love when so much about the rest of his life was still unresolved. "Running away from me again, sweetheart?"

"No!" Jade said, and tugged free. The forward momentum combined with the slippery floor sent her flying. Alec sprang forward to save her and somehow managed to put himself between Jade and the floor. He landed on his back, Jade on top of him. They were half in, half out of the laundry room. Breathing heavily, Jade lifted her head to stare at him. Simultaneously, Alec clamped his arms around her back, and held tight. Now that he had her, he wasn't going to let her go. Not until they talked.

"Let me go."

He rolled so that she was beneath him. "Oh no, sweetheart. Not until we talk about what just happened upstairs."

"I don't want to talk about it," she said stubbornly. "Dammit, Alec—" Her voice caught as he settled his weight over hers and caught her flailing wrists, pinning them to the floor on either side of her. She squirmed in an effort to get free of him, and suddenly it was all too much.

The softness of her body beneath his, the trembling of her breasts, her bare pliant mouth—suddenly, Alec knew it would never be enough to have a short, transitory love affair with Jade. Waking up and finding her gone had shown him that.

He wanted more than that. A great deal more. But first, he had to get her comfortable with the idea of them as lovers.

"We made love, Jade. And it was great—"

Jade shut her eyes and shook her head. "Wrong, Alec. We had sex. And we shouldn't have, not when it meant absolutely nothing to you, or—or to me," she finished in a choked voice, tears streaming from her eyes.

Nothing? How could she think it meant nothing to him? Unless she'd come to that conclusion because it had been so fierce...and swift. Had she stayed, he would have made love to her again, slowly and tenderly. Well, they were together again now.

Deciding there was only one way to show her how he felt, Alec threaded one hand through the hair at the nape of her neck and tilted her head back in a way that gave him maximum access to her full soft mouth. "You call this having sex, Jade? I call it making love." Ignoring her gasp of protest, he lowered his lips to hers and kissed her thoroughly. To his dismay, she remained stiff and unbending beneath him. Determined to get past her emotional barriers, he kept up the sensual assault, coaxing her with his lips and tongue. Gradually, as he had known she would, she melted beneath him.

Satisfaction flowing through him in effervescent waves, Alec slid a hand beneath the hem of her sweatshirt, his fingers moving over the slenderness of her ribs, to the lower slopes of her breasts. As he had suspected, she still wasn't wearing a bra. Still kissing her deeply, he palmed her breast, capturing the entire weight of the silky globe in his hand. She trembled, and the nipple pressed urgently against his palm. As he felt the hunger in her body, all rational thought flew from his mind. He closed his thumb and fingertips around the tender point and worked it to a tight bud. Stretching sinuously beneath him, Jade moaned soft and low in her throat and arched her head back even more.

"Alec—"

"I know, sweetheart," he whispered back as he kissed his way down her neck. He wrapped his arms around her and held her tight. "I missed you, too. You can't begin to know how much." He'd never wanted a woman so completely.

He found his way back to her mouth and kissed her again, ravenously this time, without restraint. Their tongues twined in a mating dance as old as time, while lower still, a fire raged. Knowing he had to touch her again or go mad with desire, Alec tugged her sweatpants down over her hips. Her panties followed. He swept his fingers through the dark curls and found her center slippery with desire. Her passion ignited his own. Over and over he caressed her, until she was strung tight as a bow, arching against him, and falling apart in his arms. His kiss stifled the cry of exultation that rose in her throat, but nothing could check the elation he felt as she reached the pinnacle of release she sought. His own body humming with pent-up desire, Alec kissed Jade until she had stopped trembling, then drew back and gazed lovingly down at her flushed cheeks.

They needed time, and a better place. "I want to make love to you again," he said quietly. "All day and all night. But not here. Let's go upstairs again, to my bed."

Jade's eyes, which until that moment had been glazed with desire, widened. New color flooded her cheeks and she looked at him as if she couldn't believe they'd almost made love again. "No."

Alec blinked, sure he couldn't have heard right. *"What?"*

"You heard me." Using both hands, Jade tugged her pants back up over her waist. While Alec leaned back, she struggled to a sitting position, looking totally panicked. "This shouldn't have happened." She pushed away from him and stood. Her pants and the back of her sweatshirt were soaked with both suds and water. Alec's own clothing clung to him wetly, but he didn't give a damn about his ruined business suit. He cared about Jade.

She met his eyes. Her fingers were shaking as she shoved them through her hair and tried to restore order to the dark corkscrew curls. "What happened upstairs was also a mistake."

"Now I suppose you'll tell me you're sorry," Alec presumed sarcastically, aware he was hard as a rock and nowhere near getting the release *she'd* just enjoyed.

"As a matter of fact, I am, although I wasn't going to say it." Jade clipped the baby monitor back onto her waist and then speared him with that laser look again. Her green eyes were dark and unrepentant. "I never should have let it go that far just now, not when I knew I had no intention of—well, you know."

"Easing my ache?" he supplied less than graciously as he got to his feet.

"Look, Alec," Jade told him wearily, "it's bad enough we had the lack of foresight to make love when you first got home. But now we've got other problems we have to deal with, too."

"Such as?"

"Such as the washer broke during midcycle, we're almost out of clean diapers, and we're light-years away from finding that wild, irresponsible sister of mine. We can't afford to do something this foolish."

Alec regarded Jade, attempting to tamp down his resentment. "I don't think our making love could ever be foolish," he said curtly, although inwardly he was already acknowledging that this was as much his fault as it was hers. He shouldn't have rushed her.

Unnerved by the hot intensity of his gaze, Jade averted her eyes from his. Motions brisk and purposeful, she got down on her hands and knees to finish mopping up the sudsy water with what was left of the stack of clean towels.

"And we will find Nicole eventually because Jeremy Packard is still on the case," Alec continued.

Jade dropped the last damp towel on the stack of soaked ones in the corner. "This is hopeless," she said curtly in a way that let him know the discussion of their possible involvement was closed. "I'm going upstairs to change."

Knowing nothing could be gained by forcing her to stay there with him, Alec watched her go. So they hadn't made love again right away. It would happen, he reassured himself firmly. He would make it happen. And he would start by showing Jade just how hopelessly outdated her romantic notions were.

JADE TURNED THE SHOWER on full blast and stepped into it, her emotions in a whirl. Too much had happened today, too quickly. She had hoped to finish cleaning the laundry room, shower and change, all before Alec had woken up again. But of course it hadn't worked out that way.

She'd had to face him, when she was feeling her most vulnerable, her most irritated with herself. It wasn't like her to behave foolishly. Yet whenever she was around Alec it was as if she had been robbed of her common sense.

She could blame the first time they'd made love on her fatigue and her loneliness. As for the second time…it annoyed her to realize how easily she'd nearly been swept away again. Fortunately, his calm discussion of the best place to make love had been all she had needed to wake her up. Maybe Alec's frustration over her action was good, too. If he thought she were a tease instead of just confused, perhaps he would stop giving her the full court press, and concentrate his considerable energies on finding Nicole and getting that mess straightened out. Once that happened, Jade could go home again. Get back to a normal life. Or as normal a life as she would ever have, after Alec.…

Feeling like she had a grip on things again, when she finished her shower, Jade dressed and went back downstairs. To her surprise, the laundry room was empty save for a tidy stack of damp towels in the corner, but she could hear the dishwasher running, which was strange, as she hadn't turned it on and Alec never did housework of any kind. "Why is the dishwasher on?" Jade asked Alec, knowing it had been empty the last time she looked.

Alec continued making a pot of coffee—the one domestic skill he did well. "I put the diapers in there to rinse."

Jade blinked. "You're kidding, right?"

He shook his head no. "It was easier than going to the Laundromat." He cast a sideways glance at the dishwasher, which was still churning noisily. "It's working pretty good so far, though I may have to wring the diapers out by hand before I put them in the dryer. In the meantime, I found a couple of extra clean diapers up in my bedroom so we're set if Andy wakes up and needs changing."

"Efficient, aren't you?"

"You don't know the half of it, sweetheart." He grinned and switched on the coffee maker. "I also took care of the washer. The repairman will be here within the next thirty minutes."

Jade did a double take. "On a Saturday evening?"

Alec gave a satisfied shrug. "I offered to pay him double-time if he could fix it this evening. He was all too willing to come by."

"Or in other words," Jade said sarcastically as she ventured another look at the laundry room and remembered clearly what had just happened there, "everyone has their price."

"Right," Alec volleyed right back, "and yours is marriage."

Jade stepped back, reeling from the verbal blow. She had known he was unhappy with her, she hadn't figured he'd attack her. "Look, if you're trying to put me in the same league as my sister," Jade began hotly.

Alec stepped closer, his expression calm. "I'm merely pointing out a few facts. You've got a pay-or-play attitude, too. If I gave you an engagement ring, declared my unending love and asked you to marry me, you'd be back up in my bed in ten seconds flat."

Jade stiffened. She hated his unemotional, unromantic view. "I hardly think expecting a man to love me before he makes love to me is criminal—"

"Maybe not criminal," he cut in, disagreeing softly, "but certainly unrealistic."

Jade forced the memory of his kisses and caresses, and her

passionate response to them, from her mind. Alec was wrong here, and it was up to her to show him. "You're the one who's being unrealistic if you think any worthwhile woman would accept anything less than total love and commitment from you, as a prerequisite to marriage or even just plain sex, Alec," Jade countered coolly. "My mistake was in letting myself be seduced into lowering my standards. I assure you," Jade thundered, "it will not happen again!"

Silence fell between them and stretched out interminably. Jade's heart pounded. Her pulse skittered and jumped. Finally, Alec grinned as he drawled, "Guess we got that out in the open, didn't we?"

Jade could tell by the cocky male confidence in his glance he still hadn't given up on getting his own way. "As long as we understand each other," Jade said uncomfortably, wishing he was a little less determined. It was the determined Alec she had the most trouble saying no to.

"Oh, I hear you, loud and clear," he said softly, looking deep into her eyes. He grinned without warning. "And believe me, I'm already planning my next move."

"Exactly what I was afraid of," Jade retorted.

Fortunately, they were saved from further conversation by the arrival of the washer repairman. He promptly replaced the faulty rubber water hose. Alec paid him while Jade tossed all the damp towels into the washing machine and switched it on.

"Hey, come here and look at this. My way worked," Alec announced, as he lifted the soggy but clean diapers from the dishwasher and wrung them out by hand.

Jade rolled her eyes. "Will miracles never cease."

"You're just ticked off 'cause you didn't think of it first." Alec carried the clean wet diapers in and tossed them into the clothes dryer.

"I have to admit, it never would have occurred to me to rinse them this way." Uncomfortable with what had happened there earlier, and the potent images of their tryst that kept coming to mind, she said, "I'm going up to my bedroom to check on Andy."

"I'll go with you."

So much for being saved by the baby, Jade thought.

Andy was still sleeping as soundly. "What do you think?" Alec asked Jade quietly. "Should we wake him now for his scheduled feeding or let him sleep?"

Jade bit her lip and tried to decide. "I don't know. He's had such a rough few days. Maybe we should just let him sleep. In fact," she stated quickly, deciding it would be prudent not to give them any more time alone, "I think I'll turn in now, too."

Alec looked disappointed she wasn't going to be with him for the rest of the evening, but made no comment about the early hour. "It's my turn to take Andy."

"Fine."

"But if we move him, we might wake him."

"Then I'll take him again tonight." The sooner she had Alec out of her bedroom, the better. She started shooing him toward the door.

"That hardly seems fair, since you've had him the last thirty-six hours without a break," Alec whispered back. He stood in the portal and refused to budge. "I'll tell you what. I'll bunk in here for the night. You can take one of the other guest rooms."

Jade flushed at the thought of Alec sleeping in her bed, with or without her. Now she'd be imagining him in the romantic four-poster bed, knowing he slept only in those sexy silk pajama pants, knowing what a beautiful body he had, and what a wonderful lover he was. Knowing he still wanted her...

Dammit, they were not going to become lovers. She wasn't going to settle for anything less than total love and commitment from the man in her life. Like it or not, Alec was just going to have to accept that. Either he came around to her way of thinking, as she still hoped he would, or they would let it end now.

"About Andy," Alec said quietly, breaking into her thoughts.

"I'll take him again," Jade asserted, fairly shoving Alec out the door. "But if he wakes up and stays up, I'll bring him to you. Fair enough?"

"You've been more than fair about the baby," Alec said. "It's the two of us you haven't given a fair shake."

"I'm not changing my mind, Alec," Jade whispered.

"We'll see."

Chapter Eight

"We've done a county-to-county search of the birth records in both California and Pennsylvania, Mr. Roman," Jeremy Packard told Alec over the phone the first thing the next morning. "There's no record of a Nicole Kincaid giving birth to a baby in either state."

Alec swore, and put aside the papers he'd been studying while he drank his morning coffee. He'd been afraid of this. Portable phone in hand, he walked grimly to the refrigerator and helped himself to one of what must have been a dozen freshly baked breakfast-sized muffins Jade had left for him. "Have you checked every hospital?" he demanded impatiently.

"And every private birth, even those attended by midwives. Nothing, Alec. I'm sorry."

"A woman can't have a baby without someone helping her," Alec muttered. The question was, who had helped Nicole?

"I'm willing to do whatever you decide," Jeremy said, "even if it means checking each of the other forty-eight states, Canada, and Mexico, but I also must warn you that an undertaking like this is very time-consuming and expensive, particularly when it drags on without result."

Not to mention frustrating, Alec thought as he bit into one of the muffins. He tasted a delicious combination of oatmeal, apples, and walnuts. Maybe this healthy food Jade kept urging him to eat wasn't so bad after all.

"Do you want us to keep going?" Jeremy continued.

A couple of days ago, Alec would've said yes, unequivocally. Now he wasn't in quite the same hurry he had been before. "No, I don't. Just keep trying to find Nicole."

Alec was in no rush to get Jade out from under his roof, particularly now that they had made love. He still wasn't sure whether their future would involve marriage or just a passionate love affair, but he knew they'd have something. There was no way he was letting her get away from him.

"What's up?" Jade asked as soon as Alec hung up the phone. She breezed into the kitchen, Andy in her arms.

Trying not to notice how pretty Jade looked in her chic red knit dress, Alec filled her in briefly. Jade's eyes darkened to a deep emerald. "Why don't you want Jeremy to keep going?" she asked in a low, troubled voice.

Alec shrugged. "Because there's no guarantee Jeremy would find anything. She could have had the baby under an assumed name...in fact, she probably did, because of the morals clause in her Ingenue soap contract. It's just a waste of time and money, as is. And I never waste either."

Jade shot him a look that all but accused him of being a traitor. "I see."

Did she? Alec put aside his unfinished muffin. "Jade—"

Jade handed him Andy, blanket and all. "Look, I've got to go out of town for the day."

Alec had been counting on Jade to keep the home fires burning while he went into the office today. Finding out she wasn't available to him was a rude shock. "Now?" he asked incredulously.

Jade brushed past Alec and Andy in a whiff of enticing floral perfume. She stood on tiptoe to get a coffee mug from the cupboard. For the first time that morning, Alec noticed how short Jade's skirt was, and was reminded of what he already knew—how those three-inch heels she wore made the most of her spectacular legs.

"I have to meet with someone in Baltimore."

Alec watched her pour herself a half cup of coffee. As she drank, he struggled with an unexpected wave of jealousy. Andy squirmed in Alec's arms. He shifted Andy to his shoulder, holding him the way Jade did, so Andy could see past his shoulder to the room beyond. Andy settled down immediately, once he could see out the kitchen window.

Forcing himself to sound casual, Alec asked, "Who's the client?"

"It's business," she replied in a short, clipped tone, and stubbornly offered nothing more.

"Jade—"

But she was already striding purposefully past him, to the coat, gloves, and handbag she had left looped over the dining-room chair. "In the meantime, Alec, Andy is all yours."

That, Alec didn't mind. He did mind Jade lying to him, if only by omission. And he knew from the knot in his gut that she wasn't telling him anywhere near the whole story about where she was going today or what she planned to do when she got there. "How are you getting to Baltimore?" Alec asked, noting there was no briefcase among her possessions. *Business trip, hell,* he thought.

"By train," Jade replied.

"How are you getting to the train station?"

"I was going to call a taxi."

"Let me drive you."

"Really, there's no need—"

Alec pretended not to notice the brief flare of panic in her eyes at the idea of him tagging along for even part of her trip. "I insist," he said pleasantly. "I have to go into the office today anyway."

"Wait a minute," Jade interrupted. "What about Andy?"

Alec shrugged and shifted Andy on his outer arm. "I'll take him with me."

"To the office?"

"Why not? All I need is a little help packing the diaper

bag,'' Alec said, stalling for time. ''If you'll do that for me—''

Jade blew out a breath and shook her head in exasperation. ''I know you haven't had all that much experience with babies, but you're telling me now you can't pack a diaper bag?''

Alec shrugged, feigning incompetence. ''I'd just hate to forget something important. Like Andy's medicine for his ear infection, or his formula—''

Jade hazarded another glance at her watch. ''All right, all right,'' she interrupted impatiently. ''I'll bundle Andy up and pack the diaper bag, but you have to call Dr. Merick and make sure it really is okay to take Andy to the office with you today.''

Alec grinned and handed Andy over to Jade, the first of his mission accomplished. ''No problem.''

A SHORT TWO MINUTES later, Alec had Dr. Merick on his private line. ''Is it safe for Andy to travel yet?''

''Not by plane,'' Dr. Merick said.

''What about by train?'' Alec asked.

''That's fine, as long as he has no fever—''

''It's been gone for forty-eight hours now,'' Alec said.

''And isn't spitting up—''

''His stomach is fine. The new medicine did the trick.''

''Well, then he can go. Just be sure and keep him nice and warm.''

Alec promised he would and hung up.

Jade was standing in the doorway to his study. She was already in her coat and scarf. She had Andy in one arm, a fully loaded diaper bag on the other. ''Ready to go?''

Alec folded his cellular phone and put it in the pocket of his coat. He shrugged into his own overcoat of black wool and strode forward to take Andy. ''Let's roll.''

''It isn't necessary for you and Andy to drive me to the train,'' Jade said, as they climbed in the Jeep. Her dress hiked up slightly as she settled Andy in his car seat and fastened him in securely. To Jade's irritation, Alec made no secret he was enjoying the view.

"Hey, I want to do it—if only to get a bird's eye view of the best set of legs in America," Alec teased.

"I mean it, Alec, I've still got time to get a cab."

"Meeting a lover?"

"No!" But she blushed and looked guilty anyway.

"A secret agent then?" he continued to tease.

"I told you," she repeated, turning her glance away in what Alec considered further indication of her guilt. "It's business."

"Yeah, I know," Alec said. "And don't worry about us driving you to the train station, Jade." *We're going there anyway.* "It's the least we can do, after all you've done for us. Right, Andy?"

Even if you aren't being straight with us, Alec thought. Was it possible Jade had found Nicole? he wondered as he backed out of the garage, and drove down the drive. Or was all this secrecy really because she was meeting another very eligible male client and didn't want him interfering the way he had with Johnson the other day?

"How long will you be gone today?" Jade asked casually, once they were en route.

Alec was glad to be able to concentrate on his driving, and not the beautiful woman beside him. "As long as it takes to straighten things out," he replied absently, thinking she wasn't the only one who could play at this cloak-and-dagger game. He turned to look at her as they reached a stoplight. "What about you? When will you be back?"

"I'm not sure." Jade hesitated and bit her lower lip. "Tonight, I hope. But it's possible I could get stuck there for a little longer, depending on how things go, so…"

Her voice trailed off. Alec felt another flare of jealousy and mistrust. Again, he told himself to put it aside. If she was trying to put something over on him, as he half suspected she was, then she wasn't worth worrying over. If she wasn't, then it was going to be a lot of hoopla over nothing and a waste of time, too. One way or another they would know soon.

He drove the rest of the way to the train station in silence. "Andy's getting sleepy," Jade remarked as Alec pulled up to let her off.

"Being in the car tends to do that to him."

Suddenly, it was time for her to go. Alec realized, crazy as it was, that he didn't want her to leave his side. "You've got the number for my private line?"

Jade nodded.

"Call me if you run into any problems."

Jade looked into his eyes, in that flirtatious way of hers, and teased, "Since when do I check in with you, 'Dad'?"

Okay, Alec admitted, maybe he was coming on a little strong today, but this caring about a woman was new to him.

Not about to let her know how much she was beginning to mean to him, though, until he was sure he could trust her, Alec said, "Since we started sharing care of Andy, that's when."

Jade looked into his eyes for a long moment, her expression skeptical. "Right." Then she released her seat belt and leaned over the front seat and bent down to kiss Andy tenderly. At the touch of her lips against his forehead, Andy's blue eyes lit up. He let out a cheerful gurgle and waved his tiny fists. Jade kissed him again, and paused to look at Alec. "Thanks for the ride," she said in a voice that reminded him of all that was good between them, of all that could be, if only Jade would give them half a chance.

Acting on impulse, Alec gripped the lapels of her coat and pulled her close. Their mouths meshed in a configuration of heat and tenderness. Jade was trembling when he released her. She touched the back of her hand to her lips, as if to memorize the feel of their kiss and take it with her through the day. Her eyes were dark and misty with passion.

"Always have to have the last word, don't you, Alec?" she said, but she didn't look half as irritated as he'd expected.

He grinned at her. "Seems to me we're both guilty of that infraction," he drawled.

She leapt out of the car. Alec watched her move toward the station, his feelings in turmoil. He wanted to believe in her. Her kiss just now said he could. He just wasn't sure. He knew he would be devastated if he found out she had betrayed him. Whether with another man, or her sister, it wouldn't much matter. The end result would be the same. Not that brooding about any of it would help. Only time, and her actions, would tell the truth.

Alec waited until she had disappeared inside, then parked the Jeep. He scooped Andy up—diaper bag, blankets, and all—and headed toward the rear of the train, to the private compartment he had booked for himself while she was upstairs packing the diaper bag. Jade was only two cars down. When she got off the train in Baltimore, so would he and Andy.

"LOOK, DR. XAVIER, you must know more than you think," Jade said as she followed the sexy plastic surgeon across the lobby of the Johns Hopkins Sheraton Inn.

He gave Jade a dazzling smile, his deep California tan looking oddly out of place in the cold Baltimore winter. "Is that so?" he asked flirtatiously.

For the sake of her sleuthing, Jade made a concerted effort not to grit her teeth in any noticeable way. *He's going to put the moves on me. It's what you wanted, isn't it—to snare his interest and loosen his tongue?*

She'd come all this way. She couldn't leave here empty-handed.

"Do you know you're even sexier than your sister?" Xavier asked, sliding his hand around her back.

No, nor do I care, Jade thought as Xavier pulled her uncomfortably close. "How kind of you to say so," she said with her best come-hither smile.

"Well, it's true." Kurt Xavier steered Jade into the adjacent lounge and tightened his hand on her waist. "She may

be the model in the family, but you've got the bone structure."

And she'd thought Alec was a playboy. He had nothing
on this guy. "Thank you," Jade said as the two of them
slipped into a booth. She tried not to wince as Kurt nudged
her thigh with his. "About Nicole—"

"I'd like a drink," Kurt interrupted, still sizing her up in
a way that made Jade distinctly uncomfortable. "How about
you?"

It was only two in the afternoon. She hadn't eaten much.
Any alcohol she drank would probably go straight to her
head. On the other hand, any alcohol he drank might loosen
him up. She sensed she was going to need whatever extra
help she could get to worm any information out of him. "I'll
have what you're having."

He ordered two glasses of California Chablis then turned
back to her. "So what can I do for you, Jade?"

"It's about Nicole. I need to find her. Even though the two
of you aren't still dating, I was hoping you could help me."

"Why would you think I know where she is?" he asked
evasively.

He knows something, Jade thought. *Something he doesn't
want me to know.* "Because I know she's been in trouble."

"I wouldn't exactly call it that," Kurt disagreed.

"Then what would you call it?"

Kurt shifted away from Jade slightly. "Look, this is her
private business—"

"But you know about it."

Kurt studied her sagely. "And you don't," he guessed
grimly.

Uh-oh, time to flirt big-time. Jade put her hand on his arm
and increased the pressure warmly. "I know more than you
think," she whispered flirtatiously.

Kurt held her gaze, his demeanor suddenly all business.
"Then you also know why I can't discuss Nicole with you."

"It's not as if you were *actually* her physician." Jade pretended to pout.

"Officially, no, I wasn't," Kurt said carefully. "But I helped her when she needed it, when no one else would. And for that I expect she'll always be grateful to me."

Jade stared at Kurt Xavier. "Are you telling me you were the one who delivered her baby?" she asked incredulously. Was all this secrecy on his part not due to friendship, but medical ethics?

He blinked, for a moment looking as confused as she. "I'm not telling you anything about Nicole," Kurt declared impatiently. "Don't you get it? *Under the circumstances, I can't.*"

Jade studied him. "You *were* my sister's physician, weren't you?"

"Jade, I thought I had just made it clear. I can't and won't comment on that," Kurt stated firmly.

Jade understood enough about medical ethics to know she wasn't going to get anything further out of Kurt by demanding he tell her everything. She lowered her voice persuasively, and looked at him beseechingly. "Kurt, I have to see my sister," she whispered. "Please. You've got to help me find her."

"I'm sorry." He frowned. "I don't know where she is, and even if I did, I wouldn't necessarily be at liberty to divulge that information to you. Though I understand your frustration with your sister for dropping out of sight," Kurt continued compassionately.

Jade looked at him, feeling her hopes for a quick resolution to this problem fade. "You're not going to tell me anything, are you?"

"Nothing, except that there were very good reasons for Nicole doing what she did, the way she did it," he said.

"We're back to the morals clause in her Ingenue soap contract again, aren't we?" Jade guessed grimly.

"Look, Jade, your sister has been in a difficult situation the past few months. It wasn't easy for her to decide what to do, but now that she has, she's coping with the...after effects...of that situation, the best way she can."

"What the heck is that supposed to mean?" Jade cried, upset.

Kurt sighed his aggravation, too. "Look, enough about Nicole," he said, abruptly pulling her so close she was practically sitting on his lap. "Let's talk about you and me, Jade, and where we go from here. What do you say after we get our wine, we—"

"Jade's not going anywhere with you, Xavier," a low male voice growled.

Jade closed her eyes, almost afraid to look, and slid from Xavier's side. When at last she dared, it was every bit as bad as she had expected. "Alec."

"I CANNOT BELIEVE you followed me all the way to Baltimore!" Jade stormed as she strode across the lobby.

Alec followed close on her heels, Andy in his arms. "Well, that makes us even, honey, because I cannot believe you were almost sitting in that guy's lap!"

"I was not!" Jade said heatedly, a primitive anger flowing through her veins. Just because Alec had made love to her once did not mean he owned her.

"Oh really?" Alec's black brows lifted in feigned astonishment. "Looked that way to me."

Jade shut her eyes and fought for control. She did not want to have a screaming brawl in the lobby of a Baltimore hotel. "I didn't plan for that to happen," she said tightly. She had figured she would be able to control Kurt Xavier better.

"Really," Alec rejoined sarcastically. "I didn't see you punching him in the nose."

"If it's punching you want to see, Roman, then you're in luck," Jade retorted, her voice rising almost to a shout, "because I'm about to deck someone right now!"

Alec glared at her. Jade glared back.

Tired of fighting with him, especially over something so ridiculous, Jade propped both her hands on her hips and took a deep breath. "Look, Alec. Do you want to know what I found out just now or don't you?"

He stared at her grimly. "It had better be good." He took her arm, and propelled her through the front door. There was a limo parked at the curb. Seeing Alec, the driver got out and hurriedly opened the door. Jade knew exactly how the driver felt. Alec certainly was in a don't-mess-with-me mood. She'd never seen him behave so irascibly, except for that day he'd walked in on her and Tim Johnson, and even that didn't come close to the cold fury emanating from him now.

Alec handed Andy to Jade once she was safely inside, then followed her into the limo. "Okay, I'm listening," he said curtly, as soon as they all were settled. "Out with it."

Feeling a little like a witness on the stand, Jade crossed her legs at the knee and tugged her skirt down as far as it would go. Sure she had Alec's full attention, she said with a great deal more tranquility than she felt, "Kurt Xavier all but admitted he was Nicole's doctor."

Something akin to respect gleamed in Alec's sable eyes. "Did he say he delivered her baby?"

"No, he said he couldn't discuss her 'situation' with me for obvious reasons, but that I shouldn't be angry with her for dropping out of sight, because there were very good reasons for what she had done, and she was just trying to cope with her current problems as best she could."

Alec frowned. His anger with her forgotten, he nudged closer. "What the hell does that mean?"

"I don't know...exactly." Jade let her shoulder rest against Alec's for a second, then turned toward him earnestly. "But I think he feels some sympathy for Nicole because she can't have a baby out of wedlock and still be the Ingenue soap girl that every young man in America wants to date."

"You're saying you think she'd give up all claims to Andy just to keep her job as spokesmodel with Ingenue soap?" Alec asked, his expression thoughtful.

"All *public* claim," Jade corrected, absently caressing Andy's hand with her own, "and the answer is yes, I think she might. And," Jade amended with a sigh, "considering the millions of dollars involved, and the fact she would be a single mother—which is something my wild sister is smart enough to know she's ill-equipped to handle—well, I can't say I blame her.''

Alec quirked a disapproving brow. "You wouldn't give up your child for any amount of money," he said softly.

True, Jade thought, feeling for a moment that she could drown in the depths of his sable brown gaze. She shrugged. She refused to let herself pass judgment on Nicole in this instance. "Nicole and I have different priorities. Maybe giving up Andy, to you, was the best, most unselfish thing Nicole knew how to do."

"Yes," Alec said unsympathetically as the limousine he had hired pulled up in front of the Amtrak train station. "Nicole takes care of herself and you take care of everyone else." He grabbed her elbow and steered her past the ticket line. "You don't need to buy a ticket. I already have one for you."

She stared at him in surprise. "I had no intention of leaving you here with Dr. Suave," Alec explained.

Hearing the jealous note in Alec's low voice, it was all Jade could do not to smile. Maybe Alec Roman wasn't as footloose and fancy-free as he thought he was. Though actually getting him to admit he might be falling in love with her was another matter entirely. Her spirits soaring anyway, Jade hoisted the heavy diaper bag on her shoulder and lengthened her steps to keep up with Alec's long strides.

"If I'd wanted to stay, Alec Roman, there's no way you could've stopped me," she said calmly.

"Don't bet on it," Alec muttered just as confidently as they climbed onto the train. "If I had wanted to stop you, I would have found a way."

"Probably," Jade tossed back tartly as she followed Alec through the narrow passageways that led to the private compartments, "but there'd have been hell to pay if you had."

He surprised her with a laugh. "Probably," he agreed, looking as if he would even savor such a clash. And why not? Jade thought. Whenever they clashed they invariably ended up kissing, too.

As they entered the compartment Alec had reserved for them, Andy woke up and began to fuss. "He's hungry," Alec concluded.

Her attention immediately diverted, Jade shrugged out of her coat and took Andy into her arms. She hadn't realized until this moment just how much she had missed the tiny baby who had so swiftly claimed her heart, but she had. And Alec, too—much as she would've preferred not to admit that. "He's probably exhausted from all this traveling as well," she said quietly.

"I don't see how he could be." Alec rummaged through the diaper bag for a bottle of formula, and a clean diaper. "He slept the whole way."

"Do you want me to feed and change him?"

"Sure." Alec sat down in his own seat, while Jade got busy with the baby. Suddenly, he felt very old and very tired. Tired of living a life that was all business. Tired of living a life without emotional or physical intimacy. Tired of living a life without Jade. Maybe he shouldn't want her, but he did. And he sensed winning her was going to be a struggle, if not an outright impossible task.

Alec stared out the window as the train left the station. Overhead, the sky looked very bleak and gray. Wintry. Like a storm was rolling in. Good thing he'd taken his jeep to the station in Philly. They might need the four-wheel drive on the way back to the estate, he thought.

Bored with the scenery, Alec turned to Jade. The sight of her fussing so tenderly over the baby gave rise to a wealth of other thoughts. How it would feel to have her fuss over him, touch him and kiss *him* ever so gently on the cheek? That was followed by an image of Jade, sprawled beneath him on the laundry-room floor, her clothing askew, her arms wrapped tightly around him.

Alec closed his eyes. This wasn't helping. Nor was the

short, formfitting red knit dress she had worn. He had to think about anything else...anything but making love to her....

"ALEC, WAKE UP!" the soft voice said.

"What?" Alec muttered grumpily, struggling to hold onto his dream as the train rumbled slowly to a halt. He and Jade were making love. Slow, beautiful, incredible love in his bed....

"We're here." That voice again, gentle but insistent. And there was a hand curving around his shoulder, Alec realized drowsily. A warm, supple, feminine hand. And the lulling motion of the train had mysteriously stopped.

Alec straightened slowly and opened his eyes. He found himself looking into Jade's enormous dark green eyes. She was a bit disheveled from the running around she'd done all day. She'd never looked more beautiful to him.

Alec winced as he tried to sit up on the padded bench seat. His back, neck, and shoulders were unbearably stiff. "How long was I asleep?" he asked, glancing around their private compartment and finding all was still in order.

"Almost the whole way back to Philadelphia." She gave him a curious look, as if wondering what was on his mind. "You were talking in your sleep."

Oh no. "What'd I say?"

"Nothing I could understand." She smiled a bit. "It looked like you were having a good time, though."

I was. Now if only that could happen in real life... Deciding enough had been said about his dream, Alec looked out the window. "Hey, it's snowing."

"I know. It looks like there's already a couple inches on the ground here."

"Good thing I brought the Jeep this morning."

The drive home from the station was every bit as slow and treacherous as Alec expected it to be, given the weather.

"You drive very well in the snow," Jade commented, after he had successfully negotiated a particularly tricky spot in the road that seemed to have all the cars ahead and behind them fishtailing as they hit it.

"Thanks. The four-wheel drive makes it easier but even that isn't going to be enough to help us get around safely if the underlying layer of snow turns to ice, as the weather service is predicting."

"I just want to get home," Jade said.

Alec nodded. "So do I." He reached over and squeezed her hand. "We're almost there."

Jade's fingers curled tightly beneath his.

Not about to take any chances with his precious passengers, Alec withdrew his hand from hers and put it back on the wheel.

"Alec?" Jade said, still watching the road ahead of them every bit as intently as he was. "About today. I should have been honest with you. I should have told you I was going to see Xavier in Baltimore."

Her confession was like a balm to his soul. Afraid to let himself appear too vulnerable, he ground out, "Why didn't you?"

"I was afraid of what I'd find out about Nicole, I guess. If it was bad..." Her voice trailed off.

Alec shot Jade a quick glance. She was biting her lip, and her cheeks were pink. "You still care about your sister, don't you, even after all she's done?"

Jade sighed heavily and looked him straight in the eye. "Can you honestly tell me you don't?"

"Right now I don't feel much of anything for Nicole except extreme irritation that she hasn't been as honest with me."

"Wait a minute. Heaven knows I'm no champion of Nicole—"

"Thank heaven for small favors—"

"But you're not exactly a marrying man."

"I'm no ogre, either. I deserved a chance to do right by Nicole."

Jade regarded him curiously. "Would that have included

marrying Nicole, if she'd come to you early on and told you she was pregnant with your child?''

Alec had no idea what she wanted him to say, but he knew it was a test. The best he could do was be honest.

"I don't know," he said slowly, keeping his eyes on the road. Only two more miles and they would be home. "I would have seen to her financially. Probably, knowing her history, I would have demanded blood tests to verify paternity."

Out of his peripheral vision, Alec saw Jade bite her lip again. "And if it was proven Andy was your son?" Jade asked. "What then? Would you have married her?"

Alec shook his head as his fingers tightened around the steering wheel. The snow was coming down harder now. He figured he had twenty yards' visibility, at best. "I'd have taken care of her financially for the rest of her life. I'd have treated her with respect and kindness. But no, I wouldn't have married her," Alec told her as he spotted the gate to his estate, and turned the jeep into the driveway. "I wouldn't pretend to be compatible with someone if I wasn't, and the bottom line is, Nicole and I just aren't compatible, Jade."

Jade was silent. He knew she appreciated his truthfulness. What she thought about his pragmatic attitude was another matter, however, as her expression remained unreadable.

"Thank goodness we're finally back to your place," Jade said, as Alec opened the garage door with the automatic opener and guided his jeep into the appropriate slot.

He put the jeep in park and cut the motor. From the back, Andy stirred and let out a sleepy murmur of protest. Alec grinned. "Andy thinks so, too."

Jade carried Andy inside. Alec followed with the diaper bag. For a moment, it all seemed so normal and domestic. He let himself fantasize about what it would be like to be married to someone like Jade, to have a baby with her, to live in the home he had grown up in. To have laughter and love fill the house. Then he pushed the thought away. That hadn't happened yet, and it wasn't damn likely to, not with Nicole in the picture.

Jade stopped dead in the center of the kitchen and turned to him. "It seems a little cold in here, doesn't it?"

Alec nodded. It was cold, a lot colder than it had been when they had left that morning. "I'll turn up the heat and build a fire," he said, glad to have something to do to occupy his thoughts and keep them away from Jade. He cast a worried glance at the baby in her arms. "In the meantime, better keep Andy bundled up."

"IT'S NOT GETTING any warmer, is it?" Alec asked warily as he brought another stack of wood in, dropped it next to the fireplace, and shook the snow off his coat.

"I think we're losing heat every minute, despite the fire," Jade agreed. She paced back and forth, her coat still on. Andy was bundled up like a mummy in her arms.

"Damn," Alec cursed. He brushed a thick sprinkling of snow from his dark hair, then reached into a cabinet behind his desk and withdrew a flashlight. "I'm going down in the basement to check the furnace."

He returned, looking grimmer than when he left. "I don't know what's wrong, but it's sure not working properly. I turned it off completely, rather than risk it catching fire."

Jade admired his prudence even as her worries began anew. "What are we going to do?" She and Alec might be able to manage a few hours without heat, but Andy needed to be kept warm and snug.

Alec frowned and unbuttoned his cashmere overcoat. "Normally, I'd just take you and Andy to a hotel, but with the way it's coming down now..." He stalked to the window, the tails of his coat flapping against his legs as he walked, and stared out at the thickly falling snow curtaining them off from the rest of the world.

It was so dark and still outside, Jade thought, she might well have imagined her and Alec and the baby to be all alone in the world, instead of in the heart of one of Pennsylvania's major cities.

He sighed. "I can't see more than a foot or so beyond the window."

Neither could Jade. "No wonder the national weather service has posted a traveler's advisory. These are blizzard conditions, Alec."

Hearing the panic in her voice, he walked back to her side. "Look, the house is big but it's well insulated. I've got a couple of large electric space heaters upstairs that I keep on hand for emergencies. If we close up the study and run both of those, and keep the fire going, we should be able to keep it plenty warm in here for Andy, at least seventy-six degrees or so. That system's worked for me in the past."

Jade stared at Alec incredulously, amazed at how calm he was even as she was suffused with a feeling of dread. "This has happened more than once?" she asked, as a worried shiver moved down her spine.

Alec shrugged, as if such breakdowns were very commonplace. "It's an old house, and the furnace is pretty ancient, too. I was going to have a new one installed last September, but I was so busy starting construction on my new lab in Raleigh and negotiating that deal with the Japanese that I never got around to it."

"Who would have thought such an oversight on your part would have turned out to be my loss?" Jade quipped wryly, as much to herself as to him.

He grinned back at her, all easy male charm. "Somehow I knew you'd see it that way."

Alec smiled over at Andy then turned back to her and chucked her under the chin. "Cheer up, baby. By morning, the roads should clear enough for us to get someone out here to either repair the furnace or install a new one."

"And in the meantime?" Jade continued to regard him warily.

"In the meantime, the three of us will be warm and cozy in here."

She was going to have to spend the entire night with Alec and the baby in one room, Jade realized. Andy, of course had his Portacrib to sleep in. As for the two of them...

Chapter Nine

"It's all arranged. The furnace repair service will be out as soon as the roads are cleared," Alec told Jade as soon as he hung up the phone in his study.

"Good." Morning couldn't come soon enough for Jade.

Alec came over to stand next to her. "What's the latest on the storm?"

Jade turned away from the television set, Andy still cradled in her arms. "It's going to continue to snow most of the night and probably won't stop until near dawn. Road conditions are supposed to be extremely treacherous, and worsening by the minute." She handed Andy to Alec. "It's time for his bottle. I'll go heat it up and see about fixing us some supper, too."

"You want me to come with you?"

She shook her head. "Stay here where it's warm and take care of Andy."

"See out there?" Alec said to Andy as she left the room. "That's snow. And it's the most wonderful, cold, wet, packable stuff. When you're a little older, I'll take you out and teach you how to make snowmen and snowballs."

And in the meantime, Jade thought as she stepped into the chilly kitchen, *the three of us will have this time all to ourselves.* The image of her and Alec cuddled together before the roaring fire was even more disturbing than the winter storm raging outside.

With effort, Jade turned her thoughts back to warming a bottle for Andy, and making a quick supper of soup and sandwiches. She darted out once to deliver the bottle, made a side trip upstairs to her bedroom to change out of the red knit dress and into something warm, and then returned to the kitchen. By the time she returned to the study, dinner tray in hand, Andy was sound asleep on Alec's shoulder. The two of them looked so sweet, sitting before the fire. So perfect together. *I don't care if he is a playboy,* Jade thought, *Alec would make a wonderful father. And if he could be a wonderful father, maybe he could be a wonderful husband, too.*

"You didn't have to do this," Alec said.

Jade shrugged. "Couldn't exactly make a trip to McDonald's for dinner tonight now, could we?" she prodded dryly and was rewarded with one of his sexy grins.

"Guess not," Alec said.

He glanced at her claret wool slacks and V-neck sweater with approval.

"Not only did I change clothes, I changed into clothes that match," Jade teased.

Alec's eyes lit up in amusement. "Are you making fun of my habit of wearing only one color?"

"Nah." Jade grinned back at him.

"Speaking of getting comfortable," Alec said after a moment. "This sofa is only big enough for one and I don't know about you, but I've never been particularly fond of sleeping on the floor. It'd probably be a good idea if I went upstairs and brought a mattress down for us to sleep on." He laughed at the expression on her face. "Don't look so panicked, Jade," he said gently. "Nothing's going to happen tonight that you don't want to happen."

Sure it isn't, Jade thought, as she drew her feet up beneath her and relaxed back into her corner of the deep leather sofa. "Then why do we need a mattress down here?" she queried lightly.

Alec swiftly adopted a look of choirboy innocence. He settled back in his corner of the sofa and shrugged. "Because it's been a long day, we both need some sleep, and I had the feeling you wouldn't let me join you on that sofa.''

Jade shot him a wry look. ''Your feeling about that was right.''

''I'm not sleeping on that floor.''

She guessed it was inconsiderate of her to expect him to stretch out on the hardwood floor. She studied him silently for several moments, liking the way the soft light in the study highlighted the masculine planes of his face, and brought out the raven darkness of his hair. ''I'm all for togetherness, Alec—''

''Oh yeah?'' His eyebrows lifted in interest.

''But couldn't we build a fire in one of the bedrooms upstairs?'' she asked, aware once again that she was far too attracted to Alec Roman for her own good. The evening had barely started, and already her mind was rife with fantasies of Alec making love to her on the floor before the fire, on the deep leather sofa, in a chair... ''That way we wouldn't have to drag any of the mattresses around.'' *And we'd be on different floors.*

''We could,'' Alec agreed, ''if any of the fireplaces up there were open, but they were bricked over years ago in order to conserve energy.''

''Even the one in the master bedroom?'' Jade asked curiously.

''Even that one,'' Alec confirmed.

''Oh.'' Now *that* wasn't a very playboyish thing to do, Jade thought. A fireplace in the master bedroom would be an excellent seduction tool. Surely Alec knew that. Though maybe, with the way he kissed, he didn't feel he needed it.

''Though recently I've been thinking about opening it up again.''

''Oh,'' Jade said.

Without waiting to discuss his plan further, he took off. Long moments later, he returned carrying a double mattress. Then he left again and brought back several pillows, a single set of sheets, and two warm comforters. He shut the door behind him to keep in the heat. The study suddenly looked small, confining.

Her heart pounding, Jade watched as he moved the double mattress between the fireplace and the sofa, then efficiently set about placing linens on it. "I should have known making up a bed would be the one domestic skill you'd be adept at," Jade said lightly, trying not to feel so much like a schoolgirl, anticipating her first kiss on her first date. This was silly. There was nothing for her to get worked up about here. Like Alec said, nothing was going to happen here tonight that she didn't want to happen.

Or was that the problem?

Alec bowed in mock formality. "I'll have you know, Miss Kincaid, that bed making is one of my many skills that I learned during my formative years in prep school."

"And what, pray tell, were the others?" Jade quipped back, determined to keep this evening light and playful.

He waggled his eyebrows at her. "Come closer and find out."

Jade inhaled deeply but maintained her composure. "Mmm, no, I don't think I will."

"Why not?" he asked, his dark eyes challenging her. Aware she was surreptitiously watching every move he made, he covered the pillows with clean cases, placed the second pillow he'd brought beside the first, then smoothed a fluffy down comforter over the crisp clean sheets.

"You know why not," Jade said quietly.

Her emotions in turmoil, she pivoted away from him and stalked over to the huge bay window that ran the width of the room. Once there, she stood staring out at the increasingly high drifts of snow. There had to be at least a foot of snow on the ground now, maybe more.

She could hear him moving closer. "What's wrong, Jade?" he asked from a short distance behind her.

Jade found her heart was pounding. She had that weak, fluid feeling in her knees again, the feeling she'd had every time Alec had kissed her.

"I just don't want you getting any ideas," she answered pleasantly, whirling to face him. That bed he had just made up looked perfect to make love on.

"What kind of ideas?" He tried, but couldn't quite quell a grin as he closed the distance between them in a single stride and anchored a possessive arm around her waist.

Jade stepped back, out of the warm circle of his arm. Safely out of reach, she pushed aside the tide of sensual longing she felt whenever he was near. "You know what I mean, Alec."

"I'm not sure I do. Perhaps you'd better spell it out for me." The roguish amusement in his eyes deepened.

Jade pointed to the bed and returned his challenging grin. "One of those pillows belongs on the sofa, with another comforter."

He inclined his head to look at her, taking her in from head to toe. "We could do it that way," he drawled with comically exaggerated seriousness, "but it'd be warmer if we slept together."

His use of logic on her to get her in his bed again was the last straw. Fighting a curious roller coaster of unbearable tension and thrilling anticipation, she lifted her chin and said, "It's plenty warm in here right now and you know it, Alec Roman."

"So you noticed that, too." His sable eyes glittered with an ardent light as he stepped close once again.

Noticed! She was burning up! "Get this through that thick head of yours, Alec Roman," she countered, putting a hand flat against his chest. "I don't care what happened between us when you returned from California, I am not going to sleep with you tonight."

Alec went very still. The teasing glow left his eyes, but his body seemed to grow even warmer beneath her hand. "Who said anything about that?" he said with another devil-may-care grin. "Although for the record, I don't think it's a bad idea."

Jade flushed. "Look, Alec, don't play games with me. I

know how you like to turn every situation to your advantage and—''

"And what?" he interrupted. "You think I'm such a playboy that because I made love to you before that I won't be able to control my baser urges tonight?"

"You said it," she retorted lightly, spinning away from him. "Not me."

Alec braced his hands on his waist, watching as she paced back and forth. "Only because you were thinking it, and for the record, it's a ludicrous assumption on your part," he countered calmly.

"Is it?" Jade's face flushed. She'd felt how aroused he was just now. Eager to have this out with him, she marched toward him, stopping just short of where he stood. "Why else would you have brought that mattress down here and made it up and put two pillows on it?"

Alec demonstrated his exasperation with the release of a gusty sigh. "I did that as a joke, to see how you'd react."

"Well now you know!" Her whole body thrumming with pent-up feeling, she tried to step past.

"You're deliberately taking my actions the wrong way here," he said, using his body to block her way.

"Can you blame me?" Jade shot back. She was afraid the argument she was composing against making love again would go out of her head in an instant if he touched her. "Unless I want to freeze to death, and I don't, I'm stuck here with you, in this one room, for the night."

"Yeah, right," he agreed sarcastically as he loomed over her. He put both his hands up in a mock gesture of surrender. "I confess, Jade. You found me out, all right. I deliberately arranged for the worst winter storm we've had all season to happen tonight and then—just to make matters worse—I fixed it so the damn furnace would break. All so I could set up some space heaters, brave a raging snowstorm to bring in enough wood to keep a fire going all night, and then drag a mattress down here and have my way with you on it!"

Put that way, her accusations did sound ludicrous. She stared at Alec, barely able to breathe.

Alec's probing gaze gentled. "Do you really think I'd do all that just to seduce you?" he asked softly.

Jade swallowed. Her feelings had never been this confused. "I don't know what to think." Her heart said trust him.

"Well, I do." He stalked her slowly, sensually, backing her up against the wall, putting his arms on either side of her, his body against her. "If I had wanted to seduce you, Jade, I wouldn't need a snowstorm. All I would have had to do was this," he whispered tenderly, then lowered his mouth to hers.

His lips moved over hers, and though Jade's mind was still fighting him, fighting this, her body had long ago stopped. "Alec—" she whispered. Longing swept through her with disabling force.

"Just love me, Jade," he whispered back against her mouth, holding her close. "Just let yourself go and love me. This once."

Just let yourself go and love me. The words spun round and round in her mind until she could think of nothing else. Was it possible? Could she forget everything? She had never in her life experienced such sweet, invigorating kisses and she feared she never would again. That knowledge alone was enough to make her want to continue. Who was it who'd said you only live once…?

Alec slid a hand beneath the hem of her sweater and began to gently caress her back.

"The baby—" Jade said weakly, summoning up the last of her resistance.

"Andy is sound asleep in his bassinet over in the corner," Alec whispered back, his hand ghosting over her ribs and moving ever upward, toward her breasts. "If he slept through our arguing, he'll sleep through our making love."

He paused and looked deep into her eyes, the desire he felt for her as potent an aphrodisiac as the way he caressed her breast, delicately bringing the nipple to life in his palm.

"Come on, Jade, let yourself go. This once. Enjoy the fact we made it back from Baltimore okay." His lips moved down her neck, eliciting tingles of fire wherever they touched. "And though we may well be stuck here tonight, we're safe and warm."

Laughter bubbled in her throat at his assessment of the situation. "Safe?" Jade echoed dryly. "I don't think so." She ducked her head against his shoulder, aware she had stopped fighting completely. Why pretend they weren't going to make love when she knew he was right, it was what they had both wanted. She lifted her head and allowed herself another look in his eyes. The breath soughed out of her mouth in a tremulous rush.

"But warm, definitely," she allowed.

His grin widened. "You are without a doubt the sexiest woman I ever met," Alec said. Wordlessly, he gathered her into his arms, scooped her up, and carried her over to the bed he'd laid before the fire.

He came down on top of her, and resumed undressing her with single-minded concentration. "Sure of yourself, weren't you?" Jade asked, referring once again to the cozy bed he'd made up before the blazing fire.

Again, his eyes met hers. "Not sure at all," he confessed softly, then, having removed her V-neck sweater, slid his hand beneath the silk of her camisole top. "But I knew what I wanted. This." He circled her breast, then cupped the weight of it with his palm. "And this." He flicked the nipple with his thumb, then stripping her of her camisole, too, bent to pay homage with his lips and tongue.

Jade closed her eyes and arched against him, the warmth and light of the fire spilling over them in great, glorious waves. She touched his hair with fingers that trembled, then arched again and opened her eyes as he wound his way down her body, his lips moving from her breasts to her ribs to her waist. The next thing she knew he was lifting her with one hand, unzipping her slacks with the other. He pulled them down over her hips, gently rolled down her tights, so that all that was left was one tiny scrap of claret lace embroidered with satin hearts. "And you teased me about being color-coordinated," he said.

"Alec—" Her voice caught as he captured her with his mouth, kissing her first through the cloth with maddening intensity. And then he stripped her of that, too.

She wanted him to wait so she could touch him, too, the way he had just touched her. But it was too late, he was already pushing her past the edge, sliding up over her body. She heard him release his zipper, then a quick rustling movement of his clothes.

She gasped as he entered her with his hot, hard length. Desire both overwhelming and driving her, she arched up to meet him, new demand welling up inside her. She couldn't get enough of him. No one had ever made love to her like Alec, she thought. No one had ever demanded as much or given as much. Moaning, she clasped her arms tightly around him and urged him on. Her heart soaring, she answered his intensity with her own, urging him on, delighting in her feminine power over him, until at last his control faltered and he soared higher than she ever thought he could go, taking her with him.

THE PROBLEM WITH PASSION, Jade thought wearily early the next morning, was that it always ended. And harsh reality returned. As wonderful as Alec's lovemaking had been, as incredibly wonderful and satisfyingly intimate as his weight and strength still felt wrapped around her, she couldn't ignore the fact there were still many things keeping them apart, not the least of which was her own family situation and the possible romantic triangle they faced.

She wasn't a child anymore. She knew she had been a fool to make love with the man who had fathered her sister's child, when what she had really wanted all along was her own man to love.

Her emotions in turmoil, she slipped from Alec's arms and began to dress.

He stirred drowsily. As she looked down at Alec, she realized he had never looked more content. And why not? They'd had an entire night of perfect lovemaking. A night she would remember and hold dear the rest of her life, no matter what happened.

He propped himself up on his elbow. "Where are you going?"

"Upstairs." Jade slipped her camisole on inside out and wished she felt a little less foolish. It wasn't like her to behave so impulsively, with no eye to the future. Though Alec Roman was a wonderful, tender lover, he wasn't exactly husband of the year material.

"There's no heat upstairs," he reminded her with a lazy frown, looking irritated that the sensual aftermath of their lovemaking had ended so abruptly.

"I don't care." She tugged her sweater over her head. That was inside out, too. Feeling calmer but very self-conscious, Jade said, "I have to go somewhere I can think."

He was on his feet in two seconds, his hand clamped around her upper arm. His voice quiet in deference to the sleeping baby, he said, "If you think I'm letting you run from me again after what just happened here last night, sweetheart, you've got another think coming." His grip on her arm tightened possessively. "If there's a problem, Jade, we're going to talk it out *now*. No more running away. No more hiding your feelings or being afraid of mine."

But what were his feelings? she wondered. Did he love her, or just desire her? As much as she'd come to care for Alec, and she did care for him, with all her heart, she knew she would never be happy if all he felt for her was simply desire.

But she didn't want to get into that with him this morning, either. Feeling much too tired and confused to argue, she levered a hand against his chest. "Let me go, Alec."

Alec's jaw set stubbornly. "Not until we've talked."

Jade angled her chin a notch higher and kept her eyes on his. What was wrong with her? He had just made love to her,

driven her to a completion that was soul shattering in its
intensity, and already the desire had started welling up within
her again. Already, she ached for his touch, his kiss. Already,
she ached to be a part of him. They'd only had a few days
together and one perfect night, but she could hardly bear the
thought of giving him up. What would it be like if they made
love again and again throughout the days to come, and then
he tired of her and went back to his playboy ways? Or worse
yet, suddenly decided that because of Andy, he had some
obligation to Nicole to try to make their relationship work on
more than a one-night stand basis. If either of those things
happened, she would be shattered.

She would have to find a way to survive this before she
got in any deeper, before the hurt got any worse. Dammit,
why had Alec done this to her? And how could she have
been such an utter fool? She might as well have asked to get
kicked in the teeth, because that was exactly how she was
going to feel if Alec eventually went back to his womanizing
ways.

"There's nothing to say," Jade said angrily, still disturbed
with herself for behaving so foolishly. What had seemed so
right, during the firelit darkness of the night, now seemed so
confusing in the first pearly gray lights of dawn.

Alec's hold on her arm tightened. He was still naked, and
gloriously aroused. "I think there's a hell of a lot to say.
Neither of us planned this, Jade."

Jade turned her eyes from the obvious immediate resur-
gence of his desire for her. It was clear what his agenda was
right now—get her in the sack again. "The mattress you oh-
so-conveniently dragged down here says otherwise."

"But it would have happened anyway." When she
would've interrupted yet again, he continued bluntly, "Nicole
is just going to have to understand that."

"Why did you have to pick now to bring her up?" Jade
asked quietly.

"Because she seems to be bothering you!" he flung back.

Jade rolled her eyes. "As if Nicole were the whole problem

here. But as long as you mention Nicole, I'll tell you how she'll react when she gets wind of what we've done. She'll think it's revenge, for Clark."

Alec dropped his hold on her arm and stepped back. His voice hoarse, he asked, "Is it?"

"I don't know," she answered honestly, her emotions in turmoil. She tugged on her panties, and then her tights. "It didn't feel like it at the time," Jade continued in a voice that quavered slightly and was filled with regrets as she tugged on her slacks. "But—" she swallowed hard as the brunt of her shame hit her with full force "—what if it was?"

Alec reached for his pants. He jerked them on, then sized her up cruelly. "You're telling me you don't know? *You're telling me I'm just another lay to you?*"

"It's not that simple, Alec."

"It is to me." He stepped closer, his commanding look intensifying with every second that passed. "Why did you sleep with me?"

The only possibility that came to mind was the thought that she might, however rashly, be falling in love with him. But she wasn't about to tell him that—what she'd already done had complicated things enough. Jade shrugged and said, "You're very sexy."

Her answer didn't bother Alec at all, playboy that he was. He began to relax. "And that's a problem for you?" he asked gently as he buttoned his shirt.

"No," Jade retorted dryly, determined to put him in his place, "your reputation is a problem for me." *And my own response to you. I can't live my life with a man who has one foot out the door, a man who's unwilling to make a commitment.*

"Listen to me, Jade. I'm not nearly as irresistible as rumors would have it. Roman Computer is my mistress, and has been for a long time now. Any women that have been in my life since my divorce, including Nicole, have been temporary diversions, and that's all."

"It's nice to know I'm in such good company," Jade dead-panned, as she searched around for her flats.

"I wasn't including you," Alec protested as he tucked his shirttail into the waistband of his slacks.

"Really." Jade propped her hands on her hips. "Then where do I fit into the steady stream of women in your life?" She wanted to believe Alec would change his mind about marriage someday. She wanted to believe they could have a future together. She just wasn't sure she should.

Alec frowned. "I would think that would be obvious."

"Well, you're going to have to spell it out for me."

Alec sat on the sofa and pulled her down beside him. He laced a comforting arm around her shoulders and drew her into the warm curve of his body. Jade knew she should protest his move immediately, but it felt too good to move away. "You've already proved you're more a mother to Andy than your sister will ever be," Alec continued persuasively. He covered her right hand with his right hand. "We get along most of the time, and the sex between us is great."

He was acting as if he were negotiating a business deal. Jade resisted the urge to jerk out of his arms only because she wanted to see where all this was leading. "So you want to do what?" Jade asked calmly, although inside she felt as though her heart was breaking. "Continue on as is?"

"Yeah, I do," Alec admitted, his arm tightening around her shoulders possessively. "You could move your business here. We could stagger our business trips so we're never both away from Andy at once, and be together when I'm in town. It'd be perfect."

Obviously, Jade thought, he felt he'd hit upon the perfect solution.

She extricated herself from his arms graciously, crossed to the mantel, and stood with her back to the fire. "Perfect? I think the word you're really searching for here is *convenient,* Alec. I will not be your live-in mistress and nanny all in one." Her expression hardened defiantly as she advised, "So keep looking, Casanova."

Alec stood slowly. He faced her like a warrior preparing for battle. "You're doing it again," he said calmly.

"Doing what?"

He folded his arms in front of him and continued to study her. "Twisting everything I say."

Jade tugged a hand through her tousled corkscrew curls, pushing them off her face, only to have them tumble right back down again. "Look, Alec, as much as Nicole may deserve to have her potential husband stolen the way she stole mine, I can't and won't put myself right in the thick of her messes again. What I've already done is bad enough," Jade continued.

"For the record," Alec interrupted grimly, "I don't think you owe Nicole anything in this situation. And you haven't taken anything from her because there was nothing to take. I don't love her, never did, and never will. But if it bothers you that much—"

"It does bother me," she admitted.

Jade had started out wanting her own man to love and she still wanted that. The only difference now was she wanted that man to be Alec—even though she knew her desire was unrealistic. He didn't want to marry her. He didn't want to marry anyone. And she knew she'd never be satisfied with less, even if he was. But not about to let him know that, she let him think her conflicted feelings were all about her sister. "It bothers me a lot."

"Then we'll just stop looking for her," Alec concluded with a shrug.

Chapter Ten

Jade stared at Alec incredulously. "You can't do that!"

Alec strolled to the mantel and lounged against it. "Why not?" he asked, his attitude one of complete, utter confidence.

"Because Nicole is Andy's mother!" Jade said in a voice that was soft with outrage.

"Some mother." Alec's sable eyes glittered in the faintly lit room. He thrust his hands casually in the pockets of his trousers. "She leaves her baby on the doorstep and then takes off."

Her breath coming hard and fast, Jade advanced on him. "Listen to me carefully, Alec, for I am getting very, very tired of saying this to you."

"Then don't say it."

"I will not compete with my sister for you! Not tonight. Not tomorrow. Nor anytime in the future."

Alec's outward demeanor remained calm, but his voice was a dangerous purr as he challenged, "Who asked you to?"

"You!" Jade leveled an accusing finger at his chest and advanced another hot-tempered step. "By putting me in the middle of your quarrel with her!"

Alec sighed and rubbed a jaw that was shadowed with a day's growth of beard. "First of all, Jade," he retorted warily, "I don't know Nicole well enough to have a quarrel with her!"

"And yet you share a son with her."

Alec scowled as if his patience was being tested to the limit. "I explained all that. We were thrown together, halfway across the world."

Jade arched her brow at him. "Kind of like you and I were thrown together tonight?" she asked sweetly.

Without warning, he reached out, grabbed her arms and tugged her close. The length of her body made contact with his. He was still rock hard with desire, and Jade found her body was singing the same impossibly sweet tune. "This is different, sweetheart, and you know it," he said, very low.

"Right." Jade struggled to put her weight back on her own feet, instead of against him. "For all your power, you haven't yet been able to arrange snowstorms—"

"Finally, I'm getting through to you."

More than you know, Jade thought. Her chin angled up contentiously. "That doesn't mean you couldn't take advantage of being snowbound, once it happened, though."

He released her as suddenly as he had tugged her close, leaving Jade to fall back on her heels. "What the devil's that supposed to mean?" Alec demanded.

Her outward composure recovered, even if her emotional equilibrium was not, Jade threw him a grim glance. "You're the one with the allegedly broken furnace, Casanova. You figure it out!"

IF I LIVE TO BE a hundred, I will never ever understand women, Alec thought as he went upstairs to shower and change.

At least business made sense.

Making love to a woman did not. For the first time since his divorce he had offered to share space with a woman. And where did it get him? The doghouse, that's where.

He'd thought Jade would have been delighted after they made love. He knew it had been good for her...there was no faking that response. Okay, so maybe he pushed it a bit, making love to her all night long, but dammit, he had wanted her, and he still wanted her, and he knew she wanted him.

The chemistry they shared was a once-in-a-lifetime passion. But did Jade appreciate that?

No, Alec thought as he switched on the heat fan in the bathroom. She'd thrown it in his face.

What kind of game was she playing? Responding to him one moment, shutting him out the next. Was she trying to drive him crazy with her feminine wiles, or was she just afraid to commit to an ongoing relationship with him?

Alec had no answers to his questions. At least they still had electricity and hot water, which meant he could have a hot shower in a warm bathroom. Maybe the steam would help clear his head.

When he'd finished, the snow had stopped. By the time Alec had dressed and gone back downstairs, at seven-thirty, the furnace repairman was there.

While the repairman went down to the basement to check out the furnace, Alec fed and diapered Andy. Jade went upstairs to shower and change. Alec had just put Andy back to sleep when Jeremy Packard called.

"Good news. I'm closing in on Nicole," Jeremy told him.

Alec swore. Having Nicole back in his life was the last thing he needed right now. He wanted to straighten things out with Jade. Then they'd deal with her wild sister. His priorities established, Alec said curtly, "I want you to stop looking for her."

"*What?*"

"I've changed my mind," Alec declared. "I don't think I want to find her just yet."

He had come to several conclusions during his shower. He was falling in love with Jade, and whether she realized it or not, she was falling in love with him. That was the only thing that would account for her behavior. To bring Nicole back into the picture now would be to muck things up permanently.

"Too late," Jeremy declared matter-of-factly. "She's already surfaced. Haven't you seen *USA Today?* No, I guess not, since you're snowed in there, but Nicole's front page news. Ingenue went ahead and renewed her contract as spokesmodel for another five years at *double* the rate she was receiving before.''

Well, that ought to make Nicole happy and maybe save him a few bucks, too, Alec thought. "Where is she now?"

"Myra Lansky said she went back to Pennsylvania for some cross-country skiing before the new contract begins. I figure I'll be able to locate her by noon today."

Great, Alec thought. He was so close to getting everything he wanted.... "Look, don't tell anyone else what you've discovered," he ordered swiftly. This latest development would not interfere with his ultimate goals. One way or another, he was going to have Jade in his life.

Jeremy paused. "Not even her sister?" he asked after a short, confused silence.

"Especially not Jade," Alec instructed heavily.

"I HATE TO BREAK it to you, Mr. Roman, but you need a whole new furnace."

He'd been expecting this. "How much?" Alec asked, more concerned with figuring out how to keep Nicole out of their lives for at least one more day than with the cost of a new heating system. Beside him, Jade nearly fainted at the reply.

"How long will it take?" Alec asked.

"Several days minimum," the repairman said.

Alec gave the orders.

"We're going to have to take the baby to a hotel, aren't we?" Jade asked. Staying in the house during the blizzardlike conditions had been one thing. Staying after the roads were cleared for travel was another matter entirely.

Alec nodded reluctantly, trying not to show how much he minded the idea of he and Jade leaving the place where they'd first made love. "That'd be best, yeah." For all of them. He'd almost frozen to death taking a shower in his frigid bathroom, even with the hot water running full blast and the heat fan blowing overhead. And he knew Jade had been equally uncomfortable.

They packed quickly, motivated by the cold.

"It's a shame to waste all this snow," Alec said as he lugged the first of Jade's four heavily packed suitcases down to the front door. He wondered what all she had in them. They weighed a ton each.

"I know." Jade sighed and looked longingly out at the thick blanket of white covering the grass, shrubs, and trees. Icicles hung from the tree branches and the overhang of the roof. She shook her head in obvious regret, and held Andy, who was well bundled for the increasing chill of the house, against her chest. "I haven't been skiing in so long."

"Neither have I," Alec admitted. His next thought formed with stunning rapidity. Normally, he was a forthright person, but that blunt honesty was getting him exactly nowhere with the highly romantic Jade Kincaid. Maybe it was time he came up with a few surprises of his own. One way or another, he was determined to sweep Jade off her feet, to make her see that the two of them could have a future if only she would allow herself to believe it. And there was no better place to start than the morning after the best snowfall of the season.

"I THOUGHT YOU SAID we were going to a hotel," Jade said, her expression perplexed as Alec turned his four-wheel drive Jeep onto the recently plowed interstate highway. The gloom of the day before had given way to bright sunshine, gentle breezes, and temperatures still well below freezing. It was a beautiful winter day, the most beautiful day they'd had in a long while, and Alec was determined they all enjoy it to the fullest.

Tomorrow they'd have to pay the piper and meet with Nicole. Fortunately, he'd arranged their accommodations so they'd be nearby but not at the same lodge as Jade's sister—whom Jeremy had now located, but as per Alec's instructions, not contacted. The trails from the two lodges were a good fifteen miles apart, and separated by private property, so there was no chance they'd run into Nicole accidentally, no chance he'd see her before he was ready to see her. And he wouldn't be ready to see Nicole, Alec decided purposefully, until he had settled his future with Jade. But that would happen, Alec promised himself resolutely, and it would happen tonight.

Alec shot Andy a glance in the rearview mirror. He was bundled up and sleeping soundly in his car seat. Satisfied, Alec flashed a smile at Jade.

"We are going to a hotel," he said mysteriously, in answer to her question.

Jade's brow furrowed. Because of the glare of the sun on the snow, she too was wearing sunglasses. "Is your sense of direction as bad as your domestic skills?"

"Hey!" He shot her a grin, his mood remarkably buoyant, considering all that was at stake. Only his whole life. Only his sole chance to have a loving, happy family of his own…a beautiful wife and son to come home to at night. "I resent that."

"No doubt you do," she returned dryly, the corners of her mouth taking on a speculative curve that was sexy as hell. "But Alec, unless I miss my guess, we're *leaving* the city."

"Yeah, I know." He prayed she wouldn't get too upset when he told her what he was up to.

She turned to face him, angling her body as far left as her shoulder harness would allow. "Why? Most of the hotels are in the city."

Deciding she was much too lovely a woman to study with any chance of driving safely, Alec turned his eyes back to the recently cleared road and the sparse traffic on it. "You remember me saying it was a shame to waste all this snow?" he asked casually.

"Yes…."

"Well, we're not going to." Jade ducked her head slightly and waited for him to go on. "I haven't been getting much work done the past couple of days and neither have you, so I figured why not enjoy ourselves while we wait for your sister to be found."

As always, Jade frowned at the mention of Nicole. "And

what if she's not found anytime soon?'' she challenged, her full lips tightening into a pretty pout.

Thank God, Jade hadn't had a chance to go by a newsstand or see the latest copy of *USA Today,* Alec thought with relief. According to Jeremy, Nicole's picture was on the front page.

"Then we'll go back to work, as usual," Alec promised.

He had twenty-four hours to make this thing work. If he blew it, he knew in his gut it was all over.

JADE WALKED INTO the lodge, followed closely by Alec and Andy. She stopped short as they approached the reservation desk. "Dr. Merick?"

The kind, gray-haired physician, who was standing beside an elderly woman, smiled back at her. "Hello, Jade."

"What are you doing here?" She knew it wasn't simple happenstance.

Dr. Merick shot Alec an amused glance from behind his silver-rimmed glasses. "Alec didn't tell you?" Dr. Merick drawled.

"No, he didn't." Jade looked at Alec.

"It was a surprise," Alec explained. Suddenly, he wasn't so sure this plan of his wouldn't backfire on him.

"And a big one," Jade agreed, tongue in cheek.

The Mericks grinned at the sparks flying between Alec and Jade. "I knew we needed a baby-sitter," Alec supplied. "Someone we could trust to watch over Andy while we got in a day of skiing."

"And you agreed," Jade surmised.

"I can't resist babies," Mrs. Merick confided as she picked up Andy. "As far as I'm concerned, the younger the better. And this little man is just darling!"

Dr. Merick winked at them and laced an arm about his petite wife's shoulders. "We'll just see if she's still saying that when the three a.m. feeding rolls around," he teased.

"Oh, honey, you're taking that one," Mrs. Merick quipped, and they all laughed.

Jade turned to Alec. "You really thought of everything."

He wasn't sure it was a compliment, but he pretended that it was. "Well," he defended himself with a genial shrug, "Andy was sick. If we were going to be four hours out of Philly, I wanted to have a doctor nearby."

"Now, stop worrying about that son of yours," Dr. Merick interrupted. "And start worrying about how to get this pretty young lady to marry you."

Jade blushed.

The color in her cheeks made her look even prettier, Alec thought.

"You've got twenty-four hours to yourself, son," Dr. Merick told Alec, relieving him of Andy's suitcase and diaper bag. "Then the rest of this vacation is all mine. I've got some romancing of my own to do."

"They're a very romantic couple," Jade said as she watched them walk away moments later. The two were fussing over Andy as if he were their own grandchild.

"Amazing, isn't it?" Alec said in wonder.

Astonished by the underlying note of sentiment in his voice, Jade turned to Alec. "Why do you say that?"

Alec shrugged, his expression turning a bit sheepish. "They've been married nearly thirty years, raised four kids, and still love each other as much, if not more, than the day they were married." He took off his sunglasses and looked her straight in the eye. "To me," he finished softly, "that's amazing."

To me, too, Jade thought. Together, they carried their suitcases to the second floor. Alec had reserved two rooms for them, one in each of their names. "I'm surprised you didn't get adjoining rooms," she remarked, only half-teasing. She was used to the full-court press from him. Finding him suddenly more reserved in his approach, she didn't know what to think.

He lounged in the doorway of his room. "Across the hall was the best I could do." *Believe me,* Alec thought, *I tried.*

"How long are we planning to be here?" Jade asked curiously.

"I wish we had about a month," Alec admitted, surprised he could even daydream about leaving the business for that long. But then, since meeting Jade, his priorities had changed. He still revered work and cared passionately about Roman Computer, but he wanted more of a personal life now, too. He wanted...Jade.

"I wish we had a month, too," Jade said, linking hands with him. She tilted her head back to look up into his eyes. "But we don't have that long."

"We'll be here as long as it takes, then," Alec murmured determinedly to himself, then realized from the amused lift of her brow, Jade understood more of what he was thinking than he had realized.

Knowing it would scare her off if he let on the true extent of his determination to make her his, not just temporarily, but forever, Alec allowed finally, "Depends on the furnace, I guess." He looked into her eyes and smiled as he reminded her, "We can't go back to my house until the heat's on."

Jade inclined her head and bantered back sexily, "It seems the heat's on here."

Alec captured her other hand with his. "Yeah, well, brace yourself, sweetheart, because it's going to get even hotter," he promised her.

"You don't say," Jade drawled, her green eyes lit with anticipation. And a yearning to trust.

"I do say," Alec said very, very softly.

Jade's pulse pounded. She had never been wanted this passionately. It was wildly exhilarating. Terrifying, but exhilarating. Jade stared at him, shocked at the tender intimacy in his eyes. Was it possible he was falling in love with her, too?

"In the meantime," Alec said, studying her lazily, his romantic intentions clear, "what do you say we cut loose and just enjoy the heck out of ourselves?"

She grinned at the deliberate joie de vivre in his tone. She didn't know much about him, but she knew this: he knew how to get the most out of absolutely everything he did. "Last one down to the lobby pays for dinner tonight."

"You're on, sweetheart." This plan of his had to work!

"WHAT A DAY," Jade lamented satisfying hours later. She leaned forward to tenderly massage her calf beneath the table in the lodge dining room. "I'm sore in muscles I didn't know I had."

"Yeah." Alec grinned. "I'm a little stiff, too." *In places you don't want to know about, sweetheart.* His eyes met hers, held. At that moment, he thought he had never been more crazy about a woman in his life. He had never wanted to touch a woman as much in his life. In keeping with his decision not to rush her, he had kept his hands to himself all day.

"But it was fun, wasn't it?" he asked quietly.

"Tons." Jade dipped her spoon into the whipped cream dotting her pecan pie, and lifted it to her lips. "You're not half-bad company when you're recreating."

Alec watched her draw the cream from the spoon, his manhood tightening even more. "Gee, thanks."

"Anytime," she said magnanimously. She dug into her pie again. "And you're even more fun when you're paying for dinner plus dessert."

Alec grinned. Didn't she know there wasn't any price he wouldn't pay to be with her? "Hey, I told you." He made a great show of protesting because he knew it would make her smile if he did. "That was not fair. One of my suitcases was in your room."

"True." Jade's eyes glowed with teasing lights. "You still lost the wager."

"Want to make another?"

She looked at him suspiciously over the rim of her coffee cup. Today had been the kind of day dreams were made of. Funny, romantic, exciting, full of adventure and fun. She had known from the first moment she had met Alec Roman, what a sexy, determined, accomplished man he was. But she had never realized until today how unstintingly unselfish he could be. "What kind of wager?"

Alec leaned back in his chair. "Well, we'll have to make it something easy."

"Please."

He eyed her contemplatively. "I'll bet I can throw a snowball farther than you."

Jade blinked and set her coffee cup down. She had showered and changed into a black knit dinner dress after skiing. "Now?"

"Why not?" Alec continued to lean back in his chair. His brow quirked in silent challenge. "Unless you're afraid?"

Jade curled her fingers around her coffee cup. "I'm not afraid," she corrected sternly. But the unpredictable side of Alec already had her trembling. Her eyes lifted to his. "I'm not exactly dressed for a snowball fight, either."

He grinned at her, all lazy charm, and shrugged. "Then go upstairs and put on something warm. I'll wait."

He was up to something. She just knew it.

"If I were smart I think I'd bail out now," she remarked dryly, already pushing her chair back from the table. She knew in accepting his dare she was playing right into his hands, but if she backed out, she'd be a coward. Worse, she'd never know the reason for the too-innocent smile tugging at the corners of his sensual mouth. "But then, I never have been smart when it comes to you, have I?"

Alec tossed her a satisfied grin. "I'll sign the check and wait for you out by the front desk."

Minutes later, they met in the lobby. Jade's cheeks were pink with excitement. Alec knew it wasn't a snowball fight she was going to get when she stepped outside, but something even better.

"All ready?" she asked.

Alec gestured grandly toward the door. "After you."

Moonlight glimmered on the snow. A crisp icy breeze filled the air. Taking her hand in his, Alec pulled her down a path. "Wait a minute." Jade dug in the heels of her boots. "I thought we were coming out here to have a snowball throwing contest."

"I know you did." Keeping a tight grip on her hand, Alec kept his pace brisk and kept her moving.

Their breaths made wreaths of frosty smoke in the cold night air. "Alec, where are we going?" Jade demanded.

"You'll see," he promised mysteriously. And Jade's heart pounded a little harder.

They rounded a corner and stopped in front of an old-fashioned horse-drawn sleigh, piled high with lap robes.

"Evening, Mr. Roman." The stableboy nodded at Alec respectfully, then handed over the reins. "She's all yours. 'Til midnight anyway."

Jade turned to Alec, her mouth a round O of surprise. "At last I finally succeeded in leaving you speechless," he teased gently. Taking her chin firmly in hand, he lowered his mouth to hers and delivered a long, drugging kiss that turned Jade's knees to water and her heart inside out.

"I think we'd better get going on that sleigh ride," Jade said shakily. Otherwise, they'd never make it. They'd go straight back to her room.

She didn't know how she felt about his all-out attempts to seduce her. He might be acting like a playboy...but nothing about the day had felt ungenuine to her. Rather, it had been a miracle of kindness, love, and attention. She couldn't believe he had done all this simply to get her into bed. And yet by the same token she knew full well the direction they were headed.

"Is it working yet?" Alec asked, tongue in cheek. He guided the horse around the bend, reins in hand.

"Is what working?" Telling herself her actions were motivated only by a desire to keep warm, Jade snuggled closer to Alec, the heavy velvet lap robes drawn tight around her, her side pressed against his.

He drew the horse to a halt, and turned toward her. His face was silvered in the moonlight. He had never looked more handsome. "Have I won your heart yet?" he whispered.

In that moment, she knew what she'd been trying to deny for days now. That, like it or not, Alec was the man for her.

They might not have much time together, but they did have today, and tonight. Was it possible she could be content with that? Jade wasn't sure. She only knew if she didn't kiss him again she would die.

"Oh, Alec." Giving in to the tender feelings flooding her heart, she threw her arms around his neck and kissed him long and hard. They were both trembling when she drew back.

"If that's an I-don't-know," he teased gruffly, holding her possessively, "then I can wait for a yes."

IT WAS AFTER midnight when they got back to the lodge and tiptoed up the stairs to their rooms. "I think I'm frozen everywhere it's possible to be frozen," Jade complained.

"Then let me order some hot mulled cider up to my room to warm us," Alec suggested.

Jade paused in front of her door. She knew what would happen if she joined him in his room. The only choice was whether or not she wanted to be with Alec, really with him, tonight. She found she did. "All right," she said softly, her mind made up. "I'll come in. Just for a while."

Every room in the lodge had its own fireplace, and a good supply of logs inside. Alec knelt before the hearth and expertly began making the fire. By the time it was roaring in the grate, room service arrived with their tray. Jade signed for it, then carried it in. Alec dragged the love seat from the corner, over right in front of the fireplace, then took a couple of the thick winter quilts from the bed. Jade poured the cider and they cuddled together on the love seat. "This has been, without a doubt, the best day I've had in a long time," Jade admitted.

"I'll go one better," Alec said, setting his mug aside, and putting an arm around her shoulders. "It's been the best day of my entire life, Jade." He took the nearly empty stoneware mug from her hand and drew her onto his lap. "You're the best thing that's ever happened to me. I want you to know that."

"Oh, Alec," she breathed.

Looking very much like he wanted to make love to her, Alec swallowed hard. "About tomorrow—"

Jade had an idea what he was going to say. He probably wanted to tell her he couldn't make any promises about what would happen when her sister was found, but for once she didn't give a hoot what her sister did or didn't do, or how any of it might affect her. All Jade cared about was this moment in time. And right now and right here she wanted to make love to Alec so very much.

Taking his face in her hands, she leaned into him and kissed him sweetly on the lips. "Make love to me," she whispered tenderly when the slow, languorous kiss had come to a halt. "And I'll make love to you."

"Oh, God." Alec's breath was released in a tremulous rush. "Jade—" He compressed his lips together tightly, looking as if he felt guilty for what was about to happen.

She touched a finger to his lips, compelling him to silence. "Forget tomorrow," she whispered. "I want you. I want you so very much."

She felt his entire body soften in relief. "Oh, Jade," Alec whispered as he pulled her close and buried his lips in her hair. "I want you, too."

If the first two times they'd made love had been driven by passion, the third time was driven by tenderness. Their ragged breaths meshed as one. Their kisses were sweet, their caresses filled with longing. "About time I got you out of these clothes and into my bed," Alec said as he helped her undress then kicked off his pants, tugged off his sweater and joined her beneath the covers.

"About time I was here," Jade teased him back gently as she reached for him with open arms. She lifted her mouth to his. He plunged his tongue deep inside her mouth, tasting, tempting, teaching her what it was to love, not just with her heart and her soul, but through touch, with her body and her hands and her lips.

She was just as insatiable as he. Touching him everywhere.

Following with kisses. Again, and again, until she had driven him wild with desire.

"My turn," Alec said, as he covered her body with his.

"I'm ready *now*," she whispered, lifting her mouth to his.

Alec grinned even as he kissed her. "You just think you are," he whispered back against her mouth, then kissed her again and again until she whimpered and twisted and ached. He skimmed her body with his fingers, filled his palms with her soft, hot flesh, until even the moonlit glow of the room faded and all she could think about, feel, or see, was Alec, looming over her, loving her with all his heart and soul.

Only when she shuddered and cried his name did he lift her hips and bury himself inside her. Only then did he take her as he had wanted to take her from the first touch, the first kiss, the first tender caress. The fire he'd started flamed swiftly out of control, yet Alec savored the sensation, drew it out, let her subside from quick, raspy moans to soft, release-filled gasps, only to start all over again. He allowed their passion to build and build, and this time he joined her at the edge. They rode the crest, clinging together like two survivors of a storm, then lay together, spent. An hour later, he reached for her again. And then yet again.

Hours later, they cuddled together, a tangle of arms and legs. Though no words of love had been spoken, Jade had never felt more cherished.

"I was wrong about something," Alec confided as he stroked her hair with gentle fingers.

Jade stirred in his arms, every inch of her exhausted and straining toward sleep, every inch of her resisting it, for fear morning would come too soon and their time together would end. "What?" she asked, moving so she could see his face. He looked tired, but happy—as happy as she felt.

"When I first opened my door and saw that basket on the doorstep, I thought Andy was my Valentine's Day present. I was wrong, Jade." He lifted her hand to his mouth and pressed a kiss into her palm. "Andy wasn't my Valentine's Day present. You were."

Chapter Eleven

"Marry me, Jade."

The words Jade had longed to hear sent an arrow of pain to her heart. Their romantic night together had ended, and morning had come, as she knew it would. It was time to get back to reality. It seemed they were landing with a thud.

"I can't, Alec." Jade bent down to finish fastening her snow boot. They had just finished breakfast, and were preparing to go down to meet the Mericks and pick up Andy. "At least not right now." Maybe later. If they were able to work everything out.

Alec put down his coffee cup and came to join her. Today he was dressed all in black. Black pants, silk turtleneck, wool ski sweater. The stark color, combined with the intent hungry look on his face, made him seem all the more dangerously male, and dangerously set on having his own way.

"Why not?" he asked, his sable eyes glimmering with hurt.

Jade gulped around the pain in her throat. She wished he didn't look so good in the morning. She wished he didn't kiss like she was the only woman on earth for him. She wished...she wished he had never slept with her sister, but dammit, he had, and like it or not they had to deal with the consequences. "Our situation here is very complex," Jade replied in a strangled voice.

"Forget Nicole. She has nothing to do with this," Alec advised tersely.

"She has everything to do with us," Jade said, deciding to deal with their situation calmly, even if Alec wouldn't. "And so does Andy." She hobbled around the room, searching for her other boot, with Alec fast on her heels. "Maybe if we find her...if she has no interest in getting back with you," Jade continued as she searched behind a chair. "Then we can talk about us."

Alec clamped both hands on her shoulders and forced her to face him. "Don't I have any say in this?" he demanded angrily. "Or does just Nicole get to say whom I marry?"

Jade found his sarcasm completely unnecessary. After all, he was the one who had created this mess, by wooing and seducing both Kincaid sisters, not her. She shrugged out of his light grasp. "I told you, Alec," she said evenly. "I am not competing with her again." Finally locating her boot next to the television, Jade snatched it up and went to the bed so she could sit down and put it on.

Hands braced on his hips, Alec loomed over her. "I repeat, who asked you to?"

"You did." Jade stood and shoved him aside with the palm of her hand planted on his chest. "Right now."

He caught her arm when she would have stalked past him and swung her around so swiftly she collided with his chest. "No, I'm not."

His touch had her pulse racing. "If we knew where Nicole was, things would be different," Jade explained to him. She understood why he was upset. She didn't want their love affair to end, either.

"No, they wouldn't," Alec disagreed calmly.

"How can you say that?" Jade shot back tartly.

Alec was quiet a moment. "Because I know where Nicole is," he said reluctantly, looking like he wanted to be anywhere but there at that moment, to be saying anything but that. He clenched his teeth and then continued heavily, "I've known for the past twenty-four hours."

Jade stared at him in shocked dismay. Twenty-four hours! The whole time they had been at the resort. Was that why he had rushed her out of town so fast? "Wait a minute," she began slowly, feeling a little sick inside as the depth of his duplicity sunk in. And she'd thought Nicole was the only person in her life who heartlessly used her! She wet her suddenly dry lips. "You knew how to contact my sister and you didn't tell me?"

"I didn't want to ruin things for us. I wanted last night, Jade."

So did I, Jade thought. "Where is she?"

"She's at a lodge up the road a bit, enjoying a little cross-country skiing holiday, just like we are."

Jade's heart pounded. There was so much at stake here. She wanted everything—Alec, marriage, the baby. And with so much at stake, there was so much that could go wrong. "How do you know that?"

Instead of answering her directly, Alec opened his suitcase, dug around under a stack of clothes, and brought out a copy of *USA Today.* Nicole's picture was on the front page, under the caption, Ingenue Soap Signs Spokesmodel To New Contract. Jade read the article with mixed feelings. She felt family pride, because she knew how hard such spokesmodel contracts were to get. And she felt regret. Once again, her baby sister was arriving on the scene just in time to steal the spotlight and spoil Jade's romantic life. Dammit, she had wanted more time with Alec!

"So, she managed to get her Ingenue soap contract after all," Jade said slowly, working to keep her expression unreadable.

"Which in turn tells us a little about what she's thinking." Jade turned to Alec and he went on, "She won't be able to acknowledge Andy as her child and keep that new contract. She signed the new contract…and left the baby on my doorstep…."

For a moment, a tiny flicker of hope flared in Jade's heart. "You think she's going to give him up to you? Is that it?"

"Don't you?"

Jade was silent. If Nicole didn't want Andy, Jade and Alec did. Alec had already asked her to marry him. Maybe not because he was wildly, irrevocably in love and couldn't live his life without her, but he was definitely on the right track. One of these days he would realize he loved her, just as she loved him, and when that happened she would marry him. Jade would have to make Nicole realize that for the first time in her life, Jade was going to fight for the man she loved. And she wasn't going to stop until he was hers, heart, soul, and marriage license.

Jade pressed her lips together determinedly. Far too much time had been wasted as it was. "I want to see my sister," she said.

"Now?" Alec asked, stunned.

"Right now."

"AREN'T YOU GOING to come with me?" Jade asked as she paused in front of the elevator in the lobby of the lodge where Nicole was staying. No matter what her sister said or did, she intended to stick to her guns. Alec was hers.

Alec shifted Andy in his arms, so Andy could look over his shoulder. "I think the two of you need to talk without the distraction of having me and Andy around. I'll bring Andy upstairs and talk to Nicole when you're through."

At the mention of her sister, Jade frowned again. "All right, I'll see you in a few minutes." She bent to kiss Andy and Alec goodbye, then stepped into the elevator. Jade took the elevator up to the fourth floor. She knocked on Nicole's door. After a moment the door was opened. Nicole was in ski clothes. She looked ready to hit the slopes.

"Jade." All the color left Nicole's face.

"Hello, Nicole," Jade said quietly.

"Come on in."

Jade walked in. Her face felt flushed as she watched Nicole remove her ski jacket and toss it onto the bed. She still didn't want to be here, but she knew it was past time she and her sister confronted one another. Nicole put her hands on her slender hips and regarded Jade warily. "How did you know I was here?"

Jade swallowed. "Alec hired a private investigator to track you down."

"I see."

Silence fell between them, more awkward than ever. There was something different about Nicole—she looked terrific, better than she had in years. Thinner, younger. "Why haven't you been in touch with me?"

Nicole lifted a pale brow. "It seems to me I could ask you the same question," she replied.

Jade knew she hadn't exactly behaved impeccably in the past year. She struggled with guilt. No matter what had happened between them, they were still the only family each other had.

Nicole combed her fingers through her pale blond hair, and said with what sounded like genuine regret, "Look, Jade, I know running off that way with Clark was wrong, but you're not the only one of us who has suffered the past year because of it."

Jade stiffened. "I didn't come here for an apology."

"Maybe not, but I owe you one, and it's high time I gave it to you. I really am sorry, Jade."

Jade was so overcome with emotion to have this feud of theirs ending, it was a moment before she could speak. Even then her voice sounded shaky. "You look great."

"Thanks."

"You've lost weight."

Nicole's expression was perplexed. "How did you know I gained?"

"Myra."

"Oh." Nicole paused. She walked to the vanity, picked up a brush and tugged it through her hair with smooth gentle strokes. "Well, like I said," she said on a sigh, "it was a hell of a year for me."

Jade moved to stand beside her younger sister. Jade had

missed being the older sister she knew Nicole leaned on. "First with Clark and then Alec Roman," Jade sympathized.

Nicole set down the hairbrush and turned to Jade, her eyes serious. "Alec was just a fling."

Jade swallowed around the knot of emotion welling up in her throat. "Fling or no, Nicole, you had Alec's baby." And that meant there was a bond between them and always would be, even if Nicole didn't want to admit that now.

Nicole shook her head, her expression bewildered. "You keep saying that," she complained.

Jade sighed her exasperation. She was through playing games. And she had thought, until this moment, that Nicole was, too. But Andy was very real. "And you keep denying it," Jade replied.

Nicole regarded Jade for a long moment, then strode away from her, a restless look on her face. "Look, I admit I was on a downward spiral when I hooked up with Alec last spring. Things hadn't worked out for me and Clark the way I thought they would. You were no longer speaking to me. The Ingenue soap people were wondering if they should renew me or dump me for a younger model. The jobs that used to be so plentiful two years ago were barely trickling in."

Nicole sighed heavily, the pain on her face unmistakable. "Between what I owed my roommates and my creditors, I couldn't begin to pay my bills. By the time August rolled around, I was in a real crisis. I wanted to talk to you—" Nicole shot Jade an accusing look "—clear things up, start fresh, but you still wouldn't talk to me."

"I'm sorry about that," Jade said.

"You really hurt me when you did that!" Nicole accused.

"Well, you really hurt me when you ran off with Clark!"

They stared at one another in stubborn silence. The silence gave way to sheepish smiles. "I guess that makes us even, doesn't it?" Nicole offered, showing Jade she wasn't the only one capable of forgiveness.

"I guess so," Jade admitted. She clasped her sister's hand

and squeezed it tightly. After a moment, Nicole went on with her story.

"Anyway, I pretty much hit rock bottom last fall. My life was in a shambles and I had no one to blame but myself. So I decided to take a few months off, get away from New York, try and get a handle on my problems, and investigate the possibility of new careers like Myra suggested."

"Is that when you went to Los Angeles?" Jade asked gently.

Nicole nodded. "Acting was a lot harder to break into than I'd been led to believe, though. I went to a few parties, dated a few men, but mostly just kept to myself and tried to remember what it was like to lead a normal life. It was strange, not modeling, but it was good for me, too, because I realized how much I loved my career, and how much I wanted to continue it."

"And that's why you decided to leave your baby on Alec's doorstep, because you wanted to continue modeling?" Jade persisted, still trying to understand.

"Will you stop saying that!" Nicole cried, incensed. "I did not have a baby! And I did not dump any baby on Alec's doorstep!"

Jade stared at her sister. She saw the truth in her eyes and finally began to believe there might be hope for herself and Alec yet. "But you gained weight—"

"Because I was overeating!" Nicole defended hotly.

"And became a patient of Kurt Xavier's!"

For the first time that morning Nicole looked frightened. Wary. "Did he tell you that?" she demanded suspiciously.

"No," Jade said. "But you were his patient, weren't you?"

Nicole started to bite her lip, then stopped, and crossed her arms at her waist instead. She studied Jade for a long moment. "Can I trust you to keep a secret?"

A trickle of unease slid down Jade's spine. What was Nicole up to now? "Of course you can trust me to keep a secret," she said.

"Kurt did my surgery," Nicole whispered.

"What surgery?"

"He removed the bags beneath my eyes. Gave me lip implants. He even built up my chin and tightened my jaw a bit." Nicole turned so Jade could see her in profile. "Why do you think I look so good?"

Jade blinked. "You had plastic surgery?"

"Of course! How else was I going to convince the Ingenue people to sign me up as their spokesperson and prolong my career for another five years? I'm competing with fifteen-year-olds now! I have to look good! Damn good!"

Jade felt for a chair and backed into it. "Why didn't you just tell me that?" she asked weakly, as her bottom connected with the seat.

Nicole stared at her. "On the phone?" she echoed in chagrin. "And chance some long-distance operator accidentally overhearing it? Are you crazy? I'm supposed to look this way because I follow a natural beauty routine, and use Ingenue soap on my face, not because I had plastic surgery. If word got out I'd had plastic surgery, Ingenue would drop me in a minute. That's why it's imperative *no one know a word of this, Jade.* Promise you won't tell."

"You have my word of honor." Jade paused, relief flowing through her in great calming waves. "So Andy really isn't your baby?"

Nicole sent Jade a vaguely pitying look. "He really isn't," she said firmly.

"Look, the two of them are up there probably working things out as we speak," Alec told Andy as he carried him around the lobby of the busy ski lodge. "There's no reason for me to be nervous. Nicole will give you up. Jade will agree to help me raise you. It's the perfect arrangement."

Andy gurgled and waved his tiny fists. Alec groaned. He had never been more miserable in his life. Or felt less hope for the future. "Oh, who am I kidding?" he whispered to Andy, as he pressed a kiss into his sweet-smelling hair. "Nicole's never done an unselfish thing in her life. And Jade isn't about to forget the fact I once had a fling with her sister. That stupid mistake will always stand between us.''

Eyes wide, Andy stared up at him.

''I know, I know,'' Alec continued as he paced back and forth in front of the huge picture window that ran the length of the lodge. ''Casual sex is for the birds. I should have figured it out sooner. But I didn't. Anyway, how could I regret anything that ultimately gave me you and made me realize how much I want to have a wife and child?''

Andy smiled and kicked his legs enthusiastically.

''I'm meant to be a dad,'' Alec continued. ''And Jade is meant to be a mother.''

And suddenly Alec knew what he had to do.

''THAT'S ALL THE TIME the two of you get,'' Alec announced without preamble as he walked into Nicole's suite.

''Well, hello to you, too, Alec,'' Nicole said. She looked down at Andy. ''Cute baby.''

''About time you thought so!'' Alec exclaimed.

Jade stepped forward and put a hand on Alec's arm. ''Alec, he's not Nicole's baby. She wasn't pregnant.''

For a moment, Alec was too stunned to say anything. He stared at Jade, wanting to give in to the relief threatening to swamp him at any moment, but almost afraid to, for fear what would happen if he let down his guard for even one second during this showdown between the three of them. Alec turned to Nicole slowly. ''You weren't?'' *Hallelujah!*

''Nope.'' Nicole smiled. ''So there's nothing standing in the way of you two getting together, least of all me.''

Jade flushed self-consciously. ''Let's not be hasty.''

''Let's,'' Alec said, blocking her way to the door. He eyed her determinedly. ''My proposal still stands.''

''Why?'' Jade challenged. Her chin lifted another notch. As much as she wanted to say yes to Alec, as much as she wanted to share her life with him, he hadn't yet said the words that would make a real marriage between them feasible. He hadn't yet said he loved her. "Because I'd make a good mother to your son?" she queried softly, repressing her hurt.

"Because I love you," Alec corrected. "I love you with all my heart, even if you are the most stubborn and exasperating woman I've ever laid eyes on."

"We'll be down in the lobby for the next fifteen or twenty minutes, taking a walk." Nicole took Andy from Alec. "This is where I exit," she whispered in the baby's ear, then shut the door behind them.

Completely alone in the room, Jade stood before Alec, tears shimmering in her green eyes.

"Aren't you going to say anything?" he asked thickly. A week ago he hadn't believed in love, hadn't believed in anything but building his company. Now it was all that mattered to him.

"What?" Jade asked shakily, the tears spilling from her dark lashes and running down her face. "That I love you?"

Despite her tears, she had never looked more happy. Alec knew exactly how she felt. He was damn near being completely overcome with emotion, too. "Something like that, yeah," he muttered gruffly, aware Jade's eyes weren't the only ones that were now getting a little wet.

He took her in his arms and held her tight, the soft surrender of her body against his a balm to his soul. "Of course I love you," she said softly. "I think I've loved you from that first day you barged into my office."

He threaded a hand through the hair at the nape of her neck, tilted her head back, and lowered his mouth to hers. Whatever happened next, he wanted there to be no doubt in her mind about his feelings for her. She kissed him back ferociously, until there was no doubt in his mind, no doubt at all, that the two of them were going to have the kind of incredibly happy and satisfying married life he had never imagined was in the cards for himself.

Finally, the passionate caress came to a halt. Still holding onto her tightly, he prodded, "Does this mean you're saying yes, Jade?'' It had better! If it didn't, he was prepared to persuade her personally for as long as it took.

"Yes," Jade whispered as she reached up to gently caress his cheek with her fingertips, "I'll marry you, Alec." Her eyes glistened luminously. "I'll be a mother to Andy, as well as the best wife possible to you."

Alec hated disappointing Jade. He knew how much she had grown to love Andy, but there was no getting around it, now that Nicole had finally told the truth.

Hating to let Jade go, even for a moment, he drew back slightly, regret and trepidation mixed in his heart. "Wait a minute."

"What?" She looked up at him expectantly.

"We've got a slight problem there, Jade."

"Why?" Jade shot Alec a curious glance even as they heard a key turn in the door.

"Because if Nicole didn't have that baby—" Alec continued quietly, still holding Jade tightly.

"I didn't," Nicole declared as she walked in with Andy. She handed Andy back over to Jade.

"Then there's no other woman who could have had my child," Alec said, holding the little baby close.

Jade looked as shell-shocked as he'd felt when he'd discovered Andy in that basket on his front porch. "Meaning what?" she asked, aghast.

"Meaning," Alec replied reluctantly, "as much as I love the little guy, I am definitely not his father." He was sorry he'd lost out on the chance to be biologically connected to a child he'd grown to love, but not sorry at all that there was now no other woman, no past love affair, standing between him and Jade.

The three exchanged astonished glances among themselves, then turned their attention back to Andy. For a long minute the silence in the room was palpable and heartrending. "Then whose baby is this?" Jade said.

DADDY TO THE RESCUE

Chapter One

Pennsylvania Turnpike
April, 1993

"Are you trying to get yourself killed?" Jack Rourke jumped from his car and strode toward the beautiful young woman pacing the narrow sidewalk next to the curving tile wall. "You can't park your car in the middle of a tunnel!"

"I did not *park* my car!" the slender blonde in Amish clothing shouted back. Her posture was defiant as she struggled to be heard above the roar of the cars that were zooming by, one after another, in the unobstructed left lane. "It just *stopped,* and now it won't start!"

A truck approached directly behind their cars, switched lanes at the very last second and then zoomed by at teeth-rattling speed. "Look, we've got to get your car out of here before there's an accident." Jack directed the young woman toward the passenger side of her car. He jerked open the rusty door. "Get in, and put your car in neutral."

"But—"

"I'm going to push your car out of here with mine. As soon as you're out of the tunnel, steer the car over onto the shoulder and park it. We'll deal with the malfunctioning engine when we can do so safely."

Her face white, she slid across the seat to the driver's side. Jack got behind the wheel of his rental car. As soon as she put her car in neutral, it began to slide backward, down the incline. He inched his car forward. There was a jolt as the bumper on his car connected with hers. Jack gunned his engine, hoping that the Ford Mustang he'd rented had enough power to push her aging Chevy Caprice uphill.

In his rearview mirror, he could see two cars coming up on them, going side by side in the two-mile-long tunnel. They were travelling fast. At the last minute, the car directly behind Jack saw his flashing emergency lights, braked with a squeal and cut in behind the other car and in front of yet another eighteen-wheel truck. Sweat on his brow, Jack Rourke pushed the Mustang accelerator all the way to the floor. For one long frustrating second, he thought he was not going to be able to push the Amish woman's car out of the way, but finally the Chevy began to move forward.

As soon as they were out of the tunnel, both cars were pelted with rain. Above, the lightning flashed and the night sky rumbled with thunder. She steered her car onto the shoulder and hit the brake. Jack tucked his car in behind hers. He left his flashing lights on, as did she, then circled around to the passenger side of her car and opened the door. "My name's Jack Rourke, by the way." He motioned her out. "Come on. I'll take you to a phone."

"Thank you, Mr. Rourke, but you've assisted me quite enough for one evening. You may be on your way now."

Right, Jack thought, like he could just leave her here, stranded on the side of a road. She couldn't have been more than twenty-three or twenty-four at most. And though she didn't look quite as innocent and sheltered as most of the Amish women he'd met the past few weeks, she was also not nearly as streetwise as she seemed to think she was. "You can't stay here."

"I can't leave my car."

Jack was getting drenched, standing there in the rain. Lightning flashed and thunder pounded like cannons in the black night sky overhead. "Look, Miss—"

"Lindholm." She sent him a challenging smile, as if she

was just waiting for him to try to talk her into something she didn't want to do.

Jack had a feeling this woman was more than a match for him. "Is there a first name with that?" he drawled.

She kept her eyes on his. "Rebecca."

Damn, but she was distracting, Jack thought. He cleared his throat. "There should be a service center up the road, at the next turnpike exit. We can call for a tow truck from there."

Rebecca frowned. "I don't have money for a tow truck."

Jack shrugged. "Then I'll put it on my credit card and you can pay me back later. Or not. It really doesn't matter."

He had always wanted to rescue a beautiful damsel in distress. And she was very beautiful. He'd never seen such delicate bone structure or light blue eyes. Rebecca Lindholm was definitely of Scandinavian descent. Her skin was fair, flawless and looked as soft as silk to the touch. Her cheeks were a natural pink, as were her soft, incredibly kissable lips. And even though her hair was tucked up underneath a white organdy kapp, he could see enough of it to know it was a natural white blond. It, too, looked soft and silky to the touch. So soft and inviting, in fact, that he found himself wanting to take that kapp of hers off, her hair down, so he could sift his fingers through it and see how it looked resting on her slender shoulders...

Rebecca shook her head, cutting short his romantic imaginings. "You don't understand. I have to deliver these quilts to a store in Philadelphia first thing tomorrow morning."

Jack glanced behind him and for the first time noticed the stacks of quilts in the back. "Then I'll drive you the rest of the way to Philadelphia tonight, after we get your car to a service station. I'm heading to Philadelphia anyway to catch a flight back to Los Angeles tomorrow afternoon, so it's no trouble." Even if it had been out of his way, he would have taken her.

"Thank you, but I'll stay here and wait for another Amish family to come along and offer their assistance."

The chances of that happening were next to nil, Jack knew. Few Amish drove cars. Even fewer would be foolish enough to be out on the road on a night like tonight. And Rebecca Lindholm, for all her fragile blond beauty and feisty strength, was a walking target in her plain blue Amish dress, black apron, thick black stockings and thick black spinster shoes. But there was no reason to scare her with stories of other stranded motorists who'd come to unfortunate ends. Better to coax her into cooperating, Jack thought. "Why wait for someone who may or may not come along when you've already got me here, ready and willing to help you out?"

Rebecca looked at Jack a long moment. Evidently deciding that she could trust him enough to get into the car with him, she said slowly, "You're sure it would be no bother to drive me to Philadelphia?"

Jack did the best he could to hide his relief. "None at all. I'll even call for a tow truck."

"Oh, there's no need for that. I'll come back for my car tomorrow," she said.

So much for talking sense into Rebecca Lindholm, Jack thought, then decided to take it one moment at a time. They'd deal with tomorrow, tomorrow. The first order of business was transferring those quilts from her car to his.

She had no raincoat. Neither did Jack. Both were drenched to the skin by the time they had finished moving the quilts. "I'm surprised your family permits you to be out driving alone this time of night," Jack said as he guided his Mustang back onto the turnpike.

She shrugged carelessly. "My grandparents know I can take care of myself."

He took his eyes from the road to look at her. Her soft, bare lips were set in a stubborn line. "And they don't worry about you?"

"I'm a capable driver, before dark or after," she said.

He noticed she was shivering from the damp and the cold.

He turned up the car heater and adjusted the vents to blow the majority of the warm air her way. He relaxed as she began to look more comfortable. "What about your husband?"

"I no longer have a husband."

Which meant she was probably a widow, Jack thought. The Amish didn't believe in divorce. "Your beloved then," he corrected.

Rebecca sent him a wry glance, as if secretly amused that he should be so curious about her love life. "I have no beloved, either. So. What are you doing in Pennsylvania if you don't live here?"

"I'm a screenwriter. I came back for a couple of weeks, to do some research for a movie on the Amish." Jack paused, wondering just how sheltered this woman was. "You do… know what movies are?"

"Yes," she said quietly, in a way that let him know she had taken offense. "I do."

"Sorry," Jack apologized reflexively as he tried not to notice how the sunny, springlike scent of her filled up his car and invaded his senses. "I didn't know how strict a sect you are from. I guess, since you're driving a car, you must be from one of the more progressive New Order sects." Jack knew from his research that the bishop for each community made rules that varied greatly from place to place. Obviously Rebecca Lindholm had more access to the outside or "English" world than most Amish women. In his view, that made her all the more fascinating. "Did you make all those quilts?" Jack inclined his head in the direction of the back seat.

"No. I'm the sales agent for all of the women in my community. Once a month, I take the quilts in to Philadelphia for sale."

Jack noted by the highway signs they were getting close to Philadelphia. Soon it would be time to drop her off. He wished his time with Rebecca Lindholm wasn't so limited. Then again, maybe it was just as well. He was leaving tomorrow. What was the point of starting something that had no future? "Do you have reservations at a hotel?" Jack asked.

Rebecca nodded her head and to his sharp disappointment—wasn't it his dumb fool luck to finally meet the woman of his dreams, only to have to promptly say good-bye?—she began to give him directions.

"I'M SORRY, Ms. Lindholm, but your reservations were canceled when you did not arrive by 4:00 p.m."

Rebecca sighed. This night was turning into an unmitigated disaster. She had thought she was doomed when her car quit midway up the tunnel through the mountain. Having Jack arrive to rescue her was like something out of a movie. But then, he said he wrote movies. Maybe he enjoyed acting like the forceful heroes he undoubtedly wrote about.

"Another room then—" Jack said.

"The Penn Relays are going on this week," the clerk explained with an efficient smile that said no matter how much he wanted to help them, there was nothing he could do to change the situation. "We're fully booked. Have been for months now."

"Want to try someplace else?" Jack turned to her, towering over her.

Rebecca looked up into his dark blue eyes and nodded. She normally didn't give much thought to a person's looks one way or another, but in Jack Rourke's case, she just couldn't help it. He was tremendously good-looking in a rough-hewn way that appealed to her on a very physical, very fundamental level. Unlike her own fair complexion, his skin was golden brown, hinting at year-round exposure to the sun. His jaw was ruggedly chiseled and clean-shaven, his lips masculine and firm. His eyes were direct and probing, and sincere.

He had a protective manner she liked, shoulders that were plenty wide enough for a woman to lean on and strong enough to do any of the hard physical labor required on a farm. His chest and stomach looked just as muscled. Lower still, she could see the firm outlines of his long, muscled legs beneath the fluid material of his much-washed jeans. As for the other, well…there was no way she was going to look there. She was much too tempted already. Which meant the sooner they found a hotel room for her, and they parted company, the better.

Unfortunately it wasn't that easy. Three hotels later, they were forced to confront the truth. With one of the world's largest track meets going on in Philadelphia, finding a hotel room after midnight was an impossible task.

She was about to suggest he drop her at a train station or the airport, and she would spend the night there, when he said in obvious exasperation, "Look, it's not getting any earlier. I'm staying at a friend's place. Alec Roman, you may have heard of him. Roman Computers…" He shook his head at her blank look. "Never mind. Anyway, you're welcome to come home with me. There's no one else there and the place is big enough. If you want to stay there, I'll get you wherever you need to be in the morning."

It was a matter-of-fact invitation, casually delivered. Yet her heart was pounding. Rebecca forced herself to draw a calming breath. "I couldn't possibly impose," she said, even though part of her wanted to.

"It's not an imposition," Jack said, smiling at her in a very inviting way.

Rebecca hesitated. "You say Mr. Roman would not mind?" She searched his eyes, looking for some selfish purpose there, but to her relief could find none.

"Alec's in Japan, and no, he wouldn't mind." Jack touched her shoulder gently and turned her in the direction of the lobby door. "Alec and I are old friends. That's why I'm staying there instead of in a hotel."

Rebecca allowed Jack to open the car door for her. Staying with Jack seemed safer than spending the night in the train station. "I'll stay there, then," she decided.

His relief that the matter had been settled evident, Jack drove to Alec Roman's mansion on Society Hill. They entered the open wrought-iron gates and drove up the circular driveway in silence.

Located in a picturesque area with cobblestone streets and plentiful parks, the three-story redbrick home boasted a mansard roof with dormer windows. Pine green shutters adorned every window. The front door was painted a glossy white. Smokestacks had been built at each end of the house. Tall hedges and an abundance of mature trees provided privacy while adding greatly to the elegant, pastoral setting.

As Jack parked the rental car in front of the brick mansion, Rebecca worked hard to keep her face expressionless, but inwardly she was reeling. This home was incredible...and unhappily, a lot like the home of her ex-husband's family. Memories of her tumultuous romantic past assaulted her.

Jack grabbed his own suitcase and Rebecca's satchel. Together, they headed up the walk. Inside, the ivy-covered century-old mansion was everything Jack would have expected it to be. A sweeping staircase dominated the marble-floored front hall. A chandelier sparkled overhead. To the right was a banquet-size dining room. To the left, a formal living room filled with antiques. To the rear of that, a paneled study with a huge fireplace and a gourmet kitchen with every electric appliance imaginable.

They walked back to the front hall, after the brief tour. Rebecca knew what was next. A tour of the second floor, where the bedrooms were. That, she suddenly did not want to do. "The quilts—" Rebecca said, her heart suddenly pounding again.

"They'll be fine in the car," Jack reassured her bluntly.

Rebecca shook her head in disagreement. "They were dampened with the rain. I need to dry them."

Jack strode to the front door and looked at the rain, which was still coming down in buckets.

"Perhaps if you pulled the car into the garage," Rebecca said.

"Can't. It has a separate security code, and Alec forgot to

leave it to me. If I try to open it from the inside, the alarms will go off. It's not a problem. I'll carry them in."

"I'll help." Once they'd brought everything in, Jack helped her spread the quilts out to air-dry. When they'd finished, he turned to face her, his expression bemused. "Hey," he teased, touching a finger to the tip of her nose. "You're all wet."

Rebecca looked at the raindrops glistening on the strands of his thick chestnut hair. "So are you."

As he watched her shiver, his expression became concerned. "You'd better change into something warm and dry before you catch cold."

Rebecca frowned. "I've only got one other dress and apron with me, and I'll need those for tomorrow."

Jack nodded. "I understand that you want to look nice when you go to do business at the department store, but you can't stay in wet clothes."

Nor could she change into her nightgown, and still be around him. And she wasn't quite ready to go to bed yet. She wanted to talk to Jack, find out more about him, and his life in Los Angeles. "My clothes will dry eventually," she insisted.

"Faster," Jack pointed out, "if they're in the dryer."

Unable to help herself, Rebecca shivered again. Jack went to the thermostat and kicked it up from sixty to seventy-two. "This place takes a while to heat up." He frowned as she turned even paler. "Much more of this chill air in those damp clothes and your lips will be turning blue. I'll get you some clothes to change into. And something hot to drink."

REBECCA'S FINGERS trembled as she removed her black apron and then her long blue dress. Her underclothes were similarly drenched. Hesitating only a moment, she removed everything including her long black socks, then stood cradling the men's clothing Jack had given her. What would her family think if they could see her now? she wondered, then decided it was too cold to dawdle. She slipped on the soft gray cotton sweatshirt and pants. They were baggy and too long on her, but very warm and thick. Next came the thick white men's socks—also too big—and then a thick navy blue robe made of terry cloth. She belted it around her awkwardly, then picked up her wet clothing.

She hadn't worn English clothing since she'd been married. She had forgotten how comfortable it could be. Just as she'd forgotten what it was like to want to be kissed and held by a man. But that wasn't going to happen tonight, she told herself firmly. She might be attracted to Jack Rourke, but they were worlds apart. She couldn't let herself forget that. Her emotions tightly in check, she picked up her bundle of wet clothes and headed downstairs.

Jack was in the laundry room off the kitchen, tossing damp clothes into the electric washing machine. He had changed into a dark blue corduroy shirt and blue jeans. He was wearing thick white socks, like the ones he had given her, and a pair of running shoes. "There you are," he said with a smile. "I was beginning to wonder if maybe you'd fallen asleep up there."

Rebecca shook her head. "Though I probably should be in bed, considering the late hour."

"It's been a stressful evening. We probably both need to unwind." He took the clothes from her and tossed them into the machine. "We ought to be able to wash them all together on cold," he said. "Except for these." He brought out a handful of hand-sewn white linen underthings. "These had probably better be washed out by hand or on the delicate cycle."

Rebecca flushed to her roots, despite herself. "I agree."

"Perhaps you'd like to take care of them?" he said gently.

She nodded self-consciously. Jack showed her where everything was, then left the room. "I'll be in the kitchen, making us something to eat," he said over his shoulder.

Rebecca quickly rinsed out her underthings in the laundry-room sink and put them into the dryer to dry. It took a moment, but she figured out how to use the dials and switched it on, then joined him in the kitchen. He was completely at ease at the stove. A tray was set up on the counter beside him. Seeing the thick sandwiches and tall glasses of milk, Rebecca was reminded of how long it had been since she'd eaten.

"Let's go in the study, by the fire," Jack said when he'd finished pouring steaming soup into two mugs. "It's warmer there."

The study was a large room, filled with books, and a desk and a computer. There was a coffee table in front of a large leather sofa. Jack set the tray down and sat on one end of the sofa. Rebecca sat on the other. "Do you always travel at night?" Jack asked, handing her a sandwich on a plate and a mug of soup.

Rebecca balanced her plate and mug on her lap and wondered if this whole evening felt as much like something out of a movie to him as it did to her. She frowned as she lifted the mug of soup to her lips. "No. I should have left earlier."

"Why didn't you?" Jack asked, his dark blue eyes taking on a concerned gleam.

"I wanted to see my friend's new baby." Rebecca paused and took a sip of the hot, delicious soup. "I didn't mean to stay that long. But she was so cute and sweet..."

"And you adore babies."

"And I adore babies, and I got to talking." Rebecca sighed her lament. "I always lose track of the time when I'm around babies and I get to talking."

Jack grinned at her as if he understood perfectly. "So when were you supposed to arrive in Philadelphia?"

"Long before dark." She couldn't begin to describe the panic she had felt when her car had broken down in the middle of that tunnel. All those trucks thundering past, the storm raging outside... And then her hero came charging in to save her. The more she looked at Jack, the more she realized he was a hero—a flesh-and-blood, real-life hero, even though he might not realize it.

"Will anyone be worried about you?" Jack asked gently.

"No."

"Your grandparents—"

"Will think I am at the hotel where I am supposed to be."

"Do you want to call them?"

Rebecca turned to him, unable to help but notice the way the soft light of the study gilded the rugged lines of his face. "They don't have a telephone, nor do any of my neighbors. I'll just explain what happened..." *Most* of what happened, Rebecca amended silently, "when I get home again."

Jack nodded. "And home is where?"

"A farm in Blair County."

Jack finished his sandwich. He leaned back, looking remarkably content. "Well, I'm glad we met," he said as he put his plate aside and picked up his mug.

"Why?"

He sipped his soup and regarded her warmly over the rim of his mug. "Because you're the type of person I'd like to count among my friends."

Unnerved by his assumption there could be something more between them than tonight, Rebecca stood and moved restlessly to the fire. She had taken her kapp off upstairs, because it didn't seem to go with the sweats, but left her hair in a braid. Unfortunately her hair was still damp and it was beginning to bother her. Without looking at Jack, she began to undo the braid. "We have nothing in common, Jack."

"Maybe more than you give us credit for," he said as he closed the distance between them languorously and lounged against the mantel.

Rebecca looked away from the disturbing heat in his eyes. She combed her fingers through her hair, aware she was suddenly breathing so fast she felt a little dizzy. And hot. "Such as?"

"You're naturally curious, just like I am. I saw it in your eyes when we walked in, the way you looked around. And you're headstrong, independent to a fault. You'd have to be to be out driving alone on a night like tonight."

Rebecca gazed into the fire and tried to ignore the tantalizing way her insides warmed at his nearness. Or the way she tingled with anticipation. He smelled so good. Like a pine tree, surrounded by freshly fallen snow. Being with Jack was like being in a warm wonderful dream that had little to do with the harsher realities of life.

"And you're an artist," Jack continued, withdrawing a small comb from his back pocket and handing it to her wordlessly. "You'd have to be to design one of those quilts."

Rebecca tugged the comb through the thick, damp waves of her hair. Jack watched, his eyes dark with desire.

She was aware she was playing with fire here, but she couldn't seem to stop herself. She had been alone for so long now, and she knew, given the way she felt about all the eligible Amish men she knew, she was likely to stay unmarried, too. Without warning, Jack stalked away from her. He crossed to the desk and stood riffling through a stack of papers.

"Listen, anytime you want to go up is fine with me. I'll stay down here and put the clothes in the dryer."

Rebecca hated the look in his eyes right now. So distant, and aloof, as if he wanted to be anywhere but here with her. And though she knew he was wise to pull back before anything happened between them, a part of her, a deeply feminine part, resented his ability to walk away from her when she couldn't seem to walk away from him at all.

She put the comb down and crossed to his side. "Don't, Rebecca," Jack replied tersely, but wouldn't look her in the eye.

"Don't what?" she whispered.

He lifted his head and turned to face her. "You shouldn't push this," he said, his eyes hard, warning her away. "Because I can't guarantee what'll happen if you do."

"You think I'm so innocent—" she murmured as he tilted her face up to his, so she had no choice but to look into his dark blue eyes. And he was so wrong. She'd been married, loved... She knew what was happening here. And she was feeling reckless enough to want it to happen.

"Dammit, Rebecca, you *are* innocent, at least by my world's standards," Jack insisted on a ragged breath as he laced his other hand protectively around her waist, holding her apart from him.

"No—"

"I'll show you," he said, pulling her close, as if he meant to teach her a lesson, to show her more of the world than he thought she already knew.

Rebecca was braced to resist his high-handedness, but as his mouth touched hers, everything changed. A jolt of passion surged through her like an electric current. It was followed swiftly by incredible longing, the kind she had only dreamed about, and a wealth of erotic sensations. In an instant, Rebecca felt she knew what it was to be loved and wanted, and she struggled to give back as much as she was receiving, opening her mouth to his strong, demanding kisses, twining her tongue with his.

The sudden flare of passion in Rebecca, the way she trembled in his arms and surged against him, confirmed Jack's masculine instincts. He could hardly believe it, but it was true; she wanted him as much as he wanted her. And that knowledge, as well as his own burgeoning ardor, swamped his senses. He had always felt that somewhere there was a woman for him, a woman who would captivate and enthrall and drive him mad with desire. At last, he thought, he had found her.

"Rebecca—" he murmured, reaching for the belt on the borrowed robe she wore. His robe. He released it, slid his hand inside, beneath the hem of the sweatshirt and up over her waist, her ribs, to the softness of one very round, very full breast. She gasped as he palmed the soft curves and caressed her nipple. It budded tightly in response as she shivered and sagged heavily against him. "I want you, Rebecca."

"I know," she whispered, drawing back to look up at him. Her light blue eyes were filled with wonder and longing. "I want you, too."

Her soft words were all the encouragement he needed. Jack

swung Rebecca up into his arms and headed for the stairs to the bedroom where he'd been staying. Inside was a big four-poster bed. He hadn't really appreciated the romance of it, until now. Rebecca made no protest as he laid her gently down on the center of it. "Still time to change your mind," he said as he covered her body with the warmth of his. Whatever happened next, he wanted her to be sure.

But Rebecca didn't want to change her mind, any more than she wanted him to leave. She laced her arms around his neck and with the pressure of her fingertips against his nape, brought his head back down to hers. He covered her mouth in a deep, lingering kiss. He was rewarded with an arch of her body, and a low, soft moan that streamed across his senses like soft, warm rain. His lower body throbbing with anticipation, he nudged her legs apart and slid between them. Tucking a hand inside the waistband of her sweats, he found the softest part of her and sought to discover every velvet curve.

As he stroked her intimately, she began to writhe. He eased his fingers into her damp heat, and felt her arch again. Over and over he stroked, until she clung to him almost mindlessly, whispering his name, clutching his shoulders, and suddenly, he couldn't hold back, either. His lower body swollen, hot and aching, he struggled out of his clothes and helped her out of hers. The next thing he knew she was urging him into her, holding him tightly sheathed inside. Almost beside himself with pleasure, Jack groaned and slipped his hands beneath her. His whole body throbbing and demanding satiation, he lifted her up into his thrusts. Their mouths mated as intimately as their bodies, and long moments later, when their climax came, they were still kissing as deeply and intimately as ever. Only when their bodies relaxed, when their trembling and shuddering had ceased, did they slowly, languorously move apart.

"Rebecca—" He hesitated, not sure he could find the right words to explain the depth and intensity of his feelings for her, not sure she would believe him if he did. And yet he wanted so much to say them.

"I know, Jack," she whispered, reaching for him once again. "I know..."

JACK WOKE TO FIND the first rays of daylight streaming in through the open draperies. After their wild night of truly incredible, absolutely unforgettable lovemaking, he had expected to find Rebecca still in his bed, curled up against him. Instead, she was gone. He thought about going after her, then decided against it. She obviously wanted it to be over. And although that wasn't what he wanted, he would do the chivalrous thing and respect her wishes.

Chapter Two

11 months later
Blair County, Pennsylvania

Jack Rourke glanced down at the adorable infant in the car seat beside him and wondered for the millionth time how Rebecca Lindholm could have deserted their baby. So maybe she hadn't wanted a child born as the result of their admittedly reckless one-night stand nearly a year ago, but did that mean she had to put the two-month-old Andy in a heart-shaped red wicker basket decorated with stenciled cupids and a white satin bow, and then just leave him on Alec Roman's doorstep on Valentine's Day?

And what about that note she'd left with Andy—*"To Andy's father...Own up to your mistakes!"* Could she really consider Andy, with his cherubic angel's face, long-lashed big blue eyes and dark curly hair, a mistake? Jack sure didn't. *He* had fallen in love with Andy the instant he'd flown in from Los Angeles and laid eyes on him. And the two of them had been happily bonding in the forty-eight hours since.

So how was it that Rebecca, who'd evidently had custody of baby Andy for the first two months or so of his life, had been able to just abandon their baby on a doorstep? Had she felt so overwhelmed by the responsibility that she'd had no choice but to take Andy to the place where she and Jack had spent that one magical night together and just leave him and hope for the best?

Granted, because of the clandestine way she had walked out on him that night last spring, Rebecca had had no other way to contact Jack except through Alec. But ringing the doorbell and leaving Andy on the doorstep still seemed a little heartless, no matter how desperate for help Rebecca had been.

But then again, Jack thought, it fit. Rebecca had run from Jack once. Maybe she had just been running from Andy, too. Maybe that was how she coped with stressful situations.

"I guess we'll find out what your mom was thinking soon enough, though, won't we, sport?" Jack told Andy as he turned his rental car off the Pennsylvania turnpike and into the restaurant parking lot. "Because like it or not, your mom's time for running is over. We're going to deal with this situation the way we should have from the very first, as a family."

At the sound of Jack's determined voice, Andy kicked and gurgled in response.

Deciding his son probably needed a diaper change after the long drive to Blair County, Jack unbuckled his seat belt and reached for the diaper bag. Leaving the car engine running and the heater on, he unstrapped Andy and lifted him out of his combination carrier/car seat. Pushing that aside, he laid Andy gently on the seat beside him. Quickly he unzipped Andy's white cashmere bunting outfit, and lifted him out of it.

The back door opened just as Jack laid Andy gently back on the seat.

"Are you trying to ruin me?" Rebecca Lindholm demanded in a high, agitated voice as she slid into the back seat of the sedan and shut the door. Jack understood her concern. From where they were sitting, they could be seen by anyone coming and going in the late February afternoon. Fortunately the combination gas station, restaurant and gift shop was crowded with more travelers just passing through than locals interested in gossip.

"No, of course I'm not," Jack said, hardly able to believe he and Rebecca were together again. So many times he'd thought he'd dreamed, or perhaps just enhanced his recollection, of the electricity between them. But he saw now it wasn't true. Even with her Nordic blond hair tucked neatly beneath her white organdy kapp, her fair cheeks pink with embarrassment, Rebecca was every bit as angelically beautiful as he recalled.

Merely looking at her made his pulse quicken and his lower half tighten with desire. Just as merely thinking about what she'd done made his heart twist with pain. He met her temperamental glance and struggled to hold on to his own soaring emotions. He knew he hadn't exactly played fair, tracking her down through her work just to see her again, but she hadn't given him much choice.

"Then what do you call getting my address from the Philadelphia department store where I market quilts?" Rebecca demanded.

"The act of a desperate man. Not to worry, Rebecca. I told them I wanted to commission a quilt. Nothing more."

She sucked in a quick, agitated breath. "And is that what you really want from me, Jack?"

"No, of course not," Jack replied harshly.

"Then what?"

"I want you to own up to your responsibilities," he corrected quietly.

"What responsibilities?"

"To Andy here!"

Rebecca spared baby Andy a brief puzzled glance. Andy gurgled and cooed at Rebecca with unabashed delight, which just proved to Jack that Andy remembered his mother...if not the way she had abandoned him.

"Whose child is this, Jack?" Rebecca asked.

As if she didn't know! Jack thought. "Mine," he said roughly. *And yours.*

"Oh." Rebecca stared at Andy again, this time...in shock?

Mindful that Andy was beginning to get a little restless,

Jack unsnapped Andy's light blue sleeper with the embroidered bunnies on the front, removed the soggy diaper and replaced it with a fresh disposable diaper.

He started to fasten the adhesive tape on the side. "You forgot the baby powder," Rebecca pointed out in a low, dull tone.

Jack lifted a brow at Rebecca. He found it ironic she was giving him advice on how to properly care for their son after the way she had behaved. "Thanks for the reminder," he said gruffly, "and the baby has a name."

Rebecca stiffened. "I'm sure he does. However, as I've never seen him before in my life, I wouldn't know it."

"Yeah, right," Jack agreed dryly. How much more of this innocent act did Rebecca really expect him to buy? He reached for the powder, and while Andy continued to coo and kick, he sprinkled his bottom, then finished the diapering task. "The next thing you know you'll be telling me you've never seen me before, either."

Rebecca flushed as she watched Jack refasten Andy's sleeper and rezip his bunting outfit. Evidently satisfied he had done the job properly, she returned her fiery gaze to his face. "I wasn't aware you had a baby, Jack."

"Neither was I until two days ago."

Rebecca's shock deepened, then recognition dawned on her face. "Is that why you've come to see me? Because you need a nanny for your son and you remembered how much I love babies?"

"Actually, Rebecca, I had in mind a lot more than that."

"I have no interest in working for you or your wife, Jack."

"I'm not married."

Rebecca leaned forward. "Then where is this child's mother?"

"I was hoping you could tell me that," Jack retorted dryly.

"How would I know where this child's mother is?" Rebecca asked, incensed.

Jack glared at her. "You're really determined to play this game until the bitter end, aren't you?"

"What game?" Rebecca hissed right back. "You're the one who is playing games with me. Why, I don't know. Unless…" Rebecca paused. "You're angry because of the way I left you that night last spring."

Now they were getting somewhere, Jack thought. "Wouldn't you be?"

"Okay, so maybe I shouldn't have left the way I did, but…the way things were…it seemed like the best thing to do."

The best thing? For whom? Jack wondered, recalling his consternation when he'd woken up alone.

Jack put on Andy's hat, then grabbed a bottle from the diaper bag. "You couldn't have stayed around long enough to get my address and phone number? Because you know if you had, you would've been able to contact me personally, instead of dumping this in Alec Roman's lap. And I'm going to need to go into the restaurant to get this bottle warmed for Andy." Jack got out of the car, a squirming Andy in his arms, Rebecca fast on his heels.

"I don't know what you're talking about," she whispered as she glanced furtively around them to make sure no one was watching or listening to their conversation. "I never met Alec Roman."

Jack strode nonchalantly toward the front door of the diner. "Only because you ran before Alec could answer the doorbell," he remarked.

Because Jack's arms were full, Rebecca held the door for him and Andy, then fell into step after Jack as he walked toward a booth in the back.

Loud enough for the others in the diner to hear, she said to Jack, "I think it would be possible to commission a series of quilts, but we should talk first, to determine what colors you would prefer, Mr. Rourke."

"That would be fine, Miss Lindholm," Jack said, just as loudly, then sat down, Andy in his arms. Rebecca sat opposite him. The waitress brought them menus and she left with Andy's bottle, promising to warm it carefully.

Alone with Jack again, Rebecca removed her bonnet and her cloak. She smiled at him superficially. "Let's start at the beginning. Why do you think I should know this baby? And what responsibilities are you talking about? I have no responsibilities to you!"

Jack had to hand it to her, she was quite an actress. His mouth tightened in a mixture of contempt and disapproval. "What about your responsibilities to Andy?"

Rebecca leaned across the table toward him. The pink color highlighting her high, delicate cheekbones grew even pinker. "I have none to him, either. Furthermore, I resent your coming here to see me this way."

"Well that's just too bad, Rebecca," Jack murmured back, keeping his voice deceptively casual to keep from alarming Andy, who was already squirming anxiously, awaiting his bottle. "Because I'm not going away, and neither is Andy, until we've settled things between us. And while we're on the subject, I resent the way you've been behaving, too."

"You cannot continue talking to me like this in a public place," Rebecca whispered, casting a furtive glance around them. To her relief, no one in the crowded restaurant was paying the least attention to them. She was just another Amish woman in a state crowded with Amish, talking to an English man. "It might get back to my family."

Jack glanced pointedly down at Andy—who was sitting so happily in his baby carrier—then back at her. How any woman could turn away from such a darling baby, he didn't know. But it hurt him to think that she had. "Like the fact you had my baby won't," he pointed out wryly.

"What are you talking about?" Rebecca's hand flew to the bodice of her starched blue cotton dress. "I haven't had a baby!" Jack merely quirked a brow. Her blue eyes narrowed suspiciously. "Where did you really get this child, Jack?"

"As if you don't know," Jack retorted sarcastically.

Her cheeks went from pink to scarlet. She drew her black wool cloak closer and cast another furtive look around her. "Listen to me, Jack. I do not want to play games with you."

"Fine. Then stop the innocent act and start dealing with the plain and simple facts of the matter."

"I will, just as soon as you start explaining what you think—erroneously, I might add—is going on here."

Because Andy's dark brow furrowed with every increasingly emotional syllable he and Rebecca spoke, Jack took a deep breath and attempted a softer, more conciliatory tack. "Look, Rebecca, I can understand why you'd want to keep Andy's birth a secret. Your community would shun you if they knew. But ignoring our child is not going to make him or me go away."

Rebecca rolled her eyes. "Oh, I can see that."

"There were better ways to deal with this, Rebecca," Jack continued softly but firmly. He leaned toward her earnestly. "You should have tracked me down as soon as you discovered you were pregnant," he said as Andy gurgled happily beside them and waved his hands in front of his face. "I would have come back and done the honorable thing."

Rebecca smiled at Andy, then turned back to Jack and glared at him as if he were nuts. The waitress appeared with Andy's bottle. She stayed only long enough to take their order—coffee and pie for both of them—before disappearing again.

Jack uncapped the bottle and tested it on his wrist. The formula was lukewarm. Perfect.

Rebecca watched as Jack picked Andy up out of his baby carrier and settled him comfortably in the crook of his arm. Sure Andy was settled comfortably, Jack turned his glance back to Rebecca. "If you'd rather do this—" he offered. "After all, as his mother, you have every right."

Abruptly, Rebecca looked like she was about to explode. She leaned toward him and hissed, very, very quietly, "For the last time, Jack, Andy is not my baby. Furthermore, I don't know why you would think that he is."

"Oh, I don't know," he drawled. "Maybe the fact that Andy was left on Alec Roman's doorstep, which coincidentally happens to be the only place you know to contact me.

Maybe the fact that we had one night of incredibly wild, wonderful sex approximately eleven months ago, and this baby is approximately two months old. And maybe the fact he has curly dark hair, like my mother's, and your incredible blue eyes.''

Rebecca released a short, exasperated breath. ''All fair-skinned babies are born with blue eyes, Jack! They don't necessarily stay blue. By the time the babies are six months old their eyes can be brown, or green, or gray.''

''Nice try, Rebecca,'' Jack said dryly.

''It's true! The fact he was born with blue eyes means absolutely nothing!''

''Okay, maybe it doesn't,'' Jack allowed. ''But all babies don't have your chin. Come on, Rebecca.'' He leaned toward her urgently. ''Own up to your mistake, just as I've now owned up to mine.'' Jack noticed half of Andy's bottle was gone. It was time for a burp. ''I can forgive you.''

Rebecca's face flooded with color as Jack lifted Andy to his shoulder. ''For the last time, Jack, Andy is not my baby. Now leave me alone.'' Giving him no chance to respond, she slid out of the booth, turned on her heel and marched defiantly out of the restaurant.

THE DOOR to the restaurant shut quietly behind her, but inside Rebecca was quaking. She couldn't believe Jack had come back into her life now, after all this time. Initially, yes, she had wanted to see him again, even though she knew their love was impossible. But he hadn't come to see her, and gradually she had given up hope of their ever meeting again. Only to have him show up now—with a baby, for heaven's sake!

If her grandparents heard about any of this…they would be so hurt. And if Jack didn't keep a lower profile, they might also be publicly embarrassed, and she couldn't let that happen. Not again. Her grandparents had already been through the pain of watching her marry one fickle Englishman. She couldn't put them through the same thing again, not when she knew how poorly mixed marriages fared in the real world.

Jack had romanticized her, and while that was flattering, it was also dangerous. She was not the pure angel he had first envisioned her, any more than she was the heartless baby-deserting mother he was accusing her of being now. She was human. And, as her unprecedented fling with him attested, all too impulsively romantic for her own good. She had to be sensible now, and that meant, sadly, walking away from him and this crazy notion he had gotten into his head. Andy might be Jack's baby—with another woman—but he was definitely not Rebecca's baby! Jack was going to have to understand that. Hopefully he already did.

In the meantime, she had quilts to collect for her monthly trip in to Philadelphia at the end of the week. The fickle February weather permitting, it would be another banner month for the women in her community, and the profits from the quilts would pay for their spring seed.

"REBECCA, come in and meet our visitor."

Rebecca stood in the doorway of her family's home, unable to believe what she was seeing. Her feet felt as if they had turned to stone.

"This is Jack Rourke, and his son, Andy. He is visiting the area to learn more about the Amish."

Rebecca looked at Jack. He was sitting in a straight-backed chair, a sleeping Andy curled contentedly against his broad chest. He couldn't have looked like a more loving, devoted father to his infant son had he tried. And worse, he had obviously swiftly won over her grandparents, too.

Seeing Jack so cozily ensconced in the light blue and white parlor made Rebecca want to faint and scream simultaneously. And darn him, he knew it, too. If Jack wanted a scene, however, he was going to be disappointed, Rebecca thought. She was just as determined to keep her grandparents out of this mess as Jack was determined to bring them into it.

Carefully Rebecca placed the two colorful quilts she had

just collected for the month's sale on the shelf, and then removed her cloak and hung it up in the closet next to the door. Her emotions under control, she turned back to Jack with a reserved nod. "Good afternoon, Mr. Rourke." *I should have known you wouldn't give up so easily,* she thought resentfully.

Jack looked at her pointedly, in a frank easy way that made her heart race. "You know, I did some research here last summer. Perhaps we met—?"

"I do not recall your coming to our farm," Rebecca said, wishing she didn't recall with such utter clarity what it had been like to be held in those strong arms of his.

"No, I guess I didn't," Jack conceded reluctantly, his dark blue eyes never leaving hers. "Although I probably should have. Perhaps if I had met with your family then," he continued with a forthright smile, "I wouldn't have so many questions now."

Rebecca didn't know what game Jack was playing with her, but she did know two could play at it. "I'm not sure what we could tell you that would be of interest," Rebecca murmured as she breezed past him, to the kitchen at the other end of the open first floor.

"Oh, you'd be surprised," Jack retorted.

"Mr. Rourke is looking for a place to stay while he is in Blair County," Ruth said. Rebecca shot her grandmother an uneasy glance. Ruth was a very loving woman. But unlike Rebecca, she had been protected all her life from the outside world, and hence tended to be too naive for her own welfare.

"And we've agreed to let him stay with us," her grandfather, Eli, said.

"It's important the information I get be one-hundred percent correct," Jack said. "I want to make sure everything I've written to date, as well as any rewrites I may do in the next few weeks, are as accurate and truthful as I can make them."

Rebecca turned to her grandfather numbly.

"I am sure we can show him everything he needs to know about being Amish," her grandfather said.

"How long are you planning to be here, Mr. Rourke?" Rebecca asked. Her heart pounding, she walked to the cupboard, picked up a glass and poured herself some of the lemonade her grandmother had made.

"As long as it takes for me to find out what I need to know," Jack said, his dark blue eyes narrowing as he watched her gulp the drink swiftly, then put her glass into the sink. "And in exchange for your grandparents' hospitality, I have agreed to help with any and all chores assigned to me," Jack said.

Her grandmother glanced tenderly at the sleeping baby in Jack's arms. "Isn't he sweet?" Ruth said softly, reminding Rebecca how much her grandmother wanted great-grandchildren of her own.

Rebecca nodded, her thoughts in complete disarray. This was like a bad dream that would just not end. She swallowed and affected a normal tone. "I'll start dinner."

Jack rose after her, his expression implacable as he bent and gently settled a still-sleeping Andy into the hand-carved wooden cradle the Lindholms had provided him. "I'll help."

"MEN DON'T COOK in an Amish household."

Jack looked at Rebecca. He wasn't surprised by her home. The prosperous farm boasted several white barns, two silos and a neatly tended white frame house that looked at least half a century old. Her grandparents were warm, loving people. New Order Amish, they didn't seem the type to throw Rebecca out on her ear if she had revealed to them she was pregnant. But then, he thought, maybe appearances were deceptive in this case. Or maybe she just hadn't wanted to disappoint them. Maybe she hadn't come to terms with the fact she'd had a fling. Whatever the reason for Rebecca's strange behavior, he was determined to get to the bottom of it.

Aware she was still waiting for him to voice a reason why

he should be permitted in her kitchen, Jack shrugged and said, "Well, I'm not Amish, and I do cook."

"I would appreciate your not helping me," Rebecca hissed. She glared at him in stubborn silence.

Jack regarded her calmly, letting her know with one look that if it was a waiting game she wanted to play, he would win.

"Is there a problem in here, Rebecca?" Eli's voice boomed from the other end of the room.

Her cheeks pink, her slender shoulders stiff with tension, Rebecca slowly turned to face her grandfather. "I don't wish to have Mr. Rourke help me in my kitchen," she stated plainly.

"How else will I learn the ins and outs of Amish cooking?" Jack asked casually, as he gently rocked Andy's cradle.

"My grandmother can show you, just as soon as she gets back from the root cellar," Rebecca said, giving both Jack and their son a wide berth as she stepped closer to the refrigerator that was, as far as Jack could see, one of the few modern conveniences Rebecca's family allowed themselves.

Eli cleared his throat and stepped closer, stroking his bearded jaw with one hand. Like Rebecca and his wife, Ruth, he was dressed starkly in plain black trousers and a simple blue shirt. "Perhaps it would be best if you started your chores here with something simpler," he said. "Have you ever gathered eggs?"

Jack grinned. "Can't say that I have."

To Jack's surprise, Eli looked at Rebecca. "Perhaps you can show him where the henhouse is, then, and help him get started before you come back in to begin cooking dinner with your grandmother."

"YOU'RE ANGRY with me for showing up here," Jack noted as the two of them stepped outside into the cold winter air. The sky above was a glum gray. Patches of half-melted snow dotted the ground here and there in a dismal-looking reminder of the last snowfall. Yet, despite the gloomy weather and his cool reception from Rebecca, Jack could never recall feeling more alive. Or enthused about the future. Maybe if Rebecca saw how determined he was to have her in his life again, she would open up to him.

"Don't pretend to be surprised about that!" Rebecca stormed angrily as she rushed past him, her black cloak flapping open in the wind. "I can't believe you actually talked my grandparents into letting you and your baby stay at our farm. Have you no conscience at all?"

"My conscience, Rebecca, is what brought me back here. I want our baby to have two parents. I would think you would want that, too," Jack said.

"He is not our baby, Jack, and no amount of wishing will ever make that so."

Jack noticed how the blue of Rebecca's dress brought out the blue of her eyes. The plain black apron, black stockings and schoolmarm shoes shouldn't have made her look sexy as hell, but they did. And that was making it hard for him to concentrate. "You're denying you left Andy in a basket on Alec Roman's doorstep on Valentine's Day?"

Rebecca's cheeks flooded with a healthy color that was, Jack felt, only partially due to the brisk winter wind. "Yes, Jack, I am," she said firmly.

He studied her upturned face. She was either a very good liar, or she was telling the truth...sort of. "Then who put Andy there for you, Rebecca?" Jack asked coolly.

Rebecca shook her head and rolled her eyes. "You are impossible!" she whispered emotionally.

Holding her voluminous skirts in both hands, Rebecca whirled and marched across the yard, through a fence and into a barnyard that was amazingly still and devoid of life. Jack followed at a leisurely pace, enjoying the view. More so, perhaps, because he knew beneath that prim dress beat the heart of a very passionate woman, a woman who had just given birth to his child, and who obviously now—despite all her protestations—wanted him and Andy back in her life.

Otherwise, why would she have left Andy with Alec? Why not just raise Andy on her own?

Rebecca threw open the doors of the henhouse. Chickens squawked and flew every which way. While Jack watched, she scurried them along outside with swooping motions of her hands. Most of them went gratefully, anxious to be out in the yard. She followed the chickens back out, announcing, "We'll feed them now, too."

She took the lid from a can in the corner of the chicken yard, scattered scoops of grain liberally around the yard and watched in mute satisfaction as the chickens fell on it. She headed back inside the henhouse, leaving Jack to follow.

"The eggs are in the nests," Rebecca explained, making no effort to mask her impatience both with Jack and the task assigned her by her grandfather. She picked up an egg and put it in a wicker basket. "Gather them all, put the chickens back in the henhouse, close it up and then bring the eggs back inside the house. We'll wash them in the kitchen." She turned, offering him her back.

"Wait a minute," Jack said, grabbing her arm, beginning to panic. He was a city kid, always had been, always would be. What did he know about rounding up chickens? He tightened his hold on her. "You can't leave me here."

Rebecca disdainfully removed his fingers from her arm. "I have to start dinner."

He stepped to bar her way out of the barnyard, fully prepared to hold her in front of him with both hands if necessary. "Dinner can wait," he said, setting the baskets down for a moment. "What about Andy? Don't you think you have some explaining to do?"

She looked past him toward the house, her expression more aggrieved than ever. "I've already said everything there is to say."

"You can't possibly mean that," he said, aghast.

Rebecca looked down her pretty nose at him. The brisk winter wind brought even more color to her high, graceful cheeks. "I mean that with my whole heart and soul," she retorted.

Seeing the stubborn denial in her eyes, it was all he could do not to haul her into his arms and kiss her senseless. But he knew he had to try reason first. "We have a child, Rebecca," he said softly, determined to make her come to terms with the situation. "A beautiful child. I know you're afraid, but I can fix everything." After all, Eli seemed like a reasonable man. Ruth was certainly loving. They would want what was best for Rebecca, he was sure of it. And what was best for Rebecca was being with him and Andy.

"You can fix everything," Rebecca repeated sarcastically. She planted a hand on his chest and arched a coolly disarming brow. "Including your runaway imagination?"

Jack couldn't help it, he laughed. Then he caught her hand, and pulled her ever closer. Close enough so that she could feel the strong, steady beating of his heart beneath the corduroy shirt and open leather bomber jacket.

For a moment Rebecca's eyes widened with shock. Her lips parted with desire. Recovering swiftly, she jerked her hand away. "I don't know where you got that baby, Jack." Her eyes flashed blue fire. "Or even if you truly think that I am his mother, not some other woman you encountered in your travels—"

"You can't palm this off on some other woman, Rebecca, so don't even try," Jack warned.

"Fine, I won't try to explain anything to you," she said, just as furiously. "But in return I want something from you, too, Jack Rourke."

Jack had the sinking feeling her request was going to be impossible to fulfill. "What?" He bit out the word, then emotionally braced himself for the worst.

Rebecca stomped nearer. "I want you to take your adorable little baby and leave this farm and all of Blair County forever, so I can forget my reckless affair with you ever happened!"

"YOU BROUGHT NO EGGS in with you," her grandmother reproached the moment Rebecca walked in the door.

Rebecca went straight to the kitchen sink and began washing her hands. "Jack Rourke can gather them and bring them in."

Her grandmother walked back and forth, baby Andy swaddled in blankets and cradled lovingly in her arms.

Ruth paused by Rebecca. Rebecca looked down at the baby in her grandmother's arms and just for one second felt her heart catch in her throat. Andy was a beautiful baby. And now that she looked at him closely, she even thought she could see some resemblance to Jack...in the straight nose and the pronounced line of his cheekbones. Andy's hair was several shades darker than Jack's and curly where Jack's was straight, but those qualities could have come from Andy's real mother...whoever she was.

Noticing Rebecca's gentle perusal of him, Andy gurgled in delight and beamed a toothless smile up at her. Rebecca smiled back. As always, when around a baby, her yearning for a child of her own intensified mightily. And Andy, bless his little heart, picked up on that, too. His smile broadened and his big blue eyes telegraphed a willingness to be held by Rebecca, too.

"Do you want to hold the baby?" her grandmother asked.

Rebecca thought about what Jack Rourke would make of that and shook her head.

"You don't like Jack Rourke much, do you?" Ruth said.

Rebecca shrugged. Her grandmother had always been able to see far more than she wanted her to see. If Jack stayed, her grandmother would realize there was something between them, or had been, Rebecca amended hastily to herself. "I hardly know him," Rebecca said.

Maybe it was foolish, but she much preferred to keep her mistakes to herself, and loving Jack had been a mistake. His crazy story about the baby, his showing up here now, proved that. Dear Lord, did he actually think she would give her own child away? Perhaps, had Jack been willing to listen to reason, she would have explained that to him. But one look at his face and she had known—now that he had a baby he suddenly wanted her back in his life. Not because he loved her and couldn't live without her, but because he thought Andy needed a mother. And that, she knew, was no reason for them to get together. No reason at all.

Ruth continued to study Rebecca. "It's not like you to be rude to someone, Rebecca," she chided softly.

Rebecca felt her jaw thrust out stubbornly as she struggled to contain the temper and quick tongue that always threatened to get the best of her. "I just don't think he should be here," she said finally.

"Better Jack Rourke be here, where we can watch over him, than out roaming around the countryside at will," Eli said, walking in to join the two women. "A young man that handsome and charming would have no trouble at all seducing our young women, I am afraid."

He's already done that, Rebecca thought mournfully.

"Does your dislike of Mr. Rourke have anything to do with what happened in Florida?" her grandfather asked gently.

Rebecca felt her spine stiffen. "I thought we had agreed we weren't going to talk about that anymore."

Her grandfather tucked his hands around his suspenders. "Normally you know I would not bring it up."

"But Jack Rourke is English, too," her grandmother added gently, coming around to pat Rebecca on the arm. "And you seem abnormally uncomfortable around him. We thought, perhaps because of the memories of Wesley..."

Her grandmother didn't finish, but then, she didn't have to. The memories of her time in Florida were largely bad ones. But that didn't mean they had to dwell on them now, Rebecca thought fiercely. Always an intensely private person, she found she was even more so now. "I don't know what it is about Jack Rourke that gets under my skin exactly, I just know he does," she said, not bothering to mask her temper.

Eli frowned. "I suppose someone should check on Jack and the hens."

Not me, Rebecca thought fiercely. She was not going to be alone with Jack Rourke again.

"No need for that," Jack said cheerfully as he appeared in the kitchen door, his shoulders reaching from one side of the portal to the other. He had two baskets with him, each brimming with a surprising number of brown-shelled eggs. He looked at Rebecca, challenge sparkling in his eyes, but his voice was pleasantly mild as he asked calmly, "Where should I put these?"

Darn him for taking the egg-gathering in stride, Rebecca thought. She had hoped it would make him turn and run. "In the sink, for washing," she said with a bright smile, mocking his relaxed tone to a T.

Eli cast a look out the window, at the increasingly dusky sky. "I'll see to the rest of the stock," Eli said. He left via the back door.

Ruth looked at Jack. "I noticed a moment ago that your baby needs changing. I'd be glad to do it. Where are the diapers?"

"In the bag I brought with me," Jack said.

He pumped water at the sink, and washed his hands in the cold water. Seconds later, Ruth and Andy exited. Jack and Rebecca were alone once again. He lounged against the sink beside her, deliberately standing too close. "How many more tests am I going to have to pass?" he asked.

He's not ever going to give up, Rebecca thought as she inhaled the brisk wintry scent of his after-shave. A shiver of excitement went through her. She had been pursued by boys ever since she could remember, but never like this. Never so intently. "About a million and a half," she said tartly, refusing to let the way he was pursuing her now, after nearly a year's absence, go to her head.

"Just want you to know I'm looking forward to it," he quipped. "And one more thing."

Now he was setting conditions, Rebecca thought mournfully. "What?"

Jack's gaze darkened, just the way it had before he'd kissed her, but this time he kept his hands, and his lips, to himself. "Keep in mind I give back as good as I get," he whispered softly. "This isn't over, Rebecca, not by a long shot."

Chapter Three

"Do you need any help preparing Andy's baby food?" Ruth asked as the last-minute dinner preparations were made.

"Thanks," Jack said as he stirred formula into the rice cereal specially made for infants, and then placed it in the hot water warming dish, next to the apple sauce already warming, "but I think I've got it."

He had certainly impressed her grandparents with his parenting know-how, Rebecca thought. "You seem to know a lot about taking care of babies," she said.

"I baby-sat my psych prof's son while I was in college," Jack said. He plucked Andy out of the cradle and joined the others at the table. Eli said grace. Conversation resumed, with Jack taking the lead.

"There's a lot about the Amish I still don't understand," Jack admitted as he tied a bib around Andy's neck, and tossed a hand towel over his shoulder. "For instance, is shunning still practiced in your church? And is it really as cruel a punishment as it sounds?"

Rebecca fixed Jack with a quelling gaze from beneath her lashes. She wanted him to stop this right now. Unfortunately he was so busy getting Andy settled on his lap so that he could feed him, he didn't seem to get her message. Or maybe, Rebecca thought, Jack just didn't want to get her message.

"First of all, Jack," Eli said matter-of-factly as he ladled mashed potatoes onto his plate, "shunning is not so much a punishment as an attempt to bring the sinner back to the fold.''

Rebecca swallowed hard as she busied herself spooning beef and noodles onto her plate. She was not sure how she was going to make it through this entire meal, never mind the entire night, if Jack didn't stop playing master detective in search of a clue.

''What kind of sin are we talking about here, Mr. Lindholm?'' Jack asked as he spooned cereal into Andy's mouth.

Jack frowned as Andy pushed half of the cereal back out again with his tongue. Jack caught the excess with the edge of the spoon, and pushed it right back into Andy's mouth. This time, Andy swallowed it, and then smiled as if the cereal tasted great.

''Are we talking about stealing?'' Jack continued as he gave Andy another bite. ''Murder? Coveting another man's wife?'' Jack paused long enough to look briefly at Rebecca. ''Not honoring the wishes of one's father and mother?''

Next, Rebecca thought, Jack was probably going to bring up the sin of making love to someone other than one's marriage partner. Just what she needed to make this whole miserable, thrilling, exciting day complete. ''You are blunt, aren't you, Mr. Rourke?'' Rebecca said sweetly as she ladled lima beans onto her plate.

Jack paused and waited until she looked at him. When she did, he returned her gaze evenly. ''I guess I am blunt, but I don't know any other way of ascertaining the truth,'' he said quietly as he looked deep into her eyes, his words imparting his secret strategy.

''And I do want to make sure I understand the Amish before the filming of my new screenplay is finished,'' Jack continued as he gave Andy another bite of apple sauce, ''while there's still time for me to rectify any mistakes *I might have made last spring,* while I was researching and writing the first draft.''

Rebecca's heart pounded as she again caught the double meaning of his words. What did he mean by rectify, anyway?

Was he really here to marry her because of a baby that wasn't even hers? Or did he just want another brief fling with her, one that was every bit as passionate as their last had been? Recalling what a powerful effect his kisses had had on her before, she turned her glance away from Jack and his adorable little baby. She couldn't let herself be ruled by her emotions or her attraction to this very sexy English-man.

Ruth smiled at Jack and said, "Your attention to detail is laudable. So many writers have painted us as a backward society, without talking to the New Order Amish such as ourselves, as well as the Old Order Amish. Our community is much more progressive in our thinking."

"I can see that, just by your willingness to accept me into your home," Jack said. "So back to the shunning, is it still practiced?"

"To a point, yes. We don't force a member out of the community, though. Rather, we work with them to try to put them back on the right path," Eli said.

Jack looked reassured by that, Rebecca noted dispassionately. "What if a woman had a baby out of wedlock?" he asked her grandfather matter-of-factly as he gave Andy another spoonful of rice cereal. "What would happen then?"

Eli shrugged, and said, just as serenely, "She would either marry the baby's father, or give up the baby to an Amish family to raise. And then she would go on with her life, and one day marry and have a family of her own."

"I see," Jack said as he shifted Andy a little higher in his arm.

"But that rarely happens," Eli continued with a fatherly complacence that had Rebecca squirming in her seat. "We keep a good eye on our young women. And couples tend to marry early, when they are still in their teens in most cases."

"The Amish are a loving, nurturing society, Mr. Rourke. Not a cruel one," Ruth said gently.

Rebecca saw him sizing up her family and knew he believed that about the Lindholms, at least. "Still, giving up a baby would be hard," Jack said, after a moment, as he gently wiped Andy's mouth.

"No harder than raising a child on your own," Rebecca interjected quickly, afraid of what might be revealed inadvertently if Jack kept this up. Lowering her lashes slightly, she gave him a look that told him quite frankly to cease this line of questioning here and now.

Jack ignored her. With Andy still on his lap, he began to eat his own dinner.

"What happened to Andy's mother?" Ruth asked. "You didn't say, Jack."

Rebecca tensed. Jack caught Rebecca's expression, frowned, then said, "She left me."

"After the baby was born?" Ruth gaped.

"Before Andy was born, actually."

"Are you divorced?" Eli asked.

"We were never married," Jack admitted reluctantly. "I would have married her, had I known about the baby, but she didn't tell me she was pregnant."

"How did you find out about the baby?" Ruth asked.

"The baby's mother left Andy on the doorstep with a note advising me to own up to my mistakes. I'm trying to do that," Jack said.

"Any chance you'll get Andy's mother to marry you now?" Eli asked.

Jack cast a casual look around. His gaze lingered briefly on Rebecca as he said, "I'm hopeful everything will get worked out and that we'll be a family, but only time will tell."

Rebecca caught her breath as her grandmother began doling out slices of apple pie. Jack was a fool if he thought he could get his way so easily, Rebecca thought, pressure or no pressure.

"When will that be decided?" Ruth asked.

Deciding too much time had spent dawdling, Rebecca got up and began to clear the table. Another mistake. As soon as she was on her feet, Jack's eyes were following her around the room.

"In a couple of weeks," Jack said, leaning back in his chair so that Andy was snuggled against him and the fabric of his corduroy shirt stretched across his broad shoulders and the hard muscles of his chest. Unable to help but look at him as she came back to the table for another stack of dishes, Rebecca could almost feel Jack against her as he had been that night, skin to skin, all hot and taking, urging her on...

Oblivious to the licentiousness of her thoughts, Jack shifted Andy a little higher, so Andy had a better view of the adults around him. "What happens if a young person decides to leave the Amish faith these days?" Jack asked. Rebecca knew he was trying to find out what would happen if she left with him.

"We don't like to see our young people leave the faith, but it happens, even in the best of families," Eli said. He and Ruth exchanged a look full of both shared memories and compassion. "In fact, it even happened in ours. Rebecca's mother married an Englishman and she lived in Ohio most of her adult life."

"And you allowed this?" Jack asked, surprised.

"We didn't have much to say about it," Eli answered Jack with a shrug. "Every young person has to decide for his or herself whether to stay or to go. Our daughter Elizabeth chose to leave the faith." Just as I did, Rebecca thought.

"It didn't mean we didn't love her," Ruth added gently as she got up to help Rebecca clear the table.

"She came to visit from time to time," Eli said.

"And wrote often," Ruth said.

"So how did Rebecca end up here?" Jack asked, his interest in her past intense.

Again, Rebecca fought a flicker of unease, that in his determined probing Jack might find out things about her she'd rather he not know, now, or ever. She faced him with a brisk, purposeful smile. "Ruth and Eli took me in when my parents were killed in a car accident," Rebecca said shortly, in a way that let Jack and everyone else know the subject was closed for discussion. Anticipating his next question, she sent him a quelling look. "And I was happy to be here."

Jack shifted Andy to his other arm. He regarded Rebecca silently for a long moment, then turned to her grandmother. "When I was in town, I saw some young Amish girls running around in tennis shoes, instead of the usual plain black shoes. Is that allowed?"

Ruth nodded. Passing by Andy, she chucked him on the chin and was rewarded with one of Andy's delighted smiles. Ruth held out her hands. Andy lurched toward her happily, and Jack, looking grateful for the respite, handed him over.

"Young people are encouraged to make their own decisions about clothing as well as their faith," Ruth said as she walked Andy around the room, patting him gently on the back all the while. "We encourage them to dress plain and simple of course, but a little rebellion at that age is to be expected."

"I see." Jack looked at Rebecca, as if wondering if her night with him had been just a simple act of youthful rebellion on her part.

Wordlessly Jack stood and carried his own plate to the sink. Rebecca had already used the old-fashioned pump to half fill the sink with cold water straight from the well outside, but she had to heat the rest on the stove, and as she waited for it to heat, she railed at the impractical side of the Amish way of life. Self-reliance was great, but honestly what was wrong with a little dependence on some sort of water heater—even a solar generated one—if it sped up their chores?

"What did you do when you were a teenager?" Jack asked Rebecca.

Rebecca turned her back to him, feeling guilty about her rebellious thoughts. It wasn't up to her to question the validity of their community's ways. She continued watching the water in the kettle on the huge black wood stove with more than necessary care. "Nothing out of the ordinary," she said.

And that was true, as far as her life here in Blair, Pennsylvania, had gone.

Despite the utter blandness of her words and her noncommittal expression, Jack saw through her evasive statement. To Rebecca's dismay, he leaned against the sink, folded his arms in front of him and continued to prod her mercilessly. "You didn't ever want to leave or break free of the constraints here? Sorry," he said, lifting a hand in a gesture of goodwill to both Ruth and Eli. "I mean no offense. I'm just curious, because I know teenagers rebel, no matter what circumstances they live in. It just seems to be a normal part of growing up."

"Indeed it is," Ruth agreed with a cheerful smile. Seeing Andy was beginning to be a little restless, she went over to get him a rattle.

"So I was wondering how Rebecca handled it," Jack continued easily as he slanted Rebecca an appreciative glance. "She seems to be a strong-minded young woman."

"She is at that," Eli agreed. He, too, glanced at her and smiled. "But she came back to us, like we knew she would," he concluded with familial pride.

"Back?" Jack asked pleasantly, his dark blue eyes sparkling as if he had just picked up on some extraordinarily interesting tidbit about her. "Where was she?"

"I was in Florida," Rebecca answered swiftly before either of her grandparents could say a word. Grabbing the pot holders, she carried the heavy pot of boiling water to the sink and carefully added it to the soap and water there. "I took a job as a maid in a bed and breakfast there when I was seventeen."

Jack had moved back to allow her room to work. Now he closed in on her again. His brisk masculine scent stirred her senses in a disturbing way, and lent a rubbery feeling to her knees. Rebecca drew a silent breath, telling herself to calm down. He was only a man, after all. And she had been around men all her life. She could handle this, if she just kept her emotions—and her temper—tightly reined.

"Why did you go so far from home?" Jack asked softly, still watching her carefully.

Because I was a fool, Rebecca thought, the steam from the sink rising to bathe her face.

"We wanted her to see more of the world, before she decided whether to go or stay," Eli said, answering for her.

Jack looked at her again, his gaze narrowing attentively. Rebecca had the feeling he was learning more than he let on, not just about her, but her entire family. Knowing what havoc his interest in her could cause made her heart pound.

"And you came home?" he said.

"The following year," Rebecca replied, keeping her gaze averted. But it was too late. She had already noticed how sexy he was, with his thick chestnut hair all rumpled, and the faint shadow of evening beard now lining his stubborn jaw.

"Was that when you married?" Jack asked.

"About the same time," Rebecca said as she slipped on a pair of rubber gloves and began to wash the dishes, again with more than necessary care. She would get through all Jack's questions, all his probing, and then Jack would leave. He would take his baby with him and forget about her; they'd both go back to their normal lives. As if nothing had ever happened. All she had to do was get through the next few days.

"And it can also be necessary sometimes, especially for young people like Rebecca, to do something different from time to time," Ruth added, still walking Andy around. "That's why she went to Indiana last summer to work at a bed and breakfast in Indiana."

"How long did you work there?" Jack asked Rebecca, his dark blue eyes filled with sudden interest.

"A few months," Rebecca mumbled, wishing fervently the subject had never been introduced.

"Longer than that," Eli corrected, like the stickler for detail he was.

Ruth nodded. "You left in June and came back right after Christmas. Remember, Rebecca?"

Again, Jack's face lit up.

The clock struck six in the adjacent living room. "Oh, dear," Ruth said. "You're going to be late for your singing tonight if you don't hurry," she said.

Seeing an escape route from Jack, Rebecca hurriedly added more dishes to the soapy water in front of her. "Don't worry. I'll be quick," she promised. And then I'll leave.

Again, Jack looked intrigued. "I've heard about singings, but I've never been to one," he said, then probed her with a decisive yet innocent look. "Mind if I tag along?"

Rebecca knew what Jack was up to now; he wanted to ask her about her stay in Indiana. She was about to say, "As a matter of fact, I do," when her grandmother interrupted.

"That's a splendid idea!"

"But—" Rebecca sputtered, the last of her dishes scrubbed and put on the drainboard to dry.

"I will take care of the baby," Ruth said as Andy beamed up at her adoringly.

"Great." Jack smiled victoriously at Rebecca. "Then it's all set."

A shiver of anticipation and unease went through Rebecca like a lightning bolt. Darn it all, she did not want to be alone with this man.

"I'll hitch up the buggy," Eli said, getting to his feet.

Jack smiled at her grandfather. He, too, reached for his coat. "I'll come with you," he offered and followed Eli out the door.

"WHAT'S WRONG, REBECCA?" Ruth asked gently the moment the men had left.

"Nothing," Rebecca fibbed. She hated lying to her grandmother but she couldn't tell her the truth, either—that her grandparents had just given Jack information that was going to have him jumping to conclusions and asking all kinds of questions. "I'm just worried about being late for the singing."

"Worried about being late, or worried about being alone with Jack Rourke?"

Rebecca turned away, wishing she had never been so foolish as to sleep with Jack Rourke. "You heard how nosy he is," she complained. "Asking questions about everything, personal questions."

Ruth nodded as she continued to pace back and forth, Andy in her arms. "You don't want him to know about your past."

Rebecca shrugged, not above confessing to this much. She met her grandmother's glance. "I'd rather he didn't."

Ruth patted an increasingly drowsy Andy on the back. "Jack seems like a nice man," Ruth said.

Rebecca frowned. She knew she couldn't come on too strongly here or her grandmother really would suspect something was up. "There's no doubt he's handsome and charming. But it takes more than being handsome and charming to be a good man."

"You distrust him?" Ruth studied Rebecca bluntly.

Rebecca reached up and checked her hair. As she had suspected, a few errant strands had escaped her kapp. She tucked them in as best she could and tried not to think about the loving, gentle way Jack had sifted his fingers through her hair both before and after they had made love, as if her hair were the finest treasure he had ever found.

Finished restoring order to her hair, Rebecca clamped her lips together. "I don't want to talk about this."

Ruth looked down at Andy, who was almost fast asleep in her arms, then back at her granddaughter. "Is there something your grandfather and I should know?" she asked quietly.

Rebecca looked down at the sweet, innocent Andy and shook her head. It was killing her to know that Jack had slept with another woman sometime either shortly before or after he had made love to her...and to know that other woman had had Jack's baby and then abandoned Andy. What kind of woman had Jack slept with, anyway?

Not that it mattered now, Rebecca thought, since she was out of Jack's life, and had been for some time. But Rebecca couldn't confide any of that in her grandparents. Knowing how they had suffered with her both before, during and after her disastrous marriage to Wesley Adair, she had since made a firm practice of keeping her mistakes to herself. She wouldn't veer from that course now. It was enough that she'd had a fling that had turned her own world topsy-turvy. She wouldn't let the same happen to the people who loved her most, too.

Swallowing hard, she forced herself to put on a cheerful front. "No. I am just in a mood," she explained with a rueful wave of her hand, and a woman-to-woman look. "It's probably just the time of year. I'm tired of the snow, anxious for spring." And anxious for Jack to leave.

Chapter Four

"You had the baby in Indiana, didn't you?" Jack said as he helped Rebecca into the covered black buggy. "That's how you managed to keep it a secret."

With a decisive snap of the reins, Rebecca started the horse on the way. "Good theory, Jack. Only there's one problem with it. Where was Andy when I returned to Blair County right after Christmas?"

"How should I know?" Jack settled back in his seat. "Maybe you brought him with you and secretly cared for him here at the farm."

"Then why didn't my grandparents put two and two together and know you were the father the instant you showed up at the farm, Jack? Why didn't they read you the riot act, if that were the case?"

Jack frowned. Rebecca had a point. "So maybe Ruth and Eli didn't know about the baby or the pregnancy. Maybe you arranged for someone else, someone in Indiana, to care for Andy."

"Then how did Andy end up on Alec Roman's doorstep?" Rebecca asked scornfully, looking even more beautiful in the moonlight filtering down through the trees than she had inside the house.

"I don't know." Jack shifted restlessly in his seat as the buggy bumped along the paved road. "Maybe you changed your mind and decided to make me own up to my mistakes. Maybe you wanted me to come after you.''

''Oh, absolutely,'' Rebecca agreed dryly. ''I really wanted my quiet life here disrupted, my grandparents shocked, hurt and dismayed, my reputation ruined.''

Jack frowned. ''So I can't figure out exactly how you think—yet. I will.''

Rebecca shook her head. ''That'll be the day,'' she murmured beneath her breath. With every bounce of the buggy, she seemed to slide a little closer to the middle of the seat and to Jack. ''How much farther?'' Jack demanded as she slid toward him a little more and they finally made contact from hip to knee. Sitting this close to her was agony.

Rebecca slanted him a quelling sidelong glance. ''Another five miles or so.''

Five miles! Jack scowled. He had wanted to be alone with Rebecca, but not like this, freezing to death in an unheated Amish buggy, without even a lap robe to keep them warm. He regarded her meditatively, unable to help but admire the competent way she handled the reins. ''You're still angry with me for showing up here, aren't you?'' he said softly, wishing with all his heart that she wasn't, because if she wasn't so angry, maybe she would be more willing to talk honestly and unreservedly with him. But he also knew that Rebecca had every reason to be annoyed with him. By invading her home, he had overstepped his boundaries. Of course she was mad.

Rebecca lifted her eyes heavenward. ''Your keen skills of observation amaze me,'' she remarked drolly.

He ignored the reproach in her voice and pointed out politely, ''You know, it would have been faster to take my car.'' And more comfortable, too.

Rebecca slanted him yet another sassy look from beneath her thick golden lashes. ''Being from Los Angeles, I would think you would appreciate the environmental soundness of our ways. Or perhaps you like smog?''

Most of the Amish Jack had encountered during his research expedition last summer had been blissfully ignorant of the world outside their own. Not Rebecca. "You sure know a lot about the world for an Amish woman," he drawled, finding he would do just about anything to hold her attention, even if it meant baiting her almost continuously. As for the true story of what had happened while she was in Indiana last summer and fall, he would have to wait until she trusted him completely before he'd have those questions answered.

Rebecca concentrated on the winding road ahead of them. "My downfall, I am sure. The other," she added tartly, "was ending up in your bed."

Jack smiled. "Ah, so you do remember," he murmured in delight. Leaning closer, he regarded her with a comical leer. "I was beginning to wonder."

Rebecca gripped the reins a little tighter. "A night like that would have been hard to forget," she said in a strangled tone of voice.

"Impossible to forget," Jack corrected. He leaned forward, pressed his lips to the back of her hand, and felt her tremble. "The memories of that night have been driving me wild the past few days, Rebecca."

"What happened that night was a foolish mistake," Rebecca shot back as she jerked her hand away, the hurt in her low voice as palpable as her scorn. "We have to forget we ever behaved so recklessly."

"Even if there's now a baby involved?" Jack asked.

"That baby isn't mine, Jack, and if it weren't for Andy, you wouldn't have come back for me at all."

Jack was silent.

"It's true, isn't it?" Her voice was thready with hurt. "You're only here because of the baby."

"I thought that was what you wanted, for me to get lost and stay lost."

"It was!" Rebecca insisted, color flowing into her cheeks in a way that made her delicate bone structure all the more pronounced.

"But just because I abided by your wishes doesn't mean

I stopped thinking about you, Rebecca. I've thought of you more times than you'll ever know. But I respected your privacy and your different way of life and I stayed away, until Alec found Andy on his doorstep. And then I had no choice. Andy needs his mother every bit as much as he needs me."

"But I'm not his mother!" Rebecca protested.

"So you keep saying."

Her light blue eyes narrowed on him in a way that made him decidedly uncomfortable. "And you keep not wanting to believe it's true," she said.

Jack shrugged, not about to back down now that he'd come this far. "I know what I feel in my heart, Rebecca, but you're right. We shouldn't keep talking about Andy's parentage, since that always leads to heated discussion. Let's talk about each other instead. While we were out hitching up the horse, Eli told me you were never so glad to come home as when you came back from Florida."

"So?"

Jack ignored the irritation in her voice. He continued to probe. "Eli made it sound like you regretted ever going there. I just wondered why. Were the working conditions bad?"

"No. They were fine."

"Then what didn't you like about it?" Jack persisted.

Rebecca shrugged. "I missed my family and friends here. We wrote letters to each other, of course, but it wasn't the same as being here and visiting and going to weddings and seeing the new babies born and weathering every hardship together and sharing every joy. I felt cut off from all that in Florida," Rebecca continued softly, a faint note of reverence and appreciation creeping into her tone. "There's a closeness of family and community here that doesn't exist out in the English world."

"Maybe you just didn't meet the right English people, Rebecca. I have plenty of very nice, very caring friends in California."

He watched as Rebecca transferred the reins to her right hand, and used her left to draw her thick black wool cloak closer to her slender form. She must be as cold and uncomfortable right now as he was feeling.

Rebecca glanced at him. "What about you, Jack? Are you close to your family?"

Jack thought about all the things he and Rebecca still had to learn about each other. "I never knew my father. He didn't stick around long enough to marry my mother." Crazily enough, that fact still hurt and angered Jack, even though he'd had years to deal with his abandonment. "As for my mother," Jack continued, picking his words carefully, "she died several years ago, so it's just me these days. Or at least it had been until Andy came along. Now I've got family again, a child to love. And I couldn't be happier about that, Rebecca. It's what I've wanted for a long time."

"Then I'm happy for you," Rebecca said in a voice that sounded thick with suppressed emotion, but sincere, too. "And I'm sorry about your mother," Rebecca continued softly, surprising Jack even more. She reached over to grip his hand tightly in hers. "I know how hard it is to lose a parent."

Jack squeezed back, and then released her hand reluctantly. "I guess we have that in common." Hers was a small gesture of comfort, but one he appreciated.

Looking ahead, he saw they were approaching a sprawling farm. Several other buggies were coming from the opposite direction. Another cluster of buggies was already parked in the yard, in front of the plain white frame house. "What's going to happen next?" Jack said, as Rebecca guided the horse to a halt.

"We'll go inside," Rebecca said. Jack stepped down from the buggy then reached up to lend her a hand. As he helped her down to the ground, they were flanked by two young men—Jack estimated them both to be in their early teens—in Amish garb. They looked Jack over, taking in his leather bomber jacket, corduroy shirt, jeans and running shoes. "What have we here, Rebecca?" the taller one asked.

"A friend," Rebecca said. "This is Jack Rourke. He's

staying with my family. Jack, I'd like you to meet Levi and Dieter Hoffer. They're family friends. I've known them forever. They're like my little brothers.''

"Not so little anymore," Dieter corrected, proudly sticking out his chest. "We're fourteen."

And definitely feeling their oats, Jack thought. He could tell by the dancing lights in their light blue eyes that the two were already plotting some sort of mischief for the evening.

"Nice to meet you both," Jack said.

"Nice to meet the latest Englishman who is sweet on Rebecca," Levi said with a wink. Both boys laughed. Rebecca flushed with embarrassment and glared at Levi until he and Dieter took her not so gentle hint and ran off.

"What did he mean by that?" Jack asked.

Rebecca avoided Jack's eyes altogether as she shook her head in silent aggravation and dismissed the comment with a wave. "The boys are just at that juvenile age where they think it is great fun to annoy me until I lose my patience."

"Does that happen often?"

"Sometimes. Not to worry." She gave Jack a significant look. "I get them back, when necessary."

Jack grinned. This was a side to Rebecca he hadn't seen before. "How?"

Rebecca leaned forward and spoke in a confidential whisper. "One day not too long ago when they were being particularly pesky, I played a reciprocal prank on them."

"What'd you do?"

Rebecca smiled smugly. "I told them I saw a moose in the woods by the covered bridge."

Jack frowned. "I didn't know there were any moose out here."

"There aren't." Rebecca grinned, delighted with her roguery. "It took Levi and Dieter almost an hour to discover the curious tracks I'd laid were false and that they'd been sent on a wild moose chase. They've been trying to get back at me ever since."

"Get back at you?" Jack asked.

"By embarrassing me, what else?" Looking unconcerned by the teenage boys' antics, Rebecca took Jack's arm just above the elbow and urged him toward the house. "Come on. We're going to be late for the singing."

Jack enjoyed the blending of voices as he and Rebecca stood shoulder to shoulder among the other young, single people there and sang the lively German hymns. The hymn singing was followed by refreshments and a square dance in the barn. Jack had just linked arms with Rebecca when Levi passed by again. "Better watch yourself with the Englishman, Rebecca," he warned, suddenly only half joking. "You know what happened before—"

"Levi." Rebecca glared at him like a chastising older sister. "Cut it out. I mean it." Giving Levi no chance to comment, Rebecca grabbed Jack's arm and dragged him off in the direction of the dancing. Wordlessly she tugged Jack out onto the middle of the barn floor. Not about to waste the opportunity to have her in his arms again, Jack swung her round and round to the invigorating tune the group of Amish fiddlers were playing. It had been cold in the barn when they'd first entered, but now, with the dancing and the crush of people, it was warming up fast. Just as he was.

"So what is it you don't want Levi to tell me?" he asked, flattening his hand possessively against her waist. He saw the temper flare in her clear light blue eyes.

"Nothing," she said.

Jack tightened his grip on her, determined to get to the bottom of this mystery whether she helped or not. "Try again."

She smiled at him cantankerously. "I will not."

"Then I'll ask Levi myself," he said, and started to release her.

Rebecca gripped him, hard. "That won't be necessary, Jack. Levi is just teasing me."

And pigs read books. "About what?"

"My...looks." Her floundering for an answer gave her

away more than the pink color creeping up her throat, into her jaw.

"What about your looks?" Jack asked. Then, as the dance ended, he took her hand and led her resolutely over to a bale of hay stacked against the far wall, sat down and pulled her down beside him.

Rebecca smiled out at the dancers, looking to all the world as if she were enjoying herself. "My hair gets very white in the summer. It always seems to attract a lot of attention from the summer tourists."

"There are plenty of Nordic blondes in this part of the country, Rebecca."

"True," Rebecca said as she tapped her foot to the beat of the music. "And it happens to other young single women here, too. Englishmen see us. The next we know, they are taking our pictures. Trying to talk to us. Lure us on dates with them."

Levi was talking about more than just gawking tourists; Jack would bet his life on it. Something had happened to Rebecca. "So?" he said.

"So the young Englishmen seem to think that just because they are drawn to us that we are drawn to them." She glared at him rebelliously as the fiddlers began another spirited song. "They are wrong," she said flatly.

The double-edged meaning of her words did not escape him. And though he knew she wasn't telling him the truth, at least not all of it, he also knew he wasn't going to get any more out of her now.

"So what are you going to do about Andy when you return to L.A.?" Rebecca watched as Levi and Dieter joined the dancing, too, leaving her and Jack the only two people on the sidelines. "Now that you know I won't be coming with you and the baby."

Jack shrugged. "I'll raise Andy by myself."

"You make it sound so easy," Rebecca lamented softly.

"And you make it sound so overwhelming," Jack replied.

"That's because it is an overwhelming prospect to me. I

don't know that I could manage a baby all on my own, particularly if I had no family around to help out, and I had to earn a living, too. That's a lot to take on, Jack.''

Jack shook his head. She was making too much of this again. ''I've got a job that allows me to work at home ninety percent of the time, and enough money to pay a good nanny to help out when I need help. If all else fails, I'll take some parenting classes, too. One way or another, Andy and I will get along.''

He was really determined to do right for his son; Rebecca obviously found that very appealing. Jack began to relax. Maybe things would work out between them after all.

''When are you going to tell Andy about his mother? When he's old enough to understand?'' Rebecca asked.

Jack shrugged again. ''Hopefully I'll have convinced his mother to marry me and live with us by then.''

''And if you haven't?'' Rebecca asked.

Jack grabbed her hand and pulled her through the shadows, and back, into the tack room. It was as dark as night. Jack pushed her inside, moved her back against the wall and took her into his arms. ''Come back to L.A. with us, Rebecca, and we'll never have to worry about that. Andy will already have us both, watching over him and loving him.''

Rebecca closed her eyes; she looked like he had just offered her the impossible. ''Oh, Jack,'' she whispered in obvious dismay. ''Jack, don't—'' Her breath caught as he molded his body to hers.

''I want you,'' he said, lowering his head and brushing his mouth across hers. ''I've never stopped wanting you.''

Rebecca gasped as he kissed her again, hard. Jack knew he was going too fast but he couldn't help it. Being with her seemed to bring out the caveman in him. All he wanted was to make things right between them. He was ready to make amends, to court her properly, if she'd let him. ''I want to start over with you, Rebecca. Please, say you'll give me another chance, for Andy's sake. For ours.''

Rebecca paused. She wanted to start over with Jack, to

begin again in a more conservative, normal way. But she was afraid for so many reasons that it was already too late. Sooner or later Jack would realize what she already knew: that she was not Andy's mother. And then, Rebecca thought, he would want to find Andy's real mom and reconcile with her.

She had walked away from Jack once. That had been hard, but it hadn't been nearly as difficult as it was going to be for her to walk away from him now that he'd come back into her life once again and she'd gotten to know him a little better.

"Just think about it," Jack urged gently as he slowly, reluctantly released her. "You don't have to give me an answer now."

That was good, Rebecca thought, because she didn't have an answer for Jack. The only thing she knew for certain was that the more she was around him, the more she wanted to be around him.

Jack spent the rest of the evening propped up against the barn wall, watching Rebecca dance with other Amish men. No matter how much he looked at her, he couldn't get his fill. Rebecca was beautiful, incredibly beautiful, in the plain clothing. And very popular with the young Amish men. But he couldn't help but remember how she had looked with her hair down, waving gently, as thick as silk...the heavy fragrant weight of it spread over his pillow.

He felt his body tighten painfully. How long, he wondered, before she was back in his bed where she belonged? How long before he could convince her to marry him? It wasn't as if she had never lived English before. It wasn't as if her grandparents wouldn't understand; they would. All she had to do was tell them she loved him. But first, he would have to get her to trust him again. After that, admitting she loved him would be easy.

Around ten, the dance ended. Goodbyes were said and coats and bonnets gathered. Jack escorted Rebecca out to the buggy. He could tell by the way she avoided looking him in the eye, and the stiff set of her shoulders that she was still confused and on edge.

Jack conceded silently that she had a right to be upset with him for kissing her in the tack room. Anyone could have walked in on them and carried the news of their kiss back to the community. It wasn't like him to be so reckless and short-sighted. But that, too, was going to change, Jack promised himself silently. For every moment he spent with Rebecca was a moment invested in his and Andy's future. He wanted his son to have a mother.

He climbed up into the buggy after her and while she was getting settled, he took the reins.

"What are you doing, Jack?" Rebecca pivoted to gape at him. "You don't know how to handle a horse, never mind one reined to a buggy."

Out of his peripheral vision, Jack could see both Dieter and Levi loitering next to their two buggies, watching Jack and Rebecca quarrel over the reins. There had never been a better time to assert his mastery over the situation, and not so coincidentally, over her. Besides, maybe it was time he stopped trying to convince Rebecca to return to the English way of life with him, and instead concentrated on showing her that they all could live in both worlds with equal chances of making a successful go at becoming a family.

"You know, you're right," Jack teased Rebecca gently, "it is time I learned how to handle a horse." Fortunately Jack had paid enough attention to what Rebecca was doing earlier, to be able to start the horse up and turn it toward the lane. Once that was done, the horse fell into line behind the other vehicles heading toward the road. "And a woman," Jack continued glibly, "if the jokes Levi and Dieter were telling about me every time they thought I was out of earshot tonight are to be believed."

Rebecca flushed and sat farther back in the buggy. She folded her arms in front of her defensively. "You're talking nonsense, Jack."

Jack only wished that were the case. "Am I? This is a

patriarchal society. Maybe if I'd been more masterfully dictatorial with you in the first place, Rebecca, you never would have left me the morning after.''

Rebecca leaned forward, checking both ways as they headed out onto the main road. "If you'd been any *more* dictatorial, I never would have stayed with you that night."

Satisfied, she leaned back in her seat, keeping more to her corner of the buggy than she had en route there. Jack didn't need a crystal ball to know why. The way she kept raking her teeth across her lower lip told him she was thinking about their kiss in the back of the barn...maybe wanting another one, somewhere en route home?

Jack was glad to see Rebecca direct him to take the road north, when almost everyone else was going south and west. He guided the horse through the turn, holding the reins just as he'd seen her do. When they were headed straight again, he settled back in his seat and asked what had been on his mind for what seemed like forever. "Why did you stay with me that night, Rebecca?"

Rebecca folded her arms in front of her. "I don't know."

Jack wasn't buying her innocent act. Beneath that demure Amish clothing beat the heart of a very passionate woman. She might say she still wanted nothing to do with him, but the way she'd returned his kiss tonight said otherwise. "Yes, you do," he disagreed gently.

She held herself so still for such a long moment that he thought she wasn't going to answer. Finally she shrugged and said softly, "The whole night seemed a little unreal to me, like something out of a story someone made up. I knew how much you desired me and I got caught up in those feelings, all right?" She lifted her chin and glared at him. "I was a fool to behave so recklessly!"

Jack shook his head. "No, Rebecca, you weren't a fool to love me."

"If I hadn't, I wouldn't be in this mess right now."

Jack tugged on the reins and brought the horse to a halt. The moon was so bright, the terrain so flat and wide open, that anyone within a mile of them would've seen them stop, but he didn't care. He turned to face her, his knee nudging her thigh in the process. "What mess?"

"Your chasing after me, invading my home." She started to reach for the reins, but he wouldn't let her have them. Instead, he wrapped his left arm around her waist and hauled her against him, so she was half sitting on his lap.

"You know what I think, Rebecca?" Jack whispered, dropping the reins altogether so he could slip his free hand between her black bonnet and the side of her face. She gasped as he gently caressed her cheekbone. "I think you resented my reappearance into your life at first, but now that you've seen how much I already love our son and could love you, given even half a chance, I think your feelings have changed. I think you want me to chase after you," he said, kissing her temple, and then her nose, her chin, her ear. As she trembled in his arms, he drew back just enough to look into her eyes again. "And you know what else? You kiss me like you *want* me to catch you again, too!"

Rebecca sucked in her breath and flattened both her hands across his leather jacket. Her eyes were huge, her lips parted softly, her breathing erratic. "Jack, Jack, don't—"

Her voice was like velvet, sliding over him, drawing him in deeper and deeper. He tightened his arms around her, wanting her so badly. "Don't you get it, Rebecca?" he whispered, all the longing he felt for her pouring into his low voice. "I'm here because I want you back in my life. I don't want another brief fling with you, but a chance, a fair chance this time, at forging a real relationship with you, as two parents who are as committed to being good and kind and decent to each other as they are to loving their son."

"Oh, Jack," Rebecca said in a voice that was choked with emotion. Her eyes welled up, too.

"Tell me you want Andy to be happy, and loved, by two parents," Jack commanded gruffly.

"I do," Rebecca said.

"Then that's all I need to hear." Jack bent his head and

kissed her again, tenderly this time, and with every ounce of restraint he possessed. If he did more than that they were going to end up making love right here and now. And that they couldn't do. He'd already put her through enough.

With a sigh, he released her slowly and picked up the reins. She sat back in her corner of the buggy, a look of utter confusion on her face, and released a shuddering breath. "You're making me want to be Andy's mother, do you hear me?" she whispered.

"I hear you," he said, smiling. And that was exactly what he wanted to happen.

They'd barely gone another half mile when the sound of rapid hoofbeats and the clatter of wooden wheels on rough pavement sounded behind them. The buggy had no rearview mirror so Jack had to stick his head around the canvas side to see what was going on. To his amazement, two black Amish buggies were coming at him, hell for leather.

"What the—" he muttered, his irritation getting out of hand as quickly as the buggies were gaining on them.

"Don't panic, Jack," Rebecca said. Their horse, hearing the commotion coming up right behind them, spooked and took off at such a breakneck pace that both Jack and Rebecca were knocked back in their seats. "It's only a buggy race."

Only a buggy race? "They could have at least waited until we got out of the way," Jack said. He spared a glance at the deep ditches on either side of them, the covered wooden bridge up ahead, the flat terrain speeding past.

Knocked sideways, Rebecca fought the back and forth jolting of the buggy and struggled to sit up. "They're racing *us*, Jack. And I told you not to panic!"

The buggy hit another rut, jolting them so hard that Jack lost his grip on the reins and dropped them. One flopped outside the buggy and dragged along the ground. Rebecca lunged for it just as they approached the bridge. She caught it, and managed to stop their runaway horse, just as the other two buggies overtook and then blocked them. Jack wasn't at all surprised to identify the drivers of the other two buggies:

Levi and Dieter. Of course. He knew the young teens had been yearning to get into mischief all evening.

"Saw your buggy stopped. Been doing some sparking on the way home, Rebecca?" Dieter teased, with a bratty younger brother type of wink.

"Ja," Levi drawled, "we thought there might be some problem."

"No problem," Rebecca lied smoothly as she straightened her spine. "I was just explaining to Jack the fine points of driving a buggy."

"Ja, well, the first thing you perhaps should explain to him is how to hold on to the reins," Dieter teased with a chuckle, then clicked to his horse and headed off in the opposite direction. Levi turned his buggy behind them. The two continued to lead their horses and buggies back and forth, in front of and behind Rebecca and Jack. To Jack's amazement, Rebecca seemed to take the boyish harassment in stride. "This foolishness doesn't bother you?" Jack asked.

Rebecca met his eyes and again handed Jack the reins. "Young Amish men are known for their pranks. It's generally referred to as 'cutting up' and it's the way they let off steam. They're just horsing around. They probably thought I was driving, when they came up behind us like that. They know that I know how to handle a horse. I've had carriage races with them before."

Jack's frown deepened as he anticipated the rest. "Who won those races?"

"I did, of course."

"Of course," he mimicked dryly. "But that still doesn't excuse the way they spooked our horse and nearly forced us off the road."

"Perhaps it doesn't," Rebecca said with another uncaring shrug, "but it's still a better way for a young man in his prime to let off steam than seducing young women."

Jack slanted her a glance. "I didn't seduce you, Rebecca," he reminded her flatly, as Levi and Dieter finally gave up and Jack was able to start their horse off on the path back to the

Lindholm farm once again. "You came to my bed willingly."

For a moment, she was very still, neither arguing nor admitting to his claim. "It is time we got home," she said quietly, looking as afraid to risk her heart as Jack was afraid not to risk his. "That baby of yours will be wanting his father."

Chapter Five

"It's a good thing I bought you a couple of those blanket sleepers before we left Philadelphia," Jack told Andy several hours later that same evening. "Because it's cold in here tonight."

Andy's tiny brows knitted together, as if he were concerned about the situation, too.

"I also should have asked how to work the wood stove before everyone went to bed," Jack continued, speaking quietly so as not to wake the others.

Andy's brows rose again in silent question. He waved a fist in the air and cooed. "Trying to tell me you're hungry, aren't you?" Jack soothed as Andy clumsily aimed his fist at his mouth. Finally latching onto it after the third pass, Andy sucked noisily on his fist. "Well, not to worry," Jack continued, "ye olde midnight snack is on the way. There's only one small problem. I don't have the slightest idea how to heat this bottle for you."

Andy blinked and took his fist from his mouth. "We don't even have hot running water I could set the bottle in," Jack murmured. "And I hate the idea of waking anyone else up at this time of night."

"Too late," Rebecca said softly, from behind him. "You already woke me up."

If she was still upset with him for the way he had kissed her, both at the barn dance and after, she wasn't showing it.

She seemed more amenable to their becoming friends. And that, Jack thought, was a start. Encouraged, Jack smiled at her. "What about your grandparents, are they awake, too?" Jack asked.

"No." Rebecca avoided locking eyes with Jack by gazing tenderly down at Andy instead. Basking in her obvious admiration, Andy immediately beamed her back a toothless smile, then giggled and cooed. Rebecca bent and pressed a kiss to Andy's tiny fist. She smiled again, then reluctantly released his hand.

"But then," Rebecca continued as she gave Jack a cursory look, "my grandparents sleep more soundly than I do." She brushed past him. "I'll stoke up the fire for you."

"Thanks," Jack said. Andy still cradled in his arms, he followed Rebecca to the wood stove. Rebecca's gentleness with Andy appealed to Jack on a very fundamental level. And she appealed to him physically as well, never more so than at that moment. She was wearing a high-necked, long-sleeved white flannel gown that swept the floor. She had tied a navy shawl around her shoulders for warmth. Her hair was down and she wasn't wearing a kapp. She had never looked more beautiful, and he had never wanted her to be part of his life more than he did at that moment, not just in a fleeting, physical or practical sense, but in a more permanent way, as the mother to his son.

Flushing slightly under the intensity of Jack's gaze, Rebecca opened the stove door and added several small dry logs to the fire. Jack watched as she added water to a small pan and put it on the burner, and then set Andy's bottle down inside the pan. "It'll take about two minutes to heat."

"Thanks. I'm sorry we woke you. I don't know why he's awake."

Rebecca tossed Jack a wry look that made her seem even prettier. "Andy's probably hungry," she said, moving close enough to gaze tenderly down into Andy's face. Andy blinked up at Rebecca, then began to smile as if he not only recognized her, but welcomed her gentle, feminine presence.

Jack leaned against the kitchen counter, enjoying the cozy scene. Being with Rebecca this way seemed meant to be. "I meant Andy doesn't wake until three o'clock now, if we put him to bed at ten. At least, he didn't at Alec's," Jack said. Jack frowned as he shifted a squirming Andy higher in his arms, then patted him gently on the back. "I think he realizes he's in a strange place."

Rebecca nodded, looking distinctly uncomfortable with the intimacy between them, an intimacy that appeared whenever they were together for any length of time. She glided away from Jack, the voluminous white flannel gown she wore doing nothing to hide the enticing roundness of her breasts, the slenderness of her waist, the enticing flare of her hips, or the sleek, slender lines of her thighs.

Just watching her, Jack felt his body tighten. He knew she wanted him. He'd felt it in her kiss, in the way her body instinctively softened against his whenever he held her in his arms. He didn't understand why she wouldn't surrender to that desire, to the inevitability of their being together. He didn't understand why she wouldn't admit they'd had a child together, so they could go on with their lives, become a family. What was really holding Rebecca back? Maybe it was time he dug a little deeper and tried to find out how Rebecca felt about being a mother, period.

"Then again—" Jack met Rebecca's long-lashed gaze straightforwardly "—maybe where Andy and I are doesn't have anything to do with Andy's wakefulness at all. Maybe he just wants his mother." Holding her gaze, he stepped even closer, so she could inhale Andy's fresh baby scent, and he could surround himself with the sunny, springlike scent that was Rebecca. "Why don't you hold him?"

Rebecca blinked, then stepped back and away. "I don't think so," she said, edginess in her voice giving her away. She stepped past him, removed the bottle from the pan and tested the formula on her wrist.

Unable to take his eyes from her, Jack moved a little closer. The heat from the stove that emanated around him did noth-

ing to alleviate the aching he felt in his loins. "Why not hold
him? He doesn't bite. Not yet anyway."

Rebecca handed Jack the bottle of formula. "I'm not afraid
of Andy, Jack," she said tersely, even more color flowing
into her cheeks as she dropped her gaze, inadvertently sweeping the front of his pants, then lifted it back to his face. "I
just don't see any reason to get close to him."

"Why not?" Jack studied her delicately boned face as he
gave Andy his bottle. "What are you afraid of?"

Rebecca moved to the far side of the kitchen. "You," she
said in a voice barely above a whisper.

Beneath the gown, Jack could see her nipples tighten.
"Why would you be afraid of me?" he asked, as his body
tightened more in response.

Rebecca paced back and forth, her silky blond hair flying
out around her shoulders. "Because you want what you want
without any thought to the future or to the consequences."

"You're wrong about that, Rebecca. I've given the future
and the consequences a lot of thought, and it'd be a crying
shame for Andy to have to grow up without a mother, and a
real home."

Rebecca folded her arms in front of her defiantly and
whirled to face him. "That's not my problem, Jack."

"Isn't it?"

Her bare lip thrust out stubbornly. "No, it isn't."

Jack closed the distance between them in a few smooth
steps. He offered her the nursing baby. "Just hold Andy,
Rebecca, just for a moment."

She shook her head and kept her arms clamped in front of
her. "Your plan is not going to work, Jack. Andy is adorable.
But my affection for him is not going to make me fall in love
with you."

Jack studied her in growing frustration. "Why can't you
at least give us a chance?" he whispered.

"Because I have a life here, Jack, a good life, with grandparents who love me unconditionally." Her pretty jaw tight-

ened. The air between them crackled with suppressed physical energy. "I'm not going to mess that up."

Jack quirked a brow. "Your grandparents seem very understanding to me."

"Trust me." Rebecca glared at him. "They wouldn't understand about our night together in Philadelphia, and I won't hurt them that way." She brushed past him, the silkiness of her hair catching him in the face. "Now, if you'll excuse me, I'm going back to bed."

After she had gone, Jack settled in the rocking chair next to the fireplace in the living room. He sighed heavily as he looked down at the innocent baby in his arms. "Well, Andy, I guess she told us. She doesn't want us back in her life. Not that you should take this personally, you understand. It's not that Rebecca doesn't love you, or couldn't grow to love you, you understand. Just that she's afraid right now, and to be perfectly honest, so am I."

Jack paused, shifting Andy in his arms. Noting Andy was starting to get a little squirmy again, Jack sat Andy up so he could burp. While he patted Andy gently on his back, Jack continued to explain the situation. He didn't know how much of this Andy was getting, but he knew he felt better just talking about it.

"So much in my life has changed in the past few days. Prior to Alec's call last weekend, all I had in my life was my work." Andy gurgled, and Jack turned him around to face him, so they were looking at each other, man to man. He smiled fondly down at his son. "Now all I care about is finding a way to bring your mom back into our lives without causing her undue heartbreak and shame in the process."

Andy finally burped and Jack settled him back into the curve of his arms. He began giving him his bottle again. "Considering the fact that having a baby out of wedlock is still treated as a problem here, rather than the badge of honor it is in Hollywood, we've got our work cut out for us."

"WELL, ANDY, looks like we're having soup for the noon meal," Jack remarked the next day as he walked into the kitchen and found both the Lindholm women hard at work.

Ruth looked up from the chopping board. "Indeed we are. How did your visit with Cornelius Glassenheit go?"

"Fine. I learned a lot about the ninety different types of Amish buggies currently being made. Choosing a new one must be as difficult as choosing a new car."

Ruth smiled at him indulgently while Rebecca worked pointedly to ignore him. "Would you like a cup of coffee or some sugar cookies as a morning snack?"

"Thanks, but I think I'll just sit here in the rocking chair and watch how the two of you go about your daily chores, if you don't mind."

"Not at all," Ruth said, though Jack could tell at once by the tense set of Rebecca's shoulders that she minded his presence in their kitchen a lot. Ruth wiped her hands on a plain white dish towel, and looked around. "Oh, my! I forgot the carrots! I better go down in the root cellar. Rebecca, do we need anything else while I'm down there?"

Rebecca smiled at Ruth. "Not that I can see, Grandmother," she said in the soft, deferential voice she always used around her grandparents.

"I'll be right back." Ruth tossed the words over her shoulders as she hurried to the cellar stairs. Her heavy black shoes clunked as she made her way down.

Alone with Jack, Rebecca glared at him. With Andy in his arms, Jack moved closer to her, watched as she filled the old-fashioned wringer washing machine with warm sudsy water and clothes that needed laundering. Once they were in, she moved a lever back and forth to work the agitator.

"Why don't you use one of the gasoline-powered washing machines?" Jack asked. He had seen some in his visits to other Amish homes, the previous spring.

"Because it would be foolish to spend money on one when this works just fine." Rebecca leaned over the washer, rinsed the clothes one by one, using the hand crank that activated the wringer.

Jack knew this was the way the Amish did things, and part of him even admired the Amish's self-sufficiency, but another part of him, the creative part, resented it. Rebecca was a talented designer. The variety and beauty of her quilts proved that. She could be working full-time on her quilts, if she didn't spend so much time doing chores that could easily be done completely by machines.

"Will you stop that?" Rebecca hissed as she put the last of the clean clothes through the wringer.

"Stop what?" Jack asked. Aware Andy had gone to sleep, he put him in his cradle and tucked a blanket around him.

"Stop watching me," Rebecca hissed at him under her breath as she passed by Jack, a laundry basket braced on her hip.

She looked so provoked, he couldn't help but tease her. "Why, when you're so pretty?"

"I am not."

"Oh, yes you are," Jack said, and he meant it. Rebecca might be dressed plain, but the blue chambray dress with the round collar, and long sleeves, and full, fitted skirt, the black apron, did for her figure what a designer gown did for Michelle Pfeiffer. He was even beginning to like the kapp she wore on her head, though he still preferred her hair down, the way it had been last night.

Rebecca scowled at him. She put her laundry basket down, next to the back door, and then returned to the washer to start a second load of clothes. "We both know the only reason you are still here is to bother me, not to research your movie."

"You think so?"

"I know so!"

Her words should have made him feel guilty. They didn't. Maybe because Jack knew his motivations here were noble, even if Rebecca did not. He wanted to own up to his responsibilities. He wanted to do right by her and Andy. If only she would let him. "Well, it's just too bad you don't want me here," Jack whispered back as he put his hand next to hers and moved the lever back and forth to work the agitator on the washer for her. "Because I'm here to stay."

Rebecca glared at him from beneath her thick blond lashes. She removed her hand from beneath his, stepped back slightly and smiled up at him sweetly. "I'm sure you'll give up eventually and go away."

Jack held her stormy blue gaze. "Don't count on it." He was rewarded with another glare, followed swiftly with the sound of footsteps on the stairs. Ruth came up, three large carrots in her hand. "Think this'll be enough?" she asked Rebecca.

"Plenty." Rebecca smiled at her grandmother as she went to retrieve another clothes basket.

"I want to hear more about this story you are writing, Mr. Rourke," Ruth said. "You said last night it was about a Robert and Jill—"

Jack smiled as Rebecca returned with an empty basket and set it down beside the washer. "Romeo and Juliet."

"Yes." Ruth nodded encouragingly, then frowned her dismay. "I did not understand that remark."

Noting the clothes were clean, Jack began transferring them to the adjacent rinse water, one at a time. "Romeo and Juliet was a play by Shakespeare. It was written a long time ago and is very famous. In it, two young people fall in love, but their families don't approve of the match and they come to a tragic end."

"Oh, dear. I hope your story does not come to a tragic end."

Jack slanted a glance at Rebecca who was taking the clothes he was rinsing, and putting them through the wringer. "Not if I can help it."

"Is your story set in modern times?" Ruth asked as she peeled the carrots with slow, arthritic movements of her hands.

"No." Jack shook his head as Rebecca left his side and disappeared into the pantry. "It's a turn-of-the century historical romance about the love between an English con man on the run and an Amish girl.''

"You know a lot about con men?'' Rebecca asked, innocently enough, as she emerged from the pantry, a big bag of wooden clothespins in her hand.

Jack finished the rinsing and put the last of the clean clothes in the laundry basket, just as Rebecca had done before, with the first load of laundered clothes. He straightened slowly. "Not so much, really. But I've got a lively imagination and I can see how a people that were so pure of heart could be taken in by someone not so pure,'' he said. Finished with the laundering, he dried his hands and rolled down the sleeves of his burgundy corduroy shirt.

Rebecca stomped to the door and reached for her black wool winter cloak. "We Amish are pure of heart, not naive.''

Jack followed her to the coatrack and shrugged on his leather jacket. "I never said you were naive, Rebecca,'' he corrected softly. He helped her on with her cloak, his hand brushing her slender shoulder inadvertently. "Still, I can readily see the inherent problems in an English-Amish romance and how falling in love with an Amish woman would change a man forever.''

Her cheeks flushed, Rebecca shrugged away from him and bent to pick up a load of the wet clothes. Jack started to follow her, then stopped. It bothered him to see Ruth struggling with the soup on a day when the arthritis in her hands was clearly acting up, just as it bothered him to see Rebecca washing clothes in a wringer washing machine. He turned to Ruth.

"You know, I have a food processor, an electric cutting devise that swiftly grates cheese and slices vegetables, that could do all that in three minutes.'' Jack paused, not wanting to offend, yet needing to ask. "Doesn't it ever bother you, knowing your life could be a lot easier than it is? That you could do things faster, without so much labor?''

"Not really.'' Ruth shrugged and offered an accepting smile. "But then, I've never lived any other way than this.''

She looked at her granddaughter sympathetically. "I know it's different for Rebecca, since she lived English until she was ten."

Jack looked at Rebecca, who was suddenly not looking at him. "I'm going to take these clothes out and hang them on the line to dry," she said, and slipped out the door.

Jack looked at Ruth. "If you'll keep an eye on Andy for me, I'll give Rebecca a hand."

"Of course I will." Ruth smiled at Jack.

Jack picked up the other basket of damp clothes and went out to join Rebecca at the clothesline that ran across the yard at the rear of the Lindholm home. The day was sunny, and unseasonably warm for February, the temperature almost up in the forties. "I can do this by myself," Rebecca said stiffly.

"I insist." Aware his heart was pounding, Jack asked, "Why didn't you ever tell me you lived English until you were ten?"

Rebecca shrugged and kept her glance averted. "You never asked."

"You knew I assumed differently." His anger, already simmering, began to boil. He didn't understand how Rebecca could give so much of herself, physically, to him, and so little, emotionally. For him, the two things had always gone hand in hand.

Rebecca didn't so much as blink in the face of his anger. "So?"

"So," Jack explained, working hard to contain his feelings of betrayal and hurt, "all along I've been thinking that you would have to live a whole new life in order to be with me and Andy, only to find out it's not such a sacrifice for you at all. That you've already lived a great part of your life as an English person!"

She grabbed him by the front of his jacket and pulled him farther back into the rows of freshly hung clothes, so they were concealed from sight. "Look, Jack," she whispered fervently, her fear of discovery obvious, "I never said I didn't feel half English. You just *assumed* my parents died when I was very young, because no one said otherwise when the subject was brought up briefly at the dinner table last night. You just assumed that I had no memories of living English, that I only recalled living Amish. But that's not true, okay? I do remember a lot of things, like…going to the mall to get a new dress, talking on the phone to my other third-grade friends, having a dishwasher and a washing machine and everything else that goes with that kind of life!'' That said, she started to let go of his shirt.

He caught her hand with his, and held it, inside the front of his jacket against his chest. Now that she had finally started to open up to him a little, he wasn't going to let her just run off.

''It must have been hard for you, losing your parents and having to make such a drastic life-style change all in one fell swoop,'' he said softly, his heart going out to her and all she had been through as a child.

Rebecca swallowed, looking briefly undone by the compassion she heard in his voice and saw in his eyes. ''Yes,'' she admitted to Jack. ''It was hard, at first. Very hard. But my grandparents loved me and were very understanding of how difficult it was for me to have to live without hot running water and so forth after always just having it, and so given time…I adapted.''

''Why didn't you tell me that last night?'' Jack asked, hurt that she hadn't found some way to work at least a little of that information into their conversation.

''Because I didn't want to discuss it, that's why, and certainly not at the dinner table, when my grandparents might take something I said about the frustrations I feel sometimes about Amish life the wrong way and get their feelings hurt.'' Rebecca tugged on her hand, reeling back slightly when Jack let her go. ''Besides, I learned a long time ago that people think what they want to think. And it's not up to me to correct any misconceptions you might have about me, Jack!''

Jack held the clothespins for her while she resumed hanging up the clothes. He studied her. Part of him was very glad the gloves were off, and they were speaking with gut-wrenching honesty at long last. "That's not why you didn't tell me," he drawled.

Looking slightly flustered, as if having him stand directly next to her damp underclothes embarrassed her, Rebecca planted both her hands on her slender hips and challenged, "Then why didn't I tell you?"

That was easy, Jack thought. "Because you didn't want me to know how much more we had in common than I initially thought," he said.

Rebecca picked up a pair of Eli's black trousers. "We have nothing in common," she seethed.

Jack reached around her deliberately to apply the clothespins this time, trapping her deliberately between his body and the wet clothes. "Says who?"

Rebecca ducked beneath his outstretched arm, the soft swell of her breasts bumping his arm in the process. "Says me!"

It was all Jack could do at that point not to drag her into his arms and give her some of the tender loving care Rebecca was so sure that she did not need from him. "What about our baby?"

Rebecca whirled on him so suddenly her kapp fell halfway off her head. Flustered, but no less angry with him, she reached up to catch it with one hand. "I don't care what kind of mess you've gotten yourself in, Jack Rourke, I am not going to take responsibility for that child, and that's final!"

Jack could understand her walking away from him last spring. After all, they'd been strangers who had just met, from different parts of the country. They'd had completely different life-styles. But the baby they'd made changed everything. They had a responsibility here. To his continuing disappointment, she refused to see it. "If that's the case," he said in a low accusing voice, "then you really are a heartless wench!"

Her temper exploding, she lifted her hand to strike his face. Jack caught her hand before it could connect with his skin.

Exerting pressure, he forced it down between them. Her display of passion was more encouraging than she knew, he thought in silent triumph. "Maybe you're more English than you think, Rebecca," he taunted softly, determined to get her to admit her feelings. He tightened his grip on the silky soft skin of her wrist as she started to struggle. "A real Amish woman would never strike anyone, no matter what they said or did."

Rebecca stilled and regarded him coolly. The ice maiden again. "You would try the patience of a saint, Jack Rourke, and I am no saint," she said quietly.

Jack's frustration with her mounted. His lips curled bitterly. "How well I know that."

Rebecca stepped on his foot, deliberately. "I want you out of here!" she said.

Jack accepted the punishing weight of her foot with stoic grace. "And I told you before, I'm not leaving, not until you own up to your responsibilities," he countered, then ever so slowly, ever so reluctantly, let her go.

For a second, all was still between them. Jack felt the winter sunshine beating down on his head. He heard the soothing sounds of the country…the gentle neigh of a horse, the flapping wings of the chickens in the barnyard, the slow, gentle whir of the windmill next to the barn.

He could see the pulse beating madly in her throat. See the fear and the desire and yes, even the pain and the loss, in her light blue eyes.

For another long moment, Rebecca continued to stare at him grimly. Wordlessly she spun around on her heel, picked up the empty laundry basket and marched into the house. Jack picked up the other basket and followed behind her. Whether Rebecca wanted to admit it or not, he had gotten to her this morning. And that was the first step.

Chapter Six

"Don't forget the soup for Mrs. Yoder," Rebecca said, following her grandmother and grandfather to the door, a quart jar brimming with homemade vegetable soup in her hand.

"We'll be back before dark," Eli promised as he added the soup to the basket of home-cooked food Ruth had already packed.

"I'll have supper ready and waiting," Rebecca said. "Jack can help me see to feeding the animals. And tell Mrs. Yoder I hope she is feeling better soon."

"With your grandmother's homemade soup, who wouldn't be?" Eli teased. His hand on her grandmother's shoulder, he escorted Ruth out the door.

Rebecca turned to see Jack leaning over Andy. He had just taken off one disposable diaper and put on another. She watched as he quickly snapped Andy back up into a clean warm sleeper. Unlike most of the Englishmen she had met, Jack was a man who was very comfortable around babies. It seemed there was nothing he didn't know how to do. She admired that about him, just as she admired the kind, respectful way he treated her grandparents.

Jack lifted Andy out of the bassinet and held him against his broad chest. Watching Andy bounce his tiny fist off the muscular chest, Rebecca felt a thrill of desire surge through her, and center in the most womanly part of her. Although she had tried to forget, she could still recall all too well what it was like to be held against that hard male body of his. He not only knew how to love and care for a baby, but he also knew how to love and care for a woman, too. And that made it doubly hard for her to turn away from him, but turn away she must.

"You know we could wash diapers for Andy while you're here, if you like," she said inanely as she went hurriedly back into the kitchen.

Jack followed her lazily, Andy still in his arms. He didn't stop until he was close enough for her to smell the spicy scent of his after-shave, or notice how closely he had shaved. He grinned laconically, his dark blue gaze drifting down to her mouth before returning to her eyes with determined male intent. "I don't figure on being here all that long," he said softly.

Rebecca's breath hitched. Needing something to do—anything was better than being mesmerized by Jack's sensuality—she filled the teakettle and put it on the back burner. Her back to him, she repressed the hurt the thought of him leaving brought and remarked casually, "I thought you were staying until I agreed to be Andy's mother."

Jack followed her as she moved restlessly over to the tea canister. "I don't figure that will take all that long, either," he said softly.

He was standing so close to her, she could feel the heat and tension in his tall, strong body. She whirled to face him. Her back against the counter, she stared up into his face with unmitigated frustration. "Then you figure wrong," she said flatly.

Jack transferred Andy to his other shoulder. "Do I now?" he asked, the challenge in his low tone unmistakable. Rebecca's heart raced. Their eyes held.

"My growing affection for Andy has nothing to do with what's going on here, Jack."

"Doesn't it?"

Rebecca looked into Jack's dark blue eyes and felt herself begin to tremble. She knew she wanted him to kiss her again and knew he wanted that, too. Swallowing hard, she looked away. Andy gurgled, muttered something unintelligible, and made a clumsy grab for the collar on Jack's corduroy shirt.

Jack tore his eyes from hers and beamed like a father whose child had just won the Nobel prize. "Hey, did you hear that?" he said. "Andy just said a word."

Rebecca measured tea into the china teapot. "He did not."

"He did, too. Say it again, Andy. Say 'play' for Rebecca. Come on, be a sport for daddy and say 'play…play…'"

Andy beamed a toothless grin up at Jack and mumbled something that did sound a little like play after all, Rebecca noted with equal parts admiration and exasperation. "See?" Jack crowed triumphantly. "He said it again. He's a genius!"

Not wanting Jack to get too carried away and give the baby a swelled head before he was even out of diapers, Rebecca lifted her eyes heavenward. "You have some imagination, Jack."

Jack put Andy down in his infant seat, strapped him in and then closed his hands around an infant-sized rubber rattle. "My imagination, hmm?" He put the infant seat on the center of the big kitchen table, so Andy had a good view of the kitchen, then sauntered toward Rebecca.

He took her by the shoulders and held her in front of him when she would have bolted. "I'll tell you one thing I didn't imagine, Rebecca," he said in a low soft voice that sent shivers of awareness coursing through her at a madcap rate. "I didn't imagine the chemistry between us or what happened that night last April…"

Another thrill went through her, this one more potent than the last. She had known when Jack showed up in Blair County that there was going to be trouble. And that feeling had been confirmed the moment she had looked into his boyishly handsome face. "Jack, please—"

Jack's palms slid down her arms, past her wrists. He captured her hands in his and linked fingers with her in a very intimate way. "Who's going to hear us, Rebecca?" he taunted her softly. "Your grandparents are gone. Andy can't exactly tell anyone what we're saying, even if he did give a hoot, and—'' Jack cast a look over his shoulder at Andy, who was busily inspecting the rattle in his hand ''—I don't think he does.''

Rebecca drew a shuddering breath and, gathering all her courage, lifted her face to his. ''You're talking nonsense, Jack,'' she reprimanded sternly.

His dark blue eyes only darkened more as he took her into his arms and held her against him. ''Our feelings for each other aren't nonsense, Rebecca,'' he said, taking off her kapp and tugging down her braids. He sifted his fingers through her hair, freeing it in exactly the same way he had the night they'd first met and made love. He gazed down at her tenderly. ''We both know we felt something special that first night we met,'' he whispered fervently, lowering his mouth to hers, kissing her sweetly, lingeringly. ''We still feel that way, whether you admit it or not.''

Her lips tingling, her senses awash in sensation, Rebecca pushed him away. She couldn't, wouldn't, let herself dwell on the rightness of his body pressed up against hers. ''No, Jack,'' she said breathlessly, recalling the easy way he had let her go…until he erroneously thought he had a child with her. ''We don't.''

But Jack was not to be dissuaded. ''Don't we?'' he countered softly, pulling her close again, so close that their bodies fit together like pieces of a puzzle, hardness to softness, maleness to femaleness. He threaded his fingers through the hair at her nape, and forced her head up to his. ''Then tell me why it feels so good when we kiss.''

He touched her face with the back of his hand, caressing her from the uppermost curve of her cheekbone to her chin. He rubbed his thumb across her lower lip, stared deep into her light blue eyes. ''Do you know I still remember the way you felt against me that night, all soft and warm and giving? And I think about the way you looked when you were in my bed.'' His hand glided down her throat, over her collarbone, to the uppermost curve of her breasts. "How the sheet draped your soft, womanly curves—"

Rebecca's breasts tightened into aching pinpoints of pleasure. "Stop it!" She pushed away from him.

He moved in behind her, wrapping his arms around her waist, clamping his palms together at her navel. Her buttocks were nestled in the hard curve of his hips. Lower still, she could feel the swelling evidence of his desire. There was no denying he wanted her as much as she wanted him.

"You were naked that night, Rebecca," Jack whispered, trailing his lips through the softness of her hair. She turned her head sharply to the side. His lips trailed lower, to the exposed slope of her neck. One hand stayed locked around her waist. The other moved up, inside the black cotton apron, to cup the swell of her breast through her sensible blue dress. Her nipple hardened even more.

"Wonderfully naked and you let me carry you up to my bed and take all your clothes off and make wild passionate love to you." Without warning, he turned her swiftly around to face him. "And no amount of denying it on your part is going to make those memories go away."

She shoved away from him, hard, her whole body throbbing. "That night was a mistake!"

"Was it?"

Rebecca was saved from having to answer that by the whistling of the teakettle. Her shoulders stiff, she marched to the stove, slipped on a quilted oven mitt and carried the kettle to the counter. There, she added steaming water to the teapot, and put on the lid to let it steep.

Jack waited until she had finished. The moment she had, he came up behind her again, wrapped his arms around her waist and kissed his way down her neck. "Don't run away from me, Rebecca," he urged softly, his hands sweeping down her hips, over her thighs and back up again, to the most womanly part of her.

Rebecca twisted in his arms, afraid if he touched her there

she really would be lost. She wedged her arms between them, for protection. "I have to."

"No, you don't." He looked down at her, his expression brimming with tenderness and passion. "I can take care of you," he whispered fervently. "We can be together, you and me and our baby."

"For the last time, Jack, Andy is not my baby!"

"What are you telling me?" he asked, his voice clipped.

It hurt Rebecca to say the words, but she knew they had to be said. Jack had to start facing the truth. "I'm saying," she said flatly, "that baby belongs to you and another one of your women. Not me."

"If Andy doesn't belong with you, then he doesn't belong with either of us, Rebecca."

"How do you know that?"

"Because there hasn't been anyone else in my bed, Rebecca. Not for a long time."

Rebecca wanted to believe that. But the facts said otherwise. Someone had left Jack that baby, telling him to own up to his mistakes. Jack's willingness to assume responsibility for his son, the easy way Andy and Jack had bonded further substantiated the claim. If it were true, it meant Jack had been with another woman, in roughly the same time frame he had been with her. And that hurt. Still, curiosity made her want to listen to his defense. "Why not?" she asked tersely.

Jack shrugged. "It doesn't matter." He bit out the words, his expression closed and unreadable.

Rebecca busied herself getting down the plain white teacups and saucers. "I think it does."

Jack's jaw turned rigid. "You want to know my romantic history, is that it?"

"It seems to me you've certainly done enough prying into my life."

Silence fell between them. Not caring if the tea was properly steeped or not, Rebecca sloshed some in two cups and carried them to the table. Jack followed her. Seeing she wasn't about to give up on her quest for information, he turned a chair around backward, sat down opposite her and hooked his arms over the back of it. "Okay, there's never been anyone serious in my life."

Rebecca sat primly in her chair and folded her hands on her lap. As the silence strung out between them, she sized him up quietly. "Why not?" she asked in a tight, clipped voice. She picked up her tea and sipped. It was very hot and too weak.

"Because it was just never right, that's why," Jack said gruffly, looking her in the eye. "There was always something missing and I knew it. I felt it in here." He palmed his chest emphatically.

Rebecca took another sip. She knew he meant the words to comfort her. But in truth, they did just the opposite, because they told her a reality she had been dreading, that Jack was the type of man who drifted from one highly romantic affair to another. No doubt he moved on as soon as the passion faded. "Then you must also feel that I am no different from the others," she retorted simply, testing his devotion.

Jack released a quick, impatient breath. "Wrong, Rebecca," he said shortly. "You are different."

"Why? Because I'm Amish?" The bitter words just slipped out.

"Because you're you."

Her face burned. Her eyes were hot and dry. Inside, she just felt empty, scared and afraid. Afraid because she knew how easy it would be for her to drift into a dead-end love affair with Jack. Besides, what kind of relationship could they have if he wouldn't trust her? How could she possibly get involved with a man who wouldn't believe her when she told him Andy was not her child?

Finally she shook her head.

She knew Jack was trying to be honest with her. That didn't, however, mean he had a good grasp of the cold, hard reality of their situation, or could separate what he wanted to be from what really was. "You say all the right words, Jack," she said with a certain weary resignation. "That is probably what makes you such a successful writer."

Jack's jaw tightened. For a moment, he looked as hurt and upset as she felt. "You don't believe that I could make you happy over the long haul, do you?" Jack asked bitterly.

What could she say? There was no point in denying her reservations. No point in pretending that Jack's temporary dream could ever be a lifelong reality. Not when the only reason he had even come to her was the baby, and the baby wasn't hers. She looked him straight in the eye. "No, Jack," she said simply, "I don't."

Because if he had felt they had something even half as special as he claimed, he wouldn't have let almost a whole year go by without contacting her again.

HE SHOULD HAVE KNOWN it would happen this way, Jack thought as he fed the chickens and gathered the eggs. All the time he was growing up in Philadelphia's seamy inner city, struggling to find a way to survive, a way out, there'd been no one who had ever believed in him. He'd said he was getting out of there one day, and taking his mother—who'd worked two minimum wage jobs just to keep their heads above water—with him. His friends had laughed. His mother had wanted to believe it, but still doubted his dreams could ever come true, and that, too, had hurt.

He'd said he was going to college. His friends had laughed again. And kept right on laughing, even as he got a scholarship to one of the state's most prestigious prep schools, and gone on from there to Penn. The Ivy League university hadn't proved much easier on him, despite the support of his two best friends, Grady and Alec. Yet he'd kept going, knowing one day he would make it. He'd attended UCLA grad school. From there, had gone on to work as a junior screenwriter for one of the major studios.

Those first few years as a paid writer had been very lean indeed. For every one person who had encouraged him, there'd been ten who had told him he'd be better off selling real estate or hawking used cars than trying to make it as a writer. But he'd persisted, and eventually he made it. He'd managed to move his mother into her dream home before her death. So how had it come to this? he wondered in frustration. How had he come to be here, chasing a woman who wouldn't even admit she'd had his baby?

"Need a hand there, son?" Eli asked as Jack shut up the chicken coop and walked out.

"Thanks, Eli, but I think I'm finished here," Jack said.

"The cows—?"

"And horses have all been fed, watered and brought in for the night."

"Good job."

"Thanks."

Eli fell into step beside Jack as they headed toward the house. "Rebecca's in a mood," he said.

"Yeah." Jack sighed. "I know."

"What happened?"

Jack shrugged. What could he tell Eli? That he had tried to put the moves on Rebecca, in order to prove to her that she not only had feelings for him but still harbored a remarkable, once-in-a-lifetime-kind-of-passion for him, too, and she'd resisted? That he'd tried to talk to her, and she'd stymied his efforts there, too? None of that could be said. And yet Jack respected Eli enough to want to tell him the truth, or at least what he could of it. "She doesn't want me here," Jack admitted, finally. "I think I ask too many questions."

Eli grinned and stroked the snowy white beard that covered his cheeks and chin but not his upper lip. "It is true, Rebecca does not like questions."

Jack paused on the back steps leading into the house. "She's always been like that?"

Eli nodded and turned his collar up against the cold. "Rebecca is a very private person."

So Jack had noticed. "Is she able to talk to you and Ruth, at least?"

"Sometimes." Eli frowned. He stepped inside the back porch, noted the woodpile was getting low and motioned Jack back out again. Jack paused long enough to set the eggs inside the back door, then followed Eli back out again.

"We wish it were all the time," Eli continued as he headed toward the woodpile at the other end of the farmyard. "But...sometimes she has spells where she needs to be independent of others."

"Like when she went to Florida?" Jack said, hoping to learn more about this marriage of Rebecca's, and when and exactly how it had ended.

"And last year," Eli affirmed with a nod as he picked up a piece of kindling that needed to be split and set it on the stump, "when she went to Indiana. She never told either her grandmother or me what was wrong but we knew something was bothering her."

"How did she look when she came back?" Jack asked casually as he reached for the ax. Stepping up to the stump, he split the first log, then picked up the pieces and handed them to Eli.

Eli shrugged as he cradled the kindling in his arms. "Better. Healthier. Like she was eating again."

Again, Jack's heartbeat sped up as he thought about the first symptoms of pregnancy. Skipped periods. Moodiness and lethargy. Morning sickness. "She wasn't eating last summer?" Jack asked as he selected another piece of wood to split into stove-size sections.

"Not much. She said her appetite was gone. We were worried, so we made her see the doctor in town."

Jack had to struggle to keep his soaring emotions in check. He was irritated, because Rebecca had almost, *almost* had him believing Andy wasn't her baby. And he was concerned that she had felt she'd had to go through her unexpected pregnancy alone. "What did the doctor say?" Jack asked casually.

"He suggested a change of pace for her."

Nice and vague, Jack thought. Probably at Rebecca's request. "Did he tell you that?" Jack asked.

"No. Just Rebecca. And I begin to see why you might have irritated my granddaughter, Jack Rourke," Eli said with a censuring grin. "You do ask far too many questions."

"Sorry." Jack struggled to keep his emotions in check. "It's just…" He paused again, wanting to be as truthful with Eli as he could. "Rebecca's such a mystery to me."

Eli nodded. "Rebecca is a mystery to all of us sometimes, but that is her right, Jack. It is her way."

"You're right, of course," Jack said. There were some things that were private. He understood Rebecca's wanting to keep an unplanned pregnancy to herself. He was just sorry Rebecca had felt she couldn't come to him.

Eli continued to study him. "You wish she were more talkative about herself, don't you?" Eli prodded.

Jack gave Eli a veiled glance, then went back to splitting kindling. "I wish she felt she could trust me." *I wish she would allow me to own up to my mistakes and make a home for her and our child.*

"Perhaps she will," Eli said, "in time." He held out a hand to Jack, signaling they had split enough wood to keep the stove going for the rest of the night. Jack put down the ax.

Jack picked up his own armful of wood. "I hope she does open up and talk to me about her life here," he said. *I really hope so.* Because if she didn't, he would never get her to leave Pennsylvania with him. They would never have a chance at any kind of future, even as friends. And the thought of that was almost more than he could bear.

Chapter Seven

"Hey, did you see that? Andy reached for his rattle and picked it up all by himself!" Jack said. Excited, he called the others over to the infant seat. They all gathered around to watch just as Andy whacked himself in the nose and let out a startled, hiccuping cry.

"Whoops. Sorry, buddy." Jack picked him up and cradled him close, looking every bit the devoted father—to Rebecca's continuing dismay.

"What he needs is something soft," Ruth said, patting Andy gently on the head.

"Like a stuffed animal?" Jack asked.

"Or an Amish doll." Ruth turned to Rebecca with a smile. In a panic—she already felt far too involved with Jack and his problems as it was—Rebecca tried to ward off her grandmother's next words with a glance. To no avail. "Why don't you make Andy one?" Ruth asked.

Because that is a motherly thing to do, Rebecca thought, *and I am not Andy's mother.* But, unable to say that for the questions it would prompt, she suggested brightly, "I could, of course, but it'd be faster to buy one in town."

Eli frowned his disapproval. "Since when do we buy what we can make ourselves? Besides, those dolls are for tourists. Jack and Andy are our friends."

Rebecca was amazed at the speed Jack had ingratiated himself with her grandparents.

"Normally Amish dolls are made for a child by his or her mother, aren't they?" Jack asked, with a pointed look at Rebecca.

Her heart pounding, not so much in fear he'd give their love affair away, but fear he would try to pick it up again, Rebecca nodded. "Yes," she said tightly, and went back to finishing the supper dishes, "they are."

Ruth held out her arms to Andy. The baby smiled at her and went willingly into her soft arms. "But in the case of a child who has no mother, a friend or relative would step in to do it," Ruth continued, smoothing Andy's downy soft hair, which, Jack had noted, seemed to be getting lighter every day now. "I'd sew one myself but my fingers aren't as nimble with a needle as they used to be."

Rebecca hung up her dish towel. Clearly Jack was not going to give up on this. Besides, they still had a long evening ahead of them...several hours, and this would help her fill up the time. "I'll do it," Rebecca said. "In fact, I'll get started on it right away."

Rebecca went upstairs to her bedroom and knelt at the chest at the foot of the bed where she stored the scraps of clothing and bolts of fabric she used for her quilts. She quickly picked out scraps of dark blue, black and cream fabric. Jack came in behind her and admired the quilt in progress on her frame. "This what you're working on now?" he asked gently. Pale blue diamonds radiated outward from the center, in ever-escalating sizes. Within each diamond, there were collages of many colors, braided over and through one another in what at first glance seemed a random design, but on closer observation, was instead a very well-planned, very complex pattern.

"It's beautiful. What's the pattern called?"

Rebecca didn't want his praise any more than she wanted his company. But figuring it was to her advantage to keep him talking on something less personal than the two of them, she said, "It's called a Log Cabin, Barn Raising Design, and I learned it while I was in Indiana."

"Right. Last summer," Jack said.

A chill slid down her spine. Rebecca closed the top of her cedar chest, but remained where she was, kneeling on the floor in front of it. She had an idea where this conversation was going. "We've already talked about this, Jack," she warned.

"Yes, but I didn't know then what I know now." Jack knelt next to her. He put the fabric she had just taken out aside and took her limp, lifeless hands in his. "Eli told me you were moody and upset when you left for Indiana, but that you wouldn't talk about what was bothering you."

"That's right, Jack, I couldn't," Rebecca whispered unhappily. "Not without revealing what I'd done...how I'd gotten involved with you. They wouldn't have understood, Jack."

Jack clasped her hands gently. "Are you sure about that, Rebecca? Ruth and Eli seem very understanding to me."

"Somehow I just can't envision them approving of my having a tryst with a man who picked me up on the side of the road."

"How about forgive, then?"

She wrested her hands from his and rose jerkily to her feet. "You've got to stop this, Jack."

"Stop what?"

"Fantasizing. Pretending everything will go your way just because you want it to!"

He was silent, studying the heightened color in her cheeks, and the ever-escalating panic in her eyes. Rebecca could see he had already made his mind up about what had happened. "Then why did you go, if not to have the baby?" he asked curtly, careful to keep his voice low. "Why were you in a mood? Why did you lose your appetite? Why did you go to the doctor in town before you left?"

Rebecca glanced past him, to the open door, to see if anyone was within earshot. Seeing no one, hearing nothing, she turned back to Jack, stood on tiptoe and whispered, "I went to the doctor in town because my grandparents made me go. And I went to Indiana because I needed to get away."

"To have my baby?"

"No! To get my thoughts straight!" Frustration bubbled up within her. Her hands in fists, she leaned closer and hissed, "I was confused!"

"Why?"

Rebecca whirled and went to the window. She stood looking out at the farm she had grown to love. A farm that was more home to her than any other place on earth, a farm Jack would have her leave. Aware he had followed her and was now standing just behind her, Rebecca spoke in a monotone without turning around. "It bothered me, what we'd…done. I—I'm not like that, Jack. I don't do things like that. I didn't know why I'd responded the way I did. I needed time to think about it." She turned around to face him, her back to the windowpane. "So it wouldn't happen again."

He was silent, staring down at her. She knew she had done nothing to convince him that she hadn't had his baby during her self-imposed exile in Indiana, but she also knew that if they dallied any longer someone would come looking for them. "I've got to go downstairs."

He put a hand on her arm. "Eli sent me up to look for the checkers. He's challenged me to a match."

"Oh. They're in the next room, I think." Rebecca led the way to the bedroom next to hers. She opened the closet door. She could see the checkers but couldn't reach them. Wordlessly Jack got them down for her.

"Where's Andy?" Rebecca went back to her room for the fabric and her sewing kit.

"With Eli and Ruth." Jack paused. "I've never seen two people who appreciate children more."

"All Amish do."

He stopped her as she started to brush past him. "Hey, thanks for making the doll. I'm sure he's going to love it."

Rebecca refused to let him read anything into her actions. He was imagining far too much as it was. "We'll see."

GET 2 BOOKS FREE!

MIRA

To get your 2 free books, affix this peel-off sticker to the reply card and mail it today!

MIRA® Books, The Brightest Stars in Fiction, presents

The Best of the Best™

Superb collector's editions of the very best books by some of today's best-known authors!

GET 2

HOW TO GET YOUR
2 FREE BOOKS AND FREE GIFT!

1. Peel off the MIRA® sticker on the front cover. Place it in the space provided at right. This automatically entitles you to receive two free books and an exciting surprise gift.

2. Send back this card and you'll get 2 "The Best of the Best™" books. These books have a combined cover price of $11.98 or more in the U.S. and $13.98 or more in Canada, but they are yours to keep absolutely FREE!

3. There's no catch. You're under no obligation to buy anything. We charge nothing – ZERO – for your first shipment. And you don't have to make any minimum number of purchases – not even one!

4. We call this line "The Best of the Best" because each month you'll receive the best books by some of today's most popular authors. These authors show up time and time again on all the major bestseller lists and their books sell out as soon as they hit the stores. You'll like the convenience of getting them delivered to your home at our special discount prices . . . and you'll love your *Heart to Heart* subscriber newsletter featuring author news, horoscopes, recipes, book reviews and much more!

SPECIAL FREE GIFT!
We'll send you a fabulous surprise gift, absolutely FREE, simply for accepting our no-risk offer!

5. We hope that after receiving your free books you'll want to remain a subscriber. But the choice is yours – to continue or cancel, anytime at all! So why not take us up on our invitation, with no risk of any kind. You'll be glad you did!

6. And remember...we'll send you a surprise gift ABSOLUTELY FREE just for giving THE BEST OF THE BEST a try.

Visit us online at
www.mirabooks.com

® and TM are registered trademarks of Harlequin Enterprises Limited.

BOOKS FREE!

Hurry!

Return this card promptly to GET 2 FREE BOOKS & A FREE GIFT!

Affix
peel-off
MIRA
sticker here

YES! Please send me the 2 FREE "The Best of the Best" books and FREE gift for which I qualify. I understand that I am under no obligation to purchase anything further, as explained on the back and on the opposite page.

385 MDL DRTA   185 MDL DR59

FIRST NAME

LAST NAME

ADDRESS

APT.#

CITY

STATE/PROV.

ZIP/POSTAL CODE

Offer limited to one per household and not valid to current subscribers of MIRA or "The Best of the Best." All orders subject to approval. Books received may vary.

▼ DETACH AND MAIL CARD TODAY! ▼

THE BEST OF THE BEST™ — Here's How it Works:

Accepting your 2 free books and gift places you under no obligation to buy anything. You may keep the books and gift and return the shipping statement marked "cancel." If you do not cancel, about a month later we will send you 4 additional books and bill you just $4.74 each in the U.S., or $5.24 each in Canada, plus 25¢ shipping & handling per book and applicable taxes if ^ny.* That's the complete price and — compared to cover prices starting from $5.99 each in the U.S. and $6.99 each in Canada — it's quite a bargain! You may cancel at any time, but if you choose to continue, every month we'll send you 4 more books, which you may either purchase at the discount price or return to us and cancel your subscription.

*Terms and prices subject to change without notice. Sales tax applicable in N.Y. Canadian residents will be charged applicable provincial taxes and GST. Credit or Debit balances in a customer's account(s) may be offset by any other outstanding balance owed by or to the customer.

If offer card is missing write to: The Best of the Best, 3010 Walden Ave., P.O. Box 1867, Buffalo, NY 14240-1867

BUSINESS REPLY MAIL

FIRST-CLASS MAIL   PERMIT NO. 717-003   BUFFALO, NY

POSTAGE WILL BE PAID BY ADDRESSEE

THE BEST OF THE BEST
3010 WALDEN AVE
PO BOX 1867
BUFFALO NY 14240-9952

NO POSTAGE
NECESSARY
IF MAILED
IN THE
UNITED STATES

"LOOK, ANDY, Rebecca made you a doll," Jack said an hour and a half later. Tired from their long day of work and visiting, the older couple had gone to bed at nine-thirty. Rebecca had stayed up to finish the doll and help Jack see to Andy's 10:00 p.m. feeding. Although Jack protested otherwise, she still had a feeling he wasn't comfortable cooking on the wood stove. "Isn't it neat?" Jack said.

Rebecca watched in dismay as Andy stared at the faceless Amish doll she had made disinterestedly, then shoved it away with a spastic movement of his arm and turned back to his duck-shaped blue plastic rattle.

"Andy?" Jack shook the doll back and forth, but Andy paid no attention to the replica of a little boy in a blue shirt and black pants and suspenders.

Rebecca closed the lid on her sewing basket. Her spirits, which had already been low, plummeted even further. Her grandfather was right: she was in a mood. And it was all due to Jack and the pressure he continued to exert on her. And now Andy as well.

Rebecca touched Jack's arm, took the doll and put it aside. "Let him go after the rattle, Jack. He obviously prefers it."

I can't even make a doll to please an English infant, Rebecca thought tiredly. What chance would she ever have of pleasing a thoroughly English husband like Jack in the long term? He was enamored of her now, yes, but she knew all too well how that would change once marriage vows were said and he tried to settle into a normal married life with someone like her. He would swiftly tire of her outdated Amish ways, and at the same time, she wouldn't be English enough to suit him, either.

"I'm sorry Andy hurt your feelings."

"He's just an infant. How could he possibly hurt my feelings?" Rebecca retorted.

If she was upset, and she admitted she was, it was because, being around Jack every day, she couldn't help but fantasize about what it would be like to *really* be the mother of his child. After all, it was clear Jack would make a wonderful father, and perhaps one day a wonderful husband as well. And she knew it was dangerous to be thinking this way when she wasn't Andy's mother, and never would be.

What would happen when Jack finally realized that? Rebecca wondered sorrowfully. Would he leave Pennsylvania again, without her? Or would he ask her to go back to California with him anyway so they could marry and make babies of their own? And if Jack did…was she up to that? Did she really want to leave her family again?

"Andy could upset you," Jack explained carefully, "by rejecting the doll you made for him."

Rebecca shrugged. She had accused Jack of fantasizing too much, but she was now doing it, too. "Face it, Jack, your son likes things that are shiny and plastic, not soft and cuddly."

Jack thrust his hands into the pockets of his jeans and studied her in silence. "Is that what happened before? Andy rejected you? Is that why you gave him up?"

Rebecca flushed as she went to heat the bottle for Andy. "Give it a rest, Jack."

He lounged against the kitchen counter, his arms folded in front of him. "Not until you tell me the truth."

This was like trying to move a boulder with a sewing needle. "I have told you the truth!" Rebecca protested.

Jack quirked a disbelieving brow. "All of it?"

Guilt flooded Rebecca without warning as she thought about her marriage. Jack still thought she was a widow. She'd done nothing to correct that mistaken assumption because she didn't want him to know about the terrible humiliation she'd suffered by getting involved with another Englishman. "Look, you can handle the bottle for Andy. I'm going upstairs now."

He caught her arm just above the elbow, as if they were square dancing, and swiftly reeled her in. Her full skirts swirling around her legs, she collided with the hardness of his chest. His body was just as immovable as his will. Even through the layers of clothing, she felt the beginnings of his desire, and the fire storm of passion it created in turn.

"Don't walk away, Rebecca. Not from me, and not from your son."

He lowered his head and his mouth connected with hers. It started out as a simple kiss, just the sweet steady pressure of his lips against hers. But that was all it took for her to recall the predatory claim of his hands, the gentle possession of his lips and tongue. Her lips parted and she sighed as he deepened the kiss with masterful strokes of his tongue. She was surrounded with the warm male scent of him, seduced by the strength of his arms around her. Heat pooled between her thighs. Her body melted in surrender and it was all she could do not to succumb, not to make love to him then and there, but the thought of her grandparents just upstairs soon put a damper on her ardor.

She pushed away from him, chest heaving. "I have to go, Jack."

He gave her a sexy grin, as if he thought he was winning this battle of wills. "For now?" he asked with a shameless grin.

Rebecca blushed all the hotter despite her decision not to. "Yes."

"Why?" He drew back just enough to give her room to breathe, not enough room to escape.

She leaned as far back into the counter, as far back away from him as she could. "Because when you kiss me like that I can't think straight," she admitted on a tremulous sigh.

He braced a hand on either side of her. "And that's bad?"

"When I lose sight of reality, it is."

Jack met her level gaze affably and gave her another coaxing grin. "The reality is that you, me and Andy could all be together as a family one day."

Her heart aching, Rebecca traced a line down the middle of his chest with her fingertip. She wanted to believe that. But the cold hard facts of the situation kept reminding her otherwise. "Is it? You wouldn't even be here, Jack, if that baby hadn't been left on Alec Roman's doorstep. You never would have even seen me again.''

Jack straightened. "Don't be so sure of that."

Rebecca lifted her head in surprise. "You had plans to come and see me again?''

He frowned and didn't reply.

"Just as I thought!'' Rebecca lifted a braced arm and stormed off.

He caught up with her just as she reached the living room. Circling around her, he cut off her path to the stairs and the safety of the second floor. "What does it matter how things were? We're together again now."

"But for how long, Jack?'' Rebecca shot back as she propped both her hands on her hips. "How long before you realize this baby really doesn't belong with us, but to some-one else?''

"You mean that, don't you?'' Jack asked slowly.

Rebecca nodded. Her heart constricted painfully in her chest. "I didn't believe you at first, either. I thought that you were just here because you guessed I was Andy's mother. Then, I thought you stayed because you had decided I'd be a good mother, anyway, even if I wasn't the biological mother. But now I've been around you enough to believe you when you tell me there was no other woman in your life at the time we met...and if that's the case, then Andy really doesn't belong to either of us! And if that's the case, Jack, someone is missing an adorable two-month-old baby. And if that's true, then you better go back to Philadelphia and try to find Andy's real parents!''

"I'M GETTING TO BE an old pro at this. Know that, kiddo?'' Jack asked as he lifted Andy out of the shallow basin that was serving as bathtub and wrapped him in a towel.

Andy stared up at Jack, his blue eyes happy and alert, as Jack carried Andy over to the double bed. He had everything laid out—baby powder, nighttime diaper, clean undershirt and blanket sleeper. "I bet I could even dress you in the dark with both hands tied behind my back," Jack teased.

Andy gurgled in response and tried to bat his way out of the towel Jack had wrapped him in.

Jack grinned and freed his son from the towel. "Okay," he allowed, "make that in a dimly lit room with one hand tied behind my back." He slid the diaper beneath him and then powdered Andy's bottom. "The two of us have bonded faster than I ever imagined we could. You and I are family, Andy. Family."

But what if they weren't? Jack thought uncomfortably as he fastened Andy's diaper and reached for his T-shirt.

The note left with Andy hadn't named a specific name. It had just said, "To Andy's father." Andy had been left on Alec Roman's doorstep, not Jack's. Most damning of all, Jack knew what Rebecca did not. That Alec had already mistakenly claimed Andy as *his* child for almost an entire week before Alec had figured out that Andy wasn't Alec's baby at all...and called Jack. The two of them had quickly consulted their calendars and decided Andy was Jack's baby. Jack had hopped the first flight to Philly, picked up Andy and tracked down Rebecca in short order.

But now everything was falling apart, Jack mused silently as he slid first one of Andy's wildly waving arms into the T-shirt, and then the other, then snapped it in the front.

Jack smiled at his son and chucked him under his cute chin. "Rebecca adores you, sport, I know that," he said softly as he reached for Andy's thick, soft blanket sleeper. "But the more I'm around her, the more I think that maybe, just maybe, she might be telling me the truth about your not being her baby after all. And that scares me," Jack admitted as he zipped Andy into the nighttime sleeper.

Andy's expression turned as glum as Jack's. He kicked Jack on the thigh, once and then again, demanding silently, it seemed, to be picked up.

Deciding some prebedtime cuddling was in order, Jack picked Andy up, and then scooted back on the bed until he was propped up against the headboard. "This better?" Jack asked as he turned his son onto his tummy and then placed Andy on his chest. Andy banged a fist on Jack's chest and made a sound that indicated agreement. It would be a few minutes before Andy was ready to go to sleep. He liked to be talked to or sung to in the interim. Jack figured he might as well continue his verbal theorizing.

"Okay, so where were we?" Jack asked Andy. Remembering, Jack sighed, "Oh, yeah, we were talking about whether or not we should believe her when she says you're not her baby."

Andy gurgled and frowned, then looked at Jack as if he wanted Jack to go on with the story.

"As I said, part of me does want to believe her. After all, how could I care about a woman who lied to me about something as important as this? And I do care about Rebecca, Andy, very much. Besides, just look at the facts. Rebecca is headstrong, and impulsive, but she wouldn't leave you on a doorstep and walk off and leave you with a complete stranger, would she?" Jack asked.

Andy pushed himself up, thumped his fist on Jack's chest, then shook his head restlessly from side to side.

Jack grinned at Andy's seeming rejection of that theory. "My thoughts exactly, buddy," Jack said. "On the other hand, whoever did leave you on Alec's doorstep on Valentine's Day did wait until Alec got home before he or she put your bassinet on the front stoop and rang the bell. Whoever left you cared what happened to you. And we know that Alec's house was the only place where Rebecca knew to reach me…so she could have done it."

Jack fell silent a moment. Tiring, Andy dropped his head back to Jack's chest and cuddled against him. Jack continued to gently stroke Andy's back with tender, sleep-inducing motions.

"And," Jack continued softly, "we also know that Rebecca went off to Indiana for six months and that just before she left, she was very upset, withdrawn and physically ill…so ill that Ruth and Eli insisted she see the doctor. All that, my good buddy, points to a pregnancy.''

Jack looked down at Andy and saw his son was fast asleep. He was reluctant to let him go. Jack had yet to get over the wonder of holding a baby close, of feeling the love and tenderness that poured out of him whenever he was around Andy.

''The last few days have changed me, Andy,'' he said softly. Just like the week that Andy had spent with Alec had changed Alec. Fatherhood had brought a dimension of happiness to Jack's life that he hadn't known was possible. And Jack didn't want to give that happiness, or Rebecca, up. And yet, if Rebecca was telling the truth about Andy truly not belonging to her...

Jack held Andy close and breathed in the baby-fresh scent of his skin and hair. How could Andy not be his and Rebecca's child? he wondered desperately. Andy had big blue eyes, and fair, flawless skin, just like Rebecca's. He had curly dark hair, just like Jack's mom. Or did he?

Maybe what he saw as proof was nothing more than coincidence, no matter how much he wanted to believe otherwise. There was no other reason Rebecca would tell Jack that the baby wasn't hers, or suggest not so subtly that Jack needed to be away from Blair County and out looking for Andy's real parents, unless...

Jack winced as the next idea struck.

No. It couldn't be...could it? She wouldn't do that to him. *Would she?*

''I THOUGHT YOU WOULD have been packing to leave by now,'' Rebecca said first thing the next morning when she encountered Jack in the kitchen, heating Andy's bottle.

''I just bet you did,'' Jack drawled agreeably. ''Unfortunately for you, Rebecca, I am not in the mood to go off hunting any wild moose.''

Rebecca flushed in a way that made Jack sure she was guilty. ''What are you talking about now, Jack?''

Jack leaned closer and whispered in her ear, "I'm talking about the way you successfully got rid of Levi and Dieter when they were pestering you unbearably. You laid some false tracks in the woods and then sent them off on a wild moose chase. Only I'm not falling for it, Rebecca, and neither is Andy."

Rebecca's blue eyes widened with amazement. "Is that what you think I did?" she asked dryly.

Jack shrugged, not about to let Rebecca throw him off with another display of innocence. "It's the only explanation that fits, when you and I both know Andy is our child."

Rebecca tossed Jack an exasperated glance. "You've got everything figured out, haven't you, Jack?"

Jack shifted Andy a little higher in his arms. "I even know why you were so desperate to have me out of here that you'd do such a low-down thing," he confided assuredly.

Rebecca's chin took on a stubborn tilt. She turned away from both Jack and Andy and stirred the kettle of oatmeal cooking on the stove. "And why is that, Jack?"

Jack watched Rebecca add chopped apples and raisins to the cooking cereal. The long night had given him a chance to come to terms with her actions, and put them into perspective. It had also given him time to decide that he wasn't going to leave here before he'd made Rebecca own up to her mistakes. "You want to get rid of me," Jack whispered in her ear, aware they could conceivably be walked in on at any minute, "because I've made no secret of the fact that I want to tell your grandparents everything, and you're not willing to do that."

Rebecca set her spoon down with a thud and turned to face Jack. Her expression was fierce. "I told you, before, Jack, I do not want to hurt them."

"What about me?" Jack asked. "What about Andy? Don't our feelings count?" He stroked a hand through Andy's dark curly hair.

Rebecca reached up to gently stroke Andy's downy soft

cheek. "I don't want this baby hurt, either," she whispered, really seeming to mean it.

Jack sighed and took another step closer to her. "Then why don't you stop using all your energy to push the two of us away," he asked softly, "and instead, start concentrating on overcoming the logistical problems of merging our two very diverse lives? Because once you do that, Rebecca," Jack murmured encouragingly, the three of us will finally be able to become the family we were meant to be."

"WE'RE GOING TO NEED more tea and more sugar for the frolic today," Ruth said, several hours later.

Jack looked up from the notes he had been making on Amish homes. "Do you want me to stop in town and get supplies before I drive out to the Yoders?" He owed the Lindholm family a lot. They had not only been gracious hosts, but extremely generous in sharing their knowledge of Amish ways.

"That would be a help to us," Eli said, "as I would like to be one of the first to arrive at the Yoders. The young men need us older men to help get them organized."

"And if you wouldn't mind, Jack, I'd like to take Andy with us," Ruth said.

"She wants to show him off," Eli joked with a teasing glance at his wife. He watched as Ruth bundled Andy up in a snowsuit, cap and blanket. "You're acting as if he's your own grandchild."

"I am not. Well..." Ruth allowed with a blush that was almost girlish in its innocence. "Maybe just a little, but I can't help it. It's been such a long time since we've had a little one in this house to love...you know we never really had you at that age, Rebecca, except for the occasional visit."

"I know."

"I missed watching you grow up."

Rebecca smiled back at her grandparents. "Well, you've got me now."

"That I do. So Jack...the baby?" Ruth asked.

"I'd be honored if you'd take him with you," Jack said. "That way I'll have my arms free to help Rebecca at the store."

"We'll see you at the Yoders then." Eli and Ruth went on, Andy in Ruth's arms.

Jack turned to Rebecca. "Ready to go?"

Rebecca nodded at him curtly. "Just as soon as I get my bonnet."

They went outside together. Jack gave Rebecca a hand up into the buggy. "You going to let me drive today?" he asked as he slid in beside her.

Rebecca gave him a sidelong glance. "Do you want to?"

Jack shrugged. "If I'm going to become Amish, I need to learn basic survival skills."

Rebecca gave him a sharp look as he took up the reins. "I told you not to toy with me, Jack."

"I'm not." Jack paused, then continued softly, "It occurred to me last night that I was asking you to give up everything and offering nothing in return." Jack frowned. "Maybe it's time that changed, Rebecca."

Rebecca regarded him suspiciously. "What does that mean? What are you trying to tell me?"

Still feeling a little unsure of his ability to drive a horse and buggy, Jack tightened his grip on the reins as the buggy headed out into the main road. "If Mohammed won't come to the mountain, then the mountain will go to Mohammed," he said.

Rebecca gaped at him in surprise. "You would do that for me?" she whispered. "Actually move here, and perhaps even become Amish, to be close to me?"

Jack shrugged. "If it's the only way to get you to admit to being Andy's mother and give us a chance, sure, why not?"

Rebecca scowled and folded her arms in front of her. "You're talking nonsense again."

"Yeah, but it's a nonsense we both understand," Jack said.

He cast her a sidelong glance. "What are we doing at the Yoders today?"

Rebecca looked relieved at the opportunity to talk about something else. "The widow Yoder needs a new roof, so we're having a frolic—a day of unpaid labor—to help her. Everyone in our community is going to be there."

"It sounds like fun," Jack said.

"It will be," Rebecca promised.

And it was. The men spent the morning tearing off the old roof. By the time they stopped for the noon meal, they had a new layer of plywood subroofing on. They stopped for dinner as the sun rose high overhead, the men eating first at long plank tables that had been set up outside. The food was hot and delicious, the company entertaining, but Jack had eyes only for Rebecca as she moved easily among her friends and neighbors, never quite meeting Jack's eyes, but never quite taking her eyes off him, either.

"YOU'RE SURE YOU WANT to take Andy home with the two of you?" Jack asked Ruth and Eli.

Ruth nodded, looking completely content with a snugly wrapped Andy curled up in her arms. He was sound asleep, and had been for at least half an hour—and no wonder. There hadn't been a moment all day when the women hadn't been fussing over him appreciatively. The way things were going, Andy was going to grow up thinking he was the most adorable baby on this earth. And why not? Jack thought. He was.

"You and Rebecca can stay and visit with the young people a few extra minutes," Ruth told Jack with a smile as she settled back in the covered black buggy. "It'll give you a few minutes to gather more research for your movie."

"Thanks, Ruth." Jack smiled. "I appreciate your thoughtfulness."

Half an hour later, they were finally on their way. "You must be tired," Rebecca said quietly.

Jack slanted her an amused glance. The truth was, he was a little stiff and sore. He wasn't used to standing on a roof for hours on end. But he'd gotten the hang of it quickly enough. Even Eli, one of the toughest taskmasters there, had been proud. "Think I'm not tough enough to handle a day of roofing?" he drawled.

"Correct me if I'm wrong," she teased back, "but you rarely spend an entire day wielding a hammer."

"True. But I'm not in such bad shape that I can't take a day of hard physical labor. Being sent on a wild moose hunt, now that's another matter," Jack snapped back as he transferred the reins to one hand.

"What I told you last night…about Andy possibly being some other couple's baby…was sincere, Jack."

Seeing the covered bridge up ahead, he stopped their buggy just inside. Jack dropped the reins and turned toward her. "Sure you weren't just trying to get rid of me because I've been so pesky lately?"

"I admit I've thought about it, but no, I haven't."

"Right," Jack quipped, as he took her all the way into his arms and kissed her thoroughly. She resisted at first. He didn't care. He wasn't letting her shy away from their feelings this time. After a moment, the only sounds in their buggy were the ragged gasp of their breaths, the soft sighs, the rustle of clothing. When he released her at long last, they were both trembling.

"I want you, Rebecca," he said softly, lifting her chin. "I want you so much it hurts. Not just physically, but in my life. In my home."

For a moment, she looked like she wanted to say something to him, too. What exactly, he didn't know. But the moment passed and she turned her eyes from him. He was about to take her into his arms again and kiss her senseless one more time when the sound of another buggy approaching behind them made him pick up the reins and reluctantly resume their journey.

Rebecca peered around the edge of the buggy. She hugged her arms close to her chest. "You shouldn't have done that," she said. "It isn't even dark yet. Someone could have seen us."

"I don't want your reputation in the community hurt on my account, but as for the rest of it, Rebecca, I don't care who knows we have a lot to work out."

"About the baby," Rebecca said, her expression going from wistful to deeply troubled in a matter of seconds.

"And us," Jack confirmed. "I know we began our relationship the opposite way we should have. But we can't go back and change that, Rebecca. All we can do is start again."

Rebecca paused, her expression uncertain. "The baby aside...you really think we could do that?"

"I know we could," Jack said firmly. Around them, darkness continued to fall, and they passed other buggies on the road. "Especially now that I've met your family. Ruth and Eli like me. And they love Andy as they would their own grandchild."

Rebecca's mouth tightened. "I don't want to be some Amish trophy you've collected in your travels, Jack."

"I never said you would."

"But you are fascinated—at least for the moment—with our quaint Amish ways. And don't try and deny it."

"I admit I am fascinated by the self-sufficiency of the Amish, the sense of community, the way you take care of your old people and one another. But that's not all it is."

"I know," she said in a flip tone of voice. "With me, it's sex."

"Making love," Jack corrected, his own temper heating up at Rebecca's continued obstinacy, her refusal to even give them a chance to live as a couple, as a family, with their son. He slanted her a deliberately rapacious glance. "And that's not so bad, either, judging from your passionate response the one night you spent in my bed. Or were you making up those little moans you made when I—"

"I told you I did not want to discuss that!"

Jack watched Rebecca flush a bright pink. So she hadn't forgotten her response to him, he thought victoriously.

"Don't expect me to ever let you forget it. Particularly," he added forcefully when she was about to interrupt, "since your family is no longer standing in the way of us. Not in any real sense."

"My family does not make my decisions. I do." There was no confusion in her light blue eyes as she looked at him. Sensual awareness, yes. Wavering of opinion, no.

"And I think you're a bad risk," Rebecca continued stubbornly, her soft pink mouth taking on a determined pout. "One I have absolutely no intention of taking. You're wasting your time here, Jack. When are you going to get that through your thick head?"

Chapter Eight

"Jack did well at the frolic today," Ruth said as the two women washed the dishes a scant hour and a half later. The men were outside, tending to the animals. Baby Andy was in his infant seat, his rattle clutched tightly in his hand as he followed the two women around the room with his eyes.

"Yes, he did," Rebecca said, and unable to help herself, she screwed up her nose at baby Andy, who broke into a wide grin. Gurgling at her, he enthusiastically waved his rattle around in front of his cherubic face.

Ruth patted Andy's sleeper-covered foot. "Little Andy needs a mother to love him. It's a shame Jack is not Amish. If he were, there would be plenty of women around to love and nurture Andy. I am afraid that is not the case in California."

Rebecca dried the last dish and put it away while her grandmother began wiping the counters. "I'm sure Jack will find someone to take good care of little Andy while he works."

Hearing her voice, Andy grinned at her again. He waved his rattle excitedly, and bumped himself in the nose. At the contact of blue plastic against his face, he let out a startled cry. Rebecca scooped him up in her arms and held him close. "There, there now," she soothed, breathing in the fresh baby scent of him. A wave of contentment swept through Rebecca. Sometimes she thought this was what life was all about.

Watching, her grandmother looked sad. "It's hard for you, isn't it?" she said softly. "Not having a child of your own."

"Maybe I will someday," Rebecca said, pushing the longing she felt away.

The truth of the matter was she could have Andy now, if she really wanted him. All she had to do was claim him as her own. Jack would marry her. Instant family. She even sensed, if she absolutely insisted, that she might be able to get Jack to stay in the area, perhaps even become Amish himself. At least for a while. But she also knew that he would eventually tire of their quaint ways. He was no different than the tourists who flocked to see the Pennsylvania Amish every summer. And sooner or later, the truth would come out about the baby, too. She couldn't live a lie, any more than she could live as the principal player of some romantic fantasy on Jack's part.

"Are you and Jack going to go skating on the Danhof's place tonight?" Ruth asked.

Rebecca shrugged and shifted the baby to her other shoulder. "I haven't asked him," she admitted. And for good reason. Aware her grandmother was watching her thoughtfully, Rebecca continued, "I don't even know if he knows how to ice skate."

"Sure I know how to ice skate," Jack said as he and Eli trooped in to join them. He warmed his hands next to the stove. "I grew up in Pennsylvania, remember?"

"Still, it's been an awfully long day," Rebecca said.

His eyes met and held hers. He bent and kissed his son on the cheek. "It sounds like fun."

"It will be," Ruth said. "All the young people will be there."

Jack cast another look at Rebecca, and his expression gentled even more. She realized she still had the baby in her arms. He was looking at the two of them as if they belonged together, not as temporary caretaker and child, but as mother and son. She felt herself flush. She knew she was holding

Andy tenderly, and with great joy, but she knew no other way to hold him.

Jack's glance cut back to Ruth. "You're sure you don't mind watching Andy?"

"Not at all," Ruth said. She held out her arms to Andy, who went to her happily.

Jack turned to Rebecca. "Do you have any skates I could borrow?"

"You can take mine," Eli said.

"Thank you. That's very kind of you," Jack said. He turned to Rebecca. "Let's go."

"I WASN'T KIDDING earlier," Jack said as the two of them strolled side by side down the path that led to the Danhof's pond. Because it was right next door to the Lindholm farm, they had elected to walk. "I'm seriously thinking about giving up my home in Los Angeles and moving to Pennsylvania. And I'll do it, too, if it's the only way I can have you."

His words caught her by surprise. She didn't like being pushed into anything. Jack's determination left her feeling a little trapped. "Do you always have to have what you want?" Rebecca asked lightly. She picked up her pace, so she was walking slightly ahead of him.

"In this case, yes." Jack caught up with her, dropped his skates into the snow and took her into his arms. Before she could move to extricate herself, he had clamped an arm around her waist. Her thighs tensed as they nudged his. Lower still, she could feel his arousal as her pulse pounded in her throat, and her hunger for him inundated her with tidal-wave force. Her fingers tightened on the knotted shoestring that connected her skates.

"Being with you again has made me realize what I think I knew in my heart all along," Jack confided in a low, compelling voice.

Wordlessly he wrested her skates from her hands and dropped them beside his. It was a simple action. Innocent almost. And yet nearly as sexy as undressing in front of him had been.

Rebecca could hear the jerky sound of her breathing, feel the traitorous tensing of her body as his thumb traced the line of her jaw, then moved up to brush across her lower lip. His smile softened tenderly. "You and I are destined to be together, Rebecca," he confided hoarsely, his eyes darkening to a deep Aegean blue, "we have been from the very first."

Rebecca had expected him to put the moves on her again, but not this soon. She knew she shouldn't let him kiss her again, but even as his head was lowering, her eyes were closing and her lips were parting. She drifted toward him, against him, aching with need, awash with anticipation. The first touch of his mouth against hers flooded her with dizzying waves of desire. Rebecca had never felt anything like what she felt with Jack. Never wanted this way. Never needed. Never even dreamed feeling this way was possible.

Unable to stop herself, she moaned low in her throat and went more fully into his arms, lacing her hands around his shoulders and pressing her body close to his, until they touched from breastbone to knee in one unbroken line. And still they kissed, until she was weak with wanting him, weak with need. Until he was all she could think of, all she could feel....

Slowly he drew away. Rebecca looked up at him, her gaze misty and bewildered. "I don't need an answer now," Jack told her softly, gazing down at her and caressing the side of her face with the back of his hand. He had never felt skin so silky soft. "I just want you to think about it, Rebecca, to know the possibility of my moving here to be with you exists."

As what? she wondered. His mistress? As a live-in nanny for his son? Because that was all he seemed to be offering her. Steadying a bit, she forced herself to step out of his arms. Wordlessly she picked up her skates and handed him his.

"You're awfully quiet." Jack cast her an interested sidelong glance. Moonlight filtered down through the trees, as bright as any electric porch light.

That's because I'm trying not to fall in love with you, Rebecca thought as she tightened her gloved hands into fists to stop their trembling. "We're going to be late for the skating party, Jack," she said, deliberately sidestepping any more attempts at intimate conversation. "We had better hurry." Not waiting for him to reply, for fear if she did he would use the opportunity to kiss her again, she turned and hurried down the path, all too aware he was just half a step behind her.

Unfortunately they were the last to arrive at the Danhof's farm. As Rebecca had predicted, her tardiness was noted by all. "Hey Rebecca," Levi said, crossing to her side immediately. He was wearing a forbidden bright red sweatshirt beneath his black Amish coat. "What took you so long?"

"I wanted to help my grandmother with the dishes before I left." Rebecca sat down on a log before the pond's edge to put on her skates. Times like this, when she was forced to be outdoors in the winter in a dress and black wool stockings, instead of warm wool slacks, she resented some of the restrictions of Amish life. But she supposed that came from all the time she had spent early on, and then again later, living English.

"Sure that's all that was keeping you?" Dieter sat down on the other side of her and Jack. Like Levi, he was wearing a forbidden item of clothing as an open sign of his youthful rebelliousness. In his case, it was a bright orange-and-black knit Cincinnati Bengals cap. He wrapped a teasing arm around her shoulders and looked into her face. "Your cheeks are a little pink."

"You know what I think?" Rebecca shot back, ignoring the way Jack was glaring at Dieter and the possessive arm Dieter had laced around her shoulders. "I think all the skating you have done tonight has addled your brains, Dieter." Rebecca tugged the laces of her skates tight.

"Maybe, but then I'm not the one head over heels in love with you," Dieter remarked. He stood and pulled some wintergreen breath mints out of his pants pocket. "My cousin Levi is."

Laughter erupted from the group quickly gathering around them. Levi gave Dieter a teasing poke in the ribs. Dieter poked back. The next thing Rebecca knew the two teenage boys were wrestling around on the snowy ground. Lifting her glance heavenward and shaking her head in silent remonstration, she headed for the ice.

Jack was fast on her heels. To her dismay, she found he was an excellent ice skater. No matter how swiftly she skated, he kept pace with her, easily overtaking her with his long smooth glides. "The teasing upset you." Hands behind him, he skated around her in a lazy figure eight.

Rebecca shrugged as at the other end of the ice, Dieter and Levi picked up a pair of hockey sticks and a round plastic disk. "Dieter and Levi are always clowning around."

"They're also both in love with you."

Rebecca inclined her head slightly to the side. "Not according to Dieter."

"You know what they say about boys that age. Their actions paint a truer picture than their words, and those two are devoted to you."

Rebecca couldn't argue that. Since she had returned to Pennsylvania after her divorce, those two boys had appointed themselves her honorary kid brothers. And like all kid brothers, they could be bratty and rude and fiercely protective. Right now, they still hadn't figured out if Jack was friend or foe; all they knew for sure was that he had an unusually strong effect on Rebecca. She shrugged again. "They have girls they are courting."

"But only because you won't give them the chance."

Rebecca grinned at Jack. There was no reason for him to feel jealous. But she was kind of enjoying seeing him act that way, anyway. "They're too young for me."

"I agree." Jack laced his hand through her elbow, then pushed her forward with his other hand, just in time to avoid a flying hockey puck. "You need someone a few years older than yourself, like me."

Rebecca extricated her arm from his and skated forward. It was a cold night, but she felt warm all over. "Stop it," she said in a low voice.

"Stop what?" He gave her a look of comically exaggerated innocence.

"Courting me so obviously!" Rebecca hissed back, as the flush that had been rising in her neck travelled to her cheeks as well.

Jack matched his glides to hers. Half his mouth crooked up in a rueful grin as he put his hands behind him again. "Why?"

Rebecca did a swift about-face that made her skates cut a swath in the ice. Almost beside herself with the attention they were earning, she put her hands on her hips. "Because I've never been very good at hiding my feelings!" she blurted out in exasperation, before she could think. Jack's grin widened mischievously. "That's what got me into trouble with you in the first place," she said sternly, regarding him with a challenging glare. "One look into my eyes, and you know exactly what I'm thinking and feeling."

"Not always," he disagreed, wishing he could take her hand in his the way he had in the woods. But that would cause a scandal. Even linking his arm through hers had been over the line....

"I am going over to talk to the other girls," Rebecca said, doing another fast about-face and skating off. Jack was about to follow her, when Dieter and Levi skated up to him. One on either side of him, they more or less commanded him to the pond's edge, and the picnic table of refreshments that had been set up there. "We want to talk to you," Dieter said.

Big surprise there, Jack thought as he helped himself to a cup of hot chocolate from the gallon thermos. Steam rose from the cup as he lifted it to his mouth. "What about?" he asked.

"We don't want to see Rebecca get hurt," Levi said.

"Ja," Dieter agreed, "she was hurt enough by her first marriage to that other Englishman."

Jack tore his eyes from Rebecca and the group of young women she was standing with. *Rebecca had been married to another Englishman?*

"Ja," Levi continued. He tapped his index finger against Jack's breastbone in a threatening manner. "We don't want any other Englishman marrying her and then dumping and divorcing her like yesterday's outgrown clothing."

Jack stared at them in shock. "Rebecca was married to an Englishman?" he asked, irritated to be hearing it from them, and not her. And for that matter, *why* hadn't she told him this?

"When she was in Florida," Dieter affirmed.

Levi stared at Jack suspiciously. "You're telling us you didn't know?" he said.

"That's putting it lightly," Jack said through his teeth. Once again, everything he had thought about Rebecca was a lie. She wasn't a widow. She was divorced. She hadn't married a nice Amish boy from around there, as her grandparents obviously would have preferred, but an English man, in Florida. His temper spinning out of control, he wondered what else he didn't know.

JACK WAS ODDLY SILENT as they started home. Rebecca didn't know what Levi and Dieter had said to Jack when they'd been drinking hot chocolate, but whatever it was had upset him.

"You must be exhausted," Rebecca murmured as she and Jack walked through the woods that separated the Danhof property from the Lindholm farm. In the past hour, a winter storm front had begun to move in. The stars were no longer visible and the sky had grown cloudy. Tiny flakes of snow had begun to fall. The woods were hushed and quiet. "First the frolic, then the evening chores," Rebecca recited casually, not wanting to admit how Jack's continued silence and brooding looks were unnerving her. She drew a shallow breath. "Ice skating after that."

"It's not fatigue that's bothering me," Jack said shortly. His mouth tightened even more.

Rebecca shivered in a way that had little to do with the cold night air, and dug her hands even deeper into the pockets of her cloak. "Then what is it?"

Jack turned and gave her a measuring look. "The deliberate deceptions."

Rebecca's heart stopped, then resumed a tense jerky rhythm. She forced herself to keep walking, to look straight ahead. She estimated they had another half mile or so to go before they reached the edge of the woods. "What do you mean?"

"I mean..." Jack suddenly took her by the shoulder and backed her up against a tree. He braced a hand on either side of her, effectively pinning her in place, and for the second time that night, he tossed both their skates aside. "Why didn't you tell me your first husband was an Englishman? Why didn't you tell me you were divorced? Why did you let me think you were a widow?"

Rebecca swallowed hard. She had never seen him look so angry. Pretending a calmness of spirit she couldn't begin to feel, she kept her hands in her pockets and stared up at him. "I never said I was a widow. You just assumed, Jack."

He clamped the edges of his teeth together. "But you didn't bother to correct me."

It was all Rebecca could do to hold his gaze. Telling herself that she owed Jack nothing—this was her private life after all—she tipped her head back even further. "I didn't think my marital status was any of your business when we first met, so no, I didn't correct you then." She had expected him to be annoyed if and when he found out the truth about her marriage; she hadn't expected this blazing mistrust and resentment. "Besides, you were bound and determined to think what you wanted to about me anyway," she said with a shrug.

Jack dropped his arms and stepped back. "What the hell gave you that idea?" he demanded.

Rebecca straightened against the tree trunk. She propped her hands on her waist and faced him contentiously. "Because I saw the way you looked at me."

He leaned closer, until she had no choice but to inhale the spicy scent of his cologne. "And how, pray tell, was that?" he asked ever so softly.

Rebecca's pulse jumped. Her thighs went a little more fluid. But she held his gaze with all the guts of a prize fighter stepping into the ring. "The same way every Englishman looks when he sees a pretty Amish girl," she said. "You romanticize me. You look at my clothes and assume I'm a pure angel straight out of another time. Well, I'm not. I'm human. I have flaws and faults, just like everyone else. I—make mistakes."

Without warning, Jack's face changed. He girded his thighs and folded his arms in front of him. "Like giving away your only child because you didn't want to face the scandal that trying to raise a baby on your own would cause?"

"I didn't—"

"I know you didn't mean to hurt me." His voice gentled unexpectedly. "And it means a lot that you didn't try to take my child from me, but rather gave him back to me to raise. But—"

"Jack—" Rebecca said wearily.

"You're more selfless than you think, Rebecca."

She shook her head in both bewilderment and chagrin and studied the toe of her sturdy black shoes. If she were selfless, she wouldn't be allowing him to still entertain these fantasies that the baby he'd found was their baby. She'd be working harder to convince him he was wrong about that, and that he had to leave. That he had to go off and find the baby's real mother. But she wasn't. And why?

The simple truth of the matter was she didn't want Jack to leave. She wanted him to stay right there, pursuing her for all he was worth. She wanted to see where all this lunacy on his part would lead. If he really would relocate to Pennsylvania and try to live Amish, even for a time. And that was wrong of her.

She shook her head glumly in silent self-recrimination. "Right now, I don't feel selfless, Jack. I have no reason to feel that way."

To her surprise, he didn't argue with her, but rather picked up their skates and, taking her hand in his, continued down the path. "Tell me about your divorce."

"Why?" Rebecca tried not to think about how good it felt to hold his hand this way.

Jack was quiet for about ten paces. "Because I think what happened in your marriage has directly affected your feelings about having a relationship with me now," he said softly.

"You're right about that," she said sadly.

"So tell me what happened. How did you end up marrying an Englishman to begin with?" he asked gently, tightening his grip on her hand.

"I was seventeen. I was asked to join the church, but I wasn't really sure whether I wanted to do that or not. Part of me longed for my old life, the life I'd had with my parents. My grandparents understood my need to decide for myself how I wanted to live my life, and they also knew I needed some time apart from them in which to make the decision, so they arranged for me to go to Florida and work at a bed-and-breakfast inn that hired a lot of Amish as contract workers during the winter months, when there's not a lot to do on the farm." Rebecca paused. This part was not so easy to explain. "Soon after I arrived, I caught the eye of the wealthy charming son of the owners."

"And he seduced you," Jack interrupted.

"No." Rebecca fiddled with the knotted string tying her skates together. "He didn't seduce me. He did pursue me in a hot and heavy way, though, and I'm ashamed to say I got caught up in it." Her mouth tightened and she blushed. Knowing there was no graceful way to say it, she decided to just spit it out. "I confused a lusty romance with love, and I eloped with him."

Again, Jack was silent, taking the information in. "Then what happened?" he asked as their footsteps continued to crunch along on the snow and ice-encrusted path.

"We crash-landed into normal life," Rebecca replied dryly. "He went back to law school in Miami, and I moved in with him. And that's when everything began to fall apart." Pain laced her heart as she remembered. Rebecca shook her head. "I just couldn't please him. It wasn't that hard for me to become English again, but after seven years of living with my grandparents, I wasn't quite your everyday new bride, either. To make things worse—" Rebecca's lip curled bitterly "—without my Amish ways, I wasn't the pure young innocent maiden Wes had married. And now my Amishness was an embarrassment to him."

"The marriage fell apart in a few months, despite my best efforts to hold things together for both our sakes. It was quite frankly a disaster and I do mean a disaster, and so when Wesley told me he wanted a divorce, I didn't argue with him. I just returned home to my grandparents. I talked to the community about what I had done—"

"Or in other words, you confessed your sins," Jack said.

"Right." Rebecca nodded, at peace with the understanding way she had been taken back into the community. "And they accepted me back, almost as if nothing had happened. Ever since—it's been almost six years now—I've lived Amish. And while it's not a perfect life, sometimes far from it, I also know I am safe and loved and unconditionally accepted here. That's something I never felt while I was in Florida." She gritted her teeth together and glared a warning. "I'm not going to make the same mistake again, Jack—marry someone who has idealized me into his fantasy figure of goodness and purity."

Jack didn't comment either way about that. Tightening his grip on her hand, he asked gently, in a low voice laced with understanding, "Why didn't you tell me any of this sooner?"

Rebecca sighed. How could she explain how foolish just remembering that time of her life made her feel, or how scared she was of repeating her mistakes again? "Because I am and have always been a very private person. Besides, there's no point in me rehashing the details of my failed marriage ad nauseam. It's over. And I want it to stay over, especially now that I'm back where I belong." Jack stopped moving abruptly but kept his grip on her hand. Rebecca stopped, too.

"But do you belong here, Rebecca?" Jack asked softly, looking down at her with all the love and affection she had ever wanted him to feel. "Or do you belong with me and with your child?"

Once again, Rebecca was flooded with guilt. She really should have tried harder to make Jack understand that Andy was not her child. Her heart pounding, she regarded Jack cautiously. "What are you trying to say?"

He lifted his shoulders in a careless shrug. "Simply that the way you've behaved is beginning to make sense to me now. You tried marriage to an Englishman once, and it didn't work. Naturally that made you wary of trying it again. Yet single Amish women do not raise children on their own. So you went to Indiana and had the baby there, and then made arrangements to leave the baby with me—through Alec—instead."

Rebecca released a lengthy sigh. Before she could say anything, Jack rushed to reassure her gently, "It's okay, Rebecca. I understand now. I forgive you."

"There's nothing to forgive," Rebecca muttered.

"Says you. I think there's plenty to forgive. For starters, robbing me of the chance to marry you months ago, watch my baby grow inside you and see my child born."

Her frustration with Jack and his powerful imagination mounting, Rebecca shook her head at him. "Jack. Please. For once, listen to me. Andy is not my child."

He frowned impatiently. "I can't believe, after all you've just told me, that you would still deny it!"

And it was then that Rebecca realized it didn't matter what she said. Jack wasn't going to believe her. He already had his mind made up. What was the point of trying? She'd only be wasting her breath, and both their time.

"Fine. You're right, Jack. The baby is mine," Rebecca said sarcastically, moving forward until they stood toe-to-toe. "I confess, you found me out. I did it all to protect myself. I concocted a crazy story about needing money to fix up my broken down car so I could go off and have the baby in secret in Indiana. I left Andy on Alec's doorstep only because I was too lazy to go all the way to Los Angeles and leave him there. Or maybe I just couldn't recall your last name. Who knows what motivates a selfish, lying, cowardly woman like myself?" In a fury, she stomped off, her ice skates swinging from her hand.

Jack caught up with her. Hand on her shoulder, he swung her around to face him. "Rebecca—"

She started to struggle. He pulled her close. "Don't you understand what I'm trying to tell you? It's all right. I'm here and I'm going to take care of you—"

His head lowered. His mouth hovered just above hers.

"Aha!" a low male voice chortled from behind them. "I told you he'd be sparking her in the trees!"

Jack and Rebecca turned to see Dieter and Levi creeping up behind them. They were still a good ten feet away, but it was obvious they'd managed to see plenty.

His mouth thinning, Jack pushed Rebecca behind him and took a step toward the rowdy teenage boys. "You two are going to have to find something else to do," Jack warned. "Because Rebecca and I are *very tired* of being spied on."

As far as Rebecca was concerned, Dieter and Levi had come just in the nick of time. If they hadn't appeared when they did, she might have gotten just as caught up in all Jack's romantic notions as he was.

"Speak for yourself." Rebecca pushed Jack aside and stepped out in front of him. "Hi, guys," she said flirtatiously. "I was wondering when you two ruffians would show up."

Dieter and Levi grinned back at her mischievously. "Hello, Rebecca," they echoed back in a teasing singsong voice.

"Want a lift home?" Dieter asked.

Rebecca grinned. "You two haven't got a buggy with you," she reminded. It wasn't possible to take a buggy through the woods. The path was only wide enough for walking.

"Ah, but we've got something better! Our brute strength!" Dieter replied. He and Levi rushed forward and lifted her up off the ground.

It didn't take Jack long to realize that Rebecca was enjoying herself. He frowned as the two teenagers carried a laughing Rebecca down the path toward the Lindholm farm. Short of chasing after all three of them, there was nothing Jack could do to stop the shenanigans of the boys.

Well, there wasn't any point in that, Jack thought. Rebecca clearly wasn't in a mood to listen to him. Nor did she seem ready to tell him the whole truth about the baby, at least not yet.

The problem was, he mused, picking up her skates as well as his and sauntering slowly down the path, she still didn't believe he cared about *her* at all. He had hoped his mere presence here would prove that was the case. And if not that, his kisses. Obviously it just wasn't enough.

Maybe she needed more tangible proof, he thought. Like a serious proposal and an engagement ring. *Was he ready for that?* Or maybe she just needed to be loved again, as thoroughly as he had loved her the first time.

The question was how could he make that happen. They were never alone very long. And when they were, they generally had the baby with them.

Of course, they'd have to get used to that. Interruptions would probably be par for the course from now on. The trick would be in making the most of the time they had. As for tonight...well, Jack thought as he watched Dieter and Levi put Rebecca down near the Lindholm farmhouse, Levi and

Dieter had definitely thwarted his efforts to get close to Rebecca tonight.

Rebecca had gone along with them to prevent any more intimate discussions of what she had done in the past or might do in the future. So she'd been saved this time. Temporarily. But she wouldn't be saved the next, Jack vowed. Because one way or another, they were going to work this out. He was going to get close to her again. And from there, who only knew what would happen?

Chapter Nine

"I knew you wouldn't be able to stay away from him indefinitely," Jack said just before noon the next day.

Rebecca whirled away from the cradle. Her cheeks were pink with embarrassment, even as the soft sound of her singing and Andy's delighted gurgles echoed in the room. "I was just singing Andy a lullaby," she said defensively. "I didn't think you'd mind."

Jack closed the distance between them and wrapped an arm around her waist. "Of course I don't mind," he said, loving the way she felt against him, so soft and warm and womanly. He bent his head lower and breathed in the silky floral essence of her hair. "I want you to be close to our son."

"Jack!" Rebecca chided, twisting away from his seeking mouth.

Jack put a hold on the kisses, but he didn't let her go. "There's no one here but us," he said. Unfortunately he hadn't been able to take advantage of that fact until now because he'd been away most of the morning, too, checking out a "modern Amish" dairy operation, two farms up the road.

"My grandparents will be back from town at any moment." Rebecca drew herself straight and eased from his arms.

Jack let her go reluctantly, then followed her to the stove, where dinner was cooking. As always, she was wearing a freshly starched and ironed blue cotton knit dress and black cotton apron. And though there was nothing impure about her clothes, there was plenty impure with the way she looked at him whenever she thought he wasn't looking and/or no one else could see.

"Admit it, Rebecca," he coaxed softly. With the tip of his finger, he traced one of the white organdy kapp strings that fell onto her shoulders. "As much as you try to keep your distance, you can't help but love our baby."

Rebecca turned and gave him a brisk smile. She went back to the table, where she had laid out all sizes of fabric in a mesmerizing, clever and eye-catching patchwork design. Scattered across the living room were stacks of other patches in all sorts of colors, layers of soft white cotton that would serve as the middle layer of the quilts. "Your imagination is working overtime again. And I really don't have time for it this morning. We're having a quilting bee here this afternoon. The ladies will start arriving by one."

Jack frowned. Just what he needed. Another day with very little chance to be alone with Rebecca. Soon the nonfiction article he had been commissioned to write to promote the movie would be finished. He couldn't stay away from the set forever. As screenwriter, it was his job to be available for any rewrites that came up during the filming. "How many ladies?"

"Anywhere from ten to twenty, and their children, depending on who shows up," she said. She paused. "Would you mind going upstairs and bringing down the wicker basket that contains all my thread?"

"Not at all," Jack said, "provided you first talk to me about your feelings about our baby."

Rebecca stiffened. "There's no special love in my heart for baby Andy, Jack."

"If I believe that, I would have left days ago. Besides." Jack pulled a chair out, turned it around backward and sat down next to the table. "I saw the way you looked at him just now."

Rebecca glanced up from her work. "To me, Jack, all children are special."

"I don't understand why you won't admit he's yours, then," Jack said, not bothering to hide his frustration with her and her secrets. "Dammit, Rebecca, I've come back for you. Doesn't that count for anything?" he demanded gruffly.

Before Rebecca could reply to that, the sound of the horse and buggy outside had her rushing to the window. "My grandparents are back."

Seconds later, Eli and Ruth came in, carrying two bolts of fabric and a can of kerosene for the lamps. To Jack's surprise, their expressions were grim. "What is it?" Rebecca asked immediately.

Eli removed his black hat and took off his heavy wool overcoat. He motioned for Rebecca to sit. "I don't want to upset you, Rebecca, but there was some talk in town. Dieter and Levi said they interrupted a...well, a private moment between the two of you in the woods last night. Is this true?"

For a second, the silence in the room was so intense you could have heard a pin drop. "Jack and I were talking," Rebecca admitted. She sat straighter and put both her hands in her lap.

"They made it sound like more than that," Ruth said, her expression worried as she sat down at the table beside Rebecca.

Eli's frown deepened. "Someone else said they saw the two of you parked in a buggy inside a covered bridge before the frolic at the Yoders yesterday."

Jack felt a pang of guilt. He wondered if they had also seen him kiss Rebecca. Rebecca got up and went to the stove. She stirred the stew. "I've been teaching Jack to drive the buggy," Rebecca said as she put the wooden spoon back on the ceramic spoon rest.

"Unfortunately," Jack cut in protectively, "I'm not very good at it. Yet, anyway." He was determined to do what he could to protect Rebecca.

"So there's nothing between the two of you?" Ruth asked.

"No," Rebecca said swiftly and she looked straight at Jack. "Nor could there ever be."

Her words were quiet and almost expressionless, but Jack felt them like an arrow to the heart. He looked back at her. Now was the time to level with her grandparents. Or was it? What if he told them how he felt about their granddaughter and they asked him to leave? What then? If he no longer had the Lindholm family's support in the community, he wouldn't even be able to see her.

"You still need to be careful," Eli warned Rebecca. He poured himself a cup of coffee from the pot simmering on the back of the stove. "You know how talk can spread, Rebecca."

She nodded, chastened. Her face was pale. "I'm sorry if any of this upset you," Jack said to Ruth and Eli. He looked them both in the eye. "I never wanted to bring any harm to your family."

"I know that," Ruth said. Beside her, Eli remained ominously quiet. Rebecca checked the whole-wheat bread baking inside the oven. Again, silence fell over them like a funeral pall.

For the first time, Jack realized what a scandal an illegitimate pregnancy would cause in the community, particularly if the unwed mother were Rebecca, and he the father. People had seen the two of them in a compromising position, not even kissing, and already the community was buzzing with talk about the two of them. Rebecca's past marriage to another Englishman made things all the worse.

The sound of a car outside interrupted Jack's thoughts. He moved to the window and saw a Federal Express delivery van parked outside. He swore silently to himself. He needed this like he needed a hole in the head. "It's probably for me," Jack said with a sinking heart as he stepped outside. He had told the studio where he could be reached, but he hadn't wanted them to contact him here.

"What is it?" Rebecca asked, long moments later, after Jack had taken the package inside and studied the pages inside thoroughly. He spoke without looking up. The stress of the moment forgotten, his mind was all on his work. "It's the studio. They've decided they need another scene written immediately. What they want isn't all that difficult, but it's going to require a lot of concentration." He looked up, his mind already speeding ahead, estimating the number of hours he thought it would take to complete the scene. Eight, he figured. Ten, at the very most. It would depend on how many interruptions he had. "Can I use your phone?"

The Lindholms grinned in unison. "We have no phone," Rebecca reminded him patiently.

It was all Jack could do to stifle a groan.

He looked at the new quilt she was piecing together on the kitchen table, then down at the pages in his hand. "I'll have to go in to town and make the call from there, then," he said, irritated to have to leave Rebecca again, when he'd already been gone all morning, but there was no helping it. He crossed to the cradle, then saw Andy had just fallen asleep.

"We'll watch the baby," Ruth said. "That way you won't have to wake him."

"Thanks," Jack said. "Andy gets really cranky when he doesn't get to finish his nap."

"Does this work you received mean you're going to have to go back to California sooner than you thought?" Eli asked Jack.

Her face white, Rebecca turned away. But not before Jack had picked up on the raw disappointment in her eyes. Rebecca doesn't want me to leave, either, he thought. His spirits lifting at that small sign of encouragement from her, he turned back to Eli and said, "I hope not." A trip to California now would undercut everything he had accomplished. "But right now it's too soon to tell."

"I PROMISE I'LL HAVE the new scene faxed to you by 9:00 a.m. tomorrow morning," Jack said, struggling to be heard above the clatter of buggies and automobiles in the streets.

"Jack, we need you here," the director said.

"I'm wrapping things up out here as quickly as I can," Jack said, irritated his fantasies of sweeping Rebecca off her feet hadn't begun to come true. She might still desire him, but she wasn't about to marry him, never mind admit the two of them had a baby together.

"By the end of the week," the director stipulated firmly, "or I'm hiring another writer to finish the film for you."

That didn't give him much time, Jack thought, frowning. He was going to have to work faster than he'd planned.

THE LINDHOLM'S YARD was crowded with buggies when Jack returned a scant half hour later in his rental car. He'd intended to take his portable computer into one of the upstairs bedrooms, but he changed his mind when he entered the kitchen and heard the noise level inside the house. There were quilts, women and children everywhere. Rebecca was in the center of the activity, directing work on one quilt, admiring another. Ruth had baby Andy—who was awake again—in her arms and was busy showing him off to all their guests. "Did you get your business worked out?" Ruth asked.

Suddenly all eyes were upon him. Jack saw a few speculative smiles, a few more blushes, and knew from the way some of the women were trying not to giggle that they'd all been talking about him—and probably Rebecca—before he got back. "Sort of," he said, feeling ill at ease in the midst of so much female activity. "I'm going to have to write a new scene." A new love scene. "I wonder…" Jack cast Ruth a hopeful glance. He knew he would never make his deadline if he didn't have help with Andy. "If you wouldn't mind watching Andy for a few hours more…"

"It's no problem. I enjoy taking care of the little one," Ruth said.

"Well, then, I'll just find a quiet place to work," Jack said. Apparently it was not going to be anywhere inside the plain white clapboard farmhouse. Jack looked at Rebecca. "Any suggestions?"

She smiled back brightly, the look in her eyes too innocent to be believed as she suggested softly, "I suppose you could rent a room in a nearby inn."

"I'd rather stay here," he said. With you.

"Then you might try the barn."

"REBECCA IS DOING THIS to me on purpose," Jack told the cow in the stall below as he carried the laptop computer and then two thick quilts up the ladder and into the spacious loft. He descended the ladder again and headed for the express package containing his notes. "Trying to make me want to leave, or at the very least take Andy and move to a hotel where I could work in comfort, but I'm telling you it is not going to work."

The cow looked at him with big liquid-brown eyes and went on chewing her cud. "Okay," Jack said as he paused before the stall, "so maybe it's a little crazy, me working out here like this when I have a luxurious home with a fully outfitted writing studio at home, but I've always said a true writer can work anywhere. This isn't so different from working on location. I once wrote a scene in the middle of a jungle. Did I tell you that? No, guess not." And what am I doing talking to a cow anyway, he thought as he headed for the ladder once again and climbed up into the loft. He sighed as he tried to get comfortable.

"Maybe Rebecca's right. Maybe I am losing it," he said softly to himself. The only thing he knew for certain was that he wasn't leaving here until he'd made Rebecca admit her feelings for him, and for their baby, and he didn't care how long it took. So long as he accomplished his mission by the end of the week, in time to get back to his job.

Down below, the cow let out a soft moo. Ignoring his surroundings, Jack spread out one blanket, wrapped the other around his shoulders and began to type. The words came slowly at first, but soon picked up speed.

"IT'S BEEN HOURS since you took Jack his dinner," Ruth said worriedly to Rebecca as 9:00 p.m. approached. "Maybe you should go out and check on him."

"I'm sure he's fine. He's just working hard on his writing." In fact, he had been so absorbed in his work he had hardly noticed her, Rebecca fumed. He'd merely mumbled a distracted thank-you as she handed him his supper tray, and then resumed typing.

"Well, I'm going to bed," Eli said.

"I'll be up in a minute, too," Ruth said. She turned back to Rebecca. "Do you think we should take the baby up with us?" She looked at Andy, sleeping peacefully in his cradle.

Rebecca thought about taking care of the baby herself, then recalling the assumptions Jack had jumped to when she'd simply sung a lullaby to him, decided against it. "I think that would be a good idea," she said firmly. She stood and went to get her black wool cloak down from the coatrack next to the door. "In the meantime, I'll go out and check on Jack. There's really no reason for him to continue working in the barn now, when it's so quiet in here."

Ruth nodded. She and Eli ascended the stairs as Rebecca lit one of the kerosene lanterns and headed out to the barn. The cadence of the tapping computer keys continued unabated as she hung the lantern on a hook near the center support post, climbed the ladder and moved into the loft. "I would've thought you'd be finished by now," Rebecca said. "But then I had no idea you'd be building yourself an office out here."

Jack swung around to face her. He, too, had hung a lantern up on a peg so he could see. In the soft glow of the lamp, he looked a little like a pirate, his hair all tousled, an evening beard shadowing his face. Rebecca would have died before admitting it to him, but she was glad he had done more than grunt at her this time.

"Like it, hmm?" Jack asked.

She stepped inside the "room" he'd made by stacking bales of hay three high around the perimeter. The stacked hay effectively blocked any drafts and made a cozy work space.

Additional bales of hay, stacked one and two high, served as his writing chair and desk. He had covered both with a quilt, and laid another one on the loft floor. "You've been busy since I was out here at suppertime," Rebecca said.

"Yeah, well, it started getting cold when the sun went down, but I was on a roll, so I really didn't want to move. I just went with it, you know?"

Rebecca nodded. "I feel the same way when I'm blocking out a quilt," she said. "When I begin to see a new design in my head, I want to lay out all the pieces, fast, and baste them together, before I forget. If I can't do that, then I draw a sketch."

Jack grinned. "You do understand. I guess our work isn't so different after all."

Silence fell between them. Rebecca glanced at the portable printer next to the portable computer. "Is that hard to work?"

"Nope. Want me to teach you?"

Yes, Rebecca thought, but she knew it would be frowned on. Computers weren't Amish, even New Order Amish. She frowned, wondering if she would ever stop feeling caught between two worlds.

Jack continued to regard her silently as he took the red correcting pen he'd stuck behind his ear and tossed it down into the hay. "What time is it, anyway?"

"After nine. My grandparents have already gone to bed. They took Andy up with them."

"He was asleep already?"

"The quilting bee wore him out."

"I can understand that," Jack teased. "You women were a noisy bunch."

Rebecca grinned, looking at the several small stacks of paper he had lined up on his makeshift desk. "You're still not finished yet?"

"No." He frowned and stretched his long legs out in front of him. "But I am due for a break."

Rebecca felt odd standing when he was sitting. She perched on the edge of a bale in the corner and folded her hands primly in her lap. "I never imagined writing would be such hard work."

"There are days when it isn't and days when it is." Jack rubbed the tense muscles in the back of his neck. "Today is one of those days when it is."

Rebecca looked back at the pages. She couldn't help it. She wanted to read them and see what he had written. She contented herself with asking a few more questions instead. "You said you had one more scene to write?" Jack nodded. "How many pages is one scene?"

"For this particular one, about ten pages."

Rebecca blinked. "It took you that long to write only ten pages?"

"No." Jack shook his head and sighed again. "It's a love scene. I'm having trouble getting the words right. So I keep doing it over and over. When I get one I'm completely happy with, I'll send it on to Los Angeles."

"I see," Rebecca said quietly.

Jack doubted that. In fact, he was sure she had no idea how tough it had been for him, hanging out here most of the day and all of the evening, trying to keep his mind on the characters in his movie when all he could really think about was Rebecca and how much he wanted to make love to her up here, the required revisions of the pivotal love scene for the movie be damned. Worse, he was stiff and sore from the hours spent hunched over the hay in the cool barn, working under primitive conditions so he wouldn't have to leave Rebecca. So she wouldn't think he was running off and deserting her again.

"What are you thinking?" she asked quietly.

"How glad I am that you came out to interrupt me again," Jack teased. "And I'm sorry I didn't pay you any attention earlier."

Rebecca glanced at his empty dinner tray. "I see you ate your dinner anyway."

"One of my many talents, eating and typing at the same time," he said with a grin, wishing she didn't look so damn good. He got up to see if there was any more lemonade in the thermos she'd brought out. There was just enough for half a cup each. He poured his into his glass and hers in the cup that topped the thermos. Walking over to hand her the cup, he sat down next to her on the hay. With the black cloak wrapped around her shoulders, feathery wisps of blond hair escaping from beneath her kapp, her cheeks pink with embarrassment, she had never looked prettier, or more ripe for seduction.

"So..." he said as she sipped wordlessly from the cup, "what brings you out here?" It was funny, but he had never seen her look so shy, so like she wanted to simply be with him.

Rebecca swallowed. "I came to check on you before I went to bed." She stood hastily, as if just remembering she had interrupted his work. "I can see you're fine," she continued briskly, bending to put the cup aside, "so I'll be leaving."

"Wait a minute." He caught her wrist and pulled her down onto the quilt beside him, on the makeshift bench seat. "I've got a question for you—on the Amish." He wished he could take her hair down again. He loved the way it felt in his hands, silky soft, deeply waving...

She regarded him suspiciously. Beside him, he felt her thigh tense. "What kind of question?"

Jack sighed inwardly. He could tell by the look on her face that all her defenses had just snapped securely back into place. So much for wooing her, at least tonight. And since that was the case, he might as well get back to work. "Have you ever bundled with anyone? You know, carried on a courtship on opposite sides of a bed?"

Rebecca's fair brows lowered like thunderclouds over her light blue eyes. "Bundling went out of use years ago for most Amish sects."

"How come?" Jack interrupted.

Rebecca drew in a deep breath that lifted her breasts and let it out slowly. She looked past him, toward the sturdy beams overhead. "Many of the bishops felt it led to amoral behavior."

It sure did in the movie scene he was writing, Jack thought. Too bad it wouldn't here. But, as long as she was out here, he might as well make use of the chance to have someone help him visualize what he was trying to write. He drained the thermos and put it aside. Taking her hand, he guided her to her feet and led her to the center of the blanket he had laid out on the loft floor. She looked down at the quilt he had rolled up and stretched lengthwise in the center of the blanket. "Don't tell me," she drawled, "this is your bundling place."

He grinned back at her, feeling ridiculously happy despite the poor work conditions and the pressure of having to write such a pivotal scene under incredible time pressure. "You catch on quick. Anyway, since I'm having such a hard time trying to envision this bundling scene I was hoping you'd help me out."

"Help you out how?" Rebecca ground out.

"All you have to do is pretend to bundle with me for a little while, up here in the loft," Jack explained. The moment the words were out, he knew his motives were less than pure. From a technical standpoint, he really didn't need to see Rebecca stretched out beside him on the quilt to be able to write the scene. But he did need another kiss. Or maybe two or three…

"You know, Jack, I thought you were crazy before but now I'm sure of it," Rebecca said. "You have taken leave of your senses." She started to step past him.

Again, he caught her wrist and tugged her close. "Afraid bundling with me would lead to amoral behavior?" he teased softly, taunting her with his gaze.

As he had expected she would, the challenge in his voice got to her. "Don't flatter yourself, Jack," she said stiffly. "I was a fool once. I do not intend to be one again."

He studied her flushed cheeks. He wasn't sure whether this was the time to get her to admit her feelings for him or not.

He did know they were running out of time. And they had damn few chances to be alone. This opportunity had been handed to him as if it were a gift; he'd be foolish not to use it. Particularly when it might lead to her accepting the inevitability of their love. Or admitting to him the truth about their Andy.

"Then prove you're immune to me," he taunted softly, keeping his eyes on hers, "and bundle with me for a little while."

She sucked in a quick angry breath. "This is ridiculous."

Jack just shrugged. The gauntlet had already been thrown down, it was up to her to pick it up. She didn't disappoint him. "Fine. We'll bundle," she said tightly. She stepped to one side of the quilt he had spread out over the loft floor, and reclined next to the rolled-up quilt in the middle, her body as stiff and straight as a stick. "This is my side." Rebecca pointed to the right. "That's yours."

Jack wasted no time taking his place on the other side of the "bundling bed" in the loft. Hands folded behind his neck, he lay back on his side, a grin on his face. "So," Jack said, wondering what the hell people did talk about in those days, "how did the quilting bee go?"

"We finished five more quilts. They'll each bring about two hundred dollars at market—"

"Is that all?" he interrupted, rolling onto his side. He propped his elbow up and rested his head on his hand. "They'd bring at least three hundred and fifty, maybe more, in Los Angeles."

"Yes," Rebecca corrected him with exaggerated patience, "but I don't live in Los Angeles."

"Well, there you're in luck, Rebecca, because I do."

"It's not going to work, Jack," Rebecca huffed as she hastened to sit up. Her expression was tense and accusing as she twisted around to face him. "You're not going to trick me into going out there with you."

"Hey." Irritated to be falsely accused, Jack caught her and rolled so she was beneath him. "I am not trying to trick you into doing anything," he said, bracing his arms on either side of her and staring down into her face.

"Aren't you?"

"No," he said quietly, threading his hands through her hair, pushing her kapp back, off her head. Needing to see her hair down, just for a little while, he began undoing the braid. "I'm not. I would never hurt you. Don't you know that?" he asked softly, combing his fingers through the silky white blond strands.

Rebecca's lower lip trembled. "Oh, Jack." Tears of regret and longing filled her eyes. "I wish things were different. I wish things could work for us, but they can't," she said in a choked voice as she struggled to get up once again.

He pushed her back. They'd come this far. She wasn't backing off now. Not if he had anything to say about it. "You haven't given us a chance to work things out," he said firmly, "but it's high time you did."

In a flash, she knew what he intended. And he knew what she intended. Before she could so much as try to scramble away from him again, he had both her wrists in his hands, and had pinned them above her head. Her breath caught in her chest. Her heart raced. Lower still, there was a mounting tension deep inside her. "Jack, don't—" She struggled against him, to no avail.

"Don't what?" he asked as his lips touched her cheeks, her brow, her eyes. He had never known he was capable of such tenderness. But around Rebecca, around Andy, all he felt was the incredible overwhelming desire to love.

Rebecca drew in a tremulous breath. "Don't...do...this."

"Don't do what?" Jack asked as he felt her body soften in surrender against the length of his. He kissed her eyelids shut, then worked his way down her cheek to her lips. His mouth hovered above hers as her eyelids fluttered open once again. "Don't kiss you?" His lips touched hers lightly, rubbed across them sensually, then withdrew. His smile widened rapaciously. "Or don't French-kiss you?"

"Jack—"

He cut off her gasp with a deep, sensual kiss. Electricity leapt and sizzled between them. "Tell me you don't want me," Jack challenged as the aching in his groin intensified and he kissed his way down her throat, to the collar of her dress. "Tell me you want me to leave this farm right now, leave and never come back, and I will." Ready to make good on his promise, he let go of her wrists. Bracing his weight on the forearms he'd planted on either side of her, he looked down into her face.

"Or, tell me you want me, that you've always wanted me, and we'll figure out a way to be together from now on." He paused, silently willing her to do the right thing for them both. "It's your choice, Rebecca. You decide."

Her eyes held his. Now was the moment of truth, Rebecca thought. And as she looked into his dark blue eyes, she knew she couldn't evade him any longer. "I should tell you to go," she said as her heart took up a slow, deliberate rhythm in her chest. She touched a hand to his thick chestnut hair. "But I can't." A familiar bittersweet longing filled her soul. "Not until I kiss you one last time." It might not be much, she thought miserably, but it was all she was going to have in the lonely days to come. The moment she had seen Jack get that express package she had known that he would be leaving her. It was just a matter of time now.

Jack's eyes darkened, as if he knew all she felt, and more, felt the impending loss, too. "Then one more kiss is what you've got," he said softly, lowering his mouth to hers.

The cautious part of her meant to hold him at bay, keep him from deepening the kiss unnecessarily, or going any farther than that, but the moment his lips touched hers again all was lost. All Rebecca could think about, all she could feel, all she could want, was the wonder of his mouth, and the incredibly sensual, incredibly giving way it felt, moving over her lips. She had never felt so much a woman, as she did at that moment, never wanted so much to be one with a man, and that made it all the harder to draw away.

Disappointment coiled sharply inside Jack as Rebecca

slipped from beneath him. Tensing with an immediate, galvanizing sense of loss, he reached out and curled a hand around her waist. "Don't go, Rebecca," he said softly, feeling both surprised and annoyed by the raw need he heard in his own low voice. He'd thought he'd stopped being vulnerable the day he'd been old enough to realize that his own father had walked out on him and his mother without so much as a second thought. But here he was, again sounding like a needy kid. "Please."

Rebecca struggled into her cloak. She looked very close to tears herself. "I have to. My grandparents might wake. And if they do, they'll wonder what's been keeping me."

Jack sighed. Things weren't exactly simple now, but they could be, he thought, if only he and Rebecca had the courage to be completely honest with her grandparents. "Then let's tell them," he said.

Chapter Ten

"Are you crazy?" Rebecca asked, her voice rising emotionally in the silence of the loft. Down below, a sleepy cow
mooed in irritation.

Rolling his eyes at the interruption, Jack continued to regard Rebecca seriously. "Ruth and Eli should know we care
about each other."

Rebecca gave him a searing look. "We don't, not in the
way you seem to be implying," she corrected as she
smoothed the rumpled layers of plain cotton chemise, blue
dress and black apron. Love was something that came after
years of knowing someone, after you'd seen them at their
best and their worst and still cared deeply what happened to
them. She and Jack hadn't even known each other a week,
all told.

"No?" Jack countered, just as acerbically. "Then what do
you call what's been going on here?"

She should have known he would ask that! Rebecca
glanced around for her cloak, wondering where she had left
it. "Infatuation!"

Jack shook his head. He watched her snatch up her cloak,
then caught her hand as she tried to pass him. "We feel a lot
more than a simple infatuation for each other, Rebecca," he
corrected sternly, swinging her back around in front of him
as if she were a partner in a barn dance.

Rebecca tipped up her chin belligerently as her knees collided with the muscular solidness of his. "No, we don't, Jack. You're just too much of a romantic to admit it at the moment." He quirked a brow at her; she quirked hers back, even more haughtily, then withdrew her hand from his and stepped back. "I am sure you'll come to grips with the reality of the situation in due time. Maybe as soon as you leave Pennsylvania." Jack gave her another quelling look that flamed her temper even more. Unable to help herself, Rebecca added caustically, "At least until another unclaimed child of yours appears on Alec Roman's doorstep."

Jack moved to the left, blocking her exit from the makeshift office. "That was uncalled for, Rebecca."

"Hey." She tapped an index finger against her breastbone, then pointed it back at him in an accusing manner. "I'm not the one sowing my seed all over this country."

Jack's mouth tightened in a grim warning that would have made a less spirited woman back off, but not Rebecca. "That was also uncalled for," he said, closing the distance between them swiftly.

Before she could do much more than mutter a protest, he took her into his arms again and held her close. Warmth flowed through her, followed swiftly by desire. Her blood quickened at every pulse point. It would be so easy to let herself be seduced into making love with him again, Rebecca thought. Too easy.

Sighing wearily, she lifted her chin to his. Light blue eyes met dark blue. "Let me ask you a question, Jack," she said, prefacing it with silent reassurances that she was adult enough to handle the answer. "Are you going back to Los Angeles?"

Jack's eyes darkened to a midnight-blue and he frowned, his reluctance to talk about that underscored only by his reluctance to let her go. "I'm going to have to, in a few days," he said, making no effort to spare her from harsh reality. "But you could come with me and Andy," he continued swiftly. "You could visit—"

Visit. Her heart sinking, Rebecca twisted out of his arms. "Maybe if you lived in the next county, Jack," she said in weary resignation, trying her hardest to be adult about all this. "But you live all the way across the country."

Jack watched her distance herself from him even more. He followed her over to the quilt where her kapp had fallen, watched as she took a seat on the bundle of hay and began to smooth her hair with her fingers. Jack removed the comb he habitually carried in his back pocket and flipped it onto her lap. "Well, we all don't drive buggies, you know," he reminded her in a deadpan voice. "You could hop a train or a bus. Hell, you could even live dangerously and hop a plane."

"And pay for it with what? My family is barely getting by as it is. They're going to need every cent I can bring in from the sale of my quilts just to buy the spring seed."

Jack paused. "I had no idea..." he said in a low, worried tone.

Rebecca put both hands out in front of her to ward off any further sympathy or comment. "I shouldn't have said anything. I'm just frustrated because it's getting increasingly hard to make a living off the land. Our taxes go up every year. Some years it's all we can do to pay them."

"Then why do you stay?"

Rebecca ran the comb through her hair, then began to pleat it into a single braid at the back of her head. "Because it's my home."

Again, Jack shook his head. His jaw hardened pugnaciously. "Home is where the heart is, Rebecca."

"Meaning what?" Rebecca secured her braid to the back of her head with a pin, then put her kapp back on. "I'm supposed to move to L.A. with you until you tire of me?"

"I will never tire of you," he stated. "But that's the gist of my proposal, yeah."

Rebecca couldn't believe he thought she had so little going in her life that she would just drop everything to be with him until he tired of her. This wasn't a movie he was scripting. "Well, forget it!" she stormed back.

"Why?" he asked again in a low mesmerizing tone, laced with quiet reason.

"Because it's not going to happen, Jack." She could not remember ever feeling quite so melancholy. "I desire you." Her lower lip trembled. "I admit it. But I'm not going to let you romanticize this," she said, her low voice gathering strength as all her self-protective forces moved firmly into place. "I'm not going to let you romanticize us, Jack."

He was silent, studying her thoughtfully. "The way your ex-husband did?" he asked gently.

Rebecca slipped her cloak on with stiff, jerky movements. "His intentions were honorable in the beginning, too."

The aggravation she'd seen on his face earlier was back. "Don't assume Wesley Adair and I are the same just because we're both English," he said.

He was acting as if her view of the situation was the only problem they had to surmount. "Then you stop romanticizing me and see me as who I really am."

"And who are you, Rebecca?" Jack demanded without quarter, his expression pensive. "Are you Amish or English or half of both? Admit it, Rebecca, you're not just confused about us, you're confused about you."

His words hit home. She sensed admitting the truth in them, however, would leave her at a distinct disadvantage. "Why would I be confused about myself?" she asked coolly. She sat perched on the edge of the bale of hay. She had been away from the house too long, but this was a conversation better held here, and she could tell from the look on his face, Jack wasn't about to let it go.

He sat beside her on the bale of hay. He lifted her hand and put it on his thigh, his warm strong fingers covering her cold limp ones. "Because you've always straddled two worlds, really belonging in neither place," he said softly, his dark blue eyes as persuasive as they were probing. "Part of you must rail at some of the hardships of Amish life."

Rebecca's hand tensed in his. She swallowed around the knot of growing emotion in her throat. As always, Jack was seeing far more about her than she was comfortable with. "So what?" she retorted quietly, her low voice echoing in the stillness of the barn. Shadows from the kerosene lantern hanging on the hook danced on the sturdy walls and rafters. "Everyone has frustrations."

Jack gently touched the back of his hand to her cheek. "But not every Amish woman makes reckless love with me." The silence strung out between them. His voice lowered a seductive notch. They looked at each other, each struggling to understand the other's feelings and needs. "I'm not asking you to give up all that much," he said finally.

Wasn't he? Following him to Los Angeles would mean giving up her entire life here, and that was a risk she just couldn't take. The people in the community had forgiven her for making a fool of herself over an Englishman once. If she did it a second time, to the same result, she'd be considered a woman of loose morals. And though she might not care so very much what other people thought about her, she knew her grandparents did, and she couldn't bear to see them hurt like that.

Rebecca stood and restlessly moved away. The loft felt cold and damp. As lonely and desolate as her heart. She stared at the shadow of herself on the wall, and the outline her cloak made. When she had regained her composure, she turned back to face him. "This isn't a movie, Jack. It's real life, with real people, all of whom stand to be very hurt if this thing blows up in our faces."

"How do you know?" He got to his feet in one slow, smooth movement that in no way undermined the intensity of his gaze. "I think your grandparents would understand why the three of us need to be together now if we just leveled with Ruth and Eli and told them the truth. In fact, I think under the circumstances they'd want us to be together."

"You're wrong, Jack. My grandparents would think I was a fool if I ran off with you. And they'd be right," she said, moving closer as she pleaded her case. "Things don't work out neatly just because the writer in you thinks they should."

"Oh, I don't know about that," he quipped lightly. "I think I scripted this last scene up here pretty well."

Rebecca's face burned as the sensual memories returned. She refused to let him get her off the subject at hand. "You have to face it, Jack," she continued. Melancholy flooded her once again. "As much as we desire each other, a love affair between us would never work long-term because of the differences in our life-styles and our backgrounds."

His brows rose in the equivalent of a shrug. "Says you," he disagreed.

"I am not going to have another failed marriage," she said flatly, her temper flaring as her attempts to reason with him failed.

Jack folded his arms in front of him. He waggled his eyebrows at her and grinned as if he'd just won a major battle. "So you're thinking marriage, huh, Rebecca?" he teased. "I take that as a very good sign."

Rebecca stormed past him and gathered up the dinner tray. "This is all a game to you," she said bad temperedly, annoyed he had gotten her to reveal so much more about her feelings for him than she had ever intended. Annoyed he had made her hope they might have a future together one day after all.

He stepped aside to let her pass. His eyes gleamed in the shadows of the barn. "It's not a game, Rebecca. It's real life, just like Andy is a real baby, not a figment of my imagination."

Her back stiff, Rebecca halted in her tracks.

"I'm not giving up on you," he said as she turned around slowly to face him. He gave her a steely look. "Nor on us. Not now and not ever. And the sooner you accept that the happier you'll be."

"So, YOU SENT YOUR WORK back to Los Angeles?" Ruth said the next morning when Jack walked inside.

Jack shrugged out of his leather jacket and took a seat next to the quilt the women had spread out on the floor. Andy was lying on his back, his head turned to the Amish rag doll Rebecca had made for him. Only it wasn't the same doll he had seen the other night. Rebecca had embroidered two blue eyes, a turned-up nose, pink circle cheeks, a smattering of freckles and a big smile on the doll. She'd also used yellow yarn for hair, and made a black felt Amish hat to go with the blue shirt and black overalls on the boy doll. It was an Amish version of Raggedy Andy. And Andy seemed as taken by the love she'd put into it as he was. "Yes," Jack answered Ruth in a distracted tone. He paused to smile at Rebecca's grandmother over his shoulder. "I just faxed it."

"Your employers were happy with your work?" Ruth asked.

"I hope so," Jack said. The pages were among the best he'd ever written. After Rebecca had left him alone last night, it had only taken him another hour to polish the dialogue he'd already had and add the finishing touches such as scene direction. He'd wanted to be available to Rebecca today and spend time with her again. Unfortunately she wasn't sparing him any attention.

Instead she was busy blocking out yet another quilt at the kitchen table. This one was a series of triple chains and random stars and octagons. She'd used every color of the rainbow in the design. Ruth kept glancing at Rebecca's work, intrigued, and Jack knew exactly how she felt. He couldn't seem to stop looking at the quilt Rebecca was designing, either. It was almost too pretty, too unique to be used as a comforter on a bed. He felt it should be hanging in an art gallery somewhere.

Rebecca met his gaze equably. "I imagine you're about ready to go back to Los Angeles then."

"On the contrary," Jack said, mocking her almost too pleasant tone, and saw the change in her eyes. "In fact, I'm thinking of staying a few more days. That is, if it's all right with Ruth and Eli."

Ruth smiled back at him as she finished filling a wicker basket with jars of home-canned peaches. "Of course it's all right, Jack.'' She shut the lid on the picnic hamper and reached for her black cloak and matching bonnet. As she tied her bonnet under her chin, she said, ''We've enjoyed having you here. Now if the two of you will excuse me,'' she said, noting that Eli had parked the horse and buggy just outside the back door, ''I've got to take these peaches and the strudel Rebecca just baked to Mrs. Good.''

Rebecca continued arranging quilting squares long after her grandparents had left. Jack let her revel in the silence for several minutes as he played with the son he'd spent precious little time with the past twenty-four hours. Finally he decided it was time they cleared the air. ''Still mad at me, aren't you?'' he said.

Rebecca threaded a needle and then began the process of basting the squares together with long smooth stitches. ''Anger is a waste of both time and energy, Jack.''

Jack stood and sauntered over to the table. ''So you're happy with me then?'' he teased.

She gave him a droll look he found greatly encouraging.

''Come see our son,'' he said. Taking her by the hand, he tugged her to the edge of the blanket where Andy was still playing contentedly. After a moment's hesitation, she dropped her eyes from his and glanced at Andy. He was curling his tiny fingers toward the doll she had made for him. He batted it frantically, finally curling his fingers around the doll's hand. ''See how much he likes the doll you made for him?'' Jack asked softly, tightening his own grip on Rebecca's hand, noting that she hadn't moved to extricate herself from his hold—yet.

Rebecca sighed. The sound was wistful in the quiet of the room. ''He likes the face I sewed on it,'' she said in a clipped tone of voice.

Jack tugged her down so that they were both sitting picnic style on the edge of Andy's quilt.

''I wish someone had sewed me a doll like this when I was a kid.''

Rebecca's light blue eyes widened curiously. "What kind of toys did you have?" she asked.

Jack shrugged. Maybe he shouldn't have started this conversation. "Just things you could buy in a store. Bats and balls, stuff like that."

Rebecca's teeth scraped the softness of her lower lip. "That's the first time I've ever heard you say anything about your childhood."

Now Jack knew he shouldn't have started this. "Not much to tell."

Rebecca's glance held with mesmerizing intensity. "Not much to tell or not much you want to tell?" she asked.

Touché, Jack thought. "What do you want to know?" he asked gruffly, wishing this weren't so hard for him.

Rebecca's blue eyes narrowed speculatively. "Did you have a happy childhood?"

Jack held himself very still, wondering if he should give her the cheerful version he had cleaned up for strangers or the ugly, unvarnished truth. He looked into her eyes and decided on a point in between. "What I remember most about the early years is being very lonely. I think that's why I became a writer. I didn't have a lot to occupy myself, so I had to use my vivid imagination to keep myself entertained."

"No brothers or sisters?"

"No," Jack said, aware the two of them had that in common, being only children. "Though I've got a couple of friends—Alec Roman and Grady Noland, who feel like brothers."

"What was it like for you, growing up?"

"Finances were really tight. My mother had to work two jobs to support us, which in turn meant I rarely saw her. If it hadn't been for the scholarship to prep school, and the one to Penn after that, who knows where I would've ended up?" Jack looked at Andy, who was still gazing contentedly at his Amish doll, and promised his son would have a better life than he'd had.

Rebecca studied Jack with compassion and understanding. "But you're happy writing, aren't you?"

"Very."

Her expression turned troubled. "What's it like to live in California? Los Angeles is very trendy, isn't it?" Jack nodded, not sure where this was going. He was sure he didn't like it. "Fashions change constantly, don't they?"

Jack shrugged. "I guess. I always dress pretty much the same. Jeans, shirts, leather jacket. Sometimes I add a bill cap or vary the shoes, but—" he held his arms akimbo "—what you see now is pretty much what you get, at least as far as my wardrobe is concerned."

She flushed and looked irritated again. "You know what I mean."

Jack touched his son lightly on the cheek and watched him smile, then drew a deep breath. "I think I know what you're getting at. I think you're trying to convince me you wouldn't fit in there. You're wasting your time, Rebecca. Because I think you would." Still sitting on the edge of the quilt, he lowered his mouth and kissed her sweetly. She was trembling when they drew apart and Jack knew exactly how she felt. He wanted nothing more than to say to hell with everything and everyone and make love to her then and there. Only Andy's playful gurgling reminded him they couldn't.

He released her slowly and turned his attention back to his son. The son Rebecca still wouldn't claim.

She was already getting to her feet. Her steps brisk and purposeful, she moved across the kitchen to get her cloak. He watched her take the car keys off the hook next to the back door. "Please keep an eye on the stew," she said.

Jack tensed as beside him Andy kicked and flailed, trying to get the doll to do the same. "Where are you going?"

Rebecca turned to face him, her expression brisk and purposeful. "It's my day to pick up quilts. I'll be taking the car."

Jack picked up Andy and the doll and held both cradled

in his arms. "I could drive you," he offered. Andy would probably enjoy riding in a car again.

Rebecca looked at him. "No, Jack," she said softly but firmly, "you can't drive me. There's too much talk about us already."

"SHE SHOULD HAVE BEEN back by now, shouldn't she?" Jack asked as seven o'clock came and went.

Eli and Ruth looked as disturbed as he felt. "It isn't like Rebecca to miss supper with the family," Eli agreed.

Ruth paced to the window. A light snow had begun to fall. "Perhaps the bad weather is slowing her down," she said.

"Or perhaps she is having trouble with her car again," Eli said with a frown.

"Why?" Jack asked, the anxiety of not knowing what had happened to Rebecca almost more than he could bear. "What's wrong with her car? She's got snow chains on it, doesn't she?"

"Of course she has snow chains, as well as snow tires." Eli frowned. "But the radiator has a leak in it. We patched it last month, but...it is possible the cold weather has ruined the patch."

Might have ruined the patch? It was all Jack could do not to swear as he imagined the many calamities that might have befallen Rebecca. His heart racing, he handed Andy over to Ruth. "I'm going to go out and look for her," he announced, already reaching for his leather jacket. He shrugged it on then searched his pockets for his keys. "Do you have any idea which roads she might have taken?"

Eli nodded. He seemed glad Jack was taking action. "I'll write you a list," he said.

Minutes later, Jack set out in his rental car, the map in his hand. The snow made it almost impossible to see more than a few feet in front of him. Worse, because of the weather, few cars were on the road. What if he couldn't find her? What if her car had broken down somewhere and she had been mugged trying to fix it? What if she had been in an accident? He had to stop this, he schooled himself firmly.

Finally he saw her old station wagon. It was pulled over to the side of the road. The emergency flashers were on but it was apparently otherwise intact, he noted with relief. Eli had probably been right. It probably was the radiator.

He parked behind her, turned on his emergency flashers and got out. He strode to the car window, the snow pelting his face. Before he got to her side, Rebecca had opened her car door and stepped out. "Jack!" She looked happy but not particularly surprised to see him. It irritated him to see that she was as calm as her grandparents had been. They were all acting as if this kind of calamity happened every day. Then again, considering the antiquated condition of the car she drove, it probably did.

"What happened?" he asked, not sure whether he wanted to shake her or kiss her. Only that he was very glad to see her all in one piece.

"What do you think?" She scowled at him in obvious irritation as tiny snowflakes pelted her fair cheeks. "My car quit on me."

Jack's frown deepened at her flip tone. It irked him no end that Rebecca never seemed to sense when she was in danger. For a woman her age, she had a serious lack of street sense. Whereas he, having grown up in a very bad part of Philadelphia, had an overabundance of it. "Why didn't you tell me the radiator on it was bad when you left this afternoon?" he demanded irascibly.

She sighed, exasperated, and planted her hands on her hips. "Because it was working then."

"But not now."

She shot him a deadpan look. "Obviously not or I wouldn't be sitting here on the side of the road not moving now, would I, oh handsome rescuer?"

Jack couldn't help but grin at her teasing description of him. He rubbed a hand through his hair. "I see that tart tongue of yours is still in working order," he said finally.

"Yep."

He glanced at the back of the station wagon. As before when he had rescued her, the car was piled high with hand-sewn quilts. "I suppose you want to move the quilts from your car to mine?" he said.

"We're leaving my car here?" she asked in surprise.

"I'm no miracle worker with cars and I can't tow it with this rental car. So yeah, we'll have to."

Rebecca frowned, but made no further complaint. They worked in silence, rushing back and forth. Finally they finished and she got in the passenger side. He slid in beside her, behind the wheel. His heater was going full blast. It was warm and cozy inside. "You're lucky I came along," he said as he jerked off his gloves and tossed them onto the dash.

Rebecca took off her black wool bonnet and dusted the snow from the brim. "It seems to me I've heard this speech before, Jack Rourke. Someone would've come along eventually."

"A nice Amish family?"

"Of course."

"And if they hadn't?"

She shrugged. "I would have either bundled up in the quilts and waited until morning, or bundled up in the quilts and walked to the next farmhouse, depending on the weather. But first, I simply waited to be rescued."

Her logic was plain and simple. Unfortunately they lived in a complicated, often messy and dangerous world. "Dammit, Rebecca, you need to have a more reliable car if you're going to be driving around alone like this," he said, in no hurry to get back to the Lindholm farm now that he'd found her.

Incensed, she shifted to face him. "You have no right to lecture me this way."

Jack ignored the light layer of snow dusting the windshield. "I have every right."

"Because you've appointed yourself my temporary knight in shining armor?" she retorted through tightly gritted teeth.

"Because I care about you," he corrected roughly.

"That doesn't matter." She reached for the door handle and started to push from the car.

"The hell it doesn't," Jack said. He pulled her back in his arms and reached past her to shut her door all the way again. "I want you safe." Without warning, he was suddenly fed up with the tension, the waiting, the pretending they didn't want and need each other desperately. "Don't you understand, Rebecca?" he asked hoarsely. "I can't go on like this—worrying about you, how you feel. You're my world, Rebecca," he whispered, his voice catching just a little, before he clamped down hard and got control of it once again. "My whole world."

He lowered his mouth to hers and delivered a searing kiss, putting all that he felt for her, all that he had been searching for, in that one caress. He expected her to fight; she surrendered. He expected her to protest; she brought him closer and whispered his name. He shifted her onto his lap, thinking they could handle a few more kisses. But nothing in his ever-present and all too vivid imagination had ever prepared him for the touch and feel and taste of her, the sunny springlike scent of her. Nothing had ever prepared him for the highly romantic, supercharged experience of kissing Rebecca while the snow fell all around them. Their mouths blended in desperation, in joy, in longing.

Finally Rebecca broke off the kiss. "We can't go on this way, Jack," she said in a voice that trembled. "I'm not cut out for sneaking around. If someone were to drive by and see us and word of this got back to my grandparents—" She compressed her lips together. Heat flooded her face as she shook her head in wordless displeasure. "It would be just too humiliating, not just for me, but for my whole family."

Jack was silent, unable to argue with her about that. It had been years since he'd been reduced to sneaking around and stealing kisses like a love-struck teenager. "I admit I'm not comfortable with the situation, either," he said gruffly. "But there is a solution, Rebecca."

"What?" Rebecca asked, flushing as his gaze fastened on the throbbing pulse in her throat.

Jack gently tucked a hand beneath her chin, lifted her face up to his and looked deep into her eyes. "We could get married."

Chapter Eleven

"Now I know you're crazy!" Rebecca said, moving all the way over to her side of the car.

Jack turned on his headlights, switched off the emergency blinkers and backed up slightly. "Because I want us to be together?" he asked as he eased the rental car back onto the road.

"Because Andy is not my baby," Rebecca said, clamping her arms around her waist. She stared straight ahead. He sighed and braked as they approached a four-way stop.

"I told you before, Rebecca. Sending me on a wild moose chase is not going to work."

"I am not trying to get rid of you."

"Aren't you?" Jack asked as snow continued to pelt their windshield. Rebecca fell silent. "I'm sure Andy is my son, Rebecca, and no amount of clever tricks or skillful dissuasion on your part is going to convince me otherwise."

Jack checked to make sure the intersection was clear, then continued on, driving slowly and carefully as the weather warranted.

Rebecca looked out the window at the blur of white landscape passing by. Her feelings were in turmoil. She couldn't understand why Jack would not let go of this theory, that Andy was his child. Unless…

Jack had accused her of fibbing about Andy's parentage. For the first time, Rebecca began to wonder if maybe the reason Jack was so certain that Andy was his, was that Jack was the one who was fibbing here, and had been all along.

Was it possible he'd been with another woman shortly before or after he'd made love to her? Rebecca wondered. Some woman not so suited to motherhood? Some woman capable of leaving a baby on the doorstep for Jack? Was it possible, she thought, beginning to feel a little ill, that Jack had made love to another woman during the weeks he'd been staying at Alec Roman's Philadelphia mansion last spring?

"Let me ask you something, Jack." Rebecca swiveled toward him as Jack continued to drive slowly and carefully in the direction of the Lindholm farm. "If Andy weren't your child, and you realized that, even belatedly, would you get help from the authorities and try to discover who Andy's real parents were?"

"Of course I would," Jack said, sounding a little aggrieved that she even had to ask!

"Even though you've obviously fallen in love with him and would like nothing better than to raise him as your own," Rebecca continued bluntly.

Jack frowned and upped the windshield wipers' speed another notch. "I have no interest in stealing someone else's child from them," Jack said in an annoyed voice. He braked as they reached another four-way stop, then paused to regard her impatiently. "What's this all about? Why the questions?"

Rebecca hugged her waist. "I just needed to know, for my own peace of mind." And now she did. Jack had latched onto Andy because Andy really was his child. And since Andy wasn't her child, then Andy had to be the result of another fling, with another woman.

Had Jack come to Rebecca because he believed she was the mother? Perhaps he didn't want to own up to the fact that he had sired a child with a woman who wasn't loving and nurturing, and had come to Rebecca just because he needed a mother for Andy and figured that she fit the bill. Maybe he had been so desperate to find a mother for his son, so that Andy would not grow up with only one parent the way Jack himself had, that he was willing to do anything to convince Rebecca to step in and fill the shoes of the woman who had abandoned Andy on Alec's doorstep.

Rebecca wasn't about to be used by Jack, any more than she would marry him just so she could mother his son and have her own child to love at long last. Furthermore, Jack hadn't said anything about actually loving her, Rebecca thought. Just that he cared about her and desired her and enjoyed being with her. He had probably thrown in the idea of marriage tonight only as a last resort.

Jack braked again as they approached the next intersection. When the car came to a complete stop, he rested an arm on the steering wheel and turned toward her. "Look, Rebecca, I know having to hide the way we feel about each other is upsetting to you," he said softly, thinking erroneously that this was the reason she was so disturbed. "It's upsetting to me, too. That's why I suggested we tell your grandparents about us the other night. They already love Andy. They like me. If they knew you and I had a romantic past, too, that we wanted to make a home for Andy—"

"Hold it right there, Jack! There is no way I am publicly claiming Andy as my child," Rebecca said. "Not if that means ruining *my* reputation and the reputation of *my family* in the process!"

Again, Jack glared at her in silent frustration. "Not even if it means saving Andy from the stigma of having to grow up as an abandoned kid?" Jack asked hoarsely. He shook his head, his own painful memories surfacing once again. "I know what that's like, Rebecca. I grew up that way, too, without a father. It was hell, having to tell every single teacher I ever had that I had no idea where my father was, or if he was dead or alive, working or not. The teachers pitied me, the kids taunted me mercilessly. Is that what you want for Andy?"

"No," Rebecca said, empathetic tears spilling from her eyes. "Of course that's not what I want for Andy! No baby deserves that!"

"Then help me out here," Jack pleaded emotionally, gripping her hands with both of his. "Go to Eli and Ruth, tell them we made love last spring, that that was why you were so upset last summer and had to go away and then claim Andy as your son. Let them say they're his step-grandparents. They don't have to tell anyone in Blair County what's really going on. Just claim Andy as your own legally, so he'll have the mother that he deserves, publicly, in Los Angeles."

Rebecca moaned softly. "I can't lie about something like this, Jack."

"I'm not asking you to lie, just not tell the whole truth," Jack retorted soothingly. "We could make this work," he said softly, "if you'd give us half a chance."

Rebecca stared at Jack, unable to believe he was so naive to think they could get away with such a convoluted plan, never mind try to explain to her grandparents what had happened between Jack and her on that dark, stormy night last spring. Particularly when they didn't even really understand how it was they had fallen into bed so quickly themselves!

Jack let go of her hands abruptly and rested his arm along the back of the seat. "Look, Rebecca," he said with growing frustration, "I admit our situation has been a little mixed-up from the get-go."

"That's putting it mildly. I still can't believe I...we..." She flushed, unable to go on.

"Made love that night last spring?" he supplied softly.

"Yes!" Rebecca lowered her gaze from his.

He lifted his hand to the side of her face and gently caressed her cheek with the backs of his fingers. "Don't you see?" he asked softly in a low husky voice that sent shivers of excitement down her spine. "The speed with which we got together is proof of the fact we were meant to be together, Rebecca. And the way you feel about Andy...the way he openly responds to you and adores not just you but your entire family...is even more proof that we should be a family."

Jack made a persuasive argument. Rebecca remained on

her side of the car, for a moment simply savoring the sight of him and the wonder of being alone with him in the softly falling snow. But her feelings of desire and love for him were tempered with the cold practicality in her heart, and the fear that he was using her.

She sighed as her inner anxieties obliterated the last residual feelings of pleasure she felt just being with Jack. "I confused the excitement of romance for love once Jack, and the heartbreak was almost more than I could bear. I married without a foundation of true love once. I'll never ever do it again."

"What about Andy?" Jack asked in a strangled tone. He looked even more distressed.

Rebecca steeled her heart against his emotional pleas. "I won't ruin my own family's reputation," she warned.

He touched her hair, stroked it gently. "Just think about accepting the responsibility for Andy and raising him as your own for a few more days before you give me an answer, Rebecca," he said softly. "That's all I ask."

"WHAT DID ABRAHAM SAY?" Eli asked when Rebecca and Jack returned to the farm late the next morning. They'd spent the morning having her car towed to an Amish neighbor's barn while Ruth and Eli stayed home, saw to the chores and took care of Andy.

Rebecca slipped off her cloak and hung it on the hook next to the door. She met her grandfather's eyes, hating to be the one who always had to deliver the bad news. "He said that I am going to have to buy a new radiator if I want to fix my car," she said quietly. Beside her, Jack shrugged out of his coat, too. He walked over to check on his son, who was cozily ensconced in Ruth's arms, drawing on a bottle of formula.

Ruth looked up from the baby in her arms and sent Rebecca a worried glance. "How much will that cost?"

Rebecca bit her lip. "Five hundred dollars." As her grandparents' faces grew ashen, she hastened to add, "He'll do the labor for free."

"Unfortunately," Eli said with another frown, "we don't have five hundred extra dollars to spend on the car."

Nor a way to get her quilts to market, Rebecca thought, and without the money the sale of the quilts would bring, there would be no way to buy the spring seed.

"I know a way you could get it," Jack suggested.

Everyone turned to look at him. "I've got a friend in California, Russ Saunders, who owns an art gallery that specializes in regional folk art. He's got a group of women in Appalachia who supply him with quilts on a regular basis."

"I don't see what that has to do with us," Rebecca interrupted.

"You could sell your quilts there for twice the money you'd get in Philadelphia," Jack continued. "You'd probably have enough to buy the spring seed and fix your car."

"But how would I get them there?" Rebecca asked. Shipping things was expensive. And risky. Packages on trucks had been known to get damaged. For some of the women in her quilting circle, one quilt, and the profits from it, was all they had. Others, like Rebecca, had three to five handmade quilts each to sell.

Jack appeared thoughtful as he stared down at his son, who seemed to be getting sleepier by the minute. "I have to go back to Los Angeles anyway." He paused and looked up at Rebecca. The gentle protectiveness in his eyes stirred her more than she wanted to admit.

"I could accompany you, see you got there safely and put you on a plane back home. I know," Jack hastened to add, as he turned to Eli and Ruth, seeking permission. "Normally flying isn't encouraged among the Amish, but it is permitted under special circumstances."

Ruth looked at Eli.

"Surely this qualifies," Jack continued persuasively. And just that quickly, it seemed, it was all arranged.

"YOU CHANGED CLOTHES," Jack said with a frown when Rebecca emerged from the ladies' room in the Philadelphia airport the next morning.

Rebecca grinned back at him smugly. She was wearing faded straight-leg jeans, a plain navy blue turtleneck and a bone-colored stadium jacket. She'd taken off her kapp and brushed her hair down. She wore Keds and plain white socks on her feet.

This was more of a test than he knew. "Feeling your fantasies fade, Jack?" she taunted as she switched her old-fashioned valise to her other hand.

Jack put a hand to the small of her back and guided her toward the gate. "I didn't know you had clothes like this."

Rebecca slanted a glance at Andy, who was securely strapped into a sling-style baby carrier that Jack wore like a backpack in front of him. He was wide-awake, and curiously looking around at the activity in the airport. Catching Rebecca's glance, Andy beamed her a toothless smile. Like his father, she thought on a wistful sigh, baby Andy was all charm.

Aware Jack was still waiting for an answer about where she'd gotten the clothes, Rebecca glanced up at him. "I told you I lived English the entire year I was married."

"You kept the clothes even after returning to the farm?"

"Waste not, want not, you know. Besides," she shrugged, "I always figured I'd use them in a quilt or something someday. But they were really too nice to cut up."

He seemed to be thinking that her keeping the clothes after all this time should be telling her something, but to her relief he didn't voice his thoughts out loud. One by one, they passed through the metal detectors. When they emerged on the other side of it, he said softly, "I always wondered how you'd look in jeans. Now I know." His eyes darkened sexily. "You look great."

That threw her. She had expected him to be disappointed. He wasn't. "Sure you don't like me better in a dress?" she goaded lightly.

He grinned and leaned down to whisper in her ear. "I like you best in nothing at all." He straightened, his blue eyes twinkling merrily. "I just haven't seen you that way in awhile." But he would, his grin seemed to say.

Rebecca concentrated on getting to the right gate. When they had, she got out her ticket. "Is Andy a good traveler?"

"He has been so far." Jack paused. His glance turned serious. "Why did you change clothes?"

Rebecca sighed. "I don't like being stared at, and I have a feeling my Amish dress would earn me plenty of stares in California."

For a moment Jack looked like he wanted to disagree with her about that but the moment passed without comment from him. "While you were in the ladies' room, I talked to my friend, Russ Saunders. Everything's set for your showing at the gallery tomorrow night, but I have to warn you, Rebecca. He's made a big deal about the fact that you're bringing authentic Amish work with you. He's going to expect to see you in Amish clothing."

Rebecca burned with sudden resentment. She scowled at Jack as they boarded the plane and settled in their seats. "Then he's going to have to be disappointed because I'm no one's public exhibit, or Amish fantasy."

But Jack only grinned again. "You're wrong about that," he said, leaning down to whisper in her ear. "You're my fantasy, Rebecca. And you always will be."

Silence fell between them. The next few minutes were taken up with getting in their seats. Jack settled Andy into his infant seat, in the seat next to the window, then sat down in the middle seat, so that he was between her and Andy.

As soon as he was settled, he took her hand in his and held it tightly. "I'm glad you came with me."

Rebecca looked into his dark blue eyes and saw only sincerity. She regarded him warily. "Why?"

He smiled gently. "I want you to see my home out there."

Rebecca stared past Jack and Andy, out the window, as the big commercial jet backed out of the gate and began the slow taxi toward the runway. "You think I'll be tempted to stay in California, don't you?"

Jack waggled his eyebrows at her and gave her hand another squeeze. "A guy can always hope," he quipped.

She shook her head and sent her glance heavenward. She knew this was all still a fantasy to him. But life wasn't like a movie. There were no easy answers, and often, no happy endings. Not for people like them. "Jack, you are such a dreamer."

His eyebrows climbed. "And you're not, I suppose."

Rebecca shrugged, aware it wasn't fear she was feeling now so much as excitement to be with him. "I'm not in a league with you," she said lightly, instructing herself to keep her defenses up. Though she sensed that was an activity more easily decided than accomplished.

Jack studied her with detached thoughtfulness. "Then why did you decide to come with me?" His glance narrowed faintly as he waited for her answer.

Because I want to make love to you without fear of interruption, or discovery, Rebecca thought. But she was also afraid that if she did make love with him she would be in over her head...

Hours later, they landed at LAX. Rebecca held Andy while Jack collected their luggage and the boxes of quilts, found a skycap to help him load everything on a cart and went out to long-term parking to pick up his car. Rebecca stood at the curb, Andy in her arms, the warm sunshine swirling around them. If this was a dream, she thought, feeling ridiculously happy and relaxed and free of curious public scrutiny, she didn't want to wake up.

The skycap turned to her with a friendly grin. "You folks glad to be home again?"

Not wanting to get into the story of her life, Rebecca nodded.

"Where you all traveling from?" the skycap continued.

"We flew out of Philadelphia," Rebecca said.

The skycap made a comical face. "Whoa. Cold out there, isn't it?"

"Very," Rebecca said. Although Jack hadn't seemed to mind the weather. Traveling by horse and buggy...now there was another matter.

"Well, you got a cute baby and a pretty nice looking husband," the skycap said as Jack pulled his Mercedes SL Coupe up to the curb. "A very nice car. And great weather here in Los Angeles. What more could you want?"

Indeed, Rebecca thought as Jack popped the trunk, and he and the skycap began the process of loading everything into the car. "You and your husband have a good day now," the skycap said after Jack had tipped him.

Jack got into the car, grinning hugely. "Husband?"

"I didn't want to go into long explanations," Rebecca said, pink-cheeked.

"This is what it would be like, you know," Jack said in a deep, satisfied voice. "The three of us, traveling around. Together. With every luxury imaginable."

Yes, Rebecca thought, but would you love me, Jack? Not just today or tomorrow but forever? That was what she really wanted to know. If she could believe it, then everything would be different. If she could believe it, she just might take the leap, chuck everything familiar once again and marry an English-man.

Chapter Twelve

"So what do you think?" Jack asked as he shifted a sleeping Andy a little higher in his arms.

Rebecca looked around his trilevel home in the Hollywood Hills. She had expected his home to be luxurious, and it was. She just hadn't expected it to be this cozy or welcoming. Like her grandparents' farmhouse, this place had wood floors that were polished to a golden glow. Area rugs were scattered here and there. There was a massive fireplace with a field-stone hearth in the family room, a sunny well-equipped kitchen with a dishwasher and a microwave, four bedrooms—three of which were completely empty—and three bathrooms. His study ran the entire length of the house, and had two computers, several printers, a fax machine, copier and...a Nordic track? She turned to him in surprise.

"When I get blocked, a little exercise helps," he said.

Rebecca nodded. Aware he was waiting to hear her reaction, she said, "Your home is beautiful, Jack."

He grinned, pleased. "Ah, but the question is, can you see yourself living here?"

Her throat dry, her pulse racing, she smiled. "You're pushing me, Jack."

He merely raised a brow at her soft-spoken warning. "And you're evading."

She strode nearer, aware her nipples were beading beneath the T-shirt and bra. She told herself it was because she wasn't used to being in air-conditioning. Cupping her hands beneath opposite elbows, she said, "Don't you have to go to the studio?"

"Tomorrow morning." Jack placed a sleeping Andy in his Portacrib, then walked to her side. "Tonight is all ours." He came up behind her, his front to her back, and put his hands lightly on her shoulders. "So what would you like to do?"

Rebecca knew they had to do something or they'd end up in his bed in about two minutes. She turned around to face him. Her heart was racing. Lower still, she tensed in all too familiar anticipation. "I'd like to see one of your movies."

Jack dropped his hands with a frown. "I don't have anything in the theater right now, but I've got them all on videotape—"

Rebecca smiled. "Sounds perfect," she said.

SIX HOURS, three feedings, four diaper changes later, Andy was finally ready to go to bed for the night. Jack put him down while Rebecca finished watching his Western, *Beneath a Blazing Sun.*

It had been a long day, starting with the drive from the farm to the airport, then the flight, then the trip back to his place, the rigamarole of getting settled, ordering dinner in. Jack knew he should be tired. He wasn't.

He felt as if he could go another twenty-four hours. Looking at Rebecca, who showed no signs of drowsiness, he guessed the same was true for her.

Jack switched off the VCR and, pretending not to see the tears running down her face, he took her hand and led her out back to the deck that ran across the entire width of the house. It overlooked both his lagoon-style swimming pool and the heavily populated canyon below. The night stars shone above. Jack was achingly aware that they had less than forty-eight hours left together in California. Then she'd be on a plane back to Pennsylvania. He'd have to decide whether to follow her back or cut his losses and stay here, alone with Andy.

He hadn't changed his mind about wanting her to be a central part of his life. That would always remain the case, he suspected. But he wasn't sure if she would ever allow herself to trust him. And trust was something he couldn't live without.

Jack looked down at Rebecca. She was still choked up, tears running down her face.

He grinned, remembering he'd felt the same aching sadness when he'd written the screenplay. Perhaps the two of them weren't so far apart in their thinking after all, he thought, encouraged by that sign of oneness. Perhaps all Rebecca needed was time to gather her courage, so that she could go to her grandparents and tell them the truth, and then claim her son, marry him, and move to Los Angeles, permanently.

"Come on, the movie wasn't that sad," he teased, taking her into his arms.

To his delight, Rebecca didn't fight him. She leaned into the solid male warmth of his chest. At that moment, her life in Pennsylvania seemed very far away to Jack.

She gazed up at him, her expression serious, admiring to the point of utter devotion. Jack felt another thrill slide through him. She respected his work. That was one barrier down.

"You're a very talented writer, Jack," she said softly.

He grinned, wondering if there was ever a time she didn't look beautiful, and wiped away a tear with a thumb. "So they keep telling me," he drawled, trying without much success not to let her heartfelt praise go to his head.

"You could never give it all up, could you?" she said.

Jack tensed as he realized this conversation was leading to the question of whether he could live in Pennsylvania indefinitely or not. He already knew, from his conversation with the director and the studio head yesterday, that they expected him to be more readily available during the filming of future screenplays than he had been the last week or so.

Marrying Rebecca and moving to Pennsylvania would ultimately mean living a bicoastal life-style he wasn't really sure would be good for any family. Deciding to keep things simple for the moment, he only shrugged and said, "I'm a writer, Rebecca. I can write anywhere. Even in a loft, if I have to. I thought I'd proved that."

"Yes," she said calmly, still studying his face with relentless scrutiny, "but that was very uncomfortable."

"True." Jack nodded briefly, recalling first the hours in the cold, drafty loft, then the hour or so he'd spent with her, alone up there. At that memory, he couldn't help but grin. "Until you arrived on the scene, anyway," he teased.

"Don't mock me about that."

"Who's kidding?" Jack said earnestly, still holding her against him, length to length. "You fulfilled any number of my fantasies that night."

Rebecca inhaled sharply. Her thighs trembled against his. "You dreamed about kissing a woman in a hayloft?"

Jack threaded his fingers through her hair. "I dreamed about kissing *you* in a hayloft. Now the car..." He couldn't help but grin rapaciously again at the delicious memory. "The car caught me by surprise."

She flushed, embarrassed by the frank, sexual talk, then shook her head in silent, mocking reproof. "You're incorrigible," she said sternly.

"Insatiable," he corrected quietly, bending his head to kiss her softly, sweetly. "I'll never get enough of you, Rebecca. Never."

Their mouths mated again in a tumultuous kiss.

The next thing Rebecca knew she had been swept up into his arms. Jack was carrying her up the stairs to his bedroom. And she knew even before he laid her gently on the bed that she wasn't going to stop him. Not this time. Not the next.

Jack hadn't intended to make love to Rebecca during her stay in Los Angeles. Just kiss her and hold her and remind her how much they had meant to each other, one night, one very special night, long ago. But the moment her lips warmed beneath his and her mouth opened to receive his tongue, the moment her body turned all soft and fluid and giving, he knew he wasn't going to stop with just one kiss or even two. He was going to make love to her, if she let him, and it seemed very much as if she was going to let him. He pushed his knee between hers, parting her legs, then shifted his weight inside the warm cradle of her thighs.

"I want to make love with you again," he whispered as he touched the satiny curve of her waist, the subtle drape of her hip. "I want to kiss you everywhere, touch you everywhere…and in every way," he said, rolling so they were lying side by side on his bed, facing each other. He slid a palm down her thighs, between her knees and felt her quicken restlessly against his touch as her torment and pleasure tangled. "But if I'm going too fast for you, all you have to do is say no," he promised in a low whisper, gently caressing the tender area between her knees, deftly but slowly urging them apart as he unzipped her jeans, "and I'll stop."

But to his pleasure, she didn't say no, not when he touched her intimately, smoothing his palms down her hips, between her thighs, not when he touched and kissed her breasts. Not when he gave in to the urgency driving them both and gave up the pleasure of simply caressing her and slipped inside her. Desperate for more, she reached for him. He held her tightly, one arm anchored firmly around her hips, lifting her slightly. His mind awhirl with the torrent of need flowing through his veins, he deepened his possession of her. She moaned soft and low in her throat and moved restlessly against him, but Jack remained as he was, buried deep inside her. He couldn't take much more, not without losing control. And though he wanted that, he wanted to find a way to pleasure her first, a way that would give her the ultimate release.

"Jack," she said again, stirring against him, writhing in pleasure, shuddering with release as he touched her there. And then she was gripping his hips, moving against him. The fragile thread of his control snapped. The passion that had been suppressed exploded into an eager kiss. She moaned again, willing him on, meeting each demand with one of her own. Until his hips rocked urgently against hers, infusing her with shuddering sensation. And it was only then, when he knew she had experienced the complete wonder of their love anew, when her eyes were cloudy with desire, that he let his own passions govern.

Surrendering to a desperate hunger, he braced his weight with his hands on either side of her, buried himself to the hilt and rocked against her slowly, so slowly, wanting to draw their loving out forever even as he pushed them both toward the edge. Her face lifted to his, she inhaled sharply, and their mouths met in a searing, sensual kiss. Again and again, they drew from each other, pouring out all that was in their hearts and in their souls, pouring out all the things they wanted to say, and still had no words for.

Until that night, Jack hadn't known his control could be so easily lost, but it was. He hadn't known she could want so desperately, but she did. He groaned as their tongues twined urgently and his body took up a primitive rhythm all its own. The bedroom grew hot and close. Their clothes, half on, half off, crushed between them. And yet, mostly he was aware of Rebecca, the welcoming power of her love, the soft, sweet, wild yearning he felt rising inside her.

But it wasn't only Rebecca that was experiencing this wild flood of pleasure. He was feeling it, too, the incredible intimacy of their lovemaking almost as overwhelming as the sheer luxury of having her in his arms again. He was aware of every soft, warm inch of her, inside and out. Every pulsation. Every sigh of desire and whimper of need. Burning with his need for her, savoring the sweetness of her unexpected acquiescence to his body's demands, he shut his eyes, and let himself go where she led. Lost in the maelstrom of pleasure, lost in everything but the sunny, springlike scent that was her and the soft yielding of her body, he went deeper, deeper yet.

Whimpering slightly, she clutched him closer and rose to meet him. Drunk on the power of their love, overcome with need, he plunged higher and found her hips lifting in an effort to take him even higher. His control shattered, he hurtled into the sweet oblivion of release. She went with him, rushing headlong into the storm.

When it was over, he held her close, wishing they could stay that way forever. "This is just the beginning for us, Rebecca," he whispered in a low, tender voice that warmed her from the inside out. "Just the beginning." And as he possessed her again, heart, body and soul, she began to think it was.

FINALLY EXHAUSTED, they lay in each other's arms. Rebecca had never felt so content or so free. This night, this whole week, had been something of a miracle for her. She wasn't used to losing track of her common sense. She wasn't used to giving herself over to reckless heartfelt abandon. But she had done just that with Jack, not just once now, but twice. Was the fact she couldn't seem to stay out of his bed some sort of sign they were meant to be together, as Jack insisted, or was it a sign of her own lack of character?

"I keep telling myself not to get involved with you," she admitted with a sigh. She wasn't sorry they'd made love, yet neither was she one hundred percent at peace about it. If not for the baby, Jack wouldn't have come back to her. And that bothered her more than she wanted to admit.

"That's funny," Jack said softly, "'cause I keep trying to figure out how to get you involved."

Rebecca propped her chin on her hand and studied him. She wanted to believe he was serious about her, not just for now but for all time; she just wasn't sure she could. But maybe it was time she started to find out. "Could you live in Pennsylvania?" she asked finally.

He smiled at her, laced a hand through the hair at the back of her neck and brought his mouth back to hers. "I think the real question is, Rebecca," Jack said as he bent his head to kiss her thoroughly once again, "could you live in Los Angeles?"

JACK'S QUESTION stayed with her long after they made love again, and then fell asleep, and it was still with her the following morning when Jack, Rebecca and Andy arrived at the movie set. The warehouse-like soundstage contained numerous sets. An Amish store, the inside of an Amish home. An Amish school. The three of them stood in the foreground as the actors did a scene. It looked fine to Rebecca but the young, bearded man in the director's chair was far from satisfied.

As soon as the director yelled "Cut!" another man in a bill cap hurried toward them. He had a clipboard in his hand and a worried look on his face. "Jack, glad you're here. We need some work on the dialogue. Listen to the run-through, and see what you can do to make it a little snappier..."

Rebecca stepped back, Andy still in her arms. Aware she was in the way of cameras, crew, makeup people, she roamed farther away from the activity. Andy was sleeping now, curled peacefully against her breast. Holding him close, inhaling his sweet baby scent, she felt a certain serenity, and a temptation to claim him as her own. "If only you were mine," she whispered as Andy began to stir against her. Things would be so much simpler. She would know what to do: marry Jack.

Her hand rubbing Andy's back, she moved farther away from the action, and came upon a set resembling the inside of a barn.

It was different from theirs, of course. Longer, wider, more old-fashioned, with a dirt floor instead of cement, but the hayloft was the same, the ladder leading up to it the same.

Footsteps sounded behind her. Rebecca turned to see a young woman with a clipboard coming toward her. Seeing the sleeping baby, she smiled at Rebecca and whispered, "Jack asked me to check on you."

Rebecca whispered back, "I was afraid Andy was going to wake. I didn't want his crying to interrupt the filming."

"Good thinking. Cute kid. Someone said he was Jack's?" The question hung in the air.

Forcing herself to retain a cheerful expression, Rebecca nodded. "And yours?" the young woman continued.

I only wish, Rebecca thought. She shook her head. The young woman lifted a skeptical brow but said nothing. She turned to the loft. "Nice, isn't it?"

Rebecca nodded. "They filmed the pivotal love scene there, yesterday. You know, the one Jack just rewrote. It was pretty good. Sensual anyway."

Without warning, Rebecca felt as if she could hardly breathe, but somehow she found her voice. "Did he say why he rewrote it?"

The young woman nodded. "Yeah, he said his fantasy had always been to make love in a hayloft. Guess since it had never happened, he wrote it instead."

Don't bet on that, Rebecca thought bitterly, and with great depth of feeling. They hadn't actually made love, of course, but they had talked intimately and kissed each other passionately.

Recalling how she had revealed her innermost feelings to Jack that night, she felt ill inside. Like she'd been used in the most heartless way possible. She'd thought Jack was different, but he was just like Wesley, looking for a pure and innocent girl to make his dreams come true. Someone to help him visualize and at least begin to act out the pivotal love scene he'd been having such trouble writing.

"Jack mentioned you're from Pennsylvania?" the young woman continued.

Again, Rebecca nodded. It was a struggle to retain her smile, but she was determined not to be any more humiliated in public than she already had been by Jack in private. More than ever, she was glad she hadn't worn her Amish clothes.

"He said he had to go back to do research last week," the young woman continued, shaking her head in remonstration as she confided with an indulgent laugh, "but of course we all know he was just having a good time."

At that, it was all Rebecca could do not to hunt Jack down and slay him. "A good time?" She choked out the words.

"Yeah, soaking up the local color. He's always been like that. Did he ever tell you about the year he worked on the updating of *The African Queen?* He got so far into the research all he wanted to do was go on safari-style river trips. Fortunately for all of us, he eventually got it out of his system and moved on to another project. Otherwise we probably never would have gotten another screenplay out of him."

Bitterness welled inside her. Her eyes felt hot and dry. The inside of her chest was one massive ache. "How long did it take?" Rebecca asked calmly, feeling oddly detached, as if she were too numb inside to be truly devastated…yet. The numbness would wear off in time.

The young woman shrugged. "I can't really remember. A couple months maybe—"

In the distance, there was a round of laughter from the set. The young woman smiled. "Sounds like they got it right that time." She moved off in the direction of the soundstage where the action was being filmed.

Too bad she and Jack hadn't, Rebecca thought.

"YOU'VE BEEN AWFULLY QUIET. Are you nervous about tonight?" Jack asked as Rebecca met him in the foyer of his Hollywood Hills home.

She was wearing a plain emerald-green dress, another leftover from her married life. She shook her head. "Just anxious to be leaving," she said coolly.

Jack had already said goodbye to the baby-sitter he'd hired and to Andy, so he followed her down the walk to the car. He shoved his hands into the pockets of his trousers, and matched her steps. "I'm sorry it took so long on the set today."

"I'm not," Rebecca said tightly. "I learned a lot."

He narrowed his gaze. "Did someone say something to you?"

The pulse pounded in Rebecca's throat. If she hadn't been so angry with him, she would have appreciated how handsome he looked in the sophisticated navy blue suit, striped shirt and tie. But she was angry with him, and she wasn't going to let herself forget why.

She tilted her chin up at him and stopped walking. "What could anyone have said to me to make me angry with you?"

He lifted his hands in mute speculation and held her level gaze. "I don't know," he said brusquely, his confusion evident. "But everything was fine when we got there. Since we left the studio, you've barely been speaking to me."

Suddenly Rebecca didn't want to get into it. "I told you," she repeated impatiently. "I'm anxious to be leaving."

Jack trapped her between the car door and his body. His shoulders were rigid with tension. "And I think it's more than that."

They regarded each other like two prize fighters about to step into the ring—or two lovers about to kiss and make up in bed. Rebecca suddenly decided it was politic to change the subject. She drew a deep breath and asked calmly, "Who is this woman who's sitting for Andy tonight?"

"The director's mother. Don't worry. Andy will be fine."

Rebecca turned toward the car and waited for him to unlock and open the passenger door for her. "Why would I be worried? He's your baby."

Jack leaned against the car, and gave her a hard look. "You know," he drawled, his dark blue eyes glittering dangerously, "if Russ Saunders hadn't gone to such lengths to show your quilts this evening, I'd pursue this here and now."

"Lucky for me he did, then."

"Don't think it's over, because it's not."

Oh, yes it is, Rebecca thought. As much as I don't want it to be, it is.

The gallery was packed. Russ was as disappointed as Jack had said he would be that Rebecca wasn't in Amish dress. "I thought...well, it would've been good for business," he said, "had you worn one of those hats and—"

"Kapps and aprons," Rebecca supplied wearily. She really did not want to get into all this now. She just wanted to sell her quilts and get out of here.

"Right," Russ said.

She looked into his eyes again and saw only kindness. Guilt swiftly followed. In a gentler, more polite tone, she explained, "While I'm out here in Los Angeles, I'd prefer to just blend in."

Russ frowned. "Isn't that against Amish beliefs?"

"Rebecca's always been at least half English," Jack supplied hastily.

"Oh." Russ smiled at Rebecca as if nothing further needed to be said. He took her arm above the elbow. "Come on, let me introduce you around," he offered amiably. "There are a lot of people here who want to know about the unique designs. Jack tells me you've designed many of the quilts yourself—"

The rest of the evening passed in a blur. Rebecca talked until she was almost hoarse, explaining which quilts were done in traditional Amish patterns, and which were unique.

"Is it true Jack found you on one of his trips east to research that new movie he's working on?" a woman asked as she got out her checkbook and prepared to pay an astronomical sum for a quilt to hang on her wall.

"She's not a souvenir," Jack said. He looked irritated.

"Sorry," the woman said. She stammered and turned pink. "I meant—"

"We know what you meant," Rebecca said smoothly. She turned to Jack, giving him a bright, accusing look only he could see before she finished with all the noncombativeness the general public had come to expect from the Amish. "And I guess in a way, I am a souvenir."

She just didn't want to be one.

Chapter Thirteen

"How long are you going to stay angry at me?" Jack asked as soon as they had walked the sitter out to her car and watched her drive away.

Clamping her hands against her middle, Rebecca turned and started up the pebbled front walk to his door. "Probably forever, but that's okay, since I sold all of the quilts and made quite a profit for the folks back home."

He slipped inside the house, and closed the door behind them. "Careful, you might sound mercenary."

She whirled to face him, the depth and breadth of her anger sending her emotions into high gear. "Better than sounding hopelessly cruel," she shot back.

Irritation flashed in his glance and his jaw turned to iron. He put a hand on her shoulder, turned her around and marched her toward the deep sofa in the living room. "Now that remark you are going to have to explain," he said as he sat down beside her. His dark blue eyes searched hers with laser accuracy. "What's making you so angry?" he asked gently.

Her cheeks burned with humiliation and suddenly she found she couldn't look at him after all. "You used me," she said in a low, shaky voice.

He tucked a finger beneath her chin and guided her face back to his. His expression was perplexed. "How do you figure that?"

Rebecca's heart was racing. Looking into his eyes, she could hardly believe it was true, but all she had to do was remember back to the hayloft set she'd seen at the studio, to realize the way she had been duped. And that realization made her feel sick inside. "Because I heard all about the way you operate," she said in a quavering sigh, her eyes dry but burning with both anger and shame. "I heard about the way you really 'get into your research' while you're writing your movies." Unable to bear his nearness any longer, she propelled herself to her feet. Arms folded and pressed tight against her waist, she paced back and forth. "I heard all about that love scene they filmed in the hayloft set the day before we arrived—"

"Hey." Jack bounded to his feet and cut her off. He arrowed a thumb at his chest. "That love scene was written way before we got together. I *sold* that screenplay based on what happens in that scene."

She believed he *had* imagined being in a loft with an Amish woman long before it had happened. That was what made it all so terrible, the thought that the romantic interlude they'd shared wasn't nearly as spontaneous as she had believed. "And once it was written, sold and filmed you decided to experience a bit of romance yourself, is that it?" She had been such a fool! "You decided to use your tryst with me to add the finishing touches to the scene you'd already written?"

Jack stiffened uncomfortably, but his gaze never wavered from hers. "Kissing you up there was in many ways like a dream come true for me. But if you're accusing me of bundling with you that night only to work out some problem in the writing of that scene or fulfill some romantic fantasy I had then you're wrong."

"Am I?"

"Yes." His mouth thinned to a tight white line. He strode forward, closing the distance between them in two quick strides. Hands on her shoulders, he held her in front of him.

"I kissed you that night because I wanted to be with you," he said softly.

How she wished things were different, Rebecca thought wistfully, even as feelings of torment welled inside her. How she wished they had met at some other time, some other way. But they hadn't, she reminded herself firmly as she struggled with the melting desire that filled her every time she was near him. And like it or not, it was time to take a good, hard look at their love affair, and that's all it was. A love affair. He was willing to marry her, of course, because of Andy, but Andy wasn't even her child.

She pivoted away from him, feeling lost. And hurt. And scared. The only cure she knew for that was to be held in Jack's arms. And that she couldn't allow. So she couldn't stay, she thought simply as she raced up the stairs to the bedroom.

He was fast on her heels, taking the stairs two and three at a time, catching up with her as she raced into the bedroom and grabbed the valise she had packed earlier. "Now where are you going?" he demanded, putting himself between her and the door.

Ignoring him, Rebecca walked over to the phone and picked up the receiver. She stared down at the number she had looked up earlier and written on the pad beside the phone. She had known she had to leave as soon as they returned from the showing. Before they made love again. "I'm going to call a cab," she said flatly. She turned her gaze away from his, struggling hard to keep the hurt and the disappointment she felt out of her gaze.

He stepped closer, every inch of him gentling as he neared her. "Why?" he asked softly.

Without warning, hot angry tears burned her eyes. She blinked them back. "Because it's time for me to go home," she said in a strangled voice.

"Wait a minute," he said. "Your flight doesn't leave until tomorrow."

"Then I'll spend the night at the airport."

He regarded her grimly. She knew in that moment she had just hurt him as deeply and effectively as he had hurt her. "You're that anxious to get away from me?" Jack said. In the distance, Andy woke and began to wail.

Rebecca swallowed and began punching numbers on the phone. "I'm that anxious not to be hurt," she said.

"LOOK, ANDY, it's not as if we didn't try," Jack said in the lonely silence that fell after Rebecca left. He put the empty bottle of formula aside and held Andy upright against his shoulder. "We tried our hardest. But Rebecca just wouldn't listen to us. We have to accept that and go on, alone. We can make it without a mom."

Andy gurgled in response and butted his head against Jack's shoulder. Jack took that for a sign of dissension on his son's part, and lifted Andy a little higher, so they could look at each other man-to-man. "I get the point," Jack said. He lowered his son back to his shoulder and patted Andy gently on the back. "You don't want to be without a mom. But honestly now, what choice did we have but to let her go? I can't keep invading her home in Pennsylvania. And she refuses to stay here one minute longer.

"Hell, she won't even admit that she's your mom. In her heart, sport, I know she loves you every bit as much as I do. And that puzzles the heck out of me. If ever I'd met a woman I thought was honest and blunt-spoken to a fault, it was Rebecca."

Jack frowned.

Andy burped loud enough for them both to grin.

"You don't suppose Rebecca could actually have been telling the truth all along, do you?" Jack put Andy down on his lap again.

"Nah," Jack said. "'Cause if that were the case, why wouldn't she have absolutely insisted I call the police and find your real parents?" Jack sighed. He had no answers for anything. He only knew that he had never felt lonelier or more bereft in his life.

Andy wrapped his fist around the end of Jack's index finger as Jack continued glumly, "I know what you're thinking, kiddo, that there must be something more I can do. But there just isn't. I've done everything I could to prove my love to her. Your mom—for whatever reason—just didn't buy it." Jack heaved a sigh of regret and looked down into big baby blue eyes that suddenly didn't look as much like Rebecca's eyes as he had initially thought.

"I need a woman who believes in me, who trusts me to do the right thing and not hurt her." Jack continued pouring out his troubles to his son softly. He frowned his irritation. "Rebecca doesn't even think I'm smart enough to know the difference between infatuation and love. She thinks what I felt for her is all part of my powerful imagination, my getting caught up in writing the new screenplay."

Andy stared up at Jack, let go of Jack's finger and waved both fists in the air. Looking down into his tiny cherubic face, Jack explained, "It's not as if there's anything else I can do to fix things."

Andy crinkled his brow, as if to disagree.

"We have to let her go," Jack said sadly.

Or did they?

REBECCA STOOD IN LINE at the airline counter. She had changed back into her jeans and sneakers. She wasn't sure why, but she just couldn't bring herself to resume her Amish life again yet. There was much she loved about it, and much, if she were perfectly honest, that she could easily do without. The good parts included the love of her family and friends, the security inherent in knowing that little of their life there would ever change. The bad parts including doing everything the hard way and the boredom that came with knowing that everything was going to be the same day after day after day. Rebecca liked the city. She liked driving a car. She liked the excitement of never knowing what was going to happen next. She just didn't like experiencing it all alone.

If she and Jack had worked things out...

But they hadn't.

She frowned, feeling both disappointed in herself and accepting of the truth. Maybe it was the fact that she'd spent the first ten years of her life in an English home, but there was a part of her, she realized now—the part that was most closely linked with her parents—that would always remain forward-thinking to a fault. And there was another part of her, the scared little orphan in her, that liked clinging to the safety of old ways.

The line at the airline ticket counter inched ahead slowly. Rebecca sighed. Waiting in line was one part of English life she could do without.

The lady behind her looked equally fed up with the standing around. She had curly white hair, pale green eyes and glasses. She was dressed in a magenta running suit that zipped up the front, and comfortable shoes. "Traveling alone?" she asked Rebecca.

Feeling in need of some human comfort, Rebecca nodded.

"So am I. There was a time when I would've had my whole family here with me. Kids, husband, even the family dog. Now there's just me." The other passenger smiled a little sadly, then continued to explain, "My kids are all grown now and my husband died last year."

Rebecca nodded, taking it all in. "What about your dog?" she asked, shifting her valise to her other hand.

The woman behind her picked up her carry-on bag and moved forward. "He went to live with my son."

Rebecca absorbed that. "You're not going to get another?"

The woman waved a work-worn hand. "I'm too old to chase a puppy around. Maybe if I'd gotten one before Harry died, but..." She smiled wanly once again. "Time marches on, whether you want it to or not."

How well Rebecca knew that. Only now time would march on without Jack.

The other passenger glanced down at Rebecca's hand, and

quirked a brow. "You're not married." She sounded both sad for her and surprised.

"No, I'm not," Rebecca said, beginning to feel herself get a little prickly again.

"A pretty young thing like you should be," the woman continued.

Rebecca's shoulders stiffened. "I'm waiting for the right man to come along," Rebecca said, shifting her bag to her other hand.

The woman sighed and sent Rebecca an indulgent look. "Now you sound like my daughters," she said.

The line inched forward slowly once again. Rebecca looked ahead and counted. She was now three people back from the counter. Which meant she had another five- to ten-minute wait. She looked back at the other passenger, glad she had someone to pass the time with. Though she would have much preferred it to be Jack and Andy. "Your daughters aren't married, either?" she ascertained.

The woman shook her head. "Not that that is any big surprise," she confided. Her voice dropped to a conspiratorial whisper. "They're always finding fault with the men they date. One little snafu in a relationship, one wrong or crossed signal—" the woman made a slashing gesture across her throat "—and they're out the door like a shot."

For the second time in as many minutes, Rebecca felt her shoulders stiffen again. "Maybe they had reason to leave," Rebecca said, eyes front as they all moved forward once again.

"And maybe, just maybe, if my daughters had just looked hard enough, and long enough, they would have discovered the problem wasn't such a dilly after all. Maybe they would have discovered they had a reason to stay."

Rebecca suffered a flash of guilt. Had she looked long enough? Had she really taken time to consider the consequences? Or had she just run away rashly?

The woman nudged her. "It's your turn at the counter, honey."

"Oh. Thanks." Rebecca picked up her valise and marched ahead. Her mind still awhirl with guilty thoughts and lost possibilities, she handed over her ticket. "Going back to Philadelphia this morning?" the airline agent asked with a welcoming smile.

Rebecca nodded and wished she could feel as happy about returning as she ought to feel. After all, she was going back home to the old-fashioned farm and grandparents she loved. Normally, after any time at all away, it would make her very happy to be going home again. But not this time. It just wasn't going to be the same without Jack. And she knew she would miss Andy, too, even if she never had quite gotten Jack to believe that that adorable baby wasn't hers.

"Did you have a nice stay?" the agent asked as she typed the numbers on the ticket into the computer, confirming Rebecca's presence at the airport and her seat on the plane.

"It was short," Rebecca said cryptically. *Too short.*

The agent smiled. "Couldn't you extend it?"

Rebecca sighed. "I wish it was that simple—"

Maybe if my daughters had just looked hard enough, they would have discovered the problem wasn't such a dilly after all. Maybe they would have discovered they had a reason to stay…

Did she have a reason to stay, Rebecca wondered. Was she cutting her losses too quickly? Giving up before it was time? So Andy wasn't her child. So what? She knew in the deepest recesses of her heart that Jack's wanting her had nothing to do with finding a nanny for the baby. He had fallen for her the moment they'd met on that dark, stormy night almost a year ago. And if the way he made love to her was any indication, he was still head over heels in lust with her. But was that enough to actually sustain a relationship over the long haul?

He hadn't actually said he had loved her until after the baby had appeared in their lives. But he had kissed her from the very beginning as if he did. More to the point, he had chased her halfway across the country, insinuated himself into

her home and her heart. Not because he really needed a
mother for his infant son—he was handling Andy just fine
on his own—but because he wanted her. But what about his
fantasies? a little voice inside Rebecca prodded. What happened when the movie was over, his last-minute revisions on
his screenplay finished? Would he move on to someone else,
someone who was in some way related to his next project,
or would he still desire her, the way she still desired him?

More to the point, how would she feel? Rebecca wondered.
The answer was simple. She would continue to love Jack no
matter what. She would continue to desire him. And if she
found out...for certain...that Andy was Jack's son, a son
he'd had with another woman in another one-night stand at
Alec's place, during that same research stay in Pennsylvania
last spring, what then?

Could she forgive him that?

If he told the truth about Andy's parentage, if he admitted
he'd made a mistake in either deliberately or erroneously mis-
leading her about the situation, Rebecca knew she was capable of forgiving Jack, of looking beyond their past and even
current mistakes to the future.

The agent paused. Accurately reading the indecision on
Rebecca's face, but mistaking the reason for it, the agent said,
"It's only a twenty-five-dollar charge if you want to change
the return, you know. We can do that for you very easily,
even at this time."

Rebecca tightened her hand on her valise. Heaven knew
she was tempted to throw caution to the wind and give it
another try. Attempt to make Jack level with her. But even
if that happened...if Jack admitted that the baby was his and
not hers, Rebecca didn't know if Jack would be willing to
try to sort things out again and start over. Rebecca didn't
know if there would be a workable way for the three of them
to be together and still protect her grandparents but suddenly
she wanted to try. "I think I'll—"

"Hold it right there, Rebecca!" Jack said.

Rebecca turned to find Jack standing behind her, Andy

cradled in his arms. "You're not leaving!" Jack said as Andy grinned at Rebecca and waved at her sporadically with both hands.

Joy burst inside Rebecca's heart with the suddenness of a rocket launch. "I'm not," she echoed wryly, amused to find she and Jack were suddenly of one mind after all. Even if he hadn't yet realized it.

"No, you're not," Jack repeated, his firm voice overriding hers. He cupped a possessive hand around her shoulder. "I let you run away from me once. I am not letting you run away from me again. I love you, Rebecca. Not because you're Amish. Not because the passion we share is unlike anything I've ever felt or even dreamed I could feel. But simply because you're you."

The words she had longed to hear sent tears of relief streaming down her face. And Rebecca knew she had been right to give him a second chance.

"I know I've handled this all wrong, right from the start." Jack hastened to finish his confession. "I hurried you into something you weren't ready for—"

Rebecca wiped her damp cheeks. "It takes two to tango, Jack," she said, taking her half-processed ticket back from the agent and stepping out of the line. He wrapped his arm around her. She picked up her valise and leaned into his embrace. "I hurried, too." Andy leaned toward Rebecca, expecting a kiss. Rebecca touched her lips to his brow, and was rewarded with another toothless smile.

Together, she and Jack moved to the wall opposite the passenger check-in counter and took up a deserted spot. "And what you said about you being my fantasy," Jack continued huskily, still holding both Rebecca and Andy close. "I admit that is true," he said softly, his eyes lovingly roving her face. "You are my fantasy woman, Rebecca. You're everything I ever dreamed about. You're the woman I've been writing about and longing for all these years. And that is not going to change, no matter what screenplay I'm working on at the moment. I'm still going to want you, too."

Rebecca dropped her valise, and mindful of Andy, who was still in Jack's arms, wrapped her arm around his other shoulder and hugged him as best she could, considering he was still holding his son. "Oh, Jack, I love you, too," she whispered fervently. That said, she tipped her face up to his. He lowered his mouth and kissed her with a thoroughness that left her trembling and weak and made all her doubts about him seem inconsequential.

"Next point," he said gruffly, moving back at long last, while Andy watched them both in grinning, wide-eyed wonder. "I want us to have a life together. And to that end, I'll do whatever it takes. I'll move to Pennsylvania, do my writing there. We can even live half Amish if you want. I don't care what I have to do. I just want to be with you."

Rebecca paused. "What about Andy?"

"Is he yours, Rebecca?" Jack asked hopefully, holding Andy all the closer.

Rebecca shook her head sadly. Tears filled her eyes. "I wish he was," she admitted in a thready whisper as her heart leapt to her throat. "You don't know how much."

Jack's face fell. He looked as crushed as she felt while Andy tossed perplexed looks from both Rebecca to Jack, as if wondering what in the world was going on now!

Rebecca looked at Andy's upturned cherubic face, so sweet and angelic, and felt her heart swell with love. Suddenly it didn't matter to Rebecca who Andy's mother was. "You could tell me if he belongs to you and another woman, Jack," Rebecca said gently. Her gaze meshed with his. "It won't make any difference in how I feel about either of you. I mean that from the very bottom of my heart," she whispered, standing on tiptoe to kiss them both.

"I know you do," Jack said thickly, looking as if he might be blinking back tears at any minute, too. "That's what makes dealing with this so hard."

"Dealing with what?"

"The fact Andy isn't my son." Jack tightened his arms possessively around Rebecca and Andy both. He looked down at Andy, who was curled contentedly against Jack's shoulder. "I've grown so fond of our little slugger here that I really wish I were his daddy," Jack said sadly. Jack looked back at Rebecca. "But if he isn't yours he isn't mine, and now that I know that for certain...well, we'll have to do something about that."

Rebecca was filled with relief, now that she knew for certain that Jack had not been with another woman. Suddenly it was Andy's future that was hanging precariously in the balance. "I guess that means Andy really was abandoned," Rebecca murmured, her heart twisting with the pain as she voiced the possibility.

Again, Andy's brows shot up, as if he just knew he was at the heart of this discussion, even if he couldn't understand all the words.

"So we'll adopt him and bring him up together," Jack said. "That is, if it's okay with you."

"It is."

They were all silent a moment. Andy reached for Rebecca's hair and grabbed a thick strand with his fist. Rebecca grinned at him and gently extricated Andy's hand from her hair.

Jack sized up Andy's crankiness. "Juice time," Jack said as he guided Rebecca and Andy over to a quiet corner of a waiting area. He sat down and removed a bottle of apple-pear juice from the diaper bag he had slung over his shoulder. "Try this, slugger."

Once Andy was happily settled in his arms, Jack looked up at Rebecca and smiled. "We'll get out of here, just as soon as he's finished his juice."

Rebecca sat next to Jack and Andy. She rested one hand on Jack's shoulder, the other twined with Andy's tiny fist. "Jack?"

"Hmm?"

"Did you really think that Andy was my baby until just a few minutes ago?" If so, that explained so much about his behavior.

Jack nodded. "It really threw me when you denied being Andy's mom...I mean I was so sure...I guess I just wanted so much for us to have a reason to be together." Jack sighed. "And yet, I think somewhere deep inside my heart, I half suspected you might really be telling the truth. I kept trying to tell myself he looked like you, that our being from two radically different life-styles was reason enough for such an adorable little baby being abandoned on Alec's doorstep, but I think I always knew that you had too much love in your heart to ever have deserted our child. Not that way. Not on a stranger's doorstep, even if Alec was home."

"You're right," Rebecca said softly, glad they were finally in accord on this much. She looked up at him tenderly. "I wouldn't have done that. But if you sensed Andy wasn't mine...then why did you stay in Pennsylvania, why did you bring me back here to Los Angeles?" Had it been just to make love to her, to convince her to move out here and be with him again? Was a love affair still all he was offering her?

Jack's eyes darkened. "I stayed because I half believed that he was your child. I wanted to give you the time you needed to sort out your feelings. And I also couldn't bring myself to leave you, not if there was even the slightest chance that the two of us might end up together." Although his arms were full of Andy, Jack leaned over to press a kiss in her hair. "I want you to marry me, Rebecca, just as soon as we can get everything arranged."

Rebecca gulped around the sudden lump in her throat. For the second time in the space of five minutes she found herself crying. She'd never been so absurdly happy in her life. "Yes, I'll marry you," Rebecca said. They sealed their engagement with a kiss, then slowly drew apart. And as Rebecca looked into Jack's eyes, the rest of her doubts slowly faded away. They could make this work. She knew they could.

"The road ahead of us will be tough—" Jack warned.

"My grandparents will understand," Rebecca countered softly. "They know and love you already. And they'll also understand when I tell them I am moving out here to live with you, that it's time for me to resume the life I would've had had my parents never been taken from me when they were."

"You're sure?" Jack paused, a look of concern on his face. "It's a lot to give up."

"We'll still visit. And I can still design quilts, and help support the family in that way. But it's time for me to move on, Jack. To make a life of my own. The kind I want."

"You name it," Jack whispered, leaning forward to kiss her again, "and it's yours."

He kissed her again, and would have gone on kissing her if Andy hadn't let go of his bottle of apple-pear juice and reached up and twined his tiny fist around Rebecca's hair. Rebecca winced as he tugged it. She carefully extricated her mouth from Jack's, and Andy's tiny fingers from her glorious blond locks. "Looks like someone wants out attention," she quipped, amused.

Jack grinned back at her, and then at Andy. An affection-filled moment passed. Finally Jack sighed, "Which brings us to the next question."

"I know," Rebecca said. She cast Jack a worried glance. "What are we going to do about finding Andy's real parents? Where should we start?"

"I've got a friend, Grady Noland, on the Philadelphia police force. He'll tell us how to start the search."

As soon as they got back to Jack's place, Jack dialed Philadelphia. It took several minutes, but finally Jack got Grady on the line. While Rebecca paced back and forth with Andy in her arms, Jack briefly explained their dilemma to his old college pal. "Anyway, Grady, I was thinking we could start our search by talking to someone in Missing Persons, seeing if any babies have been reported missing in the Philadelphia area."

"That won't be necessary," Grady replied abruptly.

"It won't?" Jack blinked in confusion and shot Rebecca a stunned look.

"I know whose baby this is," Grady said.

TOO MANY MOMS

Prologue

The phone was ringing when Grady Noland let himself into his apartment. He set his bags down next to the door and propped his skis against the wall. Figuring it was the Philadelphia police department wanting him to come back to work a day early, he grabbed the phone in the kitchen and spoke in a tone that was all business. "Grady here."

"Hey, Grady," Jack Rourke greeted him amiably, an underlying tenseness to his low tone. "I need a favor."

Grady dropped almost two weeks' accumulation of mail on the table and shrugged out of his coat. "Name it," Grady told his friend as he dusted a light covering of snow from his shaggy, sable brown hair and lanky six-foot-four frame.

"Well," Jack sighed, "you're not going to believe this, but...a two-month-old baby was left in a heart-shaped red wicker basket decorated with stenciled cupids and a huge white satin bow, on Alec's doorstep, on Valentine's Day."

"Wait a minute. That was over two weeks ago," Grady pointed out with a frown. He pulled a small, leather-bound book from his pocket, picked up a pen and began to make notes as Jack talked.

"Yeah, I know. The first week Alec thought the baby was his," Jack explained.

"And the second week?" Grady asked.

"I thought the baby was mine," Jack said, as if that explained everything. "So I had him."

"Is this for real?" Grady interrupted. The three of them had a history of playing practical jokes on each other.

"You better believe it," Jack said seriously. "And so is the beautiful baby in Rebecca's arms right now."

In the background, Grady could hear a baby gurgling and soft feminine laughter. It did sound like Jack had a woman and a baby with him right now. A happy baby.

"Where are you?" Grady asked.

"Los Angeles," Jack said, "but we're heading back to Philadelphia later this afternoon to see if we can't track down Andy's real parents. Initially, there was a typewritten note left with Baby Andy. It said, and I quote, 'To Andy's father, own up to your mistakes!'"

Grady continued writing. This sounded serious. Like the mother was furious with the baby's father. "Did Alec know who the baby's mother was?" Grady asked.

"Alec thought he did. He thought because of the way the baby was handed over to him, like some fabulous Valentine's Day gift, that Baby Andy was the result of a one-night stand Alec had with a model. It took Alec and the model's sister, Jade Kincaid, a week to find Nicole. When they did, they discovered Nicole wasn't Andy's mother at all, which meant Alec wasn't the father."

"So how did you get involved?" Grady asked with a frown.

"Because Alec called me. This wasn't a random abandonment, Grady, but a well-thought-out ploy to get the baby's father involved in bringing up the baby, and it looked like the mother thought Andy's dad could be reached at Alec's place. Alec had checked his calendar for last year and knew that I had stayed at his house last April while I was gathering background information for a screenplay I was writing."

Grady recalled getting together with Jack while he was in town the previous spring. "That movie about the turn-of-the-century Amish?"

"Right. And while I was there I had what has since turned out to be a lot more than a fling with a beautiful half-English, half-Amish woman. But at the time, I thought a fling was all I was going to ever have with Rebecca.''

"And now you know differently?'' Grady guessed.

"The lady's just agreed to marry me,'' Jack said happily. Grady grinned. "Congratulations!''

"Thanks. Anyway, because Rebecca had no other way to contact me except through Alec, I erroneously assumed the baby left on Alec's doorstep was mine, left out of sheer desperation. And for the last week I've had Andy with me while I tracked Rebecca down, but now I know, as much as we've both come to love Andy, that Andy's not our child, either,'' Jack continued.

"That's too bad,'' Grady said as his eye caught a postcard from France sticking out of his stack of mail. He picked it up. It read *Just Married!* on the front, and was signed, "Having a wonderful time, Alec and Jade,'' on the back. "Hey, is this postcard from Alec for real?'' Grady asked disbelievingly. *"Alec's married?''*

"Yeah,'' Jack confirmed, "he eloped right after he turned Baby Andy over to me. He and I tried to call you, but the department said you'd left town on the fifteenth to go skiing in Sun Valley. We figured the news could wait until you got back from Idaho. They're planning another wedding for family and friends on their return from Europe.''

"Wow, that's really great,'' Grady murmured, still feeling a little stunned to hear Alec had ended his days as one of the country's most sought-after playboys.

"Anyway, Grady,'' Jack continued, picking up the threads of their conversation, "I was thinking we could start our search by talking to someone in Missing Persons, seeing if any babies have been reported missing in the Philadelphia area.''

Grady sighed as his cop's mind went to work on the case. He looked over all the facts he had assembled so far. Abruptly, all the pieces fell into place. Alec and Jack weren't the only ones who'd made reckless love last spring. And anyone who knew Alec, Grady and Jack also knew how close the three of them were, and had been since their college years together at Penn. To get in touch with any one of them, all you had to do was contact one of the three.

"That won't be necessary," Grady said, as the realization hit him with gut-wrenching force. Slowly, he put down his pen and notebook. He had wanted children for a long time, but given up on ever having any of his own. Feeling a little dazed, he said, "I know whose baby this is."

"Don't tell me." Jack paused as the baby continued to coo and gurgle in the background. "You had a fling late last April, too," Jack guessed.

"Two, to be exact," Grady admitted reluctantly as he rubbed the tenseness from the back of his neck. "One was…well, it started during a party at Alec's mansion and ended at my place later that same night."

"And the other?"

Grady groaned aloud as he thought about the possible ramifications there. "Was with my ex-wife."

Chapter One

"Andy is my baby!" Jenna Sullivan proclaimed.

"No," Clarissa Noland stated just as passionately. "He's not. He's my baby."

Grady Noland stared at one beautiful woman, then the other, feeling like he'd walked smack into the middle of a nightmare from which it was impossible to wake up. And then it hit him. The relief he felt was staggering. He relaxed his broad shoulders and flashed them a sexy smile. "I gotta hand it to you," he drawled admiringly. "Alec and Jack have really outdone themselves this time." *They'd really had him going there for a minute. They'd had him completely, utterly buffaloed. But no more.*

"Alec!" Clarissa sputtered indignantly, working hard, Grady thought, to keep up the ruse.

"Jack?" Jenna appeared confused. "What do either of them have to do with this?" Her soft pink bow-shaped lips formed a pout that contrasted nicely with the angelic innocence in her wide, dark green eyes.

Grady frowned. As amusing as this had been, he refused to be played for a fool one instant longer. He tore his distracted gaze from Jenna's creamy complexion and thick, long eyelashes. "The joke's over, ladies," Grady said flatly. He was as amenable to a little mischief as the next guy, but it was time they put *this* farce to bed.

Jenna blinked again, looking completely nonplussed.

"What joke?" she asked warily, her soft, throaty voice barely above a whisper.

"C'mon, stop playing games with me," Grady urged impatiently, as he folded his arms in front of him. He had known from the first night he'd met Jenna last spring that she was a damn good sport and a lively companion. Hell, she hadn't even thought twice about stealing a bottle of champagne from Alec's kitchen and ducking out the back door so they could ditch Alec's business-with-pleasure party and walk over to Grady's place. But he'd never figured her for a practical joker, which went to show how much he knew.

"I am not playing games with you," Jenna said, carefully enunciating every word as she took in his squared shoulders and girded thighs.

"Neither am I," Clarissa stormed.

Yeah, right. Grady wished Jenna had worn some other scent. The delicate lavender fragrance was evoking all sorts of erotic memories, none of which it was wise to recall, at least not right now, with his jealous, neurotic ex-wife standing so close by.

Because Jenna seemed the more passionate of the two and the least likely to pull such shenanigans, Grady approached her with a come-on meant to make her cry uncle. "If you want to toy with me, Jenna," Grady drawled sexily as he lifted a hand to tangle in the rich, strawberry blond waves brushing her slender shoulders, "you're going to have to find some other way."

Grady's ex-wife stepped between him and Jenna. "You scoundrel!" Clarissa said.

"I agree," Jenna said to Clarissa. Then she turned to Grady, pushing his hand from her shoulder. "You are a rake and a hellion—"

"Tsk, tsk. Such old-fashioned words." Grady teasingly waggled his eyebrows at Jenna, enjoying the way the color rose in her delicately sculpted cheeks. He stepped even closer. "For such a newfangled prank."

"For the last time, Grady Noland," Jenna ground out between clenched white teeth, her full breasts rising and falling with each aggravated breath she took. "This is not a prank!"

"It has to be," Grady replied confidently. There was no way two women could both truthfully claim to be the mother of his son.

"Only a hopeless bounder like you would think so," Jenna retorted tightly, flushing all the more.

Enjoying the emotion simmering between them, Grady teased, "Give me any more compliments and you'll turn my head."

Jenna ignored his stab at humor. "Not that I should be surprised you've landed me in such a predicament," she said, shaking her head in self-remonstration. "All along I knew you were an irresponsible, no-strings kind of guy."

"Only since his divorce from me," Clarissa said. "Prior to that he was *very* commitment oriented."

"Well, I've changed," Grady said, meaning every word.

"And perhaps not for the better," Jenna muttered.

Her carelessly uttered words hit a nerve. Grady pushed the second thoughts he'd secretly been having about his new lifestyle away. "Look, you can't both be this baby's mother," he said reasonably. "So this is either the most elaborate practical joke Alec and Jack ever played on me, or—"

"One of us is lying," Jenna finished.

"Right," Grady said uncomfortably, wishing Jenna weren't so damn beautiful. In tight, faded jeans, boots, a long white thigh-skimming sweater and open navy-blue full-length wool coat that made the most of her tall, willowy figure and long lissome legs, she looked sexy. And intriguingly inaccessible.

Clarissa, on the other hand, seemed to have recently gained a little weight. Realizing that made Grady all the more uncomfortable.

Jenna folded her arms in front of her and regarded Grady contentiously.

"Well, as it happens, one of us *is* lying," Clarissa said.

"Yeah, and guess which one," Jenna baited him sarcastically.

Grady always had liked a challenge. Just as he liked Jenna's breezy girl-next-door good looks. She was the kind of woman who'd probably been a varsity cheerleader *and* captain of the debate team in high school, the kind who'd had half the boys in love with her and didn't even know it. Had he gone to high school with Jenna, Grady knew he would have taken one look at her perfect smile, creamy complexion and long-lashed dark green eyes and fallen madly in love with her on the spot. But they weren't in high school anymore.

He released an exasperated breath, shoved his hands through his hair. Apparently, they weren't done with this game, so he figured he might as well play along. "Don't you think I've already tried?"

Jenna quirked a brow at him. "Apparently not hard enough," she said.

"Jenna's right," Clarissa agreed. "You're a police detective. It should be easy for you to figure out what's going on here."

But it wasn't, Grady thought, discomfited. "What I want to know right now is which one of you left this baby on Alec Roman's doorstep with this note."

Jenna accidentally nudged his arm with hers as she looked over his shoulder at the slightly worse-for-wear typewritten note he held in his hand. "To Andy's father, own up to your mistakes," Jenna read in a baffled voice.

Grady looked at his ex-wife. "Did you do it?" As much as he hated to admit it, even to himself, he could see Clarissa abandoning his child. After all, she had never wanted kids. Her promise to consider having them the last night they were together had been a last-ditch effort to save their failed marriage. Was it possible she had stopped taking the pill before she faked her domestic emergency and tricked him into showing up to save her? Had she gotten pregnant on purpose, then not told him about her pregnancy as punishment because he no longer loved her? If he ever really had.

Clarissa drew a deep breath. "Of course this baby is mine!"

"Oh, stop lying," Jenna snapped, completely losing her patience. "You know as well as I do, Clarissa, that Andy is my baby."

"You left him on Alec's doorstep?" Grady asked Jenna. As hard as he tried, he couldn't see that happening. Jenna's whole adult life had been devoted to rescuing abandoned children. The fact that they were both really into public service and helping others was the reason they'd hit it off so well that night they'd met last spring at Alec's party. But it wasn't the reason they'd left the party early and ended up in his bed, making wild, passionate love. That had all been due to chemistry. Had it been up to him, he never would have ended it the next morning. But Jenna had made it clear she wasn't interested in flings. She wanted marriage. Children. And from bitter experience Grady had known then, as he did now, that cops and marriage didn't mix.

"Look, Grady, things were crazy two weeks ago," Jenna began nervously. She paused and raked her lower lip with the edge of her teeth. "The bottom line is Andy never should have been left at Alec's. He should be home with me. And that's where he's going."

Her tone ticked Grady off, big-time. He'd had a hell of a shock when Jack had called him from California. Since then, he'd taken an emergency leave, completely rearranged his life, gotten his hopes up that at last he was going to have the baby he'd always wanted, and for what? To be the victim of a practical joke that should have ended days ago.

Oblivious to his thoughts, Jenna tossed her rich, full mane of wavy strawberry blond hair out of her face and continued to stalk purposefully around Grady's Philadelphia apartment. Grady watched as she swiftly gathered up blankets, diapers and bottles of formula as if she really was preparing to take the baby home with her. Her dark green eyes averted from

him, she stuffed everything she had gathered into the over-
flowing diaper bag with a determined steadiness of purpose
Grady found even more annoying.

In contrast, Grady's ex-wife of almost a year, Clarissa Noland, seemed in no hurry at all to leave. He watched as she
shrugged out of her long white mink coat and dropped it with
studied insouciance on the sofa next to the portable crib.

Clarissa caught Grady's eyes, smiled at him sexily, then
turned to the baby sleeping contentedly inside the crib. Her
pretty, aristocratic features lit up into a soft, pleased smile.
She reached down and stroked the baby's tiny hand wonderingly, looking for a moment like she had just won the million-
dollar lottery. But that, too, had to be fake, Grady surmised
quickly, because Clarissa had never had a maternal urge in
her body. That was part of what had made their marriage
break up.

So it was back to his original premise. This had to be a
gag. Hell, Grady sighed, considering he'd had the bad sense
to sleep with both women in a two-week period, he probably
deserved it. It didn't matter that neither interlude had been
planned. He should have had better sense than to sleep with
Clarissa out of pity, or go off with Jenna when they were
both still on the rebound from their all-too-recent divorces,
even if the attraction he'd felt for Jenna had been the most
powerful attraction he'd ever felt for a woman in his life.

Jenna brushed past Grady in a whiff of lavender-scented
perfume. She stooped to pick up a rattle that had fallen on
the floor, stalked to the kitchen sink and washed it off thoroughly.

Grady started toward Jenna. Clarissa moved to cut him off
and at the same time block either of their paths to the crib.
"Hold on just a minute. You can't just walk out of here with
my baby."

Jenna quirked a strawberry blond brow at Clarissa and
stared at her in stunned silence. She dried off the rattle,
marched to the diaper bag and put it inside, along with a
stuffed bear. "You know, Clarissa," Jenna drawled, "if I

were you, I'd think twice about making some outrageous claim here that you'll regret later.''

''What's outrageous about having a baby with my ex-husband?'' Clarissa retorted, in the same highly miffed tone. ''Particularly when we never should've gotten divorced?''

Jenna narrowed her eyes at Clarissa. Her eyes flashed with a quick burst of temper. ''I'm warning you, you lying troublemaker—'' Jenna said. She took a warning step toward the crib. Clarissa stubbornly held her ground.

Jenna set the diaper bag on the floor beside her, her actions slow and deliberate. Straightening, she planted her hands on her waist. ''Okay, we'll play it your way and go back to square one. Since when is this not my baby?'' Jenna asked Clarissa very, very softly.

Clarissa tossed her head and folded her arms in front of her. ''Since…always, of course.''

Jenna grabbed a fistful of Clarissa's cerulean blue silk jumpsuit and brought her up short. ''Listen, you. The last two weeks have been sheer hell for me. I'm about at the end of my patience—''

''As well as your rope,'' Grady put in, enjoying the show immensely.

Jenna let go of Clarissa's jumpsuit and stomped closer, not stopping until she and Grady were nose to nose. ''I've about had it with you, too!'' she warned him. Angry color washed her cheeks.

''Oh, have you now?'' Grady taunted right back.

''Yes!''

Grady caught Jenna's hand before she could deliver a stinging slap to his face.

Behind her, Clarissa gasped and said, ''Now that is going too far! I think you ought to arrest her, Grady!''

Grady wanted to do a lot of things to Jenna now that she had come back into his life again. Arresting her was the least of them. He forced her hand down between them. The skin of her wrist felt like hot silk beneath his palm. ''Okay, Jenna,'' he schooled easily. ''Enough drama.''

"I couldn't agree more." Jenna's pretty chin jutted stubbornly. "And if you'll just let go of me—"

"That depends," Grady interrupted, "on whether you try to hit me again."

"And that depends," Jenna retorted, her wrist trembling slightly in his grip, "on whether you let me walk out of here with my baby or not."

Grady tried not to think how soft and hot her skin felt against his palm. How accessible in a very sexual way. Or how much he wanted to kiss Jenna again, Clarissa or no Clarissa. "And if I don't?"

"Then *I* might call the police," Jenna threatened, trembling a little more.

Grady gauged the temper in Jenna's eyes and saw it was cooling, coming under control again. Reluctantly, he released his hold on her. "Who does the baby belong to?" he asked firmly.

"I already told you! Andy is my baby!" both women declared in unison, then glared at one another as if they wanted to punch each other out.

Grady sighed. "The note said it was my baby."

"No, it didn't." The two women again spoke in unison. Clarissa picked up the note and read aloud. "All this typewritten note says is, *To Andy's father, own up to your mistakes.* It doesn't say you're the father at all."

"Right," Grady agreed sarcastically, "which is why, according to the lore being handed me, Alec and Jack both claimed Baby Andy as their own, too." He shook his head. This situation was too crazy to be real. "I'll give credit where it's due. You all really had me going."

"For the last time, Grady Noland, this isn't a joke," Clarissa said stiffly.

"Yes," Jenna agreed, taking Clarissa's side unexpectedly. She moved to stand next to her, both of them blocking Grady's way to the crib. "Andy is very real."

"Besides, you called me, remember?" Clarissa reminded as she gave him a steamy look that indicated she would be all too happy to adjourn immediately with him to his bedroom. "Just like I knew you would. We belong together, Grady," she continued softly, her pale blue eyes lifting persuasively to his. "I knew it before today and I certainly know it now."

Jenna stepped around them. "I'm glad the two of you have each other," Jenna said dryly. "And now that you do, Andy and I will leave you two to your reconciliation."

"Wait a minute. There isn't going to be a reconciliation," Grady said firmly, wanting there to be no illusions on anyone's part about that. He moved to bar Jenna's way to the crib. "Clarissa and I are divorced and we're going to stay that way."

"Not if I have anything to say about it," Clarissa said with a sly smile. She kept her eyes on his as she glided toward him and tucked both her elegantly manicured hands around his forearm. "That baby deserves two parents, Grady."

"Oh, I don't know about that. I think he could manage fine with just me," Jenna muttered as she buttoned her coat and looped the stuffed diaper bag over her shoulder. "And since Andy happens to be my baby—" she palmed her chest authoritatively "—I have the final say."

Clarissa continued to hang on Grady's arm. "Don't listen to her, Grady. You know as well as I do that can't be true."

Ignoring them both, Jenna picked up the tiny infant. He woke instantly. Looking at Jenna, Andy blinked, then gurgled happily at the sight of her and beamed her a toothless smile.

"Oh, precious," Jenna whispered to Andy. She bent and pressed a sweetly tender kiss on his forehead and whispered, "I have missed you so much, sweetheart. You just don't know…"

Grady watched tears stream down Jenna's face. Again, he was taken aback, both by the ludicrousness of the situation and the emotional force of Jenna's response. It was crazy. He almost wanted Andy to be Jenna's baby. And his. Even though they'd just been together that once. Even though everything in him told him this was all a little too loony to be true. And too loony not to be true…

"You see? He even knows me," Jenna whispered triumphantly through her tears.

"This proves nothing," Clarissa said hotly, "except that you have a way with children and an incredible imagination!"

"You're the one with the imagination, Clarissa." Jenna turned to Grady and sent him a stormy, accusing look that filled him with regret. He never should have walked away from Jenna the way he had after only one incredibly wonderful, incredibly perfect night together. "How can you not know whose baby this is?" she demanded of him.

"I think the answer to that is obvious," Clarissa said smoothly as she sat down and crossed her legs elegantly at the knee. "Grady and I still have feelings for one another. And the truth of the matter is, Jenna darling," she finished gently, "we always will."

"Now hold on a minute there, Clarissa," Grady said impatiently. He had been through this with his ex-wife, not once but many times.

As usual, Clarissa ignored him. "Why else would you have slept with me that night last April, just before our divorce became final?" she continued optimistically.

"Perhaps because your house had just been burglarized and you were scared out of your mind," Grady said. *And because I was a fool. A fool who felt guilty as hell because my marriage had failed.*

Clarissa shook her head at him, silently discounting his theory. "You're a cop, Grady. You don't sleep with all the women you rescue." She paused dramatically, gave him another telling look—one he was sure was meant to warn Jenna off. "Or do you?" she finished sweetly.

Grady gave his ex-wife a sharp glare. His patience was wearing extremely thin.

"The question is," Clarissa continued, rummaging through

her bags and bringing out a pack of cigarettes, "why did you sleep with her?" She pointed to Jenna.

"Yes, Grady, I'd like to hear the answer to that myself," Jenna said softly. Her expression was stormy. "Why *did* you sleep with me that night?"

"The same reason you slept with me," Grady retorted gruffly. *Because I wanted you more than I ever wanted anyone in my life.* "Because we both concluded that fleeting love affairs with no strings were better all the way around."

Only they hadn't turned out to be, Grady admitted to himself in irritation. One night with Jenna, and it had spoiled it for him with every woman since; he'd probably want her the rest of his life. But he'd also known he hadn't a chance in hell of ever making a real go of it with Jenna, or any other woman, not if he wanted to stay a cop. So when she'd walked out, he had done as she asked and not pursued her, even though he knew in his heart that he should have.

His gaze gentled as he regarded Jenna. "Why did you sleep with me that night?" he asked softly. "Was it because you were on the rebound from your divorce? Or was it something else?" Since she hadn't pulled any punches, he didn't feel required to, either.

Jenna continued to hold Andy tenderly in her arms, and for a second their glances meshed. Grady felt the familiar electricity leap and sizzle between them.

Realizing what was about to happen, Jenna dropped her gaze and shook her head. She backed away from him, looking as if she wasn't about to go into that, now or at any other time. "None of this matters," Jenna said firmly in a flat, weary voice. Avoiding looking into his eyes again, she said, "I'm taking my baby and going home."

"Wait a minute!" Clarissa said. Grady turned to his ex-wife. For a second, he'd been so caught up with Jenna, he'd forgotten Clarissa was even in the room with them. "There's no proof that baby is yours, Jenna," she continued.

Color rushed into Jenna's cheeks, highlighting the delicate womanly curves of her cheekbones in the oval frame of her face. "I showed up to claim him, didn't I? More to the point, Grady didn't even have to call me to tell me to come and get Andy, as he did you."

Which was another reason Grady still wondered whether this was a practical joke. It was all unfolding a little too neatly and unexpectedly.

Clarissa sent Grady a sharp look. "You're not seriously listening to all of this, are you?" she asked.

Grady rubbed his jaw. "At this point, I don't know what to think," he drawled. "What kind of proof do you have, Jenna? A birth certificate?"

"Of course I have a birth certificate," Jenna cried.

"Then let's see it," Grady demanded tautly.

"That's not possible," Jenna said.

"And why, pray tell, is that?" Grady asked.

"Because it's not here. It's back at my farmhouse in Hudson Falls, in upstate New York," Jenna explained.

Clarissa rolled her eyes. "Likely story," she muttered beneath her breath.

Jenna arched a strawberry blond brow. "I don't see *you* handing over any legal proof, Clarissa."

Clarissa smiled at Jenna sweetly. "That's because I didn't bring mine with me, either. But then I didn't know about you, Jenna. If I had…" She lifted her slender shoulders in an elegant shrug. "Suffice it to say, I will produce all the necessary records just as soon as I can get back to my family home in Long Island to get them."

Grady turned to Clarissa with a frown. He wasn't sure the depth of emotions simmering within the two women could *all* be feigned. Which led him to wonder how much of what was going on was a put-on and how much was the truth. If there was anything he had learned in the course of his police work over the years, it was that almost nothing was exactly the way it first seemed.

Fortunately, his experience as a detective had taught him how to dig to uncover the truth. "You had the baby on Long Island?" he asked Clarissa.

"Don't tell me you actually expected me to go through something this traumatic alone?" Clarissa said.

Grady had no intention of getting into an argument about that with her. Ignoring his ex-wife's accusatory question as well as Jenna's temper-laced glare, Grady said, "Assuming this is true, why didn't either of you call me, and let me know you were pregnant? Why did you just dump him on Alec's doorstep with that note?"

"Because Alec was home," Clarissa was quick to point out before Jenna could speak. "You never are, Grady. You're always out working on a case."

"Alec thought the baby was his!" Grady replied.

"Well, that's certainly not our fault!" Jenna said cantankerously.

"Yes, but leaving the baby on the doorstep was. Why did you do it, Jenna, assuming it was you?"

She looked away evasively. Her soft lips tightened mutinously. "It's a long story. I really don't feel like going into it now," she muttered.

"Don't feel like going into it or can't—because it never happened?" Clarissa challenged.

Jenna glared at Clarissa. Grady shrugged. "It's a good point," he said.

"How kind of you to say so," Jenna flared, giving him another withering glare.

"See?" Clarissa said victoriously. "She has no proof, Grady, none at all."

"I have the most valid proof of all," Jenna said, looking at the baby cuddled so peacefully in her arms. "Andy loves me. He wants to be with me."

"That's no proof," Clarissa disagreed with an unfriendly sneer. "He loves me, too. And I'll prove it to you."

"Fine," Jenna said, her expression determined. "Go ahead. Show us how well you've bonded to my son." Reluctantly, she handed Andy over.

Andy went into Clarissa's gentle arms with wide-eyed wonder. Clarissa cooed at him softly. As he had with Jenna,

Andy beamed her a toothless smile and cooed right back at her.

Jenna swore and ran a hand through her strawberry blond hair. "It's been so long since I've been with him I almost forgot. Andy is extremely sociable. In fact, he never met anyone he didn't like."

"Of course you would say that now," Clarissa harumphed.

Jenna turned to Grady desperately. "Look, I'll prove it to you, Grady," Jenna said. "I'll have a DNA blood test."

"So will I," Clarissa quickly volunteered.

"I can't believe this," Grady muttered. "You're both going to stand there and continue to claim this baby?"

The corners of Jenna's mouth curved up in a grim parody of a smile. "Looks that way, doesn't it?" she said.

"Okay, Alec, you win," Grady said as soon as the long-distance operator had patched him through to Paris. "This is without a doubt the very best practical joke you and Jack ever played on me."

"What joke?" Alec said, sounding genuinely confused.

Grady sighed. He was getting very tired of spelling everything out. "The baby. Your marriage."

"Baby Andy is no joke, Grady. Jack and I are seriously looking for his parents," Alec answered. He paused. "Jack told me you were sure Andy was your son."

Alec sounded concerned, Grady realized uncomfortably, then pushed the thought aside. "I also told him there were two candidates for his mother."

"Neither claimed Andy?" Alec guessed.

"Both claimed him," Grady said.

Alec started to laugh. "You're kidding, right?"

"Don't pretend you don't know anything about this," Grady advised shortly.

"I only wish," Alec said wistfully.

Grady paused. Neither Alec nor Jack had ever been shy about claiming victory, he realized uneasily. Hence, Alec's confusion could only mean one thing. He muttered an oath.

"You swear on the sacredness of our friendship this is no joke?" Grady demanded.

"I swear," Alec said firmly. "My marriage to Jade is real enough, though. Jade, say hi to Grady."

A soft, melodious voice came on the phone. "Hi, Grady."

"Hi, Jade," Grady said.

"Believe me now?" Alec asked as he got back on the line.

"Yeah, sure," Grady said. So that was one down. "Jack—"

"Is not in on it, either, Grady," Alec said.

"How do you know?" Grady demanded.

"Because both Jack and I already went through what you're going through now," Alec said calmly. "Listen to me, Grady. This is no joke. If it were, I would have owned up to it right away. You know that."

Yeah, Grady did, that was what was so troubling. Another silence fell. Aware both women were watching him and hanging on his every word, Grady ran his hand through his hair and swore softly.

"Sounds like you got yourself in a heap of trouble there, pal," Alec said. "So. What are you going to do?"

Grady turned to see both Jenna and Clarissa glaring at him. Only Andy was smiling and gurgling happily, maybe because he intuited that three people were fighting to take care of him. "The only thing I can do," Grady said grimly, as the realization of just how big a mess he was really in sank in. "I'm going to the hospital and taking those blood tests."

"How long before we get the results?" Jenna asked the lab tech at Philadelphia General Hospital impatiently. She couldn't believe Clarissa was still continuing the charade. She'd thought the other woman would give up before the blood tests were taken. But no, Clarissa had brazened her way through the tests just as if she really had delivered Andy herself. Part of Jenna could almost understand why. Clarissa was still deeply in love with Grady, even though Grady didn't appear to be in love with Clarissa now. If he ever had been, she thought. Somehow, she just couldn't see the two of them together. They were all wrong for one another.

"I'll put a rush on it, but it'll be a few days, at the very least," the lab tech said. He was young, efficient and, to Jenna's dismay, completely gaga over the elegant Clarissa.

"Great," Grady muttered, looking more impatient than ever to know what was really going on.

"In the meantime, I'll keep Andy," Jenna said quickly.

"No, in the meantime, I'm keeping Andy," Grady corrected.

"How?" Jenna shot back. "You have to work, remember?"

"Easy." Grady's intent gray-blue gaze meshed with hers. For a second, Jenna wished she wasn't so attracted to him. But the simple truth of the matter was there wasn't an inch of Grady Noland's tall, broad-shouldered frame she didn't find altogether too attractive. She liked the way he dressed—in jeans, oxford cloth shirts—today's was light blue—Harris tweed jackets—today's was gray—and boots. There was nothing soft or easy about him, and yet he was capable of great tenderness, especially in bed. "I've already called the station and arranged for an emergency leave."

Jenna looked into his intent gray-blue gaze. "You can't seriously expect me to let you keep my baby?" she said, and saw the hollows beneath his cheekbones grow more pronounced.

Grady shrugged indifferently. "The way I see it, this baby was abandoned to my care, if not directly, then indirectly, so yes, Jenna, that is exactly what I expect." His eyes probed hers relentlessly, searching for any signs of playfulness or duplicity. "Unless you can produce proof that he's yours between now and then?"

"No problem," Clarissa was quick to put in. "In fact, I'm going home to Long Island to get my proof right now."

"Fake birth certificates can be made up anywhere," Jenna said. She was beginning to feel really uneasy about all of this. Particularly since she knew her own "proof" wouldn't stand up to anyone's scrutiny, never mind the scrutiny of a crack Philadelphia police detective.

"Honestly, Jenna, you are so suspicious," Clarissa said. She turned to Grady as proprietorially as if she still was his wife. "My proof won't be fake," Clarissa reassured her ex-husband bluntly, with a great deal more confidence than Jenna felt.

"Mine isn't, either," Jenna promised. Though how the hell she was going to deliver on that promise, she didn't know. She really should have thought this all out beforehand. But then, hindsight was always better, particularly in complicated situations like this, she reassured herself.

"I'll be the judge of the proof," Grady said, giving both of them a hard look. "In the meantime, Andy and I bid you two adieu."

"I KNOW what you're thinking, kid, you're thinking this is all my fault," Grady said to Andy as he drove them both to his apartment. "That I'm just getting a dose of my own medicine. And you're right. I never should have slept with Clarissa that night, even if her apartment had been broken into. But she was so damn needy and vulnerable, and I hadn't been with anyone in so long… Okay, so that's still no excuse. Or even an explanation. But I'm not sure how I can explain how I felt at that time. Lonely. Sad that my marriage to Clarissa was over. And guilty as hell, because I felt I'd let her down. She needed me that night, and I thought my being there for her might somehow make up for my not loving her, only I was wrong. Dead wrong. It only made things worse. When her apartment was burglarized again, I sent someone else to check it out. Shortly after that, she moved back to Long Island to be with her parents. And that was that, or so I thought," Grady finished with a sigh.

Andy gurgled and waved his rattle. Grady grinned at him. He was glad the little guy, with his cherubic face, bright blue eyes and fuzzy dark brown hair, was such a trooper. "Okay. Enough about Clarissa. You want to know how I got involved with Jenna, don't you? Well, it was like this. I met her at a party at Alec's. You know Alec, don't you? Anyway, it was one of those stiff formal business parties where everyone drinks very little and eats even less and talks business the whole night long and I was not in the mood to mingle.

"So I was trying to sneak out the back way and I found Jenna also trying to sneak out the back way. Damn, she was beautiful. We got to laughing about how dull Alec's party was and we took a bottle of his champagne and we walked to my place and talked about how fed up we both were with marriage, the institution, and what a good thing it would be just to sleep with someone because you felt like it, and not worry about tomorrow, or the consequences of your actions, and the next thing I knew we were in my bed...." Grady sighed again. "When I woke up the next morning, she was already gone. She left me a note—seems that woman is big on notes—saying that it had been fun, but she wasn't looking for a relationship. She asked me not to call her or try to see her." Grady parked in front of his apartment and got out, Andy in his arms.

"That was a hard one," Grady continued conversationally as Andy gazed up at him attentively. "I wanted to see Jenna again. Boy, did I ever want to see her again. But I also knew I was all wrong for her," Grady said as he walked up the steps and paused to check the mail. "Even though Jenna said she had concluded she wasn't the marrying kind, her eyes, those beautiful dark green eyes of hers, said nothing but marriage was ever really going to do for a woman like her. And I had already proved that cops and marriage don't mix."

Grady stuffed his mail into his pocket, then shut the mailbox. "She couldn't be telling the truth, could she? She couldn't really be your mother?" Grady asked and looked at Andy briefly before he unlocked the door to his apartment. Withdrawing the key from the lock, he shifted Andy in his arms. "I mean, none of this makes sense to me. I can see Jenna having you by herself because that's just the type of gutsy woman she is—but I can't see her leaving you on

Alec's doorstep, even if it was Valentine's Day,'' Grady continued as he went inside.

"You're right,'' Jenna said softly, stepping from the shadows of his apartment. Her eyes were smudged with tears, and more desperate than he could ever have imagined them being. "I wouldn't have done that, Grady. I would never have left Andy alone like that, even for a second.''

Grady took a moment to register the fact that Jenna was in his apartment, uninvited this time. He didn't want to think about how fast she'd had to drive her rental car to get here ahead of him, or how much she'd had to bribe the superintendent to get into his apartment. "Then how do you explain it?'' he asked, part of his heart hardening at the duplicity she'd had to employ to get her way.

"Simple,'' Jenna said. She looked at Grady beseechingly and took a deep, bolstering breath. "Andy was kidnapped.''

Chapter Two

"What do you mean Andy was kidnapped?" Grady said.

"Exactly what I said. He was taken from his crib while he was sleeping."

Grady took Andy out of his snowsuit and placed him in the crib. He gave the mobile music box a few swift turns. Andy gurgled as the Disney characters began spinning round above him.

Satisfied the baby was content for the moment, Grady turned to Jenna. She had taken her coat off this time. She looked pale. Stressed out. And scared. Like a kidnapping really had occurred. But that was impossible, wasn't it? "Where were you when this happened?" Grady bit out impatiently.

Jenna wrung her hands in front of her nervously. "In the office on the first floor of my family's upstate New York farmhouse." Her voice was quiet, subdued.

"And Andy was—"

"Upstairs, in the nursery."

His thoughts spinning, Grady walked into the kitchen. He grabbed a cold Coke Classic from the refrigerator and popped the top open. He offered one to her. She shook her head. Grady took a long sip and lounged against the counter. "Let me get this straight. Someone just came into the house—"

Jenna's chin tipped defiantly. Some of the color came back into her cheeks. "Yes!"

Grady quirked a brow in quiet disbelief, but kept his voice neutral. "And you didn't hear anything," he surmised.

"No."

The seconds strung out tensely. "How is that possible?" Jenna shrugged and looked away. *She's holding something back.* "Were your doors unlocked?" Grady persisted.

Jenna stalked back and forth, scowling at him. "No. Of course not."

Grady took another long swallow of Coke. "Then how did this kidnapper get in?"

"I don't know." Jenna shrugged and spread her hands in front of her helplessly. "I suppose he had a key."

"Which he got where?" Grady asked.

Jenna's straight white teeth raked across her unglossed lower lip. Grady could tell from the way she hesitated that she was considering not answering that. He continued staring at her, waiting. She bit her lip again, looked away and said finally, "Maybe from the fake rock in the flower garden, among the real rocks."

"Are you guessing that or do you know for sure?"

Jenna clamped her arms in front of her like a shield. "I know for sure."

Grady took another long drink. "And this happened when?"

"Midmorning, Valentine's Day."

Grady paused, working hard to marshal his emotions. "Did you call the police?"

Again, Jenna shook her head. "No."

"Why not?"

She lounged against the opposite counter and regarded him wearily. "Do we have to get into this?"

He inclined his head. "Only if you want me to believe your story."

She was silent, thinking. Finally she dragged a hand through her hair and admitted in a low, troubled voice, "I didn't call the police because I knew it was an inside job, probably by some well-meaning member of my family."

Grady put his can aside, aware—even if Jenna wasn't—
that this was suddenly getting very serious. "How did you
know that?" he asked brusquely.

Jenna's full lips tightened. She lifted her glance and regarded him with obvious resentment. "A couple of things.
When I moved out to the farmhouse last summer, I had a
security system installed. It was that morning Nanny Beth—
that's Andy's governess—left the house to go into town on
errands."

"And you confirmed this with Nanny Beth?"

"Actually—" Jenna paused again "—I haven't been able
to talk to her since the kidnapping."

Grady's pulse picked up. He had the feeling this was about
to get a lot more complicated. "Why not?" he asked mildly.

Jenna treated him to a careless smile. "I don't know where
she is."

Grady paused. So much of what she'd already told him
simply didn't add up. She said she'd recently had a baby. Yet
she was reed thin, and judging from the fit of those tight jeans
and long white sweater, in fine physical shape. She said her
baby had been kidnapped over two weeks ago, yet she hadn't
called the police, hadn't even come to see him until now, and
she said he was the father! More, she had known all along
that he was a cop and could have helped her locate the baby.
More incriminating still, she seemed to think she was in the
right here. And that didn't add up, either. "You're telling me
you think your nanny is the kidnapper?" Grady asked calmly.

"Of course not! Nanny's been with my family for years."

"Where is she now?"

"I don't know."

"Did you fire her?"

"No."

"Did she quit?"

"No, but—" Jenna hesitated. "She may have taken a few
days off."

"Wouldn't she have told you if she was going to do that?"

"Normally, yes—"

"But?"

Jenna shrugged. "But she didn't this time, that's all."

"I'm going to have to put out an APB on her."

Jenna grabbed his arm. "No, Grady, don't." He looked at her. "Can't you just look for Nanny unofficially?" Jenna pleaded softly. "I'm sure she didn't do anything criminal."

"And how do you know that?" Grady drawled.

Jenna's chin took on a stubborn tilt. "Because I know her. She loves me and she loves Andy very much. She would never do anything to hurt us."

Grady paused. "I'm going to have to talk to Nanny anyway before this is all over," he warned.

"All right." Jenna sighed. "I'll help you find her. But in the meantime, we've got to try to figure out who kidnapped Andy from the farmhouse." Her dark green eyes looked directly into his. "Whoever broke into the farmhouse knew the code to turn off the security system. They used it to get into the house without setting off the alarm."

Grady picked up his can of Coke and drained it. "Who else knows the code?" He set the can on the counter with a thud.

"My father, my brother and his wife, and Nanny."

He folded his arms in front of him. "Why would they want to kidnap Andy?"

Jenna shrugged and looked evasive again. "Because they thought they were doing me a favor by getting Andy's father involved?"

Grady decided he'd played good cop long enough. It was time to crowd her and put on the pressure. He pushed away from the counter and, arms still folded in front of him, towered over her. "How do you figure that?"

Jenna swallowed hard and rummaged in her purse. "By this note that was left."

Grady unfolded the paper. He had to step back a pace to study it. Like the note left with Andy when he arrived at Alec's, this was typewritten in capital letters. It read, "Every baby needs a father, Jenna. The responsibility for Andy is not yours alone." There was a postscript. "Don't worry and don't call the police. Andy'll be well taken care of until he is reunited with his father."

Grady folded the note. "Mind if I keep this?"

Jenna glared at him. "That all depends on what you're going to do with it."

He slipped the note into his pocket. "Am I making you nervous, Jenna?"

"The fact that you're a cop is making me nervous."

"Why? You say you didn't do anything wrong."

"I didn't," she said quickly.

"Then—"

"Look." Jenna released a frustrated breath. Her fingertips trembled as she rearranged her strawberry blond hair. "I've explained the situation to you. Regardless of what that note says, Andy is not your responsibility."

Grady smiled mirthlessly. "There we differ, babe."

"Excuse me?"

"If Andy's my child, then he damn well is my responsibility."

"Fine, then he's not your child."

"It's a little too late to be saying that, don't you think?"

Jenna released another frustrated breath. The color in her cheeks turned from a pale pink to a dusky rose. "All I want to do is take my baby and go home, Grady." She spoke as if underlining every word.

"Not until we have proof that he is your baby," Grady stipulated softly, "and maybe not even then."

It was Jenna's turn to stomp closer. "Why the hell not?"

Grady held his ground, despite the fact they were now uncomfortably close. Close enough for him to smell the flowery fragrance of her hair and skin. Close enough for him to see the luminous depths of her dark green eyes, and the kissable softness of her lips and skin. His mood grim, Grady stared down at her. "Because there's still a lot I don't understand," he said gruffly.

Jenna's lower lip thrust toward him contentiously. "Such as?"

Grady's lower body was thrumming. He braced his legs a little farther apart and fought his attraction to her. "Such as why you let a whole two weeks go by before you came to see me today," he said softly.

Jenna turned away and moved to the end of the counter. "I told you." She gripped the edge of the counter tightly with one hand. "I thought someone in the family had him, and I was looking for him myself."

She's hiding something, Grady thought. "But if you knew the kidnapper planned to take Andy to me and I'm Andy's father—"

"The kidnapper didn't know you were his father!" she interrupted emotionally, pivoting to him once more. "No one did. I had 'unknown' put on the birth certificate."

Grady blinked. "You did what?"

"You heard me."

"Heard you, yes," Grady replied between gritted teeth. "Understand you, no."

Jenna smiled. Her look was deliberately provoking. "Exactly why I didn't call you," she said sweetly.

"You could have let me know you were pregnant," Grady accused tightly. His muscles were rigid with suppressed anger and resentment. Hurt.

"Why?" Jenna shot back without missing a beat. Her eyes glittered hotly as she reminded him softly, "You made it very clear to me that night we were together that since your divorce, you were no longer the marrying kind."

"As I recall at the time, neither were you."

"Right," Jenna said flatly. She moved away from him with an insouciant shrug. "Andy didn't change that."

"*Au contraire,* babe." Grady stepped around her quickly and blocked her exit from the galley kitchen. "Andy here changes everything. If he's your child."

"What's that supposed to mean?"

"It means I'm still not convinced you're telling me the

truth.'' She hadn't presented nearly enough facts to substantiate her story. In his years as a police detective, Grady had learned to trust only the facts, not people's heartrending stories or one-sided views, or even his own emotions, which in this case were jumping up and down with joy at the thought of having a child of his own at long last.

''If you didn't tell anyone who Andy's father was, then how could they figure out who to take Andy to?''

''I presume by going through my files, checking out my social calendar and putting two and two together.'' Jenna swallowed hard. ''The night Andy was conceived, I was in Philadelphia for Alec's party. Alec's address and phone number were written down as the emergency contact number I left with my office. Obviously, someone put two and two together and figured Alec Roman was the father because that's where I'd been exactly nine months before Andy was born. Only I wasn't with Alec that night, I was with you.''

''How well do you know Alec?''

Jenna shrugged. ''I met him several years ago at a charity fund-raiser for the Children's Hospital. He was interested in my work with the Children's Rescue Foundation and has even loaned me the use of his jet a couple times for foundation business.''

''So it's possible someone would think you to be—''

''More than friends, yes. We're not.''

''What kind of proof did you bring with you to substantiate this theory?'' Grady asked.

Again, she paled. ''Proof?'' Jenna gulped and stepped away from him uneasily.

''Yeah, proof,'' Grady repeated impatiently.

''I showed up here today to get Andy.''

''A good two weeks after the alleged kidnapping,'' Grady agreed. Silence fell between them. It was thick with tension. And Jenna was a million miles away from him, in her thoughts. Grady didn't recall Jenna behaving so mysteriously last spring. ''Why didn't you call me sooner if you had figured all this out?'' he persisted.

Jenna glared at him. "I tried to get in touch with you earlier."

"When?"

"On Valentine's Day. I called you at the station shortly after I realized Andy was missing. I was pretty hysterical at the time. I told your buddies there that it was an emergency."

Grady frowned at the simmering resentment in her eyes. "And—?"

Jenna paced to the refrigerator, to the stove, the dishwasher, and then back again. "And they laughed at me." She yanked open the refrigerator door, pulled out the Coke Classic he had offered her earlier and popped the tab. "They said that everyone was having 'romantic emergencies' that day, but you were out on a case and *my* 'romantic emergency' with you would just have to wait."

Her words had a disturbing ring of truth. "I never got your message."

Jenna glared at him. Her eyes were an icy green. "Never got it or just decided not to return my call?"

"Never got it!" Grady said.

She shook her head and took a long draft of Coke. "And you expect me to believe that?"

"If I believe you, yeah, I do," Grady shot back. "Besides, your call should be easy enough to trace. All calls to the station are logged in by computer."

Jenna lifted her gaze and inclined her head slightly to one side. "Meaning what? My word alone isn't good enough?"

"Your story has more holes than a sieve."

She wanted to retreat. Deciding against that option, she shifted away from him and took another long, thirsty drink. "I want my baby back."

"You're going to have to prove he's your baby first." *And then,* Grady amended silently, *you're going to have to prove to me you didn't abandon him.*

"I'm not leaving here without him."

Grady looked at her mouth, which was damp and soft. He wanted to drag her into his arms and kiss her again, reason be damned. He wanted to take her to his bed and make wild passionate love to her again, and then, only then, when they'd exhausted themselves, run the gamut of their feelings for one another, only then deal with this mess. But that was impossible.

He still had Clarissa to deal with. And Andy...

"Or, if you'd rather, I'll stay here with you and I'll help you take care of Andy until we get the results of the blood tests back," Jenna offered.

"No," Grady said.

Abruptly, she looked exhausted and close to tears. "Grady, please," she whispered. "Don't do this to me. Don't take my baby from me."

Regardless of what Jenna might think about him, he did not want to see her get down on her knees and beg. Nor did he want to forcibly part her from her child—if Andy was hers. He tugged a hand through his dark brown hair. "Look, Jenna," he began wearily, "it's been an incredibly long day—"

Jenna blinked rapidly and recovered her composure. In a voice thick with emotion, she predicted, "Knowing Andy, it's going to be even longer." Their glances meshed, and Jenna continued informatively, "He doesn't sleep through the night yet, remember? And there's something else."

Grady regarded her warily, his heart working like a trip-hammer in his chest. "What?"

Jenna released a worried sigh. Her eyes lifted to his. "We can't forget Andy was kidnapped once. I still don't know who did it."

Grady searched her face. For months, he had told himself memory had exaggerated her stunning good looks, the creamy complexion, perfect smile and long-lashed green eyes. Not so. She was even better now. Her cheekbones were more pronounced, her voice throatier, her mouth softer, more tempting. So tempting, in fact, he was having trouble concentrating on the business at hand.

"Assuming I'm able to solve this mystery for you, Jenna,

do you want this kidnapper prosecuted?'' he asked. He was curious to see what her reaction would be. If she was making it all up, the answer would of course be no. On the other hand, she could easily be out for vengeance, her target anyone from her ex-husband to a neighbor she didn't like. In his years as a cop, he'd seen it all.

Jenna drew in a wavering breath. "I want to make sure it doesn't happen again. To that end," she said slowly, "a promise and a confession from the meddlesome abductor will do."

"I see," Grady said slowly. "And what if that's not good enough for me, Jenna? As the baby's father, I certainly should have some say."

She drew in a second unsteady breath. "You don't want any trouble here, either, Grady." And suddenly he knew she was holding back at least as much as she had already told him. He'd never had much patience with people who told less than the truth, either before or after he became a cop.

"What makes you so sure of that?" Grady asked silkily as, without warning, the anger that had been building in him all afternoon took off like a rocket hurtling into space.

Dammit, if Andy was his baby and Jenna's, as she had just claimed, Jenna had robbed him not only of the chance to marry her and save their child from being born illegitimately, but she had also deprived him of his own baby's birth and the first eight weeks of his son's life. Hell, he might have gone to his grave never knowing he had a child. His son would have been similarly uninformed, senselessly hurt and denied a dad. And for what? So Jenna wouldn't have to sacrifice her pride?

"Maybe I like trouble," he speculated brashly. And maybe it was time she learned that she couldn't shut him out that way, not out of his own child's life and maybe not out of hers, either. Not if he wanted in. And right now, as it happened, he did. If he had a child, he was damn well going to be around to raise it. Even if it meant sharing that baby, as well as the whole parenting process, with her.

He stepped toward her, his decision made. She stepped back.

"Grady, don't," she said shakily.

"Don't what?" Grady asked. They continued their silent two-step until her back was against the wall. Grady was directly in front of her. She attempted to move past him, but this time he wasn't about to let her go, not until he had the whole truth and nothing but the truth from her. He put a hand out to block her escape and stared down at her grimly. "The way I look at it, if everything you've just now told me is true, you owe me big time for this, Jenna."

Hot, angry color flared in her cheeks. "Everything I've told you is true!" she shot back emotionally as Grady braced a hand flat against the wall on either side of her. "But that doesn't mean I owe you anything," Jenna continued.

Grady uttered a mirthless laugh. Their bodies weren't quite touching, but he could see her trembling. He could recall with stunning clarity the soft give of her slender body. He quirked a brow. "Oh, no?"

"No."

"Meaning what? That you never would have told me we had a child together had Andy not been kidnapped? That you would have let me go to my grave never knowing I had a son?"

Jenna swallowed and stared up at him. She didn't know what she had expected, coming back to see Grady this way. She had only known she couldn't leave Philadelphia without her baby. And she couldn't gain custody of Andy with Clarissa around, foolishly muddying the situation and insisting on *her* rights. So she'd doubled back to Grady's apartment after the DNA tests, figuring that a little one-on-one conversation with him would give her the opportunity to explain as little as was humanly possible about what had transpired in the last two weeks in order to get her back her baby.

She had known, of course, that it wouldn't be easy. Grady was stubborn and opinionated to a fault, just as she was. Furthermore, he had every right to be angry and resentful because she hadn't told him about the baby. He thought it was because she'd been selfish and hadn't wanted to share their child, but she knew in her heart just the opposite was true. She'd been trying to protect her child, and herself, from rejection the best way she knew how. She hadn't wanted to force Grady into fatherhood, even from a distance. Particularly when she knew full well how he felt about marriage. Her breasts rose and lowered with every quick, shaky breath she drew. "I don't see where my telling you or not telling you enters into this," Jenna retorted stubbornly.

"Answer the question, Jenna!"

"All right!" Her palms flattened against his chest, holding him at bay. "I had decided not to tell you."

Grady tried not to think about how it felt to have her touching him again. He tried not to recall what a sensual, giving lover she had been and instead concentrated on his hurt at having been shut out of the most important experience of his life. "Why?"

"Because," Jenna explained. She tilted her head against the wall and her voice rose emotionally as she spoke. "It wasn't necessary for me to drag you into this, not when Andy already had me, and a home, and enough money to buy him everything he ever needed or wanted."

Grady's exasperation mounted until he felt as though he was going to explode. He studied her silently. "He still didn't have a father, Jenna."

To Grady's consternation, Jenna refused to admit she'd done anything wrong. "We could have worked around that," she insisted stubbornly.

"Oh, yeah?" Grady said grimly, as his frustration mounted. "Well, let's see how well you work around this, Jenna." Beyond all thought except the desire to bring her back to some semblance of reality, he tunneled his hands through her hair and lifted her face to his. Ignoring her soft, muted gasp of dismay, he lowered his mouth to hers and then did what he had been wanting to do since the first moment he'd laid eyes on her again.

He kissed her like they'd never been apart. He kissed her to remind her what they had shared, and what they could share again, given half a chance. He kissed her because he had missed her. Because they'd let so many things drive them apart.

She fought him at first, using her hands to push against his chest. He persisted, parting her lips with the pressure of his, nudging his tongue inside, tasting the sweetness that was her, tormenting her with lazy sweeps of his tongue again and again until she trembled. He deepened the kiss pleasurably, and Jenna moaned. Her whole body softened. The pressure of her hands on his chest turned from a show of resistance to a bittersweet caress.

Satisfaction rushed through Grady as he felt her knees give out, just a little. The next thing he knew her arms were wrapped around his neck, pulling him close, and she was kissing him back with utter abandon.

His thoughts spinning, Grady struggled to keep the upper hand in their ongoing battle of wills. Kissing her was just a way to make a point, he told himself sternly. To let her see firsthand what it felt like to have an intimate part of her life decided without her prior knowledge or consent. He couldn't let this embrace get out of hand.

But before he knew it the tide had changed again. Her body molded to his, and her kiss turned even sweeter, more seductively compelling. Waves of desire arced through him. Hungry for more of her, needing more of her, needing more of this, he pressed even closer. He knew the risk in his action, even as his heart pounded and the blood rushed into his groin.

Making love to Jenna was about as safe as stepping out onto a ledge of a high rise without a safety rope, but then, Grady thought as he uttered a contented sigh and dove even deeper into the passionate embrace, he had always liked living on the edge....

He wrapped an arm around her and pulled her closer yet.

Without warning, Jenna broke off the kiss and pushed him away. "You shouldn't have done that," she said, trembling.

Grady saw her response and grinned in male satisfaction. "You're right, I shouldn't have," he said without apology, then quirked a thoughtful brow at her. "But now that I have...now that you know nothing about our attraction to each other has changed, maybe now you'll understand why you should leave."

Jenna lifted her eyes heavenward. Abruptly, she was her old sassy self. "Look, Grady, if you think one little kiss—"

"One long, steamy kiss," he corrected.

Jenna ignored him and plowed on determinedly. "Is going to have me darting out of here like a scared child, you have another think coming."

He regarded her with a look of utter male supremacy. "Is that so?" he drawled.

"That is definitely so," Jenna said. She might not have made love with anyone at all except Grady outside of marriage, but that didn't mean she couldn't be adult about it. So they'd succumbed to temptation and slept together a year ago. It had happened, but it was over. Both were smarter now. And she, at least, had learned her lesson and was a hell of a lot more restrained, as she had just proved to herself by breaking off their fiery kiss, instead of allowing it to lead her into his bed. Courageously holding Grady's gaze, Jenna continued flatly, "Because I'm still not going anywhere without Andy."

Grady sighed and stepped back. "Come on, Jenna," he said, suddenly making no effort to hide his complete exasperation with her, "I don't want to have to get ugly here and throw you out."

The truth be told, Jenna didn't want that, either. She took a deep breath and called upon all the powers of feminine persuasion she possessed. She had already proved to herself that she couldn't get to Grady, person to person. She might, however, be able to get to him woman to man. It was a risk, of course, but one she was willing to take. "If you do what I want," she promised throatily, "you won't have to."

Grady stared at her in complete fascination, stunned into

silence by her abrupt change of mood. His eyes took a slow, studied tour of her body, then returned with sensual deliberation to her face. "If this is the kind of proposal I think it is, you'd better spell it out, babe."

"If we leave now, and drive all evening, we can be at my farmhouse by midnight," Jenna proposed with as much serenity as she could muster.

Grady's steely blue glance narrowed suspiciously. He folded his arms and leaned against the counter. "Why would we want to do that?"

Jenna held his gaze with effort. She fixed him with the sort of smile she usually saved for recalcitrant contributors to her foundation, the Children's Rescue Foundation. "You said you wanted proof Andy is mine," she reminded pleasantly.

"That's right," Grady replied amiably as his expression hardened implacably. "I do."

"Well—" Jenna shrugged "—the proof is there." *And Clarissa is not.*

Grady shifted and stood even straighter. His steely blue gaze grew even more probing. "What kind of proof?"

"His birth certificate and baby footprints, for one thing. The nursery where he's slept since he was born. The pictures of him as a newborn. Even the clothes he's already outgrown. Please, Grady. Just come with me," she urged.

Once he was there, he would see what a good mother she was. He would know it was okay to leave the baby in her very capable care. He would know she had done what was best for all three of them from the very first, and that was not to force them into any domestic arrangement that was destined to make them all miserable, just because they'd been blessed with an unexpected surprise.

"We can turn my rental car in on the way out of town and then drive up to Hudson Falls," Jenna continued persuasively.

"In my car."

"Yes. It won't be quite as fast as flying but it'll be easier in the sense that we'll be traveling with a baby and able to stop whenever or wherever we need to."

"This better not be a wild-goose chase," Grady growled.

Jenna's spirits soared as she realized Grady was finally of a mind to cooperate with her. "It won't be," she promised.

Chapter Three

"How much farther?" Grady asked wearily several hours later.

"About fifteen miles."

He glanced at the rolling countryside on either side of the two-lane country road. Trees were plentiful. Farmhouses were few and far between. "You really are out in the country," he said. A city guy himself, he had never understood the allure of living out in the sticks.

Jenna smiled and settled back in her seat. She hadn't put Andy down since she'd given him his bottle. And though he had long since fallen back to sleep, seeing how utterly contented Jenna looked, just holding the sleeping baby in her arms, Grady didn't have the heart to suggest she put him in his car seat, even if it would be a more comfortable way for her to travel.

"I know." Jenna sighed as she dipped her head and pressed a tender kiss on the top of Andy's head. She laid her cheek against his soft, dark hair and breathed in his baby scent. "That's one of the things I like best about the area. The complete absence of city noise and traffic."

"Why did you move all the way out here?"

Jenna shrugged and tucked Andy's blanket around his sleeper-covered feet. "Baxter and I put our house in Albany on the market at the time we divorced. When it finally sold last June, I needed a place to live."

"Surely you could have bought another house in Albany."

"I could have. But with my family's Hudson Falls farmhouse standing empty and me needing a break from public life anyway, it made sense for me to go there. Particularly since I was pregnant and unmarried." She gave him a steady look and pointed out the next turn. "I did not want to bear the brunt of a scandal."

Grady shrugged. Even if Jenna hadn't wanted to marry him, and he admitted he hadn't been a very marriageable guy a year ago, he and Jenna still could've been together. "These days—"

Jenna shook her head and shifted Andy closer to her breast. "It doesn't matter to my father what anyone else does. He cares about me. Unwed pregnancies are not de rigueur in my family."

In Grady's, either, he realized uncomfortably. "You could have asked me to marry you," he pointed out evenly. In fact, part of him wished she had.

Jenna smirked and pointed out yet another turn. "With or without a shotgun?" she asked wryly.

He ignored her as he turned onto a country road that was barely wide enough for his car. "I would have done the honorable thing."

"That's just it, Grady. I didn't want you to do the honorable thing. Besides," she continued confidently, "I had it all worked out."

Grady's hand tightened on the steering wheel. Irritation colored his low voice. "Worked out, how?"

"I was going to tell everyone Andy was adopted. They know I see a lot of orphaned children in the course of my work for the foundation. Everyone knows how softhearted I am. I don't think it would surprise anyone to see me adopt one of the children the Rescue Foundation has aided."

Grady swore silently at her naïveté. "What about me?"

"You'd be off the hook."

Grady exhaled slowly. "Don't you think that's a decision

I should have made?'' He glanced at her in the dim light of
the dash. Jenna's mouth tightened.

"Maybe I would have let you make it had you ever called
again."

Touché, Grady thought. She pointed out another turn, this
one at a mailbox at the end of a long country lane. "You
know why I didn't," Grady said as he guided the car onto
the driveway that led to a plain white farmhouse a good half
mile back from the road. "We agreed before we ever went
to my place that night that it was only going to be a one-
night thing."

"It didn't turn out that way for me." Jenna glanced out
the window.

"Yes, but I didn't know that."

"It doesn't matter," she said and held the baby closer.

There she was very wrong. "It does to me," Grady said.
He parked in front of the farmhouse and cut the ignition. He
turned to her, no longer sure if this was a bad dream or a
lifelong fantasy come true. He only knew for certain that if
this was his baby, he wanted Andy's mother to be Jenna.
And if it wasn't their child, then…then he still wanted Jenna.
He wanted to make love to her at least one more time.

Kissing her had stirred something deep inside him, something he had thought was dead. And though he wasn't sure
that such wild passion was good for anything except getting
him into trouble, he still wanted to experience it again. Hell,
after five hours of being confined in a car with Jenna, smell-
ing her perfume and listening to her soft throaty voice, he
wanted to kiss her again, and would have if she hadn't been
holding the baby like a shield in front of her.

Jenna studied his face a moment longer, then sighed wearily. "Let's just go inside. I'll put Andy down in the nursery,
and then I'll show you the birth certificate and so forth."

Grady shrugged and warned himself not to get his hopes
up. "The hospital ID bracelet would also be nice," Grady
said. He got out of the car and rushed around to help her.

Jenna carried Andy up the walk while he followed with

the diaper bag, her purse and several suitcases. "Um, I wasn't in a hospital, exactly."

He leaned against the portal as she punched in a security code that would shut off the silent alarm and then another that would unlock the door. "Where did you have the baby?"

Jenna waited until the panel blinked okay, then pushed open the door. "Here," she said.

"You're kidding, right?"

Jenna gave him a placating smile, which only annoyed Grady. "There wasn't time to get to the hospital," Jenna said calmly.

Shifting Andy higher in her arms, Jenna stepped across the threshold. Grady followed. The house was cozy, warm, with an abundance of chintz and overstuffed furniture—just the type of place he would've expected Jenna to live. "The nursery is upstairs," she said.

Grady followed her up the stairs. "If you'll just get the door for me," Jenna whispered, "I'll put Andy down in his crib and then we'll talk."

"Sure." Grady wanted to talk, too. He stepped around her and opened the door. They stared at the room. It was completely empty.

"I DON'T BELIEVE THIS," Jenna muttered, distressed.

"Why am I not surprised?" Grady drawled, feeling his patience with the baffling turn of events fading fast. He had ruled out the practical-joke theory when he'd talked to Alec, but he hadn't ruled out a feminine-revenge plot. If it turned out Clarissa and Jenna were conspiring together to get back at him, he was going to be royally ticked off. Come to think of it, Jenna didn't look so happy herself.

She glared at him. "Don't tell me you're in on this, too!" she accused.

Grady frowned. "In on what?"

Jenna stalked past him with a glare and went to the master bedroom down the hall. While Grady lounged in the portal, she laid Andy down on the center of the bed. Taking pillows, she boxed the baby in a protective square to keep him from rolling off the bed, then covered him gently with a blanket.

Not wanting Andy to waken when so much still needed to be explained, Grady followed Jenna wordlessly downstairs and into the den she had converted into her foundation office. It had two computers, a copier, a fax machine and a three-line phone. Jenna jerked open the door on the desk and pulled out a manila file. To her relief, Andy's birth certificate was still inside. "Here," she said triumphantly. "Here it is."

The town listed on the birth certificate was Hudson Falls, New York, all right. The birth date listed was December twenty-sixth of the previous year. But the name on the birth certificate was not Jenna Sullivan. Grady gave Jenna a long-suffering look. "What is this supposed to prove?"

"That Andy is my child, of course."

Grady sat on the edge of her desk. His years as a cop had taught him to keep his emotions in check. "You're not Laura Johnson. Are you?"

"Of course not. That's just the name I gave the doctor in Hudson Falls."

Grady struggled for patience. "Why did you give the doctor a fake name?"

"Because I wanted Andy to be born to Laura Johnson so that Jenna Sullivan could adopt him. I've always wanted a child of my own to love. I've even thought about adopting. It wouldn't surprise anyone, least of all my family, to know I'd adopted a child. This way I figured I could spare my family from questions and gossip. This way, I figured, everyone would win, and no one would be hurt."

"Except the father, who didn't even know he'd brought a child into this world," Grady said heavily.

Jenna was silent. Suddenly, she looked every bit as guilty as Grady wanted her to feel.

He lowered his glance to the paper in his hands.

"Jenna, this birth certificate isn't legal," he pointed out with a great deal more calm than he felt at that particular moment.

"So?"

"If you based an adoption on a birth certificate that wasn't legal, then the adoption wouldn't be legal, either."

"So what? The adoption was all for show, anyway. Either way, Andy was my child. I was just trying to prevent him from bearing the brunt of any gossip."

Grady eyed Jenna contemplatively. Her logic had a sort of convoluted charm, made more appealing because all she had been trying to do was protect those she loved. Still, the day had been a long one, and Jenna was definitely showing the signs of it. Her thick, strawberry blond hair fell in rumpled waves to her shoulders. Her face was pale, her dark green eyes rimmed with fatigue. And yet there was something so sweetly vulnerable in the way she was looking at him that called forth a protective response from him that was ludicrous under the circumstances. For all he knew she was simply loony.

Grady sighed and folded his arms in front of him. "Let me get this straight. You had a baby here at home and put him in a nursery that does not exist—"

Jenna frowned. "The nursery did exist, until two weeks ago," she interrupted.

Grady decided to let that one pass. "Then you went into town and registered Andy's birth under a false name."

"And had him checked out by the town doctor. Don't forget that." She wagged a finger at him, adding, "He was in good health."

"What about you?"

Jenna's expression suddenly became closed and unreadable. "I'm fine," she said.

Sure you are, Grady thought. He cleared his throat. "You said you run across a lot of babies in your line of work?"

Jenna stiffened, knowing exactly where this line of questioning was leading. "I did not kidnap Andy from anyone else, if that's what you're implying," she said tightly.

In his years as a police officer, Grady had seen stranger things happen. "What about your ex-husband? Is there any chance this baby is his, or that he claimed the child he felt was his?''

Jenna glared at him as twin spots of pink appeared in her fair cheeks. ''Unlike you, I do not make a habit of sleeping with my ex.''

Deciding this conversation needed to be lightened up, pronto, before Jenna got hysterical on him, Grady feigned a blow to the chin. ''Ouch.''

''You deserved it,'' Jenna muttered under her breath. She lowered her glance.

Maybe, maybe not, Grady thought.

Jenna sighed. She circled the desk, faced him beseechingly. ''Look, I can see you don't believe me,'' she began softly.

Grady had never been seduced into looking the other way when it came to anything illegal, and he wasn't about to start now. ''Going on proof alone, there's not much reason I should,'' he said.

''Nanny Beth could tell you otherwise.''

''If you knew where she was,'' Grady said, recalling that much from their previous conversation.

''She'll show up eventually,'' Jenna said confidently.

Jenna might not think her nanny was a suspect, but Grady had been trained to think more objectively. ''Tell me more about Nanny Beth. How long have you known her?''

''As long as I can remember.'' Jenna pulled up a chair and sank into it. ''She not only raised me from infancy when my mother died, but she stayed with me during my pregnancy and helped deliver Andy. I've always thought of her like a mother, and I daresay she thinks of me as her daughter.''

Grady quirked a brow. ''All the more reason she might want Andy to have a father and you a husband,'' he said thoughtfully.

Jenna leaned forward and unlaced her ankle boots. ''Nanny Beth would never traumatize me like that,'' she said firmly. She curled her sock-clad toes several times and then stretched her long legs out in front of her.

Grady studied Jenna and tried to ignore the unconscious sexiness of her spread legs. "Are you sure?"

Jenna buried her face in her hand and barely stifled a yawn. "Yes."

"Was she here that day the baby disappeared?"

Jenna shook her head. Slouching a little lower in her chair, she stretched her arms wide on either side of her. "I told you before. She went into town to do some shopping."

"Before or after the baby disappeared?"

"Before." Jenna released a long breath, then got slowly to her feet. She bent and picked up her boots, carried them over to the doorway and set them down neatly on the other side of the portal. "I don't like the direction this conversation is headed, Grady," Jenna warned. She spun around, her back to the jamb, and regarded him patiently.

Grady found himself wishing she didn't look so sexy in the jeans and long, thigh-skimming sweater. "Too bad."

She kept her eyes on his and placed her hands behind her. "I told you before. I'll tell you again. Nanny Beth is not a suspect."

Grady decided it was high time he started taking notes. He whipped his notepad out of the inside of his tweed sports coat and turned to a fresh page. He wrote *NB* at the top of it. "And you say you haven't seen her since?"

Jenna continued to watch him, her face expressionless. "No."

"Was she scheduled for any sort of vacation?"

"No," Jenna said, "but that doesn't mean she wasn't persuaded to take one by one of my well-meaning relatives."

"The kidnapper," Grady said.

"Yes. It could be that Nanny was talked into cooperating."

"What if she didn't cooperate?" Grady asked. "Would anyone in your family hurt her?" Jenna shook her head. "Fire her?" Jenna paused. "I still want to put out an APB, just to make sure Nanny is okay," Grady said.

Jenna bit her lip, for the first time looking worried. "Could you do it in an unofficial way?"

Grady knew he shouldn't agree to this. But the silent plea for help in Jenna's eyes soon had him acquiescing. "All right. I'll call in a few markers. But if we don't find Nanny by the end of the week, we're going the official route."

Jenna nodded. "In the meantime, I'll look, too. I'll call my father and some of Nanny's friends, but that will have to wait until tomorrow morning."

Grady studied Jenna. Nanny Beth was like a mother to Jenna. She had been there for the birth of Jenna's baby and had left on the day of the alleged kidnapping. And then had simply left, unannounced, coincidentally while Jenna's baby was still missing? Something was out of place here. Ten to one, Jenna knew what it was. "None of this strikes you as odd?" he probed quietly.

Again, Jenna averted her gaze.

"What aren't you telling me, Jenna?"

"Nothing."

And pigs fly, Grady thought, but figuring he'd pushed her hard enough for one day, he said nothing more. He'd check out this nanny himself.

"Look, I'm exhausted. As much as I'd like to talk to Dr. Koen tonight, we can't really go to see him until morning."

"I agree." Grady paused. "Just to make sure no other mishaps occur while we're out here, the baby stays with me tonight," he said.

To his surprise, Jenna didn't argue, merely looked deep into his eyes. "You promise me you won't walk off with him?" she asked anxiously.

"I promise," Grady said softly.

"LOOK, JUST LET ME do the talking," Jenna said the next morning as Grady parked in front of Dr. Koen's office in Hudson Falls.

"I'll let you start," Grady agreed. He circled around to her side of the car, opened the door for her and helped her and the baby out. "I'm not promising not to ask any questions." He was ticked off enough that they were still unable to track down Nanny Beth, despite numerous phone calls on both their parts.

Jenna regarded him with obvious irritation. Her glance gentled. "Just don't embarrass me, okay?"

Grady frowned and didn't promise anything. As far as he was concerned, Jenna's story was implausible, at best. She did have one thing going for her, and that was the way Andy responded to her. Like the two of them were perfectly in sync. But then, as Jenna had pointed out the previous day, Andy had never really met an adult he didn't seem to like. He was such a cheerful, easygoing infant, he would've adapted to anyone, and Jenna had been fussing over him all morning.

To Grady's relief, the clinic seemed to be clean and well-run. The doctor who had allegedly taken care of Jenna was a young guy, in his late twenties. Probably fresh out of med school, Grady thought.

"Dr. Koen, this is Grady Noland. A friend of mine. It's a long, complicated story and I won't bore you with the details, but he'd like to ask a few questions."

"Sure." Dr. Koen gestured for both of them to take a seat.

Grady opened the manila file he'd brought in with him and slid it across the desk. "Were you the doctor that signed this birth certificate?"

"I sure did. This little guy was in such a rush to be born that Laura and her nanny delivered Andy all by themselves, out at that farmhouse." Dr. Koen grinned at Andy, who was snuggled contentedly in Jenna's arms. "They did a great job, too."

Grady resisted the urge to take out his pad and scribble a few notes. He could do that later. "When did you see them?" he asked.

"I got there shortly after the birth. I suggested Laura and her baby might want to go to the hospital at least for a day or so to rest and recuperate, but Laura was happy where she was, so I saw to her, made sure that she got the aftercare she needed, checked out the baby, wrote out the birth certificate, and that was pretty much that. Andy was due for his shots two weeks ago, you know.''

"I know. I'm sorry," Jenna apologized. She smiled at Dr. Koen earnestly. "Things have been a little crazy. I'll take care of it."

"You can vouch that Laura here had a baby, though?" Grady asked.

Dr. Koen gave Grady an odd look, but answered anyway. "Oh, yes, there's no faking the aftermath of a birth." Dr. Koen paused. "Why do you ask?"

Grady shook his head. "There's been some confusion." Declining to reveal anything more, Grady stood, signaling the interview was over. He shook hands with Dr. Koen. "That's all the information I need for now." Grady paused to glance at Jenna, who was still studiously avoiding looking at either him or Dr. Koen. "But I may be back."

Dr. Koen cast Jenna a concerned look, then turned to Grady. "I'll be glad to be of any help I can," he said.

"Satisfied?" Jenna asked as they trooped out to the sidewalk.

Grady shook his head. "Not even a little bit." He wished to hell this mess could be cleared up so easily.

Jenna whirled on him. Her strawberry blond hair gleamed more red than gold in the morning sunlight. "Why not? He told you I had a baby."

"He also thinks you're Laura Johnson." Grady hustled Jenna and the baby toward the warmth of the car. "You've got a false name on the birth certificate. A nanny and a nursery full of baby furniture who've both disappeared. There are a lot of questions here, Jenna. A lot."

She swallowed and looked uneasy again as she got into the car, Andy still cradled in her arms. Grady circled to the driver's side. She watched him get in. "Where do you want to start?" she asked warily.

"With Nanny Beth, of course." Grady started the car and paused to let it warm up. "Do you think she could've taken the baby furniture out of your farmhouse?" Assuming, Grady added silently, there ever was any baby furniture there to begin with.

Jenna turned to him. "No, of course not."

"Then how and why did it disappear?"

Jenna bent her head and rummaged through the diaper bag for a bottle of formula a contented Andy didn't really need.

"Either you tell me or I'll find out myself," Grady threatened.

Jenna shot him an ominous look. "Must you play cops and robbers with my life?"

Grady told himself not to be distracted by the heightened color in her pretty face or the lively sparkle in her dark green eyes. "That all depends," he said silkily, watching as Jenna uncapped the bottle and tilted the nipple toward Andy's mouth. "Do you want to raise this child or not?"

She knew he meant it. She smiled at Andy, who was holding onto the bottle of formula with both hands while he nursed. "My father probably took the furniture."

Now they were getting somewhere, Grady thought with satisfaction. He worked to keep his expression impassive. "What makes you say that?"

Jenna studied the dashboard in front of her. "If you knew him, you wouldn't have to ask."

"Well, I don't know him," Grady grumbled, wishing Jenna hadn't worn that lavender perfume of hers.

Jenna glanced up to confront him. "I love him, okay? Get that straight first." Her chest rose as she drew in a deep breath. "But he's very overbearing and he hates scandal of any kind. At the first hint of any kind of scandal, he sweeps it under the rug."

Grady had known all along Jenna was holding something back. Now that they were edging toward it, his pulse began to race. "Did he know you were pregnant?"

"No."

"How'd you explain your weight gain?"

"I didn't. I didn't see him at all during that time."

Grady paused and began to feel uncertain again. "And he

accepted that?'' If Jenna's father was as protective as she seemed to indicate, the explanation didn't make sense.

Jenna shrugged. ''He knows I'm as busy running my foundation as he is running Sullivan Shoes. Besides, we talk on the phone frequently, and fax each other almost daily, so it's not as if we're not in touch.''

Grady wasn't one to dispute the value of a letter, phone call or fax. But there was something about being there in person, too. ''What about Christmas?''

Jenna swallowed and began to look anxious again. ''I told him I had to be in Sweden, on foundation business.''

That made sense, if she hadn't wanted anyone to know about her pregnancy, Grady thought. He studied her relentlessly, in no hurry to leave now that they were sitting in the warm car. ''When were you planning to tell him about the 'adoption'?''

''As soon as I was strong enough and had handled all the legal details,'' Jenna said briskly.

''Which would have been when?''

''About the time Andy was kidnapped, actually. I was just getting ready, mentally and emotionally, to tell him then. You know, rehearsing what I was going to say to him and all that.''

''Not much of a liar?''

''Apparently not.''

Silence fell between them. Grady wished she didn't look so damn vulnerable, as if he was the villain here, torturing her with his endless questions. Telling himself sternly to get back to business, to not let Jenna's sensitive nature affect him, Grady said, ''Did you go to him when you realized the baby was missing?''

For a moment, Jenna was very still. ''Yes,'' she said quietly.

''And?''

Jenna swallowed and lifted her head to meet his gaze. Twin spots of color appeared in her cheeks. ''He was confused, to say the least.''

"Then what happened?"

Jenna settled back in her seat and looked at the roof of the car. "You know, I really don't want to get into this."

Grady realized he was clenching his jaw. He sat back and made a concerted effort not to be so tense. "Why not?"

"Because my relationship with my family is none of your business, that's why. Besides, it'll all be cleared up in a few days, when the blood tests come in. Then you'll know Andy's my child and yours, and that'll be the end of it."

"Not quite," Grady said.

"What do you mean?"

"If what you've told me is true, Jenna, and I'll tell you again your story has more holes in it than a sieve, then our baby was kidnapped."

Jenna rolled her eyes in exasperation. This was not exactly news to her. "Great going, Sherlock. So what? He's safe now."

"But for how long?" Grady questioned impatiently. "Until we know for sure who took him and why, Andy won't be safe, Jenna, and neither will you."

For the first time in two days, she looked frightened. Her face paled. "What are you saying?"

"That I plan to continue this investigation until I get to the bottom of this mess." He didn't think Andy had been taken for ransom, but he couldn't be sure of it. And until he was...

Jenna started to look panicked, which made Grady suspicious again. What else hadn't she told him? She clutched his arm. "Grady, you can't—"

"I not only can, I will," he corrected with a ruthless, determined smile. He was going to discover the truth with or without Jenna's help. "And I'm going to start by talking to your father."

Chapter Four

"I don't understand why you have to talk to my father," Jenna said irritably as they entered her father's Albany, New York, home.

Grady stepped into the imposing front hall, Andy cradled in his strong arms. Jenna watched as Grady surveyed the luxurious interior of the home she had grown up in, taking in the gray-and-white marble floor beneath them, the sweeping staircase in front of them and the chandelier overhead. With only a passing glance at the formal parlor to their right, with its high ceilings, expensive Oriental rugs and glossy antiques, he handed her the baby and shrugged out of his trench coat. "For one thing, your father can verify your story about the baby being kidnapped on Valentine's Day."

"It wasn't a story," Jenna told Grady hotly as she handed him the baby and shrugged out of her own coat. "It was the truth!" Grady shifted the sleeping baby in his arms a little higher and gave her a skeptical glance.

"Why can't you just take my word?" Jenna whispered as she braced herself for the inevitably difficult confrontation with her father. He wasn't an unkind man. But he wasn't the easiest man to confide in, either. Even though she knew Lamar Sullivan loved her dearly.

Grady followed Jenna down the hall, past a wall of family paintings, to her father's study at the rear of the house. "I learned a long time ago to rely only on hard, cold facts.'' His voice was close, hushed. His warm breath brushed her ear.

Jenna swallowed, slowing her pace as they neared her father's study. She tilted her head to better study Grady's face. ''In your police work, yes—''

He looked at her, his slate-blue eyes darkening decisively. ''In my personal life, too,'' he said firmly.

Jenna drew in a jagged breath, aware her pulse had picked up marginally. ''What does your heart tell you?'' she asked.

''What my heart does or doesn't tell me is completely irrelevant,'' Grady said.

He looked so right, so natural, standing there with his baby in his arms. For a second, Jenna let herself fantasize about how happy an occasion it might have been, under other circumstances, if she and Grady had brought their baby home together to introduce him to the family.

Jenna released a wavering breath and knew a second's deep regret. If only she had never cooked up this ruse to begin with. If only she had been brave enough to be honest with everyone from the first, then she wouldn't be in this tangled mess that was bound, after their joint interview with her father, to become even more complicated and potentially damaging than it already was. Unless she could just prevail on Grady's goodness and get him to be on her side before they entered the study. She tilted her head a little farther and drew another, deeper breath. ''Why can't you follow your heart, Grady?'' she implored softly. *Please,* she thought, *just this once, put all the facts aside and just help me.*

He lifted his free hand to cup her face. ''Because it's when I let my emotions get in the way of my thinking that I get into trouble, that's why.''

His mesmerizing touch sent a blazing warmth into her skin. Determined not to be sensually distracted, Jenna stepped back and folded her arms in front of her. Her plan to save herself from further humiliation thwarted, her temper rose. ''Well, I think that's ridiculous,'' she snapped.

Grady's gaze took on a lecturing quality. He stepped back,

too. "Your emotions can only mess you up in a situation like this, Jenna," he warned flatly.

"I disagree," Jenna said. "Furthermore, I think you'd be a lot happier if you'd just let your heart guide you here."

Half his mouth curved up in a disbelieving smile. "And what do you think my heart is telling me?" he asked.

Jenna drew herself up straighter, so that the top of her head almost reached his chin. "It should be telling you to trust and believe in me, facts or no facts."

Grady sighed. "I can't do that."

She had been afraid of that. Jenna released a wavering sigh and shook her head in silent regret. "Then I can't be with you," she said.

"I don't recall asking you to be with me again," he pointed out dryly. But the sexual glimmer in his eyes said it was only a matter of time before he did.

"You'll get around to it, once you find out Andy really is your son," she predicted in a depressed tone.

He smiled at her again, looking just as intrigued, just as filled with a distinctly male satisfaction, as he had the night of Alec Roman's party. The night when this all began. "You think so?"

Her emotions in turmoil, she stared at him in silence. She wanted him to desire her again, just as she desired him. But she didn't want her life turning into a soap opera. She didn't want to risk losing her child.

Aware he was waiting for an answer from her, she finally nodded. "I know your type, Grady Noland."

"Do you, now."

"Yes, and unfortunately for me, you're noble to the core."

"Why is my being noble unfortunate for you?" he interrupted.

"Because," Jenna said, and felt her voice catch just a little. She swallowed hard, fighting back the tears she felt gathering in her throat and glimmering in her eyes. "You'd die before you let the chance pass to do the right thing." Reaching for her baby, she gently insinuated her hands between his blanket-wrapped form and Grady's strong arm. Grady's body was taut with self-imposed control. "The trouble is, the right thing in this case is not destined to bring us anything but more heartbreak."

Grady released a long breath and jammed his hands on his waist. The action pushed back the edges of his gray Harris tweed sport coat, revealing the flatness of his abdomen beneath the starched light blue crispness of his oxford cloth shirt and the faded, soft, torso-hugging Levi's jeans. "You've got my life all planned out for me, don't you?" he accused cynically.

"I only wish," Jenna muttered. Finding his slate-blue glance a bit too probing, too knowing, for comfort, she turned away from him uneasily. She had an idea what he was thinking. It was as clear as the reluctant, wary expression on his face. The more he thought about her claims, the more ludicrous they sounded. The capper, of course, had been storming the nursery at the farm, only to find it empty. He had started to believe her up to then, at least to the point where he would humor her and investigate her claims. But now…now at least part of him thought she was a nut. Again.

In the study, footsteps sounded on the parquet floor. Her father came out into the hall. Lamar Sullivan's gaze went from Jenna and the sleeping baby in her arms to Grady, then back again. "Jenna." Briefly, he looked stunned.

Jenna knew exactly what he was thinking, too. She hoped she could count on her father's love of personal privacy to keep him from revealing too much to Grady about what had been going on in their family in the past few weeks.

Lamar cast a wary look at Grady. Frowning, he turned to Jenna. "What are you doing here? I thought you were still at Pinehaven—"

Damn, Jenna thought, Pinehaven was the one place she had not wanted mentioned in Grady's presence. She feigned nonchalance. "I decided to leave," she announced as if it was no big deal, when in fact it had been a very big deal.

Her father blinked. "They allowed that?" Lamar asked with a frown.

"Why should Jenna need permission to leave Pinehaven?" Grady interjected, obviously confused.

"Why else? I'm a very popular person," Jenna temporized quickly in a jovial voice, hoping she didn't look as utterly and completely panicked as she felt. *If Grady found out about Pinehaven, it really was going to be all over.* "It's not important. Dad, we can talk about Pinehaven later. I'm here to talk about Andy—"

"The baby," Lamar said slowly. Reaching behind him, he sank down onto the glossy antique parson's bench located just outside his study door.

"Yes, this is Andy, Dad. *You know, the baby I told you about when I was here a couple of weeks ago.*"

To Jenna's distress, Lamar paled even more. "Where did you get that baby, Jenna?"

Grady turned to Jenna suspiciously, his police antennae on full alert. "Yes, Jenna," Grady echoed her father pleasantly, his slate-blue eyes anything but innocent, "where did you get that baby?"

Jenna turned to Grady in irritation. He knew full well where she had gotten Andy. She gave Grady a quelling look, then walked over to her father. "It's a long story, Dad," Jenna said gently. She put her hand on Lamar's shoulder and looked into his eyes. "We can talk about it later." Her father nodded, picking up on her hint that not everything was supposed to be discussed in front of Grady. "In the meantime," Jenna continued smoothly, "I want to introduce you to someone. Grady Noland, Grady, my dad."

Recovering as quickly as she had hoped he would, Lamar got to his feet and shook hands firmly with Grady. "Grady, nice to meet you," Lamar said in the overly polite tone he used with strangers.

"Why don't we all go in your study," Jenna suggested.

"Certainly," Lamar said.

Once they were all cozily ensconced in the paneled room,

Lamar behind his desk, Grady, Jenna and Andy in the twin leather wing chairs in front of it, Jenna continued much more confidently than she felt. "Grady wants you to verify something, Dad."

"What?" Lamar Sullivan said suspiciously.

Jenna pressed her lips together briefly and prayed for strength. She lifted her chin. "That two weeks ago, on the afternoon of Valentine's Day, I came to see you here at the house and told you I'd had a baby and that the baby had been kidnapped."

Lamar frowned at Jenna the same way he had when she'd gotten after-school detention for being late to class. His hands flat on the desk, he surprised her by turning to Grady. "You're going to have to excuse Jenna," he said kindly, following his reluctantly-voiced statement with a man-to-man glance. "She's not well. In fact, she was hospitalized recently for accumulated stress and emotional exhaustion." His dark green eyes gentled with sympathetic understanding. "Apparently, her divorce from Baxter was harder on her than all of us knew."

"Dad!" Jenna said.

"Well, it's true, honey," Lamar said gently. He got up from behind his desk and came around to stand beside her chair.

Afraid she would wake the still slumbering baby because she was so upset, Jenna got up and handed Andy over to Grady. "Look, we don't have to get into that right now," Jenna said sharply.

"Speak for yourself, Jenna. This is getting very interesting," Grady quipped.

Ignoring Grady studiously, Jenna turned to her father. She crossed her arms. Suddenly, everything was so much clearer. She didn't know why she hadn't seen it right away. It all made perfect sense. "You removed the nursery furniture from the farmhouse, didn't you, Dad?" *Because you thought I was crazy, too!*

"I don't know what you're talking about," Lamar said stiffly.

"Oh, no? Then what about Nanny Beth? I suppose you're going to say you don't know anything about *her* disappearance, either!" Jenna shot back hotly.

"Actually, I *did* have a hand in that," Lamar admitted quite freely. "I gave her a five-thousand-dollar bonus and sent her off on a much-needed month-long vacation. I could tell when I talked to her on the phone February fifteenth that she'd had her hands full, caring for you."

Jenna fought to keep control of her emotions. Only the fact that she knew she was responsible for at least part of what had conspired, and the fact that Grady was taking in everything, kept her from completely blowing up. "What did she say when you gave her the news?" Jenna asked, as serenely as possible.

Lamar shrugged and straightened his silk Perry Ellis tie. "She was worried about your being able to cope alone, of course. I told her we knew about the baby situation and that everything was under control...the family was taking care of you."

Which explained, Jenna thought, why Nanny Beth would have left her. She knew Jenna had been planning to tell her father about Andy the following day. She would have assumed Lamar Sullivan had welcomed both baby and daughter into his home. Nanny Beth had left town never knowing Andy had been kidnapped, or that anything at all was amiss. "Where did she go?"

"I don't know. She said something about maybe taking a cruise."

"That's all you know?" Jenna asked, exasperated.

"Sorry," Lamar said.

"At least it's a start," Grady said. He looked at Jenna. "I'll call the station and have them start checking the cruise lines right away. With any luck, we'll find Nanny in a few days."

Jenna nodded and turned back to her father. Still trying to

contain the damage and limit how much Grady was able to discover, Jenna gave her father a weary look laced with both gentleness and affection. "Look, Dad, I know things are a mess between us. A lot of it is my fault. I should have confided my troubles in you earlier, but I didn't. I can't go back and fix that now. Nevertheless, I'm asking you to trust me. There *really* was a baby, and Andy is that baby."

Lamar looked at the darling baby sleeping so peacefully in Grady's arms. "Is the baby Baxter's?" Lamar asked.

Jenna flushed to her roots. "Dad, please."

"I think that I have a right to know, since any child of yours is my grandchild," Lamar countered.

"Well, I'm not ready to tell you. When I am, I will."

"I see," Lamar said slowly, his expression thoughtful and intent. "What about Mr. Noland? Does he know who the father is?"

Jenna doubted her father was ready to hear about her fling with Grady, so she said simply, "Grady is a friend of mine, and a policeman. He has agreed to help me discover who took Andy from the farmhouse. He's as eager to get to the bottom of this situation as I am."

Again, Lamar frowned. He sat on the edge of his desk. "You called in the police?"

"Only in an unofficial capacity," Jenna soothed. Knowing that it was her family's loathing of any scandal that had precipitated this mess she was in now, Jenna looked her father directly in the eye. "There will be no public scandal if I can help it," she promised.

Lamar breathed an audible sigh of relief, then looked at Grady sternly. "Can you verify that this infant is my daughter's child?"

Grady shook his head, looking completely natural, sitting in the wing chair, the eight-week-old baby cradled in his powerful arms. "Not yet," he told Lamar, meeting the eyes of the man who under different conditions might have been his father-in-law. "Jenna took a DNA test, at her own request, but we won't have the results back for a few days."

"I see." Lamar's expression grew even more worried, heightening Jenna's dismay. "Can you verify for me this baby was actually kidnapped, then?"

"No, sir," Grady said, his frankness with her father unabating. "I can't."

Fierce emotion welled up within Jenna. She clasped her hands in front of her tightly, and worked to keep her voice low. "Dammit, Grady, you know he was." *You have to know that in your heart!*

But Grady only shook his head in calm disagreement, looking every bit the hardened city cop at that moment. "No, I don't," he said, as their eyes held and clashed. Jenna's heart pounded with equal parts fatigue and nerves. Maybe she should have told Grady about her brief hospitalization before coming here, and made him understand what a ridiculous mix-up it had all been.

Grady looked past Lamar to the family photos lining his desk. "No other grandchildren?" Grady asked, zeroing in immediately on the lack of infants or children in family portraits.

"No." Lamar frowned, making no effort to hide his disappointment in that to either Grady or Jenna. "My son, Kip, and his wife, Leslie, can't have any. Of course, Jenna here wanted children. But she was divorced, as you probably know, early last year, so—"

"Enough talk about my personal life, Dad," Jenna interrupted.

"I suppose you're right," Lamar said. "By the way, Jenna, your station wagon is still here."

Jenna nodded. "I'll drive my car back to the farmhouse when I leave today," Jenna said. "Grady and Andy can follow in his car."

An uncomfortable silence strung out between them, reminding Jenna of all that had been left unsaid. Grady still had a lot of questions.

Her father looked at Grady. "Is my daughter in any legal

trouble here?'' Lamar asked with a contemplative frown.
"Does she need a lawyer?''

"As far as I know, there's nothing criminal going on that
Jenna could be charged with,'' Grady said. Looking as restless as Jenna felt, he got up from the chair, Andy still in his
arms, and began to pace the length of floor next to the bookcases.

Jenna turned away from Grady's tall, imposing form and
back to her father. She knew Lamar loved her, even if he
hadn't ever known quite what to do with her. "You swear to
me you had nothing to do with that nursery furniture disappearing from the farmhouse?''

"I swear it,'' Lamar said softly, putting his hand over his
heart. Without skipping a beat, he said, "You swear to me
you're well enough to be out of the hospital?''

Their glances met and held. "Yes, Dad,'' Jenna said
gently, "I am.''

"Sir, if you wouldn't mind watching the baby for a few
minutes,'' Grady said, interrupting them. His expression was
intense enough to give Jenna pause. "I'd like to talk to Jenna
alone.''

Chapter Five

"I hope you're satisfied," Jenna grumbled cantankerously as she led the way to her old bedroom upstairs.

"Not yet," Grady drawled, "but I hope to be soon."

She raised a red-gold brow as he shut the door behind him. "You have completely shocked my father," Jenna complained.

"He's not near as shocked as he's going to be when he finds out you and I may have had a child together," Grady pointed out reasonably.

"We *did* have a child together, Grady."

He let that one pass and touched the quilted top of the frilly pink-and-white gingham bedspread. "This where you slept as a kid?" The canopy bed suited her somehow, he thought. In fact, the only thing he didn't like about imagining her in it was that it was a single.

"Yes. Not that it matters."

"You're right," Grady said, swiftly getting himself back on track. "We do have more pressing things to discuss, like precisely when you were hospitalized."

Jenna's spine stiffened. "I don't see why that matters," she retorted in a voice laced with pride.

Grady had expected a lack of cooperation on her part. "Fine," he said calmly, turning toward the door. "I'll just go down and ask your father to finish filling me in."

Jenna sprinted forward, closing the distance between them

in three quick steps. She grabbed his arm. "All right, I'll tell you the whole story, but you have to promise me that you'll keep an open mind and not jump to any conclusions."

Grady tried not to let her touch, so soft and womanly, distract him. "Don't I always?" he said, holding himself very still.

Jenna dropped her arm. "Not so far, no."

He frowned. "Start talking, Jenna. I want to hear the details."

"I was admitted to the Pinehaven hospital around midnight on Valentine's Day."

"Is that here in Albany?"

"No, it's out in the country."

"Never heard of it," Grady said flatly.

"You're not supposed to have."

"Why not?"

Jenna shrugged again, her slender shoulders moving with enticing femininity beneath the jade cowl-necked sweater she wore over the long, flowing jade wool skirt. "It's extremely private, expensive."

Grady paused, Lamar's words ringing in his ears. *She's not well. In fact, she was hospitalized recently for accumulated stress and emotional exhaustion. Apparently, her divorce from Baxter was harder on her than all of us knew.* "And you agreed to this?" he asked slowly.

"Not exactly."

His muscles taut with the depth of his unease, Grady paced closer. He curved a hand against the side of her face, forcing her to look at him. "What does not exactly mean, Jenna?"

With a jerky motion, Jenna drew away from the warmth of his touch. Crossing her arms, she offered him her back. "It means I wasn't enthusiastic about the prospect," she replied through set teeth.

"But you agreed to be admitted anyway, knowing your son had just been kidnapped." Or was it *because* Andy had been kidnapped that Jenna had gone over the edge? Grady wondered. To accept that premise as gospel, he would have to take a lot on faith, maybe more than he was prepared to. And yet, something in him railed against the image of Jenna falling apart emotionally. Despite the feminine vulnerability in her nature, she seemed stronger than that. More determined, somehow.

Jenna whirled to face him, her jade wool skirt swirling around her in a drift of lavender-scented perfume. "Of course I didn't *agree* to be hospitalized!" she said angrily.

Grady blinked, a little taken aback by the depth of her emotion over this. "You just said—"

"You're not going to rest until you know the whole truth, are you?" Jenna demanded angrily.

"Probably not," he drawled. Feeling he might as well be comfortable, Grady sat down on the edge of her bed.

Jenna glared at him and continued to pace the length of the room. She waved her arms as she spoke. "When I couldn't find Andy, I was pretty upset, but I held it together until I got here. You see, initially I was sure my father was behind the kidnapping—"

"Why?" Grady interrupted with a frown. Having just met Lamar and seen how lovingly and protectively he treated his only daughter, Grady would not have come to the same conclusion.

"Because that's the way my father operates when he thinks I need protecting. He just charges in and does what he thinks is best for me. That's why I didn't tell him about the pregnancy. I was afraid he'd try to hunt down the baby's father. For my own good, of course." Jenna sighed.

"Is that the only reason you thought your dad had taken the baby?" Grady asked calmly.

"No. I knew my father had been worried about me living alone at the farm." Her eyes met Grady's. "My father had been asking Nanny Beth a lot of questions every time he called. I was afraid that Nanny Beth might have let something slip inadvertently, that my father might have discovered I'd had a baby somehow, reacted emotionally, and decided to do what the note had said and find Andy's father. I mean, it was such an old-fashioned, *male* thing to do, find the guy responsible for impregnating your daughter and make him pay up.''

Grady admitted to himself that had it been his daughter he might have reacted the same way. ''So when you drove into Albany that day and accused your father of kidnapping your baby, it was because you thought Nanny Beth had unknowingly clued your father in to what was going on with you,'' Grady said. ''And that Lamar had acted the outraged father and taken it from there.''

''Right,'' Jenna nodded. ''Only I realized as soon as I started talking to my father that he knew absolutely nothing. Nanny Beth, bless her heart, hadn't clued my father in on a thing. And that, of course, meant my dad didn't have Andy, either...because if he'd had the baby, he would have admitted that to me and then given me a stern lecture on everything he thought I'd done wrong. But he didn't. Which in turn could've only meant one thing, that he didn't have Andy, either. And so I just totally freaked out.''

Grady frowned. ''Who did you think had the baby at that point?''

''I didn't know. That's why I wanted to call the police.''

Grady felt himself being sucked in by her story, despite his initial cynical reaction to her claims. He struggled to remain as objective as he would in any police investigation. ''And did you call the police that night?''

''No.''

''Why not?''

Jenna swept her strawberry blond hair off her face. She looked aggrieved, remembering. ''Because my father wanted to call Baxter first.''

Grady paused, recalling Lamar's comment about Andy possibly being Jenna and Baxter's baby. Jenna had denied it vigorously. Grady still felt almost sick with jealousy at the thought. Struggling to put his emotions aside, he asked with a lazy indifference he couldn't begin to feel, ''What does your ex-husband have to do with any of this, Jenna?'' Was Jenna still in love with this Baxter?

"My father knows I'm not the type to have affairs, so he assumed my ex-husband was the father of any child I had. It only made sense that Baxter might have taken the baby, if he had somehow found out about my having a baby in secret."

"But you said Andy is our baby," Grady pointed out.

"Right," Jenna said. "Andy is our baby, Grady. But no one else knew that at that point, and I was so panicked I was willing to concede anything might have happened."

"Was there any other reason you suspected Baxter of the kidnapping?"

Jenna nodded. "One of the problems in my marriage was that Baxter, like my father, always felt that he knew what was best for me. And Baxter had been nosing around in my personal life, pursuing me... You see, Baxter never wanted the divorce. So it made sense that if Baxter had found out about the baby, Baxter would have viewed the baby as an impediment to our getting back together and maybe done something about it."

"What happened when Baxter arrived?"

Jenna's lips thinned to a soft rosy line. "Baxter denied kidnapping Andy, or even knowing I'd had a baby."

Grady swallowed, hating to ask the next question, but knowing he had to. "Was there any chance it was Baxter's baby, or that he might have thought Andy was his child?"

"No."

"So why does your father still think it might have been Baxter's child?" Grady pressed.

Jenna was silent.

"Why does he think that, Jenna?" Grady repeated.

Jenna sighed. "Probably because of what else Baxter said to me that night," she said diffidently.

"Which was?"

"That we never should have gotten divorced. 'Clearly,' Baxter said, 'I wasn't meant to manage on my own and this just proved it.'" Just recalling the scene made her livid, Grady noted with satisfaction.

"What did you say to that?" Grady asked, resisting the urge to take Jenna in his arms and offer comfort.

"I told Baxter he was an arrogant jerk and I didn't want him trying to manage my life, from near or far."

Good for you, Grady thought fiercely. "How'd Baxter take that?"

Jenna released a shaky sigh. "He gave me a pitying look. My father looked like he wanted to sink through the floor—he hates emotional scenes, and this one was getting very bitter and recriminating."

"What happened next?" Grady said impatiently. Feeling a little edgy himself, he folded his arms.

Abruptly, she pushed away from the bed and began to pace again, her hands knotted into fists at her sides. "My father insisted I drink a little bourbon to calm down."

"And?" Grady stood and moved closer.

Jenna paused before the window overlooking the formal gardens, which were cloaked in a thin layer of dwindling winter snow. "I admit I felt like I needed a drink by that point, so I took the drink he gave me and went off to try to reach you again. Your buddies at the station said you were out working a case."

Grady remembered what he had been doing on Valentine's Day very well. "I was."

Jenna turned to face him. Her eyes leveled on his, and Grady suddenly found a great deal of feminine resentment heaped upon him. "Yeah, well, they made it sound as if you weren't," Jenna said tightly. "And that only upset me all the more."

"And then what happened?"

"It hit me...I mean, it *really* hit me that Andy was gone and I had no idea who had him, or even if he had actually been taken to you. So I started to cry and I couldn't stop." Jenna teared up, recalling. Her voice shook as she continued. "My father found me and became even more distressed because I was so completely distraught. Then Baxter left us alone, saying he would make a few phone calls to see what he could discover on his own about the baby. When Baxter returned, he said he had found some people who could help us figure out what was going on, and he wanted me and my father to go see them.'' Jenna took a deep breath and composed herself again. ''*I* thought he meant detectives or something—Baxter meets all sorts of people, from his practice— and even though I suspected Baxter was just doing this to kiss up to me and my father and prove to me that I still needed him in my life, I said okay.''

''Did you know what Pinehaven was?'' Grady asked quietly.

''No.'' Jenna shook her head regretfully. ''I'd never heard of Pinehaven. I could tell it was a hospital when we drove up.'' Remembering, Jenna began to tremble. ''But I thought...well, I thought maybe Andy was there, that there had been an accident and Baxter knew about it because he was a doctor and had been calling the hospitals, to see what he could find out. So I went into the emergency room with them. We identified ourselves at the desk. And then a nurse took me to a room.''

Grady was silent, absorbing the details of her story. If everything she was saying thus far was correct, then she had been through a real trauma. He took her hand in his and drew her to the canopied bed. He sat and guided her wordlessly to sit beside him. ''When did you realize you were being checked in?''

''When they gave me a hospital gown to put on.'' Jenna's lips tightened mutinously. ''I tried to leave, but they wouldn't let me. And as you can imagine, the more I insisted I wasn't crazy, the more they believed that I was.''

''So your father just left you there even though you insisted you were fine?'' Grady asked disbelievingly.

''He thought he was doing the right thing.''

''I can't imagine why he would think that,'' Grady disagreed, ''if you were even half as lucid as you are right now.''

Jenna pushed away from the bed. Unable to sit still, she paced back and forth. ''You have to put yourself in his shoes to understand. All Dad knew was that I had been acting strangely for months. Hiding out at the family farm, refusing to see anyone or even come home to spend Christmas with the rest of the family. Devoting myself entirely to my work, calling my childhood nanny out of retirement to act as my housekeeper. To make matters worse, I hadn't told him of either my pregnancy or Andy's birth. So when I finally showed up at his home on Valentine's Day and accused him of kidnapping a baby he hadn't even known I'd had, my father was *very* worried."

Put that way, Grady thought, it made sense that Lamar had acted as he had. "Worried enough to call Baxter," Grady surmised.

"Right. Dad trusted Baxter's medical expertise because Baxter is an excellent physician. And he trusted him with the confidentiality of the situation because Baxter was family, or had been."

Grady was quiet for a minute, thinking. It was true that hell had no fury like a woman—or man, in this case—scorned. "Do you think this could have been some sort of twisted plot for revenge on Baxter's part, a way of getting back at you or getting you under his control?" Grady asked quietly. Was this Baxter's way of seeking revenge on an ex-wife who no longer loved him?

"I don't know," Jenna said slowly. "Generally, Baxter is very straightforward in his attempts to control my life, but that approach wasn't working anymore."

"So you still consider Baxter a suspect in this, in your own mind?"

"Yes, I guess I do," Jenna said slowly. Her eyes were troubled as she looked at him. "But I also know if he did it, he didn't act alone. He was with me and my father at the very time Andy was left on Alec's doorstep."

"Any idea who might have been his accomplice?"

Jenna gestured helplessly. "The only other person who seems to have it in for me, at least openly, is your ex-wife."

"You think Clarissa and Baxter are in cahoots?"

Jenna was silent. "As far as I know, Clarissa and Baxter don't even know one another. But...I can't figure any other reason Clarissa would claim Andy was her baby, Grady, unless it's to keep us apart and win you back. And Baxter wants the same thing."

"But would Baxter really want to take your baby from you?" Grady asked.

"I'm not so sure that was the point of this, so much as to show me what a louse you are."

Grady showed his affront.

"Well, look at it from the kidnapper's point of view," Jenna continued. "For all he or she knows, you abandoned me, but foolish me, I was still pining away after you."

"Were you pining away after me?" Grady grinned.

Jenna flushed. Recovering, she shot him an arch look. "You'll never know."

Grady grinned again. Maybe there was hope for him and Jenna, after all. "I think we need to talk to Baxter," he said. "Do you know how to reach your ex-husband?"

Jenna nodded and gave Grady the number. Grady spoke to Baxter's secretary for several minutes. Finally, he hung up the phone. He felt frustrated, but he also knew they were making progress in the investigation. "Baxter's in surgery. He's got two operations scheduled, back-to-back. I've left word with his secretary that I want to see him first thing tomorrow morning to discuss you."

Jenna winced at Grady's choice of words. "He's probably not going to like that."

"Tough. I don't like my baby being kidnapped."

Neither had Jenna. The stormy look was back in her eyes. "I'd like to be there, too."

"Fine with me." Grady paused and reviewed his notes. "Okay, we've established a motive for Baxter kidnapping Andy, but we haven't established how he got your father to cooperate. How did Baxter convince your father that you needed to be hospitalized?"

"Easy. He just acted like the doctor he is and made a

medical assessment of my behavior when my father requested his professional opinion.''

Grady scowled. ''Was this in front of you?''

''Heavens, no. If he'd done it in front of me, he never would have gotten away with it. It happened while I was off calling you at the station, Grady. While I was trying my hardest to get in touch with you, Baxter was telling my father that he thought one of two things had happened. I had either gone over the edge because of the divorce and my thwarted desire to have a child and had been suffering from a hysterical pregnancy—''

''An illness where a woman wants a baby so badly she imagines she's pregnant,'' Grady summarized.

''Right. Only in my case Baxter thought I'd taken it one step further than the average person and also imagined the birth and the kidnapping.''

Grady had seen cases like that before, where women had wanted a baby so badly they stole someone else's...and then, through some mental aberration, came to believe it really was their own.

Jenna continued. ''Or, Baxter theorized, it was possible I was just suffering a delayed reaction to the divorce and was simply emotionally exhausted and a little confused. All I needed was a few weeks of utter luxury and pampering, and someone to talk with me about my problems, and then I'd be back to my old self.''

''And Lamar bought it,'' Grady guessed.

''As did the psychiatrist at Pinehaven Baxter talked to,'' Jenna affirmed furiously.

''How long were you in the hospital?'' he asked casually.

Jenna's slender shoulders stiffened. ''Why does that matter?'' she asked as she messed with some of the antique silver picture frames on her dresser.

''It matters,'' Grady said, sensing she was evading again. ''So answer the question.''

She glared at him, resenting the third degree. ''Two weeks,'' she said flatly.

Grady lifted a brow. One day he could understand, if she had been misdiagnosed, maybe even two—but two weeks! "Why didn't you get in touch with me and let me know?" he asked calmly.

"I tried to call you at the station the day after I was admitted."

Grady thought back rapidly and was immediately filled with regret. "I wasn't at the station on the fifteenth."

"I know," Jenna said. "I talked to your partner. He said you weren't coming in that day, that you'd called in and said something about a new baby in the family,…and that you were taking time off to get acquainted with the little tyke."

"That was my sister's baby, not mine," Grady said, incensed.

"Yes, but I didn't know that," Jenna said, clasping her hands to her chest. "I had no idea until yesterday that Andy had ever been delivered to the wrong man at the wrong address. I thought the new baby you had told your partner about was Andy, that somehow someone had done what I never would've thought possible and gotten Andy to you. I asked your partner how you had sounded when you called in, and he said, 'Damn happy, but then Grady's always liked little kids.' He asked me if I wanted to leave a message if you called in again, and I said yes, and left my name and number at Pinehaven."

Grady regarded Jenna as she moved with angelic grace around the cozy bedroom. He wasn't sure whether it was a good sign or not, but this was all beginning to seem very plausible again. He could feel his guard letting down. "Did you explain to my partner that you were in a hospital?"

"I figured it was enough to leave the hospital number and try telling you one-on-one what was going on in my life, and with our baby. Only you never called back, Grady," Jenna said in a voice that was soft with accusation. She turned hurt eyes to him. "So I tried again and again. Each time you were out. I asked if you were still busy with the new baby, and your partner said, 'That and some family thing.' Your partner was also under the impression you had your hands full."

"I did," Grady confided ruefully. "My sister and her husband own a small ski lodge in Sun Valley. They've also got two other kids, both under six. She and her husband were pretty overwhelmed with everything. I went out to lend a hand at the front desk, help watch the kids, help take care of my new niece and get some skiing in. It was kind of a vacation and family reunion all in one."

"Sounds fun."

"It was." Only Grady didn't think he would have had any fun at all had he known what was happening to Jenna at the same time. Grady paused. "Did you leave another message for me?"

"Yes, the same one, several times. Again, my calls weren't returned. I figured you weren't calling me back as payback— because I hadn't told you about the baby. Finally, after about ten messages in three days, your partner explained to me that it was pointless to leave any more messages because you weren't calling in for them. If you had wanted me to know where you were, he said, you would've told me where you were going to be vacationing yourself. So if I wanted to talk to you, I was going to have to wait until you got back in town March first. So I comforted myself with the fact that you apparently had Andy and had welcomed him into your family, and perhaps wanted me to sweat it out awhile. I knew we had a lot to work out, you and I, but I figured it would wait until we could talk face-to-face," Jenna said. "But you don't have to take my word on that, Grady. You can verify it simply by calling the station, checking your messages and talking to your partner."

The part of Grady that had already loved Jenna told him it wasn't necessary to check out Jenna's story. The cop in him said it was. Wordlessly, Grady picked up the phone. A short talk with his partner later, he had his confirmation. To his enormous relief, everything was exactly as Jenna had said.

"Satisfied?" Jenna said, when he hung up.

Grady frowned. "There's something else I still don't understand." And it was a biggie. "If you weren't sick, why did you stay in the hospital two weeks? Why weren't you able to get released right away?"

"I wasn't exactly what you'd call a model patient, going in," she admitted reluctantly. "I was very upset about being admitted over my protestations that I was not crazy, and I tried to escape a couple of times."

In her place, had he been incorrectly diagnosed and locked up in a psychiatric facility, Grady probably would have done the same thing. "Couldn't they tell you'd just had a baby?" he asked, fighting to put aside his empathy and retain his objectivity.

Jenna made another helpless gesture with her hands. "After six weeks, my body was entirely healed."

Grady forced himself to ask the questions he desperately needed answered, even though he knew they were a major invasion of her privacy. "How do you know?"

Irritation flashed in her jade eyes. "Because I had just had my six-weeks postpartum check-up the day before Andy was kidnapped."

"There must've been some signs you'd just had a baby," Grady said.

Jenna fixed him with the sort of smile a saleswoman reserves for her most difficult customers. "Maybe, if I'd still been nursing, but I had stopped that after four weeks," she said coolly. "So I had no milk in my breasts, either."

"Still, there must have been other signs," Grady persisted.

"Right." Jenna leaned toward him, her aggravation apparent. "And every single damn one of them worked against me!"

Grady narrowed her eyes. "What do you mean?"

Jenna rubbed at the back of her neck. "To be perfectly frank, Grady, I was a wreck. I was run down, emotionally and physically. I hadn't been sleeping enough, so I had circles under my eyes. I hadn't had enough exercise. I was still carrying ten extra pounds. And I was fighting the usual postpartum depression. I know, on the surface at least, that I must have looked like I was in terrible shape—at least compared to the pulled-together way I usually looked, pre-pregnancy."

Grady couldn't imagine Jenna ever not looking beautiful. Even now, with her strawberry blond hair in windswept disarray, her cheeks flushed with the heat of her humiliation and rage as she described all she had been through, her lips bare of any lipstick, she looked incredibly desirable. Incredibly womanly. And in charge of herself. So in charge of herself, in fact, he was having trouble believing she had ever not been in total control.

Grady paused. "Didn't your family know you were okay, though, when they talked to you the next day or the day after that?"

Jenna's fingers gripped the top of the dresser on either side of her. "My father would have, had he been allowed to talk to me."

Grady focused on her hands, with their neat unpolished nails, slender fingers and soft white skin. "But Lamar wasn't allowed to talk to you," he guessed.

"That's not so out of the ordinary, Grady. Initially I was very angry with Dad and Baxter for checking me into that place," she explained pragmatically. "I was not exactly shy about making my feelings known. The staff concluded seeing my family would only upset me further, so they asked them not to visit for the first couple of weeks. To keep track of my progress by phone calls to the doctor, instead."

Grady recalled the photos he'd seen on Lamar's desk. "What about your brother? Was he a part of this?" Was there a disputed inheritance at stake?

"Kip and his wife have been vacationing in Hawaii. I'm not sure Kip knows even now I ever was hospitalized."

"Your father wouldn't have told him?"

Jenna shook her head firmly, sure about this much. "There was nothing Kip could have done except worry, and my father was already doing enough of that for both of them, I'd wager. So he probably just decided to tell Kip when Kip and Leslie got back from Hawaii.''

Grady released a heavy sigh. ''Back to your stay in the hospital. What happened after that first night? I mean, I assume you saw a doctor—''

''Yes, and I demanded she let me out of there, pronto, so I could contact the Philadelphia police and find my baby. As you can imagine, that was probably the worst thing I could've said, since she initially thought I was suffering from a hysterical pregnancy and possibly delusions of motherhood. She didn't believe I'd had a baby any more than my ex-husband or my father did.''

''Did she try to verify the birth anyway?''

''Yes, she checked with Dr. Koen in Hudson Falls. But I was so upset I forget to forewarn her that I'd had the baby under a false name, so all she discovered was that someone named Laura Johnson had allegedly been staying at my address and had had a baby. Finally, the second day we faxed Dr. Koen a photo of me. He verified that the woman in the photo was Laura Johnson, and that's when the tide began to turn in my favor.''

''So what happened next?''

Jenna shrugged again. ''I tried to reach you through the department, and that's when I learned you had the baby...at least I thought you had the baby. But you didn't return my calls. I was afraid to leave Pinehaven by then, for fear you'd try to get in touch with me in the interim and then we'd miss each other. And I didn't know where either you or Andy were. So I stayed another day. The third day I learned you weren't coming back with Andy for a couple of weeks, so I thought about everything that had happened and I weighed my options. I realized that I *was* incredibly run down and burned out emotionally from the stress of dealing with an unplanned pregnancy while simultaneously trying to hide out from the world and juggle the demands of the work I love. I decided to stay at Pinehaven and make good use of the opportunity to get my thoughts in order and my strength back before I tried to deal with you face-to-face and tackle single motherhood again.

"So I ate and slept and exercised...and slept and slept. And I talked to my doctor about the emotional pressure I'd been under, and the fact that I really hadn't been handling it as well as I thought I was."

"And so your stay in the hospital helped?" Grady asked.

"A lot," Jenna confirmed honestly. She shrugged. "On the whole, except for the rocky beginning, my stay at Pinehaven wasn't all that different from going to one of the plush rejuvenating spas. Of course, it would've been a different situation entirely had I suspected, even for a second, that Andy was not with you. But I really thought Andy was with you and everything was okay. That it wasn't going to make any difference if I came back sooner, because in or out of Pinehaven I probably wasn't going to get Andy back from you any quicker, and what I really needed to do was pull myself together, which I did."

Yes, she had, Grady thought. In fact, everything Jenna had done thus far was beginning to make sense to Grady. Too much sense for his own comfort. He was supposed to be objective and impartial here, but he had hardly given a thought to Clarissa's claims. And that wasn't like him. Usually he was thorough and impartial to a fault. "When did you get out of Pinehaven?" he said.

"Yesterday. I timed my release for the day you'd be back in Philadelphia."

Grady thought of Lamar Sullivan's reaction when his daughter had walked in the door. "And yet your father didn't know you'd been released?"

"I specifically asked my doctor not to talk to either Baxter or my father about the fact I'd really had a baby or was being released until I'd had a chance to talk to you and clear things up. My doctor understood I had been unfair to you, that I wanted to rectify that. As soon as I was released, I rented a car and drove straight to Philadelphia to see you."

Grady hesitated, aware he had never heard a crazier string

of events explained more logically in his life. He was also aware he wanted very much for every word Jenna had said to be true.

"If all this is true, then you've been through a lot," Grady said. And for that alone, his heart went out to her.

She regarded him hesitantly, then sat down beside him on the bed, so close they were almost touching. She took his hand in both of hers. "Enough to make you stop doubting me?" she asked softly.

It still bothered Grady that Lamar Sullivan hadn't had any idea his daughter was pregnant. It also bothered him that Clarissa was claiming this baby, too. "*If* Andy's yours—" he began cautiously.

Jenna dropped his hand. "If?" She stood and looked at him as if he was a serial killer.

Grady released an exasperated breath. "What do you want me to say, Jenna?"

Without answering him, she set her lips firmly and started to step past him. Not about to let her run away, Grady stood and fastened an arm around her wrist and pulled her beside him.

Furious at the way he held her still so effortlessly, she glared up at him, the full brunt of her temper shining in her dark green eyes. "Let me go."

"No. Not until we've settled things, and we haven't finished talking."

"This isn't fair, Grady," she said angrily.

Grady tightened his hands on her wrists and felt the smooth, warm burn of her silky skin against his. Desire welled up deep inside him as his eyes locked on hers. "I'll tell you what isn't fair," he returned, not bothering to hide his resentment any longer. "The way this whole thing has unfolded, bit by incriminating bit. I don't like being played for a fool, Jenna. I don't like finding out by accident that I've brought a child into this world!"

Guilty color illuminated her cheeks, bringing out the delicate aristocratic bone structure of her face. "Well, what did you expect?'' she ground out, struggling to free herself, to no avail.

Grady fought the potent desire that seemed to increase with every twitch and flail of her slender body. ''Maybe the truth, the whole truth and nothing but the truth right from the start,'' he stormed, still holding her close.

Her eyes flashed with temper once again, then shone with hurt. ''And how was I supposed to deliver that?'' she whispered emotionally. Her soft, bow-shaped lips tightened in misery. ''I didn't even know if you cared.''

Grady ignored the guilt her words roused and concentrated only on all *he* had lost. Witnessing the birth of his first and only child. Being there for her when she needed him. ''I cared, all right,'' he said, his low voice gruff with hurt. ''You just never gave me a chance to show you.''

With a sweep of her thick red-gold lashes, Jenna averted her eyes. ''Maybe about the child,'' she asserted, ''not about me.''

Grady felt his temper rise another notch. ''That isn't true!''

''Isn't it?''

''No!''

''Then why didn't you ever call me?'' Jenna cried.

She had a point there. What she didn't know was that he had thought about calling her, countless times, and never more than when he'd been in Sun Valley with his sister and her family. Because it had been brought home to him, like an arrow to his heart, how much he was missing by not having a family of his own. He had begun to rethink his decision never to marry again. And once that decision had started to fall by the wayside, the first—hell—the only woman that had come to mind was Jenna. But he knew to tell her that now would sound like a damn lie.

''You're right. I should have called you, Jenna.'' He searched her eyes with his, saw the softness, the hurt, the feminine mystery that was all Jenna. Giving in to instinct, he lowered his mouth to hers. ''I really should have,'' he whispered.

She had time to evade, if she had wanted to do so, but she didn't. She merely stared up at him with a mixture of wide-eyed wonder and wariness that made Grady feel all the more tender and protective of her. His lips caressed hers, gently this time, wonderingly. For a moment, Jenna was very still. Then she moaned low in her throat, and her arms came up to wrap about his neck. The next thing he knew she was kissing him back, not just in surrender but with an urgency that rocked him to his soul.

Passion for passion, he met her needs with his, met her desire, matched it over and over until his blood began to swim, until he knew it was either call a halt or take her then and there. He slowly ended the kiss and lifted his mouth from hers.

They sighed in unison. Both were trembling, dumbstruck. And cautious as hell. She was the first to turn away. She shook her head at him, as if silently chastising them both, swallowed hard, then slowly returned her gaze to his. "You shouldn't have done that," she said.

"*We* shouldn't have done that," he corrected.

Her face paled even more. Ducking her head again, she toyed with a button on his shirt. "Oh, Grady. Don't you see you're just confusing things more, kissing me that way?" she whispered.

Grady tucked a hand beneath her chin and guided her face to his. He knew it was crazy, that it was likely to complicate his investigation unnecessarily, but part of him just didn't care. "Or maybe I'm just clearing them up," he said. He knew, whether she wanted to admit it or not, that she desired him, too. The way she had kissed him just now proved that. And he had missed her, even if he couldn't tell her so just yet.

Jenna's soft lower lip took on a determined pout. "The desire we feel for one another doesn't matter, not unless you believe in me," Jenna asserted stubbornly, her slender body growing defiantly taut all over as she glared at him hotly. "Not unless you know in your heart that every single word

I'm telling you is the truth, whether I have any proof to give you or not!''

His lower body throbbing with unslaked desire, Grady paused. She was asking him to disregard the statements and actions of everyone else and to believe only her. Sadly, he couldn't do that, not until he'd had a chance to discover and sift through all the facts at length. ''All I know for certain is that I still want you,'' he said gruffly. ''And I'm beginning to think I always will.''

Wanting to explore more of what she had just given him, he lowered his mouth to hers once again.

''Don't.'' Jenna flattened a hand against his chest and pushed him away.

Grady let her hold him at bay, at least for the moment. ''Why not?'' he asked, his heart racing, need flowing through him like a river as he tested her once again. ''I thought you just said you wanted me to act on my feelings.''

''Only in order to help me,'' Jenna specified defiantly. ''Not to get me in trouble again.''

Unable to help himself, Grady sifted his hands through the soft waves of her hair. ''You call this trouble?'' Compared to what they had already been through, it was nothing.

Jenna shrugged off his touch and regarded him cantankerously, the desire she felt reflected in her dark green eyes. ''You're telling me it's not?''

Chapter Six

"There you two are! I thought you'd never get back!" Clarissa said.

Jenna and Grady got out of their cars. Jenna took charge of Andy and Grady took charge of the diaper bag. They met Clarissa on the front porch of the farmhouse. "How did you know we were in Hudson Falls?" Jenna asked Clarissa warily, being careful to keep Andy's face turned away from the brisk March wind. She had hoped to avoid another scene with Clarissa until after the results of the blood tests came in. After that, well, there wouldn't be much to say. Clarissa's ruse would be discovered.

"Grady left your number and address with the Philly police department," Clarissa said smugly, looking exceedingly pleased with herself for having been able to track them down.

Jenna gave Grady a look. "How thoughtful of you to make sure Clarissa knew where we could be reached at all times," she said sweetly.

Grady knew Jenna well enough to read between the lines. "I left the number here so they could reach me if they came up with anything on Nanny Beth," Grady explained to Jenna. He turned to his ex-wife with a frown. "But that doesn't explain how you got that information, Clarissa. I know you didn't get it from my partner."

"I told one of the rookies it was a family emergency," Clarissa admitted cavalierly. Grady's look narrowed even more. His disapproval was palpable. Clarissa finally had the grace to blush. "Oh, for heaven's sake, Grady," she said, "we were married!"

"*Were* being the operative word, Clarissa," Grady said shortly. "We aren't now."

"Yes, but we should be," Clarissa continued, "for our baby's sake."

Holding on to her temper, Jenna punched in the code to deactivate the alarm system. Keeping her dignity wrapped around her like an invisible armor that would protect her from Clarissa's lies, Jenna stepped wordlessly inside, Andy cradled in her arms. Grady and Clarissa followed her as Jenna switched on lights and paused beside the thermostat in the hall to turn up the heat.

All but ignoring the baby she claimed was hers, Clarissa shrugged out of her mink. Her discreetly colored blond hair was a shining cap around her head. "I brought the papers you wanted, Grady."

A cold chill spread from Jenna's stomach into her limbs. She had known in her heart Clarissa wasn't going to give Grady up without a fight. "What papers?" Jenna asked warily.

Clarissa moved in on Grady, her expensive perfume dominating the air around her. As Jenna and Andy watched from the sidelines, Clarissa pressed a manila file full of official-looking papers into Grady's hands. "Birth certificate. Signed, notarized affidavits from the doctor and nurse who attended Andrew's birth. Now that you have them, Grady, I demand that we reconcile at once for the baby's sake."

Jenna had never considered herself a very physical person. In fact, she'd gone through her entire childhood without once getting into a brawl, but suddenly it was all she could do to keep from socking Clarissa in her turned-up little nose.

As if reading Jenna's intentions, Grady stepped between the two women. "It's a bit more complicated than that, Clarissa. Jenna has a birth certificate for Andy, too."

Clarissa looked stunned at the news. "Then hers must be a fraud," she said coolly.

"As a matter of fact, it is." Grady opened the file of documents Clarissa had handed him and scanned them quickly, one after another. If he found anything amiss in them, Jenna realized with fast-growing desperation, it didn't show in his face.

"Then what are you waiting for?" Clarissa demanded.

"The whole story," Grady said. He shut the file decisively but did not hand it to his ex-wife. "For all I know, your documents are false, too, Clarissa."

Jenna held Andy a little closer to her chest. Ducking her head, she drank in the sweet, baby scent of him. She had missed him so much, the two weeks they were apart. There was no way anyone was going to separate the two of them again, and she didn't care who she had to mow down to protect her relationship with him. Andy gurgled and cooed as Jenna pressed a kiss on the top of his soft, downy hair. She caught Grady watching her, a speculative gleam in his slate-blue eyes.

"Those documents are definitely false," Jenna said flatly, unable to help herself from putting in her own two cents worth.

Clarissa curled an elegant hand around Grady's bicep. "Don't take her word for it, Grady," Clarissa put in quickly.

Jenna's temper simmered as she saw how possessively Clarissa was holding on to Grady. Like they couldn't do that somewhere—anywhere—else!

"I don't intend to," Grady told Clarissa. He extricated her hand from his arm and stepped away. "Any more than I intend to take yours." Grady looked at his ex-wife like a prosecuting attorney about to put a hostile witness on the stand.

Jenna watched as Grady ushered Clarissa into Jenna's office.

"Have a seat, Clarissa," he told his ex-wife with a dissecting smile that didn't reach his eyes. "As long as you're here, I want to ask you a few questions, too."

GRADY WAITED until Jenna had gone off to heat Andy's formula before he settled on the desk and spoke to Clarissa. He had heard Jenna's story in all its crazy entirety. He had seen her substantiating paperwork. He had seen Clarissa's. Both of them couldn't be telling the truth. Frowning, he began, "First of all, I want you to know, Clarissa, that if this is some sort of ploy to get even with me or punish me for divorcing you, it wore thin a long time ago."

Clarissa crossed her legs at the knee. The slim, short skirt of her silk dress rode halfway up her thigh. She made no effort to pull it down. "I'm surprised at you, Grady," she scolded in a low, throaty tone. "I never would've imagined you to be the kind of man who'd think fatherhood was a punishment."

Grady wondered how he ever could have married Clarissa. It was clear she was not, and had never really been, his type. He supposed it had just been his age—he'd been right out of college—and his hormones that had done him in. He'd wanted to sleep with a woman every night. That woman had been Clarissa. Now that he really knew her, knew how bankrupt her soul was, he couldn't imagine ever being in love with her. Worse, the thought she might have had his child to trap him filled him with dread.

He scowled at her and forced himself to get back on track. "Fatherhood isn't a punishment," he said, scowling even more.

"Good." Clarissa sat back in her chair and let her skirt hike up a little more. "We agree on something."

Grady studied her pretty profile. "How could you have had a child and not told me, Clarissa?" Despite everything she had said, he just couldn't imagine her being brave enough to have his child without him. Oh, he remembered the story she had told initially, about running to her family on Long Island to have her baby. He just didn't buy it. It seemed to him she would have come to him first. Unless she really was intent on punishing him. And maybe, Grady thought sadly, she was.

Clarissa ignored the skepticism on his face. "I was angry with you for telling me in no uncertain terms it was over between us after you'd slept with me again, instead of before," she explained. "I was angry with you for insisting on going through with the divorce when you knew I still loved you. And initially I was not thrilled to find myself pregnant."

Grady recalled how Clarissa had refused to have his baby while they were married. Initially, she had kept putting him off, saying they would have a family when the time was right. It was only as they approached their thirties that she leveled with him and told him she had no interest in being a mother, period. "I remember how you felt about not having children," he said flatly. "So what changed your mind?"

"Nothing changed my mind. My getting pregnant was an accident. Furthermore, if you'll just think back to the night it happened, the night my place got burglarized, the night before we signed the final papers, you'll understand how and why I might have been so careless as to let something like this happen. I was very frightened, and you comforted me."

Grady sighed, unable to mask his regret about that. "I remember," he said tersely. Clarissa had been upset as hell that night, and not just about the burglary of her apartment, but about everything. He'd felt many of the same emotions she had. He had never failed in anything, either. He wasn't happy about failing in his marriage. And he felt guilty as hell for hurting Clarissa, because he knew he never should have married her. He just didn't love her enough, not the way a husband should love his wife. So when Clarissa reached out to him one last time, he'd just said the hell with it and let himself be seduced that one last time. Only he'd felt more alone and lonely after their lovemaking than he had when they'd first split. And he had also known that, no matter how many guilt trips Clarissa laid on him, he could never love her again. Andy didn't change that, even if he was their child.

"That night was a mistake, Clarissa," Grady said heavily,

wishing it was possible to somehow discourage Clarissa once and for all, to let her know it truly was over, without hurting her feelings or enraging her.

Clarissa plucked at the silk fabric of her skirt. "I felt that way then, too, Grady."

"We agreed it would never happen again."

"Yes." Clarissa bit her lip. "But that was before I spent the last year alone." Suddenly, she was on her feet, her arms outstretched, moving toward him. "I want you back," she whispered.

"Then take him," Jenna interrupted from the doorway. Andy was no longer in her arms, so Grady concluded she had fed and changed the baby and then put him down in his crib. "Just don't use my baby to try and trick him into it."

Clarissa sent Jenna a wickedly derisive look, then turned to Grady. She ran her hand up and down his arm. The only effect it had on Grady was to make him want to pull away.

"Look, Grady, I admit I have made some mistakes, but it's silly to let my pride or yours get in the way of our being a family again," Clarissa said softly. As she looked at him, her eyes sparkled with an earnest glow. "I can handle this unexpected excitement in our lives, and I know you can, too."

Grady calmly extricated Clarissa's fingers from his arm and pointed to the chair. "Sit down, Clarissa, and finish answering my questions. How did the baby get to Alec's?"

Clarissa flounced to the chair and sat down, letting her skirt hike up even higher this time. "I told you," she pouted, swinging one crossed leg as Jenna walked over to collect the stack of unopened mail that had collected on her desk. "I left him there when I couldn't contact you. I just never imagined Alec or Jack would claim Andy as their own. I figured Alec would call you right away. And once you saw Andy, you'd realize the resemblance, you'd know..."

Jenna whirled to face Grady's ex. Her cheeks and eyes

were aglow with fiery temper. "She's lying!" Jenna said.

Clarissa arched an elegant brow at Jenna. "One of us is," she agreed coolly.

Jenna's jaw clenched. "This is my home," she announced flatly, "and I didn't invite you here."

"Don't pretend you're an innocent." Clarissa got out of her chair and advanced on Jenna. "You're just after Grady's money," she accused.

Bull, Grady thought. Jenna turned to Grady, her surprise evident. "I didn't know you were wealthy," she said.

"I'm not," he replied, wishing Clarissa hadn't brought that up.

"But his family is very wealthy," Clarissa said.

"Well, so is mine," Jenna retorted with a harumph. "I'm an heir to Sullivan Shoes."

Clarissa turned to Grady. Her theory shot to hell, she demanded of him impatiently, "How much longer are you going to let this nonsense go on, Grady?"

"Until we get the lab results," Grady said, "or someone owns up to the truth and admits they've lied here or been playing a practical joke that ceased to be funny two days ago."

"Why do we have to wait?" Clarissa demanded petulantly.

"Because," Grady said, "this situation is far too complicated for me to trust anything less than the DNA results."

Clarissa released a long sigh. She turned to Jenna with a look that seemed to say, don't think you've won here. Wordlessly, she collected her signature white mink and her purse. "Grady, I'm staying at the Americana Inn in Albany. I've also reserved a room for you there." She paused in the portal to give Grady a smoldering look that had absolutely no effect on him, but made Jenna livid. "I'll be waiting for you," she cooed.

Bloody hell, Grady thought. Wordlessly, he helped Clarissa with her coat and walked her out to her car.

"So. How was the good-night kiss?" Jenna asked the moment Grady strolled masterfully in the door a good ten minutes later.

"I didn't give her one." He paused, looking her up and down from the top of her mussed strawberry blond hair to the toes of her boot-clad feet. Still eyeing her with a depth of male speculation Jenna found greatly disturbing, Grady shifted so he stood with his feet braced slightly apart. He jammed his hands on his hips and narrowed his eyes. "Why would you think I had?"

"Oh, I don't know," Jenna replied with a lofty wave of her hand. She turned on her heel and started for the kitchen. With Andy sound asleep, now was the perfect time to start dinner. "You kissed me today. I just thought, to be perfectly fair, you'd also want to kiss Clarissa, too. You know, kind of a sampling-the-merchandise type thing, like one of those taste tests you see them doing in the grocery store on TV."

He caught her by the arm and yanked her forward until she collided with the hard muscles of his chest and abdomen. Sparks of sexual electricity exploded at every point of contact. "I don't operate that way, Jenna," Grady said.

Jenna's pulse pounded as she realized he looked like he wanted to kiss her. It was all she could do not to give in to impulse. "Really?" Jenna pushed away from him and offered him her back. "You could have fooled me."

Grady rested both palms on her shoulders. He ducked his head until it was close to her ear. "Why are you so angry at me?" he murmured.

"I don't know," Jenna said stubbornly. She tried to pull away. This time he wouldn't let her. She forced herself to go on. "Maybe it has something to do with the fact that I finally worked up enough nerve to tell you the truth, and it hasn't seemed to make a damn bit of difference."

Grady dropped his hands from her shoulders abruptly. He moved toward the kitchen sink. "I admit it's a very compelling story, very creative." He glanced out at the black night, turned to her slowly and folded his arms in front of him. "But then so is Clarissa's."

Jenna charged right after him. "I didn't tell you a story, Grady!" she said, hearing with chagrin the frustrated fury in her voice. "I told you the truth!"

"Then the facts will bear that out, won't they?" Grady retorted calmly.

Jenna glowered at him. She could feel the blood rushing to her cheeks, even as she struggled to get a handle on her soaring emotions. "Get out of my house." That said, she pivoted smartly on her heel and made for her study. Maybe if she did some work tonight, she'd be able to calm down.

As she feared he might, Grady intercepted her at the door. A sexy smile on his face, he braced a hand on either side of her and leaned over her. "If you want me to go, I'll go, but I'll have to get someone out here to watch over you and Andy first."

Jenna backed up slightly. Her heart was pounding. She was tingling all over. She told herself it was the tension causing her body to go haywire, and not his proximity. "Why?" she ground out. She let him know with a single glance she'd about had it with him.

Grady only leaned in closer. "Because if you are telling me the truth and Andy was kidnapped, then it could happen again, couldn't it? Particularly here."

Jenna swallowed, her adrenaline pumping for a completely different reason. "I think I hate you."

Grady grimaced right back at her. "If you had my baby without me, then I'm damned mad at you, too."

Wordlessly, Jenna slipped away from him. Refusing to address what she had no excuse for, she picked up the threads of their argument. "Furthermore, your ex-wife is a witch on wheels."

Grady grinned, amused by the apt description. "When I married her Clarissa was sweet and innocent and had stars in her eyes."

That didn't sound like the woman Jenna had met. "So what did you do to make her bitter?"

Grady's face changed. Some of the anger came back into his eyes. "I stayed a cop."

Jenna stared at him, her heart still pounding, aware she'd touched a nerve. And yet, as mad as she was with him, she still wanted so badly to understand him. "I don't get it."

Grady shrugged and shoved his hands through his agreeably shaggy mane of sable brown hair. "Clarissa always considered my police work nothing more than a rich boy's whim. She married me, sure I would grow out of it and take my rightful place in my father's brokerage firm on Wall Street."

Jenna studied his tall, lanky form. There was nothing soft or easy about Grady Noland. She sensed there never would be. He was who he was, take-him or leave it. Trying not to think how much they had in common that way, Jenna asked, "You never even thought about quitting—for her?"

"Nope." Grady's answer was firm and unapologetic. "Nor do I ever intend to. I'm a cop, Jenna," he said. "It's what I do and what I am, and that's never going to change."

Jenna released a slow, slightly ragged breath. It was crazy, but it reassured her, knowing that Grady was so solid inside, so sure of himself and what he was meant to be. Now if only he wasn't so sure he was meant to go through this life alone. She decided to test the waters delicately. "The night we met, you said cops and marriage don't mix."

For the first time that night she saw a hint of remorse in Grady's eyes. "I still believe that in most cases," he said expressionlessly. Their glances met and held.

"Why?" Jenna asked softly.

Abruptly, Grady looked like a trapped panther pacing his cage. "It's a dangerous job. Long hours. Low pay." He moved his broad shoulders beneath his trademark Harris tweed jacket and finished, "All that combined is hard on a wife."

Jenna frowned as she tried to imagine a life with a man so opposed to compromise on something that basic. "It'd be hard on kids, too."

"Yeah," Grady said meeting her eyes, "it would be." He

inclined his head slightly to the side and smiled. "I've seen it work, though."

Jenna found herself gliding closer to him as their voices dropped. "Does that mean you've changed your mind about having a family?" she asked.

Grady was suddenly very still. "According to you, I already have one."

Jenna's temper kicked into full gear. She wasn't used to having her word questioned. "Having a son isn't the same as having a wife and child," Jenna retorted, working to keep her voice as serene as she knew she appeared.

"Tell me about it," he drawled.

Jenna flushed self-consciously. Without warning, she had an idea what it would be like to be Grady's wife, to wake up with him every morning, to lie in his arms every night. The thought was as tantalizing as it was disturbing. Being near him was like playing near a fire. Too far away, she'd never get warm. Too close to the flame and she'd get burned. Deciding it was best to just keep a fair distance from him, she planted her hands on her hips and told him, "You cannot just run over me like a steamroller."

"I never said I wanted to."

Maybe not, but right now he looked like he wanted her in his bed again, Jenna realized with equal parts anticipation and anxiety. That was a dangerous proposition, indeed. Grady was the kind of man she could fall in love with. Indeed, part of her felt she had already fallen in love with him. Maybe would always be in love with him a little…

Turning away from Grady, Jenna went to the refrigerator. She took a package of hamburger patties and a bag of fries from the freezer compartment.

"Can I help you there?" He looked over her shoulder as she continued the dinner preparations.

"No. Thanks." Jenna added a package of hamburger buns to the food on the counter.

Grady watched as she took a skillet and a baking sheet from the cabinet. "Then what can I do?"

Jenna set them both on the top of the stove. "Find out who kidnapped Andy, and then get the hell out of my life."

Grady grinned at her unabridged version of her thoughts. "I don't think I can do that," he said as she tore off the cellophane and separated the hamburger patties with a knife.

Jenna removed the paper from the patties and slid them into the skillet. "I don't know why not."

"Oh, yes, Jenna," Grady said softly. Suddenly his hand was on her face, and he was lifting her mouth to his, ducking his head. "I think you do," he said softly, his eyes beginning to close. "I think—"

He was about to kiss her when suddenly he jerked away. Jenna frowned. What the—

Holding on to her with one hand, Grady reached for the marble rolling pin on the counter with the other. Jenna stiffened in his arms as she felt him tense. "What is it?" Her voice was panicked.

His arm sliding around her waist, Grady ducked his head a little lower and whispered in her ear, "There's someone outside your kitchen window."

Panic welled up in Jenna, fierce and unrelenting. "Oh, God," she said, already beginning to tremble.

"Relax," Grady instructed softly, his hand tightening on her spine. He pressed her possessively close as he promised, "I'll handle it."

Jenna's fingers bit into his forearms. Her slender body trembling harder than ever, she tilted her head and looked into his eyes. The feel of his strong, hard body pressed against hers was wildly sensual. And it filled her with an excitement that had nothing to do with the intruder lurking outside. "You're not going to go out there. Are you?" she whispered huskily, the protectiveness she felt for him revealed in the low tremor that was her voice.

Grady grinned broadly. "And I thought you didn't care about me," he murmured sexily, pressing her even closer.

Jenna flushed hotly as his lips tugged on the curve of her

ear, sending another frisson of sensation coursing hotly through her veins. "I don't."

Grady's steely blue eyes twinkled. "I'll be the judge of that," he said, and then the laughter left his eyes. He looked like he wanted to make love to her, there, that second. "Kiss me again," he urged roughly. "And make it look really distracting." Giving her no chance to argue, he lowered his mouth to hers. Jenna tasted the sweetness that was Grady, felt his wildness in the plundering, demanding sweep of his tongue. God, she had missed him, she thought as he continued to shower her with hot, passionate kisses and kneaded her back with hungry impatience. She had missed this.

But there was no time for further exploration. Grady lifted his mouth from hers. Gazing into her eyes, with a seriousness that let her know he was simply buying them some time to make some plans for their defense, he demanded, "Were you expecting anyone?"

Oh, God. The intruder. For a second, she'd been so caught up in Grady's kiss, she'd forgotten. Her throat unbearably dry, she shook her head and said, "No—Grady—I—"

Frowning at the edge of panic in her voice, he lowered his head and kissed her again, hard.

Vibrantly aware of the swift state of her own arousal and the way her lower body seemed to automatically mold to his, Jenna struggled to keep her emotions out of the kiss. And found, just as she had predicted, that it was a battle she just couldn't win. She wanted Grady. Always had, and probably always would. It didn't matter that these lust-at-first-sight feelings were quite unlike her. When she was in his arms, all she could think about, all she could do, was surrender. Surrender and make the absolute most of the moment given her.

Reluctantly, Grady broke off their kiss. And wished again she didn't look so damn vulnerable. "Stay calm," Grady ordered against her mouth.

Jenna nodded, letting him know she understood. She knew it was foolhardy of her, but she wished he didn't have to let her go now, just when things were really starting to heat up between them once again.

"And stay here," Grady continued firmly. He leaned forward, pressing another all-for-show kiss into her hair as he whispered his intentions softly in her ear. "I'm going around front to check this out."

The thought of anything happening to him filled Jenna with panic. "Grady, no—" Her hands clutched his shirtfront before he could step away from her. She tilted her head and looked into his ruggedly handsome face. "Let's just call the police," she said.

Grady extricated her fingers from his shirt and lifted them to his mouth. "Hell, Jenna," he said lightly, kissing her knuckles as he shook his head at her in silent remonstration, "I am the police."

The moment Grady was out the door, Jenna grabbed the phone with one hand and began dialing the Hudson Falls sheriff's office in case Grady needed backup. But even before she finished dialing, she heard a shout of alarm. Dropping the phone, she rushed to the window and saw two men tussling in the dark. Several quick moves later, Grady emerged the victor. Jenna went to the phone. She was still dialing as Grady hauled the intruder in.

"You know this clown?" he demanded breathlessly.

Jenna gasped as she got a look at the man's face.

Chapter Seven

"Do you know this guy, Jenna?" Grady growled the moment he had shoved their intruder in the kitchen door.

"Know me!" the burly man with the wavy black hair croaked as indignantly as he could, considering Grady had both his arms pinned behind his back and a nice, subduing choke hold around his neck. "She was married to me!"

Grady loosened his grip on the man's throat. Now that he took a closer look at the guy in the light, he could see he had a patrician look about him. His black hair was shot through with gray. Ditto his thick mustache. His pin-striped wool suit, starched dove gray shirt and coordinating tie indicated he was a professional person, and judging from the quality of the cloth, a highly successful one, at that. Grady loosened his grip a little more and took a wild guess. "Baxter?"

His captive stiffened. "I see you've heard about me."

"And then some." Grady thought about releasing Jenna's ex, then decided he liked the guy right where he was. He used the toe of his boot to pull a chair forward.

"Who are you?" Baxter asked.

"Grady Noland."

Baxter surmised quickly, "The detective who spoke to my secretary late today?"

"You got that right," Grady said. Keeping one hand securely on Baxter's collar, Grady propped one booted foot on the seat of the chair. "Jenna says you put her in Pinehaven."

Baxter's bushy eyebrows lowered like twin thunderclouds over his black eyes. "It was for her own good," Baxter asserted grimly.

Grady shot Jenna a look and saw her breathe a sigh of relief. He knew what she was thinking—that finally someone had corroborated her story. Of course it didn't make him feel very good to realize it had been an untrustworthy, peeping Tom of an ex-husband who'd done the corroborating, but beggars couldn't be choosers.

He made a mental note to check with the staff at Pinehaven first thing tomorrow, and to check with the New York state health department about · Pinehaven directly after that. He wanted to know what kind of reputation that place had.

Figuring he had sufficiently intimidated the pediatric surgeon, Grady removed his boot from the chair and shoved Baxter into the chair. Grady leaned over him. Calling on his years of experience in police interrogations, he leaned over Baxter and said calmly, "Second question. What were you doing snooping in the bushes?"

Baxter looked at him. Whatever thoughts he'd had about not cooperating with Grady, and Grady could tell he'd had some, vanished as he looked into Grady's eyes. Baxter swallowed hard, and his mustache quivered just a bit, but it was Jenna Baxter looked at as he answered, not Grady. "I just found out from Lamar that Jenna had checked herself out of the hospital," he said quietly. "I was worried about her."

Grady cut Jenna a glance, too. If she'd had any feelings for Baxter, he noted with something very closely akin to relief, they weren't showing now. In fact, she looked every bit as irritated as Grady to find Baxter had been snooping outside her house. "Why?" Grady asked, moving slightly to the left so that he stood between Jenna and her ex.

Baxter frowned. Grady saw arrogant self-assurance in his expression. "Because she was very sick," Baxter said.

Jenna looked at Grady as if to say I told you so. Grady had never resented a man more than he did at that moment. He wanted to throttle Baxter for having Jenna put away against her will, even for a brief time. And he could tell, just by looking at him, that Baxter was exactly the kind of guy who would do such a despicable thing.

"The only sicko around here is you, Baxter," Grady growled.

"I don't have to listen to this." Baxter started to stand.

Grady shoved him back in the seat, hard. Hands flat on the table, he leaned over him. "How long have you been spying on your ex-wife?"

"This is the first time."

"Yeah, right." Grady looked at Jenna. "I say you should have him arrested."

"What the hell for?" Baxter asked, and then flushed a bright red.

Grady straightened slowly, knowing he'd just driven home his point. "Trespassing, for starters," Grady said.

"Jenna—" Baxter looked at her imploringly. "What's going on here? Who is this?"

"This, Baxter, is my baby's father."

Baxter looked shell-shocked. Grady felt a little stunned, too. He hadn't expected Jenna to admit to it so bluntly when she'd gone to so much trouble earlier to keep her one brief fling with him secret.

Baxter's skin began to look even more mottled. "That again? Jenna, I thought we'd covered that particular delusion. If you want a baby of your own, I'd be happy to—" Baxter frowned as an infant's wail sounded in the distance. He blinked. And blinked again. "What was that?"

"My delusion," Jenna said dryly. "If you gentlemen will excuse me, I have maternal duties to attend to." Leaving Baxter with Grady, she slipped from the room. Grady saw Baxter was about to follow her and clamped a firm hand on Baxter's shoulder. "The truth. Did you have anything to do with the kidnapping?"

"No," Baxter said, as Jenna came into the room, a gurgling Andy in her arms. "Cross my heart. I didn't. I didn't even know there was a baby."

Grady studied Baxter's face. If Jenna's ex was lying, he was a hell of an actor, because the guy looked absolutely stunned.

"Well, there was a baby," Jenna retorted shortly.

"But how—" Baxter said.

"The usual way," Grady said, staking his claim.

Baxter turned even redder. Jenna glared at Grady. "It's a long story," she said. "One I have no intention of going into."

Baxter's glance went from Jenna to Grady and back again. "My God," he whispered. "The two of you really—"

"Yes, Baxter, we did," Jenna said dryly. "But that isn't an issue here right now. What's done is done. I've felt that way for a long time."

"That's why you've been staying out at the farm," Baxter mumbled, still in shock. "That's why you've been running the foundation from here!"

"Yes," Jenna said. She went to the refrigerator and removed a bottle of formula. She carried it to the microwave, slid it inside and punched the defrost button. "I wanted to keep my pregnancy secret."

"Well, you did that, all right," Baxter mused. He shook his head. "And I thought... The nursery... Oh, my God, Jenna! I'm sorry."

Suddenly it all made sense. "You took the furniture, didn't you?" Jenna asked gently.

Baxter nodded, watching as Jenna strapped Andy into the baby seat on the counter. "I came out here a couple days after you were put in Pinehaven, not sure what I was going to find. When I saw all the baby furniture... I knew we hadn't been together and you weren't the type to—" Baxter paused and threw an accusing glance at Grady "—sleep around, so I just figured...well, I just thought it was a sign of how sick you were. I had all the furniture put in storage so you wouldn't have to deal with it when you came home from the hospital."

Jenna took the bottle from the microwave, shook it vigorously, then tested it on the inside of her wrist. "You didn't tell my father what you'd found?"

"I didn't want to worry Lamar. He was already just sick about the way you seemed to have fallen apart."

Jenna sighed. Shaking her head in mute dismay, she unstrapped Andy, picked him up and began giving him his bottle.

Deciding finally that Baxter was an idiot but no threat, Grady stepped back. Baxter got up. "I'm sorry, Jenna." He crossed to her side.

"I want Andy's things back," Jenna said. To Grady's surprise, she didn't seem angry. Just resigned. Accepting. He wondered at her ability to forgive the guy so easily. In her place, Grady knew hell would have frozen over before he'd had a kind word to say to the guy.

"I have surgery tomorrow morning, but I'll make arrangements to have someone bring the baby's things back first thing," Baxter promised. He studied his ex-wife. Grady could see the guy still cared about Jenna a lot. And though he didn't like Baxter's continuing affection for his ex, he understood it. Jenna would be a hard woman to let go.

"You really are okay?" Baxter asked Jenna gently.

Jenna released a tremulous sigh. "I will be," she announced, "as soon as I figure out who kidnapped Andy."

Baxter looked at Grady accusingly. "Are you sure it's no him?" Baxter asked Jenna suspiciously.

Jenna rolled her eyes. Deciding Andy had had enough, she put him up on her shoulder and patted him on the back "Grady didn't know about the baby, either, Baxter," Jenna said.

"That must mean you're not very involved with him," Baxter guessed triumphantly.

The hell she's not, Grady thought, but figuring that sentiment could best be expressed later, in private, Grady kept his counsel.

"I love you, Jenna," Baxter said softly. "I never stopped I know we had a lot of problems—"

Now Grady felt like a peeping Tom.

"Baxter, please," Jenna said wearily. When Andy burped, she put him down in her arms and began feeding him his bottle again. "We've been over this."

"We've talked about how you feel," Baxter corrected. "Not how I feel. And I'm still in love with you, Jenna. I always will be."

Grady had had enough of *The Young and the Stupid* for one day. "Okay, time to go." Grady grabbed Baxter by the arm and shoved him toward the door.

"Jenna, don't let him do this," Baxter said, casting her a beseeching look over his shoulder.

"He's right," Jenna said. "It is time for you to go."

"You're not going to respond to what I told you?" Baxter asked incredulously.

Jenna sighed. "Baxter, your wanting me to love you doesn't make it so."

Baxter's face tightened into a mask of displeasure. "We're not through here, Jenna," he said. He stormed out.

Grady followed him.

When he came inside minutes later and set the alarm, Jenna was not in the kitchen. He followed the sounds of soft, feminine, slightly off-key singing and found Jenna in the living room. She was seated in the rocking chair, Andy on her lap.

"He's gone," Grady said.

Jenna nodded but said nothing in response. Grady thought she had never looked more beautiful than she did at that moment, with her hair all loose and flowing, her baby, their baby, cradled lovingly in her arms. He wanted to go to her and take her and the baby in his arms and tell them both he was sorry he hadn't been there for Andy's birth. He wanted to cuddle Andy for a while, and then put the baby to bed, and take Jenna to bed. But none of that was about to happen tonight, Grady realized grimly, reading the hands-off body language Jenna was giving out.

He strolled into the room and took a seat on the end of the

sofa. He figured if she had a gripe, she might as well voice it. "You're angry with me, aren't you?"

Again, Jenna shrugged and said nothing.

Frustrated that she was not talkative for once in her life, Grady clasped his hands loosely between his spread thighs and leaned closer. "Look, so I was a little rough with your ex," he began conversationally. "He deserved it for hiding in your bushes and scaring you half to death."

"It's not that," Jenna said softly. She smiled at Andy, who was gazing at her adoringly with his big, baby blue eyes. She continued to rock back and forth serenely.

Grady waited. When no other explanation was forthcoming, he said, "Then what is it?"

Jenna lifted her head. Her dark green eyes lasered into his. "It's the way you acted when he was here."

Grady felt the impact of her steady gaze like the punishing lash of a whip. He didn't know why, but suddenly he was in deep trouble here. "What do you mean?"

Jenna arched a slender brow. "Proprietary. Like you *owned* me or something."

Now that she mentioned it, that was the way he had acted. It was also the way he felt. Now that he knew the baby was in all probability his and Jenna's baby, Grady had a lot at stake. It annoyed him to find that Jenna wasn't more grateful to have him close by, to save her from jerks like Baxter. His mouth tightened as he felt his grip on his temper loosen, but he kept his voice calm. "I was protecting you."

In the soft light of the living room, her classically beautiful features—the high, jutting cheekbones, the deep-set eyes, the feminine line of her jaw—were more pronounced. As was her displeasure with him. "Did it ever occur to you I don't need protecting?" she said.

"The events of the last couple of weeks say otherwise," Grady disagreed.

Jenna glared at him, stood and handed him his son. "Here," she said tightly. "You can rock Andy to sleep."

She marched to the door, her full skirt swirling enticingly around her knees.

Grady followed her to the coatrack. "Where are you going?" he demanded.

Jenna shrugged on her coat and lifted the hair away from her neck. It spilled across her collar in glorious strawberry blond waves. "Out."

Grady shifted the warm bundle in his arms a little higher. He didn't like feeling like a jealous spouse, but that was exactly what he felt like. "At this time of night?" He regarded her with disapproval.

Jenna shrugged and refused to meet his eyes. "I've got some things to work out," she said evasively.

Grady had the sudden impression he wasn't just being held at arm's length, but pushed away. For good. The thought was damn disturbing, particularly since he hadn't figured he'd ever want to be fenced in by marriage or any other relationship-style commitment again. And yet here he was, wanting Jenna back in his bed, and in his life, for good. What kind of spell had she put on him? And what did it matter anyway, as long as it lasted? "Jenna—" His voice was soft, conciliatory.

Her reaction was not. Her fists clenched in front of her, she spun toward him in a drift of lavender perfume. "If I stay here, Grady, I'm going to explode."

Grady knew how he'd like an argument like this to end— in bed. But he couldn't engineer a solution like that for several reasons, a wide-awake Baby Andy being the least of them. When they were together again, and he was more sure than ever that they would be together again one day soon, he wanted it to be because she wanted to be with him. Because she couldn't live without him. Or at least didn't want to. "I don't like this," he said, hoping his displeasure would have some effect on her.

Again, she disappointed him. "Tough." She sent him a beleaguered smile that mirrored the turbulent emotion in her eyes. "Life is full of things we don't like, Grady Noland. Ask me. I'm an authority on that!"

JENNA DUG HER HANDS in her pockets and walked the inside fence along the property line. She had been right. The cold air and solitude had been exactly what she needed.

It had been an upsetting few days. An upsetting couple of weeks. Hell, an upsetting year. But having her very own baby to hold and love had made all the heartache worthwhile. If only things had stayed that simple. If only she had been able to go through with the "adoption" of Andy as she had planned, then everything would have been all right. But that hadn't happened, and right now things weren't all right. She still hadn't discovered who had kidnapped Andy or why. Worse, Grady now knew about his son and was behaving possessive.

Maybe that wouldn't have been so bad had Grady believed her story from the very first, but he hadn't. She had bared her soul to him, kissed him like she meant it, trusted him enough to ask him to help her find the kidnapper, and all for what? Grady had listened to her dutifully but he still had plenty of doubts about her. So the bottom line was he still didn't trust her. Never had. Probably never would. Just like Baxter hadn't trusted her when they'd been married. She couldn't live like that again. She just couldn't.

The only thing to do was go back to her original plan and stick to it. She would adopt Andy and continue on as a single mother, Grady or no Grady.

JENNA DIDN'T COME BACK for almost an hour. When she did, her cheeks were flushed with the cold. Her eyes were no less fiery, but she seemed less physically tense than when she had left. And yet there was something different about her, Grady couldn't help but note. Something aloof. It was as if she'd made up her mind about them, and there was no them. Not any longer.

She inhaled the scent of broiled meat and piping hot fries. "You've been cooking."

He nodded. "We didn't get around to eating earlier. I figured you must be famished." Grady motioned to the fax machine in her office. "You had several messages come in while you were gone. One from Switzerland, another from Ethiopia, one from Panama."

She slipped off her coat and walked over to her fax machine. Grady followed her. "Where did you go?"

Jenna glanced up from the fax she was reading, her green eyes deliberately expressionless. Grady had never seen that particular look in her eyes before. He wasn't sure he liked it.

"Is this an inquisition?" she asked.

Grady knew he was supposed to say no. "Maybe," he said.

Their glances held for another long moment. She passed on the opportunity to answer his question and returned to her reading. "Where's Andy?"

"In his crib upstairs. I figured it was time to put him down for the night."

Jenna finished reading her faxes and put them on her desk. "Time for us all to be down for the night," she said. "But dinner first. Did you already eat?"

"I thought I'd wait for you," Grady said.

Jenna looked like she had just found out she hadn't won the lottery, but she made no comment. He followed her down the hall past the stairs to the kitchen. Although he was careful to give her the correct amount of physical space, he couldn't help but track the provocative sway of her hips beneath the swirling wool skirt. With every graceful, feminine step she took, he felt the desire coil more tightly inside him. The depth of possessiveness he was feeling toward Jenna was new to him. He wasn't sure he liked it. "I think you should stay away from Baxter," he said.

Jenna looked as if she had been expecting that. She shook her head in silent bemusement, then sashayed to the refrigerator to get herself a bottle of light beer. "Why?" she quipped as she set her drink on the table, then followed it with mustard, pickles, mayonnaise, catsup, lettuce, tomatoes, onions and cheese. "This may come as news to you, Grady, but it's not up to you to decide whom I see or don't see."

But it was up to him to protect Jenna, Grady thought, whether she wanted him to or not. "Baxter's still in love with you."

Jenna shut the refrigerator with her hip. "So he said," she replied mildly.

"You're not concerned?"

Jenna shrugged. "Having an ex who won't let go seems to be a problem we share," she said, spearing Grady with a laser look. "Besides, with Baxter, it's a matter of ego more than anything else. He's had women falling over him for so long he can't believe that someone might actually not want to be with him."

Grady frowned. Jenna's blasé attitude disturbed him. He removed the plates warming in the oven and carried them to the table. "As far as I'm concerned, he's still a suspect in the kidnapping," Grady continued.

Jenna regarded Grady cautiously. Her conflicting feelings on the subject were reflected in her dark green eyes. "Baxter just told us he didn't do it."

Grady watched her pull up a chair. He got out a beer for himself, twisted off the cap and sat down beside her. "People lie, Jenna, sometimes very convincingly."

Jenna was silent a moment, thinking. Finally, she shook her head. "I know how it looks, but...I have to trust my gut feeling. You're off the mark here, Grady."

Grady paused, perplexed, wanting nothing more at that moment than to take her in his arms. "Why are you defending him when he's already proved himself to be a threat to you and our baby?"

"Our baby?" Jenna interrupted. "You just said our baby, Grady!"

Grady felt the blood move into his face. Jenna was right—he had. It wasn't like him to consider anything a fact before it was a fact. That went contrary to everything he had ever learned in the course of his police work. He had better watch his step here. Clearly, his feelings for Jenna were getting in the way of his deductive reasoning.

"You're getting off the subject, Jenna," Grady reprimanded sternly. "The man convinced your father to put you in a mental hospital."

"He did what he did regarding Pinehaven and the baby furniture because he thought I'd gone off the deep end and he was trying to help, as best he knew how. I don't know who kidnapped my baby, but as soon as I saw Baxter's stunned reaction to Andy tonight, I knew it certainly wasn't Baxter," Jenna said firmly. "And the more I think about it, the more I know I'm right. Baxter just would not hurt me that way.

"Clarissa, on the other hand, is another matter," Jenna continued, picking up steam. "Clarissa not only has a motive for kidnapping Andy, she's manipulative and devious enough to try to carry it off. I think if we have a suspect here, Grady, it's Clarissa, and nothing you can say or do is going to convince me otherwise."

Grady sat back, his arms folded across his chest. "Just so you know, Jenna," he said softly, "I'm checking out Clarissa's documents, too. I faxed copies to my partner while you were out on your walk."

"Oh." Jenna flushed and fell silent. "Does that mean you believe me when I say Andy is our baby?" she asked softly, her jade eyes shining with new hope.

Grady wanted to tell Jenna yes and put her mind at ease, but he couldn't, not without going against every bit of training and experience he'd ever had. "It means," Grady warned cautiously, and watched the hope leave her eyes as suddenly as it had filtered in, "that I'm taking nothing at face value." He knew what he hoped for—that Andy was his baby and Jenna's. But he couldn't, wouldn't, let himself count on that prematurely. "I'll know what the truth is only after all the facts are in."

Chapter Eight

"Do you have any idea what time it is?"

Jenna glanced up at the sound of the low, husky voice. Grady stood framed in the doorway of her office. He was dressed in a pair of jeans and the light blue oxford cloth shirt he'd had on the day before. His mane of shaggy brown hair was mussed from sleep, and his ruggedly handsome face was lined with a day's growth of golden brown beard. He looked like he had just tumbled out of bed, and wanted nothing more than to tumble right back into it again—with her this time. Jenna's heart skipped a beat at the realization of how much Grady still desired her.

But his desiring her again didn't mean he would have her, she thought. Getting involved with Grady would be dangerous, too dangerous for her blood. And she didn't want to be hurt again, not by Grady, not by anyone. "It's three in the morning," Jenna replied. "Go back to bed, Grady."

Grady unfolded his lanky frame from the doorway and stalked closer, his sock-clad feet moving soundlessly on the plushly carpeted floor. He lifted a stack of files from the corner of her desk and sat down. Both feet flat on the floor, his long legs slanting in front of him, he folded his arms across his chest and probed her face with a relentlessly searching glance. "Not until you tell me what you're doing up."

She reached for the telephone receiver and said matter-of-factly, "I'm making some phone calls to Switzerland."

Grady's hand covered hers before she could so much as lift the receiver off its cradle. "Couldn't you do that in the morning?"

Her pulse racing at his nearness, Jenna withdrew her hand from the warmth of his. "I won't be here in the morning." Needing suddenly to put some distance between herself and Grady, she stood and stalked to the file cabinet. She yanked open the drawer, then paused as she saw the red satin heart-shaped box inside.

"What is it?" Grady said, already sliding his hips off her desk.

"Nothing." Tired of Grady nosing into every aspect of her life while granting her no more trust than he would the suspect in one of his cases, Jenna shut the drawer. She was pretty sure, from the handwriting on the envelope and the placement of the gift, that she knew who the present was from, but she would wait to open it in private.

"Nothing, my foot." He stalked past her.

She caught his arm, delaying him. "My files are none of your business."

Grady continued moving, but made no effort to disengage her fingers from his arm. "Until we figure out who kidnapped our baby, Jenna, everything around here is my business."

Determined to hold at least part of her life sacred from his relentless prying, Jenna dropped her hold on his arm and scrambled to stand in front of him. He merely smiled, reached behind her and pulled open the drawer. He frowned at the Valentine's Day candy box and unopened greeting card.

"Baxter," Grady supposed grimly.

"Baxter or no, it's none of your business!" Jenna announced defiantly. Trapped between the half-open file drawer and Grady's tall, lanky body, she was incredibly aware of him, throbbing all over.

"I beg to differ, babe. We're rounding up suspects here. Whoever sent that gift might be one of them." Leaning in

closer, he pulled both items from the drawer. Their chests
were so close they touched. Jenna felt another tingle of desire
move through her.

"It's not from Baxter," Jenna said. She crossed her arms.
"Satisfied?"

"No. If it's not from Baxter, then who is it from?" Grady
asked as he lifted both items over her head.

Jenna remained stubbornly silent. Looking just as dis-
pleased with her as she felt with him, he held the card out to
her. "Open it."

Jenna glared at him. Grady was way off base, but it
wouldn't do any good to tell him so. "This is how it started
with Baxter, too, Grady. Little demands that soon escalated
into larger ones. I am not falling into the trap of having a
man control my life again, so when I feel like opening it, I
will, and not one instant before then."

Grady's sensual lips thinned authoritatively. He wasn't
used to having his orders disregarded and he was fast losing
patience with her. "Last chance, Jenna."

Jenna mocked him with a look. "No, this is your last
chance. You're dreaming if you think I'm going to let you
order me around in my own office!"

He shrugged, not the least bit perturbed by her lack of
cooperation. "Fine, have it your way. Then I'll open the
card." He started to tear the seal.

Jenna grabbed the card from his hands. "Like hell you
will! It's my card!"

He merely quirked a brow, letting her know with just a
look that he'd already made up his mind, too, and if it came
down to a physical struggle he'd win.

She held the card to her chest. Her fingers were trembling.
She really did not want to get into a physical tussle with
Grady, nor did she want to set a precedent with Grady like
she had with Baxter by just giving in. Irritated because Grady
could make her so edgy and angry all at once, Jenna lifted
her chin. "I'll open it when I want to, and I don't want to
right now."

Grady backed her up. The edge of Jenna's desk collided with her hips. He leaned in. Jenna leaned back, but could go nowhere. She found herself bent backward over her desk. His legs were suddenly pressed against hers. Jenna had to put a hand out behind her to steady herself and keep from falling.

Grady tossed the candy aside, put a palm on either side of her and braced his weight against the top of her desk. His slate-blue eyes roved her upturned face, dropped lower, to linger at the open vee of her satin pajamas. "What are you hiding, Jenna?"

Jenna clutched the unopened card to her chest. The hand she'd put behind her was beginning to tremble with the strain of holding her weight in such an awkward position. "My private life."

Grady's sable brow quirked again. His eyes radiated interest, but no pleasure. "Meaning what? You have another beau?"

Jenna raised a threatening knee to the inside of his thigh. He stepped back defensively. She straightened quickly and did an about-face. Grabbing both card and candy, she sat down, laid them both across her lap, scooted her chair forward until her legs were completely beneath the desk. Her back to Grady, she began typing once again.

She half expected another tussle. Grady merely watched her get comfortable, then sauntered across the room. He stretched out on the sofa with lazy disregard for her presence. As he wedged a throw pillow beneath his head, his shirt fell open even more, revealing more of his sinewy chest with the golden skin and whorls of golden brown hair. Jenna recalled with disturbing clarity how it had felt to run her hands over the solidness of that chest, how it had felt to cuddle against him and wantonly string kisses from throat to navel to...

Damn. She was never going to get any work done with him here, and she had a ton of work to do. She stopped typing but didn't turn to face him. Instead, she continued to regard him out of her peripheral vision. "Now what are you doing?" she demanded tensely.

Grady smiled at her and got even more comfortable in the deep cushions of the floral sofa. "Waiting for you to finish your letter." He turned slightly on his side and propped his head on his hand. "Then we're going to wrestle for that card."

Jenna's pulse points pounded at the heat she heard in his voice. "We are not."

He grinned at her and continued to regard her like a predator stalking his prey. "Wanna bet?"

Jenna released a pent-up breath. She swiveled her chair around so that she was facing Grady directly. "You know I divorced Baxter for this very reason. He was too controlling."

"Lucky for me we're not married then, isn't it?" Grady bounded up from the sofa and closed the distance between them with surprising swiftness. Clamping his hands on the chair arms on either side of her, he leaned down so their faces were almost touching. "Open the card, Jenna," he said softly.

Jenna wished he didn't smell so damn good, like sleep and bedclothes and warm winter nights. She wished she wasn't so familiar with the scent of his spice and sandalwood cologne, or the slightly rougher, very male texture of his skin.

"Come on, Jenna," Grady continued to provoke. He pressed a string of kisses across the crown of her head.

Jenna held herself perfectly still. She knew what he wanted. He wanted her to fight him off so he would have an excuse to tussle with her, but she wasn't going to give it to him, just like she wasn't going to open that card.

"Forget me opening the card, Grady," she said flatly.

"Why?"

Because if I do, I'll have let you seduce me into doing what you want. And that was just as bad, in her mind, as being bullied or coerced into something she didn't want to do.

"Okay." Grady moved away from her with a suddenness that surprised her. He bounded behind her swivel chair toward the phone. "I'll call your father and ask him who the candy might be from. And if he doesn't know, I'll ask Baxter. And if he doesn't know—''

Jenna stayed where she was, knowing he expected her to back down any moment. ''Then what?'' she taunted, lounging in her chair.

Grady leveled his eyes on hers and kept them there, letting her know in a heartbeat that his determination to get at the truth was every bit as unshakable as hers was to hide it. ''Then I'll take out an announcement in the *Times*,'' he said softly. Unrepentantly.

Despite her resolve not to show any emotion save bravado, Jenna felt her lips thin into a line of absolute resentment. She had to decide whether to cut her losses and give in or carry this through to the bitter end.

She stared into his eyes that had never seemed so blue to her. She supposed it was the blue in his shirt bringing out the blue in his eyes. Either that, or the subdued light in the study. But the color of his eyes and her attraction to him were neither here nor there, she thought, as she released a beleaguered sigh. Getting caught up on her work was crucial, and she would never get caught up while Grady dogged her about something that had absolutely nothing whatsoever to do with the kidnapping he was investigating.

''You're going to feel awfully silly for being so suspicious when you see who this is from,'' Jenna predicted as she tore open the card.

Grady looked at the signature inside, then looked again. ''Nanny Beth?'' he read incredulously. ''Why would your nanny give you a Valentine heart full of candy?''

Jenna reached for the candy heart and tore open the seal. ''Just to be sweet. She knew it had been a rough year for me.'' Jenna popped a chocolate in her mouth. It had a gooey caramel center. She handed the box to Grady. He selected one, too.

''Because you were a single mother?'' Grady asked.

''And because I felt I had to hide out,'' Jenna said. In retrospect, she saw that she had been wrong about that, that

with time she probably could have gotten her father to understand her decision, if not actually support her in it. But at
the time she hadn't wanted to take the risk that her father
would track Grady down with a shotgun and try to make him
do the decent thing. But someone had, anyway, she thought.
And they were no closer to discovering who had taken Andy
from his crib.

"It never occurred to you to go back with Baxter?" Grady
asked. "He probably would have remarried you, you know,
despite the pregnancy."

"Probably," Jenna agreed. She lifted a cup of coffee to
her lips. It was ironic. She and Grady had made a child together, but they still knew so little about one another's pasts.
Maybe it was time that changed, she thought. Maybe if he
knew more about her, maybe he would know she was telling
him the truth, and nothing but the truth. Certainly, if he was
less suspicious of her, the next few days would be easier on
them all.

She searched through the box and found one that looked
like a chocolate-covered almond. "But I didn't want that."

Grady helped himself to more candy, too. He studied her.
"Why not?"

"Because our marriage had already failed once," Jenna
explained.

"What went wrong?" Grady moved to the small sideboard
in the corner and helped himself to some of the coffee Jenna
had fixed earlier.

"In a word, everything," Jenna replied as she got up to
get another cup of coffee.

Grady waited until she had finished pouring her coffee,
then tangled his fingers with hers and led her over to the sofa.
He sat in one corner. Jenna sat in the other. "How did the
two of you meet?" he asked.

Jenna lifted her coffee cup to her lips and took a sip. "We
met through my work for the Children's Rescue Foundation.
He volunteered his services for some needy children in South
America. I was there during the month he did the surgeries.

I saw what a dramatic difference his skills made in those children's lives, and I fell a little in love with that. We had a whirlwind courtship and married as soon as we got back to the States. And it was then that things began to go sour between us.''

Grady downed half his coffee in a single gulp, then rested his cup on his thigh. ''Sour how?'' Grady asked gently.

''Baxter expected me to be a figurehead boss, not a real one, at the Foundation. When I refused to devote all my time to being a doctor's wife, he became very suspicious. He accused me of not wanting to stop working because I was secretly having flings with doctors and lawyers and professionals I met around the world in the course of my work. I figured that he would relax as time went on when he saw this truly was not the case. So I tried never to chide him when he called me in the middle of the night, or popped up unexpectedly to surprise me when I was on a business trip, or embarrassed me in front of family or friends or staff with some of his detective-style questions. But when a whole year passed and he was still as suspicious and controlling as ever, I knew that he wasn't ever going to change. I couldn't live that way, knowing my own husband didn't trust me. And I also knew,'' Jenna continued sadly, ''that I wasn't in love with him and I never had been. I had only been in love with what he'd done for the children. Despite everything, Baxter is a selfless humanitarian and a wonderful physician. So I asked him for a divorce.''

Grady finished the rest of his coffee in a single draft. ''How'd he take it?''

''He was angry at first—but then he just kind of dug in where he was. You know, maintained his ties with my family. Kissed up to my dad and all that.''

Grady got up to get himself another cup of coffee. When he returned, he didn't sit in the opposite corner of the sofa, but in the middle. ''And your dad bought it?''

Jenna pulled her bent knee in toward her body, so it would no longer be touching Grady's thigh. ''My dad wanted me to be married and have a family. He knew Baxter was a good man.''

Jenna went to the coffeemaker. She thought about having another cup, but decided she was too wired already. She turned the coffeemaker off, put her cup aside, and because it was the only other truly comfortable place in the office to sit and still have a quiet conversation with him, she went to join Grady on the sofa once again.

Grady waited until she had curled up in her own corner of the sofa cross-legged. ''Did your father know you weren't in love with Baxter?''

She frowned as she traced a mindless pattern on her bare ankle. ''My father has always felt I was far too picky when it came to men.''

Grady's eyes followed her index finger as it strayed to the tip of her ballerina slipper and slipped idly beneath the edge. ''Picky how?'' he persisted.

''I just want the guy I'm with to be perfect.''

''And if he's not?''

She looked up at Grady and offered him a deadpan grin. ''Then I lose interest.''

''Maybe you just haven't loved the right guy,'' he teased, but there was an underlying seriousness to his twinkling gaze that suddenly had her senses in an uproar.

Jenna struggled to retain control of her soaring emotions. ''And who would the right guy be, Grady?'' she shot back facetiously, aware her heart was pounding again in a way that had nothing to do with the caffeine she had just consumed. ''You, I suppose?''

''Maybe,'' Grady allowed, still holding her gaze.

Jenna drew a shaky breath. It was time to end this intimate little early-morning tête-à-tête. It was a tête-à-tête like this that had gotten her into trouble in the first place, she thought.

She bounded up from the sofa. ''Maybe not.''

Grady bounded up right after her. He caught her arm and pulled her gently around to face him so they were standing toe-to-toe, face-to-face. "I'm sorry you had to spend Valentine's Day the way you did," he said softly, meaning it.

Jenna suddenly found she had to swallow or not breathe. She drew a shaky breath. "I got over it," she said.

"Yeah, I know," Grady drawled. "The question is, will you get over this?" He lowered his head and delivered a gentle kiss. "Will either of us, Jenna?"

He kissed her again. Her lips parted beneath the pressure of his as his tongue swept her mouth in long, sensuous strokes. His hands circled her tightly and pressed her more fully into his arms until Jenna's whole body was alive, quivering with urgent sensations unlike any she had ever felt. She moaned and allowed him to press her closer. The satin of her pajama top was little protection against the hardness of his chest. Her nipples beaded and ached as he crushed her closer. Her abdomen felt liquid and weightless, her knees weak. And where he pressed against her so intimately, hardness to softness, there was a tingling ache. It had been so long, she thought. Too long.

Jenna wanted so badly to give in to him, to the desire seductively inundating them both. But even as he kissed her again, dipping his tongue into her mouth with practiced, honeyed strokes, she knew she couldn't give in and still keep her wits about her. And for Andy's sake, for her own, she needed to maintain her ability to think straight, to reason, to act like a responsible adult, not a lovestruck teen.

Her mind made up, she planted a hand firmly on his chest and pushed. Grady lifted his mouth immediately—well, almost immediately, she thought as her lips continued to burn and tingle and crave even more of his plundering kisses. She stepped back, aware she wasn't the only one trembling like a leaf in the wind this time. So, she thought with distinctly feminine if somewhat irrational satisfaction, Grady was having trouble dealing with his feelings, too. Good. She hoped he ached all night, because she was certainly going to!

"You insist on pushing the limits, don't you?" she asserted angrily, all too aware how close she had come to going to bed with him again. One more kiss, one touch of his hand to her breast, and she would have been his...maybe not for all time, but for tonight. Jenna groaned. It was all she could do to keep from burying her face in her hands. When would she ever learn?

Grady wrapped a lock of her hair around his fingertip. "Pushing limits is my specialty," he teased without one iota of remorse.

As if I didn't know, Jenna thought morosely. Grady's bad-boy sensuality was a big part of what had attracted her to him in the first place, that and the compassion and tenderness she saw in his eyes. But bad boys who didn't believe in marriage did not make good fathers, she told herself sternly, and Andy needed a father. "I'm not getting involved with you again," Jenna insisted flatly, meaning every word more than ever.

Grady merely looked at her. "We'll see."

"HEY, JENNA, is this an okay time?" Steve Jackson asked as he handed her the morning paper.

"It's fine." Jenna greeted her father's young assistant warmly. At age twenty-six, he was several years younger than her. Lamar had hired the MBA grad straight out of Penn's prestigious Wharton School of Business, and Jenna knew it had been one of the smartest things her father had ever done. Steve was nice and easygoing, with a decidedly optimistic outlook on life and a can-do attitude Lamar appreciated. Steve never complained about having to work overtime. No chore was too big or too small for him. On the few occasions Jenna had visited the corporate offices to see her father, she had enjoyed hanging out with Steve precisely because he was so easy to get along with. "What brings you all the way out here?" she continued.

"Your dad wanted me to check up on you before I went to work this morning, to make sure you were all right and everything."

"Well, as you can see, I'm fine," Jenna said.

Steve turned as an Acme Furniture Storage truck pulled into the drive behind his black Porsche. "You expecting them?"

Jenna frowned thoughtfully. "Baxter said he'd return Andy's baby furniture today."

Steve whistled long and low. "Yeah, I know. He sure didn't waste any time, did he?"

Jenna ushered Steve inside. She took his navy trench coat and hung it on the coatrack, then led him to the kitchen and poured him a cup of coffee. "How did you know about that?"

Steve bent in front of the baby swing and tickled Andy under the chin. "Baxter came to see your dad last night."

"Before or after he'd seen me?" Jenna asked.

"After. Anyway, I happened to be there. Your dad and I had been working on the advertising budget for the rest of the year. So I heard part of the story," Steve said. Straightening, he helped himself to a Danish and took a big bite. "I have to tell you, Lamar was pretty hot about Baxter breaking in here and putting all your baby furniture in storage without telling anyone what he'd done. He read Baxter the riot act for interfering that way."

Aware the baby swing was running out of steam, Jenna gave it another crank and a little push. Andy smiled and cooed with delight as the swing picked up speed. "How did Baxter take it?" Jenna asked, hoping there hadn't been a fight. She didn't need any more stress in her life right now.

"Well, surprisingly enough, Baxter agreed completely with your dad. He said he realized when he saw you and the baby last night that he had overstepped his bounds."

Which is why he's making good on his promise to have everything moved back so fast, Jenna thought, *because he wants me to know he is serious about making amends.*

"Was that all Baxter said?"

"Well, actually he started to say something about Pine-haven—if that means anything to you—but then Lamar shushed him up and asked me to leave, so I did."

So Steve didn't know she had been in Pinehaven, Jenna thought. Ten to one, no one except Baxter and her father and now Grady did, either. Probably not even her brother, Kip...

The sound of the doorbell brought Jenna out of her thoughts. She returned to the front door, and the delivery men began bringing things in. For the next several minutes Jenna was completely occupied as she directed them where to take the crib and dresser and changing table. Ten minutes later, everything was in place more or less as it had been. Jenna signed for the things and then watched as the van took off. She had just shut the door again when Grady walked down the steps. Just out of the shower, he looked fresh and handsome and vital. He glanced at Steve Jackson, who was coming out of the kitchen with Andy in his arms. "He was a little tired of the swing, and started to fuss, so I picked him up," Steve said. "I hope you don't mind."

Jenna smiled at Steve. "Not at all." Aware Grady was regarding them both with an interested look, Jenna made introductions, finishing with, "Steve just dropped by to check in on me." She looked at Steve, who, with his precision-cut dark brown hair and Armani suit, looked every bit the successful young executive. "I know you just had a Danish, but if you'd like to stay for a proper brunch, I'd be glad to fix you whatever you like," Jenna finished.

Steve flushed with pleasure. "Normally I would take you up on that, but your dad needs me at a meeting with the franchisers at eleven-thirty, so I better hotfoot it back to Albany unless I want to be late. I'll tell him you're looking well, though. And so's the baby."

"Thanks, Steve, I'd appreciate it."

"And Jenna?" Steve paused. "I don't know a lot about what's been going on with you lately. Your dad just said you'd had a baby and were still trying to decide what to do about...well, you know, everything. I just want you to know I'm happy that everything seems to be going so great for you. You're a great gal, and the apple of your dad's eye, but then you know that.'' Steve hung his head shyly as he ran out of steam.

"Yeah, I guess I do." Jenna smiled, touched by Steve's boyish enthusiasm. She gently touched his arm. "And just so you know, my dad is always talking about how much initiative you have. He says he barely knows there's a problem before you're doing something to fix it. He really thinks you're doing a great job."

"I really try," Steve gushed as he struggled into his trench coat. "Your dad's given me a hell of an opportunity, putting me on the fast track to a vice presidency at Sullivan Shoes. I want to make sure he's getting his money's worth."

"Well, he is." Jenna showed Steve to the door. "Tell my dad when you see him I'll try to stop by to see him just as soon as I can."

"Do you know when that will be?" Steve asked as he paused in the portal. He shot a cautious look at Grady, who was standing by politely, taking in every word.

"Just as soon as I get things wrapped up here," Jenna promised. She said goodbye to Steve.

As soon as she shut the door, she turned to Grady. "That was completely unnecessary, you know."

"What?" Grady feigned innocence.

"The way you just checked out Steve Jackson."

Grady shrugged. "Until we discover who kidnapped Andy everyone who comes in and out of this house is a possible suspect."

Jenna shifted Andy to her other arm. She could tell by the way he leaned his head against her shoulder that he was getting sleepy again. She went up the stairs and into her bedroom and put Andy in the cradle. He settled onto his tummy with nary a whimper. Jenna covered him with a blanket and crept out again.

Andy was still quiet.

She took the baby monitor and went into the bath across the hall. "This is my house, Grady," Jenna said, picking up the argument where it had left off.

Grady followed her into the bath and with a wary glance across the hall shut the door. "And that's my son," he said flatly.

Jenna had been brushing her hair into smooth waves. She paused and put down the brush, feeling a crazy mixture of emotion running riot inside her. "You sound pretty sure about that, all of a sudden," she said.

Grady folded his arms and leaned against the door. "Shouldn't I be?" His eyes met hers. Once again, he was weighing everything she said and did.

Jenna turned to the mirror. "I am not having this discussion," she said.

"Yes, Jenna, we are."

"Right." She clipped the length of her hair in a gold clasp at the nape of her neck, spritzed on some perfume and headed for the door.

Grady continued to block her way. Evidently realizing that ordering her around didn't work, he tried a different tack. "Wait a minute, Jenna—"

"No," Jenna said hotly. She waved a lecturing finger beneath his nose. "You wait a minute. You have no claim on me."

Grady put a hand on her shoulder. "If Andy's my son—" he began calmly.

Jenna removed his hand like an odious scrap of garbage. "So it's *if* now?"

Grady scowled. "You know what I mean."

"Yes, I do, and that's what bothers me," Jenna snapped. Needing to do something, anything, except look into his eyes, she leaned toward the mirror and picked up her lipstick. "If Andy turns out to be your son, then you want to get serious with me," she said, pausing to outline her lips in muted peach. "And if he doesn't, I can just forget it."

Grady looked into the mirror and watched her rub her lips together to set the lipstick. "If he isn't my son, it means you've lied to me."

Her temper soaring, Jenna spun around to face him. "That's not the point."

Grady leaned in closer. "Then what is the point?" he demanded in a tone that was just as fiery.

Jenna stabbed a finger at his chest. "The point is you should already know the truth in your heart, Grady. We should never have had to go for blood tests or wait for results. The point is you should have known the truth the first moment the words came out of my mouth." She shook her head in silent recrimination. "The fact you didn't... Well, I just can't live that way!" Pushing him aside, she was out of the bathroom and down the stairs like a shot.

He followed her to the first floor. "Jenna, I am investigating a kidnapping here."

"So that makes it okay for you not to accept anything I tell you at face value? So that makes it okay for you to make a federal case out of a simple Valentine's Day gift? I can't live this way again, Grady, and damn it, I won't!" Jenna pulled a burgundy wool reefer from the front hall closet.

Grady jammed his hands on his hips. He regarded her with growing impatience. "I'm a cop, Jenna. This is how cops operate."

"And I'm a person, Grady," Jenna retorted, echoing his harsh, pragmatic tone. "A flesh-and-blood person, with feelings!"

He watched her shrug into her coat and stomp to the front door. His lips thinned in irritation. "Where are you going now?"

"Out!" Jenna grabbed her keys and purse.

"To do what?"

My own sleuthing, Jenna thought. Because while she had been working in the office last night, she had known there was someone else they had to investigate. Someone Grady knew nothing about. Someone close to her who might have taken Andy in a misguided effort to help her. "I have to send those papers I typed up last night by overnight mail," she told him, going into the office to pick up the packages she had prepared.

Grady frowned. "Can't you fax them?"

"No."

"Then wait a bit, until Andy wakes up, and I'll go with you," he suggested.

Jenna shook her head firmly. "No, Grady, I need to be alone." She had to figure out how she felt about Grady. She had to figure out why she couldn't seem to stop kissing or wanting or dreaming about him, when he was so clearly wrong for her. Grady stopped arguing abruptly and gave her a hard look. She had the uneasy feeling he knew she wasn't telling him the whole truth, but she couldn't worry about that now.

Chapter Nine

"You look great, Jenna," her brother Kip said the moment he stepped out of the Jetway at the Albany Airport, his beautiful, dark-haired wife at his side. "But what are you doing here? Leslie and I weren't expecting anyone to meet our plane." He paused, his expression turning slightly worried. "Everything's okay, isn't it?"

"Yes and no," Jenna said tensely. Looking at Kip in his Hawaiian duds and winter suntan, a lei still wrapped around his neck, she found it hard to believe that anyone as laid-back and fun-loving as her older brother could be devious enough to kidnap Andy, drop him at Alec's, then just leave on vacation. But Kip and Leslie had been the only ones in her family who knew about Andy's birth. And they had disapproved vigorously of her decision to go it alone, so that made them prime suspects. She just hadn't wanted to face it before, because she had always felt Kip was on her side. Jenna swallowed hard. "Can we talk?"

"Sure." Looking both bewildered and concerned, Kip and Leslie accompanied Jenna over to a deserted corner of the passenger area outside the gate. Jenna noted that Leslie looked just as tanned, happy and relaxed as Kip did. Part of her was very glad about that. She adored Leslie as much as Kip did.

"So how's Andy?" Kip whispered.

"Just fine."

Kip searched her face. "No second thoughts?" he asked.

Plenty, Jenna thought, but not about having the baby, rather getting involved with Grady. So what if the chemistry between them was still as potent as ever? So what if he not only seemed to hit it off with Andy right away, but was feeling downright protective of their baby? He didn't love her. Sure, he might be willing to marry her, for the baby's sake, but she didn't want to be married because Grady felt an obligation to Andy. She wanted Grady to marry her because he was wildly in love with her and couldn't live without her. Anything else just wouldn't do.

"You know, Jenna, our offer is still good," Leslie added. "Kip and I will—" She cast a furtive look over her shoulder to make sure no one was within earshot. "Well, you know..." she whispered.

"Adopt?" Jenna supplied dryly.

"Right," Kip said.

"It's not as if we'd be doing anything we hadn't planned, since Kip and I are already on the waiting lists at several private adoption agencies."

Jenna tucked a lock of her strawberry blond hair behind one ear. "I appreciate what you've offered to do. What I didn't appreciate was the kidnapping."

Kip paled. "What kidnapping?"

Briefly, Jenna explained, watching their faces all the while for the slightest show of culpability. To her frustration, she saw none. They seemed as in the dark about everything as she was.

"Why didn't you call us?" Kip interrupted as Jenna was describing the abduction. "Dammit, Jenna, you know that Leslie and I would have come home immediately!"

Relief flowed through Jenna as she realized she could still trust Kip and his wife, that she hadn't been wrong about them. She shrugged. "I thought about it as soon as I realized Andy wasn't in the house. But then I got to thinking that maybe you two had told Dad about the baby, because you were so worried about me, and that Dad had taken him."

"We told you that your secret was safe with us," Kip said.

"Even if we didn't approve of your decision to keep his birth secret," Leslie added.

"Furthermore, you know me better than that," Kip reminded her sternly. "I don't renege on promises." He paused. "I assume you found Andy...didn't you?"

"A few days ago."

Kip did a double take as that sunk in. "Not until then?" he said incredulously.

Jenna told them about Pinehaven. Kip scowled. "Just like Baxter to muddle things up with his self-centered misdiagnosis of the situation. When is that guy going to realize the two of you aren't still married?"

Soon, if Grady had anything to do with it, Jenna thought. "So you didn't tell Dad or anyone else—anyone at all—about Andy?" Jenna persisted.

"We swore we wouldn't." Kip looked at Leslie.

Leslie looked at Kip. "Not a soul," she said.

"And you had nothing whatsoever to do with the kidnapping," Jenna continued doggedly.

"Nothing at all," Kip and Leslie said in unison.

"Then I don't understand," Jenna said, throwing up her hands in frustration. "Who took Andy from his crib on Valentine's Day? Who left that note?"

Kip and Leslie shook their heads. Obviously, they were as baffled as Jenna was. "I wish I could tell you," Kip said. "But honestly, I haven't a clue."

Jenna looked up and swore.

"What is it?" Kip touched her arm.

Jenna covered her face with her palm. Her whole life was turning into a perfect proof of Murphy's law. "Don't look now, but here comes father and son."

It annoyed her to see how right the two males looked together, like a father and son should. Grady's shaggy, sable brown hair was wind-tossed, his cheeks and nose red with the cold, his blue eyes alert and furious. Yet he carried the two-month-old infant with the tender sensibility of an old pro.

And it was clear that Andy, who was bundled up in a powder blue snowsuit and matching knit infant cap, was happy to be with his dad. Wide-awake and flashing delighted smiles at everyone around him, Andy nestled contentedly in the cozy nook formed by Grady's shoulder, chest and arm.

Four long lazy strides later, Grady joined the group. His eyes lasered in on Jenna's. "Get your Federal Express package mailed?" he asked her mildly.

Ignoring his question, Jenna smiled back just as placidly and said, "I thought you and Andy were going to stay at the farm."

Grady quirked his sable brow. "Following you seemed more interesting."

"I'll bet."

Grady smiled at her. "Aren't you going to introduce us to the rest of the family?"

"How did you know who we were?" Kip asked with a frown.

"The pictures in Lamar's study," Grady explained.

"You must be very observant," Leslie said nervously.

"He's a detective with the Philadelphia police force," Jenna said, and Leslie paled even more. "So the only surprise would be if Grady wasn't observant."

"I trust you'll remember that in the future?" Grady said.

Jenna smiled tightly. "Don't count on it," she said tartly. Giving him no chance to retort, she went ahead with the formal introductions. "Kip, Grady Noland. Grady, my brother Kip and his lovely wife Leslie."

Grady nodded at Leslie and shook Kip's hand. "So you're the father," Kip said.

Grady gave Kip a man-to-man glance. "For the record, I would have been here a lot sooner had I just known about the situation."

As Jenna had feared, Kip warmed to Grady's innate sense of responsibility immediately. "Leslie and I tried to get Jenna to tell you," he confided.

"How long have you known?" Grady asked with a frown. Spying Jenna, Andy gurgled and strained toward her.

"Since New Year's Day," Kip admitted. "Leslie and I paid a surprise visit to the farm. We tried to get Jenna to tell Dad, but she refused."

Jenna took Andy into her arms. "Having two people in the family who were hysterical about my being a single mother was more than enough, thank you very much."

Grady raised a brow.

"What she means is we tried to talk some sense into her," Kip corrected. "She knows we've always wanted to adopt."

"Andy is my child, Kip," Jenna said softly, feeling proprietorial again.

"And mine," Grady said.

Jenna's eyes widened. Without proof, Grady was acting as if his paternity was a fact. Could it be that he was listening to his heart, just as she had always wanted him to? Hope swelled in Jenna's heart as Kip looked at them both.

"Then the two of you are going to work things out?" Kip ascertained hopefully.

Grady glanced at Jenna, his expression wary but determined. Jenna had the uneasy feeling that whatever happened, Grady was not going to be very open to compromise. "We'll try," Grady said. To Jenna's disappointment, he promised nothing more.

"YOUR'RE STILL ANGRY with me, aren't you?" Grady said as he fell into step beside her.

Jenna cuddled Andy a little closer. The pink in her cheeks grew even deeper. "You didn't have to follow me all the way to Albany."

Grady steered Jenna past the crowds gathering near the baggage claim and out the front doors of the airport toward the parking lot. The winter air was brisk, and instinctively he drew her and Andy close to his side. "How else was I going to know what you were up to?" Grady asked. That morning, before the furniture arrived, he'd been coming downstairs to tell her that the doctors at Pinehaven had substantiated every single word Jenna said. Not content to leave it there, Grady had then called the hospital accreditation board. A person there had confirmed that Pinehaven was a highly respected, if very private and very expensive, medical facility. Grady was almost ready to take Jenna's story as gospel truth—until she had lied to him about going in to Albany to mail a couple of Federal Express packages. Then his doubts had surfaced all over again. Clearly, she was the wiliest, most determined woman he had ever been around, and that included Clarissa.

Jenna struggled to turn the collar up on her long, jade green reefer with her free hand. "What makes you think I'm up to anything?"

Grady reached over and gave Jenna a hand with the part of the collar she couldn't reach. As he tugged it up, the back of his hand inadvertently brushed the softness of her cheek. Grady dropped his hand quickly. He didn't want to get distracted here. "The guilty look on your face when you saw I had followed you, for one thing," he said. She'd been panicked to see him there, and he'd known she felt she had something to hide.

Jenna's pretty lips set as she marched across the parking lot to her red Volvo station wagon. "I have nothing to feel guilty about, Grady."

Grady figured he would worry about getting his car later. Right now, he wasn't letting her out of his sight. He climbed in the passenger side while Jenna settled Andy in his baby seat. "*Au contraire,* babe. You've got plenty to feel guilty about, but we won't go into that now."

Jenna finished buckling Andy in. She smiled at him and closed the door. "And I suppose you think your conscience is completely free," she retorted as she settled behind the wheel.

"Freer than yours," Grady agreed. While Jenna started the car and adjusted the heater, he moved his seat back to the farthest position. His knees were still touching the dashboard in front of him. Stretching an arm out along the seat, he swiveled to face her, "Anything else you want to do while we're here in Albany?"

Jenna gave her total attention to her driving as she backed out of the space. "I need to stop by the store and pick up a few groceries. So I'll drop you at your car, wherever you parked it, and—"

"No need for that," Grady said cheerfully. "I'll just ride along with you and Andy."

"Look, you can't just leave it here."

"Sure I can," he said easily.

Jenna paused at the end of the row of cars, her foot on the brake. She looked at him in growing frustration. "I have a lot of errands to do here, Grady. I need to go to the dry cleaner and the office supply store, too."

"Then you'll need me along, won't you, in case Andy gets fussy?"

Jenna sighed, but was unable to dispute that.

"Don't worry. We can stop by to pick up my car before we head back to Hudson Falls. But then we'll need to be getting back to the farm."

It was Jenna's turn to narrow her eyes at him suspiciously. "Why?"

Grady didn't know how she could have forgotten—he sure hadn't. "The results of the blood tests are supposed to come in today," he reminded her softly. "Phil General said they'd call us there when they did."

"LISTEN, MR. TITLEMAN—" Grady said.

"Fikleman, Martin Fikleman," the lab technician corrected.

"Are you absolutely sure about what you just told me?" Grady asked. He felt numb with disbelief.

"Positive, Mr. Noland. The results came in today."

"Is it possible," Grady said slowly, "that there could have been some mistake? Some mislabeling or—"

"I handled the lab specimens myself," Martin Fikleman replied. "Everything was done very carefully."

"Then perhaps there was a mistake in the way the DNA test was conducted," Grady said, beginning to feel a little desperate. There had to be. Andy was his child. His and Jenna's. Not his and Clarissa's.

"There was no mistake," Martin Fikleman replied steadfastly. "DNA tests are very accurate at establishing paternity."

"Have you called my ex-wife?" Grady asked. God, this was a nightmare.

"I'm about to."

"What about Ms. Sullivan? Have you told her yet?"

"No, sir. If there's nothing else..."

"Actually, there is," Grady was quick to add. "You can fax me those results." Quickly, he read Martin the number of Jenna's fax machine. "I want to see them with my own eyes."

"Yes, sir," Martin said. "Right away."

Grady hung up the phone. He felt like he wanted to punch something. Why? Because he'd done the unthinkable and let his emotions get in the way of his investigation into Andy's paternity. He'd paid little attention to Clarissa's claims and given literally all his attention to Jenna's. Not because one woman's claims were more meritous, but because of what he wanted, deep down. And what he wanted was for Andy to be Jenna's child. Jenna's and his.

And after talking to the officials at Pinehaven, meeting Kip and Leslie and hearing how they'd seen Jenna's baby on New Year's Day, he had come to believe that Andy probably was his child. He had believed it so much that he had expected the DNA results to verify it.

"Grady? Is everything okay?" Jenna asked anxiously from the doorway to her office.

"Why wouldn't it be?" Grady sat back uneasily and folded his arms in front of him.

Without warning, Jenna turned white as a ghost. "I don't know." She wet her lips nervously. "You just don't look very happy."

"That's because I'm not," Grady muttered, his anger, his sense of betrayal building to typhoon force. Right now, he wasn't sure of anyone or anything. Both women had birth certificates for Andy, but Jenna's were in a false name, and Clarissa's were in her real name. Clarissa had gained ten pounds, whereas Jenna was just as willowy as always. Clarissa seemed exactly the type to desert a baby on a doorstep. Jenna seemed the antithesis. And yet Jenna had been the first to demand a blood test.

If the lab results were flawed, and Andy really was his and Jenna's child, as Jenna kept insisting, then Jenna was not only perfectly sane, she was acting just as fiercely protective as any mother would act in a similarly crazy situation. And Grady loved and admired Jenna for that.

If, however, the lab results were true...then Andy was not her child, but his child and Clarissa's. And if that was the case, then whose baby had Jenna been pregnant with last fall? And where was that baby now? Was it possible Jenna had lost her baby during a home birth, then gone into some sort of mental breakdown and kidnapped Clarissa's child? He'd seen cases like that before, where women grieving for a lost child stole into hospital nurseries and took a baby to replace the one they'd lost, not realizing what they were doing.

Was that what had happened to Jenna? And if it turned out it had, how would he cope with that?

"What's coming through on the fax?" Jenna asked as her machine began spitting out paper.

"Phil General is faxing us the results of the blood tests."

Jenna looked perplexed. "Why didn't they just tell you over the phone?" she asked.

"They did, but I want the results in writing and I want them in writing now," Grady said.

Jenna narrowed her eyes at him, swiftly came to her own heart-rending conclusions and beat Grady to the fax. Together, each holding one side of the fax paper, they stared down at the results. Jenna blinked. And blinked again. "It can't be,'' she breathed incredulously, looking as if she might faint at any second. ''It just can't be.''

Grady stared at her fiercely. She seemed genuinely stunned.

Almost immediately, Jenna's phone began to ring. His eyes still on her face, Grady beat her to the desk and snatched the receiver from its cradle. His frown deepened as soon as he heard who was at the other end of the line. ''Yes, we got 'em. No. *Don't come out here, Clarissa.* I know. Clarissa, listen to me. I'll take care of everything here. You just sit tight. Yes. First thing tomorrow.'' He hung up the phone and was caught off guard when Jenna flew at him and pounded on his chest.

''You bastard! You set me up!''

He grabbed her fists and held them tightly in front of him. ''If anyone was set up, it was me,'' he said angrily. Furthermore, he'd had about all the manipulating he could take, from both women.

''Like hell!'' Jenna struggled against his grip and swore hotly, ''I never conspired to take your child away from you.''

''Oh, didn't you?'' he shot back in a silky voice. ''Then what do you call never telling me you were pregnant?'' If, indeed, Jenna had been pregnant with his child.

Her soft body trembled against the length of his. Her dark green eyes widened as Grady backed toward the desk and sat down on the edge of it.

''So this is what—payback?'' She stepped between his spread knees. Her eyes glimmered with unshed tears that under any other circumstances would have broken his heart. ''You want me to know how it feels to have my child stolen from me, not once, but twice?'' She slammed her palms against his chest, then spun away from him.

She got as far as the outside of his knees when he grabbed her shirt and pulled her back to him.

''Wait a minute, Jenna.'' She lost her balance, and her gently rounded bottom made contact with the hardness of his thigh. ''I had nothing to do with the kidnapping,'' he said.

Her attention caught, Jenna folded her arms in front of her, and for a moment she stayed where she was. Her chin took on a stubborn tilt. "How do I know that?"

It irritated Grady to have his integrity questioned. "Because I said so."

"It seems to me I said this was my baby and you didn't believe me."

Grady decided it was altogether too cozy, having her sit on even half his lap. He lifted her away from him, stood and circled the desk. He offered her his back as he poured himself a swallow of brandy. "That was different."

"How?"

Grady lifted the glass to his lips and took a slow sip. His eyes on hers, he said bluntly, "There was factual evidence to the contrary."

Jenna regarded him cantankerously, refusing to back down. "Well, those blood tests you fixed are factual evidence, too." Her green eyes focused on his with absolute purpose. "I want them done again, Grady."

Grady was getting very tired of playing games. He was also very tired of hotly desiring a woman he had no business wanting. "For what purpose?" he asked wearily.

"For the purpose of ascertaining the truth!" Jenna said.

Grady tore his eyes from the flushed contours of her face and finished the brandy in his glass. "All right, we'll redo the lab tests," he relented, hoping, like Jenna, that they'd show a different result. Grady sighed and rubbed the back of his neck. "But if the second set of tests turns out the way the first set did, then I want something from you, too," he finished reluctantly.

"What?" Jenna's voice was soft again, and very wary.

Grady put his glass down and turned to look at her. Damn, but she was beautiful in the soft glow of the fading daylight with her hair all mussed, her eyes bright and sparkling. He didn't want to say it, but he knew for their own peace of mind they had to be sure. "Then I want you to agree to be evaluated by a psychologist friend of mine, Jenna. And don't look at me that way. I'm not doing this to punish you.''

Jenna blinked and looked like she was going to cry again. "Then why?"

Grady drew a deep breath. "Because I care about you, Jenna," he said softly, meaning it.

Jenna was silent a long, depressed minute. Grady kept quiet, too. He wished the lab tests had turned out differently. But they hadn't. And it was time he stopped being ruled by his emotions and let himself be guided by the facts. Finally, she swept a hand through her hair, tousling the already mussed strawberry blond waves. "Listen, Grady, if the results come out the same way—and there's no way that will happen if they're done correctly this time—then I'll do what you ask and get evaluated."

Grady breathed a sigh of relief. He had half expected Jenna to fight him on this. It surprised him she hadn't.

"FORGET IT, GRADY, I'm not going to agree to another blood test!" Clarissa shouted into the phone. "I agreed to the first one. I proved what I had to prove. Now I want you and the baby back!"

The baby, Grady thought, latching onto his difficult ex-wife's every word. Not *my* baby, but *the* baby. Warning bells went off in his head. Maybe Jenna was right to want another test. *Maybe there had been a mistake.*

"Look, I just want to be sure," Grady soothed.

"Why can't you be sure now?" Clarissa asked.

Because I want Andy to be Jenna's child, Grady thought. Because Jenna acted more like a mother than Clarissa ever would. And that, in turn, made him hope—against the current physical evidence to the contrary—that there had been a mistake in the DNA tests and that Andy might really be his child and Jenna's. "Are you going to cooperate or not?"

"No way," Clarissa said.

"Fine," Grady said. "Only Jenna and I will need to retest anyway, to insure her peace of mind."

Clarissa sighed. "You're really going through with a second DNA test?"

"Just to be sure, yes," Grady said.

"Then I'll be there, too," Clarissa promised reluctantly.

Grady hung up the phone to find Jenna watching him. "It's all arranged," he said. "Clarissa will meet us in Albany tomorrow. We'll have the blood tests redone first thing tomorrow morning, and shipped out from there to a university hospital in New York City that does DNA testing."

Jenna nodded her understanding. Her relief was palpable. Grady, too, began to relax. Dinner was surprisingly pleasant under the circumstances, and they shared the clean-up efforts. When Andy woke, needing to be changed and fed, Grady helped out with that, too. For once, Jenna seemed content to let Grady handle the bulk of the baby's care.

"Look, if you'll excuse me, I'm going to turn in for the night," she said with a polite smile. "Tomorrow's already shaping up to be a full day, and I'm really beat."

Grady was reluctant to see her go, but he understood. It had been a grueling day. And because Jenna had been up much of the previous night working, she hadn't had a lot of sleep. "I'll play with Andy until he's sleepy again, and then put him down for the night."

"Thanks." Jenny gave Grady a distracted smile, then turned and went up the stairs.

Grady had fun with Andy, but by nine Andy was fast asleep. Grady put him down for the night. Jenna's bedroom door was closed. He could hear her shower running in the bathroom beyond. He went downstairs. It was only nine o'clock. The night stretched out ahead of him endlessly.

Restless, he got up and went into the kitchen. For lack of anything else to do, he brewed a fresh pot of coffee and unloaded the clean dishes from the dishwasher. By the time he'd finished, he could hear Jenna moving around quietly on the second floor, and knew she was out of the shower and wasn't any sleepier than he was.

She just hadn't wanted to spend any more time with him.

He could understand that. He had upset her life terribly, just as she had upset his. Last week his life had seemed problem-free. This week it seemed like one big problem. But soon they would have all the answers. Grady would deal with the facts, make his decisions based on those facts, and go from there.

Chapter Ten

Jenna tiptoed down the back stairs, being careful to move soundlessly in the darkness. The blue numbers on the microwave clock flashed 1:37. She only had two more loads to go, and then she'd get the baby.

She didn't want to run away, but when she had learned of the results of the first DNA tests she had swiftly realized she had no choice. It didn't really matter anymore who was conspiring to take her child from her. She only knew someone was. And if she didn't get away from here—now—she would lose her baby again.

She set her suitcases down and opened the back door. Carefully, she moved her belongings across the threshold, then shut the door behind her. Tiptoeing out to the car, she set the two suitcases next to the crib, blankets, diapers and toys. Now all she had to do was get enough food from the kitchen to last for a few days, go in and get Andy, stop by the cash machine in Albany, and she'd be all set.

Jenna shut the trunk, then moved soundlessly across the drive, up the steps and into the kitchen. She was just reaching for the refrigerator door handle when the light flicked on. "Going somewhere?" Grady asked in a cool, deliberate tone.

Jenna sucked in a breath. She turned to face him, making her expression as normal as she could make it, considering that he was glowering at her in a completely uncivilized manner. "Grady. What are you doing up?" Jenna asked cheerfully.

Like Jenna, he was completely dressed in jeans, shirt and blazer, socks and shoes. Unlike Jenna, he did not have on a winter coat. *He* wasn't planning on going anywhere.

He reached behind her and helped her off with her coat. "I thought I might ask you the same thing," he drawled mildly. His sweeping glance covered her from head to foot. "What are you doing up at this hour?"

Jenna swallowed hard. Experience had taught her that emotional arguments with Grady usually ended in a few hot kisses, or at least a sexy clinch. She could not afford to indulge in a few hot kisses. She dropped her gloves and her car keys on the countertop beside her as if she hadn't a care in the world. "Well, actually it's a really funny story," she fibbed.

Grady folded his arms, the action serving only to more distinctly outline the hard, masculine contours of his shoulders and chest beneath his powder blue oxford cloth shirt. His gaze narrowed as Jenna stalked to the cupboard in an effort to buy herself time to come up with said story. Aware of his eyes sliding impatiently over her, she took out a glass, filled it with water from the tap and drank deeply.

"So go ahead," he prodded mercilessly. "I'd like to hear it."

Jenna blew out an uneasy breath and took another drink. "I had a dream." She paused and wet her lips. Pushing her hair away from her face with a careless sweep of her hand, she continued easily, "I guess I must've been sleepwalking—"

"You always sleepwalk fully dressed with a coat on and a suitcase in each hand?" Grady walked forward until he was standing right next to her. He extended one hand, palm flat, to the cabinet beside her as he waited for her answer.

Hellfire and damnation. Now what was she going to do? She had half the baby stuff loaded in the car. Andy was still upstairs. There was no way she could still run away, and no way she could pretend she hadn't been trying to run away...

Jenna wet her lips and tried to look suitably subdued. Telling herself it was imperative she keep a grip on herself, she forced herself to return Grady's level gaze with a flippant one of her own. "I'm a very efficient sleepwalker," she said.

Grady lifted his hand from the cabinet. "And you keep forgetting I'm a cop," he growled, as he stepped back slightly. "I can tell when people are lying to me. Admit it, Jenna." He gave her a once-over that was anything but comforting. "You were trying to run away just now. And you were planning to take Andy with you!"

Jenna ignored the way his dark, dangerous, oh-so-male presence was suddenly looming over her. "All right. I admit it." Jenna set her glass on the counter with a thud. "I was running away, but only because you left me no choice!"

"Really." His eyes steady, Grady sauntered closer and picked up the glass she had set down. He took a long, thirsty drink, draining it, and then fixed her with a laser-sharp gaze that let her know she was in trouble. "And how," he said politely, "do you figure that?"

Jenna refilled the glass, then took another gulp to calm her nerves. She forced herself to meet his eyes. "Someone screwed up those blood tests, Grady. The more I think about it, the more I'm convinced it wasn't an accident."

Suddenly, the troubled light was back in his eyes. Grady released an aggravated breath and shoved a hand through his tousled, sable brown hair. "Well, we'll know shortly, won't we?"

Jenna shrugged, wishing she had Grady's faith in the system. But in the last two plus weeks, the system had done nothing but betray her. "Maybe we will and maybe we won't." She blew out a weary breath. "If the DNA results were screwed up once, they could be screwed up again." The question was, Jenna thought, by whom?

He studied her with resigned disapproval, guessing accurately where this conversation was leading. He braced a hand on either side of her. "Jenna, if I wanted to take the baby from you, I have all the evidence I need right now to do just that."

"Then why don't you?" she demanded emotionally.

Grady leaned closer in a drift of brisk, masculine cologne. The shadow of his evening beard clung to his face, giving him an even more rugged look than usual. "Because I want to be sure I'm doing the right thing if and when it comes to that, and right now I'm not sure of anything," Grady said softly. "Except that you need me and will continue to need me until this whole mess is resolved."

Tears of gratitude and frustration pooled in her eyes. She willed them not to fall, but they fell anyway. Jenna turned her back to him and felt her shoulders graze the hardness of his chest. "I see."

He put his hands on her shoulders and wordlessly turned her gently around to face him. His eyes softened as they searched her upturned face. "Do you?" he asked quietly, abruptly looking and acting as vulnerable to the fates that were conspiring against them as she felt. "I want to help you, Jenna. I want to be here for you—if you'll let me."

When he looked at her like that, when he touched her so tenderly, it was all she could do not to fall in love with him. Hanging on to her self-preservation by a thread, she shrugged free of his light, detaining grip. "I'm tired of talking about this, Grady. I'm going to bed."

He stepped in front of her, barring her way to the stairs. The implacable look was back on his face. "Not alone, you're not."

Jenna's heart skipped several beats. She swallowed around the sudden dryness in her throat. This was the dangerous side of Grady, and the one she found most appealing. "Come on, Grady," she forced herself to say wryly. "Give me a break. I'm not going to try to run away again."

"I know you're not, because this time I'm not letting you out of my sight," he countered with a knowing smile. Hand beneath her elbow, he guided her toward the stairs.

Jenna dug in her heels and grabbed the banister. She refused to go up even one step. "This is ridiculous."

"I agree," he said mildly, extricating her hand from the banister, "but I didn't start it with my sleepwalking routine."

She studied him in exasperation. He was so sure he was doing the right thing! Her chest and throat so congested with emotion that she could barely breathe, Jenna backed up until she felt her spine graze the wall. She forced herself to cross her arms and lean against the wall insouciantly. Aware he, too, was plotting his next move, she angled her chin up another notch. "Well, if you trust me so little, I want to know why you don't just take the baby everyone already agrees is yours and leave." They both knew he would have no trouble overpowering her physically, and with the evidence they had gathered so far, he could probably get the law on his side, too.

Grady propped his hands on his hips and glared at her in aggravation. "Several reasons. One, you seem to need to be near Andy for your own peace of mind."

That was certainly true, Jenna thought.

"Two—" he patiently closed the distance between them "—I don't think it'd be a good idea for you to be alone out here."

Jenna didn't want Grady's protection. She wanted his unerring trust. She glowered at him stubbornly and wished he hadn't chosen to stand so close to her. "Why not?"

"Because you're going through a difficult time, that's why not," Grady explained.

"So why not foist me off on family and friends and take off?" Jenna continued, forcing herself to be logical and cool, despite the fact she could feel the warmth emanating from his tall, muscled body beckoning to her like a soft, cozy feather bed.

"Because I care about what happens to you," Grady said gruffly. "And my gut instinct tells me that you've got feelings for me, too."

His gut instinct was right. And that frightened her more

than the botched-up DNA tests. "I told you I wasn't looking for a relationship!" Jenna stormed. And particularly not with a man who was so much like her overly suspicious ex-husband. She couldn't go through life having to prove herself and her intentions at every turn.

"Well, that's too bad because, like it or not, I'm here. And I do care about you. As a friend. And maybe—" his voice lowered another notch as he planted a hand on either side of her "—more than that."

She saw the change in his eyes and drew back, shaken and confused. "How do you expect me to trust that?" His caring what happened to her, or the baby, hadn't helped her so far!

Grady gathered her into his arms and brought her against him. "Because it's real," he said softly, the passion in his low voice fueling her own. "Just like what we feel every time we look at each other is real, too. You can call it what-ever you want, Jenna." He lifted a hand to her hair and sifted through the silky strands. "You can label it or not. But it's there."

"That's not the way it is at all!"

"Tell me that after I've kissed you, and I'll believe you." Engulfing her with the heat and strength of his body from head to toe, he lowered his head and delivered a breath-stealing kiss.

Jenna meant to fight him, she swore she would, but at the first touch of his mouth to hers, she trembled, and a low moan issued from her throat. She tingled everywhere they touched and everywhere they didn't. A melting weakness shifted through her, further weakening her resolve. He felt so good against her, so warm and strong and solid. So male. And it had been such a long time since he had made love to her, she thought wistfully. Such a long, long time since she'd felt beautiful and wanted, soft and feminine.

Grady unbuttoned as he kissed. His mouth still moving ardently over hers, he divested her of her blazer and blouse, and then her bra. Jenna offered no assistance or resistance as his hands cupped her breasts. It was everything she could do to try to hold herself and her soaring feelings in check. But when he uttered a soft, male groan of contentment as he brushed her hardening nipples with his fingertips, then bent to kiss the taut, aching crowns, desire swept through her in powerful waves. "Oh, God, Grady," she whispered.

"I know," he said, taking her breasts greedily into his hands and backing her up against the wall again.

He was hard as a rock against her. Demanding. Coaxing response after response from her with his deep, drugging kisses. Dizzy, overcome with need and yearning, she tugged the shirt from the waistband of his pants and slid her hands up the solid warmth of his back. The world had narrowed to just the two of them. All she knew, all she wanted to know at that moment, was that his skin was smooth and hot to the touch, corded with muscle. And she wanted more, so much more than a few kisses and the feel of his hands on her breasts. She wanted to know all of him, just as she wanted him to know all of her. She wanted to feel connected to him again, not just physically, but heart and soul.

Without breaking the kiss, he found the front zipper of her jeans and pushed them down over her hips to her knees. Impatient to be free of them, to tear down the emotional and physical boundaries she had imposed around herself, Jenna kicked them the rest of the way off. For the second time in her life, she was going to enjoy without worrying about the consequences. Clad only in panties, her heart pounding, she divested him of his jeans. And his Jockey shorts.

He stroked her softly through the cloth, swiftly raising her desire to a fever pitch. She moaned her frustration, and then her panties were off, too. He was straining against her, moving inside her, letting her know he wanted her as wildly as she wanted him. Pushing herself up a little higher, she arched her back and pulled him deeper still. That quickly, they catapulted over the edge. Shuddering, their breathing rough and noisy, they clung together.

"Jenna." His voice was rough against her ear, filled not with regret, as she had feared, but longing for more.

She swallowed hard as yet another thrill swept through her, tightening her breasts, weakening her knees. Her mouth was swollen from his. She could feel it, even as she longed for his kiss again. She wanted him that way, all fire and passion, no holds barred, nothing standing between them. Not the baby, not his work, not his crazy notions about cops being unmarriageable.

Maybe she had been wrong, she thought. Maybe she should have told him about the pregnancy, given him the chance to be a proper father to Andy from the very first. But it was too late now…wasn't it? Or was it?

He threaded his hands through her hair, pushing it away from her ear. "I want you upstairs," he said softly, "in my bed." And what Grady wanted, it seemed, he got. The next thing Jenna knew, she was being swept up into his arms and carried up the back stairs. Dropping her into the rumpled covers of his bed, he joined her swiftly. They kissed hotly, possessively, the passion so strong and so right and so total, it didn't feel quite real. But it was, Jenna thought, as Grady's hands swept down her body once again. It was.

AFTERWARD, they lay tangled together, their intertwined bodies exhausted, trembling, and yet still eager for more.

"I thought I had imagined how good it was," Grady said, pressing a kiss against her bare shoulder. "I didn't." He sighed his contentment and held her closer yet.

Spent, Jenna lay in Grady's arms. Now that the passion had faded, reality was beginning to return. She didn't want to lose her baby. She knew Grady would only believe her if the second DNA tests supported instead of disputed her claims. So why was she still here with him? Why had she allowed herself to make love with him that way? She had so much more common sense than that…except that Grady had gotten to a place deep inside her heart that no one had ever even come close to before. He'd made her want to lose herself completely in him, and in their lovemaking, and that frightened her. It frightened her a lot.

"I wonder what you're thinking," Grady drawled.

"I'm wondering how it is that we keep finding ourselves in these messes," she lamented wryly. Because it wasn't like her, it wasn't like her at all!

Grady groaned with comic effect, as if he understood perfectly and wondered the same. He rubbed his hand up and down her arm, from shoulder to wrist, creating frissons of warmth everywhere he touched. "Ever hear the word irresistible?" he teased, rolling so that she was beneath him once again.

The solid feel of him sent another thrill of excitement rushing up her spine. "Yes."

He framed her face with his hands and gazed lovingly down into her face. "Well, that's what you are to me," he whispered softly, looking as completely and utterly besotted as she felt whenever he touched her. "Completely irresistible."

Jenna released a wavering sigh. "To me, too," she said finally, then bit her lip. "Not that I think that is good," she amended cautiously, beginning to feel more like her normal self now that his kisses had stopped. "It's not."

Grady acknowledged her continuing reservations with a lift of his brow. "Yeah, but it felt good at the time." Grady rolled so that she was on top of him. "And I'm willing to bet it could feel good again," he said softly, as he began to make love to her once more.

AN HOUR LATER, Jenna finally slept, her soft, warm body curled against Grady's side. Grady lay on his back, staring at the ceiling. Jenna had been right. They shouldn't have made love. Not now. Not until everything was settled, and maybe not even then.

He couldn't make too much of Clarissa's reluctance to take a second blood test. And the way Clarissa kept referring to Andy as "the baby" and not "my baby" meant nothing except Clarissa was not going to be much of a parent. But baby or no, Grady knew he was not going back to Clarissa. Their marriage was over. He was not going to resurrect it.

As for Jenna...

She was a loving and attentive mother. Andy clearly adored her. Grady could see the two of them parenting Andy together. Was that, plus his desire for Jenna, clouding his perspective? he wondered uncomfortably. Making him miss clues he should have seen?

What if they retook the blood tests and the DNA results were the same? he wondered uneasily. What if it was necessary for Grady to take Jenna to see his psychologist friend at the department, and she pronounced Jenna completely loony? Could the unthinkable be true? Was he falling head over heels in love with a crazy person?

And what would he do if he was? He knew the answer to that. If that was the case, if Jenna needed help, then he'd stay with her and see that she got it.

But he didn't think that was the case. The fact of the matter was Jenna was too lucid, too loving, too determined and forthright, to be delusional. The truth was as she'd said. Andy was Jenna's child, and he'd been taken from her. It was up to Grady to prove an abduction had occurred, he thought, and then see that it didn't happen again, that both Andy and Jenna remained safe.

After that...Grady sighed. As far as he and Jenna went, they would just have to see what was possible. She kept insisting that she wasn't looking for either a relationship or marriage, and if he was completely honest, neither was he. Because frankly, he wasn't sure it was possible to be a good cop and be married.

Grady frowned. He didn't want to be without Jenna, either. Didn't want to live in two different states while they split the care of an infant son. Nor was he willing to give up his job with the Philadelphia police force. And he doubted Jenna would leave her home in New York and relocate for his convenience. So where did that leave them? he wondered. Just what kind of resolution was going to be possible here?

Chapter Eleven

"The baby's awake," Grady said softly, several hours later.

"I know," Jenna said. She could hear Andy in his crib. He was gurgling happily, probably either to the mobile that hung overhead or to one of the dolls he had brought back with him from his stay at Alec's and Jack's.

"He's going to need a bottle, isn't he?"

Jenna nodded.

"I'll go down and warm one, then," Grady said. He flung back the sheets and headed for the stairs.

Jenna shrugged on her robe. She went in to Andy, knowing he'd be wet. By the time she had changed him and put on a fresh sleeper, Grady was upstairs with the formula. "Bring Andy in here with us," Grady said. Bottle in hand, he beckoned toward the rumpled covers on Jenna's bed.

Jenna settled against the pillows Grady had propped against the headboard. Andy cradled in her arms, she proceeded to feed him his bottle as Grady watched.

Grady smiled and tickled Andy beneath the chin. Andy stopped nursing and gurgled wildly, looking thoroughly amused and thoroughly content. Jenna felt pangs of regret and longing simultaneously. It would be so nice to have more times like this. Lazy mornings, with Grady and their baby. She wanted the sense of connectedness and affection and solidarity that only family could provide. Jenna looked at Andy's wide blue eyes, so much like his father's, and wondered in frustration why Grady couldn't just see that Andy was their son, and no one else's.

Grady paused and reached out to touch a lock of her tousled strawberry blond hair. "Last night was great, Jenna." He probed her eyes. "The question is, where do we go from here?"

I wish I knew, Jenna thought. "Isn't this conversation a little premature?" she asked lightly.

Grady regarded his son fondly. He let Andy wrap his tiny fist around one of his fingers, then turned to Jenna and saw the indecision in her eyes. "I'm not giving the baby up, Jenna," Grady warned quietly.

Jenna sat Andy up and patted him on the back. "I thought you said cops made lousy husbands and lousy fathers."

"Maybe I could be the exception to the rule this time. I'm willing to try," Grady said softly, holding her gaze. "Mind if I feed him the second half of his bottle?"

"Not at all," Jenna said. This was the way it should be—two parents, equally shared responsibilities. A sense of family and love…

Jenna watched as Grady settled Andy on his lap. Andy tapped his fingers on the bottle as he sucked down his breakfast. "Supposing we get everything worked out," Grady continued casually. "Would you marry me?"

Jenna had longed to hear those words from him for months now. Ever since she had found out they were going to have a child together, she had dreamed about those words, yearned for them, wished for them. But the reality fell short of her imaginings, maybe because she knew Grady would never be proposing if she hadn't had his child.

Jenna's shoulders tensed. Her heart reverberated with hurt. With effort, she blinked back the hot, bitter tears gathering behind her eyes and kept her voice coolly matter-of-fact as she replied, "I don't want your charity, Grady."

"Then think of our baby, Jenna." Grady linked his fingers with hers. "Andy needs two parents."

Jenna withdrew her hand from his. "I married for the

wrong reason once, Grady," she reminded him stiffly. "I'm not doing it again."

They were silent for a minute. Jenna swallowed hard around the fear gathering deep inside her. "Grady, what happens if the test comes out wrong again?"

The planes of his face seemed to sharpen. His slate-blue eyes grew more alert. "What makes you think it will?"

Jenna paused, feeling treacherously near tears again. "The fact it was already messed with or switched once." Grady made no comment about her assumption. But something in him seemed to harden. Suddenly, he looked more suspicious Philly cop than contented lover.

"There's still Nanny Beth's testimony," he said. "The guys in the department are getting close to finding her."

"When do you think we'll be able to talk to her?" Jenna asked.

"I hope before the day is done," Grady said.

"THANK GOODNESS that's over," Clarissa exclaimed at Albany Memorial Hospital. "Again."

Grady sent Clarissa a censuring look. "I'll bring the car around," he told Jenna.

Jenna nodded. "I'll be out as soon as I change Andy's diaper," she promised, then disappeared into the powder room. When she emerged minutes later, she saw Clarissa chatting with Baxter. It was no surprise they'd run into her ex-husband. Jenna knew he was on staff and had patients at all the area hospitals. But it was a shock to see him looking so chummy with Clarissa.

She waited around until the conversation had apparently run its course, then caught up with Baxter. "What was all that about?" Jenna asked as she fell into step beside Baxter, Andy cradled in her arms.

"In a nutshell, she wants me to work on you so she'll have a clear path to Grady herself," Baxter said. He gave Jenna a hard look. "I'd do it, too, if I thought I had half a chance."

Jenna felt a tinge of regret. Despite everything that had

passed between them, she had never wanted to hurt Baxter. "We never should've married, Baxter," she said gently. "You know that."

"I know you think so," Baxter said stiffly.

"I don't love you."

Baxter shoved his hands in the pockets of his starched white lab coat. "Do you love Detective Noland?"

The fifty-million-dollar question. "I don't know," Jenna said evasively. Though inwardly she thought maybe she did, she just didn't want to admit it to herself.

"Yeah, right," Baxter said skeptically.

Jenna caught sight of Grady's car waiting in front of the hospital. "I've got to go." She put Andy's knit cap on his head and headed out the door.

"What took so long?" Grady asked as Jenna settled Andy in his car seat, strapped him in and then got in the car herself.

Jenna twisted toward Grady as she fastened her shoulder harness. "I saw my ex talking to your ex and I wanted to check it out."

Grady rested one hand on the wheel. He made no effort to put the car in gear, just looked at her closely. "You think they're up to something?"

Seeing Clarissa and Baxter together had struck a chord in Jenna. "Has it occurred to you that the two of them might have gotten together and kidnapped Andy?"

Grady's suspicious look deepened. "In order to keep us apart?"

Jenna shrugged, wishing Grady hadn't shaved quite so closly that morning. "Something like that."

His eyes never leaving hers, Grady thought about it a moment. "Did Baxter know that we were together last spring?"

"Not that I know of, but... He could have had me followed, Grady. Just as your ex could have had us followed, and anyone who had followed us from that party at Alec's that night would have known I spent the night at your place."

Grady frowned, but didn't disagree with her. "While you

were having your blood taken, I had a chance to talk to Clarissa out in the hall.''

''What did she say?''

''That this second test was just a formality. We'd only end up finding out what we already knew. She wants me to go ahead and marry her again, for the baby's sake.''

''And?'' Jenna waited for his answer with bated breath.

''I told her it was over between us, no matter who Andy's mother is,'' he finally said.

''Even if Clarissa was Andy's mother, you wouldn't marry her?'' Jenna asked as hope for her future flared inside her. Maybe Grady did care about her, after all!

''Why? We'd only get divorced again, probably even more acrimoniously than the last time. Clarissa and I are not compatible. You and I are, Jenna.''

Jenna drew an unsteady breath and ducked her head. He hadn't said he loved her yet. But he was on the right track.

''What about you? I saw you talking to Baxter. Has this business with Andy given you second thoughts about your divorce?'' Grady asked.

Jenna shook her head, her opinion on that unchanged. ''I told Baxter there was no hope for us getting back together,'' Jenna admitted.

''And?''

''As with your ex, the news seems to be very slow sinking in,'' Jenna said.

''ANY MESSAGES?'' Grady asked the moment they arrived at her Hudson Falls farmhouse, settled a sleeping Andy in his crib and went to the first floor.

Jenna went into her study and checked her telephone answering machine. ''Mostly work messages,'' she proclaimed after several minutes of listening.

Grady came in carrying a tray of coffee, cups and a plate of shortbread cookies and fresh fruit. He looked disappointed.

"Anything else?" He poured Jenna a cup of coffee, stirred in some hazelnut flavored coffee creamer and handed it to her.

"The receptionist at my dentist's office, telling me it's time for my six month check-up."

"I mean important." Grady poured himself a cup of coffee.

"Nope." Jenna settled on the sofa and began going through the mail that had been delivered in her absence. She and Grady had spent so much time together the last few days, it almost seemed like they were married. It wasn't an unpleasant sensation. Rather she cherished the intimacy in even the simple things. She cherished the time spent with him, and though she knew she was wearing her heart on her sleeve, she couldn't help but wish things continued on in exactly this way.

Jenna had just opened a bill when the phone rang. Because he was closer, Grady picked up the phone. "Grady. Yeah, put her through." He covered the receiver and looked at Jenna. "It's Nanny Beth."

Jenna leaped to her feet. At last, something was going her way! "Put Nanny on the speakerphone," she instructed Grady. "I want to hear this, too."

Grady did as she asked. Seconds later, Nanny Beth's high, thin voice warbled over the long-distance lines. "Jenna, sweetheart?"

Jenna smiled. "Hi, Nanny Beth," she said cheerfully, unable to hide the smile in her voice or the happiness in her heart. "Where are you?"

"In Bermuda. The police here tracked me down and said you wanted to talk to me." Nanny Beth paused a disapproving moment. "What's going on there, sweetie?"

"It's a long story, Nanny Beth, but I've got a policeman here with me, a Detective Grady Noland from the Philadelphia police force. He wants you to tell him how and when and where Andy was born."

"No hints," Grady mouthed to Jenna.

Jenna released a slow breath. Suddenly, she was very worried. What if Nanny Beth said the wrong thing, or in some way made Grady think he had been misled?

"You mean you want me to tell him how Laura Johnson stayed with you last fall and had a baby in Hudson Falls at Christmastime?" Nanny Beth asked anxiously. "And how you helped take care of Andy and then fell in love with him and then found out Laura wanted to give Andy up for adoption, because she didn't think she could care for him properly, so you told her you'd care for him, and started making plans to adopt him right away?"

Jenna rolled her eyes. Leave it to Nanny Beth to keep up the ruse past the time when it was necessary. "No, Nanny Beth. I don't want you to tell Grady about the story you and I cooked up to cover my tracks. I want you to tell him the truth, without any more prompting from me."

"All right, dear. Detective Noland, are you there?"

"Right here," Grady affirmed.

"Well, I delivered Jenna's baby. We were supposed to go across the border to Vermont because Jenna wanted to have her baby there. She thought it would be easier to keep the birth private. But her labor came so hard and fast that we didn't even have time to go into Hudson Falls! So I delivered the baby at the farm, and then Dr. Koen came out to make sure Jenna and the baby were all right. He wanted to move them to a hospital, but Jenna didn't want to go, so it ended up being a home birth from start to finish."

Grady breathed a sigh of relief as he realized that Nanny Beth's story matched Jenna's perfectly.

"I understand you finally got everything worked out with your family," Nanny Beth said to Jenna.

"More or less," Jenna said, not about to get into that. "Listen, would you mind cutting your vacation short and coming on home, Nanny Beth? I think I'm going to need you."

"YOU LOOK HAPPY," Jenna told Grady as she hung up the phone. In fact, happy didn't begin to cover it. He looked ecstatic.

"That's because I got my wish," Grady said hoarsely, taking her into the warm circle of his arms. And then his mouth came down on hers.

Jenna's heartbeat pounded like thunder against his as their mouths met with fiery demand. No one had ever wanted her like this, Jenna thought, as his lips caressed hers and his tongue probed languorously deep. She had never wanted like this, never ached so just to be touched, held, loved by a man. But it wasn't just any man she wanted, it was Grady.

He drew away from her. Her breath caught as she gazed into his eyes. As she read his intent, to make love to her here, now, in the study while Andy was still asleep, her heart began a slow, heavy beat. Bending close, he pulled her against his hard length and used his other hand to brush the hair from her nape. His warm breath touched the soft, vulnerable skin of her neck. And then his lips.

Trembling with pent-up desire, Jenna turned her head so their lips met once again. "Oh, Grady," she whispered. *I love you, I love you so much.*

He deepened the kiss and wrapped his arms around her, the pressure of his hands on her hips and back bringing her intimately close. Another torrent of need swept through her, further weakening her knees. Grady backed to the sofa. They went down in a tangle of arms and legs and came together quickly, in an explosion of passion, tenderness and need.

Afterward, replete and drowsy, Jenna melted against Grady in blissful ecstasy. "What are you thinking?" he murmured contentedly, running his fingers through her hair.

Jenna flattened her hands on the muscled warmth of his hair-whorled chest. He was so masculine. So steady, despite all the turmoil of recent days. "I was thinking that I've missed this…missed the closeness—"

"That comes with making love?" Grady asked, caressing her shoulders gently.

"And being with someone so intimately," Jenna admitted as she rested her head against his chest and listened to the steady drumbeat of his heart. She didn't know why she was suddenly being so honest, even if she hadn't exactly come right out and said it was Grady she had missed, not just someone. Anyone. Her emotions were still in turmoil where Grady was concerned. He hadn't said he loved her. Only that he would marry her because of the baby.

"I've missed being with you, too," Grady said. He turned her palm up and pressed a kiss on it.

Jenna snuggled closer. *I need to start appreciating what I have and stop wishing for the impossible,* she thought. "There were so many times I wanted to call you this past year."

Grady's hands swept down her back and tightened on her spine. "Why didn't you?" he said.

Jenna shrugged. *I was afraid it wouldn't work out. I didn't want to be rejected.* Her lips curved wryly. She propped her chin on her fist and looked at Grady honestly. "I didn't want to be told cops and relationships don't mix."

"And now?" Grady asked, tangling his hands in her hair as her lips moved against his throat.

"Now I just want us to forget everything that's happened and start all over again." Jenna kissed his collarbone. "There's only one thing standing in our way," Jenna finished with a sigh. Grady looked at her, and they said in unison, "We've got to find out who kidnapped Andy!"

GALVANIZED INTO ACTION by their mutual concern for their infant son, they dressed quickly. Jenna picked up a blank yellow legal pad and a red felt marking pen from her desk. "Okay. Here are the suspects we've pretty much eliminated so far," she said as she wrote. "My father, my brother Kip and his wife Leslie, and Nanny Beth."

Grady finished buttoning his shirt and began hunting around for his boots. "That leaves Baxter and Clarissa. We disagree about Baxter, but we both agree Clarissa could be capable of just about anything if it enabled her to get what she wanted.''

''I seriously doubt Clarissa is going to confess to any wrongdoing, unless we have solid proof against her. How's your partner doing with the phony documents she produced?''

''Still working on tracking down the source.''

Jenna frowned. ''What do you suggest we do next?''

Grady paced to the carafe of coffee he'd brought in earlier. He was in luck. The coffee was still hot. ''I think we should start by putting our emotions aside and running this investigation less like a family drama and more like an official police inquiry.'' The way he should have run it in the first place, he told himself sternly.

Grady poured himself a cup and promptly downed half of it before continuing, ''We've checked for inside clues and found little except that it was an inside job and that no one in the family is confessing to it.''

''So now what?'' Jenna said, as she helped herself to a cup of coffee.

''Now it's time we checked for outside clues,'' Grady said.

Chapter Twelve

"Nope, didn't see anything," Jenna's neighbor to the east said.

"Wish I could help you, but I was at my son's elementary school all day helping out with his class's Valentine's Day party," said her neighbor to the north.

"Maybe the third time's the charm," Grady said as he approached.

"Maybe," Jenna said glumly. And maybe they'd never discover anything at all. Maybe the only thing this guest would do was make it look as if she had engineered Andy's abduction from start to finish, just to get Grady's attention and falsely win his sympathy and then his heart. She knew it had occurred to him, just as it occurred to her. She saw it every time she looked into his eyes.

"Now that you mention it, I did notice something," Edward Frick said. A farmer, he was dressed in overalls, a green flannel shirt and work boots. "I drove by about two in the afternoon. I remember, because I was on my way into town to pick up some flowers for my wife, it being Valentine's Day and all, and when I went by your place, Jenna, I saw a man putting a baby in a car seat into the back of a car."

"How could you have seen all that just driving by?" Grady interrupted. "I mean, Jenna's house is pretty far back from the road."

"That's what was so unusual about it," Edward Frick said.

"The car wasn't parked next to the house. It was parked at the end of the drive, next to the road, just inside the property line. It just didn't make sense to me to carry the baby and that car seat all the way down the lane on such a cold day, when the driver could easily have pulled the car all the way up to the front porch."

"Unless you were trying not to be heard," Grady muttered.

Jenna looked at Grady. "That explains why I never heard a car. It's nearly half a mile from the end of the drive to the house."

"Did you get a good look at the baby or the person carrying the baby?" Grady asked.

Edward Frick pointed to Andy. "The baby kind of looked like the one you got sleeping in the back of your car right now—leastways, it was about the same size, a real little one. I wasn't close enough to see the baby's face or anything."

No matter, Jenna thought. If there had been a baby outside her farmhouse on Valentine's Day, then it had to be Andy. Now all they had to do was identify the kidnapper. "What kind of car was it?" Jenna asked excitedly. "Do you remember?"

"Sure do, 'cause we don't see many of that kind out here in the country. It was a fancy black Porsche."

His expression all business, Grady pulled a small pad and pen from the inside pocket of his tweed blazer. "Did you get the license plate?" he asked with cool police efficiency.

"No." Edward Frick shook his head in obvious regret. "Sorry."

"Any of the letters on it?" Grady persisted.

"No, not a one, sorry," Edward said.

Despair welled up in Jenna. She pushed it aside determinedly. "Can you give us a description of the man carrying the baby?" she asked.

"Well…" Edward Frick rubbed his bearded jaw. "He was wearing a navy trench coat, the kind that goes over suits."

"What color hair did he have?" Jenna asked.

"Now that I remember. It was dark brown, and he had one of them fancy city-slicker haircuts, the kind that don't seem to move at all in the wind. Oh, and he was clean-shaven, no beard or mustache."

Jenna looked at Grady. There was only one person who wore a navy trench coat and drove a black Porsche who could have had access to the security codes at the Sullivan family farm. Her smile widened. "Bingo," she said.

STEVE JACKSON looked up from the stack of papers on his desk when Grady and Jenna walked in, Andy cradled in Jenna's arms. His smile faded as Grady removed a badge from his pocket and flashed it in Steve's direction. "Mind if we ask you a few questions?" Grady said.

"That depends," Steve said nervously. He looked from Jenna to the baby and at Jenna again. "Jenna?"

"It's okay, Steve," Jenna said gently, sure even if Grady wasn't that no harm had been meant. Steve was too nice a guy to have abducted Andy for malicious or greedy reasons. "We just want to talk," she said.

Steve put down his pen. He studied Jenna's face wordlessly for several seconds, then sighed. "You know, don't you?" he presumed heavily.

Jenna nodded and continued to rub Andy's back. He had just had a bottle and was about to go to sleep again. "We've got an eyewitness who saw you loading Andy into the car midafternoon on Valentine's Day. What I don't understand is why, Steve."

Steve pushed his swivel chair farther from his desk and propped an ankle on the opposite knee. "Isn't it obvious? You and your dad have always been so nice to me. I wanted you to be happy."

"You thought kidnapping her baby would make her happy?" Grady asked gruffly. His expression ominous and unforgiving, he glared at Steve.

"I thought reuniting her and the baby with the baby's father would make her happy," Steve corrected. He got to his feet and shoved his hands in the pockets of his tailored Armani trousers. "And since Jenna was too stubborn to do it on her own…" Steve looked at Grady and frowned. "What I don't get is what *you* have to do with all this," he said.

Grady swore heatedly beneath his breath. "I'm the baby's father," Grady growled.

Steve blanched. "Wait a minute." Steve turned to Jenna. "I thought you were involved with Alec Roman!"

Jenna shook her head. Andy was beginning to feel heavy, so she sat down. This comedy of errors seemed to know no end. "Let's start at the beginning, Steve," she said gently. "How did you know I was pregnant?"

A flush started in Steve's neck and worked its way up to his face. He looked at Jenna. "Remember when I delivered that Christmas gift from your father to the farm on December twentieth and Nanny Beth answered the door?" Jenna nodded. Steve continued, "Well, you were supposed to be in Sweden for the holidays, on business. Only Nanny Beth was supposed to be out at the farm then. But I caught a glimpse of you coming in the back of the house just as I arrived, and I saw how pregnant you were, and… Well, I was worried, so I cornered Nanny Beth and demanded to know what was going on. She told me you were hiding out at the farm, not to recuperate from your divorce from Baxter, as everyone had been purposefully led to believe, but because your baby's father had told you that marriage just wasn't for him. Nanny Beth said she had tried to talk some sense into you, to get you to at least call the baby's father or tell her who it was, but that you stubbornly refused."

"Imagine the trouble you would have saved us all if you'd only listened to Nanny Beth," Grady interjected dryly as he put his pad and pen away.

Jenna shot Grady a silencing look, then turned to Steve. "I still don't get how you figured out it was Alec's baby," she said.

"I didn't. Not right away. I mean, at first I just assumed

it had to be Baxter's, because I know you don't play ar—
well, never mind.''

"We understand she's not promiscuous," Grady said.

Jenna covered Andy's shoulders with a blanket and settled
back more comfortably in her chair. "Go on with your story,
Steve," she encouraged quietly. "We want to know how and
why and when you decided to take the baby to Alec Roman's.''

"Well, I kept in touch with Nanny Beth from Christmas
on. I called her once a week, usually on some pretense or
another, but she knew what I was really worried about was
you. And she told me that instead of coming to your senses,
as she had hoped you would after Andy's birth, you were
being more stubborn than ever. And that you were also pretty
depressed about it. She said if she only knew who the father
was she'd tell him herself! So, one afternoon at the end of
January while you were in Albany on business, I went out to
the farm, and she let me go through your office files and
calendar. As close as we could figure, you'd been at Alec
Roman's party the night Andy was conceived. A glance at
your long-distance phone records showed you'd been in constant touch with him by phone ever since. We also knew,
from the news reports, what a big playboy he was. So...''

Jenna was so stunned for a moment she couldn't speak.
"Are you telling me Nanny Beth was in on the kidnapping?''

"I wanted her to be, but she refused. She said you were
going to tell your father February fifteenth, when you went
into Albany again on business. I had an idea how Lamar
would react to the news, and figured it would be better if you
had already reunited with Andy's father before you dropped
the news on your dad, so I waited for the first opportunity,
and took it.''

"How did you know the code to deactivate the alarm?''

"Lamar has it in his office safe, along with a spare key to
the front door.''

"Oh, Steve." Jenna cuddled the baby sleeping in her arms
closer to her chest and shook her head at him in regret.

Steve shot Jenna a penitent look. "I'm *really* sorry, Jenna."

"Why didn't you come forward sooner and tell Jenna what you'd done?" Grady asked. Gliding closer to Andy, he smoothed a palm over Andy's baby-fine hair.

Steve shrugged and looked confused again. "I thought everything had worked out the way it was supposed to. I mean, who'd turn their back on a woman like Jenna if they knew…"

No one, Grady thought. In fact, the more he was with her the more he knew he'd been a fool to ever let her go. Maybe his marriage to Clarissa hadn't worked. It didn't mean his relationship with Jenna wouldn't.

"I'm sorry, Jenna," Steve said contritely. "I was just trying to help. And anyway, I did check with your dad the next day."

Jenna frowned. "What do you mean?"

"I asked Lamar if he had heard from you and he said, and I quote, 'Jenna is fine. She finally came home last night, and as it happens, it wasn't a moment too soon.' I told him I had been worried about you, and he said it was easy to see why. I asked your dad if you had explained everything to him, and he said you had. He also told me not to worry, that he knew I had stumbled on 'quite a bit' when I went out to the farm at Christmas, and again in January, but that he was getting you all the help you needed to see that your situation got squared away once and for all.

"I asked him how long he thought it would take, and he just shrugged and said he hoped everything would be taken care of in a couple of weeks." Steve paused. "I thought everything was fine."

Only it hadn't been, Jenna thought, because Steve had delivered the baby to the wrong man at the wrong address. "I thought Andy had been kidnapped," Jenna said. "I accused my father of doing the kidnapping, and when he denied it, I nearly had a nervous breakdown."

"Oh, God, Jenna, I'm sorry," Steve said, his face ashen.

"I understand you were just trying to help." Jenna sighed. With her free hand, she tucked her hair behind her ear.

"Now I'm confused." Steve paused. "If Alec Roman wasn't Andy's father, why were you in constant touch with him?"

Jenna smiled. "Because last spring Alec agreed to let me use his jet to ferry kids back and forth whenever he wasn't using it."

"Oh." Steve looked more chagrined than ever.

"And at that party I had solicited a rather large donation from him—before I started talking to Grady."

Again, everyone was silent. "Well, at least we have confirmed Andy was kidnapped and no harm was done. Now all we have to do is figure out what happened to the DNA tests," Jenna said.

"I have a feeling I already know the answer to that," Grady said grimly.

"YOU KNOW what you did constitutes fraud," Grady said to Martin Fikleman, the lab tech at Philadelphia General, several hours later, after Martin had admitted switching the results.

"I know. I'm sorry." Martin hung his head. "But I was just trying to help. Your ex-wife said... Well, I guess it doesn't matter what she said, does it?"

Grady shook his head and hoisted a wide-awake Andy a little higher on his shoulder. "What happened to the original test results?"

"I kept them. In fact, I can show them to you now." Martin disappeared into the file room. He returned with a document that had been filed under *Fikleman, Clarissa*. Martin handed it over to Grady and Jenna for their perusal. "Andy is the child of Grady Noland and Jenna Sullivan."

The clatter of high heels had them all looking up. Clarissa stood in the doorway, her white mink thrown over her shoulder, her discreetly colored blond hair shining in the fluorescent light of the hospital lab. "Hello, Grady," she said in a throaty voice. She took in the furious look on Grady's face, the baby in his arms and sighed. "I guess I owe you an explanation."

"As well as an apology," Jenna said tightly.

"I wanted another try at our marriage," Clarissa said simply.

"So you produced fake documents and sworn affidavits and coerced a lab tech to switch the results of the blood tests?" Jenna asked incredulously, moving closer to Andy and Grady.

"When I did all that, I didn't think Andy was your baby, either," Clarissa said.

"It was still a lie," Jenna emphasized bluntly.

Clarissa regarded the group gathered in the Philadelphia General lab unapologetically. Her gaze sharpened as she surveyed Grady. Resignation filled her eyes. "It's futile, isn't it? You don't love me. You never did."

Grady didn't know what to say to that. Finally, he shrugged. "Maybe in the beginning…"

"But not anymore." Clarissa frowned and released a short, impatient breath. "I suppose it's just as well, because in the midst of all this, I realized something, too, Grady. You're not what I want, either. You never were." She turned on her heel and left the lab. And Grady knew that it truly was over. He was free.

JENNA ALLOWED GRADY to take her and Andy to his apartment for the night. She fed and changed Andy and settled him down in his crib for a nap while Grady put on a pot of coffee. He poured them each a cup, laced both liberally with Kahlua and topped them with generous dollops of whipped cream.

Jenna wrapped both hands around her mug and tried not to feel too cozy, sitting there with Grady at his kitchen table.

"Well, where do we go from here?" Grady asked bluntly, studying her over the rim of his cup.

Jenna shrugged, painfully aware that if not for Andy asleep in the crib nearby, she wouldn't be here with Grady at all.

She drew a stabilizing breath. "I guess we decide custody of Andy. I'm willing to take full custody but—" she took another deep breath, drawing on all her courage as she attempted to be as fair as she could about this "—I'm willing to grant you liberal visitation rights."

Grady's slate-blue eyes gleamed with a mixture of displeasure and disappointment. "I don't want to visit my son. I want him with me all the time." He squeezed her hand possessively. "And I want you with me, too."

As if it was that simple. Jenna withdrew her hand from his and tried not to be too hurt Grady had put his proposition to her so bluntly. But it was an impossible task, because she *was* hurt. She had wanted hearts and flowers, declarations of wild, impassioned love. Not this matter-of-fact discussion. "How romantic of you, Grady."

Grady leaned back in his chair and kept his eyes on hers. "I'm serious," he said softly. "Why should we have to split up Andy's care? Why can't we just get married?"

Jenna gripped the handle of her stoneware mug tightly and forced herself to take a sip of the rich coffee. The scalding hot liquid didn't burn nearly as much as Grady's unromantic proposal. "Because cops and marriage don't mix, remember?" she retorted lightly, fighting for serenity.

"Marriage to a cop and Clarissa didn't mix," Grady corrected. He leaned toward her again and traced a lazy pattern on the back of her wrist. "I have a feeling you're independent and understanding enough to make a damn good cop's wife. Besides that, we're compatible—sexually and otherwise, from similar backgrounds, with a bent for public service. We share a baby."

He talked like he was stating a business case, Jenna realized miserably.

"What more could either of us want?" Grady finished pragmatically, clearly not understanding her reluctance to be with him.

How about a love that was every bit as strong and abiding as their physical passion for one another, Jenna thought miserably. How about a commitment that had nothing to do with the child they had made and everything to do with their deep feelings for one another?

"I've got a question for you, Grady," Jenna said casually, pulling her tingling wrist out of reach, "that just may help put things in perspective for you." For both of us, she thought.

He got up, went to the cupboard and returned with a bag of chocolate-chip macadamia-nut cookies. "Ask away," he said as he sat down.

"What would have happened had I not been able to prove to you beyond a shadow of a doubt that the baby I had was yours? I mean, what if we hadn't had access to DNA tests or the results of those tests had stayed screwed up or maybe just been inconclusive, then what?"

Grady offered her a cookie. She refused.

He shot her a baffled look. "What does it matter? What does any of that speculation—and that's all it is, Jenna, speculation—have to do with me asking you to marry me?"

"Is that what you just did?"

Grady released a short, impatient breath and gave her a look that said she was making this unnecessarily hard on them both. "You know I did," he said gruffly.

"Just as I also know you haven't yet answered my question, and I want an answer, Grady. What if I hadn't proved Andy was our child? What would you have done?" Could he have followed his heart, trusted in her and his love for her and realized the truth anyway?

Grady munched on a cookie and thought about it for a moment. Finally, he shrugged, as if it no longer mattered much to him either way. "Relied on Nanny Beth's eyewitness testimony to the birth, I guess."

He was being deliberately obtuse, and it infuriated her. She needed him to tell her that he would have trusted her and loved her no matter what, before she could commit to him. Being careful to keep her voice down lest they wake the sleeping Andy, Jenna said, "You're a cop, Grady. You rely on the facts, as you reminded me dozens of times this week. Would you have felt comfortable with that? Knowing you had nothing to back it up with except my word and Nanny Beth's?''

Grady shrugged. ''Not as comfortable as now, no, but—''

So he didn't really trust her or love her after all, Jenna realized sadly. She got up so abruptly she jarred the table and sloshed coffee from her mug. ''That's all I needed to hear.'' As she had the last time she had been in his Philadelphia apartment, Jenna began gathering up Andy's things. ''No, I will not marry you, Grady. Yes, you can be Andy's father.''

''How generous of you,'' Grady retorted furiously, pushing the words through his teeth. ''But I don't want just a son. I want my baby and a wife.''

A wife, or a glorified baby-sitter cum mistress? Jenna wondered darkly. Fury engulfed her as she thought about the way he was using her. Whether he was conscious of it or not didn't seem to matter. ''My second point,'' Jenna said coolly. ''You wouldn't be marrying me now if it weren't for Andy. And that's just not good enough, Detective!''

Looking exasperated beyond belief, Grady propped his hands on his hips and regarded Jenna sternly. ''Then what would be?'' he demanded.

''That's just it, Grady,'' Jenna told him sadly, wishing with all her heart that things were different but suspecting sadly that they never would be. ''You just don't know.''

Chapter Thirteen

"I know we got off to a rocky start, and that's my fault as much as Jenna's, but I thought I'd made that up to her," Grady confided dispiritedly to the three other men seated around the table in the Albany bar. "For a while, of course, we had the baby business standing in the way of our getting together, but the minute that got cleared up, I asked her to marry me, so I could be a proper husband to her and a father to Andy."

"And?" Lamar Sullivan asked, leaning forward on the edge of his chair as he waited for Grady's reply.

"And she acted like I'd just sold her a worthless piece of swampland in Florida," Grady admitted with a beleaguered sigh. "Maybe I'm being uncommonly dense here, but I don't understand why she said no, guys, and that's why I asked you all here tonight. We all love Jenna. We all care about her. I figured if we put our heads together, we might be able to shed some light on Jenna's fury with me."

"I take it that means Jenna is still refusing to take your calls," Lamar Sullivan said with an understanding sigh.

"Won't take my calls. Won't see me, period," Grady muttered as he loosened his tie with a jerk.

"Have you tried writing her a letter?" Steve Jackson asked helpfully before he popped a shelled peanut in his mouth.

"Yes. According to Nanny Beth, she won't even open the

envelopes if she sees my names on the outside,'' Grady retorted humorlessly.

"It's only been four days,'' Kip said as he took a handful of pretzels from the bowl in the center of the table.

"The longest four days of my life.'' Grady scowled. He couldn't ever recall feeling more miserable or alone, which was why he had called this impromptu session with all the men in Jenna's life. Someone had to have a clue what to do next. God knew he was at his wit's end.

"Jenna always was high-strung,'' her brother admitted with a shrug. "Furthermore, when it comes to matters of the heart, she's never been all that rational.''

Lamar's expression sobered sympathetically. "Give her time, Grady, she'll come around,'' he said.

"What if she doesn't change her mind?'' Grady stared into his beer. Too late, he realized he should have believed in Jenna from the very beginning. The fact he hadn't was doubtless contributing to her anger and distrust of him now.

"It's up to you to see that she does agree to marry you, son,'' Lamar Sullivan said sternly. He had to strain to be heard above the jukebox.

"Any ideas how I might accomplish that?'' Grady searched the faces of the men around him.

"Tried telling her you're sorry?'' Kip asked.

"Yes,'' Grady admitted tightly as a fresh wave of frustration washed through him. *In a roundabout way.*

"And?'' Every eye was glued to his face.

Grady shrugged. "She doesn't seem to want to forget and forgive.''

"Maybe you're just not convincing enough,'' Steve Jackson speculated thoughtfully.

"I agree,'' Kip said. Everyone turned to look at him, including Grady. "Jenna's a woman with a lot of heart. Seems to me she wants a man with the same.'' Kip leveled a stern glance at Grady. "If you haven't got that, my friend, as much as we'd like you to be part of our family, you haven't got a chance.''

JENNA FINISHED TYPING the letter to the United States Embassy in Budapest, urging the speedy release of the fifteen orphans who were waiting to be adopted by their Foundation parents. Her mood still grim, she printed the letter, folded it and slid it into the envelope. The doorbell rang just as she was turning off her computer.

"Jenna, darling, can you get the door?" Nanny Beth called from the second floor. "I'm in the middle of giving Andy his bath."

"No problem," Jenna called up the stairs, her mood nowhere near as pleasant as her voice. The last few days had been hell.

She trudged to the door, looked through the viewer and frowned even more. Grady Noland. Again. Would the man never give up? "Go away, Grady," she said through the door of the farmhouse.

"You said I could see my son whenever I wanted," he said.

Jenna paused. She had promised that, damn it. And damn him for reminding her. "You're supposed to call first," she said.

"I did. Nanny Beth said it was okay."

Jenna frowned. Nanny Beth had been given strict instructions that Grady was to visit Andy only when Jenna wasn't around to see him, too.

She opened the door and ushered him in. "We're going to have to talk about this."

"I agree." Grady shrugged out of his overcoat and handed it to her. "Hudson Falls is a heck of a long drive from Philadelphia. I can't keep doing this every day."

Jenna hung his coat on the rack next to the stairs. "So borrow Alec's jet."

"Very funny."

Suddenly, he was right behind her. Close enough that she could smell the spicy, masculine scent of his after-shave. Close enough that she could feel the warmth of his tall body. Pushing the memory of the passion they had shared from her mind, she turned to face him. "Andy is upstairs with Nanny Beth."

He braced a hand on the banister beside her. "I didn't come here to see Andy," he said quietly, stepping closer and invading her space, his voice so quiet she had to strain to hear him. "I came to see you."

Jenna swallowed and stepped away. Much more of his closeness and she'd end up in his arms. "We've already said everything we have to say."

"Mmm, I don't think so."

The new determination in his tone had her pulse jumping. Without warning, Nanny Beth appeared at the head of the stairs. Andy was wrapped snugly in a thick warm terry-cloth baby towel. "I thought I heard you, Grady," she said cheerfully.

Jenna glared at Nanny Beth and Grady suspiciously. "Since when did the two of you get so chummy?" she asked as Nanny Beth came down the stairs with Andy in her arms.

"Since I told her I asked you to marry me," Grady said.

"Then you also should have told her I refused your oh-so-romantic offer," Jenna snapped back. She wished she had known Grady was coming. If she had known, she would have changed out of the snug worn jeans, white turtleneck and oversize denim workshirt and into something coolly aloof and intimidating. She would have done something with her hair, pinned it back severely or something, instead of leaving it down to flow over her shoulders in soft waves.

Grady grinned and looked at Nanny Beth. "I told you she was feisty, didn't I?"

"Always been that way, probably always will be," Nanny Beth agreed. She handed Andy over to Grady. "Want to see your papa for a moment, sugar?" she asked. Andy beamed at Grady and gurgled with delight.

Jenna stared at Nanny Beth. "Whose side are you on?" she demanded.

"Yours, of course," Nanny Beth said, unperturbed,

"which is why I think you should go out with Grady to-night."

"I'll go out with Grady Noland when hell freezes over. Now if you two matchmakers will excuse me, I have more work to do."

"Jenna, it's eight o'clock at night," Grady reminded.

"So?" She was so furious with him, so hurt for the non-chalant way he had proposed to her.

As quick as one-two-three, Grady handed Andy to Nanny Beth, cut Jenna off at the door to her office and threw an arm out to block out her way. "So, I think you can spare a few hours for me," he drawled, his smile so wicked it made her heart race.

Don't give in to him. Don't let him break your heart again.
"Then you think wrong." Jenna ducked beneath his out-stretched arm and charged into her office.

He followed her, then turned to Nanny Beth. "You're all set for tonight?" he asked her.

"Andy and I are fine," Nanny Beth said, just as mysteriously. She made a shooing motion with her free hand. "You two run along and have fun."

Jenna released an impatient sigh. Why was it that absolutely no one was listening to her this evening? "I told you, I am not going anywhere with this louse," Jenna said.

"Damn, but I love it when you're feisty," Grady said.

The next thing Jenna knew, he had closed the distance between them and swung her up into his arms. "Grady, put me down!" Jenna commanded icily.

"Gladly, as soon as we reach the limo," Grady replied. He strode past Nanny Beth with a cheerful, determined smile. "Don't wait up."

"Have a good time, darlings," Nanny Beth said with a wave.

There really was a limo outside, Jenna noted with disbelief. A white stretch limo with darkened glass and a driver who got out to open the door for Grady. "You know, Detective Noland, this is against the law," Jenna muttered as he dropped her gently onto the seat, then followed her into the car.

"Taking a woman on a date?" Grady asked innocently.

"Kidnapping a woman on a date," Jenna corrected as she started to scramble for the other side.

He made a scoffing sound and pulled her beside him. "I'm not kidnapping you."

"Are, too," Jenna insisted as the car took off and rolled smoothly down the drive to the road.

"Am not!"

They glared at one another. Jenna decided it would be undignified to struggle anymore. She would just let him say what he had to say, tell him no again, that she would not marry him, and then be done with him. She folded her arms beneath her breasts. "Okay, spit it out, Detective. Let's get this over with."

"First, open your present," Grady said.

Jenna reluctantly took the large ribbon-wrapped box he handed her only because she didn't want to prolong the argument. Inside was a beautiful red dress worthy of any screen siren. It was just her size, made by a designer she loved. Nanny Beth had to have helped him. Jenna pretended not to understand. "This is a little large for Andy," she said.

Grady threw back his head and roared with laughter. "You break me up," he said, slapping his knee.

Jenna felt a new wave of color come into her cheeks. "Right," she said dryly. She tapped a sneakered foot impatiently. "Are you done?"

"No, as a matter of fact, Ms. Jenna Sullivan, I am not." Grady reached across the seat, picked up a fragrant bouquet of red roses, and tossed the flowers in her arms. "These are for you, too."

Jenna cradled the flowers loosely in her lap. She told herself sternly that it was far too late for Grady to be behaving like the hopelessly ardent suitor she had always yearned for. No matter how many gifts he gave her, it wasn't going to do him any good. He wasn't going to be able to buy his way into her good graces. Nevertheless, without warning, she was feeling ridiculously close to tears. Getting a tight grip on her composure, she said in a harsh staccato voice, "Now are you finished?"

"Nope." Grady punched a button so that the car was filled with beautiful music and handed her another ribbon-wrapped box. Figuring she'd save them both a lot of time and energy if she just opened it—which didn't mean she had to accept the gift—Jenna tore off the ribbon. Inside was a big bottle of her favorite perfume. She knew exactly how much it cost, and he'd spent a mint on it. "I hate to tell you this, Grady, but my affections can't be bought," Jenna said dryly.

Grady ignored that and met her eyes. "How about won, then?" he said softly, so softly her heart skipped a beat.

The limo stopped in front of a popular bed-and-breakfast inn. The driver opened the door for them. Grady got out and extended a hand to her. "I don't care what else you have planned for me, I am not going to let you seduce me," Jenna whispered sternly in his ear as they started up the steps.

"I don't want to seduce you, not ever again," Grady said softly, so only she could hear. His hand tightened on hers as he ushered her through the front door of the quaint country inn. "If you come to me again, it's not going to be a reckless impulse, Jenna."

She turned to face him as she slipped inside. "Then what is it going to be?" she replied, "if not an impulse?" Until now that was the only way they had made love.

He caught her hand and tugged her close. They collided, softness to hardness, as he looked hotly down at her and teased, "You admit there's a chance for us, then?"

"I admit no such thing," Jenna said stiffly, stepping promptly away from him, but she knew he had just made his point, that deep inside she was already simmering with possibilities.

He had certainly gone to an awful lot of trouble here. Trouble that had very little to do with the baby they had made and everything to do with her, Jenna realized as she looked at the huge antique table and saw it had been set just for two. A fire was flickering warmly. Soft romantic music played in the background. The proprietress came out to meet them. "Just let us know when you're ready for the meal, Mr. Noland," she said with a charming smile. "The champagne is on ice. And the room upstairs is ready, too."

"Thank you," Grady said. Giving Jenna no chance to say a word, he ushered her toward the stairs.

Jenna told herself she was only continuing to go along with him for the pleasure of turning him down once again. "You're wasting your time here, Grady," Jenna said under her breath.

He touched a light hand to her back and guided her into the first bedroom on the right. "I'll be the judge of that."

The room was lovely, the bed a huge old four-poster, complete with canopy, lacy white comforter and crisp white sheets. Another enticing fire roared in the grate. Jenna saw a sexy red lingerie set in the same shade as the dress he'd given her in the car and carried up in the box. An old-fashioned tub stood in the corner. Grady went straight to it, turned on the water and poured a liberal amount of perfumed bubble bath under the spigot. "I'll be waiting for you downstairs," he said with another wicked smile. "Take your time. We've got all night, thanks to Nanny Beth."

I might as well be incredibly beautiful when I turn him down, Jenna thought. She locked the door after him, and then turned to the bath. It had been a long time since she'd been pampered, a long time since she'd been alone with Grady. Five whole days, in fact, since they'd spent any time together at all....

When she walked downstairs, he was waiting for her, dressed not in the casual clothing he had worn to pick her up, but in a tux. He looked freshly showered and shaved. Jenna felt her heart skip another beat. Maybe it wasn't going to be as easy to say no to him tonight as she'd thought.

"Champagne?" He got up to pour them both a drink.

Jenna struggled to contain her euphoria. "It's not going to

work," she told him again. She looked around, hoping for any distraction. "And where is the proprietress?"

"Upstairs in her private quarters. I told her I'd summon her if we needed her, but I don't expect to need her."

For the first time, Jenna noted the covered silver chafing dishes on the sideboard. Their dinner, no doubt. "Where are the other guests?" And why was her heart suddenly pounding so?

Grady stood in front of the fireplace. "There aren't any tonight. I rented out the whole inn."

He had a trust fund, she reminded herself. So even if this was costing him a mint, it wasn't as if he wouldn't eat lunch for a month because of his extravagance. Money didn't matter to him anyway, any more than it mattered to her. She met his eyes. "Why?"

"That should be obvious."

She remained on the other side of the mantel. "It's not," Jenna said stubbornly. He hadn't made it easy for her, and she wasn't going to make it easy for him.

He crossed to her side, stepped behind her and wrapped his arms around her. "Because tonight is the most important night of our lives," he whispered against her hair.

Jenna leaned against the solid warmth of his chest just for a moment. She closed her eyes and tried not to think of how much she still longed to hold him and make love to him again. "I don't know how you can say that," she said thickly, knowing that as much as she loved him—and she did love Grady Noland deeply—she never wanted to be the wife he'd had to marry because of the baby they'd made.

Grady pressed a kiss in her hair and turned her gently to face him. One arm slid around her back, holding her close. The other hand cupped her chin and guided her face up to his. "I say it because it's true," he said, all the tenderness she had ever dreamed of radiating in his low, sexy voice. His slate-blue eyes roved her upturned features. "I screwed up before, Jenna," he confessed miserably. "I thought I was being sensible, limiting myself to casual affairs, refusing to even consider marriage.''

"And then Andy changed all that," Jenna interrupted sadly. Andy. Not her.

"No, Jenna," Grady corrected sternly as he tightened his possessive grip on her waist, "*you* changed all that. From the night I met you there's never been anyone else." He bent and touched his lips lightly to hers. "Nor will there ever be again."

Tears glistened in her eyes but did not fall. Her mouth trembled with the emotions that had caused her to run from his cookies-and-coffee proposal in the first place. "You're just saying that because you want the baby," she accused.

Grady shook his head. His eyes were dark, intense. "I'm saying it because I want you. I know I wasn't romantic enough before, Jenna, and I'm sorry for that, so sorry."

Jenna shook her head in silent censure as she stepped from the warm, inviting circle of his arms. "My turning you down had nothing to do with your lack of romantic notions, Grady. In fact, romance per se can be just as deceptive as the cold, hard facts."

"Then let me tell you what's in my heart," Grady said gruffly. He tugged a chair close with his foot, sank down into it and pulled her onto his lap. "I love you, Jenna." He held her tenderly, looking deep into her eyes. "I have always loved you. Even when your actions and mine made no sense, I loved you," he said softly.

Jenna's spirits soared. Her heart did cartwheels in her chest. She wrapped her arms about his neck and pulled him closer still. "Those are feelings you're talking about now, Grady," Jenna teased.

"I know."

Jenna paused, her fingertips resting on the starched collar of his pleated white shirt. "Are you sure you can trust them?" she asked tremulously.

"Yes," Grady said softly, firmly. "I am. And you know why? Because those feelings I have in my heart will never change. I'm always going to love you, Jenna. Whether we share a baby or not, whether you wear my wedding ring or not, I will still love you.''

"That's all I needed to hear." Jenna tugged him closer, and they indulged in a long, steamy kiss that left her feeling glowing and alive.

"Better?" Grady asked, when at last they drew apart.

"Better," Jenna confided in a shaky voice. She paused as she looked at him again. "But why didn't you just tell me that back at the farmhouse?" she asked softly. "Why did you go to all this trouble?" Surely he knew he didn't have to. All she had ever wanted to know was that he loved her and wanted to marry him, baby or no baby.

Grady gave her a very smug, very male smile. "Because I wanted us to celebrate the Valentine's Day we never had, the way we should have in the first place, the way we will every year from now on," he said.

"Flowers and everything?" Jenna teased.

"Flowers, tux, sexy new red dress and everything," Grady affirmed. "I never thought I'd actually be saying this, or feeling this, but…" He shook his head as if he couldn't quite believe it. "You bring out the romantic in me, Jenna."

Jenna laughed, delighted. "And you bring out the romantic in me," she confided, lifting her mouth to his.

Grady kissed her again, deeply, lingeringly, until she was limp with surrender, tingling with longing. "Is that a yes?" he said. "Will you marry me?"

Jenna smiled up at him, knowing all was right with their world at last. "Yes, Grady," she said. "I will."

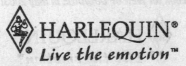

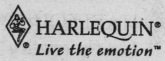

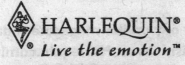

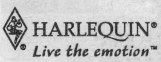